THE GREAT TEEN FRUIT WAR

A 1960 Novel

By

Jay Dubya

THE GREAT TEEN FRUIT WAR

A 1960 Novel

By
Jay Dubya

1648_21

Jay Dubya

ISBN 978-1-58909-131-3

For peach and blueberry lovers everywhere that enjoy '50s and early '60s teen culture

Other Books by Jay Dubya

Adult Fiction

Black Leather and Blue Denim, A '50s Novel
Ron Coyote, Man of La Mangia
Frat' Brats, A '60s Novel
Pieces of Eight
Pieces of Eight, Part II
Pieces of Eight, Part III
Pieces of Eight, Part IV
The Wholly Book of Genesis
The Wholly Book of Exodus
The Wholly Book of Doo-Doo-Rot-on-Me
Thirteen Sick Tasteless Classics
Thirteen Sick Tasteless Classics, Part II
Thirteen Sick Tasteless Classics, Part III
Thirteen Sick Tasteless Classics, Part IV
Thirteen Sick Tasteless Classics, Part V
So Ya' Wanna' Be A Teacher!
Mauled Maimed Mangled Mutilated Mythology
Fractured Frazzled Folk Fables & Fairy Farces
FFFF & FF, Part II
Nine New Novellas
Nine New Novellas, Part II
Nine New Novellas, Part III
Nine New Novellas, Part IV
One Baker's Dozen
Two Baker's Dozen
RAM: Random Articles and Manuscripts
Time Travel Tales
Modern Mythology
UFO: Utterly Fantastic Occurrences
Prime-Time Crime Time
Snake Eyes and Boxcars
Snake Eyes and Boxcars, Part II
The Psychic Dimension
The Psychic Dimension, Part II
Shakespeare: Slammed, Smeared, Savaged and Slaughtered
Shakespeare: S, S, S & S, Part II
First Person Stories
The Arcane Arcade

Thirteen Tantalizing Tales
PLOTS
PLOTS, Part II
THEMES
Hawthorne: Hacked, Shakespeare: Sacked, & Thurber: Thwacked
Hawthorne: Hazed, Hooked, Hammered and Hijacked
Suite 16
The FBI Inspector
Poe: Pelted, Pounded, Pummeled and Pulverized
Twain: Tattered, Trounced, Tortured and Traumatized
London: Lashed, Lacerated, Lampooned and Lambasted
O. Henry: Obscenely and Outrageously Obliterated
Homer's Odd Sea Odyssey
HOMER'S ILL ILIAD
Homer's Ill Iliad and Odd Sea Odyssey
The Timeless Time Machine
War of the Worlds
The Invisible Man
Parody Paradise
Parody Paradise, Part II
Parody Paradise, Part III
Parody Paradise, Part IV
A Christmas Carol
Bee 17, Short Stories
Bee 17, Part II, Short Stories
Bee 17, Part III, Short Stories
Bee 17, Part IV, Short Stories
Bee 17, Part V, Short Stories
Bee 17, Part VI, Short Stories

Young Adult Fantasy Novels and Stories

Pot of Gold
Enchanta
Space Bugs, Earth Invasion
The Eighteen Story Gingerbread House

Contents

Contents (Continued)

Preface

The Great Teen Fruit War, A 1960 Novel is a work of pure fiction. Any similarity to any person living or dead, or to any individual that might be content living a dead life on this strange earth is strictly coincidental. Therefore, any human being thinking that he or she resembles any certain individual in this work must also then be a fictional character.

The author remembers moving from Hammonton, New Jersey to Levittown, Pennsylvania in the spring of 1954, living at 50 Daffodil Lane, and then moving back to Hammonton in late December of '59. The author admits suffering from severe bouts of amnesia and from annoying perpetual hallucinations. Sometimes, the hallucinations are more desirable to experience than the harsh, mundane reality that exists outside the writer's body. On occasion, the author has difficulty distinguishing strange reality that seems like weird fantasy from weird fantasy that seems like strange reality. Sometimes, the author thinks that fiction is fact, and also that fact is fiction, so this makes him no different than the average American who habitually watches television, goes to the movies, or who reads the daily newspapers.

The writer has always preferred intellectual escapism to everyday boredom, preferring to live in the imagined world rather than endure the grueling drudgery and monotony associated with everyday human existence. He strongly believes that fantasizing is his vital link to the remainder of his species.

The Great Teen Fruit War, A 1960 Novel is the sequel to *Black Leather and Blue Denim, A '50s Novel. Frat' Brats, A '60s Novel* completes the "coming of age" trilogy.

Chapter One

"A Hammonton Childhood"

I was born (not hatched as some acquaintances might believe) in 1942 at the Swenson Home on Horton Street, on the north side of the railroad tracks, in Hammonton, New Jersey. The town had no hospital back then, so many other Hammontonians who were not delivered by midwives were also naturally born (or born naturally) at the Swenson Home on the "proper side of the tracks".

On December 7, 1941, Pearl Harbor had been attacked. *World War II* was in progress in the European and in the Pacific Theaters (where the war was playing). My father had volunteered his services after the Pearl Harbor attack and was away training at U.S. military camps, and later after 1943, dad had been stationed in France and in Germany during my early childhood. When pop returned from the terrible conflict, he opened a small gas station/repair shop next to the family's modest white bungalow, which was situated beside my mother's parents' Hammonton business, Square Deal Farm Market on *Route 30*, the White Horse Pike.

Grand-pop Tony had pioneered the farm market trade on that busy highway, which at the time, was the major summer tourist link between Philadelphia and Atlantic City. Gramps would often drive me around South Jersey in his black stake-body truck to various fruit and vegetable farmers, where the farm market merchant would purchase corn, peaches, apples, blueberries, cucumbers, peppers, zucchini squash, tomatoes and other locally-grown produce. Several times Grand-pop Tony even brought me to Dock Street in Philadelphia, which at the time was the area's major fresh food distribution center.

Antonio Giacobbe was a Sicilian immigrant who had come over to America via Ellis Island and settled with former Old-World Messina, Sicily relatives in Philadelphia. Gramps started-out in the American free enterprise system by vending fruit and vegetables from a pushcart, hawking fresh produce around the Italian Market on Ninth Street. In a few years, the produce hustler earned enough money to invest in a fertile five-acre tract on the White Horse Pike in Hammonton.

Italian immigrants were not too well received from the firmly entrenched and established English Hammonton WASPs. A year after my grandparents had erected Square Deal Market during the mid-1930s Depression, an influential farm family of British descent was determined to knock the newcomers out of business by building a similar farm market right next to Square Deal. When a customer would stop his or her automobile between the two commercial properties,

Grandma Annie would rush-over and nail the fresh fruit shopper before the competition ever had a chance to react to the prospective customer's arrival.

Eventually, Antonio Giacobbe prevailed and proudly bought the other market from his chief rival. My Sicilian grandparents on my mother's side had overcome 1930s WASP discrimination through hard work and personal determination. Perseverance was a good lesson I had learned at an early age. It has as much to do with human economic survival as persistence has to do with human success.

Grandma Annie Giacobbe also had a difficult childhood. She had come from a very poor Sicilian family that lived beyond the end of Pine Road in an area then known as Sandy Crossways. She had to wear her father's discarded tattered shoes with holes in the soles to school, and was often mocked by the other children fortunate enough to have wealthier parents and better shoes. Young Annie vowed to elevate herself above poverty. My maternal grandmother always remembered the emotional scars she had suffered in her impoverished childhood. After marrying Grandpa Tony, GrandMa Annnie gained self-esteem by running Square Deal Farm Market with steadfast precision and a terrific Old World work ethic.

Kindergarten was not mandatory back in 1948. I remember entering first grade at St. Joseph School on Third Street in downtown Hammonton. I managed to master the fundamentals of reading and writing in four-years of schooling, and when Grandpa Tony took me to buy produce, I soon realized at a young age that I knew how to read and write and that he didn't. Grandpa would ask me on our excursions around South Jersey to read the various billboards and signs that dotted *Route 206, Route 54, Route 322,* and *Route 30,* and I would oblige. All Gramps had mastered was how to scribble two letters, his initials "A.G.", which the farm market owner used to certify his approval on sales receipts that verified his wholesale purchases.

No matter where Grandpa would drive me, the Sicilian immigrant would always reiterate his reason for moving to New Jersey. The fat, bald-headed man knew very little English, and repeated at least ten times to, and ten times from our given destination, "Giovanni, there's too much true-bulla in Pencil-bania!" Antonio would repeat in between smoking and puffing his huge *El Producto* cigar, before coughing like a tuberculosis victim. Then. Grandpa Tony would again ask me the identification of words that puzzled him on various highway billboards. But Gramps knew his mathematics without the need of a pencil, eraser, or adding machine. The math' wizard could calculate and subtract figures in his head, and would tell amazed commission house brokers the exact total of his purchases to the penny, a task that took *them* minutes to figure-out with their modern adding machines.

When I was six years old in 1948, Mom and Aunt Frances took me one Saturday night to The Rivoli Theater on Bellevue Avenue in downtown Hammonton to watch the Otto Preminger film *Forever Amber,* starring Cornell Wilde and Linda Darnell. The movie had a very spectacular fire scene, and at six-years of age, I thought that the whole theater had been engulfed in the inferno that was being shown up on the big screen. I panicked and started screaming my lungs out, until Mom removed me from my seat; walked me to the foyer, and soothed my alarm by buying some much-needed popcorn and soda.

The *Philadelphia Phillies* had won the National League Pennant in 1950, and I recall how psyched-up I was watching them on a small-screen black and white TV play in the *World Series* against the *New York Yankees*. Joe DiMaggio hit the winning home run in game two, and then the *Yankees* cruised to a four-game sweep in spite of inspirational play by *Phillies'* centerfielder, Richie Ashburn, my boyhood hero.

During the summer months, Gramps would take me north on *206* to Indian Mills where the stand proprietor would daily buy two thousand ears of freshly "pulled" Jersey corn. Then, my escort would bury me up to my chest with corn ears, as I sat in a back *corn*er of his black Chevy stake-body truck. I got a thrill waving to surprised motorists and their car passengers passing us, going south toward Hammonton on *206*.

Grandpa Tony often took me in his black truck to the Hammonton Auction Block where the entrepreneur would buy fruit and vegetables to resell at his farm market. Post *WWII* Hammonton was an agricultural community of around ten-thousand inhabitants, with a large Italian immigrant population, and most of the farmers wore caps, flannel shirts, gray wool vested sweaters, baggy pants, and had mustaches. I recall that some older Sicilian farmers even still brought their crops to the auction "block" in horse-drawn wagons. The local growers would line-up their trucks and wagons in three lanes that passed through the "auction block". Lots were drawn to see which line would go through "the block" first, second, and third. Commission produce brokers and independent buyers like Grandpa would bid on items, after being shown "sample packages" of the fruit and vegetables up for sale.

When I turned nine, I became a friend of David Parkwell, whose family had a Farm and Garden Center across the White Horse Pike from Square Deal Market. David was two-years older than I was, and I immediately admired his mischievous nature.

"Slow John" DiAngelo was an elderly grower who owned ground behind Grand-pop Tony's five-acres of peach and apple orchards. Several times, I pretended I had been naughtily picking (stealing) cucumbers in "Slow John's" field, precisely when the gimpy farmer was riding down a sandy road on his old *John Deere* tractor. This activity would fully infuriate the partially-lame old grower. Slow John would halt his tractor; leap off, and then awkwardly chase me across twenty or so rows of cucumbers until I safely gained shelter and escape inside a nearby woods.

While "Slow John" was pursuing his elusive nemesis (who had also been wearing a Halloween Dracula mask), Dave Parkwell would exit a clump of trees from the opposite side of the field along the dirt road. Then, my friend would hop onto the *John Deere* and drive it along farm roads through pepper and tomato fields, until my co-conspirator parked the piece of machinery a mile or so away.

Dave and I would then reunite at my parents' snack bar, located inside of Square Deal Market, and we would celebrate our dual mischief with "Electrocuted Hot Dogs" and bottles of *Ma's Old Fashion Root Beer*. Then, I would furtively show Dave the neat Dracula mask I intended to wear next Halloween.

Dave convinced me to join the Hammonton Little League, which had the distinction of winning the 1949 Little League World Championship. My buddy was the star of our team, DiDonato's Bowling. I played an occasional second base or left field.

In one particular night game, a big kid named Rollie Cantrobone hit a towering fly ball to left field. I backed-up to the green wooden fence; held my glove up toward the blinding lights, and defensively searched the night sky for the obscure baseball. Incredibly, a small miracle happened. The baseball plopped-down into my open glove as was shielding my face to protect it from the descending white object. The fans on both sides of the field erupted in a boisterous cheer in recognition of my fantastic, accidental accomplishment.

I had a great time making and having friends at St. Joseph School on North Third Street. During recess, we played marbles on the hardtop playground, and yo-yos were prized possessions, too. I invented the baseball card game known as "three-way matchies". Two close friends and I would simultaneously flip to the ground baseball cards with the images of major league players on the front, and the players' performance statistics on the other side. The owner of the odd-sided flip would win "the jackpot". If two cards showed their back side, then the player that owned the face-up card would be declared the winner. My buddies and I spent hours of leisure recess time perfecting and demonstrating our various marble, yo-yo, and "matchies" skills.

I remember when I was ten that all the Catholic school kids from grades three to twelve had to attend an assembly at the Rivoli Theater. We all walked by grade level classes from the Catholic school two blocks east to the movie house on the corner of Bellevue Avenue and Third Street. All that week, the St. Joseph School Fillipini nuns and Pallottine priests had been talking about heavenly visitations from the Blessed Virgin Mary, angels, saints, and the religious teachers were hyping the newly released movie *Our Lady of Fatima.* The cinema presentation was an awesome experience to a ten-year-old kid. The film must have had a profound impact on my vulnerable subconscious. It probably also immensely sparked my fertile imagination.

Sometimes, I would sleep the night inside the spare bedroom upstairs in my grandparents' red brick home, which had been constructed behind Square Deal Farm Market. A statue of St. Anne (the Virgin Mary's mother), dressed in a macabre black robe, rested atop the brown mahogany bureau next to the bed. The statue's stern face was always peering-down at me, and I always had to go to sleep turning my body and my head in the opposite direction. St. Anne's hands held black rosary beads, suggesting that she was praying for the soul of the bed's occupant, lying beneath her presence.

Every 16th of July, the town of Hammonton celebrates the Feast of Our Lady of Mount Carmel, featuring a large traveling carnival along with an Old-World religious street procession. Statues of Jesus, Mary, Joseph, and saints from St. Joseph Church are mounted on carts with drapes covering their frames and wheels, and escorted by faithful parishioners through the major streets of the community, and then back to the Third Street church. Clusters of donations in the form of five, ten, twenty, fifty and hundred-dollar bills were hung from and adorned the statues. In the years after *WWII,* fifty-thousand visitors would attend the 16th of July Mount Carmel Festival. The pilgrims were mostly Italian immigrants, or first-generation offspring, many of whom arrived by chartered buses from Philadelphia.

Grandma Annie Giacobbe gave me a five-dollar bill to have pinned onto the statue of Our Lady of Mount Carmel. My grandparents did not trust banks, because many had collapsed during the Depression, so they stashed cash in the mattress of an old bed stored in the brick house's attic. I discovered the cache (of cash) and stole five-dollars from the attic mattress. I had received an additional five-dollars spending money from my parents, and I also had in my pocket the *Abe Lincoln* my grandmother had given me to be pinned on the Our Lady of Mount Carmel procession statue, besides the five-dollars I had been saving since May for the carnival.

I met some friends at the carnival grounds, and the four of us bought popcorn, soda, pizza, and cotton candy. Then, we played different games of chance, and tried-out various amusement rides. Before I knew it, I had exhausted all the money in my possession including, the five dollars I was supposed to have pinned on the Blessed Mother's statue.

"Did you pin the money on Our Lady's statue?" my grandmother asked. "That donation will bring our family good luck!"

"Yes," I lied, feeling quite guilty. "And the nice man collecting the money said 'Thank you'."

"Good boy," Grandma complimented. "Marie, I think your son is goin' to grow-up and become a priest. He's such a *bona, belle* boy!"

That night, I slept in the spare bedroom of the red brick house. As my guilty mind approached the drowsy state that usually comes before actual sleeping, I turned my head and thought I saw St. Anne's statue kneeling beside the bed, piously praying for my wandering, straying soul. "You must return the five-dollars you have stolen," she commanded, "or else your soul will burn in hell!"

The next morning, I didn't know what to do. I entered the small white bungalow and saw my father's wallet on the kitchen table. While dad was in the bathroom shaving, I opened his wallet that contained only ten-dollar bills and removed one. That night mom told me I had to sleep in the red brick house, because she and dad were going out to dinner.

I was tossing and turning in bed from the guilt of my third misdeed involving Dad's wallet. I had planned to go over to David Parkwell's parents' Farm and Garden business the following morning, and have my pal change the ten-dollar bill into two fives, which I would then surreptitiously plant into the stuffed attic mattress, since it contained mostly five-dollar bills.

As I feared, I opened my eyes around midnight, and St. Anne was again kneeling beside the bed. "You've been a sinful boy again," the statue said to me while sobbing and weeping. "I don't want to see you burn in hell for all eternity!" I turned my face, and when I looked back, the statue was no longer on the floor beside my bed. It was again stationed upon the mahogany bureau.

My heart and conscience were both in the same miserable quandary. How would I get fifteen-dollars to repay my debts to the Blessed Mother and to Dad? I prayed to St. Anne for a solution to my heartfelt dilemma. I was in for the shock of my young life!

The next morning Steve Van Buren, an all-pro football player for the *Philadelphia Eagles,* stopped at Square Deal Market to acquire some tomatoes, corn, blueberries, and peaches on his way to the Jersey shore. I immediately recognized the famous sports' celebrity from *Eagle* television football games and from sports news' clips I had seen at the Rivoli Theater.

I almost swallowed my tongue when Steve Van Buren and his wife approached the little candy/soda/hot dog concession where I had been standing behind the counter. The couple ordered *Pepsi-Colas* and hot dogs, which I began to prepare on the "Hot Dog Electrocutor". Then, the football star and I struck-up a brief conversation.

"Do you know who I am?" the pro football star casually asked while his wife chuckled in the background.

"I think you're Steve Van Buren, my very favorite football player!" I exclaimed.

"You're absolutely right," the tough athlete remarked. "Would it be all right if I signed and gave you an autographed picture? I have some in my car."

"Can I have one for my friend David Parkwell, too?" I begged.

"Why sure, no problem," Van Buren returned. "I'll be right back with two of 'em."

I graciously and thankfully received the two unexpected gifts. I was thrilled to death to obtain them from the *Eagle* great.

After Steve Van Buren gathered his produce and then drove-off with his pretty wife, another farm market patron made his way to the concession stand.

"Wasn't that Steve Van Buren?" the excited man asked.

"Sure was," I answered.

"He's the best fullback in professional football," the Square Deal customer elaborated. "I'll give ya' twenty bucks for one of those signed pictures. What do ya' say?"

"Okay," I replied. "But this is a big sacrifice," I stated, recalling a school synonym I had learned for the word *bunt* in baseball.

"I will cherish this picture for the rest of my life," the elderly fellow commented. "I'll even have it framed."

That afternoon, my father again was shaving. I sneaked into the bungalow's bigger bedroom, found his wallet on the bureau, and replaced "the ten-dollar loan" I had borrowed. Then, the next time I was in church, I put five-dollars in the collection basket. And finally, I replaced the five-dollars I had pilfered from the attic mattress.

'Thank you, St. Anne!' I gratefully acknowledged as I rolled my appreciative blue eyes toward the ceiling. 'Now, I'm off the hook!' And that's how David Parkwell never got his autographed Steve Van Buren photo' (which *he* never knew about).

My parents had purchased their first television in early 1953. I was forced to sit-down for a "lesson in history" and watch the boring Queen

Elizabeth Coronation in network black and white. Even at ten- years of age, I hated royal pomp and ritual. The monotonous ceremony went on for hours and hours. I thought to myself that the mere act of placing a crown on somebody's head (even a *Head* of State) should require no longer than fifteen-seconds. So, even at age ten, I had already been exhibiting symptoms of cynicism towards the artificiality of "stupid" adult traditions.

In March of '54, I received some bad news. Dad explained that the family would be moving away from Hammonton, New Jersey to a newly-constructed suburban community, Levittown, Pennsylvania. "Levittown is closer to Norristown than Hammonton is," Dad explained. "Uncle Frank got me a good job as a stainless-steel fabricator at his company, Martin and Quade."

Before 1954, my life was rather nondescript. At age ten, I was satisfied and content doing simple basic chores around Square Deal Farm Market. I felt threatened, having to abandon the security of playing Little League for DiDonato's Bowling and of leaving the familiar halls and rooms of St. Joseph School.

I had turned eleven in the spring of '54 when my family made the move to 50 Daffodil Lane in the Dogwood Hollow section of Levittown, Pennsylvania. My sister Anne was six, and my younger brother Skip was an infant. I was rather melancholy for having to break-away from all I had known and valued as a youngster, growing-up in an Italian agricultural community. I was extremely apprehensive about what to expect in my new social environment. At age ten I had concluded that some things in life just were not fair.

Chapter Two

"From Pennsy' Back to Jersey" (1959)

Before I knew it, my family had moved into 50 Daffodil Lane in the Dogwood Hollow section of Levittown, Pennsylvania. I soon realized that Dogwood Drive was a mile-long ellipse, and that all of the interior streets began with the letter D. Besides the existence of Daffodil Lane, there was Dewberry Lane, Dahlia Lane, Deepgreen Lane, Daisy Lane, Disk Lane, Darkleaf Lane and Deerfield Lane. All the inside lanes (including Daffodil) eventually connected with elliptical Dogwood Drive.

The newly-constructed suburban paradise was modeled after Levittown, New York on Long Island, which had preceded it by five-years. To avoid monotony, Dogwood Hollow had four different house designs. When all of the new city's sections had been completed, Levittown, Pennsylvania had fifteen-thousand spanking new homes. with an instant population of around fifty-five-thousand happily transplanted people.

Levittown, Pennsylvania was a rather bold experiment in suburban living. The new suburban city had been designed to be a "middle-class" community, but more specifically, Levittown was an exclusively "white middle-class community". Caucasian families in quest of a better way of life were instantly attracted there. Whites desired to escape the rampant social disorganization that was quite characteristic of 1950s' eastern U.S. cities. Levittown was a calculated social-economic gamble in suburban living, where houses, shopping centers, highways, schools, and recreations areas had been creatively engineered to harmoniously mix and blend together. My initial reaction was that Dogwood Hollow seemed like a great place to live.

In 1954, human interaction was stratified and compartmentalized in most suburban communities all over the country. Levittown, Pennsylvania was entirely "white". Blacks interacted mostly with blacks elsewhere, and whites stayed mostly with whites in both cities and towns. That brand of racial segregation "by choice" was explained to young people by their parents as "separate but equal".

Ethnic and religious separation and discrimination were also quite evident. The Kalens, who were Jewish, lived across the street from us on Daffodil Lane, and their neighbors, who were Irish and Scottish, wouldn't allow their children to associate with the Hebrew kids. Dad allowed Anne to play with the Kalen kids on Monday, Wednesday and Friday, and my sister was permitted to interact with the Irish and Scottish children the other four days of the week.

Divisions along nationality and Christian lines also existed. Catholics did not marry Protestants, and Irish Catholics did not marry Italian Catholics, and Baptists thought three times before marrying Presbyterians. Christians did not marry Jews, and Occidentals did not marry Orientals.

So, looking back to the spring of '54, Levittown, Pennsylvania was like a giant Bingo card with horizontal and vertical lines drawn in orderly rows in order to demarcate culture, religion, race, nationality, and a family's economic level. Levittown loyally reflected the inflexible norms and standards of America that had been firmly established by the rigid, century-old predominance of White Anglo-Saxon Protestantism.

I quickly made friends with Carnie, who lived two blocks away on Darkleaf Lane. The insecure kid was the son of a deadbeat carnival barker who had basically abandoned *his* family. Carnie was neurotic and resentful, and my pal's moods often vacillated between ultimate joy and extreme depression. The nervous wreck was a manic depressant decades before psychiatrists had ever popularized the term. Carnie and I came under the influence of Tinker, a vindictive nasty "greaser" with destructive tendencies. Tinker had the potential to become lethal when angered, and the delinquent's reputation for trouble preceded him wherever his nose pointed.

Older kids from the Kenwood section occasionally harassed Carnie, Tinker and me. Bruno Popeye Messina and Cummings formed a ruthless gang of rednecks, the Kenwood Kamikazes. The notorious bullies terrorized eggheads ('50s nerds), jocks, and other unfortunate greasers.

In April of '54, the Fairless Hills Steel Mill opened on the Delaware River between Levittown and Trenton. Carnie and I were rambunctious sixth-graders attending St. Mark's School on Radcliffe Street, which paralleled the *Delaware* in Bristol. A Venezuelan ship, the *Caracas,* was transporting the first iron ore shipment from South America up the *Delaware River,* sailing past Bristol towards Fairless Hills, Pennsylvania.

Students from area schools were invited to come to the Delaware River and wave linen American flags on wooden sticks at the passing vessel. The St. Mark's School nuns emphasized the significance of the event by claiming that it was "history in the making". Carnie and I crossed Radcliffe Street with our sixth-grade class and found a good vantage point in the second row of student spectators waiting to view the *Caracas* passing Bristol. Public-school kids in back of us were jabbering, jostling, and shoving.

When the giant black ship approached, four people in the front row accidentally fell over the bulkhead into the *Delaware River*. Two of them were cousins Angie Palermo and Bubbles Messina, gorgeous Levittown girls who soon blamed Carnie and me for "pushing" them into the river. I had really had "a crush" on both dolls from the first times I had seen each of them back in Levittown, and the *Caracas* incident was the genesis for future hostility with the Sicilian babes and their Mafia fathers.

Angie Palermo was my neighbor who lived at 66 Daffodil Lane. I later found-out that her dad was a drug and pornography distributor who had certain business ties to the Kenwood Kamikazes. Bubbles Messina was Angie's cousin and the sister of Bruno "Popeye" Messina, a ruthless founder of the Kamikazes. Their father, Dante Messina, was Mr. Sal Palermo's unscrupulous business partner.

In 1955, I played Little League baseball for Meenan Oil and was fortunate to make the Levittown National League All-Star Team. In our second game, we played Morrisville, Pennsylvania, which had two kids over six-feet-tall that intimidated us. Morrisville beat us in a close contest, and then went on to Williamsport and won the Little League World Series. So, I had the distinction of playing in a New Jersey Little League (Hammonton) that had won the championship in 1949, and of playing against the team (Morrisville, Pa.) that had won it all in 1955. Ironically, Levittown American League All-Stars won the Little League World Series five years later in 1960.

My pal Carnie and I were ice-skating on the Delaware Canal in late January of '57. Popeye Messina, Cummings, and several other Kamikazes approached our innocent fun. The punks roughly grabbed me and threw my frail body across the ice, which suddenly cracked and broke. I fell into the freezing-cold water, and was bravely rescued by Carnie and another friend, Robbie Wilkinson. My near-death experience was a "pay back" from the vile Kamikazes for believing that I had pushed Angie Palermo and Bubble Messina into the *Delaware River*.

Later that January, Tinker and I were hitchhiking on Haines Road on our way to our favorite hangout, the Feed Bag. Cummings and Popeye Messina stopped in the Kamikazes' familiar black '52 Ford. The two blackhearted thugs kidnapped Tinker and me; transported us to Philadelphia, and dropped us off against our wills at Broad and Erie. Tink vowed revenge on the cruel Kenwood "scumbags" for not showing him more respect while mischievously kidnapping him.

In early '57, I first met Bo Jalonec, a tall, handsome, blond-hair kid at the Feed Bag. Bo was from Junewood, but since Junewood didn't have a gang, I suggested that we form the Dogwood Diablos to protect us from the barbaric Kamikazes. Quinn became the Diablo's leader, and Bo, Carnie, Robbie Wilkinson, Tinker, and I were assigned to be on the gang's executive committee.

Bo and I had gone on a fishing expedition in Tullytown, just north of Bristol, along the *Delaware River*. Cummings, Popeye, and the Kamikazes showed-up and surprise-attacked us. My pal and I fled to an old abandoned rowboat abandoned on the Tullytown shore, and frantically paddled-out into the Delaware as quickly as we could. The destructive K's threw stones at us, and one hit Jalonec on the forehead, forming a bloody gash. Suddenly, the *Caracas* came around the bend from the direction of the Fairless Hills Steel Mill, and the high waves from its wake filled the already sinking rowboat. Bo and I had to leap into the river and desperately swim like drowning rats onto a small island lying between the Pennsy' and Jersey shores.

Soon, pranks between the Diablos and the Kamikazes escalated into life-threatening situations. Things were getting out of hand as more chips were laid on the table. The D's and the insane K's quickly became more than adversaries. Our conflicts became more personal and dangerous.

Our leader Quinn became friendly with Marcus "Sugar Ray" Spellman, a young black mechanic who often worked on the Diablo' boss's black '42 Ford coupe. Tinker was unhappy that Quinn had chosen a black kid to work on his prized '42 Ford's souped-up engine. Tinker threatened to quit the D's and buddy-up with the racist Kamikazes, and Carnie and I had to convince the young hoodlum to stay with the Dogwood Hollow guys. From then on out, Tinker demonstrated his deep jealousy by trying to undermine Quinn's authority, every chance the unstable kid had. Tink was jealous because *he* had not been selected to work on Quinn's '42 coupe, being rejected in favor of a "black grease-monkey".

Phil Jackson was the star quarterback over at Cardinal Reagan High, where Carnie, Robbie Wilkinson, and I also attended school. Jackson was a rich, spoiled jock who had every material thing his heart ever desired, including a beautiful white '56 Corvette. One night the athlete made the mistake of insulting Tinker inside the Feed Bag. The two stepped-out of the teen hangout for some fisticuffs, and Tink beat-up Jackson pretty badly in a fair fight. Three weeks later, Jackson and three of his offensive linemen attacked and injured Tinker behind the Route 13 Dairy DeLite custard stand. Soon thereafter, Tinker got revenge by stealing Phil Jackson's white '56 Corvette and then ruining the fine auto by filling its interior with at least a quarter of a ton of wet cement, after my lethal friend had temporarily highjacked a cement-mixer truck.

The Diablos "executive committee" next orchestrated a night raid on Sal Palermo's (Angie's father's) Bristol, Pennsylvania money-laundering business, *Specialty Enterprises*. Our gang discovered a cache of marijuana and pornographic literature inside the building's rear warehouse. The Diablos heisted some of the contraband for future use. Later, in May of '59, Tinker planted some marijuana and naughty pictures in the trunk of Cumming's '52 Ford and Phil Jackson's father's Lincoln, and the two amigos got into serious trouble with the police, that is, after the D's set *them* up for detective' interrogations at "the clinic."

Quinn and Cummings had a drag race on Haines Road, but Tinker, who wanted control of the Diablos, interfered with the outcome. Cummings, Popeye Messina, and the Kamikazes entered the Feed Bag after the aborted drag race. Marcus Spellman was sitting there at the Diablos' "reserved table" with Quinn, Carnie, Tinker, and me. Cummings made ugly racist insults at Marcus, but Quinn defended Spellman's integrity, and then challenged the chief K to a fight at the Tullytown quarry. It was a terrific battle, and I think that Quinn was winning. Suddenly, a police helicopter appeared overhead, beaming-down illumination from a powerful searchlight. All of the greasers and their girlfriends evacuated the isolated quarry in a hurry. Before everyone left the scene, Cummings and Popeye maliciously heaved Tinker into the man-made lake. Tink didn't know how to swim, so Quinn jumped into the quarry and saved the rotten skunk from drowning. Thankfully, a certain gang war between the Diablos and the Kamikazes had been, at least, temporarily averted.

I thought that Tinker would have been grateful for being rescued from certain death by drowning, but the arrogant moron wasn't. The vengeful rogue went on a crazy rampage and destroyed a whole fleet of Kamikaze cars. The maniac also ingeniously demolished Phil Jackson's replacement white Corvette, which the quarterback's wealthy parents had purchased to appease *his* sensitive ego. Things were getting out of hand.

A second drag race between Quinn and Cummings was scheduled to happen at a New Jersey blueberry farm on Labor Day of '59. The large plantation had a blacktop straight and narrow main road down its center, and two identical, forward and backward dirt road figure nines, led back to the central asphalt strip. Quinn and Cummings had to crisscross several times to change lanes on the blacktop strip, and then take dirt roads on opposite sides of the five- hundred-acre farm, which had gravel roads elevated twelve-feet above the enormous plantation's irrigation canals.

While the exciting race was in progress, a New Jersey State Trooper's patrol cruiser entered the blueberry farm and promptly chased after Quinn's 'black '42 Ford coupe. At the final intersection before the home stretch, Quinn and Cummings converged at the blacktop road in what amounted to a classic game of "chicken". Cummings panicked and applied his brakes. Quinn skidded onto the asphalt road, successfully negotiating his very perilous turn. Cummings' '52 Ford smashed into the speeding state trooper's vehicle that had been doggedly pursuing Quinn.

The impacted vehicles then flipped over several times, and landed in opposite canals. Tinker, Carnie, and Robbie Wilkinson rescued the trapped trooper from drowning, and Marcus Spellman was the principal savior of Cummings, before *his* totaled black '52 Ford' slid down an embankment, and landed sideways in the five-foot-deep irrigation ditch.

Phil Jackson had experienced a mental breakdown, which was mostly a result of Tinker's destruction of *his* second '56 white 'Vette. The *Notre Dame* bound quarterback left a suicide note, and then ran-away from home. Local newspapers reported that his concerned parents had offered a generous ten-thousand-dollar reward for information leading to their precious son's whereabouts.

Quinn was having some serious romantic problems with his girlfriend. Patty Van Arsdale didn't like her beau's criminal involvement with the Diablos, so to spite *her* opposition, our leader became more active in our valiant crusade against the Ks. Quinn asked me to devise a clever prank to use against the Kamikazes. I decided to employ Phil Jackson's mysterious disappearance as a basis for baiting Cummings and Popeye Messina into a clever trap. "J.W., you have the green light, as long as nobody gets hurt or killed!" Quinn cautioned.

The Diablos met the Ks inside the Feed Bag, and informed the bullies that *we* had discovered Phil Jackson's body over in Croydon, a town south of Bristol. Beginning *our* ruse, Quinn offered to share the lucrative reward money with the Ks, in order to signal a permanent truce between the two warring gangs.

The Ks followed us to Croydon on Columbus Day of '59. Amazingly, according to plan, Phil Jackson's ghost supernaturally appeared in a woods', right after the two gangs discovered *his* body along a forest trail. The Ks had been incredibly frightened by the Diablos' "trick"," and the knuckleheads rushed to their car. Worm, an ugly Kenwood punk, recklessly drove the terrified Kamikaze members onto the country road, and quickly fishtailed-down to a major highway. The speeding '59 Edsel was struck at an intersection by a tractor-trailer. The vehicle was wickedly crushed like an accordion.

Worm was instantly killed in the violent collision. His best friend Spits was paralyzed from the waist down. Cummings required hospitalization, and Popeye Messina suffered lacerations, bruises, and loss of pride.

In late October of '59, Marcus Spellman and his family moved into Dogwood Hollow at 43 Deepgreen Lane, which fed into Daffodil Lane, right across the street from Sal Palermo's residence. The presence of the new black residents greatly upset the proud adults of the formerly all-white community. The Diablos, led by Quinn's excellent example, took a stand, and defended Marcus's right to live in our neighborhood, despite the protesting of Mafia boss Sal Palermo. The Ds and the Ks finally came together on common ground by mutually accepting the black family's right to live in Levittown.

At least a hundred other things happened in Levittown from 1954-'59 between the Diablos and the Kamikazes that I have not mentioned, and those adventures are all chronicled in the book *Black Leather and Blue Denim, A '50s Novel.*

My father announced that the family was again ready to pick-up stakes and move from 50 Daffodil Lane back to the White Horse Pike. Pop had the opportunity to buy Pete's Farm Market on *Route 30* in Elm, Camden County. The business was located a mile west of Grandpa Tony's Square Deal Farm Market, on the same side of the bustling highway.

I figured that I could endure any bizarre teen conflict after what I had encountered and survived in Levittown. I had acquired personality traits from my Diablo friends that could insulate me from future teen aggression. From Bo Jalonec, I had obtained a great sense of humor along with the unique ability to make nonsensical puns and inane jokes. I had learned the value of friendship and honesty from Robbie Wilkinson, and the importance of loyalty from my paranoid pal, Carnie. Even though I despised Tinker's perpetual ruthlessness, I had acquired cunning and stealth by being associated with his devious nature. And from my hero, Quinn, I felt that I had found "cool" leadership skills, which I could skillfully practice on my new friends at Edgewood Regional High School.

On December 29, 1959, I was back in good old New Jersey. My heart was glad to leave the chaos of the Kamikazes and the venomous peer pressure of Tinker back in Pennsylvania. My mind was certain that nothing could be as dangerous as what I had recently lived-through between the Diablos and the crazy Kamikazes. That was before I became involved in the great teen fruit war developing between "the Reds and the Blues".

Chapter Three

"New Friends at Edgewood High"

My father drove me over to Edgewood Regional High School on Coopers Folly Road in early January of 1960 in his green and cream '55 Chevy Bel Air. The Tansboro, New Jersey school was only one-year old and still looked brand new. I couldn't attend Hammonton High because Dad's new business and house were in Winslow Township, Camden County, and not in Atlantic County. We had visited St. Joseph High where my folks really wanted me to attend, but the small high school did not have the same curriculum that I had been taking at Levittown's Cardinal Reagan.

The Edgewood guidance counselors explained to Dad and me that the coordinators were going to "bump me up" from a junior to a senior because if they didn't, I was already approaching eighteen, and would be around nineteen when I would finally graduate. Pop liked the idea, but I was a little skeptical of such a radical maneuver, just because I happened to be a year older than the normal junior. After filling-out some admissions' forms in the Edgewood Guidance Office, Pop was free to leave.

I discussed my educational background with Mr. Wilson and Mr. White, and the counselors devised an individualized schedule tailored just for me. It wasn't until third-period that I was able to arrive at my first class, Mrs. Murphy's American History II.

The teacher examined my "Class Admission Card; checked that I was in the right room and period on my schedule; entered my name in her roll-book, and told me to sit in the back of the class. After introducing me to the College Prep' group, Mrs. Murphy asked if I'd like to be called anything besides my regular name.

"Yes, you can call me J.W.," I politely replied.

"Okay, J.W. Here's your comprehensive History II text. It's quite a monster. Good luck in my class," the instructor pleasantly related. "Hope you enjoy doin' lots of homework and library research."

I graciously accepted the hefty textbook with a blush on my face as the other students snickered and giggled at my very obvious temporary discomfort. The history teacher then said she was going to ask the class some pertinent questions about the *Civil War.* History was one of my strong suits at Cardinal Reagan High, so I thought I could impress everyone if I would accurately answer the first challenging question.

"What important *Civil War* battle that went on for over six-weeks gave the north control of the *Mississippi River?"* Mrs. Murphy quizzed.

That answer was definitely stored inside my mental repertoire. I flung my right arm up, begging for recognition. My solicitation was quickly recognized.

"I believe I'll call on our new scholar J.W. for the correct response," Mrs. Murphy indicated as the remainder of the CP students silently turned their heads in the direction of my location in the last seat of the last row, nearest the room's windows. Everyone was curious to hear what the new kid would say.

"It was the battle of *Vicks*burg," I proudly announced, "and General Grant finally won, even without the use of cough drops!" I elaborated, deliberately attempting to be funny deftly mentioning a brand name' product while imitating my old pal, Bo Jalonec.

The class broke-out in a roar, not laughing at my silly pun alluding to a brand name cough drop, but at me standing upright beside my desk. At Cardinal Reagan High, standing was required for students when asking or answering academic matters out of respect for the priests, nuns, or lay teachers on the faculty. I had instinctively acted out of force of habit. I was extremely embarrassed behaving like a Catholic school kid in his new public-school environment.

"J.W.," Mrs. Murphy laughed. "You just have to stand in this school to recite the *Pledge of Allegiance* during homeroom announcements. This is Edgewood Regional High School, you know. It isn't Fort Dix or the Pentagon!"

The entire class again burst-out in a boisterous roar in response to Mrs. Murphy's suave diplomatic admonishment. I sank-down in my desk with my face florid, feeling excessively stupid and very foolish.

Fourth-period was with no-nonsense Mr. Andrews, a stern, inflexible trigonometry teacher. His rigid, non-smiling personality tolerated little humor or frivolity from students. I really minded my P's and Q's during my first exposure to the austere educator. I quickly realized that I was ahead of the public-school kids in English and social studies, but far behind their achievement level in advanced math' and science.

Fifth-period was cafeteria time, so I had a chance to make some new acquaintances. I dragged my tray on the metal, waist-high ledge through the food serving line and wound-up at the cashier with portions of meat loaf, mashed potatoes, and green peas. I saw an odd-looking kid sitting alone at a nearby table, eating a peanut butter and jelly sandwich in his left hand, and alternating bites of that with a *Three Musketeers* candy bar in his right. I paid the cashier and then sat-down across from the strange-looking guy, and next started-up a conversation.

"All I need is some quiet on my tray because I already have some peas," I laughed while again impersonating Bo Jalonec's inimitable wit. "Then I could have *peas* and quiet!"

"Have you been a jerk-off all your life, or is it just startin' to happen right now!" the weird-looking dude loudly exclaimed so that kids three tables away could easily hear his tirade.

"Don't pay any attention to Goose," another fellow holding his tray advised. "The ogre hates the world and everyone in it! Can I sit down here?"

"Sure," I agreed, as Goose completely ignored the new arrival. "Make yourself comfortable."

"I'm Tommy Tomasello, but my friends call me News, 'cause I know all about what's happenin' in the world. And this wise guy here is Ronald Restuccio, better known as Goose."

"Hi," I greeted. "Glad to make your acquaintance."

Goose looked at me with a mild grin and uttered, "Ya' look like a friggin' ankle biter to me! Bit any ankles lately?"

"Ankle biter?" I mildly inquired.

"Yeah, a little kid," Goose clarified. "You're probably still wet behind the ears and dry inside your dick, too."

"Whatcha' reading?" I asked News Tomasello, trying to change the subject to avoid conflict at my new school.

"*Catcher in the Rye* by J.D. Salinger," Tommy answered. "I keep it insulated in this brown book cover I made from a paper bag, so that the teachers think I'm readin' a small textbook on geometric theorems, or a scholarly collection of Shakespearean sonnets."

"*Catcher in the Rye?*" I chuckled and smiled. "Is it a biography about Yogi Berra inside a whiskey factory vat?" I gasped, alluding to the star *Yankee* catcher.

"If ya' make one more stupid-ass comment like that, I'm gonna' kick your butt good in front of all these pecker-head kids!" Goose Restuccio threatened as the unstable kid gestured his arm around the cafeteria table. "You and Tom-Tom here sound like Minnie Mouse and Tinker Bell havin' the dumbest of dumb-ass conversations."

"I actually thought your joke was pretty good!" Tommy "News" Tomasello remarked while completely ignoring Goose's exaggerated protest. "The book's really pretty neat. It's about a guy named Holden Caulfield who is innocent, immature, gullible, and naïve. Young Holden Caulfield thinks that the world is messed-up, but the misfit finds that the people in the world are basically evil, selfish, conniving, and sinful. They all *think* ..."

"That Holden Caulfield is fucked-up!" Goose interrupted. "I read that friggin' book when I was in fifth-grade. It's a doozy! Have *you* read any good books lately?" Ronald "Goose" Restuccio haughtily asked me, testing the extent of my literacy.

"Well, yes, where I used to live in Levittown, I read D.H. Lawrence's *Lady Chatterley's Lover*. It was super cool and dirty!" I proudly exclaimed.

"J.W., that's exactly what I mean," News excitedly articulated. "Miss Hunter, Mrs. Waldman, and the other English teachers just want us to read benign goody-goody stuff like *Silas Marner* and *Precious Bane*. They're afraid of a little controversy."

"How did you know my name?" I asked News.

"You don't remember, but I was in Mrs. Murphy's third-period history class when ya' stood-up and absurdly answered Vicksburg!" Tommy reminded.

"Well, News, that history class is *ancient history* now. What's happenin' in the world?" I jovially inquired.

"Well, J.W., John H. Reynolds of the University of California estimates that the universe is nearly five-billion-years-old," Tommy Tomasello stated. "His calculation is based on a meteorite found forty-one years ago in Richardton, North Dakota."

"Did Professor Reynolds use a North *Decoder* to find it?" I asked, again paying tribute to my old Levittown friend, Bo Jalonec.

"Yes J.W.," News concurred. "If he hadn't used his North Decoder, it would've been a meteor*wrong* instead of a meteor*right*."

"You two assholes are so fucked-up that ya' deserve each other! I think you two creeps oughta' get married!" Goose complained as the vulgar *student* got-up and hastily moved his tray to an empty cafeteria table.

"What's with him?" I asked News. "He seems anti-social."

"Goose is a spoiled, temperamental, Sicilian brat," Tom-Tom informed. "He's arrogant, distrustful, and has no real friends. G.R. thinks he could buy anyone, including teachers, with his Mafia daddy's loan-sharkin' money."

"Sounds like a kid I knew back in Pennsylvania, Bruno Popeye Messina," I related and shook my head in disgust.

News elaborated that Ronald Goose Restuccio was a malcontent who was resented by nearly everyone in the school. The discipline problem had a brand-new, white, four-seater '60 Thunderbird; made fun of everyone else; possessed a nasty temper, and was very vindictive. Immediately, I also connected Goose's mercurial personality traits to those belonging to Tinker back in Levittown.

Two other kids sat-down and joined our company. "J.W," News said, "I'd like ya' to meet Frankie Arena and Johnny Illiani."

"Lots of Italians in this school," I commented. "Glad to meet you guys." We shook hands, and Frankie told me his nickname was Jives, and Johnny informed me that he was often called Juice.

"Why Jives and Juice?" I asked.

"Because Jives uses a lot of cool slang when the beatnik talks," News explained, "and Juice has all the girls wantin' his sperm."

Johnny Juice Illiani blushed upon hearing News' evaluation of *his* hypothetical sexual prowess. Johnny had lived with the unusual nickname only because others insisted that the stud was a local legend with the Edgewood High girls, who generally went goo-goo over his handsome looks.

"Juice, stop actin' like Squaresville," Jives Arena criticized. "All the kinky chicks are eyeballin' ya' right now. They'd all like to rock and roll in the crib with ya', even the horny babes that are still in *cherry* condition."

"Frankie means virgins," News clarified. "Did you guys know that the musical term rock and roll is really black slang for havin' sex in bed?"

"Yeah," I concurred. "It was invented by a Cleveland disc jockey named Alan Freed. He's broadcastin' out of New York, now."

"I know the background," News affirmed. "Alan Freed used the term to give rock music a non-black image, so that white parents would think it was okay and acceptable. The real funny irony is that rock and roll really means *black sex* in bed, and white parents don't want their lily-white children to have sex at all."

I rubbernecked around the cafeteria and realized that a table of really cute girls was to my right. The chicks were all entranced by Johnny Juice Illiani's presence at my table.

"Who's the dark-skinned girl over there sittin' at the end?" I asked Frankie. "She's a real knockout!"

"That's Joanne Berenato," Jives Arena informed, readjusting the red French beret on his head. "She's a slick chick with a classy chassis. Ya' ain't the first cat that's gone ape over her! I can comprende why you're hot to trot over that radioactive broad. No guy's got dibs on that bitchin' chick. She's Venus's twin sister."

I soon found out that Frankie Jives Arena and Johnny Juice Illiani were close friends and also aspiring actors. The duo was discussing the school's upcoming play competition in March between the sophomore, junior, and senior classes. The seniors were going to have tryouts for a one-act comedy play titled, *There's Gold in Them Dar Hills*."

"J.W., ya' want to try-out for the play?" Jives Arena invited. "It's gonna' be a trip and a half!"

"Yeah," Johnny Juice Illiani verified. "Ya' have the makings of a good *thespian.*"

"I think J.W. prefers being a normal male fightin' simple acne than becomin' a homosexual female," News laughed. "Juice, you say the *queerest* things. I mean, bein' a female homo' is worse than bein' a neuter."

"Well, J.W., think it over," Johnny suggested. "The girls here at Edgewood that aren't *lesbians* love guys that aren't afraid to get-up on stage and do their thing."

"And J.W., there's gonna' be some real cookin' babes tryin' out for the play competition, who are hot to trot to share Cloud 9 with ya'!" Jives convincingly indicated.

I soon learned that Tommy "News" Tomasello's father was a peach farmer; Frankie Jives Arena's dad had a general store in Winslow, and Johnny Juice Illiani had excellent communications skills because his parents were teachers at Overbrook, another area high school. Sal Fabian Midilli, another good-looking stud, soon joined our company. The newcomer had terrific mechanical skills because according to News, "His pop owns a gas/repair station in Waterford on the White Horse Pike. The Flyin' A."

The guys then gave me a brief history of the Edgewood Regional High class of '60. Up until their junior year, the kids had all gone to Overbrook Regional in nearby Lindenwold. Then, Edgewood was constructed, and the students from Atco, Winslow Township, and West Berlin were transferred to Overbrook's recently-constructed sister school, Edgewood High.

"So J.W.," Jives piped-up. "You're about as new here as the rest of us bucks and does are. My cool advice is just stay-away from Ronald Goose Restuccio, or you'll be cruisin' for a bruisin' from most all the dudes in this here country think hole."

I turned-around and glanced at swarthy-skinned Joanne Berenato, while News was irrelevantly lecturing about sixteen-year-old boy wonder Bobbie Fischer, who had recently successfully defended his U.S. Chess Championship in New York City.

"The egghead was probably *jumping* for joy because he finally got something off his *chess,"* I awkwardly joked, as my mind wandered in and out of the table conversation.

"J.W., speaking of chess, I think ya' got your sights on *jumping* Joanne Berenato," Johnny Illiani perceptively observed as Juice observed me craning my neck toward another table.

"J.W., come on over to another cafeteria table before ya' make your feelings too obvious," Juice requested. "I want ya' to meet some of the Reds."

"The Reds? Are they from Cincinnati?" I awkwardly asked as Juice, Johnny, Frankie and I carried our lunch trays to the cafeteria's washing and cleaning waste window.

"No, but I'll give ya' the lowdown later on," Johnny told me. "I guarantee ya', the Reds like peaches, but they aren't exactly *fruits* if ya' know what I mean."

Juice brought me to a table where mostly brawny athletes were exchanging jock anecdotes about the *New Year's Day* college football bowl games. I was introduced to Chickie and Charlie Calabrese, twin brothers, who were district wrestling champions, grappling in the 150 and the 165-pound weight classes. Jack "Hoss" Gregorio, a senior, was seated next to his smaller brother, "Little Joe," an Edgewood junior. The Gregorio brothers were tough offensive guards on the winning Edgewood High football squad.

"I guess Hoss is short for Horse," I respectfully commented.

"Ya' got that right," Johnny Illiani commended. "These two brothers could be professional wrestlers and beat the stuffing out of Gorgeous George and the Butcher, if they wanted to!"

I looked at "Little Joe Gregorio," whom I estimated to be around five-feet-eight and weighing about two-hundred-and-twenty-pounds.

"Are ya' called Little Joe and Hoss after the Cartwright brothers on *Bonanza?"* I curiously asked.

"Yeah," Little Joe confirmed. "And my older brother Hoss, here, is six-three and weighs in at three-fifty. I ain't never gonna' catch-up to that monster!"

Everybody at the cafeteria table laughed and pounded the slate in front of them. That loud raucous behavior got the attention of several observant teachers on lunchroom duty. The keepers of the cafeteria peace then signaled for the athletes to stop the noise by making football referee time-out gestures.

"Hey J.W.," Hoss's voice boomed. "Do ya' know who won the Sugar Bowl over the holidays? I missed that one on TV."

Luckily, News Tomasello had joined our company and was standing directly behind me. The human encyclopedia was ready to provide the exact answer should I falter.

"Mississippi won," I stated. "I think the score was 21-..."

"Twenty-one to zip over Louisiana State," News interrupted. "And Syracuse beat Texas in the Cotton Bowl, 23-14, Georgia put it to Missouri in the Orange Bowl, 14-0, and Washington trounced Wisconsin, 44-8 in the Rose Bowl."

"How do ya' remember all that stuff? I'm deeply impressed!" Hoss Gregorio remarked to News Tomasello as the teen behemoth feigned sincerity while coincidentally showing a mild degree of admiration.

"Tommy News got a camera stored inside his head that allows him to have a photographic mind," Juice humorously explained.

At the time, I couldn't remember the names of all the other jocks seated at the table, but I later would personally know them as full-fledged "Reds". Jim "Guy" Marinella was a strong but average-looking linebacker with a big nose, and then there was Tony Passarella, whose family owned a small peach farm next to the Silver Fox Tavern, across the street from Pete's Market. Two other "Reds", Marty Ransom and Pete Clarke, rounded-out the remaining jocks sitting at the crowded table.

Everyone laughed in response to Johnny Illiani's clever comment about the cerebral camera. I then wanted to discover why the guys at the jock table, and also News Tomasello, were called "Reds", and my mouth was about to ask that question. Without warning, a sudden, very discernible disturbance erupted at a neighboring table.

A black student had sat-down across from Goose Restuccio, who then apparently had verbally insulted the colored kid. The Negro boy stood-up and loudly called Goose a "KKK' racist," and then Ronald Restuccio angrily flipped-over the cafeteria table, and the food from the colored kid's tray splattered all over the tile floor.

"Shut the fuck up, ya' friggin' mool-en-yon!" Restuccio cursed. "One nigger at my table is one nigger too many!"

"I ain't afraid of you dago, even if your Daddy is in the Mafia!" the black kid yelled.

Three teachers scurried-over to quell the heightening altercation. "Now boys, let's just simmer-down. We'll all stroll-down to the main office right now, and straighten this whole thing out," the first instructor ordered.

"Right now, it's three detentions each," the second male teacher related. "Any more words from either of you two, and it'll be certain suspensions for at least a week!" the on-duty monitor barked at the two livid cafeteria gladiators that wanted to maul and cripple each other.

"Illiani, Arena, Tomasello, clean-up this mess on the floor while I escort these two offenders down to the principal's office!" Mr. Andrews, the third teacher on the scene commanded.

Mr. Andrews followed Goose Restuccio and the black kid out of the cafeteria. I bent down and helped News Tomasello turn the cafeteria table right side up. "What's a mool-en-yon?" I wondered and asked.

"It's Italian slang for eggplant!" Tommy disgustedly explained.

Chapter Four

"Cowtail Bar"

Later that night, I learned that Goose Restuccio had been suspended for five days for being the perpetrator of the cafeteria altercation, and that the black kid, Tyrone Davis, had been given a three-day hiatus from school. Goose's outrage was emblematic of the same kind of unbridled racial prejudice I had observed in Levittown with Tinker, Cummings, Popeye Messina, and the fanatical Kamikazes.

Frankie "Jives" Arena confronted me at my locker in the S-Wing (South Wing) between seventh and eighth periods. Before I knew it, I had been double-teamed by Johnny Illiani. It is hard to say "no" to kids in a new school exerting heavy peer pressure to do something.

"J.W.," Jives began his drivel. "Juice and me think the script to the new play is pretty gear, and I know it's gonna' wind-up with us takin' some dolls out to the submarine races once the women dig that we're not from Weirdsville."

"Jives means that if ya' go out for the senior one-act play, the girls in the cast will want to party big time with us," Johnny competently interpreted.

"And none of the chicks tryin' out for the show are grungy, even if ya' check 'em out through Juice's Clark Kent peepers," Frankie agreed while specifically referring to Johnny's thick-rimmed, Buddy Holly-style glasses.

"What do ya' say?" Juice Illiani pressured. "It might turn-out to be a bash and a half."

"Look fellas', I'm used to hangin' out and smokin' weeds with greasers," I argued. "I haven't seen one black leather motorcycle jacket with zippers on the sleeves since I've been here. Where are the car and biker guys?"

"There's a few greasers over in Hammonton," Jives declared, "and the nasty punks put down any boppers they think are cubes."

"Cubes?" I asked in a puzzled voice.

"Yeah, Daddy-o," Jives answered. "Cubes, my amigo, are three dimensional squares. Ya' dig! I hope ya' don't got too much smog in your noggin'! The punk greasers over in Hammonton are the nutcase Ramrodders."

"Come on J.W., what do ya' say? Give the play a try," insisted Johnny.

"Is anybody else goin' to try-out besides you guys?" I wanted nervously to know.

"Yeah, News Tomasello and also Fabian Midilli," Johnny enthusiastically replied.

"It'll be like Cool Incorporated with the five of us Turks gettin' all the boss roles," Frankie Jives Arena maintained.

"What about the jocks?" I inquired.

"They're too stupid to realize that only horny eggheads like us and faggots with big peckers get laid in this school," Jives clarified.

"Well, all right, I'll give it a try," I agreed. "I'll call my folks and tell them I won't be comin' home tonight on the school bus."

"I got my wheels in the non-fink zone of the student parkin' lot," Jives Arena informed, "so I'll speedo ya' to your pad after practice so that ya' can make the home scene with your Neanderthals."

"Jives means he'll drive ya' home after play practice and then ya' can see your parents again," Juice verbally deciphered.

"Alright, count me in. Let's scoot. There's the bell. We're already late to eighth-period," I suggested.

* * * * * * * * * * * * * *

I stayed for play practice with Mrs. Murphy and Miss Hunter doing commendable jobs as the senior one-act play director and co-director. I had never acted on a stage before, but in the final analysis, I managed to earn a six-line part in *There's Gold in Them Dar Hills*. I was far from elated about that, but was more euphoric about Joanne Berenato getting the female lead and with Juice, News, and Sal "Fabian" Midilli getting the top male acting parts.

"What a royal bummer!" Jives Arena vehemently complained. "My only lines are that I gotta' run out on stage and yell, 'You are insane! You are insane!' Then, I cut-out off the platform like the fuzz was haulin' ass after me."

"Look, Jives," News pointed-out at stage left. "Ya' told me you're in this show because ya' wanta' get in thick with some good-lookin' girls, and now you're bitchin' that ya' don't have enough lines. What a freakin' hypocrite!"

"What's a freakin' hypocrite?" Jives demanded to know.

"It's a large box that animal trainers capture a hippopotamus in," I offered.

"J.W., ya' shoulda' been an ant colony 'cause ya' really know how to bug people," Jives criticized. "Ya' oughta' piss your brains out the next time ya' drink a six pack of brew."

"Let's go over to Cowtail Bar and celebrate our success at getting parts," Sal "Fabian" Midilli suggested. "That's the swiftest teen place around."

"Cowtail Bar?" I asked. "Will I get carded?"

"Naaa, it's a boss ice cream joint that fences shakes and sundaes for legit' money," Jives indicated. "Ya' know," Frankie Arena then said to Sal Midilli, "your mug looks more like Bobby Rydell's friggin' face than it does like Fabian's."

Fabian was not too enthralled with Frankie's critical opinion. "Jives, you're so pretty ya' could be Miss America if ya' just let your raunchy wig grow-down to your shoulders," Sal replied.

The five of us left the Edgewood High Auditorium and strolled over to the student parking lot, where we piled into Jives Arena's '57 black and white Dodge Coronet. Juice and News sat in the front, with Frankie and then Sal parking their buttocks in the back alongside me.

"Tell me more about this Cowtail Bar? Do they serve beer to snortin' bulls there?" I joked.

"No," Johnny began explaining. "Goose once said it's a front-name for an animal whorehouse where faggots screw Holsteins when the fairies run out of sheep!"

"That sounds like somethin' that *that* friggin' hiney-biter Restuccio would say," admitted Sal from his position seated behind the slang-talking driver.

"Goose ain't playin' with a full deck," Juice Illiani observed and opined, "and he's trouble with a capital T. The insane jerk is toxic. Avoid him like the bubonic plague."

"Johnny's right about Goose bein' warped," Jives concurred as the driver finally fired-up the engine. "Goose gets frosted over the smallest things, and then wants to give the nearest guy a knuckle sandwich after insulting *him* with some Sicilian pig lingo."

"Goose Restuccio once told me somethin' funny," Sal Fabian Midilli stated in defense of the totally weird kid.

"What's that?" I asked.

"Once I was comin' out of a stall in the M-Wing Boys Lavatory when the wise-ass said that I shouldn't feel bad because even President Eisenhower, Vice President Nixon, and Queen Elizabeth have to wipe their rear-ends after takin' a crap," Midilli related.

"That is sort of funny," News remarked and chuckled. "Not genuinely humorous, but sort of."

"Yeah," Fabian Midilli continued, "and then Goose proceeded to say that maybe he was wrong about Queen Elizabeth because she probably has seven servants and one Prime Minister standin' there to wipe her regal butt for her."

"That's even more into funny territory," News laughed.

"Ya' guys know who the tallest President is?" I asked while remembering something that Bo Jalonec once shared.

"No!" the other four guys yelled in unison.

"President Eisen*tower!"* He's Nick's son!" I finished.

Everyone else jeered in sheer admiration in response to my silly plagiarism of Jokes Jalonec's patented material. "You're a born- again jerk-off if I've ever seen one!" Jives shouted-out, looking in the rear-view mirror. "You and Goose Restuccio must have had the same ancestors somewhere back in the Stone Age, which really rocked," the driver added.

News Tomasello then said something rather philosophical. "I don't like guys that curse too much. Cursin' all the time is really a basic sign of insecurity."

"Tell Goose Restuccio that comment and you'll wind-up in the morgue behind Wooster's Funeral Home," Sal Midilli predicted.

Jives Arena finally pulled his wheels out of the Edgewood High student parking area and onto Coopers Folly Road, soon heading towards the White Horse Pike. The jargon-master made a left at Wooster's Mortuary, passed through *Route 30* in Atco, and then turned right at *Route 73,* just past the Atco Drive-in.

"That's the local passion pit," Sal Midilli told me. "More guys get laid there than in all of the bordellos and flea' bag hotels in Philly' and Atlantic City combined."

"Yeah," chimed-in Jives. "If you're goin' to get laid anywhere, be sure to go to the Atco Drive-in. Admission is only a greenback a carload, and for two buckeroos, a sleazy hooker is usually supplied to a Dodge Coronet full of lucky, horny jerk-offs like us."

News Tomasello got the group into a more serious mode when the verbal newsreel began discussing how President Dwight D. Eisenhower stated that the prospect of improved East-West relations was somewhat better because of "recent Soviet deportment".

"What the frig' is deportment?" Jives Arena asked as he sped around the *Route 73* Berlin Circle onto *Route 561*.

"It's a store that sells a little bit of everything," I injected. "A deportment store!"

"Ha ha!" News chortled. "Deportment is on your damned report card. It means 'conduct'. I think I'm gonna' write an article about that creative word in the *Aquilla*."

"The *Aquilla?* What on earth is that?" I wondered and mentioned aloud. "Sounds like a porcupine!"

"It's Latin for eagle," News Tomasello related. "And it's the name of the school newspaper. I'm Editor-in-Chief. It's called *Aquilla* because the Edgewood mascot is an eagle. Our football team is called the Edgewood Eagles."

"When ya' get older, change your last name to *Britannica* and write your own damned encyclopedia," Juice Illiani recommended to Tommy News. "You're more borin' than a family of hyperactive groundhogs on February 2nd."

On the final leg to Cowtail Bar the guys gave me the lowdown on "the Reds". The members were the sons of peach farmers, stretching from the area around Edgewood High seven-miles east all the way past the west side of Hammonton. News Tomasello was the only Red' passenger riding in Jives' car.

"News, ya' oughta' sit in front of the windshield so ya' could be Little *Red* Riding *Hood,"* Juice yelled and laughed.

"You should've been an enema 'cause you're a real pain in the ass," Tommy Tomasello countered, feigning false anger. "You're about as funny as the Boston Massacre times Hitler's Holocaust to the third power."

"Who else from Edgewood is in the Reds?" I asked Tommy.

"Well, there's Jack "Hoss" Gregorio and his brother Little Joe; Guy "Moose" Marinella; Charlie and Chickie Calabrese; Tony Passarella; Marty Ransom, and Pete Clarke from Edgewood. And some guys from St. Joe's over in Hammonton like Dave "Herc" Juliano; Denny "Baker" Harrison; Jake Maccarella, and Ollie "Balls" Giordano."

"I guess 'Herc' is short for Hercules. and 'Balls' means that the guy is basically crazy and will try anything," I surmised and stated.

"You guessed right on the money," Sal Midilli concurred. "And the enemy of the Reds are the Blues, who incidentally, all go to Hammonton High," News added to the strange conversation. "They're the sons of blueberry farmers on the east side of Hammonton. *Route 206* marks the boundary between sandy blueberry soil to the east of the town, and dark peach soil to the highway's west."

I asked if the Reds and the Blues had a longtime feud going. News informed me that the Reds and the Blues' parents had been bitter enemies ever since *World War II.* The hostile vendetta between the peach and blueberry farmers was two full decades old. "In the late forties and fifties, peaches were the "Queen of Fruit" in the Hammonton area, but after the *Korean War,* blueberries were giving freestones very serious market competition."

"Does somebody's father have to be a peach farmer in order to become a Red?" I asked News.

"No. If ya' have any relatives that are peach farmers, let's say uncles, grandfathers or cousins," Tommy News communicated, "then ya' can join. Also, since *you* are gonna' sell peaches at your farm market, you're eligible, too."

"My grandfather was a peach farmer," Sal Midilli acknowledged.

"My Uncle Jim and Jives's cousin Al over in Waterford are peach farmers, too," Juice clarified and revealed. "Basically, everyone sittin' in this car is eligible."

Jives Arena turned the wheel of his black and white Dodge Coronet off *Route 561,* and a half-mile down a two-lane highway pulled into the popular Cowtail Bar parking lot. The place was really hopping with teenagers representing different high schools from within a fifteen-mile radius.

A pretty blonde hostess escorted us to our round "table for five" inside a side dining room that led to a third snack bar area. Everything on the menu had a minimum of three ice cream scoops.

"Wow, look at the 'Kitchen Sink'!" I marveled and exclaimed as I examined the extensive dessert menu. "It has twelve scoops of ice cream and a half-pound of hot fudge, all topped with a pyramid of whipped cream and maraschino cherries."

"Yeah. Hoss Gregorio and Moose Marinella from Edgewood and Herc Juliano from St. Joe's once had an eatin' contest here. The gluttons each ordered Kitchen Sinks," News reported.

"What happened? Who won?" I curiously asked.

"Nobody," Tommy News answered. "Because it all ended in a three-way tie. Each of those guys must have more intestines than a large bull elephant. It was unbelievable!"

"Their English teachers must like their colons and semi-colons," I commented, as everyone else seated at the Cow Tail Bar table laughed after Jives loudly farted.

I ordered a strawberry sundae; Juice wanted a Polar Cocktail Delite; Sal selected a super-duper banana split; News decided on three dips of spumoni, and Jives preferred having "a giant root beer *float* that's not gaseous, and not left-over from last year's Hammonton Halloween Parade".

News told a thoroughly bored audience how Dolph Schayes of the Syracuse Nationals NBA team had just become the first professional basketball player to score fifteen-thousand points. Seeing that none of us had been enamored with his terrible monologue, Tommy next told us all about the *Trieste.* It was a bathyscaphe navigated by Lieutenant Donald Walsh, USN, and the fantastic diving apparatus had established a depth record of twenty-four-thousand-feet on January 7th in the Pacific Mariana Trench, sixty-miles off the Guam coast.

"News, I'd be more interested in your story if that *naughty-cal* turkey was doin' some happy muff divin' instead of deep sea divin'!" Jives Arena lamented. "Then, the goin-south dude wouldn't wanta' come-up for air 'cause the lucky stiff wouldn't surface until he had the *hole* problem licked."

"Now your dirty talk is soundin' a little too much like Goose," Johnny Illiani criticized. "But Jives, I gotta' admit. I'm getting' half a hard-on just thinkin' about goin' south on a babe."

Just then four mean-looking wise-guys, dressed in blue denim jackets and blue denim jeans, passed from the rear snack room and ambled through our side dining area. One of them stopped beside our table, and recognizing one of us, deliberately flicked his left index finger against Tommy Tomasello's right earlobe. "Hey News, you freakin' Red, make sure none of these four pussies sittin' with ya' become Reds, too! Ya' dig Punk!"

The four "tuff" looking characters then sauntered their way to the cashier, paid their bill, and slowly exited the ice cream establishment, rather proud of their most recent put down.

"What was that all about?" I inquired.

"Those four jerks are Blues from Hammonton High," News explained, rubbing his abused earlobe. "The bullies were tryin' to intimidate and humiliate me in front of my friends. And ya' wanta' know somethin', it worked!"

"What're their names?" I asked.

Tommy told us that the guy who had flicked his finger against *his* ear was Gabe Gillette, whose father owned Sandy Soil Blueberry Company on Weymouth Road, southeast of Hammonton, which was the biggest cultivated blueberry plantation in the United States. "The other three jerks were Dan Bertino, also known as 'the Hammer', Arty 'Butch' Lanza, and the huge guy was Paul 'Ox' Narducci. 'Ox' Narducci and 'Hoss' Gregorio hate one another," News related.

"If Hoss and Ox ever fought," Juice interrupted, "it would be like two Tyrannosaurus Rexes dukin' it out to the death inside a prehistoric tar pit!"

It all was a very familiar scenario to me, and I didn't savor it one iota. The Blues acted just like the Kamikazes had conducted themselves back in Levittown. The swagger, the cockiness, the lousy attitude, and the desire to intimidate and hurt others whom they resented were all quite evident in the Blues' public demeanor.

Sal Midilli and News filled us in on the "teen fruit war" that had been escalating around Hammonton for the previous ten-years. "Fabian" regretted that the Blues were more organized and much more aggressive than the docile Reds were.

"I've seen this scene all before, back in Levittown, with the warring Kamikaze and the Diablos greaser gangs," I revealed. "And I know exactly what has to be done in order to defeat the Blues, if I have to get involved and act."

"What needs to be done?" News asked.

"Well, the first thing is that *your* gang needs some sort of common uniform, like the Diablos had black leather jackets, blue denim jeans, and engineer boots," I suggested. "Notice that the Blues all wear the same blue denim jackets. Ya' gotta' make a statement, and let everybody know ya' aren't afraid to act as one machine against 'em, if ya' have to."

"The Reds need new threads!" Jives jokingly rhymed.

I then had a relevant idea. I proposed that the Reds all wear red zip-up jackets like the one worn by James Dean in the movie *Rebel without a Cause*. Sal and the others thought that my recommendation was excellent.

"That's de-luxe! Totally supreme!" Jives exclaimed. "It's bosser than boss. It's el cool! We'll throw the *Kitchen Sink* at the weirdo coneheads!"

"I saw red jackets like that James Dean one over at the Berlin Auction," Juice related. "And they only cost fifteen bucks each!"

"Great," News readily agreed. "I'll bring it up with all the Red guys tomorrow in the cafeteria. I'm sure they'll all wanta' go for it."

The cute brunette waitress brought over our bill, so I figured I would impress my new friends by impersonating Bo Jalonec.

"Doll, do you know where Cleopatra kept all of her money?" I asked the waitress.

"In the banks of the Nile!" the attractive honey responded.

"Shot down without a *'chute* on your back!" Jives Arena chided.

Everyone laughed at my general incompetence, as the pert brunette wiggled her very captivating fanny through the swinging doors, heading back into the Cowtail Bar kitchen. We all chipped-in our share of the bill, left an appropriate tip, and paid our group check at the cashier.

When the five of us stepped outside and walked over to Jives' '57 Dodge Coronet, we were in for a shock. All four tires had been deflated. A note had been conveniently placed under the right windshield wiper. I removed the message and read its threatening content out loud.

News,

Hi Zitface! Tell your four dorky pals they'd better not join the Reds. Better dead than Red!

The Blues

"Don't worry, I'll call my Pop, and he'll come-out from his gas station with an air compressor," Sal said to Frankie Arena.

"Jives, these tires look like they've just been deflated from the valves. They haven't been slashed with switchblades," News observed and stated. "I'm sorry, Man. I feel responsible for this happenin' to you."

"I'm not gonna' have a cow over this," Jives answered outside the Cowtail Bar, "because now that it's happened, I really wanta' join the Reds to enjoy some sweet revenge."

"Me, too!" Sal "Fabian" Midilli chimed-in. "I need some adventure in my dull life."

"Me, too!" Juice Illiani asserted. "Count me in!"

All four fellas' then stared in my direction. The pale moonlight made all of their facial features very visible. My conscious mind felt the weight of their intense scrutiny. My vulnerable ego felt their peer pressure.

"Me, too!" I reluctantly volunteered.

Chapter Five

"Downtown Hammonton"

Downtown Hammonton hadn't changed much since the late 1940s. Dad was away in Europe going up against Hitler's minions, so Mom would take me onto Bellevue Avenue every Friday night to do shopping. During the daytime, Monday to Saturday, my mother would faithfully wait for the daily mail to see if a letter from France or from Germany would be forthcoming. Many American kids grew up in the mid-'40s without fathers (that were in the military) around to give them guidance and discipline. So, like many other young boys during that decade, I was more exposed to female nurturing than to male naturing.

The town's early claims to fame were having presidential candidate Teddy Roosevelt's campaign train halt for a whistle stop speech, and having noted anthropologist Margaret Mead, living on Fairview Avenue during her younger days, where the researcher studied the cultural adaptations of Italian immigrants. Another important event in the town's history was when acclaimed virtuoso John Phillip Sousa and his famous touring band gave a sit-down concert for local citizens at the Hammonton Lake Pavilion.

I remember that late '40s and early '50s Bellevue Avenue was crowded with enthusiastic shoppers. There were soda fountains all over the main street. Every drug store, five and ten, and luncheonette had one. I recall Vega's Drugs on the corner of Third and Bellevue, Godfrey's Drug Store at Bellevue and Egg Harbor Road, Kern's Drugs at 2nd and Bellevue, J.J. Newberry's and Joanne's Restaurant on the main drag all having splendid soda fountains.

Grandpa Tony spoiled me rotten by taking a young J.W. to see the 4 a.m. freight train rumble past the intersection of Fairview Avenue and Egg Harbor Road, next to Vet's Bakery. My biological clock would wake me up at 3:30 in the morning, and then I would bawl and throw a tantrum until Grandpa put me in his black stake-body truck and transported me to the *Pennsylvania Railroad* tracks to see the locomotive, the counted tanker and boxcars, and finally the caboose.

When Dad returned from overseas, the war survivor opened his small gas station/repair shop next to the little white bungalow, which was adjacent to Square Deal Farm Market. One day after supper, Dad sent me on an errand. I had to fetch a bill of sale from his office' desk inside the garage. I left the building, closing the garage door very hard, and the descending object smashed-down on my left foot, crushing my big toe. I was afraid to tell Pop of the catastrophe, but since the pain was so excruciating, I finally had to divulge my self-inflicted injury.

Dad, who had seen all kinds of dead mutilated corpses in Nazi Germany, was horrified. He rushed me to Dr. Frazier Elliott's Office on Packard Street, two blocks from the center of Hammonton. Dr. Elliott was a remarkable man who inspected my ugly wound without batting an eyelash. Then, the general practitioner administered a needle and proceeded to cut the entire toenail off my big toe as if he were casually peeling a potato. Even at age ten, I had to admire the fine, dedicated small-town doctor who settled me down, calmly allayed my fears, and kept his cool under very dire circumstances.

Saturday afternoons, the Rivoli Theater at Bellevue and Third, across the street from Vegas Drugs, had matinee movies. I still vividly recollect seeing *King Kong*, *Mighty Joe Young*, *The Beast from 20,000 Fathoms, The Creature from the Black Lagoon,* and *The Day the Earth Stood Still* at the downtown movie house with St. Joseph school friends. The theater boasted an ornate ceiling with crystal chandeliers that made it a showplace for the proud, small town in the '40s and early '50s.

Most '40s and '50s businesses were little mom and pop operations like Rescignio's candy store across Third Street from St. Joseph School, and like Miller's Family Department Store on Bellevue Avenue. Then, highway custard stands began replacing main street soda fountains, and malls started sprouting-up, knocking places like Miller's Department Store and Rescignio's Candy out of business. Finally, in the early '60s, the popularity of a new medium, television, led to the demise of the glorious Rivoli Theater.

In the late forties and early fifties, Grandpa Tony would take me over to the Sons of Italy Garibaldi Lodge on North Third Street and park me on a barstool to drink all of the *Cokes* and eat all of the pretzels and potato chips I wanted. Gramps would then play an Italian fingers game with some old cronies, and if Grandpa had had a dispute with Grandma Annie, the fingers contest expert was determined to win the nightly game. After becoming victorious, Gramps would become the Capa, or Boss, and appoint a Lieutenant. Everyone else who had lost in the fingers game would have to watch Grandpa drink eleven beers on the table (paid for by the losers), and then appoint his lucky Lieutenant to drink the twelfth.

Many Saturday nights, Grandpa Tony would arrive back home drunk, and then tripped and stumbled in the dark over living room furniture on his way upstairs to bed. Later in life, his bad case of diabetes had been compounded, which eventually led to wheelchair confinement. Antonio's excessive drinking and need to be the "beer Capa", along with the nasty-looking bruises on his legs didn't help his condition any. His legs had to be amputated up to his knees.

Downtown Hammonton in 1960 was very similar to the way Bellevue Avenue had appeared in the early '50s. On Friday and Saturday Nights, the Blues from Hammonton High School hung-out on their side of town in front of Vegas's Drugs and Augie's Sub Shop and Hamburger Paradise. And across the street, the Reds from St. Joe's and from Edgewood High usually congregated in front of the Rivoli Theater. Bellevue Avenue acted as sort of a demilitarized zone separating the two rival factions. The fearsome Ramrodders greaser gang hung-out in front of the Central Café on Egg Harbor Road, three blocks away.

Certain business establishments were neutral territory, where all three teen groups would occasionally share space. Those businesses were the Gem Burger Bar on Central Avenue, a block west of Hammonton High School, DiDonato's Bowling Alleys and Royale Crown Custard Stand on the White Horse Pike, both being on the Atlantic City side of Hammonton.

* * * * * * * * * * * *

The last cold Saturday morning in January of 1960, News Tomasello drove his dad's red and white '57 Ford Fairlane to my place. Tommy had agreed to take me twelve-miles west down the White Horse Pike to Berlin to obtain my New Jersey driver's license. I had a little trouble making the K-turn, but I had a very patient middle-age inspector, who told me to attempt the maneuver one more time. "I like ya', 'cause you seem to be a polite kid," the man said as the inspector certified me. "I can't stand wise guys and punk greaser troublemakers," the evaluator personally confided.

News drove me back to Hammonton, and I was elated with my most recent success.

"Ya' know, Tommy," I began. "I drove my friends all over Bucks County near Levittown, and all over Philly' for two whole years, all without a license. Now, at last, I'm finally legal."

"Glad I could help ya' out," my amiable new friend replied. "Sounds like ya' got more balls than a bowling alley. You can really get rollin' now."

Tommy pulled into the Pete's Market gravel driveway, and Pop and Mom were busy painting the interior kitchen area of their new business, getting ready to open it in April.

"How'd you make out?" Dad asked me.

"Great! I passed. I'll be getting my permanent license in the mail in two weeks. Until then, I have this temporary one," I replied.

"Now you'll be able to drive the truck to the new Food Distribution Center in South Philly' and pick up fruit and produce," Dad happily observed and predicted. "That'll be a big help to me. Thanks, Tommy, for taking my son over to Motor Vehicles."

"My pleasure," News politely acknowledged. "Your son and me are gonna' be great friends."

"What happened to Dock Street?" I asked Pop.

"All of the commission houses are movin' into the new Food Distribution Center in South Philly', just off of the *Walt Whitman Bridge*," Dad informed. "Soon, Dock Street will be nothin' more than a fond memory of where Grand-pop used to take you when you were only knee-high to a grasshopper."

Just then, a most unexpected thing happened. Ronald Goose Restuccio pulled onto the property in his immaculate, white '60 Ford Thunderbird. The new arrival pushed-down the power window button and said, "Hi guys! Wanna' go for a ride. I gotta' collect some money from my gumball machine route, and then restock plenty of gumballs. Come along, and I'll treat both ya' turkeys to hoagies and *Cokes.* You guys look like ya' both need a good Italian hoagie with hot peppers."

"Who's that?" Dad asked me.

"Oh, a kid I know from Edgewood. He's got a bubble gum machine route and wants us to help him empty money out and put new gum balls inside," I stated as I picked-up on what Goose had said during his introductory remarks.

"Okay, you can go along, but only if ya' learn something new about business from that young man," Dad asserted. "But you'll have to spend all day tomorrow helpin' your mother and me get the market ready for opening day. Thanks again Tommy for being a Good Samaritan."

News and I hopped into the back seat, because we finally noticed Juice Illiani sitting on the front passenger side of the magnificent four-seater T-Bird. Goose raised the power window of his luxury street machine, and then took-off rather gingerly out of the Pete's Market gravel driveway.

"Ya' really got a gum ball machine route?" I asked.

"Shut the fuck up!" Goose snapped back. "I'll talk to ya' after we listen to my own personal National Anthem, 'Rock Around the Clock'. Even though it's old, it's still my favorite song!" The driver turned-up the radio's volume, and we all had to endure a very loud rendition of the still-popular tune by Bill Haley and the Comets.

When the first official 1954 rock and roll song finally ended, the driver lowered the volume to allow normal conversation to transpire. There was a short void where nothing was said.

"J.W., I just finished reading *Ben-Hur* by Lew Wallace and *The Scarlet Letter* by Nathaniel Hawthorne," News related, breaking the silent tension in the T-bird. "Ya' read any good books lately?"

I perceived Tommy's inquiry as an opportunity to mimic my old Levittown pal, Bo Jalonec. "Yeah. I just finished reading the *Diarrhea of Anne Frank,* which really stunk all the way to high heaven. Now I'm readin' *Cellophane Bathing Suit* by Seymour Hair, *The Cat's Revenge* by Claude Balls, and *Old Age Sex* by Jerry Attricks."

Even Goose's face had a smirk on it as the driver glanced-back at me in the rearview mirror. "I guess ya' also went to the movies and saw the *Beast from 20,000 Phantoms,* and *The Incredible Man's Shrinking Dick,* too*!"* Goose laughed while somewhat impressing me by making a pair of rather clever word substitutions.

Volatile Ronald Restuccio soon stopped his immaculate T-Bird in front of Vet's Bakery. A minute elapsed, and then the four of us stepped inside the glass doors. Restuccio got out a key from his shirt pocket and showed us how he emptied nickels into a heavy linen money sack, which the entrepreneur had carried into the establishment. Goose observed that the gumball machine was still over half-full, so the devious kid didn't have to open his trunk and get a new supply for the bakery location.

"J.W., how much does your old man make?" Ronald Restuccio asked.

"A little over five-thousand bucks a year," I proudly exhorted. "But after we pay off Grandpa Tony and Aunt Marie, who lent us money, he'll make at least another five-thousand from the market."

"How much did your pop pay for Pete's Market and the house?" Juice inquired.

"Thirty-thousand smackers, quite a steal!" I added. "Grandpa lent us ten-thousand; Aunt Marie ten-thousand, and Pop had the third ten-thousand saved from the house we sold in Levittown."

"J.W., that's chicken feed!" Goose gruffly countered. "Ya' can make more money with simple-ass nickels than ya' can with dollars. Ya' see these stupid-ass gum ball machines everywhere, don't ya'?"

Goose's three listeners all nodded our heads in tacit agreement out of fear of how Restuccio would react if we didn't comply. We apprehensively waited for the remainder of his lecture.

"Well, junior jerk-offs. I'm just a seventeen-year-old punk, and I already make over twenty-five thousand bucks doin' my asshole gumball route. My father set me up in this business, 'cause my old man wants me to be legitimate; learn how to launder bad money into good dough, and then do loan sharkin' on the side like him."

The four of us re-entered the White T-Bird and repeated the gumball machine emptying process at the Garibaldi Sons of Italy Lodge on North Third Street. Several Blues were in the back room playing poker, but the rich kids seemed to ignore us after the studs observed the business nature of our activity. The Sons of Italy machine required a refill, so I was assigned to go-out and get fresh bags of gumballs from cardboard boxes situated inside the white T-Bird's trunk.

"Here're the keys! Don't steal my wheels and drive to Siberia!" Goose deliberately hollered loud enough for the Blues in the adjoining room to hear him as the take-charge guy.

The four of us finally left the premises, and Restuccio drove his three disciples around metropolitan downtown Hammonton. We efficiently cleaned-out nickels and added gumballs to machines at Vega's Drugs, at Augie's Subshop Luncheonette and Hamburger Paradise, at Miller's Department Store, at J.J. Newberry's Five and Ten, at Godfrey's Drugs, at the Central Café, and at Dan's Town Stationery/Record Store.

"You guys getting hungry?" Restuccio asked.

"Getting Hungary is better than getting Austria!" I wisely answered.

"How many brain tumors do you have?" Goose shouted at me. "When I ask a serious question, I fuckin' want a serious answer! How about you, Juice?"

"I sure am famished," Johnny replied. "When do we eat?"

"I gotta' make one more stop at the Palace Diner over on the Black Horse Pike to re-supply a couple of machines that are almost empty," Goose informed. "I'll treat you three imbeciles to dinner after we get there."

The T-Bird traveled east from the center of town down Egg Harbor Road to the amber blinking traffic signal at Weymouth Road. Goose turned right at Morano's Bag Supply Company, and proceeded south along the Atlantic County country road that wove in a serpentine path through potentially hostile blueberry territory.

"Hey Goose, isn't this the road that Gabe Gillette's farm is on?" Juice worriedly asked.

"Yeah. I saw that rich asshole sittin' in the back room over at the Sons of Italy playin' cards with Ox Narducci, Butch Lanza, and Hammer Bertino. Those dick-head Hammonton High creeps are enough to ruin anybody's friggin' day!" the crude talking driver maintained. "Just the sight of 'em makes me wanta' puke my pancreas out."

"Why don't ya' like 'em?" I asked. "Have they hurt anybody ya' know?"

"Because the fact that those guys are Blues from Hammonton," Johnny injected, "and the HHS Blue Devils hate Reds that go to Edgewood and to St. Joe's. Don't be surprised if the jerks follow our asses and then try sendin' us to the emergency room at Atlantic City Hospital by running us off the road."

The white T-Bird followed Weymouth Road along the front of Gabe Gillette's family's massive and impressive thousand-acre blueberry plantation.

I remembered something Bo Jalonec once said when Carnie had driven Jokes and me past a similar blueberry farm on *Route 322* on the way to Atlantic City back in early September of '59. "Wow! I haven't seen so many bushes since a thousand naked girls chased me through the Levittown Shopping Center, because the dolls wanted to rip my birthday suit off my naked bod'!"

Even Goose thought my silly remark to be funny. "J.W. where do ya' come-up with this dumb shit ya' always seem to say? You're fucked-up, but I really mean to say that you are kind of fucked-up in a pretty cool way."

News and Juice hardily laughed in reaction to my oral description of *bushes* while the T-bird was passing by the enormous blueberry farm, and also in response to Ronald Restuccio's commentary about his appreciation of my 'secret' Bo Jalonec sense of humor.

I took a moment to inspect the back of Goose's head, which had an elliptical shape that made me imagine that his noggin looked like a comic Charlie Brown cartoon character. Goose's mouth slanted down on the left side of his face, but I dared not ask the freakish-looking driver if he had ever had some kind of debilitating palsy, or neurological childhood disease.

"Watch out for that truck!" Juice cautioned and pointed from the front passenger side. "It's gonna' pull-out in front of us from Gillette's packing house."

Goose vigorously blew his shrill horn and the two-ton farm transportation vehicle halted in its tracks. The peeved young driver gave us the proverbial middle finger as the T-Bird swiftly sped by.

"That's Marty Gillette, Gabe's younger brother drivin' that rig," Goose reported. "He's a sly bastard just like his older brother is. A bitchin' bastard at that! Hey News," Restuccio continued, "I wanta' forget about Gillette and his brother. Tell us what's happenin' in the freakin' world. Is it more fucked up than it was yesterday?"

News told us that there was a giant Payola scandal brewing in the Congressional Hearings that were going on in Washington. Prominent

DJs like Alan Freed and Dick Clark were soon to be interrogated by various legislative committees about the unethical practice of record companies giving radio and TV disc jockeys money to play *their* 45 rpm platters on the air.

"The government plans to give a five-hundred-dollar fine and a year in prison to any DJ broadcaster caught taking Payola," News related. "That's it in a nutshell."

Here was another chance for me to imitate my former idol, Bo Jalonec. "Broadcasters!" I ranted in false exaggerated fury. "How far could a *broad* caster throw a chick wearin' a bikini in the air? This country really needs more *broad* jumpers, and less *broad* casters. Then, more babes will become pregnant because of more rapes being committed by horny guys."

"Ya' know, J.W.," News said, "for once Goose is right. You *are* entirely screwed-up, but screwed-up in a pretty neat way. I'll be glad to sponsor you, Fabian, and Juice into the Reds. Hey Goose, ya' wanna' join, too!"

"Naaaa, News. Those blueberry fuckheads wouldn't dare do anything to me, or I'd have their dicks cut-off and sent to Mexico to be hung in butcher' shops alongside dead dogs and cats!"

"Goose, ya' sound tough, just like Marlon Branflakes sounded in that movie *On the Waterfront,"* I joked.

Everyone laughed, including Ronald Goose Restuccio. We stopped at a light at Weymouth Road and the Black Horse Pike, *Route 322.* The signal changed to green, and next, Goose pulled into the Palace Diner, which was a quarter-mile down the highway on the right. We first cleaned-out the nickels from the three gumball-machines; added new merchandise from the expensive car's trunk, and then locked the heavy linen moneybags, filled with hundreds of five-cent coins, inside the T-Bird's rear compartment.

A busy high school waitress paced over to take our special orders. Goose preferred having a small pizza listed on the paper menu; Juice a hamburger, and News a meatball sandwich.

"And Handsome, how about you?" the pretty waitress winked in my direction.

"Give me a *snake* sandwich with *marijuana* sauce," I said while remembering a line used by a former Levittown friend.

"I think he means a steak sandwich with marinara sauce," News clarified for the somewhat-bewildered honey. Everyone wildly laughed at my witty order. Then, we all requested large *Pepsi Colas,* and the pretty auburn-hair waitress stepped into the kitchen to place our orders.

"That was alright," Johnny assessed, referring to my original imaginative order. Very novel; almost creative!" my new friend sarcastically complimented.

"Usually, I order a cheese furburger with brunette pubes, but I figured we're already *eating out,"* I remarked, seeking the group's favor and acceptance.

"J.W., have you ever seriously considered suicide?" Juice joshed. "You'd better, 'cause the three of us are presently seriously considerin' committin' homicide."

A Palace Diner patron dropped a quarter into the jukebox slot and selected five Elvis Presley' hit songs, "Don't Be Cruel", "Hound Dog", "Teddy Bear", Heartbreak Hotel", and "Jailhouse Rock". News was inspired to ask me a pertinent question in the middle of "Hound Dog".

"J.W., what do ya' think of Elvis being drafted into the Army?" Tommy asked. "Isn't that the pits?"

"It's all a lousy government plot. That J. Edgar Hoover bureaucrat is out to destroy Rock and Roll," I stated with an air of authority.

"Why's that?" Juice Illiani inquired.

"Because J. Edgar and his right-wing FBI think that Rock and Roll is causin' juvenile delinquency and makin' white kids rebel against their parents," I elaborated.

"But why?" asked a very interested Goose Restuccio. "Music ain't fuckin' hurtin' nobody!"

I then thought about what my pal Carnie had once told me back in Levittown. "Because lots of black singers like Little Richard, Chuck Berry, and Fats Domino are getting rich, and powerful white people in the country don't like that goin' on," I emphatically remarked.

"And," News interrupted, "I read in the papers where parents don't like their kids being influenced by black rhythm and blues, and so DJ Alan Freed invented a new term for Rhythm and Blues, ..."

"Rock and Roll!" everyone yelled in unison.

"And so," I continued with my narrative, "*we'* can't trust the government that's tryin' to destroy *our* way of life. Elvis was drafted because the Washington politicians figured that if they got rid of 'The King', then Rock and Roll would disappear forever."

"Rock and Roll is here to stay, and it will never die!" exclaimed Juice, as the group's orator intentionally quoted lyrics from the '50s classic song by Danny and the Juniors.

The petite, cute Palace Diner waitress brought us our orders and being in a hurry, the big-breasted vixen got the meals a little mixed up. "I'm sorry!" she apologized.

"That's alright, Doll!" I aptly declared. "I've pulled a few *boners* in my life, too!" I stupidly finished, as I made a naughty jerking gesture with my right hand. There was a general, genuine laugh, which luckily included Goose and the slightly-embarrassed waitress.

"How do ya' think of this dumb shit so fast?" Goose wanted to know. 'Do ya' have worms for brains?"

"It just comes naturally like sperm fluid always does," I answered in tribute to my memory of Bo Jalonec.

The guys enjoyed our meals, and then Goose paid our modest dinner bills. "Hey, Honey," the distorted-face patron yelled to the cute waitress. "I'll give ya' a ten-dollar tip if ya' kiss me on the mouth for ten-seconds."

I could tell that the waitress was quite confused by the bold remark, but since Ronald Restuccio was a regular visitor to Palace Diner, the well-endowed broad came over and reluctantly obliged. I felt sorry for her, because Goose had been so rude and crude, and also because the cretin wasn't the most handsome male in the world with the best-looking mouth. Somehow, the accommodating waitress managed to overcome her sensitivity and endure the horrible ten-second experience. "Okay, Doll. Here's a ten-dollar tip for five-dollar's-worth of food. Don't spend the *Hamilton* all at one place," the ugly speaker stipulated.

"Thank you so much!" the blushing girl exclaimed in disbelief. "This is the biggest tip I've ever gotten!" the excited doll exclaimed in sheer astonishment.

It was fairly obvious that Goose Restuccio thought that money could buy anything, including love, affection, and loyalty. It was a convenient solution and substitution for the more important things in life, things that Goose often adroitly avoided and shunned.

The four of us then stepped-over to the Snafu pinball machine to waste three-dollars-worth of Restuccio's coveted nickels. We were preoccupied for at least an hour-and-a-half when the "carry out" phone rang on the main counter.

"Hey, Goose," the Palace Diner owner yelled. "Some guy wants to talk to ya'."

"Hello. Yes, this is Goose."

"Goose, what song by Guy Mitchell went to number two on the charts in 1956?" a furtive voice asked, speaking through a handkerchief into the telephone.

Hey, J.W.," Restuccio haughtily called across the near-empty restaurant. "What song by Guy Mitchell went to number two on the charts in 1956?"

"Ahhhh, yes. 'S*inging the Blues',"* I recollected and yelled.

"*Singing the Blues,* Shit-head!" Goose hollered to the anonymous caller into the telephone.

"Well Asshole, just forget the singing part, and only remember *the Blues*. Ya' got that!" the phantom voice articulated.

"Hey, who the hell is this? What's your fuckin' name? Is this some kind of friggin' crank call?" Ronald Restuccio yelled, exhibiting a bright-red face full of anger.

"Just remember *the Blues!"* Click.

Goose hastened over to the pinball machine area of the Palace Diner. "What do ya' suppose that dumb-shit crank call was all about? I was almost insulted!"

"Goose, did ya' lock your car?" Juice asked.

"I never do," Restuccio lividly replied. "Nobody ever fucks with me 'cause they know who my Pop is."

The four of us nonchalantly sauntered out of the diner after spending nearly two-hours inside the isolated eatery, built on the fringe of the Jersey pine-barrens. Goose's mouth suddenly dropped-down to his chest when we approached his white '60 Thunderbird.

"What the fuck!" the apparent victim yelled at the top of his lungs. We peered through the automobile's closed windows at blue mounds extensively heaped on the front and upon the back seats. Goose forcefully opened the driver's side door, and inside the luxurious car were small hills of frozen blueberries.

News spotted and removed a message tucked under the right front windshield wiper. He somberly read the note aloud like a minister at a funeral service.

> "Dear Ronnie Baby,
>
> Guess what, Restuccio! Your Goose is cooked. Stop hangin' with *that* Edgewood Red jerk-weed, and those other two simple dipshits, or, you'll really be Singin' the *Blues* without Guy Mitchell. Ya' got about one-hour to empty out your fancy car, before the frozen berries thaw, and then stain your precious T-Bird all over.
>
> The Blueberry Hill Boys (without Fats Domino)

"Jesus Christ!" Goose impiously exclaimed. "There must be at least a thousand-pounds of freakin' blueberries sittin' in my car!"

"I'll bet Gabe Gillette and his poker playin' buddies followed us here from the Sons of Italy," Juice Illiani theorized and shared. "Then, Gillette probably went back and got his brother Marty, who was hauling the berries from the cold storage, and…"

"And the shitheads dumped and crammed the friggin' frozen fruit into my T-Bird!" Goose angrily finished. "Sons of Italy sons of bitches! I'm so pissed that my kidneys are about to explode!"

"This horrible vandalism is a bigger pisser than the cow-type circular urinal the Phillies have in the left field Men's Room at Connie Mack Stadium!" News uttered in pure amazement.

"Hey, News," Goose stated in a melancholy tone of voice. "Could ya' sponsor another kid into the Reds?"

"Sure. Who is the lucky candidate?" Tommy Tomasello asked.

"Me!" the Blues gang victim lividly answered.

Chapter Six

"The White Horse"

The four of us pushed Goose's white Thunderbird to a pine barrens' woods, located about a hundred-feet behind the Palace Diner, and frantically tossed handfuls of at least a thousand-pounds of frozen blueberries from the car's interior. It took us a full-hour of rushed labor to successfully remove all but a few hundred tiny blueberries from on and under the seats of the deluxe white automobile.

"It's a good thing that ya' have protective plastic seat covers," Juice observed, speaking to Goose, "or your red upholstery would have been completely ruined."

"That doesn't matter," the owner defiantly said, "because even if those damned Blues had destroyed my car, my old man would just buy me a new one at the drop of a hat!"

"I think all you'll need is new rugs," News Tomasello announced. "Those blueberries that had thawed really have done a number on your red carpeting."

The four of us continued laboring until all of the frozen blueberries our eyes could see had been anxiously removed. We were all profusely sweating in our heavy winter clothes as we frenetically rushed to finish the task.

"After I get done with those cock-suckers, the dumb fucks will wish they had cunts instead of dicks," Goose promised his tired listeners. "Let's get the hell out of this rat-hole-dump and go back to Winslow Township and recuperate!"

The following day, I assisted my parents around their farm market, making preparations for its grand opening scheduled for April 10. Since it was still January, Pop figured we had plenty of time to complete all necessary repairs and improvements. I was pretty excited to wait on my first retail customer.

The next week at Edgewood was extremely brutal for me. My star shined so brightly in my English and in my American History II classes, yet Mr. Jenkins in Physics, and Mr. Andrews in trigonometry, appeared to be speaking foreign languages having different enigmatic alphabets. Their classes seemed like Tower of Physics Babel I and Tower of Trig' Babel II. I was becoming more and more frustrated with each passing day. Finally, I decided to venture-down to the Guidance Office and see my counselor, Mr. White.

"I want to transfer out of trig' class," I emphatically enunciated.

"You can't," Mr. White calmly answered. "You need that class in order to graduate. Nobody else here teaches that subject except Mr. Andrews."

"You don't understand," I insisted to the student curriculum adviser. "I'm completely lost in that class. I need a compass and an interpreter every time I leave the classroom because my head is spinning like a top. I think my brain is more messed-up and confused than Dizzy Dean."

"J.W., you seem to have a good head on your shoulders," Mr. White praised. "Why don't you give it a fresh try? You have to step back from your problem in that class and analyze the situation. Then, go back and give it your best shot."

"But Sir, I'm afraid that there's a personality conflict brewin' between Mr. Andrews and me. He liked me at first, but now that the guy knows how weak I am in his subject, he almost totally ignores me," I argued. "He's given up on me."

"Well, J.W., you'll just have to do something to get his attention back. Maybe his snubbing you is just a figment of your imagination," the guidance counselor speculated. "Maybe it's something that you feel in your mind that isn't really true at all in real life. I'll have a talk with Mr. Andrews after school," my advice mentor suggested.

I hardly heard Mr. White's promise that he would discuss the matter with Mr. Andrews. All that my mind focused on comprehending was that I had to do something bold to get the teacher's attention. The change of classes' bell rang, and the next subject on my daily schedule was trigonometry. I high-tailed it upstairs to the M-Wing, not wanting to be late for Andrews' class. I just reached my desk by the window right before the late bell rang.

"You just made it by the skin of your teeth," Andrews criticized in a martinet vocal tone. "Next time, allow yourself more latitude and get here earlier."

"I had gone down to the…."

"That's enough!" the stern pedagogue yelled. "Answer me back again, and you'll be cited for insubordination and then 'Green Carded' to the Vice-Principal!"

"I was only…"

"Knock it off!" the incensed instructor ranted like an obsessed maniac. "You're skating on thin ice!"

I slouched-down in my desk and sullenly observed some students around me snickering with their heads pointed down, touching their chins. I was pretending that I was an inhabitant of another universe. Mr. Andrews took a deep breath and partially regained his composure.

"Okay, class, we're going to try a little different procedure today," the instructor announced in a monotone voice. "Yes, a new teaching method. Arrange your desks in a giant semi-circle for intelligent group discussions on sine, cosign, tangent, and co-tangent. You must master those four, basic trig' functions and related formulas if you want to advance in mastering this very important subject."

After the twenty-three students made the prescribed semi-circle with their desks, Mr. Andrews turned one of the classroom's few empty desks around and sat-down in front, with his mean-looking countenance facing in his students' direction. I was so angry and disgusted with the man's austere demeanor that I couldn't control my defensive instincts. "We've all heard of *Meet the Press,"* I idiotically blurted-out, "so this must be our math teacher's version of *Face the Class*."

Mr. Andrews did not appreciate my allusion to popular television news' programming. The former marine pointed his index finger at me, and the rest of the class immediately comprehended his dissatisfaction and instantly stopped laughing. "J.W., I'm going to make your life miserable in this class. Go down to the principal's office. I'll send a Discipline Referral Green Card as soon as I can write one up," the teacher ordered. "You'll be sent-down to the office from this class every time you demonstrate insolence and disrespect. Is that clear? Now leave this room right now!"

I left the trig' classroom, realizing the stupidity of my immature antics and semantics. I was just attempting to break the ice with the teacher, but the tyrant understood my funny endeavor to be unwarranted defiance of *his* almighty authority. Mr. Pinkerton assigned me to two days of office detention, and the principal advised me that the next similar violation would result in a two-day disciplinary suspension.

I called home before lunch and told Mom that play-practice would be all week. I would be taking the late "Activity Bus" home from school, but I actually would be missing two days of *There's Gold in Them Dar Hills'* rehearsal because of my Tuesday, followed by my Wednesday, rendezvous with Office Detention.

That Wednesday in late January I parked my carcass at my usual cafeteria table, accompanied by News Tomasello, Juice Illiani, and Fabian Midilli.

"These school lunches are for the birds," I complained. "The Feds probably serve better grub in San Quentin. Then, the prison food must really be for jail*birds."*

Hearing my reference to a famous federal penitentiary often mentioned on *Dragnet,* Juice, Fabian, and News entered into a non-melodious musical utterance, “Dum, dee, dum dum. Dum, dee, dum, dum, DUMB!” The guys all pointed their index fingers at me when the last word “dumb” was loudly accentuated.

“That’s about as funny as a submarine with huge screen doors at each end, and with a giant water fountain in the center!” I objected.

“Don’t yell too loud or the rest of the cafeteria kids will think you’re finally being circumcised,” Juice laughed.

“What size is circum’ *size?”* Fabian joked.

“I want you two morons to know that I *have* been circumcised!” I nastily hollered-back in a mild fit of rage.

Two tables of girls turned-around in our direction; stared at me sitting there with my tray of ham and potato salad, and then broke- out into a roar at my audible, indiscreet statement. I sat there with a red face, feeling the full impact of humiliation and embarrassment.

“Hey Jack Webb and Frank Smith, thanks a lot,” I protested to my two amused companions. “Ya’ both really busted my sensitive testicles good!”

“We’re sorry, J.W., but I think we did ya’ a favor. Ya’ finally got Joanne Berenato’s attention,” Juice noticed as Johnny raised his eyebrows and head, and nodded back at the two tables of girls. “I’ll betcha’ her panties are already wet. Once a guy gets a chick’s focus, the girl’s ovaries get excited and start shootin’ out plenty of sweet-smellin’ wetness.”

“Where’s Jives Arena?” I asked, thinking to change the trend of conversation to protect my feeble psyche.

“He’s home, sick with the flu,” News informed.

“Jives should stop playing Santa Claus and stay outa’ chimneys,” I snapped. “That way, the chatterbox wouldn’t get the flue!”

Before Juice, News, or Fabian could respond to my zany pun, Goose Restuccio joined us, taking Jives’ usual cafeteria seat.

“How you three pecker-heads doin’? To tell you dick-heads the lame truth, I’ve seen better faces on slum walls that *have* already been de*faced!”* Restuccio characteristically mocked.

No one thought Goose’s remarks to be funny, especially me. I asked the weird-looking kid with the peculiar egocentric personality if Restuccio had gotten the new red rugs inside his white Thunderbird installed.

“Sure have,” Goose reported. “My Pop took care of it for me and lent me one of his Caddies until I get my wheels back this afternoon. Besides fresh red rugs, I had to get new plastic seat covers, too. But the upholstery underneath wasn’t damaged at all.”

I felt I had to assert myself and stand-up to Goose in front of Juice and Fabian. Naturally, I had to invoke the wit of Bo Jalonec. “Well,

Goose, it sounds like the Blues should've ab*stained* from ruining your red carpets, which don't sound like they were too *rug*ged!" as I intentionally stressed the pronunciation of certain syllables in the key words "abstained" and "rugged".

"J.W., I'm gonna' see what kind of brass balls ya' really got," Restuccio bristled. "And in fact, I'm gonna' find-out what kind of como se llamas all four of ya' dork-faces got!"

I figured that before I accepted becoming involved in some sort of mischief schemed-up by nefarious Goose Restuccio, I would first ask the maverick/rogue a pertinent question. 'Is your dad really in the Mafia?"

"That's right, he's above Lieutenant and just below Capa," the neurotic kid with the elliptical Charlie Brown skull replied. "Why do ya' wanta' know?"

I had to think fast and create a reason. "Because I knew two Mafia guys back in Levittown named Sal Palermo and Dante Messina. Ever hear of 'em?" I volleyed, protecting my anxiety.

Goose was impressed with the identities of my former adult acquaintances. G.R. related that he had met Palermo and Messina at a wedding in a South Philly' Italian restaurant, and that his pop had had several business dealings with both volatile Sicilians. "They was into marijuana and pornography, if I remember," Goose declared, "and they had two knockout daughters named …."

"Angie Palermo and Antoinette Bubbles Messina," I finished his thought by furnishing an appropriate compound direct object.

"Hey J.W., you're gonna' be alright! You're gonna' make a good paisan or a decent goombaaaa," Goose predicted, "unlike your jerk-off' pals sittin' here like a pair of circus bozos!"

Everyone reluctantly laughed at Restuccio's awkward attempt at Sicilian put-down humor. We all suspected that *our* only other option was sneering, which might have meant suffering, torture, death, or some other macabre aspect of the Mafia retribution code.

During the rest of the cafeteria period, I told the guys some Levittown anecdotes I remembered about Sal Palermo and Dante Messina. "And then, Sal Palermo said to me, 'You ain't gonna' get your noodle wet in my daughter Angie's crotch soup,' and I pointed to my head and told Palermo, 'This is the only noodle I ever use'!"

Goose, Juice, Fabian and News all clapped their hands in appreciation of my story. "And what did Sal Palermo say to you then?" Restuccio asked.

"He said go lick a dozen roosters, you little cock-sucker!" I had hooted the gross indiscretion a trifle too loudly.

Joanne Berenato's table went silent. The chicks all turned in my direction. Then, Joanne and all her friends erupted into a fierce female cackle, sounding a little like a hen house does when the chickens become excited over a wild rooster fight. Restuccio, Illiani, Midilli, and Tomasello also contributed their obnoxious voices to the general levity. Mr. Andrews, Mr. Jenkins, Mr. Rebeck, and two other male teachers stepped-over to our section of the cafeteria to quell the mild disturbance I had generated.

The dismissal bell was about to ring, so the five of us settled- down and adroitly feigned regaining our composure. Seeing that we had abandoned our rebellious deportment, Mr. Andrews, Mr. Rebeck, Mr. Jenkins and their colleagues moved-around to patrol other parts of the large lunch area, telling kids to clean-off their tables and pick-up debris off of the floor.

"Friday night around eight, I'll be around to pick-up you four circus clowns," Goose commanded. "And we're gonna' paint the town red," the menace related, right before the clanging dismissal signal sounded.

* * * * * * * * * * * * *

That last Friday night in January, Goose Restuccio pulled into the Pete's Market gravel driveway and parked his re-conditioned white '60 T-Bird between the farm stand and my house. The juvenile delinquent sent News up the front steps to knock at the door. I told my folks I'd be back by midnight, because the family had some serious cleaning to do to the market kitchen's tan linoleum floor, and that I couldn't wait to get started on the project the next morning.

"Where we goin'?" I asked when my body was the last one to enter the back seat of the fabulous, renovated T-Bird. I surveyed my environment and noticed Goose and Juice Illiani in the front seat, and Fabian Midilli, Jives Arena and News Tomasello illegally squeezed in the back with me.

"How's your cold?" I asked Jives. 'Been to Antarctica lately?"

"My cold's not too warm, Daddy-o," Jives replied from his weird position between Fabian and me in the four-seater T-bird having six occupants.

"Where we goin'?" I repeated.

The other five guys all ignored my innocent inquiry until Goose reiterated, "J.W., I told you while we was sittin' inside the school cafeteria that we're goin' to paint the town red!" Then, the five other T-bird occupants giggled and buckled-over in sheer delight at me being in the dark.

I felt very much out of the social loop. "How's your bout with the flu coming along?" I again sympathetically asked Jives.

"I'm still one sick dude," Frankie hoarsely growled. "But in your case, you're one sick pup. Ya' got any *Geritol?*"

A half-mile down the White Horse Pike, heading east toward Hammonton, Goose made a left-hand turn onto Walker Road. The other fellas' in the T-bird couldn't stop sounding like a small pack of laughing hyenas being tickled all over their more sensitive areas with chicken feathers.

"Isn't that the house where Joanne Berenato lives?" I inquired about the Sicilian dream girl.

"Yeah," Goose replied. "And her daddy's one of the biggest peach farmers in the area. Don't got no sons, though. Only two pretty daughters."

"Joanne's old man farms four-hundred-acres," News elaborated from the front seat. "Three-hundred peaches and nectarines; thirty-acres of apples; twenty plums; twenty tomatoes; ten corn; ten peppers, five eggplant, and five zucchini. This orchard ya' see on the right is either Rio-Oso-Gems or Blakes, I don't know which peach variety. I'm pretty sure it's Blakes, though."

"Quite an operation," I observed and opined. "I only have two acres. I got them when a Kamikaze greaser kid punched me in the testicles," I jested, as I imitated the personality of an old Levittown acquaintance. I was happy to hear everyone else appreciating what my traveling companions had thought was *my* superb sense of teen humor.

"Yeah, J.W., Joanne's old man grows, packs, and ships about two-and-a-half-million pounds of peaches each summer," Tommy added. "And several-million-pounds of the other crops, each and every harvest season."

"Goose, ya' say Joanne has only one sister and no brothers?" I queried. Before Restuccio rendered any response, the crazy driver veered his T-Bird onto a dirt road that separated Farmer Berenato's extensive Blake peach orchard from another one that had rows of barren apple trees.

"Hey, where we goin'?" I demanded as I forgot all about Joanne Berenato's family tree and her beautiful swarthy-skinned face.

"You'll see," Goose mysteriously answered with a smirk. The other four knowledgeable passengers grinned and collectively chuckled under their breaths.

The Thunderbird's headlights were then clandestinely shut-off. Goose Restuccio made a right angle turn onto another dirt road, which led directly through two peach orchards into the rear of old man Berenato's packing house, which faced *Route 30.* The maniacal driver then carefully turned his vehicle around, making sure not to get stuck in soft sand. "Everybody out, pronto!" Goose instructed.

"What the heck is goin' on?" I insisted on knowing.

"You'll soon see!" Goose promised. "Now cut the chatter until we complete *our* little prank."

The psychotic driver exited his auto and gently closed his door, and the rest of us mimicked his example on the passenger sides. Goose opened his trunk, found a can of red paint and two brushes, and then instructed his fledgling apostles to "come follow me".

"I told ya' J.W.," Restuccio lowly whispered, "we're gonna' paint the town red. Well, I was lying a little about that. We're just gonna' paint Joanne's father's precious White Horse's balls and dick red, and not the whole damned town. Don't got enough paint to do that."

Goose led his fidgety disciples down the dark dirt lane and around a green and white tin storage building, his route leading to the back of the farm's enormous packing-house. We all crouched- down and slinked and sneaked in a rather stealthy fashion around the front of the landmark White Horse Farm Market. Directly before our eyes was the farm's proud symbol, a huge White Horse, which had stood for two-decades upon an elevated wooden platform, that had been constructed six-feet above ground level.

Restuccio ordered Fabian Midilli to open the paint can with a small screwdriver *he* had brought along, and Sal did the easy task as commanded by Goose. Then, Ronald R., oblivious to the headlights and scrutiny of passing highway traffic, proceeded to paint red polka dots onto the reproductive organs underneath the artificial white stallion's posterior. After two-minutes of assiduous vandalism, Goose announced that *our* mischief would not be complete until "J.W. finishes the artwork". Restuccio handed me the half-empty can along with the still-clean second paintbrush.

Then, Goose tore off the White Horse's tail and handed-it to me and proclaimed, "Pretend this is Joanne's pussy 'cause this is the closest you'll ever come to it. Keep the tail as a sacred souvenir."

Restuccio then stood-up on the brick base below the elevated wooden pedestal, climbed-up and mounted the great White steed. Juice, News, and Fabian followed his stellar lead and clambered-up, too. The four fools pretended being drunken cowboys atop a fierce bucking bronco as astonished motorists passing-by on the White Horse Pike slowed-down and honked their horns at the totally bizarre spectacle. All the while, I was pretending to be painting the huge white horse's reproductive organs as Jives Arena stood guard.

"Okay, J.W., it's your turn to climb aboard good old Trigger here while Roy Rogers ain't around!" Goose insisted. "Give me your hand, and we'll fit your ass up here somewhere!"

I put the brush and paint can on the brick ledge and reluctantly reached-up to latch onto Goose's left-hand palm when all of a sudden, spotlights anchored in the ground illuminated the great White Horse. Before I could accurately decipher exactly what was happening, a buzzing noise was discerned, and Goose, News, Juice, and Fabian all wildly shouted a plethora of expletives. The four merrymakers clumsily tumbled-off the majestic horse, and fell into a landscaped area of azalea and yew bushes that had been planted on both sides of the highway landmark, just below the vandalized steed's wooden platform.

"What happened?" I asked as Jives and I assisted a still-shocked Juice Illiani to his feet.

"That friggin' horse became electrified as soon as the lights went on!" Johnny gasped and panted. "Joanne's old man must have rigged the horse to give-off a couple thousand volts if someone sat or even touched its back."

"You was *juiced!"* Goose exclaimed to Johnny as the instigator got up off the ground and dusted-off *his* blue jeans. "Juice was *juiced!"*

"Very funny!" Juice sneered as the aching accomplice nursed a pretty big cut on his right knee. "You were juiced, too!"

Several shotgun blasts were heard to our right as old Farmer Berenato charged from his home in our direction, hustling and carrying his deer-hunting weapon. "Let's get the hell outa' here!" Goose exclaimed in rare terror. "That blind old bastard might accidentally get lucky and kill one of us, and it's not gonna' be me!"

The six of us sprinted to the back of the packing-house, dashed past the huge green and white tin storage shed, and then scampered like Olympic athletes to the safety of the white Thunderbird. We hurriedly piled inside, and Restuccio fired-up the powerful engine. Soon, the entourage was fishtailing-down the dirt road with the sound of shotgun blasts filling the black night sky behind us.

"What the hell's wrong with my wheels? They're wobblin' like mad!" the petrified driver gasped.

"Maybe you've busted a wheel bearing or a shock absorber?" theorized Fabian. "I'll check once we escape being assassinated!"

"Goose, you've missed the turn to the left! Watch out!" News shouted from his new position in the middle of the twin front seats.

The T-bird zoomed between two apple trees, burrowed through some dirt furrows, and then ran over irrigation pipe that had still been lying on the ground since the autumn apple season. Our heads hit the roof's sash, giving the five passengers and the reckless driver instant scalp' lumps and headaches. We nearly got stuck three times in sand as the frantic driver tried finding a way out of the perplexing apple orchard maze. Finally, the T-bird's wheels made contact with the familiar asphalt of Walker Road, where G.R. stopped the vehicle. We all jumped out to inspect the possible damage.

"Oh no, a flat tire!" the driver-prankster moaned.

"Hey Goose, I'd hate to break it to ya', but you have another flat over here on this side," Sal alerted. Fabian advised us that Mr. Berenato might come-out onto Walker Road with his shotgun, so we had better leap back into the car, and slowly take the wounded vehicle to an old gas station on Route *206*.

We traveled north at five-miles-an-hour with our lights off, until we reached Union Road. Goose revolved the steering wheel as if he were guiding the *Titanic* past an iceberg, and in a few minutes, we shimmied past Oak Road; then Pine Road, and next Basin Road, which all paralleled one another at half-mile intervals. At last, the Thunderbird teetered and lurched along the Union Road shoulder, and next around the wide bend until we approached *Route 206.* Goose activated his headlights, turned right, and miraculously made it to safety, crawling at five-miles-an-hour the full mile down *206* to our destination, Morgan's Gas Station, at the busy intersection with *Route 30*.

When old Mr. Morgan took the first tire off, the mechanic discovered that it had been slashed with a switchblade. The second flat revealed the same vandalism signature. The guys were all stunned by the very apparent physical evidence.

"I'll bet the Blues did it," Goose speculated and verbalized.

"How do ya' know?" News challenged. "We have no real proof!"

"J.W., what do ya' think?" Ronald Restuccio asked. "Give me a wild theory."

I had always prided myself on being a fast thinker back in Levittown, and Quinn had commended me on several occasions for my immediate presence of mind. "Goose, I think the Blues did rupture your two front tires, and my educated guess is that either the blueberry dunces had coincidentally showed-up to paint the horse, too, and saw us there first, or the dolts simply were staking-out your car somewhere, and secretly followed us to the peach orchard road."

Goose saw merit in my "brilliant deductions" and professed that I had more brains than Einstein had.

"I hope J.W. does have more brains than Einstein does," News Tomasello interrupted, "because Albert Einstein's been dead nearly five-years now!"

Sal Midilli then asked me why the Blues only slashed the front two tires and not the rear ones, too. I had to contemplate the possibilities, but then I managed to organize a suitable hypothesis.

"I think that the thugs probably had cut the first two tires but then heard old man Berenato blastin' away with his shotgun," I conjectured and shared. "Then, the Blues hit the panic button and got out of there quick, before we all dashed back to Goose's car." Everyone concurred that my theory was feasible.

New tires were mounted onto the rims, and the gas station proprietor said that the total expense was fifty-dollars. Goose whipped out a wad of hundred-dollar bills. Inside the rich heir found two fifties. "Here," he said to old Mr. Morgan as the spoiled teen handed the amazed gent the two Ulysses S. Grants. "Ya' can keep the second fifty as a tip for helpin' me out."

After our series of harrowing White Horse Farm experiences, we all decided it was time to call it a night. I was the first one to be dropped-off.

"Well, J.W., if ya' ever get to marry Joanne Berenato, I'll bet it'll be a shotgun wedding!" Goose kidded, followed with his characteristic sarcastic laugh.

Everyone inside the T-Bird split a gut, except me.

Chapter Seven

"Winslow Junction"

After arriving home from the infamous White Horse Farm equine painting debacle, I said "*Cheerio, Wheaties,* and *Rice Krispies*" to my exhausted Edgewood High comrades. Then, I exited the white Thunderbird, entered the house, and marched upstairs to my bathroom, where I gulped-down three aspirins so that I would sleep soundly and then be able to effectively work outside the next morning, fixing up the Pete's Market kitchen. Before I hopped into bed, I placed the White Horse's tail I had sneaked into the house under my coat into an empty shoebox, and stored the container in a remote corner of my bedroom closet. Next, I visited the Sandman.

On Monday morning, I woke-up early, getting ready for school. I washed my face, brushed my long brown hair back, and then used a comb and some *Vaseline* petroleum jelly to complete the grooming. I dressed and Mom prepared me two eggs, toast, and orange juice for breakfast. After eating, I zipped upstairs to brush my teeth, shave a few whiskers off my face, and comb my hair a final time.

Finally, I donned my winter coat, said "goodbye" to Mom and Dad and walked two country blocks to the corner of Lexington Avenue and Third Street to catch the standard yellow bus. Soon, old Herman Priestley drove the half-full vehicle onto Third Street from the fork in the road at *Route 30,* and I nonchalantly boarded the school transportation device. I was almost glad to get back to the drudgery of physics and trigonometry after spending eight-hours after church on Sunday painting the cabinets, sanding the wooden counters, and scouring the farm market's tan, linoleum kitchen floor.

News Tomasello was picked-up on Spring Road, and the human talking machine sat-down next to me in the same seat. "How's it goin' J.W.? Do any more red horse paintin' yesterday?"

"I'm burned-out like a dead light bulb," I declared. "That crazy escape with Goose still has my brain warped, and then I had to work most of all day yesterday at the market. My head is still throbbing from when G.R. ran over the irrigation pipe, and we all hit our thick skulls on the roof."

"I'm not exactly a hundred-percent today either from that near-death experience," News commiserated. "But ya' gotta' admit, that electrified horse was a terrific misadventure you'll never forget."

"Yeah," I agreed. "You five idiots didn't know *watts* the matter when you all got juiced. Even Juice got juiced! I guess old Mr.

Berenato got tired of seein' his white horse highway symbol being constantly vandalized."

Tommy smiled and finally grinned in response to my comments. Then News started talking about how the House Un-American Activities Committee suspected that communists had infiltrated the American Clergy in general, and the National Council of Churches in particular. I didn't want to hear about the continuation of 1950s Wisconsin Senator Joe McCarthy's philosophy. I didn't even want to think about Charlie McCarthy, my favorite talking dummy. I simply ignored News' annoying prattle until the garrulous kid would eventually change the subject to something more interesting, or until the yellow "student dumb wagon" would reach Edgewood High.

On the seven-mile ride to Edgewood Regional High, I deeply thought about recent developments. I knew that Ronald Goose Restuccio was big trouble, and I was trying to devise a way that I could evade G.R. and not become directly implicated in his devious plots. I vowed to myself that I would seek-out the company of Juice, Jives, Fabian, and News, and try my best to evade any and all contact with Goose's instigation and influence. But sometimes, the best of intentions gets lost in the cards of reality's daily shuffle.

"And J.W.," News concluded his litany, "I understand Air Force General Dudley C. Sharp is gonna' testify before the House Un-American Activities Committee in three weeks about the dangerous communist church infiltration caper."

"News, we're almost at Edgewood," I answered as the bus rumbled down Coopers Folly Road from Atco to Tansboro, "but I sure hope that *Dudley* will *Do Right* in his testimony."

"J.W.," Tommy replied. "Goose is right about you. Either you are insane, screwed-up in the head, have cavemen for ancestors, or you're a genius with words. Maybe you're all three Betty Crocker ingredients put together."

'Thank God for Bo Jalonec!' I considered as old Herman Priestley piloted the yellow bus to the school's pavilion, located in the edifice's rear entrance, outside the cafeteria.

Lunch-time arrived before I was entirely awake from my weekend ordeals and travails, and my heart palpitated in the cafeteria line when Joanne Berenato coincidentally showed-up behind me.

"Hello," I nervously greeted the Sicilian Junior Prom Queen. "Do ya' know all of your lines for the play?" I courteously asked. "The only line I know is the cafeteria line."

"Most of them," the thin-but-pretty girl said while ignoring my second comment. "But I still have to memorize twenty more. How do you like your new school?"

"It's alright, but I miss my old friends back in Pennsylvania," I honestly replied. "This is the sixth school I've gone to since first-grade, so I really don't have any roots, or any long-time friends."

"Maybe that'll change after you finally settle into a groove here," the dark-skinned Aphrodite answered. Joanne selected a fried chicken platter while I grabbed one with two thin slabs of roast beef. And then, my light blue eyes made contact with her dark browns. "You're sort of like a tumbleweed," the prom queen strangely remarked. "A rolling stone gathers no moss. Miss Hunter explained that neat idiom to the class back in November."

"Who the heck wants to have moss all over themselves in the first place?" I joshed. "And a rolling stone is probably also a very dizzy one. Rolling Stones! Those two words would make a really great name for a rock group!"

"You're funny in a peculiar sort of way," the Italian doll said. "I thought so your first day here when you courageously stood-up and answered 'Vicksburg'. And J.W., somebody told me that you know who painted daddy's white horse with red polka dots, and stole the white stallion's tail."

"I, I don't know exactly what you're talkin' about," I stammered, "but it sounds pretty interestin'. I'm not really into vandalism, destruction, or murder. I'll keep my eyes and ears open and see if I can find that info' out for you."

"Are ya' sure you don't know who did it?" the Italian chick quipped. "There's a lot of gossip about who the culprits are!"

"All I can tell you is that *I* did not paint your father's horse, rip-off the tail," I shrewdly stated as I thought about Goose doing those mischievous deeds, and also about the furry contents of my shoebox in the right corner of my bedroom closet.

I paid the cashier my fifty-cent lunch debt, smiled and winked at Joanne, and paced over to my favorite table to await the arrival of Juice, Jives, Fabian, and News. Unfortunately, Goose Restuccio was the first acquaintance to enter the cafeteria and park his fat butt directly across from me.

'Teen life these days is really hard,' I thought. I imagined that being a friend of Restuccio's would be comparable to a wild roller coaster ride, fraught with rebellion against adult authority on one end of the teen social spectrum, and conformity to powerful peer pressure on the other. What a tremendous collision of opposite ideas! Rebellion versus conformity! And I also was well-aware that peer pressure from guys like Goose had more influence on me than did adult parental rules, or teacher expectation. It was very obvious to me that Goose Restuccio could exert great force on my personal choices; on my safety; on my need for adventure; on my inclination to rebel, and on my desire to conform. The prankster's unorthodox personality along with his Mafia' ties fascinated the heck out of my petite, vulnerable mind.

"Well, J.W., have ya' painted any White Horses today?" Goose began rather caustically. "I'm not gonna' be happy until I get ya' expelled from school!"

"That's the last time I'll *horse* around with you!" I effectively countered. "That experience wasn't even a *mane* event in my life. It wasn't even a filly lost in Philly'."

"Ha, ha, ha, you freakin' crack me up," G.R. laughed. "I mean, what we pulled the other night was pretty slick. Would ya' rather have spent the evening playin' back seat Bingo with that queer-bait, Frankie Jives Arena? That punk drives his fruity black and white Dodge Coronet through the new modern car wash, just to get a good blow job at the end!"

"I thought you're suspended from school?" I exclaimed, changing the character assassination subject.

"My old man called Mr. Pinkerton and got me off the hook, G.R. informed. "Even the school principal is afraid of the Mafia!"

Before my mind could fully digest Goose's ugly diatribe, Juice, Fabian, Jives, and News all ambled, with their lunch trays, over to *our* table. Ronald Restuccio sarcastically addressed the new arrivals. "You guys look like *Raunchy* without Bill Justis!"

"That was a great instrumental number," I barked at the repugnant troublemaker. "My friends and me listened to that song all the time in the Feed Bag."

"The Feed Bag!" Goose loudly yelped. "That sounds like a paper container to vomit your guts into! Ya' flunkies should've listened to the *Banana Boat Song* by that Harry Belafonte freak," the malcontent youth suggested, "because ya' turds are like a pack of dumb jerk-off immigrants that would insist on stayin' on the damned banana boat after it landed at Ellis Island."

"Hey, guys," interrupted Jives Arena. "I'm feelin' boss and like blastin' off ever since my bod' totally totaled the flu bug. I gotta' fifth of *Southern Comfort* I stole from my grandma's liquor cabinet. Who wants to make the booze scene, and pop the clutch with me over at Winslow Junction? We'll have some cool *kicks* out there in the hicks' sticks."

"Should I bring a football?" I joked while honoring the memory of Jokes Jalonec's plays on words.

"I can't make it tonight, but how about a rain check?" Goose requested. "If it was *Jack Daniels,* I might have considered your fucked-up offer!"

"Party pooper!" Juice facetiously accused.

"No, I think Goose poops in the toilet, and he doesn't poop parties into his toilet," I injected. "That's one time it always pays to sit down on the job."

"Where do ya' think of this weirdo funny shit!" Restuccio said in amazement. "Ya' sound like a clever idiot when ya' say those fuckin' freaky jokes."

"J.W. sleeps in the party pooper toilet!" Sal Midilli injected.

"Yeah, if I was royalty, I'd be a royal flush!" I exclaimed, again recalling a favorite line of inane Bo Jalonec.

Goose explained to the guys that he had to make the rounds of his gumball machine route over in Egg Harbor, Pomona, and in Mays Landing. The Mafia candidate also joked that he needed to buy his mother a new washing machine so that his criminal daddy could launder more skimmed, illicit Cosa Nostra money.

"I can't make it, either," Johnny Illiani confessed. "I gotta' lotta' lines I still have to learn for the senior play, and I'm way behind on my *Civil War* report. I gotta' research all the major battles."

"I can't go, either," News declared. "I promised my pop that I would stay home and help him put my miniature model area landscape together."

"What's that?" I deliberately asked. "If ya' wanta' be into models, try some stacked ones outa' *Playboy Magazine.*"

News Tomasello related how he and his dad had spent two-years making a scale model of Hammonton and vicinity on a large platform that took-up most of the space in his basement. All of the major buildings, streets, highways, train crossings, and farms were represented in great detail. The mammoth project was almost complete, and when it would be, News promised that we would all be invited over to evaluate the incredible craftsmanship.

I remembered a line that Bo Jalonec had once recited in the Feed Bag, and I thought I would hammer the guys with its profundity. "Juice, why don't ya' write your *Civil War* report in an Italian restaurant. Then, you'll be able to turn in to Mrs. Murphy the Spaghettisburg Address; that is, if ya' get any red gravy on the papers. I'm sure that Mrs. M. will love it!"

Just about everybody sitting at the table rose to express contrived dissatisfaction with my unique sense of humor. Pretentious Jives, Juice, News, and Fabian strolled from my company and found empty seats at adjacent tables. Only Goose remained stationary across from me. "Ya' oughta' change the name on your birth certificate to Frank Furter, because J.W., now you're officially one, big, stupid, shit-faced hot dog!" the ballbreaker affectionately criticized.

"I gotta' get on the good side of Joanne Berenato," I lamented, trying to be sincere for a change. "She's a knockout!"

"Well, J.W.," Goose sneered. "I think you oughta' first move fifty-miles north of New York City."

"Why?" I reflexively asked, realizing that egocentric Restuccio knew little about the abstract word 'sincerity'.

"So, then you could learn some Cunt-etiquette!" Ronald Restuccio vulgarly suggested with a stone face. "In order to get laid, ya' gotta' forget New Jersey and know all about Cunt-etiquette!"

Even though I detested Goose's foul mouth, I did have to smile in reaction to his bizarre Connecticut joke. The main difference between Jokes Jalonec and Goose Restuccio was that Bo had been naturally funny and his one-liners were usually clean. If they involved sex, the punch lines were delivered with style and class in the form of sexual allusion. Jalonec's wit always had some degree of imagination attached. Goose's jokes were just like he was, crass, gross, obscene, mean-spirited, and shallow.

I called Mom at home from the pay phone in the main hallway outside the Edgewood cafeteria and told her I was going to eat at a Berlin diner with Jives Arena and Fabian Midilli. She said, "Alright, but be home before midnight."

Frankie Arena, Fabian Midilli and I left school right after the lackluster play practice finally ended. The three of us entered the black and white Dodge Coronet, and Jives exited Coopers Folly Road and drove east on *Route 30* to Waterford. We stopped for gas at the *Flying A* station next to Sal Midilli's family's modest, white, wood-framed two-story home.

Fabian got out, pumped three-dollars-worth (ten gallons) of "petrol" into the tank, and handed the sum to his pop. Soon, the 'three musketeers' were heading west to Berlin to have burgers, steaks, and *Cokes* prior to our *Southern Comfort* engagement at secluded Winslow Junction. After seating ourselves in a comfortable booth inside the small diner, a middle-age waitress came over to take our individual orders.

"What'll it be?" the red-hair matron bluntly asked.

I was inspired by her words to use a fairly cute Bo Jalonec ploy. "*It'll be* February 3rd tomorrow," I wisely answered. "And believe it or not, the next day will be February 4th."

Fabian Midilli picked-up on my lead and put a quarter in the jukebox selector that had been installed above the side of our table next to the window. "*It'll be* three songs, all about you, Sweetheart," Sal said and winked as the handsome guy pointed to the frowning waitress.

"I'm gonna' select 'Party Doll' by Buddy Knox; 'Little Darlin' by the Diamonds, and Chuck Berry's 'Sweet Little Sixteen'."

And then Jives Arena was not to be denied his jollies, either, saying to the aggravated old waitress, "*It'll be* Adam and Eve on a boss raft without any grungy *Howdy Doody* foodies inside," Jives loquaciously ordered.

"You say ya' want two eggs on toast without any butter?" the waitress skillfully translated from Jives's recitation.

"Naaaa, I changed my mind," Frankie stated with a straight face. "Since I left my specs home, I can't use my peepers to read your oddball menu. Instead, give me a Beethoven, a Louis the XIV, and a Tchaikovsky, please."

"What on earth is that?" the frustrated woman inquired.

"It's a BLT sandwich," Jives clarified, "and be generous with the bacon from the Mayo Clinic."

Fabian ordered a super steak sandwich, and finally it was my turn. "I'll have an atomic sub with fried onions. And go easy on the uranium, and make sure the atomic *sub* is in a *torpedo* roll," I demanded with a smart-ass smile.

The other two guys broke-out into minor convulsions. "And give us three large *Cokes* before the Russians invade this place and make us order vodka, instead!" I finished. The red-hair waitress wasn't impressed with our little, rude, conversational antics.

"You three young cretins ought to comb your teeth, shave your tongues, and then gargle with arsenic!" the livid woman shrieked, and vigorously left in a huff as we continued our great frivolity.

"She called us cretins!" Jives laughed. "Dudes, that vocab' is cool as a ghoul holding his tool with a fool on a stool in an Arctic swimmin' pool."

"Maybe she thinks we live on an island near Greece," I added, "and the hussy believes that we're all descendants of the Minotaur. That would make us official *Cretans*. I'll bet there's a lot of *ancient grease* in the backroom kitchen of this greasy-spoon dump."

"J.W., ya' know almost as much junky funky facts as that knuckle head News Tomasello does," Jives pointed-out. "You're a round-trip and a half from Earth to Mars!"

The three of us then discussed that if Tommy News had been with us, the 'fact wonder' would have been boring us to death seven times over by talking about some insignificant event like Jimmy Hoffa battling propaganda back and forth with the Senate Select Committee. "Just last week," I seriously uttered, "News was concerned that the government called Hoffa 'dishonest' when *he* claimed he would rid the Teamsters Union of its criminal element."

"Maybe News would be telling us all about *Ebbets Field* bein' torn-down to make room for an apartment housing project," Sal Midilli sincerely contributed, "and now the *Dodgers* are really in L.A. and no longer in Brooklyn."

"That makes perfect sense," I added, "because the traffic in Los Angeles is so fast and heavy that pedestrians have to be dodgers, or else, get run-over all the time by speeding motorists."

We merrily ate our meals and paid our tab without generating any more public incidents. The three genial high school seniors exited the Berlin Diner, sauntered to the rear parking lot, and then climbed into the four-door black and white '57 Dodge Coronet. The next stop on our itinerary was Winslow Junction, an old abandoned train depot that had been popular with seashore-bound summer tourists in the 1930s. In 1960, the junction was especially used by several major railroads as a country train yard, to exchange and link-up freight cars and locomotives.

It was just getting dark and Jives' car radio was blasting-out "Twilight Time" by the Platters. Joe Niagara, a very popular Philly' WIBG DJ, announced "twin spins", and the second Platters' tune was the slow number, "The Great Pretender". That song allowed me to engage in some serious self-analysis while Fabian and Frankie continued making small-talk about News' supreme mastery of meaningless trivialities and irrelevant newspaper headlines. Finally, Frankie turned right onto Spring Road, passed by a newly constructed middle-class housing development, and followed the straight, paved road a mile south to Winslow Junction.

Jives turned-down the radio volume to conceal our presence to any railroad employees that might still be straggling-about Winslow Junction. Frankie Arena backed-up into a remote area, his Dodge penetrating into an open indentation in the woods. "Little Star" by the Elegants was playing softy on radio. The rambunctious driver reached under the front seat and produced an almost-full fifth of *Southern Comfort,* and after unscrewing the cap, passed the liquor bottle around so that his delighted passengers could imbibe a few healthy swigs.

"This fire water is the best booze goin' this side of Siberia," Frankie observed and opined. "It'll put us in a kookie state, and it's really better than havin' sex with a carload of chicks. Sex only lasts about ten-minutes with around five babes. This bottle will send us to Weirdsville in less than an hour. Then, we can go home and pile-up some serious Z's."

"Two weekends ago," Fabian said to me, "Goose never saw the Blues stash all the frozen berries in his car, and this past weekend, we never saw the Blues slash his tires in the peach orchard at White Horse Farm."

"That's right," I agreed. And we just have to assume that *they're* the ones that did it. I think the Blues are tryin' to discourage us from joinin' the Reds. Jives, pass that bottle over here before the last six ounces of that sweet whiskey evaporates."

Frankie passed me the fifth of *Southern Comfort,* and I told the guys that the half-full booze bottle was what Beethoven was drinking and thinking about when the eccentric composer wrote his famous *Fifth Symphony.*

Frankie flicked the radio dial to a station playing "Problems" by the Everly Brothers. No sooner had the lunatic accomplished that minor feat, in his semi-inebriated state, that the car's four doors were flung-open, and six faces covered by nylon stockings scared the living feces out of us. The treacherous assailers dragged us out of the Dodge and tossed our rear ends onto the ground. Being half drunk, none of us could accurately perceive exactly what was happening.

Having the three of us pinned-down on the cold, hard ground, the six antagonists tied our hands behind our backs; stuffed blue bandannas into our mouths, and next tied each of our left and right feet together with clothesline' ropes. One by one, we were picked-up and carried to an empty boxcar, that was attached to a train pointing due north. After my body was roughly deposited onto the boxcar's dirty wooden floor, our attackers closed the sliding door, and soon the latch clicked. We each struggled to loosen our encumbering bonds, but none of us could free ourselves as we rolled-around the stenchy straw that had been randomly strewn upon the boxcar's putrid floor.

I attempted to use my tongue and teeth to force the handkerchief out of my mouth, but was unsuccessful in my vain maneuvering. We heard a shrill whistle blast, and the next thing that could be perceived was the sensation of forward motion. It was pitch black inside the boxcar, and our ears could hear each other squirming-about and grunting, but that was all that our distorted senses could interpret. Glimmers of light would penetrate through the tiny crack between the boxcar's sliding door and the enclosure's frame, but such sensations were intermittent, depending on the population density areas that the freight train was passing through.

Forty-minutes later, I detected a slight change in the freight train's inclination, as the boxcar slanted upward, careening back and forth on the rails. I presumed that the freight was crossing a bridge, and my hunch was the Camden-North Philly' railroad span across the Delaware River. All three of us had ceased our pursuit of liberation, having exhausted most of our energy in the first twenty- minutes of confinement. All I could hear was the panting, grunting, and gasping, originating from my two companions and myself.

Soon, I became aware that the freight train had finally chugged to a halt. We were lying there in the pitch-black darkness, not knowing what the unexpected had to offer. Then, the boxcar's noisy door slid open, and we were greeted by our assaulters, again wearing their nylon stocking masks.

"Welcome to North Philly'!" one of our masked molesters sarcastically proclaimed. Three of the belligerent kidnappers clambered-aboard the boxcar; dragged us one by one to the door, and then the other three maniacs non-gently pulled us off and plopped us one by one to the ground. The six muggers next cut the ropes binding our wrists with very effective, industrial wire sheers. Our half-dozen tormentors then scurried-around a side warehouse and fled to an awaiting car. An engine fired-up, and an auto peeled out of the freight yard into the silence of the frigid February night.

I was the first to totally escape my bondage. Once my hands were free, I tugged the *blue* bandanna from my mouth that had been tickling my throat; wiggled my feet out of the bottom rope that had tethered my legs together, and crawled-over to assist Fabian and Jives. We were all relieved to have escaped what we thought would be a certain flirtation with death.

"Who the hell were those guys?" Fabian asked while breathing very heavily.

"I think those molesters were Blues," I answered as my lungs struggled to inhale much-needed oxygen. "The butt holes were wearin' blue denim jackets, and used these blue handkerchiefs to stuff in our mouths. The blue jackets and the blue bandannas are not just clues. They're Blues' symbols!"

"Who goes there?" yelled a night watchman as the yard employee held-up his lantern to his eyes, about two-hundred-feet down the track. The three of us rapidly stood-up and quickly darted as fast as our legs would carry us, running around the same warehouse behind which the Blues had hidden their escape auto. Like decathlon champions, the trio successfully sprinted-out of the freight car yard and hustled three full blocks, until fatigue had its toll on our already low stamina levels.

"I've seen this sort of crap before in Levittown with the diabolical Kamikazes," I told my fellow victims. "Things are gonna' get worse before they get better."

"I think that Broad Street is about nine blocks that way," Fabian exhaled deeply as Midilli pointed west. "We can catch a trolley or cab and go down to the bus terminal at..."

"Filbert Street," Jives finished. "I know that jazz 'cause I got some buds that jive around there in center city. And I gotta' say that those Blues are scum-bag city all the way *from here to maternity!"*

"Didn't you mean *From Here to Eternity*?" I challenged.

"Hey J.W., gotta' match?" Jives unexpectedly asked while deliberately switching gears on me. The distraught kid haphazardly reached inside his shirt pocket and distributed three cancer sticks from his crushed pack of *Camels*.

"I haven't had a match since Superman found a mother lode of kryptonite!" I mused.

Then, Jives looked pleadingly at a still very frightened Fabian Midilli.

"I've not had a match ever since Goose Restuccio laid a golden egg, pretending he was a chickenhawk guarding the hen house!" Midilli sniffed and chuckled. The three of us laughed in spite of us recently surviving several very harrowing experiences.

"J.W., who were those stupid *ass sailors* again?" Jives inquired.

"Our vile assailers were members of the Blues," I reiterated.

Chapter Eight

"The Gem"

The three weary, now-sober adventurers carefully walked through several tenement slums, and after nine monotonous blocks, we eventually found our way to North Broad Street. The exhausted and relieved trio boarded a city bus, and fifteen-minutes later, exited at City Hall. We stared-up into the cold winter sky at William Penn's statue illuminated over five-hundred-foot high atop the classic architectural landmark, and soon the valiant threesome headed east several blocks on Market Street. Jives, familiar with the area, led us to Filbert Street, where the terminal was located, to purchase tickets for a Jersey bound Public Service Bus.

I received a quick punch to my arms from each of my friends after I declared, "I hope we don't get a terminal illness while we're waitin' in this place for our freakin' bus!"

"Get serious for a sec'," Jives admonished, "or else you'll be certain to be hurtin'! Just kiddin', of course. J.W. Now that I got your stupid attention, why do ya' think those cootie-biters didn't rob our' butts blind?"

"Because Jives, "they're Blues and don't need our *poultry* chicken feed. The clowns got the big bucks and don't have to fool-around with penny-ante stuff like us."

"And besides," Sal added inside the comfort of the Filbert Street Public Service Bus Terminal. "We weren't wearin' blindfolds, so they couldn't have robbed us blind. The blindfolds were in our mouths and not around our eyes, and that shows ya' how messed-up in the head those imbecile Blues really are."

"Yeah," I agreed. "If the Blues had one more guy with 'em they could've had enough gray matter to have half a human brain."

"Say Fabian, baby, when we gonna' get that fink News to sponsor us into the Reds?" Frankie asked. "I'm ripe for the pickin'."

"As soon as possible Jives," Sal confided, kicking a few already smoked cigarette butts on the bus terminal dusty floor. "I feel like kickin' some real human butts now, until those rich Hammonton High creeps are black and *blue*."

The three of us slept for most of the hour-long bus trip back to somnolent Hammonton. I woke-up as the mass transit shore-bound vehicle neared the *Route 30* Ancora Bridge overpass, which the freight train we had involuntarily ridden had passed under four and a half' hours before. I woke-up my traveling companions and the returning triumvirate got off at Lexington Avenue, which bordered the west side of Pete's Market. Then, I drove Sal home to Waterford in Dad's dark blue "Pete's Market Special" '57 Ford truck.

"See you two pud-pullers at school," Fabian summarized. "And if ya' get kidnapped at Winslow Junction again, give me a call."

"You'll see us at Edgewood if you're lucky!" I sharply answered. "Better in school than lyin' horizontal at the funeral parlor."

"Don't do us any mucho favors! Manana amigo, y hasta Luigi, hermano!" Jives uttered as the punster deliberately butchered some common 'palabras' he had learned in Mr. Taylor's Spanish II class.

"See ya', Sal," I finished. "It's been real! But why didn't ya' get off the bus in front of your Pop's Waterford gas station? It passed right by here."

"Because, Bird-brain. I was sleepin' on the damned bus and *you* didn't wake me up until we got to the Ancora Bridge between my house in Waterford and your place in Elm," Fabian reminded me.

On the way down Spring Road to Winslow Junction, Jives and I listened to Connie Francis's rendition of "Who's Sorry Now?" on the farm market's truck's radio. I slowed-down to ascertain that no Blues were in the vicinity of the seldom-used country freight car yard. I hit the brakes and patiently waited for Frankie to enter his black and white Coronet.

"Hey J.W., those scuzzy scum' bags stole my keys," Jives reported in a quasi-astonished tone. "Zoom this tin monster over to my pad. I always keep my crib port open for emergencies. I have another set of igniters stored inside the top drawer of my bureau. Vamonos, ahora!"

"Okay, Jives, ya' make more sense in Spanish than you do in English. But you shouldn't keep your keys in your drawers," I said with a poker face. "You should always keep your car keys in your pants' pocket, instead. If ya' keep your keys in your drawers, the sharp objects might scratch-up your dingle and your minor league ballpark, too!"

"You couldn't be more-full of shit if you was the friggin' Jolly Green Giant's cesspool!" Jives vehemently responded.

I drove Frankie to his place a mile away in the village of Winslow. Arena lived in a standard, three-bedroom ranch home. The jive-talker gingerly opened his bedroom window and inelegantly clambered inside. After fumbling in the dark through his top bureau drawer, the searcher managed to locate his set of duplicate car keys. The awkward. heavy-set kid gingerly climbed outside, shut the window, and lethargically re-entered the Pete's Market Special.

I conveyed Jives back to Winslow Junction where he got out and then attempted starting his '57 Dodge Coronet. A hound dog could be heard wildly barking in the distance. Everything else was silent and eerie around the abandoned old train depot.

"No juice," Frankie related in a defeated tone of voice. "Those Blues oughta' get bent somethin' serious! They've really rattled my cage somethin' fierce by creamin' my wheels!"

"Don't get frosted! It's cold enough out here," I advised. "Let's take a gander under the hood." I removed a small flashlight from the truck's glove compartment, popped Jives' hood, and immediately identified the source of the difficulty. "Ya' have no freakin' battery!" I exclaimed.

"Those dirty scum-bags have really twisted my horns with this friggin' gig they've pulled," Jives lividly confessed. "The buffoons need to be put-down, Major League big time!"

Fortunately, Dad had a rusty chain stashed on the floor behind the farm market truck's seat. I then backed-up the dark blue, half-ton pickup's rear end, stopping directly in front of Frankie's '57 Coronet; attached the chain hooks securely to both vehicles, and then towed Jives and his jalopy back to the hamlet of Winslow.

"See ya' later alligator," I said with a low degree of animation.

"After while, you' super-asshole reptile," Jives disgustedly replied, instead of the standard 'crocodile'.

Monday rolled-around, and I met my Edgewood High buddies at fifth-period lunch in the cafeteria. I was deeply depressed and demoralized because I had just failed another one of Mr. Andrews' enigmatic trigonometry tests. "No teacher oughta' give a major test on Monday morning," I complained. "It's downright unethical!"

"Don't worry, J.W.," G.R. sympathized. "Have no fear because Goose is here. I'll fix that bastard's wagon good for ya'. He's gonna' regret ever fuckin' with *you*, I guarantee it!"

"In Levittown at Cardinal Reagan," I recalled, "if a teacher used his power and screwed-up a kid's future like Andrews' is runnin' wild with my life right now, my Diablos' pals would've poured sand and sugar in his car's gas tank and make him pay the price," I recalled and stated. "We once did that to a police cruiser, when the nasty cop gave us some static."

"J.W., that's pretty cool. I'm glad I don't gotta' take trigonometry, algebra, calculus, geometry, or any of that other advanced math shit," G.R. articulated. "I only gotta' take General Math' with Mr. Zelnick. It's a snap. I ain't gotta' go to college, but I'll wind-up makin' more dinero in my lifetime than all you fucked-up zombies put together."

Fabian busted on Goose by asking the defiant Sicilian what war General Math' had fought in. Before Restuccio could formulate an adequate reply, I remembered a Bo Jalonec line and chimed-in,

"General Math fought in the same war with General Office, General Motors, and General Electric," I indicated.

"J.W.," Jives responded, "you musta' had a jug of *Southern Comfort* for breakfast before ya' came to *Romper Room* this morning. The ice cream shootin' outa' your mouth ain't exactly *Good Humor."*

Everyone laughed as Jives effectively "busted-on, and shot- down" his new-found buddy, who had just recently safely towed *his* car out of Winslow Junction. I took the "put down" with a grain of salt, because if I had shown any signs of being insulted or embarrassed, the rest of the guys would have made minced-meat out of my tender ego.

On the night of February 3rd, Goose picked up News, Jives, Juice, Sal and me, and drove the overcrowded white '60 Thunderbird into metropolitan downtown Hammonton. It was tight quarters in the four-seater, but we managed to squirm-around and get comfortable. We passed by the Reds, predictably and faithfully standing in front of the Rivoli Theater, and the Blues, loyally stationed across Bellevue Avenue, positioned on the curb in front of Vega's Drugs and Soda Fountain and Augie's Burger Paradise Luncheonette.

G.R. cruised town in the familiar loop, steering his boss machine south on Bellevue Avenue; across the Pennsylvania Railroad tracks; took a right turn down Front Street; across the tracks again; cruising east on Egg Harbor Road, and then north through town on Bellevue to Central Avenue. Around a hundred other flashy teen cars and "customized" hot rods were cruising the town strip also, the activity being a nightly tradition in Hammonton as well as in thousands of other small towns across the country.

After superstitiously doing "the circuit" three times, "once each for the Father, the Son, and the Holy Ghoul," Goose parked his "Bird" in front of Olivo's Supermarket, across Central Avenue from the Gem, a popular local teen hangout.

"Guys, be careful in that dick-doin' dive," Goose cautioned, "because the Gem's only a block away from Hammonton High, and a lot of Blues stake-out this place."

"But the Gem is neutral territory, just like DiDonato's Bowlin' Alleys and Royale Crown Custard," Sal objectively challenged. "And we oughta' be safe in hangin' in there as long as we don't start any trouble ourselves."

The six of us entered the noisy teen joint and sat in a semi-circular booth in front of the restaurant's Central Avenue pane-glass window, just to make sure that no one tampered with Goose's "Bird" parked in front of Olivo's across the street. Bobby Darin's "Queen of the Hop" was blasting from the crowded place's rainbow-colored jukebox.

My eyes looked-around and saw Joanne Berenato and two other babes at another booth, talking to several Reds that attended St. Joseph High. News identified the three brawny guys as Dave "Herc" Juliano, Jake "The Brute" Maccarella, and Ollie "Balls" Giordano. Herc Juliano was a tall, muscular kid, who had biceps the size of cantaloupes; Jake Maccarella was a two-hundred-twenty-pound linebacker, and Ollie Giordano was also a burly strong-looking dude with a nasty temper when angry.

Tommy News explained that the Giordano family had immigrated to America from Italy; worked at Renault Winery's vineyards in Egg Harbor for ten-years, and then bought a twenty-acre peach farm in Rosedale, just west of Hammonton. At age five, Ollie had to master English as a second language all by himself.

News also described a rather interesting story scenario. One day in July of '59, Ollie Giordano was in a local grocery store. Several signs written in Spanish were posted on the walls, giving directions and information to Hispanic customers who were summer Puerto Rican farm migrants. Giordano demanded that the grocery market's cashier pull-down and then rip-up the offensive Spanish signs.

When the market clerk asked "Why?" Ollie Giordano argued that when he had come to the U.S. from Italy, he had to learn the new language all by himself without any help from store signs, and that Puerto Ricans had to learn and understand English from square one, just like he had to do. The mercurial Italian lad despised and resented cultural advantages. The market employee refused to honor Giordano's command, so Ollie became excessively hostile and tore down the signs, ripped them up, and wildly threw the debris into the store's trashcan.

"What happened next?" Juice Illiani asked News Tomasello.

"Well, a big, fat colored lady was in the store and accused Giordano of being a racist, and Giordano told the obese woman point blank," Tommy continued his unique tale by saying, "those Spanish signs discriminate against you, too, you fat black bitch, because they weren't written in good English, or in bad Swahili."

"That's a real cool story," Goose insisted, "because I don't like lowlife niggers or spics either. Those three St. Joe' guys are all right in my book."

'Fine Catholics,' I thought as I linked Goose Restuccio and Ollie Giordano with the racial bigotry that had been amply exhibited back in Levittown by Bruno Popeye Messina, Sal Palermo, Tinker, and the redneck Kamikazes.

Vivacious Joanne Berenato, her two pretty girlfriends, and the three St. Joe' Reds glanced-over in our direction, and News waved over his polite greeting to *his* fellow gang members. Then, we all gave each other the peaceful "hi sign," and the Edgewood contingent instantly felt safer sitting in the Gem and being comfortably allied with the three tough St. Joe' Reds.

"That St. Joseph guy must really be rich," Goose irreverently remarked, "because *he* owns schools and churches all over the goddamned country."

Honey Anderson approached our booth to take our orders. "What do ya' say?" the twenty-year-old buxom blonde angel asked.

"*I say* Mary had a little lamb, and the doctors were amazed!" Jives unimaginatively injected.

"I *say* words," News factually indicated.

"Do ya' have Caesar's salad?" I requested before Honey could muster-up a response to neutralize Jives and News's lunacy.

"Yes, we do," Honey answered while still reeling from Frankie Arena and Tommy Tomasello's ridiculous stupidity.

"Well, then," I added. "you'd better give Caesar's salad back to old Julius, or he might get mad and start *Roman* the streets lookin' for you!" I declared in memory of Bo Jalonec's wit.

And then sarcastic Goose Restuccio had to contribute to the perfectly contrived mayhem. "Do ya' have any bearded clams?" the Italian Stallion wanted to know.

"Look, you cross-eyed Edgewood jerk," the rattled waitress boomed in a perturbed soprano. "We don't have any bearded clams here because all the waitresses have shaved their crotches! Now what the hell do ya' really want, and for Pete's sake, don't ask me if I have elephant's thighs or friggin' frog's legs, either!"

We all got the message as everyone in the place heard what Honey had shouted, because the jukebox had just seconds-before stopped playing "Rockin' Robin" by Bobby Day. Then, the next song "Splish Splash" by Bobby Darin was spun, and we all thoroughly cooperated with standard restaurant behavior by ordering *Pepsi Colas* and burgers.

No sooner had News told us that Dave "Herc" Juliano was "one crazy sick pup" that the aforementioned guy got-down, sat on the floor, and pretended he was taking a bath, enacting the lyrics of "Splish Splash" in every minute detail. Then, zany "Herc" began bouncing-about and rolling-around on the establishment's black and white checkered tile floor, and around thirty appreciative kids stood in a circle and put their hands together in rhythmic clapping, demonstrating their satisfaction with *his* bizarre antics. When the novelty song finally ended, the entire place gave "Herc" a thunderous round of applause.

Something special registered in my brain, and since my imitations of Bo Jalonec were working so well so far in my new social environment, I thought I would next take a page out of Quinn's book. I recalled that February 3rd, 1960 marked the one-year anniversary of Buddy Holly's death in a fatal plane crash outside Clearlake, Iowa. I recalled that my Diablo hero Quinn had pulled the plug on the Feed Bag's jukebox, and then gave a magnificent speech honoring the memory of Buddy Holly, the Big Bopper, and Ritchie Valens, who all had perished in the horrible, snow storm plane disaster. Here was my stellar opportunity to impress the Gem' teen crowd by imitating Quinn's masterful Feed Bag accomplishment.

I had planned the entire strategy all out in my head. Sal Fabian Midilli would amble over to the jukebox, and at the right moment, pull the machine's plug out of the wall. The silence would immediately get everybody's undivided attention. Then, I would stand on my booth's light-green padded-leather cushion, and astound everyone with my eloquent Buddy Holly' eulogy. After everyone in my Gem' audience would be mesmerized by my magical words, I fantasized I would ask the crowd for two-minutes of silence; march to the jukebox; re-insert the plug into the wall socket, and deposit two quarters. I intended to select and play a medley of songs in tribute to the three very talented, deceased rock and roll stars.

"Sal, at the end of 'Yakety-Yak' by the Coasters that's playin' now," I boldly directed, "on the count of three, I want ya' to go over and pull the jukebox plug out of the wall socket. Then, I can give a little speech in honor of Buddy Holly's death," I suggested.

"Can't ya' get someone else to do it? I'm too self-conscious," Fabian pleaded. "What if I screw-up?"

"No Sal, you're the best guy for the job, and the only one I can trust to do it right," I sternly replied. "Do the job and I'll find you an old Dewey button to wear."

When "Yakety-Yak" finished playing, and on the count of three, Sal obediently proceeded to the jukebox and vigorously tugged the plug out of a wall socket, just after the guitar-fret opening to Chuck Berry's "Johnny B. Goode" had begun. The absence of music instantly caught the teen patrons' attention. I bravely stood-up on the booth cushion and solemnly stared at my captive audience like a pious minister or priest peering at his devout Sunday congregation.

"A year ago today, February 3rd, 1959," I began just like Quinn had done in the Feed Bag, "a terrible plane crash happened outside Clearlake, Iowa. The small airplane crashed in a remote cornfield, and it was carrying..."

"Who gives a crap?" Gabe Gillette yelled-out from *his* Gem table. Before I knew anything else, Gillette hurled a hamburger in a bun, and it hit me in the center of my forehead. That action was quickly followed by other food tosses from three other Blues' bullies, (later identified by News) Hammer Bertino, Butch Lanza, and Ox Narducci. I lost my balance standing on the booth's light-green leather padding; tumbled backwards, penetrating, and then shattering the thick pane-glass window behind me. I was temporarily knocked unconscious from the impact with the window, and also from the jolt of my fall.

The next thing I recalled was Juice aggressively slapping me across the face. I was immobile and almost comatose, lying on the hard cold pavement amidst broken glass shards. I glanced-up and hazily perceived a crowd of Gem patrons standing around me in the frigid night air, watching steam vapor escaping from their mouths and nostrils. I had never been more publicly embarrassed in my short life as I was just then.

Officers Chet Rubba and Doug Patton from the Hammonton Police Department pulled-up in their black and white Ford squad car, wanting to investigate the unique incident.

"Are ya' all right, son?" Patrolman Rubba asked. "Should we call an ambulance?"

"He has a cut on his left hand and some blood around his right ankle," Officer Patton observed and related. "I don't think any bones are broken."

Goose then took over, and apparently, Chet Rubba and Doug Patton knew who he was. "I'll take care of J.W., here," G.R. guaranteed the local cops. "He'll be okay, once I drive him home and he washes up." And then, Goose turned toward the still-shocked Gem' proprietor, Mr. Arturo Sorrentino. "How much damage was done? What do we owe ya'?"

"That front window costs a hundred-and-fifty bucks, new," Mr. Sorrentino complained. "And I'll have to board it up until I can get a decent replacement installed."

G.R. took a wad of hundred-dollar-bills out of his dungaree pocket. "Well, Mr. Sorrentino, here's three-hundred-bazookas for your trouble. That oughta' cover the window, the wood panels, and your aggravation."

"Why thanks, Goose!" Mr. Sorrentino commended as the happy hangout owner examined the three crisp *Ben Franklins* in the palm of his hand. "Thank you very much! You're a *lifesaver."*

"Goose looks more like a *Chiclet* or a *Mary Jane* than a *Lifesaver*," Juice perceptively added.

"Well, Officers," Goose Restuccio aptly continued his problem solving. "J.W. here is gonna' be all right, and Mr. Sorrentino has been fully paid for the broken window."

The officers agreed that the debt had been officially settled, and that the Gem's owner was quite satisfied with the arrangements. Their only concern was about the status of my physical welfare. I stood from my knees, and walked up and down the sidewalk in a straight line, as if taking a drunk-driver sobriety test. And then I attested to the town constables that I was "ninety-percent all right".

My eyes searched the crowd and spotted Joanne Berenato staring at me, as if I was a visiting alien from Mars. Then, the doll smiled in my direction, and that made me feel warm inside. I waved goodbye to the Italian princess, and instructed Goose to drive me home, because my head and body were both engaged in excruciating pain.

The next fifth period lunch at Edgewood, I was still suffering from "the Blues", since my abused body was still aching all over. The guys tried cheering me up and then buoying my damaged spirit.

"J.W., that was a really nifty thing you tried at the Gem," Juice Illiani began, "and I'd still like to hear ya' give that Buddy Holly speech. I gotta' admire you for ever attempting it in the first place."

Jives Arena was residually fatigued from what the jargon-talker had creatively labeled the "Gemma dilemma". "Those Blues think they're cool and everythin' the harmful shits do is no sweat. But I'm sure that old J.W. here has some nifty tricks to fix their kicks."

I tried smiling and noticed Fabian Midilli yawning and stretching his arms while sitting across the table next to Goose Restuccio. That action sent my brain waves into a hyper Bo Jalonec mode. "Knock it off, Sal," I snarled, "because the Hammonton Rescue Squad needs a new *stretcher* and you might just fill the bill."

"Yeah J.W., Gabe Gillette and his pack of degenerates nearly sent you to the cemetery," News observed and remarked. "But I hope that shattered Gem window hasn't shattered your heart. I think ya' really impressed Joanne with your failed attempted speech stunt."

I craned my neck behind me and noticed Joanne Berenato chatting rather vociferously with her sorority of gabby, bobby-sock, Edgewood chicks. Goose then assumed and rhymed that my dream girl was yakking about "the Gem *dunce* to the other cunts".

"Keep your' friggin' perverted poetry to yourself!" I hollered across the table at the semi-surprised instigator. "You have a stone heart to match your rock brain!"

"Next time ya' need three-hundred-bucks in a hurry, kindly see somebody else," Goose convincingly fired back.

"My soul is not for sale!" I argued with a rejuvenated spirit.

"I never knew four heavy deluxe hamburgers could do so much injury and damage to one person," Juice commented in almost normal

English. "It really fractures me how hairy it all was," Johnny marveled and described.

"I don't know why people call them hamburgers," News Tomasello stated in his typical academic, philosophical tone, "since ham comes from a pig and the meat in a hamburger originates from a cow. It would be more accurate callin' the edibles steakburgers rather than *ham*burgers."

"You and J.W. ought to be roommates in Ancora," criticized Goose as the wise-ass referred to a local South Jersey mental hospital. "Then, ya' two could impress each other with stupid shit all day and all night long, and not realize that each of ya' is actually a crazy mother-humpin' dick-head."

It was getting towards the end of cafeteria period and the guys had already brought our food trays back to the washing and cleaning window. Juice rose from the table and walked-over to talk to Mr. Rebeck at the lunchroom's microphone. I saw the main teacher on duty nod his head in agreement. Then, Mr. Rebeck got everyone's attention and asked *me* to step-up to the microphone and to deliver an important message to my fellow students about remembering a "special anniversary".

"Tell everybody in here about Buddy Holly," Illiani advised as Juice leaned-over my shoulder at the cafeteria table. "Give 'em the same speech ya' couldn't give at the Gem."

Almost in a trance, I nervously paced-up to the front of the cafeteria. My eyes surveyed the two hundred-fifty kids seated in the extraordinarily quiet room. I witnessed Joanne "Ginger" Berenato peering at me, her mouth open in awe with her right hand covering it. I took a deep breath and approached the lonely microphone stand. I cleared my throat and neurotically gazed at my very large attentive audience. All I could think about was Quinn's courage when my former idol had stood and had spoken his successful oration in the Feed Bag. 'I dedicate this speech to Quinn,' I thought to my conscience.

"Yesterday, February the third," I slowly began, "marked the one-year anniversary of a terrible accident that had happened outside Clearlake, Iowa". My heart was wildly pounding inside my chest cavity as I gradually gained more confidence. "A small airplane had crashed into a remote cornfield. The plane was carrying three popular recording stars, Buddy Holly, Ritchie Valens, and the Big Bopper. I still personally feel their loss, and I know like me, *you* all love their songs on the radio," I emphasized, pointing my index finger at the stunned cafeteria assemblage. "I would like to honor their memory and their music the best way I know how, with a moment of silence. Let's all bow our heads in memory of the three dead rock and roll stars."

Remarkably, even the wise guys in the crowded cafeteria felt some remorse and did not heckle or jeer my sincere request. Ten full seconds elapsed, and then I announced into the mic, "Thank you very much!" To my surprise, the entire cafeteria assemblage stood and produced a very loud and sincere round of applause. I glanced to my right, and gleefully noticed Joanne Berenato also cheering and clapping rather vigorously.

I paced to my familiar table in almost military fashion with my shoulders square. I had never felt so proud in all my life. The guys greeted me as if I were some sort of courageous war hero.

"That was fantastic!" Juice acknowledged and praised. "Everyone except Mr. Andrews loved your tribute!"

I turned to my left and saw Andrews leaning against the side, yellow cinderblock wall with his arms tightly folded in front of his chest. A definite frown was welded on his facial features. The old gent's sneer was accentuated by a row of wrinkles on his forehead.

"Don't worry J.W.," Sal assessed and stated. "The old coot is jealous of ya'. You showed him ya' got guts, and he's afraid of you challengin' him again inside his sacred classroom."

"Sal's right, J.W.," News confirmed. "Old Andrews sees *you* as a threat to his supreme authority in *his* little classroom empire. Mrs. Murphy taught us that control freaks like Napoleon and that dictator Hitler hated guys like you that can think on your own. You're a definite threat to your trig' teacher's tyranny!"

"Ya' really got that jive math' turkey basted and then frosted with his outa' sight cage rattlin'!" Jives reported. "The brutal bastard knows we're talkin' about him standin' all alone over there against the side fence in Nowheresville."

The most informative and devastating remark came from the lips of Goose Restuccio. "J.W., do ya' remember ya' tellin' the guys the other day how the Diablos had taken care of that Levittown police car by pourin' sand and sugar in the friggin' gas tank?"

"Sure do," I amiably recalled. "That was a classic!"

"Well, J.W.," Goose continued his commentary, "this mornin' I hired a couple of my Pop's hit-men to do a small job for me. While you was strugglin' through that fink Andrews' daily trig' torture this mornin', my Pop's men came on campus and poured a mixture of dirt and sugar into the gas tank of Mr. Andrews new black Ford Fairlane. That baby won't turn over in another hundred-years."

"I didn't ask you to do anything to Andrews' car!" I objected.

"Oh, no!" News Tomasello exclaimed. "Mr. Andrews and Mrs. Murphy both have identical new black Ford Fairlanes," News reported. "But I saw Mr. Andrews come to school with Mr. Rebeck. Rebeck was driving his old red and white De Soto. So, Andrews's car is probably in the shop getting serviced."

"You mean that…." Goose stammered in rare amazement.

"Exactly," News interrupted as G.R. fumbled for the precise right words to express his reaction. "Your Mafia hit-men probably vandalized Mrs. Murphy's new black '60 Ford instead of Mr. Andrews' new wheels."

Chapter Nine

"A Wild Scavenger Hunt"

Play practice for *There's Gold in Them Dar Hills* was scheduled for after school at 3:15. I was feeling despondent, realizing that I had given Goose the destructive idea of pouring sand and sugar into Mr. Andrews' gas tank. The whole matter really became ugly when G.R. unilaterally dispatched a couple of his father's Mafia goons to the teacher parking area and by accident, the henchmen sabotaged Mrs. Murphy's black '60 Ford Fairlane instead of the one owned by my dreaded trigonometry instructor.

"Are you all right J.W.?" a concerned Mrs. Murphy asked midway into the one-act play practice. "The color of your face looks like something between ashen and chalky. I don't think the nurse is still in the building to take your temperature."

"I'll be okay once I go home and drink a ginger ale or two," I softly and guiltily answered. "My stomach is a little queasy from eating too much puddin', pretzels, and potato chips at lunch time."

Esther Phyllis, Elaine Hill, and Nanette Banks soothed my sensitive soul with encouraging words. "J.W., Elaine said, "I think Joanne Berenato has her eyes on ya'. That cafeteria speech ya' gave about Buddy Holly showed everybody a real piece of your inner self. I even had tears in my eyes. Ya' definitely got what it takes. Now that you know, go for it!"

"Thanks Elaine, you're a true friend," I returned. "I'd like to ask Joanne to the March Cotillion, but I can't get-up the courage."

"Don't be surprised if she says 'yes'," Nanette Banks added with a wink. "But you'd better make your move first before someone else sends her an invitation, or calls her on the phone."

"Elaine and Nanette are right," Esther rendered her opinion. "Sometimes, guys are afraid to ask the prettiest girls in the school out because they're worried about being rejected," the second-lead actress pointed-out. "Sometimes, the most gorgeous cheerleaders and most attractive school actresses never get to go to the dances they dream of attendin', simply because they're too beautiful to be asked out by petrified guys."

I didn't have the heart to see Mrs. Murphy's vandalized car not being able to start and remaining stationary until a tow truck arrived in the teacher's parking lot. I couldn't wait for Fabian to drive Juice, Jives, News, and me home in his father's '59 white Chevy Impala. We conversed as Sal Midilli turned right in east Atco off of Coopers Folly Road at Wooster's Funeral Home, onto the White Horse Pike.

"My wheels are outa' action until Fabian puts a new juice maker in my lame Dodge tomorrow after school," Jives informed his four depressed listeners from the front passenger side. Those loony Blues are bad news that really lit my fuse."

"Those Blues really did an *assault* on your *battery,"* Juice replied in an effort to create some much-needed levity.

"Hey, look on the right!" Fabian pointed-out up ahead. "Ain't that Goose comin' outa' the Atco Sub Emporium. I'll betcha' he's collectin' some more gum ball machine money. J.W. almost made old G.R. a pauper after the Gem window incident," the chauffeur exaggerated and joked.

Fabian Midilli turned into the Atco Sub Emporium's asphalt driveway and his boss white Chevy skidded to a semi-dramatic halt. The tall, stocky, pock-faced Sicilian entrepreneur casually sauntered over to the '59 Impala. Goose never seemed to have any conscience or guilt about anything he ever did or said, and that negative aspect of his demeanor bothered me very much.

"Hey, you peasant creeps, if you're lookin' for pussy you'll have to find the nearest cat kennel," the rude excuse for a human being addressed us. "Ain't no damned hair pie around here! Hey, Sal, ya' oughta' trade this tin pig in for a real pussy-wagon!"

"Goose, we gotta' do somethin' to help-out poor Mrs. Murphy," I begged. "Her black Ford might never get over the indigestion it'll have when she turns-on the ignition and nothin' happens."

"Well, J.W., I figured that minor crime my Daddy's boys committed would be botherin' your weak heart," Goose grinned, showing teeth that looked like polished ivory piano keys out of the left side of his slanted mouth. "J.W., you're damned lucky that I sort of like ya' and even tolerate your asshole bullshit. Otherwise, I wouldn't give ya' a square inch of sandpaper to wipe your skinny butt-hole with."

I asked Goose to specifically identify how the future Mafia don planned to remedy the harsh reality of Mrs. Murphy's disabled automobile. As usual, pathetically miserable Restuccio believed that money could cure any particular human vexation or difficulty.

"J.W., here's five newly-printed *Ben Franklins*. Put them in an envelope with a typed letter apologizin' for the ruined gas line," G.R. suggested. "The gift should cover the expense of fixin' the problem, towin' Mrs. Murphy's car and her rentin' a new one until the gas tank is removed and rinsed-out, and the gas lines are thoroughly either cleaned-out or replaced."

"Goose, you think money can solve anything, don't you!" I protested, despising his ruthless, conceited, arrogant attitude. "You have no heart. Your wallet is your soul!"

G.R. threatened to withdraw his generous offer if I persisted in my "stupid, naive opposition". I succinctly shut and zipped my mouth closed and dutifully swallowed my pride as I humbly accepted Mrs. Murphy's five-hundred-dollar compensation.

"You're learnin' fast," Goose caustically commended. "Now listen-up, good! Mrs. Murphy will be thrilled to death when she'll look in her teacher mailbox at school and finds this wonderful, sudden, five-hundred-dollar windfall. She might become so excited that she'll start masturbatin' on stage in front of the whole freakin' student body."

I reluctantly gazed-down in my hand at Goose's five-hundred-dollars and acceded to authoring and mailing a typed letter containing the surprise bonanza and an anonymous brief apology. I promised my allegiance to Goose's conniving scheme, even though I abhorred the conniver's cocky disposition to the nth degree. From the doted-on kid's narrow perspective, *he* was the almighty center of the universe.

"Mrs. Murphy will be doubly excited when she gets her insurance check in her faculty mailbox and realizes that this half-a-grand is a bonus. And J.W.," Goose concluded and emphasized, "your friggin' friendship has already cost me about a thousand-bucks. Just think about the Gem broken window and Mrs. Murphy's car, and you'll know you'd have to work at least three-summers at Pete's Market just to pay-off those two huge debts."

After I had been driven home in the 'cherry' '59 Impala, I scampered upstairs to my bedroom desk typewriter. After a moment's meditation, my fingers pounded-out an anonymous brief apology letter, addressed the envelope using the typewriter; inserted the money along with the letter inside; found a postage stamp, and drove the Pete's Market Special twenty-four miles to the Pleasantville Post Office for safe delivery.

On Wednesday and Thursday, Mrs. Murphy looked somewhere between glum and lugubrious. But then on Friday, I reckoned the social studies teacher had finally received her anonymous monetary reward in her Edgewood mailbox. I noticed that afternoon that our play director was animated, ecstatic, and seemed exhilarated throughout the entire two-hour play rehearsal. Goose's money had wonderfully rekindled her dormant enthusiasm.

Our one-act play director's obvious ebullience and amiable spirit rubbed-off on me. I observed Joanne Berenato standing alone and holding her own envelope next to the plush green Edgewood auditorium stage curtains. I approached her angelic appearance with new-found zeal.

"Hi, Joanne. I've been meaning to ask ya' somethin' important for a couple of days," I forthrightly prefaced.

"Oh, hi J.W.," the swarthy-skinned, good-mannered doll greeted with a smile. "What's cookin', good lookin'?"

"I was wonderin' if," I hesitated, "I was wonderin' if you'd like to go to the March Cotillion Dance with me, if that's all right with you?"

"Oh J.W., I'd love to," the peach farmer's daughter stated. "But Elaine Hill just gave me this card and envelope from her third cousin over in Hammonton. I don't know if ya' know him or not, but his name is Gabe Gillette."

"The name does remotely ring a bell," I rather disgustedly acknowledged.

Joanne ripped-open the envelope and inside was a request from rich kid Gabe Gillette to escort her to the Edgewood March Cotillion Dance. The Sicilian beauty and I were both flabbergasted by the extraordinary coincidence.

Elaine Hill surmised that something was amiss so out of curiosity, the well-respected senior ambled-over to investigate *our* mutual crisis. Joanne explained the uncanny phenomenon to her close friend, and being a born problem solver, Elaine had a very profound brainstorm. "Why don't ya' have some sort of neat contest between Gabe and J.W. The winner will get the exclusive right to take you to the Cotillion?" Elaine suggested to Joanne.

"Well, what sort of contest?" my dream girl asked, her mind in a dire quandary. "I wish this were the Sadie Hawkins Dance instead of the Cotillion. Then, I would definitely ask J.W. Elaine, exactly what do ya' propose?"

"Well, how about something like a scavenger hunt between J.W. and my rich cousin, Gabe?" Elaine answered with a question. "Each contestant will have to drive around the Hammonton area and find, let's say fifteen items or pieces of information you give them on a planned list. The first lucky guy to get the job done earns the privilege of takin' you to the Cotillion."

"That's a great idea," Joanne commended, showing a bit of euphoria about the scavenger hunt contest. "I decree that each guy will be able to choose one person to go with him as a guide, and help in the search. Elaine, you're a *lifesaver.*"

"Yeah," I added in a disappointed tone of voice. "The *Titanic's* captain could've used Elaine Hill *after* it hit the iceberg!"

"Okay, J.W., be in front of the Gem with your partner at eight p.m. sharp on Saturday night. This is going to be really neat fun!" the Italian chick indicated, completely ignoring my *Titanic* remark. "Thanks, Elaine. You're a true friend!" Joanne exclaimed.

I figured my loyal Lieutenant should be News Tomasello. Tommy was the most qualified because he was a Harvard or Rutgers-bound brainiac; knew all kinds of facts and figures; was a whiz at advanced academics, and was the most honest and trustworthy Edgewood friend I had. I called News on the phone to alert the local geography wiz of my special preference.

"Sure, J.W., I'll be more than glad to accompany ya' on the scavenger hunt. It sounds like more fun than Milton Berle, Jackie Gleason, and Red Skelton put together," News expressed ad indicated. "I can't wait to get started. I love intellectual challenges and academic competition!"

Saturday night soon arrived, and Tommy Tomasello picked me up in his '57 red and white Ford Fairlane. Tommy turned left off of Bellevue Avenue onto Third Street, curved around Penza's Hardware Store to Central Avenue, and found a rare parking space close to the Gem. Gabe Gillette was already at the teen hangout, with his brand-new light blue Corvette parked in front of Olivo's Market, facing in the direction of the U.S. Post Office and Town Hall, a block away across from Kiwanis Triangle Park, and yellow-brick Hammonton High School.

"He's got way more speed than we have," I confided to News as we exited his Ford Fairlane. "That blue 'Vette's really hot!"

"Yeah, J.W.," Tommy grinned. "Notice what color it's gotta' be. But remember, ya' have me on your side, and my mind is worth any three blue 'Vettes on the entire planet."

"Hey, Tommy, I'm happy to see that Mr. Sorrentino has gotten his front window fixed. Looks as good as new," I happily mentioned.

News and I entered the Gem and spotted Gabe Gillette and another muscular Blue in their customary blue denim jackets and matching dungarees, talking with Joanne Berenato, Nanette Banks, and Elaine Hill.

"J.W. and Tommy," Elaine commenced, "I'd like to officially introduce you to Gabe Gillette and to Bobby 'Speed' Mortellite."

News and I professionally shook hands with our designated opponents as if we were honest and polite drivers at the Indianapolis Speedway. Any bystander could easily tell that our meeting was not exactly a mutual admiration society. Gillette and Mortellite's fathers were big-time area blueberry farmers, and *our* raunchy opponents projected joint condescending attitudes, which viewed News and me as expendable, poor, white-trash indigents.

"Okay, guys. I'm going to give each of you gentlemen identical lists," Joanne explained, "and each sheet of paper contains fifteen places you have to visit to get the vital information that is instructed in each listed direction."

"Yes," Elaine rather constructively added. "And after ya' get the information to the fifteen locations, you must solve the cryptic riddle of the scavenger hunt' clues."

Joanne finished the Gem briefing by saying that the first one to call her home phone number at 561-1445 before eleven p.m. with the scavenger hunt' riddle accurately deciphered, would be determined the winner. "Both teams now have five-minutes to study your lists."

News was smart enough to bring along three sharpened Number 2 pencils, a ballpoint pen, and an empty black and white marble Composition Tablet to take and record precise notes. Tommy's first entry was 561-1445, the aforementioned Italian goddess's unlisted, private phone number.

The fifteen locations provided on the typed loose-leaf sheet were easily recognizable and familiar to us, but the hidden riddle was much more of a mutual concern.

"The obscure message seems to be a real conundrum," Tommy News pontificated. "This is gonna' be fun to figure-out!"

"Jesus Criminizer, News. If ya' can't speak *plain* English, at least speak mountain English!" I criticized.

"Well, alright," T.T. continued his analysis. "And if we can't decode this secret encryption, then I seriously doubt if Gabe Gillette or his knuckle-head chum can interpret it, either," News whispered. "How's that for consolation?"

"Okay, guys, the official five-minutes of studying are up!" Elaine announced. "Get ready to compete!"

"On the count of three," Joanne yelled-out, "Gentleman, start your engines!"

The forty or so teens on the sidewalk outside the Gem cheered loudly in response to the famous *Indianapolis Speedway* starting signal. Gillette and Mortellite hastily exited the Gem and hopped into the custom-painted '60 light blue Corvette, with "Speed" being the assigned driver. According to prior arrangement, I jumped behind the wheel of News' red and white '57 Ford Fairlane, and my astute passenger had the responsibility of taking accurate notes, and also serving as my trusty navigator.

The blue Corvette peeled-out going east on Central. "Look at those nutcase idiots zoom," News noted. "They're probably headin' to Hammonton High School, item number three on the list. The best way to handle a list of fifteen tasks is in numerical order. That way we won't have to shuffle back and forth from item three to item fourteen, to item six. In the final review, Ben Franklin was right. Haste makes waste!"

"Well, then," I noted after firing-up the Ford's engine. "It's off to the 'Welcome to Hammonton' sign south of town on *Route 54.*"

The directions had specified that we should obtain the exact language that had been advertised by the town council on the designated billboard.

"Don't go over the twenty-five mile an hour speed limit," News prudently cautioned as I headed south through the heart of town. "A traffic ticket could be the difference between success and failure. Go slow through intersections, and especially across the railroad tracks."

The speed limit changed from twenty-five to thirty-five after we passed the First Road intersection. Another mile down *Route 54* was the "Welcome to Hammonton" sign facing north in the opposite direction. I made a skillful U-turn, and illuminated from ground-level lights the designated billboard read, "Welcome to Hammonton, the Blueberry/Peach Capital of the World". And below that testimonial the sign stated, "All Roads Lead to Hammonton".

News jotted-down *that* pertinent information into his marble composition book, and then it was time to zip-over to stop two, the United States Post Office specific address "number" on South Third Street.

"J.W.," T.T. verbally mused, "the language on the billboard read that all roads lead to Hammonton, but you and I both know that *all major highways* lead to somewhere else!"

I smiled and remembered something Bo Jalonec had once told me inside the Feed Bag. "Tommy, I think you're gonna' go to Oxford, buy the right shoes, and become a *roads* scholar," I answered as I adroitly substituted certain words.

My right foot on the brake pedal stopped the Fairlane next to the curb; News leaped-out with his flashlight, and in thirty-seconds, returned to the car. "It's U.S. Post Office Number 144," my recording secretary scribbled into his notepad with his pencil, as I again dimmed the interior lights.

"Location Number Three is across the street on Central Avenue," Tommy directed. "We need to know the date on the Hammonton High School cornerstone."

I made a left past the triangular Kiwanis Park at Peach Street, and another quick left onto Central Avenue. News again hopped-out of the Ford with his flashlight and swiftly retrieved the necessary data. My assistant returned out of breath with winter steam flowing from his mouth. "The high school was built in 1925," Tommy entered into his improvised journal.

Item four instructed us to zip across Bellevue Avenue to the corner of French Street and Egg Harbor Road where we had to glean the American Legion Post's Address Number, which turned-out to be #186. Next, we accelerated down French Street to North Third, where the fifth task on the scavenger hunt sheet was the Sons of Italy Garibaldi Lodge Number, which on the building was #1658.

"A lot of numbers in this weird scavenger hunt," I observed and shared as I headed south on Fairview Avenue to the town brewery on Washington Street.

"Number Six wants us to get what inscription is etched on the side of the brewery, and Number Seven directs us to snare the words on the front of Hammonton Packaging Company. That's good, because it's only three blocks away from the town brewery on Railroad Avenue."

The brewery inscription simply read "The Brewing Corp.," and the language on the front of Hammonton Packaging was, "Wholesale to Farms, Retail to Farm Markets."

"Do ya' think ya' now have enough words to figure out the message?" I anxiously asked News as I accelerated ahead.

"Not yet, J.W.," Tommy replied, out of breath. "Joanne is an all A National Honor Society student, so whatever the riddle is, I'm sure it's gonna' require plenty of brain power and cleverosity to unravel."

"What's Number Seven?" I demanded in a determined voice.

"We gotta' get the street address of the *Hammonton News*. That should be an easy task because it's right on Bellevue Avenue," my loyal assistant stated.

"Wrong!" I corrected. "Bellevue Avenue becomes Twelfth Street above the railroad tracks, and then *Route 54* below First Road."

"Wow, J.W., you're right!" News acceded. "And Bellevue Avenue north above the White Horse Pike becomes *Route 206*. The damned street has four different names! No wonder why the brain-dead Blues are so screwed-up living in this crazy town!"

I stopped the red and white '57 in front of the *Hammonton News*. Tommy briskly exited the auto and scampered-up to the small white-painted brick building to secure the street address. Then, my fellow explorer rushed back with a disappointed look on his face. "There's no address anywhere, either on the outside wall or on the door or window. Look J.W.! There's a phone booth next to the gas station across the street."

News sprinted across Twelfth Street; entered the Ma Bell vertical glass and metal rectangle, and flipped his fingers through the white pages of the telephone book. My search colleague scurried back with the precise information, "115 12th Street!" T.T. panted while registering the essential numbers in his essential log.

Stop "Number Eight" on the odyssey was Bruni's Pizzeria, only a block south of the *Hammonton News*. I slowed-down enough to obtain the prescribed *pertinent language* on the business's overhead shingle, "Bruni's Pizzeria, Open 4 PM-10 PM, Tuesday-Sunday, Parking in Rear".

"Well, News," I declared. "I think Bagliani's Grocery Market is just a block ahead. I believe we have to get the two words written in red on the store's main sign, if I remember correctly from the list."

"You're right J.W. It reads 'Italian Sausage', that's exactly what it says! 'Italian Sausage'. Now Number Eleven is the giant Renault Winery bottle on the White Horse Pike in Elm between Pastore Orchards Farm Market and the Ancora Bridge overpass. Again, we gotta' get the exact words off of the colossal bottle."

I took a short cut down North Third Street to *Route 30.* In another minute, we were parked below the lit-up twenty-four-foot-high, illuminated champagne bottle. "The words read," News identified, "Renault Winery, Founded in 1864, Bremen Avenue, Egg Harbor City, New Jersey, 16 Miles East-Straight Ahead."

"Bremen, isn't that a city somewhere in Europe?" I inquired as I made a quick U-turn back onto the four-lane White Horse Pike.

"Yeah, it's in Germany where Elvis was stationed," News attested, "and most of the residents of Egg Harbor, and its neighboring town of Cologne, are of German descent. Our next stop is the other Renault Winery bottle east of Egg Harbor City."

"Isn't it identical to the one we just visited in Elm?" I insisted.

"You're absolutely right!" News confirmed. "I think this is some kind of stupid trick item, or wicked detour of some kind. I'm familiar with that identical Egg Harbor champagne bottle, too. And the only difference between the two statues is that there's an arrow that points north on Bremen Avenue saying '1 Mile, instead of 16 Miles East."

"Are you suggesting that we skip Number Twelve because it's basically the same as Number Eleven?" I asked.

"Precisely," Tommy returned. "And Gillette and Mortellite will probably waste a half hour drivin' the blue 'Vette sixteen-miles all the way to Egg Harbor for nothin'. All I'm gonna' put into the book for Number Twelve is 1 Mile and nothing else. I'm sure that *we* have the right answer!"

Number Thirteen on the sheet was the *Civil War Memorial* in Hammonton's Greenmount Cemetery, nestled between 1st Road and Chew Road. Joanne's directions stipulated that we had to obtain the exact nomenclature carved onto the base of the stone memorial, which featured a Union soldier standing at rest with a rifle.

"Isn't the cemetery between 1st Road and 2nd Road?" I wondered and questioned as I sped ahead.

"That could be a mistake that Gillette and Mortellite will make," my clever associate revealed. "Chew Road doesn't become 2nd Road until after the first bend, just beyond the cemetery. This Hammonton is really a weird town as far as highways, roads, and street names are concerned."

I drove the '57 Fairlane into the dark, gloomy graveyard. It was both eerie and spooky inside the dismal cemetery, being all by our lonesome in the dark. I stopped the Ford, and News and I got out. While stretching my legs, I had to hold the car's flashlight up to the stone pedestal when my competent companion was copying-down the lengthy inscription. "Erected By the Members of General D.A. Russell, Post Number 88, G.A.R., In Memory of The Country's Defenders, Sept. 28, 1885".

We hurried back inside the Ford Fairlane, escaping out of the cold February evening. Even though the heater's fan was blowing, we still breathed-out into our hands to warm them up.

"Strange," News observed, "that when soup is hot, ya' blow into it to cool it off, and when our hands are cold, ya' exhale into 'em to warm them up."

"Only you think of cool, trivial academic stuff like that. Glad to have ya' by my side," I genuinely praised. "Only two more stops to go," I remarked as I rapidly sped-out of the dreary, lonely cemetery's gates. "I remember that the last itinerary stop will be the Oak Grove Cemetery on the Pike, but I can't seem to recall Item Fourteen. I think it is…."

"Angelo's Store on Egg Harbor Road in Rosedale, just beyond the Hammonton line in Camden County," my very knowledgeable partner keenly articulated.

Again, our assignment was to acquire the words painted on the side of a building. I stopped long enough for News to read aloud and copy-down, "Angelo's Store, Liquor Store, Beer, Wine and Ice".

Only one more scavenger hunt location remained, which was the sixth grave monument that is situated just inside the Oak Grove Cemetery entrance off of Old Forks Road.

"My folks and grandparents always called this road Cemetery Avenue. Why is it called Old Forks Road now?" I asked News.

"Because people ran-out of old used spoons and old knives to throw away," my buddy hardily laughed. "Once we get these final bits of information, we'll be able to work on decoding the mysterious secret message. It's sort of like a jumbled-up jigsaw puzzle, with a variety of pieces that don't seem to jibe."

I applied the brakes just inside the creepy Old Forks Road entrance to Oak Grove Cemetery. News very slowly counted from *one* until our feet reached the sixth tombstone. Then, my trusty associate flicked-on his flashlight and shone its beam directly upon the ominous-looking object. "Here, give me the handy torch while you write-down the required dates," I offered. "The tomb stone we're after is on the driver's side."

"Jason St. John, Born May 7, 1832, Died June 15, 1901," we both read simultaneously.

"I thought St. John was buried in Palestine or over in Asia Minor," I volunteered, attempting to break the suspense with humor. "St. John owns a lot of churches and schools, just like St. Joseph does, but not quite as many."

"J.W., be quiet while I work on solving this well-concealed hidden message," News admonished. "Now that we have all the facts and words that we need, here comes the hard part, that involves our total concentration."

"Okay, let's get-out of this ghoulish place before St. John's ghost ascends out of that grave and attacks me for makin' that horrible joke about his name," I suggested. I drove through the dark, scary graveyard with my lights out, fearing that a passing police car might notice our presence and investigate our surreptitious activity, causing us a valuable time delay. When I approached *Route 30,* a light-blue, custom-painted Corvette heading east sped by like it was a streaking bolt of lightning.

"That's crazy Mortellite and insane Gillette," News recognized and communicated. "Those low I.Q. idiots are probably going from the Renault Winery bottle down in Elm east to the Renault Winery bottle on the corner of Bremen Avenue and *Route 30* in Egg Harbor. Ya' know, J.W. It pays to have a good memory!"

"Those guys really vacillate between dumb and stupid," I agreed. "But only if your theory about the two champagne bottles havin' the same words beneath them is correct."

"The only difference is that the bottle sixteen-miles east in Egg Harbor has a '1 Mile' arrow instead of sayin' 16 Miles Straight Ahead," Tommy confidently maintained.

I turned on the Fairlane's headlights and drove three-miles from Oak Grove Cemetery to the phone booth in front of Olivo's Supermarket across Central Avenue from the Gem. I kept the Ford Fairlane's motor running so that we had sufficient heat to stay comfortable while attempting to aptly decipher the seemingly very confusing secret message.

News had the uncanny propensity to be able to think about two things at the same time. While his keen mind was absorbed in puzzle solving, my sagacious friend discussed a story Tomasello had studied in his eighth-period English class.

"J.W., I can't help but think about Oedipus and the riddle of the Sphinx," T.T. spoke while studying his comprehensive notes.

"Wasn't Oedipus an ancient Greek, and the Sphinx an Egyptian figure that guards the pyramids?" I queried.

"J.W., the Egyptian Sphinx had a man's head attached to a lion's body, but the legendary Greek Sphinx had a woman's head connected to a lion's body."

"Wow!" I exclaimed. "The ancient Greeks made the Egyptian Sphinx into the first trans-sexual in all of mythology!"

"Get serious for a minute, will ya' please!" News adamantly objected. "You're beginnin' to sound a little like Goose or Jives. In Greek mythology, Oedipus was challenged to answer the riddle of the Sphinx. 'What has four legs in the morning, two legs in the afternoon, and three legs at night'?"

"A magical hippopotamus?" I answered with uncertainty.

"No, dummy, A man has four legs in the morning because he crawls; two legs in mid-life because he walks, and three legs at night because he struggles-around in old age with a cane."

"Well, News, that's just great! But how are we gonna' solve Joanne's crazy riddle. Do you' *sphinx* you know how?"

"You're hilarious squared, which in elementary math' is hilarious times hilarious!" Tommy cynically replied. "What I'm tryin' to tell ya; is that we can't be thinkin' along conventional lines here. We have to be unorthodox, instead of linear!"

Five crucial minutes must have elapsed without a word being uttered. I opened the window a crack to avoid being asphyxiated by an excess of carbon-monoxide exhaust fumes. Then, News, mimicking Archimedes, enthusiastically yelled-out "Eureka! I think I've got it!"

"*You reek a'* stupidity!" I negatively and weakly punned. "What the heck can you be thinkin' of except being cold in frigid twenty-degree temperature? *Eureka?* Have ya' just invented a fancy new Greek vacuum cleaner?"

News opened his glove compartment and fumbled for his ball-point pen so that the academic guru could mark legible symbols on a blank page inside the marble composition tablet. Then, the math' wizard revealed something rather significant. "J.W., all of the words I jotted-down from the directions mean absolutely nothin' at all, even in any combination!" Tomasello excitedly yelled.

"Do ya' mean we did all of that riding around for nothin'?" I returned. "Do ya' want a broken *Slinky* or a decapitated *Barbie Doll* for a cheap carnival prize?"

"No Silly, none' of the words or their combinations mean anything at all. That fact leaves me to only one brilliant deduction!" News shouted in a very exuberant voice.

"And what on earth might that factor be?" I inquired, my mind being at wit's end.

"The words don't mean a damned thing, but all of the numbers we obtained in the scavenger hunt do. Here, I've written them down," T.T. excitedly indicated. "First, I'll review all of the *even* numbers."

I was momentarily dumfounded and speechless. News added together the *even* numbers 54 from *Route 54,* 114 from the U.S. Post Office, 186 from the American Legion Lodge, and Number 1658 from the Sons of Italy Lodge. The Hammonton News on 12th Street, 4 and 10 from the Bruni's Pizzeria sign, 1864 and 16 miles from the Renault Winery bottle, and 88 and Sept. 28 from the Greenmount Cemetery *Civil War* Monument were the next *even* numbers. And finally, 6th grave along with 1832 from the Jason St. John tombstone inside the Oak Grove Cemetery were cited. "The total of 54, 114, 186, 1658, 12, 4, 10, 1864, 16, 88, 28, 6 and 1832 comes to 5,872," my friend oddly declared.

I didn't say a single syllable. I was almost hypnotized by News' fantastic mathematics that still made no sense at all. All I could think about was the sum 5,872, which meant positively nothing at all to my frame of reference.

"Now, J.W., I'm goin' to focus on all of the *odd* numbers in the scavenger hunt directions and accurate answers. Here we go," News Tomasello stated as the numbers' experimenter flipped-over to a clean page of horizontal lines in the school composition marble notebook. I carefully shined the flashlight onto *his* newly formulated odd-numbers' arithmetic.

"The Hammonton High cornerstone was laid in 1925," News continued, "and the street address of the *Hammonton News* is 115. The Renault Winery arrow-sign in Egg Harbor says 1 Mile; Greenmount Cemetery is on 1st Road; the year the *Civil War* Monument was erected and dedicated was 1885; Jason St. John was born on May 7, and the sea captain died June 15, 1901. If I add together 1925, 115, 1, 1, 1885, 7, 15 and 1901 I get the grand total of.....5,850!"

"The two numbers are very close to one another!" I loudly proclaimed, "5,872 and 5,850. But what does all this mean?"

"Don't you get it?" News chided. "If you subtract the sum of the odd numbers from the sum of the even numbers, your answer is 22."

"But I'm only seventeen!" I hollered.

"Yes, that's true," News concurred, "but doesn't the number twenty-two mean anything to you? J.W., there's only twenty-two days remaining until the Edgewood Cotillion Dance!"

"News, you're a genius with a capital G!" I bellowed. "If you were inside Aladdin's lamp, you would be a *genie*-us!" I laughed.

I couldn't harness my extraordinary ecstasy, me being fully overwhelmed with joy. I rushed outside to the phone booth; fumbled in my pocket for the appropriate change, and hurriedly deposited two nickels into the slot. I very carefully dialed 561-1445, Joanne Berenato's private bedroom number.

"Hello, Joanne. This in J.W. callin'. Guess what! I think I've solved your secret hidden message!" I joyfully yelled. "The answer is twenty-two, the number of days left until the big Edgewood Cotillion Dance! Is that right?"

"Yes, J.W., that is one-hundred-percent correct," Joanne replied and verified in a somewhat *listless* voice.

"Joanne," I worriedly interrupted. "Has Gabe Gillette figured-out the fantastic riddle yet?" I curiously asked.

"No, he hasn't," the Italian honey responded in a melancholy tone of voice. "J.W., there's something pretty important I gotta' tell you," the very saddened, prom-beauty-queen informed.

"What's that?" I asked in a more sedate tone.

"Daddy says I can't go to the Cotillion with Gabe Gillette because he's the son of a blueberry farmer, and Daddy's a prominent peach grower, and you know how the blueberry kids in Hammonton hate the peach kids and vice versa....."

"Yes, I know," I affirmed. "It's sort of like *Romeo and Juliet,* with the Montagues and the Capulets despising each other. I always remember that *her* first name and her last name rhymed, Juliet Capulet. But that's totally terrific news for me. Gabe Gillette can't take you to the big dance!"

"But J.W.," Joanne moaned in what sounded like emotional distress. "Daddy also said that I can't go to the big dance with *you* either, because he doesn't know you, and because your family doesn't grow peaches."

My addled brain was in orbit. I couldn't muster-up the right words to vent my astonishment, as my voice awkwardly stuttered over the phone. "But, but, Joanne, does all this crazy type of small-town nonsense mean you can't go to the Cotillion with anybody?"

There was a long moment of abnormal silence. "J.W.," Joanne sniffed, "Daddy wants me to go to the Edgewood Cotillion with Herc Juliano, whose father's a big peach farmer on *206*. Daddy already talked to Herc this evening when he was over the Juliano' farm buying some fertilizer. I'm sorry, but it's a done deal. Goodbye J.W.," Joanne sobbed.

"Goodbye," I returned with a twinge twisting-away deep inside my stomach, and then spiraling-down to my intestines. I slowly walked back to the sanctuary of the red and white '57 Ford Fairlane, with my throbbing head crestfallen.

"What happened?" News solemnly asked. "Has the world ended without my knowledge?"

"The scavenger-hunt turned-out to be a stupid wild *goose* chase instead!" I vehemently complained as I kicked an empty, rusty tin can across the cold Central Avenue sidewalk.

Chapter Ten

"Speeding Around"

I was more than a little upset at what Joanne's father had arranged with Dave "Herc" Juliano's pop, especially since News and I had soundly vanquished Gabe Gillette and Speed Mortellite in the meaningless February 1960 scavenger hunt. I was irritated at Joanne for allowing her parents to control her life, but in tightly-knit Italian families, blood is often thicker than water, and I was the odd man out. I resented her blind submission to assumed adult authority.

There's Gold in Them Dar Hills won the Edgewood one-act-play competition, and I didn't really care one iota. I boycotted the cast "victory celebration" over at Cowtail Bar to let the leading female role, Joanne Berenato, know exactly how I felt about her wealthy agrarian family. 'Things are not at all peachy,' I sadly mused.

I promised my ego that I also would boycott the Edgewood Cotillion, scheduled for the following Friday night in early March, and I honored my solemn pledge. Juice attended the gala social with Elaine Hill; Jives with Esther Phyllis; News with Mimi Bartuccio, and Fabian Midilli with Justine Jackson. Of course, Joanne attended the ball with mental-case Dave "Herc" Juliano, who would impress all of the attendees by obnoxiously rolling, bouncing, and cavorting all over the formal event's dignified dance floor.

My options for the evening of the March Edgewood Cotillion were really limited, which meant that Goose Restuccio was the only acquaintance available with whom to commiserate. The ignoble Sicilian picked me up at my place around eight p.m. in his ritzy '60 white Thunderbird.

"What's the word, Thunderbird?" I greeted the rogue in a traditional teen slang rhyme as I opened the passenger door.

"Cut the fuckin' bullshit and get your ass in the friggin' car!" Goose reprimanded. "I gotta' stop hangin' out with rank jerk-offs like you! Ya' always try to sugar coat bull crap', ya' damned fruit!"

"Goose, you aren't going to the Cotillion shindig, either! Why?" I wondered and asked.

"Because I don't like immature high school pussy, that's why," the driver claimed. "I've been screwin' classy prostitutes and good-lookin' hard-up-for-cash magazine models, ever since I've been in ninth-grade. What the hell do I wanta' be bothered with little immature, cock teasin' high school girls for?"

"Because you're still in high school, too!" I smartly answered.

"Sometimes, ya' gotta' learn to keep your goddamned mouth shut!" Goose rankled. "If ya' had any brains, you'd understand that a prostitute gets paid to be laid; has a clean pussy, and attends special classes to know how to give professional blow-jobs. In high school, ya' just got a lot of flirty girls who are nothin' more than ball-breakers that don't put out," G.R. unconvincingly lectured. "Then, ya' got those high school scum-bag, skanky whores that give ya' bad sex for free, but then you're riskin' disease when ya' fool around with those horny young sluts," Goose elucidated. "That's why I pay for decent sex from foxy, expensive hookers, and get it over with in a hurry. Then, I could spend more time concentratin' on my business enterprises with a clear mind, and not think about stupid sex all the shittin' time."

A minute later, Goose scared the devil out of me when the malcontent said he was taking *us* to an exclusive luxury Atlantic City bordello the braggart had always frequented after emptying-out a dozen or so gum ball machines in Atco. I nearly gulped-down my larynx after hearing *that* graphic description of my soon-to-be Cotillion night's Queen of Resorts' activities, forty-miles east of the Cotillion. I didn't favor the idea of having big-time adult sex being performed out of my amateur teen league.

"J.W.," Goose promised. "After tonight, you'll never wanta' go to another damned juvenile high school dance again. And you'll never dream about that holier-than-thou' Joanne Berenato's spring-chicken pussy 'cause you'll know it ain't half as good as the hot stuff you'll be sniffin' and screwin' later tonight."

I sank-down in the passenger-side of the Thunderbird and very deeply wished I had been attending the Edgewood Cotillion with even the most-ugly female dragon in the whole damned school. I feared the all-too-real, illicit adult world in which Goose claimed to casually reside.

I sat mum all the way heading west to the Ancora Bridge overpass. Goose was obnoxiously bragging about his superhuman sexual prowess, and I evaluated that the guy was the ultimate ingrate bent on recruiting and corrupting me as a soul mate into his own personal evil crusade against societal morality.

"My problem is that I'm really a mature adult stuck in kiddy high school," G.R. related, "and I havta' hang-around with turd munchers like you until I get my diploma. I got no choice but be trapped with little kids until I get the hell outa' that goddamned manure dump."

"Maybe ya' never had a decent childhood and are afraid of what you hate," I philosophically retorted, nervously pretending to be Socrates reincarnated. "Did ya' ever consider them apples?"

“J.W., after tonight you’re gonna’ forget the stupid-ass senior play; forget the stupid-ass Cotillion; forget stupid-ass Juice, Jives and all those other dumb-shit faggots, and forget all about stupid-ass Joanne Berenato,” Goose vehemently returned while skillfully evading my poignant accusation.

Jerry Lee Lewis’ “Great Balls of Fire” was being spun on Philly’s WIBG radio, and that tune inspired Goose to raise the volume and comment, “Tonight in Atlantic City, you’ll know all about what good old Jerry Lee is singin’ about in that hit song.”

I didn’t say anything back to my egotistical chauffeur, preferring to listen to “Book of Love” by the Monotones, and Ricky Nelson’s “Poor Little Fool” on the car’ radio. ‘Goose Restuccio certainly didn’t write the ‘Book of Love,’ I mused, ‘and I’m Edgewood’s classic example of a down and out ‘Poor Little Fool.’

“Well, Goose,” I finally answered, “what do ya’ think of Joanne Berenato? Ya’ gotta’ admit she’s the cat’s meow!”

“J.W., she’s so skinny the scrawny bitch could be a guest on the Red *Skeleton* Show,” the egregious, dangerous brat snickered. “And I think you’re wastin’ your time chasin’ an imaginary rainbow with a pot of shit at the end of it,” my contemptible companion bluntly replied. “J.W., wake up to reality! “There’s a real ugly son of a bitchin’ world out there, and you’re prancin’ through an evil jungle that’s full of nasty, poisonous thorns, pretendin’ it’s only a beautiful rose garden.”

Goose piloted his ‘60 Thunderbird all over Atco, emptied-out at least a dozen gum-ball machines; restocked ten of the devices, and after completing those perfunctory tasks, headed back east off of *Route 73* onto *Route 30* in the direction of Atlantic City.

“Well, J.W., when ya’ have a fancy Thunderbird like me,” Goose boasted, “ya’ don’t have to waste your time to see the USA in your Chevrolet like that phony whore Dinah Shore sings about on her goody-goody, ha-ha TV show.”

I thoroughly detested G.R.’s narrow attitude toward life and toward other people. The deranged cynic criticized everything that the average American valued: family, education, wholesome entertainment, and genuine friendship. The arrogant, self-centered scoundrel preferred to honor money, power, and sex, and perhaps that was why I was so influenced by the magnetism of his didactic rhetoric. I really knew little about those three adult temptations that Goose purported to have absolute control over.

“So, J.W., are ya’ gonna’ spend the rest of your life watchin’ Lawrence Welk and listenin’ to the lovely little Lennon Sisters accompanied by Myron Florin on the accordion, or are ya’ gonna’ listen to my shrewd advice and be what my Pop calls 'a power broker'. What do ya' say?"

Before I could answer Goose's query, an identical white '60 Thunderbird pulled-up next to us at the *Route 30* Atco traffic light. I glanced-over and recognized that the driver was "Speed" Mortellite, and riding shotgun was villainous Gabe Gillette. I glanced to my right and saw Wooster's Funeral Home, a place which I definitely didn't want to be featured as the central focus. The front seat passenger in the twin '60 T-Bird comprehended our identities, and immediately lowered his power window. G.R. did the same.

"Hey Goose, wanta' race us all the way to Hammonton," Gillette challenged. "Your pig Bird ain't got a chance against Butch's hopped-up monster."

"You're on!" Goose yelled as the traffic light changed to green.

The element of surprise gave us a temporary advantage. G.R. mashed the pedal to the metal and our 'chariot' screeched-off like a phoenix out of Hades. The White Horse Pike curved right around Atco Lake, and our T-Bird made the fairly sharp turn at eighty-miles an hour. I craned my neck to view the rear window and observed that Butch Mortellite's white chariot was rapidly gaining on us.

"Goose, you're gonna' get us killed!" I shouted as the obsessed maniac wove in and out of Atlantic City-bound tourist traffic. "Either that, or you're gonna' get someone else killed and swiftly sent to Wooster's!"

"No sweat, J.W. We're just havin' a little fun. Those jerk-offs are thinkin' this here race is serious shit, a life and death dumb-ass war, or somethin' major like that, but I'm only toyin' with their heads. Pullin' their friggin' chains."

I couldn't believe what my worried eyes were witnessing. The speedometer was reading a hundred-and-ten and we were veering into the left and then weaving into the right-hand lanes, avoiding cars, buses, and tractor-trailers, and on three occasions, playing chicken with oncoming westbound cars heading west toward Atco. Still, Butch Mortellite was right on our tail, playing a precarious game of 'advanced chicken' as the nefarious freak tailgated us five-full-miles, soon entering Waterford.

"Goose, it's not worth it!" my throat screamed. "They're tryin' to ram us from behind! Slow-down and let them win! The Ancora Bridge is just up ahead!"

"J.W., if all guys had balls like yours, the fucked-up human race would stop existin'!" Bo laughed back toward my distressed face like a deranged madman. "You ain't lived until ya' come close to death! Count your few sperms, Good Buddy!"

“You’re insane! You’re Ancora asylum material!” I yelled as I inadvertently made an allusion to the mental hospital that was located a half-mile from the steep Ancora Bridge.

I closed my eyes as the white Thunderbird reached the overpass summit and hurtled five-feet up off the bridge’s crown, landing recklessly and blindly on the down-side. I gasped in awe of what had just transpired. “Goose, there could’ve been a car or slow-moving truck on the blind side of the bridge, and we could’ve been flyin’ up to heaven now! I haven’t been to confession lately!”

“Ha, ha, ha!” the crazed fanatic behind the steering wheel ranted. “You can go to heaven J.W., but I prefer hell. All the interestin’ people that ever lived have gone to hell! Think about it!”

“You don’t believe in Heaven?” I hollered to my left as our speeding vehicle crossed the highway’s double-yellow-line and entered approaching traffic in the third lane, heading toward Atco.

“There’re no such places as heaven or hell!” Goose reprimanded as the bedlam-case recklessly swerved back into the passing lane to evade a head-on collision with an oncoming dump truck. “They’re just things invented by friggin’ religion to keep ya’ goin’ to church on Sundays to support a lotta’ lazy, holier-than-thou priests that don’t work for a livin’!”

Our white T-Bird zoomed under the Elm railroad trestle, and Butch Mortellite’s excellent street machine finally caught-up with us again, repeatedly honking his horn behind us in the passing lane. Suddenly, Goose piloted his T-Bird into the right-hand lane, allowing Mortellite and Gillette the empty lane to our left. We were still going well-over ninety miles an hour.

Gillette was putting his power window down to mock us when Goose suddenly veered right around a *Route 30* bend at the El Motel, venturing onto North Third Street, nearly sideswiping a stationary car at the stop sign facing west.

“Jesus, Goose! You almost creamed that old lady in that ‘56 Buick!” I yelled. “You almost sent her to Purgatory! And incidentally, the old bag wasn’t a little old lady from Pasadena!”

“Just remember, J.W.,” G.R. emphasized. “Almost’ only counts in horseshoes and hand grenades, but not in near-death experiences! *Perk*atory? Is that where they make fuckin’ coffee pots?”

Restuccio soon left Elm in Camden County and next entered Hammonton via North Third Street; made a left at the traffic light onto Bellevue Avenue, and headed north toward the all-too-familiar White Horse Pike.

"Are we goin' to sinful Atlantic City now to visit the ritzy whorehouse?" I asked, wishing all the time we were heading to the Cotillion at Edgewood High.

"Naaaaa, I'm hungry. We're gonna' check-out the Midway Diner first. I just wanta' see if Mortellite and Gillette stopped there. I gotta' hunch that the fuck-heads might of."

"Look!" I yelled. "There's Mortellite's white T-Bird parked on the side of the diner! I recognize the tag number."

"That's just what I figured," Goose answered exhibiting a rare smile. "We're gonna' park this baby over at Dual Motors where I bought it. That way it'll look like it's one of the models on the display lot."

Restuccio drove a block away via Elvins Avenue to Dual Motors, the only bona fide Ford dealership in Hammonton. We exited the vehicle, which was parked next to two other Thunderbirds on the Elvins Avenue side of the dealership's display lot.

"Why all the secrecy?" I asked. "Why not park in the front of the diner up on the Pike?"

"You'll see!" the enigmatic Sicilian promised his astute listener. "There's a madness to my method!" the non-academic-scholar unwittingly transposed words.

The two of us entered the Midway Diner, and Goose brought to my attention two of his father's henchmen, introducing them to me only as nicknames Frankie Fingers and Joe Zucchini. I turned to my left and witnessed Speed Mortellite and Gabe Gillette sitting restlessly in an adjacent booth, with both Blues glaring resentful looks at the scar-faced occupants already sitting in our booth.

"I can almost see the daggers flyin' out of their eyes," I related to Restuccio as I slightly gestured with my thumb toward apprehensive Gillette and Mortellite.

"Forget those motley Bozos," Goose said with a self-satisfied smile. "Frankie and Zuck' here was the ones that sweetened-up Mrs. Murphy's gas tank, and they're both quality bone-breakers that go way back with my Old Man."

"Are ya' gonna' do somethin' soon to Gillette and Mortellite?" I naively inquired.

"Not yet; not quite yet, J.W. I'm just tryin' to put a little scare into 'em, if ya' know what I mean," Goose slyly indicated.

Reacting to Goose's comments, Frankie Fingers and Joe Zucchini let-out roars that quickly got the attention of the other diner patrons, especially Gillette and Mortellite. I immediately could tell that Gabe had animosity in his heart toward Goose and me. My winning of the scavenger hunt, along with Goose's deft avoidance of the other T-Bird at the Third Street El Motel cut-off, were probably responsible for the blueberry farm heir's apparent rancor.

At that precise moment, a New Jersey State Trooper entered the diner; looked around, and stepped toward Gillette and Mortellite's brown leather booth. "Young man, is that your white Thunderbird parked outside?" the on-a-mission trooper asked Speed.

"Why, er, yes!" Mortellite gulped in surprise.

"Well, the tires are still very hot," the state cop accused, "and the engine is really hot, too!"

"So, what's that supposed to mean?" Gillette volleyed, regaining some of his faded confidence. "Other cars out there match the same description."

"It means that you boys were racin' another white car going over a hundred-miles-an-hour all the way from Atco!" the policeman confidently charged. "I wanta' see your licenses. Then, I'll check the vehicle registration outside."

"We were racin' that ugly jerk over there!" Mortellite indicted as he pointed to Goose sitting at our booth.

"Oh then, you admit you were racin'!" the keeper of the peace grinned. "Stay here while I ask that gentleman a few questions."

The trooper strode over to Goose, who did not seem at all perturbed by *his* approach or presence. "Were you racin' those boys over there all the way from Atco?" the tall uniformed officer asked in an authoritative voice.

"No, Sir," G.R. politely lied. "I came to the diner with Frankie here in his red and white '57 Chevy parked outside! Ya' wanta' check *his* registration."

"That's right, Officer!" fibbing Frankie Fingers and Joe Zucchini collaborated in unison. "Those kids over there are lyin' their brains out," Frankie maintained. "They think their mouths can lie their way outa' anything."

"Sir," the trooper addressed Frankie, "could ya' step outside for a moment. I'd like to examine your driver's license and your car registration. And as for you two," the cop said pointing a finger at Gabe and Speed, "I'll be back to take care of you two in a minute!"

"But it's not fair!" Gillette protested to the investigator. "They were speedin' too, in the other T-Bird!"

"Maybe yes, maybe no," the curious trooper asserted, obviously disenchanted with their impotent challenge. "But the real truth is that I caught *you,* and *you* have already confessed to speeding a hundred-miles-an-hour down Route 30 from Atco to Hammonton."

Frankie Fingers and the austere trooper stepped outside into the March cold night air, and 'the fuzz' intensely scrutinized the registration to the sleek. red and white '57 Chevy. Then, the solemn-faced law enforcer walked-around the entire Midway Diner parking facilities, searching for a second white Thunderbird, but could not locate any such vehicle.

In the meantime, I gulped-down a slice of cinnamon-apple pie a la mode and drank-down the cup of hot chocolate I had ordered. Goose and Joe Zucchini were chuckling about how Gabe and Speed had been deftly outsmarted.

The New Jersey policeman re-entered the diner and summoned Gillette and Mortellite outside for questioning. I saw Speed Mortellite handing the trooper his registration and license, while gesticulating his hands wildly over his head, ineffectively complaining about the injustice of New Jersey highway law enforcement being rendered.

In another fifteen-minutes, the four content customers at my booth had eaten our desserts and had drunk our assorted hot beverages. "Fellas' thanks a lot!" Goose acknowledged to Frankie and Joe. "I'll pick up the tab!"

Fingers and Zucchini waved goodbye. Restuccio and I proceeded to the diner's cash register, and the street-smart adolescent handed the pretty hostess a brand new fifty-dollar bill. The young lady inspected the Ulysses S. Grant to make sure it wasn't counterfeit.

"Here's your change Sir, thirty-nine dollars and eighty-five cents," the Midway Diner cashier politely offered.

"Keep it, Doll!" Goose replied like the high school senior was losing a penny. "Buy yourself a new bra, panties, and girdle."

"Why thank you!" the pretty brunette grinned while either ignoring or not hearing Goose's cruel, snide remark. "Why thank you very, very much!"

On the diner's stone steps, Goose busted on Gillette and Mortellite, teasingly waving to them, since the preoccupied trooper had his back to us. The Blues sneered in our direction as the dedicated highway patrolman lectured the two violators about the perils of speeding, and how their reckless mal-conduct had endangered the lives of other White Horse Pike motorists.

I asked Goose a few pertinent questions on the brief trek back to Dual Motors. "I know ya' parked your T-Bird at the dealership's lot because ya' saw Mortellite's car sittin' on the side of the diner," I began, "but how did you know that Frankie Fingers and Joe Zucchini would be sittin' in the diner."

"That's easy," Goose replied. "I saw Frankie's red and white Chevy parked near Mortellite's T-Bird. I recognized the license plate number, so I figured that if a snooping cop came into the diner, that the boys would cover for me. And they did. It really wasn't much of a gamble."

"You sure fooled Gabe and Speed," I noted with an element of admiration. "Mortellite will probably lose his license for three months."

Goose informed me that I was "too naïve and fucked-up stupid", and that Mortellite's rich old man would pull some "power-strings" and get his spoiled son off the hook. Then, G.R. said that the state trooper was young and idealistic; was going through all of the procedures he had been taught in training, but would later become frustrated in the case, since all of his energy would be wasted, because of local blueberry money and Hammonton power politics.

"You'll see," Goose haughtily told me. "I just wanted to aggravate those two clowns as payback for the frozen blueberry incident at Palace Diner, and for slashin' my tires when Joanne's daddy was joltin' the royal shit out of my tender ass while I was riding on that freakin' White Horse statue."

"Well, I guess it's time to go to Atlantic City," I reminded my chauffeur for the evening. "Let's hit the trail."

"Naaa J.W., you're too innocent to be corrupted right now by the evils of real life," Goose declared, out of character. "I'll take ya' home so that ya' can dream about feelin'-up Joanne at the Cotillion, and then wake up; jerk- off; pop a load, and go back to sleep."

Boy, was I totally relieved to hear those particular, inviting words. G.R. drove me home via back roads to stay off of the White Horse Pike and to keep out of patrolling police scrutiny. I gratefully entered the house, dreamed of slow-dancing with Joanne Berenato at the Cotillion; hopped onto my bed, and quickly fell into a very deep sleep. My subconscious must have willed me to defy Goose's outrageous predictions, because I never remembered dreaming about anything immoral that the treacherous fiend had said I would be fantasizing about in my sleep.

The next morning, Dad confronted me at family breakfast. "Last night I heard two cars race by the house goin' over a hundred-miles-an-hour. You weren't involved in that joyriding, were you, son?" Pop asked, temporarily catching me off-guard.

"No, Dad, I would never drive that fast, and anyway, I didn't have the car last night," I creatively replied.

"I'm glad to hear you've got a level head on your shoulders," my concerned parent answered before sipping his breakfast cup of coffee and returning to his perusal of the early morning edition of the Philadelphia *Inquirer*.

The following Thursday in March of '60, I had a need to abandon my New Jersey teen problems and reunite with my Levittown past. I still had the Cardinal Reagan basketball schedule inside my room's desk drawer and decided to drive dad's '55 green and cream Chevy Bel Air over to Pennsylvania to catch a slated round-ball game. I needed to escape Goose's lunacy, and desperately felt that I had to distance myself from the strange, romantic, failed relationship I had forged with Joanne Berenato.

In the Reagan stands, I reunited with several old acquaintances from my former Levittown high school, but everyone and everything seemed foreign and different. I realized that I had a new identity in a new place, and that resurrecting my Pennsylvania past would be no substitution for living my New Jersey present at Edgewood High and around Hammonton. My March forty-mile journey to the Cardinal Reagan gym confirmed the fact that my adventurous life was destined to be continued back in New Jersey.

After the game, which the Cardinal Reagan squad incidentally won, I was invited to a small party at Carol Zella's house in Levittown's Pinewood section, and I consented to show my face at the affair. I had dated Carol several times when we were sophomores. My former girlfriend still was very pretty, but right from the get-go, it was quite obvious that she and her twin sister Barbara had found new boyfriends, and that I had been just another fella' that had revolved in and out of Carol's romantic involvement. And so, Joanne, Goose, News, Fabian, Juice, and Jives back in New Jersey seemed much more alluring on the return drive from Levittown than the group had seemed on the hour-and-a-half excursion crossing-over the *Burlington-Bristol Bridge* to Pennsylvania, just five-hours before.

As I traveled *Route 206* south toward Hammonton, I felt very melancholy, detached, and alienated. The two-lane highway was dark, quiet, and deserted. I recalled thinking that Bo Jalonec would have joked that a big college had been built at the end of the road, "*Tulane* University". The thought of Bo's sense of humor brought a much-needed comforting smile to my lips.

My mind then thought about Joanne's father's indirect rejection of me, and I recalled Goose racing Speed Mortellite from Atco to Hammonton on *Route 30*. Without any hesitation, I impulsively pressed the accelerator to the floor. The speedometer needle was buried all the distance from Atsion Lake to Hammonton, which was seven-straight-miles passing through the Wharton State Pine Barrens Forest. Everything seemed copesetic until I reached the intersection of *206* and the White Horse Pike.

As I impatiently waited for the green light, I peered into the rearview mirror and noticed a large steam cloud billowing-up into the cold night air, originating from the '55 Chevy's exhaust pipe. In my exuberance to experience intense speed that I falsely believed would cancel-out my emotional frustrations, I had ruptured the six-cylinder engine's head gasket, and water had leaked into the crankcase, causing a dense jet of white steam to be generated and then emitted. My abuse of the green and white coupe had cracked the motor block, and had damaged the Chevy's camshaft. My wild joyride had resulted in a considerable unexpected expense for Dad.

Although Pop was not Robert Young, my father often had to show me that *Father Knows Best*. Dad was a great judge of character; loyally advocated punishments for misdeeds, and he also had me easily figured out as if I was a primary school basal reading. I was forbidden to drive the '55 Chevy Bel Air out of Hammonton after his auto had received its new, re-built, six-cylinder engine.

My stupid fascination with speed had cost me the privilege of visiting my old Diablos' pals back in Levittown. Soon, I discovered that Carnie and Robbie had moved out of Dogwood Hollow; Bo Jalonec's family moved to Pittsburgh, and then, I had little motivation or desire to return to the area across the Delaware River. The only former friends remaining there were Quinn and Tinker.

I was always in awe of Quinn, and strongly desired remembering him as a superhuman legend, bigger than life. As for Tinker, I honestly never wanted to see his hideous, evil face ever again. From that moment on, I was aware that my immediate future would be lived at Edgewood High School and in Hammonton, New Jersey.

Chapter Eleven

"The Bowling Ball Caper"

I was acutely aware of how cunning Goose Restuccio's devious mind really was. The menace wasn't academically brilliant by a long shot, but he was extraordinarily gifted when it came to being street wise. The crafty dictator and his Daddy's henchmen had made Speed Mortellite and Gabe Gillette look like pathetic rank amateurs inside the Midway Diner.

The following Monday, G.R. approached me at my S-Wing locker before homeroom. Juice Illiani and Fabian Midilli were complaining and telling me all about the mediocre-time the pair had had with their dates at the formal Cotillion.

"You moron jerk-offs shoulda' been with J.W. and me last night," Goose began his evaluation. "We beat Speed Mortellite and Gabe Gillette in the coolest seven-mile race ever, and then we set the dumb-shits up for a state trooper citation at the Midway Diner. Let me tell you two Bozos, it was better than getting laid eighty-times."

"Goose, stop exaggeratin'," I opposed his narrative. "If any guy did it eighty-times in a row, he'd have to die from dehydration, exhaustion, and from loss of fluids."

"Wow!" Johnny Juice howled. "You two oughta' wear army uniforms loaded with medals and ribbons. You're big-time operators now! Wait 'til everyone hears about how you handled Gillette and Mortellite. You two brilliant guys will be local legends."

"Hey, Goose, when are we gonna' join the Reds?" Sal Midilli asked. "We better be organized, because after last night, pretty soon, those Blues are gonna' hit us with everything they got."

"I thought about that idea, you bunch of mental dingle-berries," Goose typically chided, "and I'll give ya' all the details at lunch."

I couldn't wait for the school clocks to advance to noontime, fifth-period lunch. First period gym was all right with Mr. Zardas teaching us how to use the parallel bars and how to safely dismount from the trampoline. In second period Western Civilization, Miss Hunter discussed ancient Mesopotamia and the *"Fertile* Crescent" between the Tigris and Euphrates rivers forming the "Cradle of Civilization," which generated the development of cuneiform writing on clay tablets and many ancient babies.

I got a laugh from Miss Hunter after I raised my hand and told her that many Mesopotamians didn't like to swim in one of the rivers, and the king called them "*you fraidy*-cats," and that the Mesopotamians who spoke too much too often were called *Babblelonians*. And when I said that a Fertile Crescent was a sword that reproduced easily, then poor Miss Hunter and her fun-loving class could hardly stop laughing.

Third period U.S. History with Mrs. Murphy went by without a hitch. I got a chuckle from the instructor when I related that the south had sent several incompetent spies up to a Massachusetts river looking for *ironclad* clues on how to *monitor* the *Merrimack.* Of course, Bo Jalonec's material worked quite well when *he* was not around to outshine me with his outlandish witticisms. I stayed in a gleeful mood until the next class, which I dreaded more than the perfidious Blues.

In fourth period trigonometry, I kept my mouth sealed and tried listening to despotic Mr. Andrews discuss the principal esoteric distinctions between the secant and the co-secant. 'I think Mr. Andrews needs Goose to take him to that swanky Atlantic City bordello to get his limited mind off of all this nonsensical advanced math crap,' I whimsically contemplated.

Finally, fifth period cafeteria rolled around, and after getting my serving of hamburger on a bun with French fries and baked 'farting' beans, I joined News, Juice, Fabian, Jives, and Goose at our usual rambunctious table.

"What's new News?" I asked in a jovial voice.

"Well, J.W., as you might know, Jack Parr walked off the 'Tonight Show' set last month when NBC censored one of his mild jokes," T.T. informed. "He just returned to the show last night."

"Then, it would have to be 'The Last Night Show' and not 'The Tonight Show'," Juice cleverly interrupted. "Television programs are entirely too confusing for the brain-dead public to understand."

"And the play 'Thurber Carnival' opened at the ANTA Theater in New York last week," News boringly related. "The show is based on author James Thurber's fabulous works."

"Hey, we read some of his stories in Mrs. Waldon's eighth-period English IV class," Fabian recalled and reminded us. "The ones about the ferocious family dogs were pretty neat."

"Yeah, Thurber's crib' stories are a half-shelf above Howdy Doodyville," Jives concurred, "and Hollywood's gonna' make a few of the bosser ones into crappy flicks."

"Holly Wood?" I injected. "Isn't she Natalie Wood's younger sister?"

"Hey, News," Juice yelled to his pal across the table. "Who won the Winter Olympics over in Squaw Valley?"

"Russia won the most gold medals; Sweden was second, and the U.S. came in third," Tommy glumly reported.

"There must be plenty of papooses in Squaw Valley," I joked, "and you would think that the Polish would've easily won the Winter Olympics since they have plenty of *skis* at the end of their last names."

"Where do ya' think of all this silly-ass, happy horse shit?" Goose wanted to know. "J.W., if the school has a Mr. Stupid Contest, be sure to enter it!" Restuccio added, showing an excess of fake dissatisfaction.

Then, Goose feigned being serious for a minute. The instigator disclosed that he had been speaking to fellow Edgewood seniors Jack "Hoss" Gregorio, Moose Marinella, and Chickie Calabrese about News sponsoring the guys seated at our cafeteria table into the Reds, but according to G.R., we had to pass a difficult initiation test in order to fully qualify for bona fide membership.

"What sort of initiation test?" Juice asked. "I'll try it as long as it doesn't involve murder, adultery, or suicide."

"Ya' can't commit adultery, Dumb-ass!" an irritated Goose stubbornly reprimanded. "Ya' ain't even married yet!"

"But I could be forced to have sex with a married woman against my will!" Johnny challenged.

"Then, Shit-head," G.R. chastised, "it would be adultery for the guy's wife, but only dumb-ass sex for you!"

"Keep your wild and crazy sperm in your stupid little worm and you'll have nothin' to sweat because you'll be outa' debt," Jives eloquently injected.

Goose, becoming weary of the zany adolescent conversation, held his hands over his head for silence. Soon, we all adhered to and honored his benign intention. The tall, stocky Sicilian told us to meet him at Joanne's Luncheonette next to the Rivoli Theater at six-thirty that night, where the 'local Hitler' would divulge the particulars of the Reds initiation activity.

That evening, News picked-up Juice, Fabian, Jives, and me, and then drove his red and white Ford Fairlane to Bellevue Avenue, where the peach kid parked "the wheels" behind the Rivoli Theater. We exited the '57 and strolled the block to Bellevue. I looked-up at the movie house marquee and observed that a double feature, *Gigi* and *Around the World in Eighty Days* were playing.

"Ya' can tell the movie industry is getting hard-up when two big films can't fill the theater," I commented. "The Rivoli's seen better days."

"You said it," News agreed. "Television is beatin' the crap out of small-town movie houses all over the country. It's just a matter of time until the Rivoli's death bell tolls."

The five of us entered Joanne's Luncheonette and soon sat-down at the establishment's main table that Goose had reserved for our scheduled parley. I surveyed the cozy place to see if I knew any of the other clientele.

"Glad to make the scene," Jives indicated to Ronald Restuccio. "Ya' got some good words for these bird turd pals of mine?"

Ronald Restuccio reiterated that the junior don was now determined to join the Reds, only because the Blues had dumped a thousand-pounds of frozen blueberries into his T-Bird at Palace Diner, and the rich hooligans had also slashed his two front tires in the peach orchard at White Horse Farm. G.R. next explained that he had cleared "the secret commando project" with the Reds Executive Committee, and the Sicilian brat conveyed to our ears that once *we* would complete our qualifying 'initiation assignment', all six of us would be eligible for our Reds' induction.

"But what do we gotta' do?" Juice insisted. "Why all of the suspense as if it's *Alfred Hitchcock Presents,* or some other crazy program like that?"

Before Goose could reveal the elements of "the covert commando project" that had to be performed on the Blues, Babs De Stefano came over to take our orders.

"Hey, Babs," Goose greeted. "Did you know that J.W. here lives on the White *Whores* Pike because he doesn't like colored hookers! And the new Edgewood kid likes beef jerky, especially when it's in the palm of his right hand!"

"You're very rude, crude and uncouth," Babs accurately said, "and the only reason the waitresses here put up with ya' is because you're a great tipper."

"What's the matter Babs?" Goose asked, sounding much like a first-grader. "Have your tiny tits been eaten-away by your livin' bra? Try goin' without one for a change."

The humiliated waitress knew better than to angrily answer Goose's general lack of discretion. Babs simply stood beside our table and held her order pad in her left hand and her trusty yellow #2 pencil in her right.

"Forgive his lack of culture, Babs," I apologized to my new female acquaintance. "But Goose often acts like he needs to go to finishing school, because he's never finished insultin' nice people like you."

"J.W., when are ya' gonna' evolve from pure diarrhea into a bona fide solid turd?" my new-found critic suggested, not at all being enamored with my compassionate rhetoric to Babs.

Trying to break the tension around the table, I inquired, deferring to my former friend, Bo Jalonec. "Do ya' have any sweet dough?"

"Naaa," Babs countered, "and if ya' want *dildo,* ya' gotta' go to one of them perverted sex shops over in 'Philly."

I cleared my throat as the other potential Reds all busted their guts. I politely ordered two slices of pizza and a large *Pepsi,* while the other guys all calmed-down and acted more sophisticated by exhibiting acceptable luncheonette table manners. All of us were more interested in our proposed initiation rites than we were in harassing innocent waitresses in friendly eating establishments.

After Babs De Stefano left our un-illustrious company, Goose went on a tangent by saying that most people were merely brainless "crabs in a bushel". The phony contemporary Plato expounded that folks in our great American society are trapped inside a giant imaginary bushel, and the incarcerated vistims are crawling-over each other, and are crapping on each other's heads, attempting to escape to economic freedom.

"J.W., I'm really one of the lucky ones outa' the friggin' bushel that *you* crabs are still trapped in," Goose intimated, "but I gotta' still pretend I'm an ass-hole crab, too, until I finally get the hell out of that goddamned high school."

"Don't ya' wanta' play any sports?" Juice inquired.

"Sports are just a dumb-shit distraction created by schools and society," G.R. replied, "and they've been created to keep kids from doin' what their instincts tell 'em they oughta' be doin', getting laid and getting drunk. That's the whole gig in a wrapper."

I then related to the guys the infamous Dairy DeLite telephone booth caper that my Diablo friends and I used to employ against unsuspecting Feed Bag' restaurant waitresses. Goose seemed fascinated with the fantastic technique I was describing, and I explained the entire methodology in detail. "Just say over the phone that ya' have a crazy name like Peter Small," I stated, "and the rest of the prank falls into place."

Goose Restuccio figured that the sarcastic prankster, namely him, would aggravate Babs some more with his unpolished crudeness. The '50s barbarian with the 'football-shaped head' ambled outside to a nearby Bellevue Avenue telephone booth and called Joanne's Luncheonette on the horn. Naturally, Babs answered the phone in a semi-courteous voice.

"Hello, I'd like a large tomato and cheese pizza to go," G.R. specified while disguising his trademark baritone, "and put on loads of pepperoni, too!"

"What's your name?" the skilled waitress requested.

"Peter Small," Goose professionally and confidently uttered.

A novel thought germinated inside Babs's head. A mental light turned-on, and a red flag went-up. "Well," the waitress yelled into the telephone, "if *your* Peter is Small, maybe ya' oughta' consider some kind of sex operation to make the tiny thing bigger!"

Goose Restuccio adamantly slammed-down the telephone onto the hook inside the Ma Bell booth. The five of us had heard Babs's remarkable oration, and we burst-out into a boisterous roar when we noticed G.R. demonstrably experiencing his extreme frustration outside in the corner phone booth. The defeated victim trudged back into the luncheonette with his head down, accompanied by a disappointed look upon his already-distorted face.

"I ain't tellin' ya' damned turkeys nothin' about the Reds' initiation until ya' follow me over to my place," the outsmarted phone call recipient dejectedly informed us. "By then, I will have gotten over bein' tricked by some cheap dollar-an-hour luncheonette broad."

The rest of us knew that Goose was livid since, the vulgar kid never said another curse word until it was time to pay the check.

News started describing how Missouri Democratic Senator Stuart Symington claimed that the American public was being misled about the U.S.-Russia missile gap, but T.T. could easily tell that the rest of us weren't too enthusiastic about his chosen topic of conversation. "It's mostly political, anyway," Tommy admitted, "since we have a Republican President sittin' in the White House." Then, everyone forked-up *his* own share of the bill, where ordinarily, under regular circumstances, Goose would insist on treating us by covering the entire tab.

The six of us quietly departed Joanne's Luncheonette with "The All-American Boy", sung by Bill Parsons, blasting from the juke-box speakers. The lyrics made me think of the six young warriors about to perform some wild "commando" stunt to be eligible to enlist in the Reds' peach gang, which, I presumed, was the high-school equivalent of joining a college fraternity.

"Back in Levittown," I uttered, breaking the cold silence, "ya' had to do somethin' to the police before ya' could qualify to join a greaser gang."

"We got four-hours to kill before the initiation project," Goose told us. "So, I'm gonna' treat you freaks to a double feature at the Rivoli. Then, according to my scheme, we'll be ready to officially become Reds around midnight."

The six Reds recruits sat through *Gigi* and most of *Around the World in Eighty-Days.* Several of us had been napping out of sheer boredom, but then our ill-tempered host awoke Juice, Fabian, Jives, and me and informed his sleepy listeners that it was finally time to desert the half-full theater.

G.R. was also parked in the half-empty lot behind the Rivoli Theater, and without saying a command, motioned for News to follow his T-Bird in the red and white '57 Fairlane.

"Where does Goose live?" I asked.

"On Mallard Lane!" Juice healthily laughed. "We're gonna' take a *gander* of his place soon."

"Real funny," I evaluated. "Now try bein' a little more candid."

"Over past Rosedale, a mile after the village's Angelo's Store," Johnny conveyed a little more sincerely. "It's sort of a miniature palace, and being an only child, he's sort of the coddled prince."

News followed G.R. and his three passengers west on Egg Harbor Road, and then we passed Angelo's Store. "We're officially in Rosedale, now," Tommy related. "And Rosedale's not what that Orson Welles guy kept on saying at the end of the classic *Citizen Kane* movie. If I remember right, it was 'Rose Bud'!"

I had News pegged as a serious scholar, and anything else seemed drastically out of character for him. Duane Eddy's "Rebel'-Rouser" was playing on WIBG Philly' Radio 99, my suspicious mind sensed that the instrumental tune portended some soon-to-be-known, nefarious "commando-activity" about to commence.

News followed Goose's T-Bird into a long, narrow, paved driveway that led around several bends of pine and deciduous trees. G.R. stopped his white '60 Dream Machine beside his magnificent manor house, which was a red, brick and stone, two-story mansion, that only the most successful corporate executives and Mafia' dons could ever afford.

Our secretive project organizer signaled his five disciples to follow him to the rear of the property. A large white box truck had been parked in front of the expensive estate's three-car garage. Goose opened the back panels and instructed his four fellow-inductees, plus News, to "hop inside".

"Where we goin'?" I queried. "News is already a Reds' member. Shouldn't Tommy be leading this expedition?"

"You'll find out when we get there," G.R. imperatively declared. "It'll all make sense in about half-an-hour."

The five prospective riders, one by one, grabbed a side support; lifted a leg onto a steel-stepping frame, and helped one another into the huge, empty storage compartment. Our eyes scanned both left and right walls, and noticed five empty racks on each side, ranging from knee to shoulder height, each rack being around a foot above the one under it.

"Okay, dick-heads," Goose instructed. "Next stop is Egg Harbor, thirty-minutes east from here." Then, the furtive kid closed the dual rear panels, and locked us in total darkness.

"What the hell does that lunatic have in mind?" Sal asked.

"I only hope we're joinin' the Reds and not the Mafia or the Kremlin," I replied. "I'm too young to own a death certificate!"

"We'll know in thirty-minutes," News speculated and said in the pitch-blackness. "The suspense is killin' me, and I'm already a Red."

The truck's ignition was started, and soon, the transport rumbled to a halt at the end of Goose's curvy driveway. The plotter turned left onto *Route 561,* zipped through Rosedale, and stopped next to the Fairview Avenue railroad tracks.

"We're in Hammonton," News alertly imagined and reported. "Of course, I'm just goin' along for the ride to help you guys out."

"Yeah, we just crossed the tracks," Jives agreed. "And if we get killed, at least we won't havta' D.D.T."

"D.D.T.?" Fabian wondered and asked aloud. "Isn't that some sort of insecticide?"

"No, you silly Stupid," Jives corrected. "D.D.T. is an abbreve. for 'Drop Dead Twice'!"

Our route was easily familiar to the six passengers in the dark cargo compartment. "We're heading east on Egg Harbor Road," Juice described, "and now we just passed Bellevue and we're goin' east toward the Pike."

On our bleak trip to Egg Harbor City, News began talking about Felton Turner, an unfortunate, twenty-seven-year-old black Houston, Texas resident, who had been beaten with a tire iron, and then mercilessly hung upside-down from a tall oak tree in a bizarre, southern, racial hate incident. "The initials KKK were carved with a knife on his chest by four masked teenagers protestin' the sit-down strikes that black students are havin' at Texas Southern University," T.T. disclosed.

"Well, News, who really gives a flyin' fart!" Jives challenged. "What's that got to do with this mysterious, sci-fi Egg Harbor gig?"

"Guys, Goose hates black kids. Ya' heard him call Tyrone Davis an 'eggplant' in Italian in the Edgewood cafeteria," News equated. "Maybe he's plannin' to use us five pawns the same way those four masked thugs nearly crucified Felton Turner upside-down. Of course, I'm already a Red and I'll refuse to participate."

"If that's what the rest of us gotta' do to become Reds," I nervously answered in the dark, "then I'm either walkin', or I'm hitchhikin', back to Hammonton."

Twenty-minute later, we all felt the box truck slide to the right, veering off the highway onto the road's shoulder, and then ease several-hundred-feet straight ahead. After turning left, Goose slowly advanced another hundred or so feet, and then gently applied the brakes. A minute later, the back panels were again opened, and the stars and moon were visible in the cold, clear March sky.

"Welcome to Egg Harbor City, the other armpit of South Jersey besides Hammonton," Goose greeted and mocked. "And especially welcome to Egg Harbor Lanes, in Egg Harbor City to be exact."

"What are we doin' after midnight at a bowling alley in Egg Harbor?" I demanded knowing. "Why couldn't we have just gone to DiDonato's in Hammonton at eight o'clock, instead of wasting our time watchin' *Gigi* and *Around the World in Eighty Days?"*

"Because Shit-head," Goose contemptibly said, "we're gonna' break into this cornball dump, that doesn't have a bar and a late-night crowd; steal all of the freakin' bowlin' balls, and neatly stack the round mothers on the racks situated in back of this white truck. Then, we're gonna' take the stolen balls back to Hammonton."

"Why are we gonna' do that? What does this idiotic theft have to do with me becomin' a Red?" I inquired.

"Are you a thick-headed dunce, or what?" G.R. nastily replied. "We're takin' the bowlin' balls back to Hammonton to use 'em against the dip-shit Blues. That's where *you* come into the picture, J.W. We gotta' come-up with some cool scheme usin' these stolen Egg Harbor' bowlin' balls back in Hammonton," Goose declared. "Now Fabian, you're supposed to be a mechanical wizard. Here's a special key my Pop stole from a skeleton that opens all doors, anywhere. Use it to break into this friggin' place right now."

Fabian Midilli reluctantly-but-obediently accepted the marvelous key from Goose, and we all followed the 'mechanical wizard' to the back entrance. In less than a minute, Sal had adroitly uncorked the lock, and soon the back door to Egg Harbor Lanes had been swung-open. It was cold and dark inside the building, so Goose supervised the heist with his small flashlight, the object being the only source of illumination in the entire bowling alley.

"Ya' guys can carry two balls at a time, one in each hand," the project manager grumbled. "There's about two-hundred bowlin' balls in this damned place, so I figure four of ya' only have to make about fifty-trips back and forth to the truck. I say four of ya' because one guy's gotta' stay on the truck and stack the balls neatly in the side racks."

Jives volunteered to be "the stacker", so that meant that Juice, News, Fabian, and I had to scurry back and forth with two bowling balls each round trip, while Goose verbally supervised and orally criticized our mischievous, ongoing endeavor. "Don't make any noise," G.R. instructed. "I don't have too much influence with the Egg Harbor cops!"

After an hour of assiduous labor, the five of us had worked-up heavy sweats. Perspiration was dripping-down my chest; down my back; under my wool sweater, and beneath my heavy winter coat. I was glad when the "commando theft job" had finally been completed without us being arrested. The five fatigued passengers slowly clambered back into the white truck's rear compartment, and then Goose closed the panels and again locked us inside.

On the trip back to Hammonton, the prisoned cargo riders were all exhausted and weary.

"We just committed a major felony, actually grand larceny!" News panted. "I didn't have to do anything when I joined the Reds."

"I don't know if becomin' a Red is worth the trouble, if we gotta' spend some serious time in jail," Juice added.

"Penn State has much more appeal than State Pen does," I giddily giggled in the pitch-black enclosure, as I again imitated a Bo Jalonec one-liner. My four companions also felt tired and silly, laughing incessantly in response to my goofy parallelism. Thirty-minutes later, the "Bowling Ball Express" eventually pulled into Goose's serpentine driveway.

When Ronald Restuccio re-opened the rear transport vehicle's dual doors, the five occupants were in for the shock of our lives.

"Surprise!" screamed a dozen voices in unison. Standing below us were Edgewood kids Goose Restuccio, Jack "Hoss" Gregorio, Little Joe Gregorio, Denny "Baker" Harrison, Guy "Moose" Marinella, Chickie and Joey Calabrese, Tony Passarella, Marty Ransom, and Pete Clarke. The public-school fraternity was accompanied by St. Joe' High Reds Dave "Herc" Juliano, Jake "the Brute" Maccarella, and Ollie "Balls" Giordano.

"What the hell is goin' on here?" Johnny Juice Illiani yelled-down at Goose. "Are we goin' to have a major gang war with ourselves?"

"Notice J.J. that the guys are all wearin' the Reds' zip-up jackets, like the one James Dean wore in that movie *Rebel without a Cause,"* G.R. pointed-out. "Great idea J.W., about the red jackets! I bought them all at the Berlin Auction last week."

All of the full-fledged Reds, clad in their new bright-red jackets, wildly cheered their approval. After being praised by Goose, I felt a little like a minor celebrity.

"News, here's your new jacket," G.R. hollered as the surly, self-appointed leader tossed-up to Tommy T. his own official James Dean apparel.

"But Goose, what about the two-hundred pilfered bowlin' balls?" I shouted. "We're all gonna' be thrown in the clinker!"

The dozen Reds again let-out very loud hoots, as if I had just scored a touchdown, or just hit a game-winning home run. I couldn't make heads or tails out of *their* raucous reaction.

"Not really, J.W.," Goose's voice disagreed above the levity. "Ya' see, those two-hundred bowlin' balls were not stolen like ya' thought they've been," G.R. laughed. "I actually bought them from the Egg Harbor Lanes' owner the other day at a big discount, three bucks each. He's getting' a new supply delivered tomorrow morning. So, you five jerk-weeds did some cheap labor for me tonight, and all it cost me was the price of five lousy movie tickets!"

"Then, we've passed our initiation, and we're now officially in the Reds?" Juice demanded verification.

"Not exactly," Goose directly answered. "That won't happen until after J.W. schemes-up some clever things to do to the Blues with these two-hundred friggin' bowlin' balls."

"News, were you in on this crazy trick?" I wondered and asked.

"I ain't ever tellin' this sinful caper to the priest sittin' inside the St. Joe confessional," Tommy Tomasello shrewdly answered. "I might be excommunicated twice!"

Fabian, Juice, Jives, and I looked at each other in absolute bewilderment. Then, Goose summarized everything that had occurred by saying, "Guys, the Reds have now officially admitted me into their ranks, because I've gotten them two-hundred bowlin' balls for free."

"Hoss" Gregorio threw an "extra" red James Dean jacket over the crazy Sicilian's shoulders. "Goose, welcome to the Reds!" the gigantic football tackle boisterously announced without the aid of either a megaphone or microphone.

"Thanks, Hoss for givin' me this cheap red jacket I bought for myself at the Berlin Auction," Goose immodestly replied.

Senior Class Clown Jives Arena vividly reviewed the gang's complicated Egg Harbor City bowling ball excursion by inaccurately quoting William Shakespeare, "All's swell that ends swell!"

Chapter Twelve

"Vineland versus Hammonton"

I was more than slightly jealous after I realized that Goose had become an authentic Red before Juice, Fabian, Jives, or me had ever received formal invitations to join the Hammonton peach fraternity. Hoss Gregorio, Little Joe, and the other Reds had shunned Goose only several weeks before his emergence as their strategic ally and Blues' adversary. Then, Restuccio had blueberries dumped inside his hallowed T-Bird; had his front tires slashed while *he* was committing blatant vandalism to the landmark White Horse; outwitted Speed Mortellite and Gabe Gillette in the bizarre Midway Diner' adventure, and ultimately, bribed the Reds' allegiance with two-hundred vintage bowling balls. All of a sudden, Goose Restuccio had transformed from lousiest leper in the colony to living legend.

Before homeroom the following Monday in March, I ventured into the S-Wing Boys Lavatory. I heard someone singing the lyrics to the Five Satins' "In the Still of the Night" from inside a bathroom toilet stall as I went about the mundane business of draining my radiator into a urinal. 'That singing sounds pretty good,' I thought as I was responding to nature's call. The melodious voice continued while I zipped-up my pants, flushed the urinal, and mechanically washed and then dried my hands. Just when I was about to leave the washroom, the toilet flushed, the stall opened, and a stout black kid stepped out from the enclosure.

"Hey, aren't you the guy that had words with Goose Restuccio in the cafeteria?" I asked. "That wild incident almost started a massive food fight!"

"Yeah, I got suspended because that retard called me a...."

"A mool-en-yon," I finished. "It means eggplant in Sicilian."

"You're his friend, ain't ya'?" the stocky kid inquired.

"Well, sort of," I replied rather tentatively. "But I can definitely say that Goose Restuccio is not my best Edgewood friend. My nickname's J.W.," I expressed, extending my right hand.

"I'm Tyrone Davis," the muscular black kid hesitantly divulged while giving me a firm, vice-like grip during our handshake.

I commended Tyrone on his stellar singing voice, and my new acquaintance related that he and four of his black buddies were forming a new Doo-Wop singing group, the Marvelons. Then, Tyrone revealed that he and his friends were searching-around for a manager who could "get the group a few gigs to get rollin'," so naturally, being naively entrepreneurial in a heartless, predatory, free enterprise system, I volunteered my services.

"That's real cool," Tyrone admitted. "Ain't never been no good friends with a whitey before, but ya' all seem okay to me. See ya' around school, J.W."

"See ya'," I said, and after the two of us exited the lavatory, Tyrone turned, looked me in the eyes and again thanked me for offering to be the Marvelons' manager.

No sooner had my new pal disappeared into the crowd of students down the S-Wing corridor to my right, that Goose Restuccio approached and accosted me. The prejudiced Sicilian was embittered at my apparent cordial association with Tyrone Davis.

"Hey J.W., what the hell ya' sharin' your space with a nigger for, especially with *that* nigger!" G.R. criticized.

"He's a kid that seemed pretty friendly to me," I replied, "and just because he's *your* enemy, it doesn't mean he's necessarily got to be mine, too!"

"Look J.W., if ya' wanta' be a damned nigger-lover, that's your goddamned business," Restuccio hypothesized and stated. "But if ya' wanta' be my paisan and be a nigger-lover too, then that's not ever gonna' happen in a million-years. Stop soundin' like you're a freakin' liberal Democrat runnin' for President. Ya' sound like ya' want your pecker carved on Mt. Dickmore, or somethin'!"

Goose turned his back to me and paced down the S Corridor toward his M-Wing homeroom. I thought about his discriminatory remarks and concluded that I would prefer being Tyrone Davis's distant friend than a personal colleague of Goose Restuccio, if it weren't for G.R.'s magic bankroll that had already rescued me out of several very tight jams involving the Gem's front window and Mrs. Murphy's car vandalism. 'The biased, conceited jerk that's swindled my loyalty,' I concluded.

At seven p.m. that March night, News, Juice and Fabian picked me up at my place in Sal's '59 white Chevy Impala. I was glad to be out with three of the best-looking Edgewood studs, and temporarily away from the negative influence of Ronald Goose Restuccio. Sal Midilli's destination was "neutral Hammonton territory," which was the popular Gem over on Central Avenue.

"The town's a little crowded tonight," Juice observed and commented. "That's pretty rare for a Monday."

"There's a lotta' kids from Vineland ridin' around, cruisin' the avenue," News disclosed. "And don't be surprised if there's some conflict resultin' from their innocent turf invasion."

I was well-aware of how territorial South Jersey towns like Hammonton, Berlin, Williamstown, Egg Harbor, and Vineland actually were. The local pride went beyond school spirit, pep rallies, and high school football rivalries. It was very real ethnocentric prejudice, agrarian discrimination that echoed the refrain, "Our town's better than yours." News suggested that a foreign threat was the only factor that could successfully bring the Reds, the Blues, and the Ramrodders together for a common purpose.

"Could ya' explain yourself?" Juice asked T.T. in quest of clarification. "I'm afraid you're bein' a little vague."

"Sure thing," News returned. "It's all quite simple. The only common bond the Reds, Blues, and Ramrodders have is the turf the gangs each claim in downtown Hammonton," Tommy maintained. "If guys from Vineland show-up and start flirtin' with Hammonton girls, and show hints of takin' over, then the three gangs will become territorial, just like aggressive animals on *Wild Kingdom* do when some passin' hyena clan trespasses onto lions shared property."

"I think I see," I concurred. "Dogs bark at strangers because they feel their territory is being threatened, and lions will fight other lions over boundaries, but then lions will unite with other prides, that had been former enemies in order to fight-off clans of prowlin' hyenas invadin' *their* common territory. I saw that phenomenon last week on a television special."

"You two eggheads oughta' go on *the 64,000 Question* because ya' really know your stuff," Juice commended. "You two must be the smartest hombres in the entire school. Info' like that territory remark plus one thin dime will get ya' an almost full cup of coffee anywhere in town."

"I promise to tell ya' all about *crap* after we get to the Gem," I predicted to my companions. "I'm an expert on the shitty subject."

"Don't blast through any more windows tonight," Fabian advised. "Thank goodness there's still eleven more months for February 3rd to roll around again."

Sal found a convenient parking spot in front of Olivo's Super Market. The four of us paced across Central to the Gem and were lucky to secure the last booth in the already-crowded burger haven. Johnny Horton's "The Battle of New Orleans" was on the '45 rpm record spinning-around inside the Gem's colorful Wurlitzer jukebox, and the fighting *War of 1812* song conjured-up in my mind images of possible combat between Hammonton and Vineland high school greaser students. I was hoping that my hunch was wrong, so I switched gears and asked faithful News Tomasello what interesting events were happening in the world.

"Well, J.W., I'm happy to report that Pioneer 5 is the third U.S. satellite to be orbited to go around the sun," News revealed to his rather apathetic audience. "As ya' no-doubt remember, it was launched a while back from Cape Canaveral."

"A *pie-in-ear* is better than a moist cake in the face!" I punned. No one else at our booth considered my shallow joke amusing except its insecure creator.

"What were the first two other space probes called?" Juice glibly asked omniscient Tomasello.

"Pioneer 4 and Russia's Lunik 1," News speedily related without any hesitation. "There's an intense space race goin' on, no doubt about it. Competition is what keeps science goin.' The U.S. fears Russia's getting' ahead, so we come-up with new science and technology, and then the Soviets do the same."

I was a little bored by News' presentation, so I glanced-around the burger joint and saw Joanne Berenato, Elaine Hill, Esther Phyllis, and Nanette Banks giggling and gossiping their brains out over in a distant booth in the opposite corner. Joanne spotted me scrutinizing her loveliness and was about to wave in my direction when Herc Juliano sauntered-over to announce his presence to her.

My spinal cord and entire nervous system were instantly smitten with sudden, cold twinges of jealousy. My mind's activity patterns quickly accelerated. Soon, my consciousness became rejuvenated, and my dormant personality rejoined the mediocre conversation that had been initiated and sustained by News Tomasello.

"Hey, guys," I interrupted, "all of this United States versus Russia Cold War saber-rattling that's goin' on is because of the *WWII* atomic bombs that were dropped on Japan," I cited, remembering what Quinn had once asserted back in Levittown. "And the fear of atomic war is even spillin' into the news and the movies."

"Well," Juice Illiani challenged, "explain yourself!"

I conveyed to my Reds pal that the flying saucer rage had officially begun with the suspicious Roswell, New Mexico UFO crash incident, a news story that had been blown out of proportion by paranoia about new satellites and Sputniks being developed by Soviet technology. And then, I elaborated by saying how *Hollywood* movies that featured mutations caused by nuclear radiation had spawned popular films like *The Beast from Twenty Thousand Fathoms*, *War of the Worlds*, *This Island Earth* and the incomparable *Creature from the Black Lagoon*.

"Wow!" News exclaimed in near admiration. "J.W., ya' really know your trivial facts' shit!"

"Speakin' of shit," Juice picked-up on Tommy's intro', "J.W., ya' told us in the car while we were cruisin' town that you had somethin' major to tell us about *crap*. Now's your special chance to educate us."

I was about to advance Bo Jalonec's incredible theory about the stratification of feces when Judy Salvatore, an attractive brunette waitress, came-over to take our orders.

"How are things over at St. Joe's?" Juice asked the friendly chick about her Alma Mater.

"Okay, but I'd rather go to Edgewood and get-away from those obnoxious Hammonton High Blues over there," Judy said before nodding her head in the direction of a booth occupied by formidable Gabe Gillette, Speed Mortellite, Butch Lanza, and Ox Narducci. "I'd rather work in a more placid restaurant in Atco or Berlin."

"Judy, just remember that Goose Restuccio goes to Edgewood," Juice plausibly advanced. "And he's no Charlton Heston, Elvis Presley, or Frankie Avalon, either."

"I guess you're right," Judy grinned. "The grass is always greener somewhere else."

"Juice," Judy said. "I know News Tomasello here, but who are your other two buds. Barry Cooda and Doug Dirt?" she laughed.

Johnny apologized for not introducing Fabian and me to the dark-skinned, pretty waitress, so Illiani formally performed the customary salutations. Judy Salvatore told us that her aspiration was to become an art teacher.

"Why not teach all the kids and not just Art!" I jested. "And how come ya' got the same last name that Fabian here uses for his first name? I really hope the next world's more-simple to live in than this weird one is."

"J.W., what do ya' want to drink? Have ya' made up your limited mind yet?" the cute dark-hair chick requested.

I remembered a former Levittown line. "I'm not so hungry right now, so please be so kind to get me a Michigan on the rocks," I answered.

"What on earth is a Michigan?" the doll asked in a very amused voice. 'Never heard of it!"

"Well, Judy, if ya' don't have a Michigan, then kindly bring me a *mini-soda*. And make it a *Pepsi.*"

Everyone at the table laughed at my fairly witty comment, and when I turned-around, I noticed Joanne Berenato wondering exactly what had been said at our table that would have generated the humorous reaction.

"Don't mind J.W.," Juice directed to Judy, "because he's gonna' change his name on his birth certificate to *Harley Davidson,* since he thinks he's a major league mean motor scooter."

After Judy struggled through finally obtaining our legitimate food and beverage preferences, News demanded that I share with the group my exceptional knowledge about the hierarchy of feces, of which I professed to be an authority.

"Well, fellas'," I began while impersonating the inimitable Bo Jalonec, "there are different di*stinct* levels of crap." I proceeded to explain to my Reds comrades about the lowest level is commonly known as chicken shit, which was everyday crap not worth thinking about twice. "Then, above the chicken droppings there's horse crap, which is the kind of academic trivia and stuff that Mrs. Murphy, Mr. Jenkins, and Mr. Andrews try to unload on us in their sacred classrooms every school day," I related. "Those academic ideas have no real meaning or basic importance in the real world that's existing outside the shelter of the classroom."

"J.W., ya' really know your shit!" Fabian Midilli acknowledged in an amazed tone of voice. "Give us more of your great view of the world from inside the toilet bowl, lookin' up at all the assholes fartin' around in the world."

"Well, Sal," I continued my exposition, "above horse crap there is bull crap, which every television commentator and every newspaper reporter lays on ya' to make you believe that ya' really need to see and hear what the heck they're sayin' on TV, or writin' in the papers is important," I informed. "And at the top of the dung world is serious crap. Serious crap is definitely an extremely dangerous kind of feces," I communicated. "Serious crap could even get ya' killed, like the heavy poop goin' on between the Reds, the Blues, and the Ramrodders right now. In fact, I plan to write a *feces* on the subject when I go to college. Do you guys dig my three-level-theory?"

"Holy mackerel!" Juice exhorted, almost plummeting out of the booth. "We listen to our parents to learn chicken shit; we go to school to find-out about horseshit; we watch television and read the newspapers to become experts on bullshit, and we date girls, look for fun, and fool-around with the Reds to know all about serious shit! J.W., you're a genius. That's the greatest truth my gullible ears have ever heard!"

Several tough-looking strangers entered the Gem just when the jukebox began belting-out "Western Movies" by the Olympics. After scanning the premises, the two newcomers, dressed in handsome button-down blue and red letterman's sweaters with big *Vs* sewn on the right sides above the pocket, strolled-over to Joanne Berenato's Gem' booth.

My first inclination was that the boys' outstanding-looking two-tone high school sweaters seemed like a much-needed compromise between the Reds and the Blues, but after the two foreign greasers started chatting with my dream girl and her friends, I became a tad stricken with green-eyed envy.

Johnny Horton's "The Battle of New Orleans" again was being emitted from the Gem juke's powerful speakers, and the tune's marching rhythm and war cadence seemed to be ominously signaling ominous events to come.

"Those two muscle-bound weightlifters are from Vineland," News pointed-out, "and the taller one is Joanne's cousin, Joe Lo Biondi. I think he's interested in takin' Elaine Hill out and usin' Joanne as his agent."

"Yeah," Juice confirmed. "But I don't think that Herc Juliano knows that Joe Lo Biondi is actually Joanne's cousin. This could mean…"

Before Johnny Illiani could finish his sentence, Herc Juliano and Ollie "Balls" Giordano picked-up the two Vineland jocks and hurled them at the Gem's front window, shattering the pane glass. Girls were screaming and everyone rose to their feet in response to the recent, unanticipated violence. Juice, News, Sal, and I were the first ones to rush outside to investigate the carnage.

I was quickly grabbed by three Vineland kids that were loitering outside the Gem, lifted-up, and then tossed like a rag doll through the empty space that had been made in the Gem's front window frame. I temporarily landed on top of the table situated in front of the then-empty booth. My forward momentum made me skim and skid off of the front table, and then unceremoniously crash with a thud upon the black and white checkered tile floor.

Joanne Berenato and Elaine Hill rushed-over and gingerly assisted me to my feet. Both dolls still appeared stunned by my sudden Gem reappearance, after being flung *inside* the teen restaurant through the open window space. I wasn't exactly the epitome of poise as I futilely tried regaining my equilibrium.

Mr. Arturo Sorrentino exploded out of the Gem's kitchen; looked at me; noticed his broken front window, and then scratched his head wondering why no shattered glass' floor' shards were evident on the inside of his eatery. "Boo-tana! Not this bullshit again!" the hard-working, neurotic Italian yelled-out in hysterical astonishment. I dared not correct Mr. Sorrentino that the psychotic proprietor had mistaken *serious shit* for ordinary "bullshit".

Then, benevolent Elaine Hill sedately told the teen hangout owner that a young customer other than me had been chucked through the pane-glass window from *inside* the Gem. The still semi-traumatized owner, wearing his dirty kitchen apron, staggered through the main door out to the coldness of Central Avenue to identify the victims, to learn the names of the culprits, and to assess the full property damage.

By that time, a number of fights had broken-out all over downtown Hammonton. The first was between Ox Narducci, Speed Mortellite, and Butch Lanza representing the Hammonton Blues, who were mauling the three Vineland studs that had just airmailed me back into the Gem. The Central Avenue mayhem spilled-over onto Bellevue where town police on patrol were attempting to break-up turbulent brawls in front of the Rivoli Theater on one side, and a huge melee in front of Vega's Drugs and Augie's Hamburger Paradise on the opposite side of the main drag.

Finally, a town squad car pulled-up to the Gem, and soon, two husky officers with nightsticks ran across the street to quell the disturbance between the determined Hammonton and brawny Vineland High jocks.

"All of this conflict because cousins can't talk to each other in a downtown Hammonton restaurant!" News observed and lamented. "This town is so inbred that it doesn't know there's a whole big world that exists outside its narrow borders."

Pee Wee Lucca, the Blues' answer to colonial patriot Paul Revere, came running-down Central from Bellevue yelling-out, "Vineland kids are all over the place! Vineland kids are all over the place!" As the beleaguered Hammonton cops finally separated Ox Narducci, Speed Mortellite, and Butch Lanza from mauling and maiming the three Vineland athletes. Pee Wee Lucca reported to anyone that listened that the Ramrodders had demolished the windshield of a Vineland kid's Oldsmobile.

"It all happened outside the Central Café over on Egg Harbor Road," Pee Wee panted, "and then those crazy Rodders' chased four Vineland High jocks three blocks down to the Rivoli. Two carloads of Vineland punks were parked in front of the movies, and before ya' could say Jack Robinson twice, a wild fight broke-out all over Bellevue Avenue, the fracas involvin' at least two-dozen Vineland jerks, and member of the Ramrodders, the Blues, and the Reds."

My pupils looked-over at Joanne Berenato, and her big brown eyes showed shame and guilt for what had recently transpired all over town, which had originated at her table inside the Gem. The sexy beauty glanced at me, and then looked-away at the police unit still grappling with the three Vineland High studs, who were still defending their injured egos by pretending to foolishly want a piece of Narducci, Mortellite, and Lanza.

All of that in-progress pandemonium was interrupted when Mr. Sorrentino's shrill voice screamed-out, "Boo-tana! Who the hell's goin' to pay for this damned busted window this time?"

Chapter Thirteen

"Trouble on the Home Front"

The only time the Hammonton area male teens united was when their territory was being challenged by what the area greasers perceived as a foreign threat. The "invasion incident" with the formidable Vineland High jocks clearly demonstrated that the Reds, the Blues, and the Ramrodders would form an unnatural coalition to resist any outside desecration of *their* sanctuary, downtown Bellevue/Central Avenue turf. When not feeling jeopardized by external enemies, then the three disparate factions would persist in quarreling over which group ruled downtown Hammonton.

The third week in March marked the end of the local high school basketball scene. The classic contest of the season pitted two evenly matched teams, the St. Joseph High Joeys (school mascot: a kangaroo) versus the Hammonton High School Blue Devils. The St. Joe gym on Third and Pleasant Street was packed with rabid round ball enthusiasts from the area, including a contingent of fans from Edgewood High in attendance.

The HHS Blue Devils had Pee Wee Lucca and Gabe Gillette as starting guards, Bobby Speed Mortellite and Butch Lanza as forwards, and the ever-dangerous and unpredictable hatchet man Ox Narducci at center. Ollie "Balls" Giordano, Herc Juliano, and Jake Maccarella were starters for the home team Joeys. From the outset, the game was more like a survival struggle than a sports' event. Both sides wanted to win so badly that an un-savvy spectator would believe that the losers were to be executed by a firing squad immediately following the final buzzer. The game was more like a vicious war between Reds against Blues, rather than a good sportsmanship-like rivalry of HHS devils against St. Joseph High "baby kangaroos".

"This is some terrific game!" Juice yelled at me towards the end of the fourth-quarter among the ultra-boisterous fans at one end of the filled-to-capacity, Pleasant Street St. Joe gymnasium.

"You said it!" my hoarse voice enthusiastically boomed back. "The score's 63-62 favor of HHS with only seven-seconds remaining. It'll take a major miracle for St. Joe to score and pull this baby out, but the Joeys do have the ball," I verbally indicated. "They gotta' somehow beat the Hammonton press and then throw-up an Apostle's Creed and hope that heaven is listenin'."

Then came one of the most remarkable things I have ever seen exhibited on a basketball court. Jake Maccarella in-bounded the ball at center-court to Herc Juliano, who faked a forty-foot turn-around jump shot, and then flipped the ball behind his back to Ollie "Balls" Giordano. The tough kid dribbled low between Pee Wee Lucca and Gabe Gillette's defense without committing a traveling violation, and the two HHS defenders were prudent and did not want to foul and stop the clock. When Giordano ran out of wooden floor in the far corner of the court, in desperation, the speedy dribbler dramatically hooked the basketball over his right shoulder, without ever looking at the basket. The round sphere majestically arched through the air as Giordano left the court and kept running down the steps, directly into the St. Joe' locker room, without any knowledge of his frantic shot's fate.

The basketball hit the front of the rim when the horn sounded, ending the game. The ball bounced-up; caromed off the backboard with the most optimal rotation; rose a foot above the support cable, and then plunged-down, dramatically swishing through the net. The Edgewood and St. Joe fans went wild.

"Balls was already in the locker room when that unbelievable shot swished through the hoop from the gym's rafters!" News shouted in my right ear. "Balls wasn't even facin' the basket when he released the ball."

"Never seen anything like it in my life," I confessed. "In a close game, it's better to play for a Catholic school when ya' throw up a Hail Mary like that."

"Now ya' guys know why they call Ollie Giordano 'Balls'!" Juice Illiani marveled and finished. "If he misses, everyone knows he tried his best. If the shot goes through, he's an instant hero. Then, the crazy kid gets to act nonchalant and super cool like he had planned it that way all along. That game-winner has only added mystique to his local reputation."

"I'm just glad Balls saved that lucky shot until the very end to beat Gabe Gillette and the Hammonton Blues," a jubilant News Tomasello related. "This loss oughta' put the pugnacious Blues in their place for a couple of weeks while the audacious bullies stay in their den and lick their wounds."

"Or it might make the hostile creeps more aggressive than ever," Juice cautioned. "Ya' don't know exactly how wild animals will react when the predators are wounded."

The next morning at Edgewood, I saw Tyrone Davis in the upstairs' M-Wing before homeroom. First, the black kid commended me on being the Marvelons' manager, but next, the group's lead singer disclosed something I was unprepared to hear.

"J.W., the Marvelons got us a decent promoter, but we need a couple hundred-dollars for some seed money to get our act started at area night clubs. That's where you come in!" Tyrone revealed.

"Where am I gonna' get two-hundred-dollars?" I asked. "Why can't ya' get the bread from your promoter?"

"Hey, man! You're the manager. Ya' gotta' complete deals that the promoter makes," Tyrone insisted. "Our promoter needs the money within the next week. Good luck, Cat."

I was really despondent, my mind in a total abysmal-type of quandary. The only one I knew that had enough expendable cash to finance the entertainment project was Goose Restuccio, but I dared not approach the junior loan shark because I was aware of his animosity toward colored people in general, and toward Tyrone Davis in particular. And besides, G.R. would probably then verbally crucify me daily about my proposition, if I owed him the dough.

At the lunch table, the guys were cutting-up pretty good, while my spirits remained in a distraught state of depression. News had already forgotten about Balls Giordano's amazing, game-winning hook shot that had vanquished Captain Gabe Gillette's Hammonton High Blue Devils. Tomasello was now jabbering-away about how Ohio State had soundly defeated pesky California 75-55 in the NCAA basketball championships. The comprehensive basketball conversation shifted to Wilt Chamberlain's recently announced retirement from professional round ball.

"He's the greatest scorer ever, and the man's a credit to the game," News maintained. "Those wars between him and the Celtics' Bill Russell will go down in sports history as classic match-ups. Our kids will watch them on TV, I guarantee it."

"I guess Chamberlain's career has finally *wilt*ed," I negatively stated as I equated the star Philadelphia Warriors' center to a flower being exposed to the first heavy autumn frost.

"All you freakin' guys seem to love niggers," Goose Restuccio accused. "The colored flunky makes a thousand times as much as your old man does, all because he's a descendant of some eight-foot-tall, spear-chuckin' Watusi tribesman."

"Look, Goose," Juice retorted as the good-natured senior admired his own bright-red James Dean' jacket. "Chamberlain's got great talent. Wilt's the only NBA player that can truly dominate a game."

"Look here, Dork-face," Restuccio obnoxiously responded. "First of all, Chamberlain can't shoot from the foul line when nobody's guardin' him. From the line, the shine ain't worth a damn. Second, basketball was a game invented by a short white man for dinky white kids that averaged only five-foot-ten-inches-tall," G.R. argued. "Now we got seven-feet-tall-niggers ploppin' the ball into ten-feet-high baskets. Now, to be fair to every player, I think the baskets oughta' be raised to twelve-feet, so that all those African black bastards can't dunk the goddamned thing so easily. Then, we'd see just how good those dark sons of bitches really are playin' the way the game was meant to be, below the friggin' rim."

I was appalled by Goose's deep-rooted prejudice, which I believed to be unwarranted and hypocritical. "Goose," I intrepidly stated while concealing a degree of anger welled-up in my heart, "ya' never played any organized sports. Why do ya' criticize what ya' don't really understand? Speak from experience."

"Okay, J.W.," Restuccio insisted. "I'll fuckin' speak from experience. The only reason that fuckin' Tyrone Davis is kissin' up to your butt is because he thinks ya' got money to finance his new flunky singin' group. And when your limited cash flow runs dry, be sure not to call on me to support the far-fetched, pipe-dreams of five, goin' nowhere niggers."

I wished in my heart that Goose had been dead wrong and that the talented Marvelons would emerge as a dynamic new Doo Wop sound in the burgeoning record industry. I fantasized that my two-hundred-dollar investment would blossom into a small fortune, and that someday, I would have to salvage an indigent Goose Restuccio from the throes of financial bankruptcy. But realistically, I was smart enough to keep my thoughts secret and all to myself.

"Well, men," Fabian interceded in an effort to give the contentious debate a rational spin, "I think that Chamberlain is quoted in the papers as sayin' that the white players bang him around pretty heavily under the basket, and that his body can't endure that much more punishment."

"You wait," argumentative Goose countered. "That guy's a big black crybaby. In a couple of weeks, that spook will sign a big contract and return to the NBA. He's only holdin' out for more bucks. Where else could a mool-en-yan freak like him make that kind of serious money, except in exploitin' a game that was designed for short, white college boys?"

"You're more-obscene than D.H. Lawrence ever was!" I yelled across the table at Restuccio.

"Your mouth is goin' south," Jives Arena hollered at me. "And J.W., stop havin' a cow and thinkin' you're getting' the royal shaft, just because Goose here is rattlin' your cage somethin' fierce!"

"By the way, J.W.," News Tomasello informed. "That book you said ya' read, *Lady Chatterley's Lover* by D.H. Lawrence, was ruled just the other day as not being obscene by the U.S. Circuit Court of Appeals, Judge Charles E. Clark presiding."

My sagging spirit had been reduced to rubble. I felt disconsolate and conquered by Goose and Frankie Arena's staunch opposition.

'There is only one salvation,' I thought. I had amassed the sum of two-hundred-and-ten-dollars in a savings account from working my paper route and from laboring at Hal's Delicatessen in Levittown.

That next day, Edgewood had half-sessions to accommodate parent-teacher conferences. After riding Herman Priestley's school bus home, I had been assigned by my parents to go on an errand into town to pick-up two cartons of pints for the farm market from Hammonton Packaging Company. I walked-up the stairs to my room and secured the local bank savings' deposit book from my desk drawer. I had enough time to pick-up the pints; withdraw the required two-hundred-dollars from my personal savings account, and then drive the blue Pete's Market Special back home without anyone ever suspecting my clandestine bank activity.

The bank teller gave me a very curious look when I awkwardly handed her my Account Book and made my request to virtually deplete my entire principal. The lady conferred with her supervisor for a minute. Then, the elderly woman returned to her teller's station and gave me a brief interrogation.

"Why are you withdrawing most of the money?" the bank teller firmly asked.

I had to think fast without giving away the true reason, which the bank employee might suspect being a highly-impractical one. "I just got my driver's license and need the money for car insurance," I imaginatively fibbed. "My folks say I gotta' pay my own way or not drive." I was worried that the bank supervisor would call home about the questionable transaction that I was attempting to make.

The lady again conversed with her superior, and after several very suspenseful minutes, returned to her cash drawer; made the two-hundred-dollar deduction from my savings account, and handed-over the ten crisp twenty-dollar bills.

I was elated. I folded and tucked the ten Andrew Jacksons inside my brown leather wallet; stuffed my Account Savings Book into my shirt pocket, and promptly left the marble-pillared building with a relieved mind and a slightly-guilty conscience. I was not prepared for what awaited me on the home front.

Dad confronted me at the market right after I drove the blue truck onto the property and exited the vehicle. "Son," my parent began. "I want to have a frank discussion with you." Immediately, I instinctively knew that his message was not going to be favorable. "I had just had a conference with Mr. Andrews at your school, and your math' teacher says you're failing trigonometry. Mr. White then told me that if you fail that major subject, then *you* will not be able to graduate in June, and you'll have to go to summer school. We need ya' to work at the market, and not be riding a public service bus all summer long back and forth to Haddonfield."

I didn't know what to say, or how to react. "I'm sorry," I finally uttered. "I'm really tryin' my best to pass, but I just don't understand the subject. I don't have enough higher math' background to understand and do the word problems."

"Son, I'm afraid that's not quite good enough," Pop answered. "And if ya' don't pass, then you're really goin' to be in hot water. I haven't forgotten how you blew-up the engine in my Bel Air just a few weeks ago. It's cost me two-hundred-dollars to get a rebuilt motor installed. And now you're flunkin' your math course..."

"It's not just *simple* math!" I defensively challenged. "It's advanced trigonometry. I'd like to see *you* show me the difference between secant and co-secant!"

"I'm not takin' and flunkin' the course!" Dad lividly bellowed. "You are! And besides, what are ya' doin' with your Bank Account Savings Book sittin' inside your shirt pocket?"

My pupils glanced-down through my open Diablos black leather motorcycle jacket and saw the exposed bankbook. My temper was ascending from dormant to furious. "It's my money and none of your business! I'm the one who earned the money back in Levittown, and it is mine to spend or to keep!" I snottily replied.

"As long as you live under my roof in my house, ya' gotta' answer me honestly!" Pop argued. "What are ya' goin' to do with that amount of cash?"

"How do ya' know I didn't make a deposit, and that's why I have the bankbook!" I ineffectively debated.

"Because ya' haven't been workin' to make any money to put in the bank!" Dad accurately replied. "And I feel I have a responsibility to make sure ya' spend the money in an intelligent manner, and not piss it away on some naïve investment scheme, or on some silly juvenile purchase!"

I had to really think fast. "Okay," I said. "I fell through the window at the Gem Restaurant. A friend lent me the money to pay for the damage, and now I have to pay him back."

Pop informed me that he had heard about the "window incident" in town and that a rich Mafia kid named Goose Restuccio had satisfied the debt and had *not* demanded that I pay *him* back. I was boiling inside because Dad had known the truth, and now his skeptical mind wanted a valid explanation, which I was not ready to divulge at that particular time and place, since my perceptive father would consider my motivation to finance the Marvelons frivolous.

"And I really must say that I don't approve of your choice of friends, either," my astute father communicated while indirectly condemning Goose Restuccio.

"Goose is alright!" I defiantly shouted. "He paid for the window without makin' any big deal about it!"

"You're bein' too impetuous, wanting to spend that hard-earned money so hastily," Dad directly criticized. "And I think it would be safer if you just turned it over to me." Pop had a premonition that I was going to hit the panic button; hop into the blue Pete's Market truck, and leave the property, so my interrogator opened the driver-side door and removed the keys from the ignition. "Son, I'm waitin' for an explanation, and I don't want any lie or excuse this time."

"If I have to live with you pryin' into my personal affairs all the time, then I'm leavin' and runnin' away from home!" I screamed.

Pop argued that I couldn't provide for myself and that I couldn't get anything other than a minimum wage job at best. My family prosecutor was attempting to force his dominance and to reinforce my dependency on me, and I didn't savor his objectives one bit.

"I'm leavin' right now!" I yelled back, almost in tears. "You can't run my life!"

I turned with a hurting heart and paced to our neighbor's peach orchard. I was soon off the Pete's Market premises and angrily walking diagonally through the orchard of barren fruit trees. In ten minutes, I found my way to North Third Street, and in another half-hour, I had trekked the full two-miles to downtown Hammonton.

I entered town hall on Central Avenue across from Hammonton High, still in a minor state of agitation, which had been fueled by exasperation at my father's deeply meddling into my private life. "Where's the Army recruiter?" I boldly asked one of the clerks stationed behind the Tax Department window.

"He's here only Mondays, Wednesdays and Fridays," the lady curtly replied. "Today's Thursday."

'Great,' I regretfully thought. 'I have the luck of a born loser.' "Thanks," I said to the preoccupied woman, who was already busy working on her next secretarial task.

I dejectedly left Town Hall and sneered at an Uncle Sam "I Want You" poster that had been taped onto the wall near the main entrance. As I was descending the stone steps, remarkably, a white '60 Thunderbird pulled-over to the curb. I was never so happy to see Goose Restuccio.

"Hop in Jerk-weed!" the mercurial spoiled brat commanded. "I'm gonna' treat ya' to lunch. But don't ask me for any goddamned money to float Tyrone Davis's flunky nigger singin' group."

"I'm sure glad you weren't Speed Mortellite. Where we goin'?" I wanted to know, my disoriented mind still in flux.

"Over to Augie's Burger Paradise next to Vega's Drugs," Goose related. "The Hammonton High kids are allowed to leave the school for lunch, and most of 'em go to the Gem. We'll be safer getting a bite to eat at Augie's place."

Goose explained to me at the hamburger joint that he had been in town to mail some letters at the post office and to buy some stamps, but that the town visitor had all afternoon to accomplish those minor chores. At the burger haven, we ordered steak subs and *Cokes*. Then, Goose and I had a nitty-gritty conversation.

"Ya' know J.W., I sorta' like ya'," G.R. began his monologue. "And I don't wanta' see ya' hurt in either your world or in mine. I wanta' be like a father to ya', do ya' get what I mean?"

"That's all I need is another father," I aggressively protested, before gulping-down three ounces of cold *Coca-Cola*. "One father's more than enough!"

Goose sensed that I had been encountering some problems on the domestic front, and being under extreme duress, I spilled my heart out to him, describing every specific detail of my quarrel with Dad. My alert listener quite surprised me as being very sympathetic and understanding to my dilemma. My wealthy associate promised to patch things up in a jiffy. My rich friend jotted-down my phone number; marched over to the indoor phone booth, and called Pop to inform him that I was quite safe and sound.

I heard Goose's penetrating staccato voice negotiating with Dad the terms of my delivery; that I was to go directly to my room; sleep overnight without eating dinner with the family to avoid any toxic arguments, and that I would go to school the next morning without incident.

While Goose was ironing-out the settlement terms with Pop over the pay phone, two Hammonton policemen entered Augie's Burger Paradise to have lunch. The town fuzz noticed me sitting all by my lonesome at a table, so the inquisitive cops asked me a few rather essential questions.

"Son, aren't ya' supposed to be in school?" the first officer queried. "You aren't being truant, are ya'?"

"Well," I stammered, "I have..."

"What school do you go to?" the second patrolman questioned. "I don't believe I've seen you around town?"

Goose Restuccio finished his mediation session over the phone with Pop; plunked the receiver onto its vertical holder, and then exited the booth.

"Good afternoon, officers," Goose greeted the two policemen. "This here is J.W., and he's hanging-around with me. We had only a half-day over at Edgewood because of afternoon parent-teacher conferences."

Apparently, the two cops were familiar with Goose and accepted his stated word as gospel truth. "Okay, gentlemen," the first cop commented, "enjoy your lunch." The second cop gave us a mock salute as the two town keepers-of-the-peace ambled-over to the counter to place their lunch orders.

"Do ya' control the cops, too?" I leaned-over and whispered to G.R. "Ya' sure gotta' lot of clout!"

"I'm not tellin', and that's for you to fuckin' find-out and decide," my illustrious, reprehensible companion casually replied. But cheer-up, J.W. I hear that the St. Joe sport teams are gonna' be changin' their mascot name from the Joeys to the Wildcats!"

Chapter Fourteen

"The Boatnecks"

Goose drove me home from Bellevue Avenue. I marched-up the front steps into the house and then climbed the stairs up to my room. Feeling upset and defeated, I activated my record player and listened to the Fleetwoods' "Mr. Blue," Guy Mitchell's "Heartaches by the Number," Frankie Avalon's "Venus", and to Paul Anka's "Lonely Boy" over and over for two whole hours, and then eventually dozed-off to sleep.

Friday morning, I awoke, had a quiet breakfast of buttered toast and strawberry jam with Mom while Dad silently read the morning *Philadelphia Inquirer,* hardly showing his eyes between sips of coffee and the headlines. I was very happy to leave the strong tension that existed at the breakfast table, and finally exit the house and gladly board Herman Priestley's yellow school bus.

On the way to Edgewood, News was first talking about the Tiros I weather satellite, and how it was going to send thousands of cloud and storm photos' back to earth. I ignored his standard academic prattle, worrying about my myriad teen problems. All I could concentrate on was how impulsive I had been in wanting to leave home and enlist, out of spite, into the U.S. military. News finally came-around to engaging-in normal conversation and empathized with my recent "fight or flight" behavior.

"Ya' know, J.W.," T.T. prefaced. "Ya' might not have even been able to sign-up for Fort Dix because ya' didn't graduate from high school. And if Andrews fails your butt in trig', which is probably more certain than either death or taxes, then you wouldn't even qualify for the service."

"You're absolutely right," I somberly agreed. "What I did was dumber than dumb."

After entering the school, I met Tyrone Davis in the same M-Wing Boys Lavatory and handed him the ten twenty-dollar-bills. "I knew you was the man!" the head Marvelon hooted as Ty slapped me rather lustily on the back. "We's gonna' hit the bigs, J.W. And the Marvelons are gonna' take *us* to the top!"

"That would be terrific," I answered as my confused mind weighed Dad's prediction about spending hard-earned money to close a foolish investment. 'Maybe I should've just put the ten twenties in a shoe box and set it on fire,' my suspicious instincts imagined. "Okay, Tyrone, I'm glad I could help ya' out with some seed money. Let me know when somethin' big breaks."

"Sure will. Practice is at 'The Dew Drop Inn' in Williamstown at seven," Davis related. "Can ya' make the cotton-pickin' scene?"

"No Ty. I got another appointment, but maybe next time," I lied. "Gotta' do some serious work for my folks."

"Okay, Cat, thanks a million for the two-hundred clams." Davis was the first to exit the washroom, and then I peeked outside to ascertain that Goose was nowhere in the vicinity. Then, when I determined that the coast was clear, I proceeded directly to Mr. D'Agostino's homeroom, where the short, Italian teacher would by mistake mark me absent at least twice a week. A really tall six foot-nine-inch black basketball player, Eli Washington, sat in front of me, and obscured my physical presence from the diminutive homeroom instructor's view, who would then send my absentee attendance card down to the main office.

I was really relieved to be out of the house and back into Edgewood High. The place seemed to be less hostile than the general atmosphere was with my parents at home. Even Mr. Andrews' class seemed relatively enjoyable compared to my tenuous home environment. I was almost happy to be in the strict teacher's presence, and he seemed to sense some peculiar, radical change in my demeanor.

At lunch, News Tomasello was telling us all about the Academy Awards for the 1959 motion pictures, and that *Ben-Hur* had nearly swept the Oscars in all categories. "Charlton Heston won best actor, and Hugh Griffith best supporting actor for their stellar roles in *Ben-Hur,"* News declared.

"I think that Stephen Boyd was better in that movie than Griffith was. Boyd was terrific playing Messala," I recollected and related. "*Oscar* Mayer must have been the head of the nominatin' committee. I'm surprised that Ben-Hur and Messala had chariots in the big race scene and not Wienermobiles," I added.

"Shelly Winters won best supporting actress for her performance in the *Diary of Anne Frank,"* News continued as my act-oriented friend completely ignored my astute Wienermobile remark.

"Maybe she should have had a milk farm and called her book the "*Dairy* of Anne Frank," Juice offered. "Then, that flick could've gone out to pasture where it belongs, before the film ever began milking the paying customers."

"Don't any of you jerk-offs have anything interestin' and new to say?" Goose nastily butted-in. "Maybe tomorrow, ya' all can bring your mothers' knittin' needles and together, knit one, purl two, all your tiny, shriveled-up dicks."

Frankie Jives Arena had something of merit to contribute to the mediocre bull session, so we all momentarily listened attentively to discern his lackluster drivel. "I got somethin' hot-diggety-dog to spiel," Jives began his dissertation. "I gotta' really cool cousin in the record business in New York, and the cat called me on the horn and asked if I had some good-lookin' high school, All-American stud-friends to pose for a new record album cover gig. I've already gotten the okay from Mr. Pinkerton to have the photo' shoot done on stage in the school auditorium. Who here is hip to the boss's hot sauce I've been cookin'? Who wants dibs?"

Juice was impressed with Frankie's exciting proposal, but asked the more than slightly-warped kid for clarification. Jives obliged with additional relevant information.

"The singin' group is called the Boatnecks, and their new album is bein' test-marketed next month somewhere in Montana," Frankie related in near normal English in order to get our sought-after endorsement. "The album is logically called 'The Boatnecks', and the boss hot song single is 'Ya Gotta' Believe', a slow soul-blaster-spin born right from Passionville."

"Why don't they test-market the album at the South Pole or inside Mt. Vesuvius?" Goose disrespectfully ridiculed. "There's probably more moron penguins at the South Pole and more hot wax inside Vesuvius than there are illiterate idiots taking shits in Montana."

Jives rejected G.R.'s valid critiquing and further elaborated that we all had to wear matching Boatneck shirts with horizontal blue and white, three-inch parallel stripes from shoulders to our waists for the special photo' shoot. "Cats, it ain't no problem that me, the resident Jivester, can't easily tackle in his sleep. I have six large Boatneck' shirts ordered and comin' C.O.D. in tomorrow's mail. Now, who here wants to be famous and ready for Hollywood?"

Everybody at the table raised their hands except Goose, who was generally negative about any idea that hadn't been generated from his own dark imagination. "Ya' five royal butt-heads must all go home and suck huge, wet salamis as pacifiers every night!" G.R. ranted. "That Boatneck record's gonna' only sell maybe five asshole copies in the whole-wide-world, and each of you raunchy, fucked-up jerk-weeds is gonna' buy one apiece."

With Goose's voluntary exclusion, that left Jives, Juice, Fabian, News, and me to participate in the exciting auditorium photo' session. "Ya' five guys are all freakin' gullible, piss-ant, wanna' be famous dip-shits, and nothin' more!" Restuccio mocked. "You'd have better luck if ya' just got Tyrone Davis and his nigger Marvelons to take your places for the phony photo' session!"

Jives Arena brushed-aside Goose's caustic and cynical remarks, and conveyed to the assembled Reds that the potential record mogul had a decent chance of becoming the official East Coast manager for the fledgling Boatnecks. My ears pricked-up at once, since I was already the worldwide manager of the Marvelons as designated by Tyrone Davis, and perhaps I could learn some sound fundamental advice listening to Frankie Arena's sage expertise.

The following Monday after school, Jives distributed the handsome-looking Boatneck striped shirts on the Edgewood High auditorium stage. Juice, Fabian, News, and I were all enthused about our participation in the opportunistic photo' session. Jives had even commissioned a professional photographer from Berlin to capture our charming countenances in a dozen still shots taken, from a variety of angles, and having several different lighting settings.

"We look like skilled Venice Grand Canal gondola rowers," News commented. "This record's gonna' really take-off!"

"Yeah, News," Fabian Midilli answered. "How come ya' didn't get the senior stage crew to build a gondola for us to stand in?"

After the highly successful photo' shoot had been completed, Jives Arena had some more propitious news to relate to his anxious and receptive Boatneck colleagues. "Guys, this Friday evening at seven, I've arranged a sort of early April cool publicity press gig at my pad. Come over to Winslow at seven p.m. for a pop session. And we're gonna' have a royal-ass Boatneck party, and two-hundred screamin' chicks are gonna' show-up from Jersey, Delaware, New York, and Pennsy' thinkin' we're the real Boatnecks. Be sure to wear your brand-new striped shirts to the big happenin'."

"What do we have to do?" Juice asked. "Paddle a boat to a Venetian blinds factory?"

"Just be there, mingle with the hot chicks swimmin' in the mix, sign fraudulent autographs, and drink free sodas," Jives assured. "These lady fans are gonna' go goo-goo over us new tinsel-town celebs'. Don't forget how to scribble your names between now and next Friday."

I couldn't sleep all that week anticipating the arrival of Friday evening in Winslow, and my brain fantasized the prospect of having two-hundred adoring female fans, without braces, idolizing my friends and me. 'I sure can learn plenty about promoting a group from Jives,' I imagined as I combed my long greasy hair while admiring my glorious Boatneck appearance in the upstairs' bathroom mirror. "I feel as proud as Clark Kent or the real Fabian!"

News drove his red and white Fairlane over to my place at five p.m. in order to transport me to instant fame and recognition in the rural hamlet of Winslow. When T.T. and I arrived on the scene, we met-up with Jives, Juice, and the undiscovered Fabian, who were preoccupied pouring potato chips, pretzels, cookies, and popcorn into plastic bowls set upon three tables on his front lawn, to accommodate our yet-to-arrive two-hundred appreciative, young lady guests. Signs of spring were evident with yellow forsythia flowers blooming on the well-trimmed bushes around Jives' rural house, and colorful daffodils were sprouting inside Arena's mother's neatly-kept landscaping.

Sure enough, at exactly six o'clock, plenty of cars began pulling-up to Frankie's house, and by quarter-to-seven, at least fifty of them were clogging usually quiet Hall Street near Jives's out-in-the-sticks corner residence. I was extremely flattered when a bevy of gorgeous teeny-boppers began initiating conversations with me, asking me my name, where I lived, and how long I had been a recording star Boatneck. I really was relishing the attention and the role-playing.

Juice, Fabian, and News were all good-looking fellas', and circles of doll fans were interviewing them, too. All in all, about two-hundred rabid rock and roll chicks showed-up for the event that had been masterfully contrived and orchestrated by Frankie Arena.

Just before seven p.m. Jives managed to pry News, Fabian, Juice, and me away from our infatuated audience of female admirers. "Guys, the girls want us to sing our smash hit 'Ya Gotta' Believe'. We can't let 'em down. What do ya' say?" Frankie pressured.

"But we aren't the real Boatnecks, we're just imposters!" News protested, showing a high degree of integrity. "I can't do what I don't know how to do!"

"We don't know the words to the dumb-ass song!" Juice adamantly complained.

"We can't even sing a flat note!" I worriedly chimed-in. "This is gonna' be a total disaster, far worse than the *Hindenburg* crash! The two-hundred-babes will soon figure-out we're total frauds, and we'll crash like we're a lead zeppelin!"

"No sweat," Frankie replied. "We'll lip-sync to the record. I have a fresh copy I'll play on my new *Sears*' record player I just brought from the house. I'll explain to the chicks that two of us have bad colds and are not soundin' that good. Then, they'll be happy just to see us lip sync 'Ya Gotta' Believe'."

"But I don't know the lousy words?" I yelled loud, enough to almost be heard by several attentive dolls standing close by. "This is crazier than nuts! Why don't we perform the freakin' song over at Ancora State Mental Hospital?"

"Just pretend you're havin' sex with Marilyn Monroe or Jayne Mansfield and fake it to the climax!" Jives unconvincingly replied. "It's gonna' be orgasmic, er, I mean organic! A real sex orgy with our clothes on, I'm tellin' ya'!"

The '45 rpm "advance copy" record was delicately placed onto the cheap phonograph. Jives used a microphone and an amplifier the buffoon had borrowed from a rock band friend, and everyone stopped their cheering and politely became quiet as Frankie attached the microphone to a stand. The intro' music started-up, and the two-hundred girls began shrieking and screaming in ecstasy as if Elvis had been standing on the wooden front porch instead of five artificial, phony Boatnecks.

When the singing part started after the slow-music intro', I felt really stupid trying to move my lips to the words of a song I had never heard. By the second verse, the enthralled delegation of chicks was almost in a feeding frenzy, and I began fearing for my life, standing-up on Frankie's front porch, which now was a vibrant, makeshift rock and roll stage. By the middle of the seemingly eternal-length song, my fellow Boatneck impersonators and I were actually becoming familiar with the tune's catchy rhythm, lyrics, and melody. Our individual comfort zones had finally and successfully been established.

Suddenly, a metallic blue Corvette, a white Thunderbird, and a '60 blue Buick convertible, with the top up, screeched to a halt in the middle of Hall Street, stopping opposite Frankie's home. Gabe Gillette, Speed Mortellite, Dan "the Hammer" Bertino, Ox Narducci, Butch Lanza, Pee Wee Lucca, and four other Hammonton Blues had heard about the contrived concert, and decided to crash the biggest gala event in Winslow Village's history.

The five impostors, pretending to be bona fide Boatnecks, immediately went into our panic mode, as *we* lip-synced while nervously eyeballing our uninvited visitors, with our wary eyes looking-down from the elevated porch. As 'Ya' Gotta' Believe' reached its final notes, the five of us were unexpectedly pelted from head to toe with round projectiles, that upon closer scrutiny, turned-out being frozen blueberries being blown-out of long thick straws, big enough to be used as cannibal, poison dart, blowguns.

And just as the song reached its last few sensational lines, the Hammonton wise guys whipped-out large water guns containing a mixture of blue food coloring and diluted blue paint, and the marauding Blues brazenly squirted our imperial presence, still lip-syncing up on the porch. That sudden foreign abuse generated a wild response from the appalled two-hundred outraged girl fans, who came to *our* embattled defense, and started thrashing and mauling the stuffing out of the formerly formidable Blues.

The Hammonton vandals broke free of their enraged female molesters, and wildly darted to their respective vehicles, double-parked in the center of Hall Street. In the midst of nearly being pulverized by the incensed teen females, the three cars hastily skidded south down the village's main drag, and sped out of the vicinity, safely abandoning the chaotic scene of pandemonium.

I wiped the blue gook from my eyelids and face, and then stared Frankie Arena directly into his paint-coated, azure features. "I guess this marks the end of the Boatnecks," I observed in disgust. "What a horrendous nightmare!"

"I've never felt so *blue* in all my life!" Frankie sorrowfully admitted. "I think I feel stinky wetness in the front, and also in the back of my underwear!"

"Look!" Juice aptly pointed-out with his index finger. "Most of our disgusted fans are getting in their cars and pullin' outa' here, too!"

"Those Hammonton blueberry jerks have really done it this time, ruining our fun," the fake Fabian alertly evaluated and complained as Sal wiped blue material from his active hands with paper napkins. "And right when everything was goin' super, the vandals show-up and sabotage our finest moment. The creeps demolished our glory."

The five vanquished Boatneck imitators were in an absolute stupor, completely lost for words. Then, Tommy Tomasello broke the dominating silence. "Where's your nearest toilet?" News anxiously asked Jives. "I think I gotta' use your nearest hopper from both ends of my abdomen!"

Chapter Fifteen

"Dead Man's Curve"

The Blues had accomplished their numskull objective. The abusive dunderheads had very efficiently wrecked and terrorized Frankie Arena's celebrity party, and had systematically disbanded the Boatnecks with one atrocious gang raid. A few remaining girls tried soothing our ruptured spirits, along with our rapidly fading enthusiasm for the rock and roll recording industry. The half-dozen compassionate young ladies stayed to help clean-up the scattered mess, which had made Jive's front lawn look like something between a crime scene and a war zone.

"It's a good thing your folks went out to dinner and to a movie," Juice told Jives. "Otherwise, your out-of-the-loop parents would've each had dual coronaries."

"You're a real *riot,* Juice. If they were here during the Blues' Pearl Harbor II, my folks would've had dual strokes plus twin heart attacks," Jives attested in normal English.

"If ya' think I'm a riot, you oughta' meet my older brother. He's a mob!" Johnny said in an attempt to experience some humor, while still recovering from the grips of catastrophe.

"Wait until Goose hears about this disaster," Fabian added. "He'll broadcast the incident wherever he has gum ball machines all over South Jersey. We'll be the laughing-stock of the whole area."

"Does anybody have a handful of aspirins?" News sincerely asked after returning from the bathroom. "The inside of my head feels like it's vomitin' its brains out!"

The following April Monday at school, Goose Restuccio really mercilessly busted our vulnerable chops. Naturally, his chosen topic was the aborted Boatneck party fiasco. We all first tried ignoring the risqué, loathsome ingrate, and then when those efforts failed, the guys endeavored changing the conversation to more benign subjects. Restuccio only displayed pleasure with a situation when someone or a group of individuals had made public fools out of themselves; had excessively embarrassed themselves, or when G.R. was enjoying ridiculing a victim with his filthy, acerbic remarks.

Finally, Jives got Restuccio to veer away from the humiliating Boatneck debacle by noticing something different in G.R.s normal appearance. "Hey Goose," Frankie said. "Where are ya' getting all of these stupid letterman sweater threads? Today, you're wearin' one with an M; Friday ya' was sportin' one with an H.S., and last Thursday ya' had on a letterman's sweater with an A.C. on it? Hey Dingbat, what's your dip-shit M.O.?"

"I was waitin' for one of you' half-blind dickheads to finally notice my threads," Goose replied in his classic put-down mode. "On Wednesday night, I was out with a prostitute from Atlantic City. The bitch liked havin' all-night sex with me so much that the kinky whore gave me her former A.C. high school sweater as a token of her appreciation."

"Well, Goose, what about the sweater you wore on Friday with the H.S. letters sewn on?" I curiously inquired. "What *H.S.* was it? Overbrook or Sterling High?"

"J.W, are you a dunce, or are you a retarded imbecile?" Goose snottily replied. "On Thursday night, I was out with another expensive hooker from Pacific Avenue in Atlantic City that had gone to Holy Spirit High. The prostitute liked havin' all-night sex with me so much that she gave me *her* damned high school sweater, so that I would remember havin' great humpin' and pumpin' with her."

"Okay, Goose, let me guess the big *M* you're wearin' on today's sweater," Juice volunteered. "While the Boatnecks were getting clobbered and ransacked in Winslow by the abominable Blues on Friday night, you were out with a horny harlot from *M*illville who liked your action so much that she gave you her former high school sweater!"

"No, you stupid Asshole!" Goose answered in a faked serious tone. "The friggin' bitch was from *W*illiamstown High!"

Everyone at the table roared when we all eventually deciphered the significance of Goose's great letter-inverted charade. "Long live sixty-nine!" the warped-brained son of a Mafia Don proclaimed to his delighted male audience.

That afternoon, Goose's white '60 Thunderbird pulled into the family yard with News Tomasello as the sole passenger. I was outside with Dad finishing-up putting a new door in the Pete's Market kitchen. Pop was happy to see News, but not so delighted with G.R.'s ignoble presence appearing on *his* property.

News was telling Dad how excited the peach kid was that the Boston Celtics had just won the NBA championship by soundly beating the St. Louis Hawks four games to three. "The Celtics are my favorite team," News told Pop.

"Red Auerbach is a great coach," Pop jovially replied. "And I once attended a game up at the Boston Garden. It was a really great experience."

I asked Dad if I could go-out with the guys until ten that night.

"Son, do ya' have all your homework done?" my father amiably asked. "Your academics are faltering."

"Yes," I respectfully answered. "I even did my trig' problems."

"Well, alright, but we're gonna' open the market next weekend. We're gonna' get a few shipments of spring flowers delivered, so be available for unloadin'. Also, I'll probably need ya' to take a run to Packer Street and pick-up a load of watermelons at the new Food Distribution Center in South 'Philly."

Goose had a few gum ball machines to clean-out in downtown Hammonton, and then he told Pop he would drive us out to *Route 73* to treat News and me to custards at Mr. Bill's, which had just opened for the spring/summer ice cream season.

Goose drove to Hammonton and cruised past the Town House on Third and Orchard Streets to see if any St. Joe High Reds were hanging-out there, and after not noticing any familiar faces, the 'Italian Stallion' drove down Orchard, bragging about his new Reds' James Dean jacket.

"When J.W. finally passes his initiation test," Goose announced, "I'll buy him a new red jacket just like I had bought for the other Reds. Have ya' noticed them wearin' their new zip-ups to school? Ain't they cool as a ghoul in a swimmin' pool?" Restuccio proclaimed in imitation of Jives Arena,

"Yeah," News said from the front seat. "They look pretty snazzy and jazzy. But the school administration will probably say that the red jackets are a violation of the Edgewood dress code, even though there's no offensive language printed on them."

"Hey!" I observed and pointed-out. "Look who's buyin' boards over at Crane's Lumber Company!"

"It's Gabe and Marty Gillette!" News quickly responded. "Looks like they're loadin' up enough wood to build a small garage!"

Goose impulsively turned the steering wheel, guiding the T-Bird into the lumberyard; abruptly braked his boss auto, and then boldly stared-down the somewhat-startled Blues, quite effectively using the element of surprise. Restuccio lowered his power window and politely asked, his voice sounding a little like Howdy Doody, "Hi guys. What's happenin'! Where's Clarabell, Mr. Bluster?"

Gabe Gillette ignored Goose's salutation, preferring to talk to someone on the other end of a set of Walkie-Talkies. His younger brother responded to Restuccio's inquiry.

"Just getting some lumber we need to build a new deer stand," Marty explained. "We'll get a pile of old wine-sap apples we're usin' for deer bait."

"Well Brother Martin," Goose chided. "Why the hell ain't ya' still studyin' the *A-pock-kill-lips* at the Malvern *Cementery* over in 'Pennsy!"

"Isn't deer-hunting season in December?" I innocently asked. "It's only April!"

"Who asked for your two-cents?" Marty nastily answered into the back of the T-Bird. "We kill deer whenever the hell we want. And we kill game wardens, too, if the the snoopin' assholes ever give us any static about killin' deer," Marty boasted. The younger blueberry prince then told us that he and his brother had saved a half-bushel of reject apples, and the siblings planned to throw the rotten fruit at Dennis Measley's house. The poor, destitute kid lived "out in the sticks", had a low IQ, and his old dilapidated house was often frequented as a target of abuse by the arrogant Blues.

"Well, I'm in town to clean-out a couple of nickel candy machines in the lumber-yard's office," Goose informed Marty. "Who's your' brother talkin' to?"

"Awww, just a couple of the guys," Marty nervously disclosed. "We like to keep in touch. Say Goose, where did ya' get that red jacket? I've seen a lot of 'em around lately. I hear you're now in with the peach punks."

"Sort of," Goose replied with a huge degree of pride. "It's just somethin' to do, that's all! I'm just their main adviser that's all."

"Where ya' headin'?" Marty asked.

"Over to Mr. Bill's on *Route 73,* G.R. disclosed. "I'm gonna' treat these two Bozos to some banana splits or hot fudge sundaes after I clean-out a few machines over in Winslow."

"Watch-out for Dead Man's Curve!" Marty sincerely warned. "It could be pretty dangerous."

"I promise ya', jerk-weed, I won't go-around that bend doin' over fifty!" G.R. exclaimed with a haunting, sinister sneer showing on his slanted mouth. "I'm gonna' live for as long as I can 'cause there ain't no heaven and there ain't no hell," the wise-ass bragged. "Just nothin' except an ugly, damned, empty void, if ya' know what the fuck I mean."

"You're almost cool enough to be a Blue!" Marty admitted while his older brother continued deliberately ignoring the visiting Reds, softly speaking words into the powerful Walkie-Talkie to his anonymous communicator on the other end.

"Okay, see ya' later alligator," Restuccio said, abruptly ending the superficially dishonest conversation.

News and I accompanied Goose into the Crane Lumber Company office; emptied-out several gum ball and nickel candy machines, and casually discussed how the Blues seemed fairly decent and pleasant compared to other encounters we had had with the fanatics. We left the busy lumber-yard office and then re-entered the nifty T-Bird. We next headed down Bellevue through town, crossed the railroad tracks and motored west on *Route 561* toward Winslow.

"I don't trust those sons of bitchin' Blues as far as I can shit a hard, brick-shaped turd," Goose crazily spoke in his standard jargon. "I smell a Wilt Chamberlain-size nigger in the woodpile. Most kids puke vomit, but the fucked-up Blues regurgitate veiled threats!"

"You're bein' entirely too crude and also too damned defensive," News constructively criticized. "There's a bit of good in everybody. The Blues won't bother us as long as we respect their space."

"Ya' don't smell somethin' rotten in Denmark stinkin' worse than a dirty old whore's infected pussy?" Goose argued. "Those connivin' cock-suckers are up to somethin' miss-tear-ious!"

"Marty said they were goin' to bounce some apples off of a kid's house," I commented. "That's pretty rank, don't ya' think?"

"That kid, Dennis Measley, lives out this way off of *561* between Hammonton and Winslow," Goose revealed. "And I've thrown all kinds of apples off his dinky house, too! It's common practice around these parts. And it's pretty neat scarin' the livin' hell out of him and his retarded parents at three-thirty in the mornin'."

I challenged Goose's point of view, and the future criminal was upset that I dared protest *his* omnipotent thoughts and actions. "J.W., just remember, lions kill sheep. Sheep don't kill lions. Stronger always wins-out over weaker. That's the meanin' of life, not what those friggin' lazy-ass priests and ministers preach in church on Sunday. I don't know much fuckin' science, but Darwin rules!"

I couldn't understand why Goose hated priests, hated nuns, hated ministers, and positively (negatively) hated religion. It was all an enormous riddle to me. "Were you born in a convent?" I laughed at the obsessed driver. "Were you an orphan?"

"Goose's beady eyes glared at me through the reflection in his rear-view mirror. "Do ya' wanta' get out and fuckin' walk back to Pete's Market?" the irate bigot replied. "What if I told ya' that a goddamned priest screwed my old lady, because my old man was out in Vegas getting drunk and laid with three call girls, and that I was not fuckin' born legitimate! Would ya' then believe my bullshit?" the nutcase vehemently challenged.

"Well, I don't know," I stuttered. "I'm sorry to hear *that* insane scenario had happened to you!"

"J.W., what the fuck do ya' have to be sorry for!" Goose yelled like a raving maniac. "*You* didn't pork my mother! A goddamned priest did! Now ya' know the fuckin' truth, and because of your friggin' stupid religion, ya' don't wanta' believe it!"

News turned-around in his seat and raised his eyebrows in my direction. Then, Tommy put his index finger in front of his mouth and tacitly signaled for me to shut-up. We cruised past Winslow Junction, and then sped past the landmark Winslow Brickyard, which produced a famous yellow brick that had been utilized in local area construction, including the 1925 Hammonton High School. Still, a word was not spoken until Goose made a left onto Flemington Pike, and headed in the direction of *Route 73* and popular Mr. Bill's Custard Stand.

"Slow down, Goose!" I cautioned from the back seat. "That's Dead Man's Curve up ahead!"

"Yeah, Goose," News concurred. "Slow down. There's some kind of accident up ahead. I think we're the first ones on the scene. We gotta' help!"

An old brown Volkswagen was overturned midway around the precarious bend that local residents had labeled Dead Man's Curve. Goose halted his classy vehicle, and the three of us then hastily moved to the apparent emergency, looked inside the damaged foreign car, and were amazed to observe the forms of three dazed nuns lying motionless inside.

Goose suggested that we should drive to Mr. Bill's and notify the Hammonton Rescue Squad to come out and attend to the unfortunate accident victims, but News thought that we should try and assist the helpless, unconscious occupants. "Here comes another car," Tommy indicated as Tomasello saw headlights approaching from the north, a mile off in the distant twilight. "Let's try and get the nuns out and tell that driver to go get help."

"We're lucky that a car's comin'," I stated. "This road is not too heavily traveled after five in the afternoon. I hope the three injured nuns are still alive!"

News and I managed to drag the three Sisters of Mercy out of the overturned Volkswagen, while Goose stood there and shook his head in disgust at our heroism' exhibition. All three nuns were very young, and had really attractive faces that appeared unscathed from their bad encounter with Dead Man's Curve. The three religious women were coming to, just as a familiar white '60 Thunderbird and a dark blue Pontiac sedan pulled-up to the accident scene. Speed Mortellite, Ox Narducci, Butch Lanza, Dan "the Hammer" Bertino, Pee Wee Lucca, and Al "Sonny" Perone all jumped out of the T-Bird quickly exited their respective vehicles.

Then, to our utter astonishment, the three beautiful nuns got to their knees, stood-up, whipped-off their black habits, and gave Goose,

News, and me tremendous, big, prolonged kisses on our lips. The nuns peculiar, out-of-character behavior allowed the six Blues enough time to tackle Goose, News, and me, and then wrestle us to the cold ground. Before we could defend ourselves from the shock of the nuns' unorthodox conduct, along with the ferocity of the Blues' vicious surprise attack, we found that our hands had been already tied behind our backs. Mack Martello, another psycho Blues' member, pulled up to the scene, and then Goose, News, and I were roughly tossed into the recently arrived blue Cadillac's back seat by our seven malicious enemies.

"What the fuck is this all about!" Goose ranted and raged like a psychotic mental patient. "Don't you shit-heads know who you're fuckin' with here?"

Mack Martello and Speed Mortellite were talking with a third party over Walkie-Talkies. The foreign voice was soon recognized to be that of head-honcho Gabe Gillette. "Bring the idiots to the stage-platform," the Blues kingpin's familiar voice commanded. "Those three assholes are gonna' be on the official 'Welcome to Hammonton' friendly greeting committee."

Goose was really pissed-off because the egomaniac recognized that one of the disguised nuns was, in reality, an area prostitute, cleverly masquerading as a religious personage. "I've been betrayed!" Restuccio loudly complained. "That freakin' bitch'll never get a hundred-bucks from me for a mother-f'-in' blow-job, ever again!"

"Shut the hell up in there, if ya' wanta' live more than another minute!" Ox Narducci threatened as the beast peered into the blue Caddie's backseat. "Okay, men, help me turn the VW back onto its wheels, and ladies," Narducci addressed the three imposter nuns, "you can drive the German jalopy back to where ya' got it. Gabe will show-up and give ya' each a hundred bucks for your fine help."

Narducci, Mortellite, Martello, Bertino, Lanza, Perone, and Pee Wee "the Troll" Lucca all bent-down and managed to cooperatively roll the old Volkswagen over onto the asphalt road. The three grateful prostitutes, who had been coyly clad in nuns' garb, hopped into their temporary small automobile. Soon, the motor was running, and the small foreign vehicle sputtered south down Flemington Pike in the direction of Mr. Bill's Custard Stand.

"Well asshole, Reds," Mortellite mocked as the brute bent-down and stared into the blue Cadillac. "Mack here is gonna' drive ya' to meet a good friend of ours, named Bill."

"Bill?" News reacted. "Who's Bill? Mr. Bill?"

"No, you degenerate freak," Mortellite giggled as the other Blues standing behind Speed mimicked his haughty example. "His last name is Board. Mr. Bill Board!"

"Hey, Speed, there's another car comin'!" Pee Wee Lucca hollered as the short coward pointed south. "Let's get the hell outa' here before the Winslow cops start investigating."

"You're right," Speed agreed. "We don't want anybody reportin' this here friendly meeting to the fuzz."

Mack Martello instantly hopped into the blue Caddie's driver's seat, and Ox Narducci jumped into the front passenger side. Speed Mortellite and three other Blues quickly entered the second white T-Bird, and Pee Wee Lucca leaped into Goose's coveted '60 wheels and promptly took off first.

"Where's that little runt drivin' my car?" Goose insisted on learning. "His eyes don't even come up to the steerin' wheel!"

"If I was you," Ox Narducci firmly prefaced as the brawny passenger turned toward the rear seat, "I'd worry about my damned life and not about my damned car. We've just graduated from bombardin' Dennis Measley's house with a bushel of reject apples! We might be goin' into the scrap metal business now, just like your greedy Old Man!"

The three-car caravan drove forward a half-mile north to the intersection of *Route 73* and Flemington Pike. Pee Wee Lucca waited at the Stop Sign and soon crossed the four-lane highway, made a U-turn with Goose's T-Bird inside Mr. Bill's parking lot, and then headed south back in the direction of Dead Man's Curve.

"I gotta' give ya' damned guys credit," Goose said in a rare moment of praise. "This was really a clever set-up. Ya' had used the Walkie-Talkies to communicate with Gabe Gillette at the lumber-yard, and then had the hooker-nuns ready, waitin' to scam us."

"Forget the credit," Ox Narducci laughed, "just give me cash instead. But really, you jerks have to learn to keep your damned gabby mouths shut. Everybody in Hammonton knew for a whole week that you had been braggin' and chatter-boxin' that you were treatin' some Edgewood punks to Mr. Bill's Custard tonight. That gave us enough time to get an old Volkswagen ready to put into service, and to hire the three call-girls to get your attention."

"Well, I'll be a monkey's uncle!" G.R. said in amazement. "I've been victimized by a lousy third-grade stunt. This nun-bait-shit is almost as crazy as fillin' my car with freakin' frozen blueberries."

Mack Martello and Ox Narducci amply laughed at Goose's acknowledgement that the junior don had been totally outsmarted by such a simple, elementary, decoy prank. Martello drove east on *73* from Winslow to Folsom, until the highway narrowed into two-lane Mays Landing Road. Then, at Pat's Tavern, our chauffeur turned left at the traffic light onto *Route 54,* which would lead directly into metropolitan downtown Hammonton. Martello glanced into the rear-view mirror to make certain that Speed Mortellite and the remaining Blues contingent were loyally riding behind us.

"Hey, what are you guys gonna' do with *my* T-Bird?" Goose demanded.

"You'll find out soon enough," Ox laughed from the front seat. "I don't think you're gonna' rush home and jerk-off over it!"

Mack Martello piloted the blue Caddie to Chew Road, and pulled-over directly behind the *Route 54* "Welcome to Hammonton, the Blueberry/Peach Capital of the World" billboard. The word 'Peach' had recently been covered-over with dark blue paint. "Okay, here's where we get out!" Ox Narducci ordered. "You three assholes can sit in the car and watch the initial activities!"

Gabe and Marty Gillette had already arrived at the billboard in one of the blueberry company's pick-ups *we* had seen at the lumberyard. The brothers handed Narducci, Mortellite, Martello, Lanza, Bertino, Perone, and Pee Wee Lucca hammers and nails.

"What the hell are they doin' with those two by fours?" Goose asked his fellow captives. "What the hell are those creeps buildin'?"

"A scaffold, some kind of wobbly platform," News guessed. "But they're constructin' the catwalk on the backside of the billboard and not on the front where it normally belongs."

We captives sat in the back seat like three stunned manikins with our hands manacled behind our backs. The Blues' construction crew labored for about forty-five minutes, shaping-up the structure of their secret project.

"Hey, I just thought of something that makes a lot of sense," G.R. muttered. "That's the lumber and plywood Gillette said he was gonna' use to build his illegal tree stand with. The lyin' no good, nasty bastard!"

The amateur carpenters' platform had been completed in another fifteen-minutes. The nefarious Blues stood there, proudly admiring their most recent accomplishment. In the meantime, *Route 54* traffic whizzed by, seemingly oblivious to the bizarre mischief in progress, and the motorists apparently apathetic to the three hostages occupying the blue Cadillac's back seat.

Ox Narducci then clambered-up onto the wooden scaffolding. The mammoth hulk made a fist and then punched-out three holes in the '*Os'* in the words "Hamm*o*nt*o*n and W*o*rld" that had been circled on the backside of the large sign. The brute then used a hammer to enlarge the gaping holes that he had manufactured in the plywood with his powerful, clenched fists.

"Okay, you three weasels, we're gonna' now put you on public display," Speed yelled at us. "You and your dingle-headed pals are gonna' pay for givin' me plenty of grief at the Midway Diner," Mortellite predicted to G.R.

I then remember being roughly dragged from the blue luxury car; ungently elevated into the air; turned face forward on the recently constructed wooden platform, and then having my head thrust though a large, circular cavity that had been recently formed by Ox Narducci's fearsome fist. My head projected through the first *O'* hole in "Hammonton", and News Tomasello's skull had been punctured through the second *O*. Finally, Goose's noggin' had penetrated the O in the word "World", and all three of us had been effectively incapacitated by a modern version of Puritan colonial stocks and bonds. I was afraid to squirm-around and slit my throat from the jagged pieces and sharp plywood splinters that were pinching at my neck.

"Now our dear friend, Mr. Bill Board, has three new buddies to keep him company!" Gabe Gillette hollered-up to his humiliated victims. "Next time, screw-around with people in your own league, you three dumb-shit, circus clowns!"

The Blues re-entered the light blue truck, the '60 blue Caddie, and Mortellite's '60 white Thunderbird, laughing-up a storm at our general immobility. Finally, the three vehicles flicked-on their headlights, backed-up, turned-around, and then peeled-out down *Route 54* in the direction of Hammonton.

"What the hell are we gonna' do now?" Restuccio moaned like a listless cancer patient lying on his deathbed.

"We gotta' wait for someone to see us and stop to rescue us," News declared. "That might not happen until tomorrow mornin'."

"These speeding motorists don't seem that alert," I lamented. "At least fifty cars have passed by, and not one has stopped to investigate our dire situation."

Another fifty or so automobiles zoomed past without even one noticing our rather extraordinary predicament. Finally, an old rusty black '47 Plymouth coughed and twanged by the welcoming billboard, traveling at around twenty-five miles an hour. The driver applied the brakes, and then drove the old puddle-jumper in reverse, until the relic car stopped opposite the front view of the billboard.

"Who's there?" a timid voice asked from below. "Need any help?"

"Get us down from here!" Goose screamed like a distraught child throwing a tantrum in its high-chair.

"Hey guys!" News realized and hollered as his eyes looked-up from his slanted head, tilted-down. "It's Dennis Measley!"

Chapter Sixteen

"The Jersey Devil Affair"

Dennis Measley, the least likely kid within a fifteen-mile-radius of Hammonton, came to our rescue. Even Goose Restuccio, who had admitted to maliciously bombarding Dennis Measley's dilapidated house with apples at least a dozen-times at three-thirty in the morning, was happy to see the unkempt kid show-up to save the day.

"Who did this to ya' guys?" Dennis yelled up. "Don't tell me. It was the Blues, I'll betcha'."

Dennis removed a penknife from his pocket, climbed-up on the recently constructed rear billboard planks, and cut the clothesline ropes that still bound our hands behind our backs. I told News and Goose not to try removing our heads from the plywood, since any of us could easily sever a vein or artery by attempting to wriggle a throat inside the vertical welcoming billboard.

"I'll cut you fellas' out one at a time," Dennis promised. "Stay still while I carve the loose wood from around your necks."

News was freed first, then me second, and finally Goose third. We all took deep breaths and suddenly, inhaling and life never seemed so wonderful. Tommy climbed-down from the platform and stepped to the front of the town's advertisement. A note had *been Scotch*-taped under the former word "Peach", which had been canceled-out in blue paint.

"What's it say?" Goose asked while rubbing both sides of his sore neck with his palms. "I need an Egyptian *chiro*practor bad," the embarrassed schemer mumbled.

"It says," News read, "your necks should be *kiln* you. Killin' is spelled' k-i-l-n."

"Those goddamned Blues oughta' know how to spell better than that," Restuccio remarked. "The dick-lickers must have a lousy faculty over at Hammonton High. Those retards don't even know how to spell killin'."

"Well, Goose," News said before clearing his throat passage, "k-i-l-n is an actual word in English. It means a large oven, or maybe even a furnace where things are baked in."

"What kind of things?" Goose asked in rage. "I ain't too good at fancy vocabulary words. All I know is that if you fall into a deep cesspool over your head, you can't see shit!"

"Things like expensive china, earthenware and baked bricks," I interrupted. "I think the Blues are givin' us a definite clue about your stolen T-bird."

"You said it J.W., you said it!" Tommy T. exclaimed. "Bricks. I got a theory. The Winslow Brickyard Company out past Winslow Junction."

"Let's go!" Goose demanded. "Those crazy sons of boo-tanas are gonna' regret what they've done to me tonight, I guarantee it!"

The four of us got into Dennis Measley's grimy '47 Plymouth, and the piece of rusty tin reminded me of Tinker's old junker back in Levittown. Empty soda bottles and greasy oilcans littered the smelly floor and the cruddy seats.

"Beggars can't be choosey!" News philosophically stated as my good friend tossed rubbish from the seat to the floor. I found some old newspaper pages tucked under the back seat, distributed three sections, and News, Goose, and I used the fragments to sit on to avoid permanently soiling our blue jeans.

"Look!" G.R. pointed out, "I already got some nasty stains on my James Dean' jacket from that damned billboard adventure. Those pricks are gonna' wish their asses were born in hell. I've never been so damned mad in all my life. I wanta' kill!"

"I thought you once said there was no such place as hell," I answered.

"There ain't!" Goose insisted. "I'll just change hell to a German concentration camp, so then I mean hell on earth. Religion and God are the biggest frauds ever invented."

On the slow drive out to Winslow, Dennis Measley told us a story about an encounter the victim had had with the Blues the previous week at the Gem. Gabe Gillette had bribed a well-endowed waitress ten-dollars to go up to Dennis, who had been waiting at the main counter for a carryout order. The waitress explained to Measley that she was feeling hot flashes and began unbuttoning her blouse, exposing a D-cupped bra containing a massive set of hard breasts. Dennis Measley's eyes had almost exploded out of their sockets.

"What happened next?" Restuccio asked from the front passenger side. "I think I heard this ten-dollar bribe story last week from unreliable Herc Juliano."

"Well," said Dennis. "I couldn't help but stare at those big things stickin' out from her chest. So, when my order pizza came, I became very scared. I turned to get out of there in a hurry, but fell on my face. When I looked up, everybody in the Gem was laughin' at me."

Goose said that he knew what had really happened. "While the waitress was distractin' Dennis with her big knockers, one of the Blues sneaked behind him. The blueberry punk stooped-down to the floor and tied Dennis's shoes together, while poor Measley was lookin' at the doll's super huge torpedoes."

"If ya' mean somebody tied my shoelaces when I was lookin' at the girl's big chest, then I think *that* is what really happened," Measley confirmed.

The old black '47 clunker sputtered into the main entrance of the closed-for-business Winslow Brickyard Company. To the right was a massive oven, large enough to fry a mastodon along with its extended family. The lock on the door had been sheered-off, so we slid the metal object sideways on its rollers. Goose found a light switch and illuminated the room.

"Jesus S. Christ!" G.R. irreverently cursed. Four slashed white-wall tires on rims lay in one corner to the left, and in the center of the open kiln rested the remains of one totally baked '60 Thunderbird. The white paint had been burned-off; the red interior upholstery and red rugs completely incinerated, and the entire burned hood, doors, bumpers and trunk had been battered and showed huge dents.

"Totaled!" Goose screamed in absolute distress. "Destroyed by sledgehammers and cremated by fire!" The proud rich kid who, had always shunned emotion, cupped his hands in front of his eyes to fight back tears.

Goose told Dennis to drive him home first so that *he* could report the felony to his father, who would then contact Gillette's old man to pay for the damage, or else be executed.

"What about insurance?" News asked Restuccio. "Won't the insurance company pay?"

Goose explained that an accident report would first have to be obtained from the police. The cops would want to conduct a shallow, fruitless investigation, once the local police found-out that the prime suspects were the rich-kid' Blues. The best way to settle the problem, according to G.R., would be for a wealthy elder to pay another wealthy elder the cash debt without cops and insurance companies ever entering into the picture and complicating matters.

"If old man Gillette doesn't fork-over the missin' bread," Goose conjectured, "then my Pop will have Gabe's old man castrated, crucified, and then illegally embalmed."

After we said "good night" to Goose, and after *he* said, "What the fuck is good about it?" Dennis drove past Winslow Junction to Spring Road to take News home. When the slow-learner pulled-up to Tomasello's driveway, News immediately noticed that his family's mailbox had been knocked-off its post, probably with a baseball bat or crowbar.

"I'll bet it's the Blues sending me a signal not to sponsor you, Jives, Juice, and Fabian into the Reds," Tommy theorized and revealed. "It's a scare tactic."

"What are ya' gonna' do?" I asked. "Call in the National Guard?"

"Oh, I'm more determined than ever now to make you four guys Reds," T.T. declared. "J.W., how could I get even with those damned punks? I want sweet revenge, just like Goose does."

I told News about something the Diablos had done to a wise-guy Kamikaze in Kenwood. The kid had obliterated Tinker's mailbox with a crowbar, so then Tink and I installed a new mailbox and then filled it with concrete.

"What happened next?" News asked.

"Well, when the Kamikaze fool returned a few days later to repeat his vandalism, the moron smashed the mailbox with his crowbar and broke both his wrists in the process."

"Okay J.W., you're really a resourceful guy," News commended. "I'll have a new cement-filled mailbox up in two days flat. I'm sure my dad will like the idea of stickin' the cement inside. I'll get him to notify the Hammonton Post Office to keep our mail there for the next week or so, until a destructive Blue tries demolishin' my mailbox again."

Dennis Measley drove me home to Pete's Market, which to tell the truth never looked so magnificent to my humble eyes. I thanked the over-harassed kid for his generous assistance, and said that I hoped I could fully return his favor some fine day.

"My folks are gonna' open up in a few days," I told Dennis. "Would ya' like anything to eat from the market's cold storage?" I asked him.

"Sure, a couple of nice juicy apples would be fine," Dennis strangely answered.

The next April morning at school, Goose told News and me before homeroom that his dad had called Mr. Gillette, who under pressure of mass Mafia retribution, agreed to satisfy the three-thousand-five-hundred-dollar expense incurred by *his* criminal son. "I'll have a new set of wheels by Easter, so until then, I'll have to rely on you' pecker-checkers for general transportation," the spoiled Sicilian, oversized brat berated.

During fifth period lunch, News related the tale of his disintegrated mailbox and exactly how he and his cooperative dad planned to remedy the situation. The newly-constructed mailbox would be ready for special delivery packages and junk mail within two days.

"Mung is better than those asshole Blues any day," Goose angrily described his hated foes.

"What's the heck is mung?" News inquired. "Is it foul Chinese food or somethin'? Never heard of it."

"I thought you was smart!" G.R. retorted to the intellectual genius. "Ya' know all this chicken-shit crap like *kiln,* but don't know somethin' damned important like mung!"

"Well, what the heck is it?" I joined in, defending News' sensitivity. "I'm intrigued, too!"

"Mung, M-U-N-G," Goose emphasized and spelled very slowly, "is what happens when some nasty jerk-offs like the Blues hit a pregnant lady in the stomach with a baseball bat. Mung is what the fuck comes-out of her snatch, after her belly is crushed eighteen times with the baseball bat, one time for each baseball position, and one time for each inning!"

"Sorry I asked," I answered. "I should've known it would be somethin' disgustin' and nauseous."

News was also appalled by Goose's raunchy definition and by *his* gross description of the new horrible vocabulary word "mung." Tomasello deftly changed gears and began talking-about how Arnold Palmer had just won the Masters Golf Tournament by one stroke over rival Ken Venturi.

"That's odd," I said, "because a golfer could get seventy strokes and still win a golf tournament, but only one major stroke could finish off a formerly healthy American. Strokes are sometimes worse than heart attacks, and I suppose pro golfers are immune to them."

News ignored my ludicrous commentary about how lethal strokes could be glorified, and how wonderful it was that the ice hockey dynasty known as the Montreal Canadiens had just defeated the Toronto Maple Leafs in four straight games to win an unprecedented fifth Stanley Cup in a row. Goose Restuccio didn't savor the flow of the discussion, so the self-centered egotist related a secret ambition he had had ever since the insidious Blues had bragged that they illegally hunted deer during the eleven month "non-season".

"Listen, you two guys," G.R. said in a muffled voice, like the goony kid was an international spy conferring with two secret agents. "I'm gonna' have a special huntin' expedition in the Wharton State Forest in back of Glossy Fruit Farms up on *206*. I want to see how brave J.W., News, Fabian, Jives, and Juice really are, because I think you five hambones are really only weak faggots to begin with," the still-upset Red disclosed. "Tell the three other dip-shits to be at my house at four p.m. after school on Friday. We're gonna' have an illegal deer hunt right in *their* backyard, just to show those Blues that we're just as tough as they are," Goose bragged.

At lunch, the three other guys reluctantly agreed to join our company in the pine' barrens' forest expedition, only because everyone felt sorry for the kiln fate of Goose's white '60 Thunderbird, and also for the obliteration of News' father's rural-free-delivery mailbox. G.R. described the forest gunning expedition as a "pre-initiation ritual-Reds-raid" into the Blues' sacred hunting territory. "I got permission from the Reds' executive committee to see exactly what kind of testicles you five freaks have," Goose chastised and belittled. "For all I know, you five queers might have five ovaries instead of two balls."

News and Fabian picked me up in the red and white '57 Ford Fairlane, and we met Jives and Juice in the driveway outside Goose's regal rural mansion.

"How's your Coronet runnin'?" I asked Frankie while the five of us patiently waited in the asphalt driveway for G.R. to make his grand appearance.

"Good, ever since the Winslow Junction' stolen battery thing," Jives reported. "The only reason I'm goin' along on this secret huntin' gig is because of the party crashin' those Blues had done at my pad. It put the bitchin' Boatnecks on the dust shelf for good. Now I hope with every hair on my balls that that freaky "Ya' Gotta' Believe" album tanks, and takes a mean-mother-assed, deep cesspool dive."

The massive garage door in front of us suddenly opened, and there stood Goose Restuccio, wearing a vindictive revenge frown upon his normally-gruesome facial features. "Don't just stand there, ya' five lazy dork-faces. Give me a hand with these here three sledgehammers, shotguns, and crowbars. J.W., grab that bowlin' ball inside the garage and quickly pull-down the damned door," G.R. commanded.

"What are the three sledgehammers and crowbars gonna' be used for?" Juice curiously inquired. "I thought we were just going illegal deer huntin' in the woods!"

"We're gonna' rip the Blues' huntin' cabin to shreds over in the east side of the Wharton State Forest," Goose predicted. "Then, after we wreck-up the shittin' log cabin, I'll leave this here bowlin' ball we got from Harbor Lanes inside. It'll be the only useful thing left in the whole goddamned lodge."

I returned with the bowling ball after shutting the garage door. "That's just like foreshadowing," I alluded, remembering a certain vocabulary term I had learned in English literature back at Cardinal Reagan High.

"J.W., what the fuck are ya' talkin' about?" Goose questioned. "I'm gonna' leave this here bowlin' ball inside the ransacked cabin, just to warn the ball-breakin' Blues that somethin' with bowlin' balls is gonna' happen to their crummy asses, soon in the future."

I told Goose that I was aware of the symbolic function of the bowling ball, and that I was vigorously working on a creative plan to employ the one-hundred-and-ninety-nine remaining spheres against our blue fruit enemies. "But Goose, that's precisely what I meant by *fore*shadowing!" I reiterated. "I meant exactly what you said."

Restuccio glanced-up at the setting sun. "You're right J.W." the chronic troublemaker observed and agreed. "The sun's gonna' set soon, but there's gonna' be six shadows vandalizin' the creeps' hunting cabin. Where do ya' get this shit-head *four shadow* crap?"

The five of us laughed at Goose's deficient knowledge of simple literary nomenclature. As we loaded the three sledgehammers, three crowbars, three shotguns, and the symbolic bowling ball into the two trunks, I had a few questions for Restuccio. "How do ya' know the Blues won't be at the cabin? Aren't ya' afraid of the police or forest rangers findin' out?"

"J.W., tonight the Blues are gonna' be in town at the Gem and in front of Vega's Drugs as usual. There's a rumor that the Vineland jocks are comin' back to town with reinforcements for a battle royal rematch," Goose informed. "And as far as the cops are concerned, as soon as the fuzz find that this vandalism involves the Blues and me, they'll back-off, just like Mr. Gillette did with my Pop."

I was not too keen on destroying the Blues' hunting cabin sanctuary, even though the thugs had deflated tires; stolen Jives' battery; and had kidnapped my friends and me at Winslow Junction. Also, Gabe Gillette and his punk pals had filled Goose's car with frozen blueberries; had stuck three of our heads through a *Route 54* billboard; had cremated G.R.'s T-Bird in the brickyard kiln, and had cruelly crashed Jives' hopping rock and roll party. I had had enough of out-of-control criminal activity back in Levittown, and I knew quite well that pranks would inevitably escalate into life-threatening situations, if gone unchecked. 'This is the Diablos versus Kamikazes revisited,' I unpleasantly thought, 'and it's all disguised as the Reds against the Blues.'

News drove Sal Midilli, Ronald Restuccio, and me out of the estate's winding driveway, and Jives and Juice trailed in the black and white '57 Dodge. The fact that the Blues had harassed all of us in one way or another prevented any of us from challenging Goose's clarion call for proportionate retribution.

G.R. instructed News to take Fairview Avenue to bypass possible detection by the Blues of us driving down Bellevue through the center of Hammonton. We turned right onto "the Pike", and then hung a left onto Basin Road. I sensed we were all contemplating the upcoming plundering of the Blues' revered cabin, and I was reflecting on the prospect of certain prison incarceration if we were apprehended in the act.

News broke the reigning silence by expounding that school integration in the south had only been successfully implemented in six percent of the Dixie' public-school districts, in spite of the 1954 Supreme Court ruling against racial segregation.

"Look here," Goose warned his three jittery listeners. "If ya' think we got trouble with these goddamned Blues, just wait 'til ya' see what happens once political power is given to niggers. Then, the Reds and the Blues are gonna' have to become allies, just like we did against the Vineland jock jerk-offs. Before ya' know it, those jungle bunnies are gonna' want everything for nothin', and wanta' take over the whole damned country."

"How can ya' honestly say that?" I answered. "What makes you think *that* will be true? Are ya' a prophet of the devil or something?"

"Because, the niggers are gonna' want upside-down slavery, that's why!" Goose yelled, the veins protruding from his neck and throat. "Those mool-en-yon' cunt-lappers will want us white guys to all work for them, whether any of 'em ever become rich or not. They'll want to take-over the whole damned country without workin' for anything. They'll want everything for nothin'! Darkies don't only want fuckin' equality. They not only want power. Niggers wanna' fuckin' rule our asses!"

News was becoming extremely nervous as the spiteful driver turned right onto Union Road, and swung around the bend in the direction of *Route 206.* Fabian sensed G.R.'s discomfort and paranoia, and asked Goose from the back seat the specific directions to the Blues' hunting cabin.

Tommy was directed by the expedition's organizer that we'd turn north on *206,* and about a mile past the Red Barn Farm Market, our commando raid would slow-down and ease into a dreary, dirt road that penetrated into the eastern pine barrens. I looked behind and observed that Frankie's Dodge Coronet was still tailing us.

"Why ya' so scared?" Goose asked News. "Did ya' just find out you're pregnant with triplets, or are ya' afraid of the Jersey Devil?"

"Maybe," News answered timidly, before swallowing some saliva in one big gulp. "But I'm more afraid of breakin' the law. I didn't think that your huntin' trip would wind-up bein' raw juvenile delinquency."

Everyone in the car was familiar with the legend of the Jersey Devil, who was reputed to haunt hunters and campers in the Jersey Pine Barrens all the way from north of Atlantic City to the Berlin-Atco area. Hammonton and vicinity, being the hub of South Jersey in the center of the lush pine forest, was the location for many past Jersey Devil' sightings.

"How'd this Jersey Devil bullshit all get started?" Goose asked as the '57 Fairlane rumbled-down the bumpy dirt road. Since News was so petrified that he couldn't think or speak properly, I filled in the void with the legend's origin.

"An old lady named Mrs. Leeds cursed the idea of her havin' a thirteenth child, and when the demon was born, it had the head of a horse, the legs and feet of a goat, and flapping wings to fly," I shared. "Mrs. Leeds had given birth to a dangerous monster. When the hideous creature abnormally grew in size, the miniature beast flew-out of the family chimney, and has lived in the pine-barrens ever since. It seems to prefer haunting and attacking people in the Wharton State Forest part of the pine barrens. That's where we are right now!"

"Where did this Mrs. Leeds live?" Fabian asked.

"Over in Leeds Point, not far from New Gretna and Smithville, near the mouth of the Mullica River, about ten-miles northwest of Atlantic City," I replied in a worried-but-semi-scholarly voice.

It was twilight when the two automobiles pulled-up next to the Blues deserted cabin. Goose told us that we had to act with dispatch in performing the intended demolition. I carried a crowbar, a shotgun and the symbolic bowling ball to the cabin door. Goose smashed-down the portal with five vicious swings of his sledgehammer. We trespassed into the near-dark interior, and began breaking and shattering chairs, tables, glasses, cups, dishes, cabinets, windows, and everything else in sight. The entire cabin wreckage took about five-minutes to complete. I imagined that I was a primitive barbarian, a fierce Mongol, or a savage Visigoth, as I participated in the marauding, but none of us were half as zealous as Goose Restuccio was. Th crazed dictator ravaged and devastated the cabin's interior like he had been possessed by a hundred evil demons.

"Okay, J.W.," Goose ordered after his pillaging-obsession had been satisfied. "Put the bowlin' ball in the center of the cabin so that we can have *four shadows* for the Blues to see," he honestly said. "And then there's somethin' else I wanta' do before we leave this shit hole' scumbag place. First, ya' all gotta' put your crowbars and sledgehammers back into the cars and then follow me with your shotguns and the shells I gave ya'."

Restuccio reached into his Reds' James Dean jacket and removed some additional pellet' shells, telling Juice and me to keep them to later load the new ammunition into the 12-gauge shotguns when needed. Then he said is a sinister voice, "Let's go blow the damned Blues' tree stand to smithereens."

Goose led us in quasi-military fashion to a narrow dirt trail that wound into the interior darkness of dense tall pine trees. "Up ahead about three-hundred-feet is where the Blues have their tree stand to spot bucks from," Restuccio informed. "I'm gonna' destroy that freakin' thing too before we leave this piss hole place."

"But I'm scared to death," News cried out. "Can't we just go home?"

"News is hip," Jives nervously agreed. "Too much shit won't flush down any toilet bowl, even the one owned by Hedda Hopper. Let's scoot and bug-out before the fuzz shows."

"Come on Goose," Juice chimed-in. "Haven't we already done enough damage?"

"I think a damned castrated eunuch has more balls than you' five toad turds do," Goose scolded. "I shoulda' took Balls Giordano with me rather than you friggin' cowards."

I despised Goose's constant hostility, but I truly admired News's sense of conscience and sense of basic morality. Just as I was about to cravenly turn around and scuttle back to Tommy's car with my shotgun, Goose pointed to a dim tree stand silhouetted by a gibbous moon, and gave the bold command, "There it is guys. Let's blast the goddamned thing outa' the friggin' pine tree with our shotguns."

On the command of "ready," Goose, Juice, and I all aimed our shotguns at the desolate Blues' pine tree stand, which was elevated twelve-feet or so above the forest ground. When Restuccio ordered us to "aim", I was more anxious than ever to pull the trigger, and then dash as fast as my legs would carry me back to the safety of News's Fairlane. Right when G.R. was about to yell the word "fire!", a loud growl was heard coming from the center of the forest.

A hideous-looking creature emerged with a horse's head, a devil's body, and grotesque flapping wings. The horrible thing was snorting loudly, and also swiftly moving in our direction.

Three shotguns were blasted at the approaching monster, but none of the buckshot seemed to faze the incensed creature. We all were momentarily petrified.

"Let's get the fuck outa' here!" Goose screamed in sheer panic.

"Ahhhh!" News, Jives, Juice, Fabian, and I bellowed in unison. The six of us sprinted as fast as our bodies could move, hustling the three-hundred-feet up the narrow, sandy trail, and then the four-hundred-feet down the hunting road, until we reached our two cars. News, G.R., Fabian, and I all jumped inside the red and white Fairlane. Goose was the only one still possessing a shotgun. Juice and I had dropped our weapons during our arcane contact with the supernatural phantom. News fired-up the engine, and the almost berserk driver quickly maneuvered the '57 Ford into a wild U-turn, which was soon mimicked by Jives' black and white Dodge.

"That *was* the Jersey Devil!" News screamed like an absolute lunatic. "That *was* the Jersey Devil!"

"News, keep goin' faster!" Fabian insisted. "I'm so nervous that I can't even shit my pants!"

Our pan*demon*ium was interrupted by Goose Restuccio's shrill, piping laugh. "Ha, ha, ha, ha!" the loudmouth guffawed. "This is the funniest damned thing I've ever done. Ha, ha, ha, ha!"

"What's so funny?" I shrieked from the back seat. "That ugly fierce thing *was* the Jersey Devil! We're all lucky to be alive!"

"Ha, ha, ha, ha!" Restuccio persistently screamed as the psycho buckled-over. "I think my fuckin' balls are gonna' fall off!"

"Goose, *you* are even more crazy than everyone says you are!" Fabian accused. "That was a near-death experience we had back there, and you think it was the funniest thing you ever saw! You need a long stay at Ancora State Hospital real bad!"

"Stop the car!" Restuccio ordered. "Stop the damned shittin' car right now!" G.R. dramatically hesitated for a moment; told everyone to lock their doors, and we then reluctantly acceded to Goose's cryptic, fanatical demands.

"Fellas'," the junior don expressed and laughed. "That creature was not the Jersey Devil. It was Hoss Gregorio and his younger brother Little Joe wearin' a Jersey Devil costume. It cost me five-hundred-buckeroos to have the disguise made, but it was worth every penny. Ha, ha, ha, ha!" the lunatic chortled. "That was a friggin' expensive outfit that scared the livin' shit out of you lame turkeys," G.R. again laughed." Now we're gonna' go out to *206,* swing a U-turn, and go back and get the shotguns that you weak, scared-to-death assholes dropped on the road near the Blues deer tree stand."

"But that terrible, horned monster looked so real!" News marveled and gasped. "That creature was real, I tell ya'. I saw it snortin' fire darts out of its damned nostrils!"

"I didn't give a damn about the tree stand," Goose disclosed. "I only wanted to destroy the huntin' cabin. I used the tree stand as an excuse to scare the hard turds out of *your* constipated asses."

"But the monster seemed as real as life!" I also argued. "It was too real to be fake!"

"Your eyes and your minds were playing tricks on you," Goose revealed, slapping still-flabbergasted News Tomasello on the shoulder. "Let's get the hell out and tell Jives and Juice what really happened, before the dumb-fucks both have double hernias, and die from a bad case of twisted balls."

The four of us exited News' Fairlane, somewhat-relieved from our former intense anxiety. We paced back to Jives' Dodge, which still had its windows raised and doors locked, out of fear of the savage and brutal patrolling Jersey Devil.

Suddenly, a third car's headlights could be seen as the vehicle sped toward us from the direction of the cabin. Dust was billowing-up into the night sky, the car going about fifty-miles-an-hour on the ominous, sandy, pine-barrens road. Soon, the automobile's tires slid to a halt, almost plowing into the back of Jives' Coronet.

"That ain't no forest ranger or any Blue's car," Goose recognized. "That's Hoss and Little Joe's tin tank."

"Nice goin' fellas'," G.R. congratulated as Hoss frenetically rolled-down the driver's side window. "Ya' guys were terrific masquerading in that weird, expensive, fucked-up outfit. Ya' both shoulda' seen…"

"Cut the damned bullshit!" Hoss yelled at Restuccio. "We were in our Jersey Devil disguise, ready to head toward the tree stand to scare the crap outa' you guys, when the real Jersey Devil came out of the woods and scared the livin' shit out of us."

"What!" Goose screamed. "Ya' mean to tell me that ya' never scared us away from the tree stand like we planned at the Reds' meeting! If it wasn't you, it musta' been the real…."

"Jersey Devil!" eight voices simultaneously screamed our tonsils out in absolute fright.

We all were delirious. Goose forgot all about his two shotguns that had been left behind under the Blues' favorite tree stand. The Reds eagerly jumped into our respective cars, which soon perilously sped-out of the Wharton Tract pine-barrens. Restuccio's intimidated entourage was quite happy to have escaped with our precious lives.

Chapter Seventeen

"The Watermelon Express"

Later that week in April, Dad was going to officially open Pete's Farm Market for business. Pop had already arranged to have seventy-five, Congo striped watermelons picked-up at the Levins and Sampson Commission House at the new south Philadelphia Food Distribution Center. Goose had volunteered to accompany me in the blue "Pete's Market Special", a three-year-old Ford half-ton, stake-body pickup that came along with Pop's purchase of the retail farm market. The 'Philly watermelon rendezvous had been scheduled for midnight.

I picked-up G.R. at his family's palace around ten-thirty, and the rebellious prankster suggested that I cruise into Hammonton to see if the Blues were causing any trouble. "I also wanta' buy a pack of weeds," G.R. added, "so I'll have somethin' constructive to do while listenin' to your horse-crap all the way to 'Philly. I don't know who's worse, you or that pussy-munchin' News Tomasello. Ya' both make about as much sense as me readin' an advanced Chinese physics' textbook written upside-down and backwards."

"Well, Goose," I mentioned. "News and Jives will never be the same after that Jersey Devil incident the other night. We blasted the thing with our three shotguns, but the monster still came roarin' toward us as if nothin' at all happened."

"Damnest thing I ever saw," Goose marveled and uttered. "That son of a bitchin' thing oughta' be dead as Mussolini. But it ain't!"

"It's supernatural and *immortal,"* I maintained as we cruised North Third Street heading toward Bellevue.

"What do ya' mean it's *immoral.* Of course, the freakin' thing was *immoral*", Restuccio insisted. "If it goes-around in the damned woods killin' people and eatin' high school kids for supper, then it certainly is *immoral."*

I applied the brakes and coasted the blue truck into a parking space in front of Godfrey's Drug Store at the corner of Bellevue and Egg Harbor Road. Goose hopped out wearing his enviable red James Dean' jacket. The wise-ass with the distorted mouth exchanged a few jocular comments with Balls Giordano and Herc Juliano, both of whom were idly stationed in front of the drug store, protecting the west-side of the main drag from area Blues and from Vineland High "town-crashers". After buying his *Camels* from a late-night convenience store, my volatile companion re-entered the truck, and then I crossed the railroad tracks, and cruised one full circuit of the almost-abandoned downtown area. We both lit-up smokes to make our still-frazzled emotions' nerves simmer down a bit.

"It's only Thursday night," Goose declared. "Wait 'til tomorrow and ya' won't be able to find a friggin' parkin' space anywhere on Bellevue. This is a great tradition, J.W., believe it or not."

"What is?" I asked. "Parkin' a car on Bellevue?"

"This cruisin' town Friday night thing," my ornery passenger replied. "Your lucky kids and grandkids will be doin' the exact same damned thing fifty ugly years from now."

On the way going west on *Route 30* across the Hammonton-Winslow Township line, we were approaching the infamous white horse mounted to the left of Elm's White Horse Farm Market. As we passed by, the display lights anchored in the ground faithfully illuminated the landmark' horse. Four blue-clad figures that had been seated atop the electrified stallion suddenly went flying off the horse statue in opposite directions.

"Ha, ha, ha, ha!" Goose laughed until my amused companion almost went *hoarse*. "That was Gabe Gillette and three other Blues getting the royal-ass shock treatment from old man Berenato. The gimpy peach farmer probably thinks the trespassin' jerks were tryin' to impress Joanne with their general stupidity."

I couldn't fathom a particular point, so I asked my traveling mate for detailed enlightenment. "The Blues were in the peach orchard the night we almost got electrocuted on that horse doin' the exact same thing," I recalled and shared. "How come they're so dumb tryin' exactly what we did on that juiced horse?"

"Because, the annoying pricks were in the damned peach field, and only heard old man Berenato shootin' off his good-for-nothin' shotgun. The dunces never saw the horse's lights go on, and the Reds flyin' off, as if we was sittin' in prison electric chairs without straps holdin' us down," G.R. generalized and chortled. "So, the Blues probably tried paintin' the horse's balls and dick polka dot blue; hopped on for a little joyride, and then got the freakin' shock of their lives, just like our buds did. Ha, ha, ha, ha!"

I had seen something in the fleeting moment when we had zipped by when the horse's floodlights had gone on, and I relayed my observation to Restuccio. "Did ya' see a kid fall off on the Atlantic City side of the horse?" I asked.

"No, I missed that shit happenin'," G.R. related and coughed while still splitting a gut. "I only got 20-40 vision in one eye, and my other one is 20-80. I think I should go consult a *podiatrist.*"

I told G.R. that the academic dunce had meant to say 'optometrist', but then, my bellicose rider insisted that he had originally enunciated *that* word and not *podiatrist."*

"Well, I think the kid that plunged off the horse fallin' to the east was Pee Wee Lucca," I stressed. "And the dolt had what looked like two white casts from his wrists up to his elbows on both arms. He musta' been the one who…."

"Who was ridin' shotgun in Gabe Gillette's Corvette convertible with the top down playin' mailbox-baseball on Spring Road. He musta' gone for a home run," Goose giggled, "and….."

"And unfortunately swatted a mailbox full of solid concrete," I finished, laughing so hard that tears began forming in my eyes. "What a circus that fiasco must have been!"

The two of us laughed ourselves piss-silly down Winslow Road all the way to Williamstown, where I turned onto *Route 322,* which I took until I reached the Freeway, *Route 42,* heading toward *the Walt Whitman Bridge*. Then, entering South 'Philly, I was more than slightly insulted by a remark Goose unintentionally made.

"J.W., when you was a young kid, ya' used to live in that little white house next to Square Deal Market, didn't ya'?"

His blunt statement deeply offended me. I felt that it was another attempt by G.R. to disparage my middle-class dignity. I didn't relish the way in which the term *'little house'* had been used."

I wanted to conceal the actual truth from his keen awareness. "No Goose," I prudently answered. "I spent most of my younger years in the red brick house behind my grandparent's farm market." At that moment, I was also hiding another pertinent fact from Goose's sarcastic curiosity. Tyrone Davis had asked me for an additional hundred-fifty-dollars of "seed money" so that the Marvelons could cut a vital demo' record. But after what had transpired with the rich-kid Blues at Jives's Boatneck rock and roll party, I wasn't so sure that I wanted to again become involved in any remote way with the dangerous travails associated with the unstable music recording industry.

I stopped, paid the fifty-cent bridge toll, and then Goose told me that a ferry used to transport cars, busses and trucks across the Delaware prior to the erection of the impressive, seven-lane span.

I then felt compelled to tell Goose of several Delaware River adventures I had experienced when I had lived in Levittown. First, Carnie and I had been blamed for pushing Angie Palermo and Bubbles Messina over the bulkhead in Bristol while the iron ore ship *Caracas* sailed north on the Delaware, heading up to the Fairless Hills Steel Mill.

I next related how the *Caracas* had almost drowned Bo Jalonec and me in the main channel while we were trying to escape the clutches of the Kamikazes in an old decrepit, leaking rowboat. "The waves from the *Caracas's* wake filled the rowboat with river-water, so Bo and I had to dive into the Delaware and swim for our lives to a small island in the middle of the river."

"Those bastard Kamikazes sound a lot like those bastard Blues," Goose connected and noted, "and I'm sure glad I never had to deal with those K dickheads you're describin'. The Blues are enough for me to handle."

I saw merit in Restuccio's comparison of the Kamikazes and the Blues, except that the Kamikazes were redneck, middle-class white trash, and that the Blues were wealthy white-scum. I also understood that most of the Blues in Hammonton; the Kamikazes I used to know, and also Goose Restuccio shared one common attribute: they were all white supremacists who loathed racial integration.

The blue truck pulled into the Food Distribution Center off Packer Street in south 'Philly. My eyes easily found the Levins and Sampson Commission House, and then I backed-up to the loading dock at eleven-fifty. The seventy-five melons wouldn't be ready for transfer onto the empty truck until midnight, so Goose offered to buy me some early/early morning breakfast at the food center's restaurant, located three doors down from the L and S Commission House. Naturally, me and my voracious appetite surrendered to his generous proposal.

"What the hell is News Tomasello talkin' about now besides the cleanin' the shit-stains in his underwear after bein' terrorized by the Jersey Devil?" Goose wanted to know. "He'll have to cut another asshole just to be able to shit right."

"Well, I heard him talkin' about how the black restaurant counter sit-ins in the South have been endorsed by the National Council of Southern Presbyterian Churches," I reported as if I was Douglas Edwards on national TV. "News thinks there's goin' to be a big social revolution if blacks don't soon get equal rights. The government's gonna' have to step in quickly and save the country."

"Everybody's tryin' to kiss jealous niggers' asses," Goose boisterously protested loud enough for most of the people seated in the crowded restaurant to hear. "J.W., I don't pay that much attention in history class, but I did hear Mrs. Murphy once say that the Negro got the right to vote just after the *Civil War,* and that women didn't get the right to vote until the 1920s. Niggers have been votin' a full fifty-years before white women have been votin'," Goose lectured his discrimination view. "Don't talk to me about this equal rights shit! It's phonier than a three-dollar-bill. If the blacks can't improve themselves in a hundred-years, why does it have to be *our* damned concern?"

"But I knew a black kid named Marcus Spellman who moved into Levittown, and he had…."

"I know, the rug-head had trouble because he's a nigger," Goose finished my thought in not the exact nomenclature I wished to utilize. "Tell me, J.W. How many white kids want to move into nigger neighborhoods?" Restuccio barked and ranted. 'It's only the spear-chuckers and the ghetto-slum lowlife that wants ta' live next to *you.* And did this Marcus kid's family pay for their house, or did some lily-white church group, or state do-gooder organization, put up the down payment?" Restuccio loudly argued. "This black equality bullshit is nothin' more than communist propaganda. Its aim is to destroy this country's way of life and our traditions! It's gonna' try and ruin good old white American free enterprise, and change our system to black-ass communism."

I was appalled and puzzled by Goose's persuasive-but-convoluted logic. I was about to challenge his declarations when my bigoted friend received a round of applause from the prejudiced Caucasian clientele dining at the food distribution restaurant, the robust cheers coming in response to my bigoted companion's grossly-opinionated, impromptu speech.

I glanced outside the restaurant's front window and witnessed industrious black laborers sweating like crazy, tugging heavy dollies and carts laden with heavy boxes of southern peaches, tomatoes, and fifty-pound sacks of onions and potatoes. I was going to point those particular circumstances out to Goose, but then the waitress brought our orders of ham and eggs. I thought how futile it would be to debate civil rights with such a closed-minded and cynical "know-it-all" as Goose Restuccio was, inside a busy restaurant.

During "midnight breakfast", to change the controversial subject to something more moderate, I informed my traveling partner about News Tomasello telling me that a Polaris missile had been fired from a submarine off the coast of San Clemente Island in California. Goose answered that the communists were out to take over the world, and that part of their wicked scheme was having black people revolt against white authority. "We need those goddamned missiles to fight the goddamned Russians J.W.," G.R. insisted. "And those sons of bitches plan for us to destroy ourselves from within by makin' our government spend all its money on niggers, weapons, and rockets, while fearin' a Soviet nuclear war as a cover."

Thank goodness it was time to leave the noisy restaurant, or my skull might have ruptured from too much emotional distress. Goose paid our bill and left a generous five-dollar tip on the table. We exited the eating establishment and paced-over to three piles of huge watermelons, each stack pyramided on a wooden skid. Mr. Levins walked-over and then tallied-up the bill for seventy-five melons at a dollar-and-a-half apiece, and tersely announced, "That'll be a total of one-hundred-and-twelve-dollars-and-fifty-cents. Your Dad already agreed on the wholesale price over the phone."

"Here," Goose offered after whipping out a wad of hundred-dollar bills. "Here's a hundred-and-twenty-buckeroos. Give the change to a couple of black laborers ya' have layin' around to load the damned melons on the truck."

Mr. Levins tore off my yellow receipt copy of the pink bill of sale, thanked Goose for his prompt payment, and told two black company employees to lug and stack the seventy-five Congos onto "the blue-staked truck". "You've already been tipped," Mr. Levins informed the muscular black men, so just load 'em up. We'll settle things up later on. Thanks fellas'!" the congenial commission house owner hollered to Goose and me as he waved goodbye.

I smiled when I thought about how Grandpa Tony would have instantly said, "A hundred-twelve-dollars-and fifty-cents" before Mr. Levins would even had located his pen hooked onto his shirt pocket. The blue truck was loaded in less than fifteen-minutes. I raised and then locked the tailgate; hopped inside the cab; made sure that my vociferous passenger was safely inside, and then slowly drove away from the concrete loading dock.

Soon, we reached the Walt Whitman Bridge toll plaza, where I found the exact change deep inside my jeans' pocket to pay for our passage back to New Jersey. As the truck approached the crown of the magnificent, recently-constructed bridge, my eyes glanced-down into the river and saw a familiar, huge, lit-up object making its transit south, going in the direction of Delaware Bay. "Look, Goose! There's the *Caracas* I was tellin' you about," I exclaimed to my fairly interested rider. "I'll bet it's heading back to Venezuela after deliverin' iron ore to the Fairless Hills Steel Mill."

"Is that the goddamned ship that nearly killed you and your pal Bo back in Pennsylvania?" my petulant and irascible friend inquired.

"Yeah," I verified, "but it was only an accident."

"Stop the damned truck!" Goose yelled like a hysterical, crazy, asylum patient. "Stop the fuckin' truck!"

I nervously did as commanded because I wanted to live to see and value the next sunrise. Restuccio's insane behavior was so unpredictable and so volatile that at that moment, I virtually feared for my life. The erratic nutcase was more mercurial than mercury. 'Thank goodness there's little traffic heading east towards Jersey,' I remember thinking.

The wacky, deranged Edgewood High senior leaped-out of the passenger side and methodically lifted a plump melon off of the pile stacked above the raised tailgate. Next, G.R. walked to the side of a bridge suspension cable and quickly chucked the large watermelon onto the front deck of the passing *Caracas,* which was gliding under the *Walt Whitman*. Being unsatisfied with his first exploit, the bizarre delinquent repeated the enaction by dropping a second Congo onto the massive ship's deck. "That's for nearly drownin' my good pal J.W.!" the fiendish rogue boomed-down at the titanic tanker. "If ya' fuck with J.W. again, you'll have to answer to me!" Then, the daft psychopath re-entered the Pete's Market Special via the passenger-side door, and pretended that nothing extraordinary had ever transpired.

"You might've killed two or more sailors with those heavy melons, and not even know it!" I vigorously objected.

"Naw! I aimed pretty good and missed everybody by at least five feet," Goose, who had inferior vision, falsely testified. "But I did scare the shit out of everybody lazily standin' around on the deck with their brown thumbs up their asses!"

"Are ya' sure?" I insisted. "Are ya' sure you didn't hit, injure, or kill anybody? I don't want to be seen being arrested tomorrow on Action News!"

"Yeah, as sure as there's now only seventy-three melons on the back on this damned truck," G.R. laughed.

"What am I gonna' tell Pop about the two missin' melons?" I gasped. "I can't even afford to pay for them?"

"Here's ten bucks," my passenger said, waving an *Alexander Hamilton* before my florid face, momentarily blocking my sight of the bridge lane. "Give this ten-spot to your old man, and tell him that some hungry fruit' lovin' jerks stopped us on the highway and bought two luscious melons for ten bucks. Your old man will be happier than a pig rollin' in shit!"

I then formulated a dumb pun, which Goose did not at all appreciate. "It's a good thing that Lassie wasn't ridin' aboard the front deck of the *Caracas!"* I joyfully proclaimed.

"Why the hell's that?" my sarcastic comrade inquired.

"Because then Lassie would be very melon-collie!"

"Where the fuck did you learn all this stupid shit that ya' always say?" Goose indignantly yelled. "No wonder why Mr. Andrews wants to flunk your ass into summer school! If I was him, I'd do the same damned thing to your ass as that math' teacher-Hitler is doin' to you!"

I decided to take the recently completed *I-295* cut-off-ramp to *Route 30.* I wanted to stop at a new hamburger franchise that featured dual huge golden arches on the roof above its front counter. The recently-built restaurant was called *McDonald's.*

"What the hell is this?" G.R. asked as I very meticulously eased my truckload of precious fruit into the "Open All Night" hamburger joint's asphalt driveway.

"It's a new type of restaurant that's very popular out in California," I firmly attested. "I've read about *McDonald's* in the *Philadelphia Inquirer* magazine. It's supposed to be a giant step forward in the new fast-food fad. This one we're now at must be an East Coast experimental or test restaurant to gauge the area market."

"A cheap joint like this will never replace the Gem or Augie's Burger Paradise," Goose adamantly maintained. "What kind of mystery meat could be inside a lousy fifteen-cent hamburger? Sounds like the cook's name must be Sal Minella!"

"Then Goose, you don't think that someday there'll be thousands of *McDonald's* all across the country?" I challenged and asked.

"J.W.," G.R. said. "I can't think of a worse fuckin' investment. I say that you must still believe in Santa Claus, in the Easter Bunny, and in the homosexual Tooth Fairy. There's a better chance of Mr. Andrews having his monthly period tomorrow and then passin' you in trig' class than for this piece-of-crap hamburger joint to ever become famous all across America."

"Hey, Goose," I said while reaching deep in my dungaree pocket. "Here's the hundred-and twelve dollars Pop gave me to pay for the load of watermelons."

"Keep it," G.R. surprisingly muttered as if the amount was a mere penny. "But don't spend it on those *paris-site* nigger Marvelons. And also," the future Mafia don concluded. "Don't ever forget, J.W. Ya' also owe me for the shotgun ya' stupidly lost back at the Blues' huntin' cabin."

"I didn't lose it," I argued. "I dropped it on the ground."

"Okay then, let's go back and get it right now!" my crass buddy snapped. "And also, give me back the hundred-and-twelve bucks!"

"No, I'd rather not drive back to the Blues hunting cabin, especially with all these watermelons on the back of the truck," I retorted. "We might have to sacrifice the watermelons to the Jersey Devil, if the on-a-warpath Blues don't destroy them first."

"Well then," Goose insisted with a wink of his distorted left eye. "Ya' still owe me for the fuckin' shotgun ya' lost at the Blues remote forest cabin."

Chapter Eighteen
"Blueberry Hill"

I was disillusioned. I thought that I understood people. I trusted them, liked them, and helped them whenever I could. Goose Restuccio had predicted that Dad would be thrilled to receive ten-dollars for two watermelons that G.R. had chucked onto the deck of the *Caracas.* The whole incident had been deceptively packaged as a lie to Pop, and the perverted "money kid" was absolutely accurate in his prognostication.

"You must be a descendant of Nostradamus," I told Goose in the upstairs M corridor at Edgewood, right before homeroom.

"Naaa, I don't like dumb Catholic colleges," the academic dunce truthfully answered. "My grandfather never got out of eighth-grade at St. Joe's over in Hammonton, so *he* never had a chance to flunk out of Nostradamus."

I left Goose's inelegant company at his locker and entered the upstairs M-Wing Boys Lavatory, which had become a rendezvous-money exchange venue for Tyrone Davis and me.

"Hi J.W., ya' got the bread?" the black kid asked. "I knows you'll come through with the green paper."

I felt like I was being both used and extorted by Davis, who propagated the notion that I had been wisely investing in a black harmony Doo-Wop group having great potential. "Yeah," I said, wishing I was somewhere else. "I had a hundred-and-ten, but had to scrounge-up the other forty-bucks from cookie jars, desk drawers, and pinball machine slots over at DiDonato's Lanes," I replied, as I forked over the required stipend.

"Geez, J.W.," Tyrone continued his oration, "you'll be rich and famous someday, just like the Marvelons will be. Someday, we'll celebrate this here historic lavatory meeting, yes sireee," the black kid resumed his propaganda. "And as folks always say, 'Getting to the top is really more fun than actually bein' there'."

"I'd rather be there," I frankly returned. "And quite honestly, I'm becomin' a little tired of just getting there."

"J.W., the Marvelons really like havin' ya' as our manager, the other cats really do, but if ya' wanta' do a little promotin' on your own time," Tyrone speculated and recommended, "I'm sure that our gig guy and the Dew Drop Inn won't mind the little help you'll be givin' the group."

"Okay, I'll remember that," I consented, a little too lethargically. "There's a popular Canteen Dance every month over in Hammonton. Maybe I can arrange somethin', and have the group perform a small concert there."

“That’ll be cool, J.W., real cool,” the lead singer of the Marvelons excitedly stated. “See ya’ around, and if ya’ need any more cash to finance the group, see that Goose Restuccio Mafia goon. He’s got deep pockets and lots of dough stashed inside ‘em.”

“Sure,” I answered, as Tyrone briskly stepped out of the lavatory. “As sure as cold, frost, and snow in winter.”

At lunch, Goose informed the regular table guys that *he* was going to treat us all to supper at the Gem. I was keen on the idea, but Juice was still scared about the Jersey Devil apparition, and about us ransacking the Blues’ cabin, and so was Jives and Fabian. The only other kid at the cafeteria table who showed even a mild interest in Goose’s suggestion was News Tomasello.

“Okay, crotch-breaths,” Restuccio belittled his chief apostles. “I already talked with Hoss and Little Joe Gregorio about the Gem supper tonight, and the brothers told me they’re both goin’. I need some bodyguards around for protection in case the Blues get rowdy, and I’m willing to treat the gladiators with free meals. And Jives, I think…”

“I’m not coppin’ out, I promise I’m not,” Frankie testified. “I gotta’ do some long scribblin’ under the full moon, or Mrs. Murphy will punt me in the A double scribble all the way to Dudsylvania.”

“Jives means,” Juice interpreted for the rest of the Reds seated at the table, “he needs to stay up late tonight to do a report for his American History II teacher, or she’ll kick him hard in his rear end.”

“Okay, you pathetic Munchkins. Hoss is gonna’ pick me up at four-thirty,” Goose reviewed. “J.W. and News, be ready before five for your scheduled appointments at the Gem.”

At exactly five o’clock, Hoss Gregorio’s green and white ‘59 Edsel sedan stopped in front of Pete’s Market, which was ready to have flowers and produce ready for sale the next day. I opened the back door and sat next to Little Joe and News. I noticed that Goose, Hoss, Little Joe, and News were wearing their red James Dean jackets, but since I wasn’t an authentic Reds’ member yet, I had to wear normal teen civilian clothing.

“Gonna’ open the market soon?” Little Joe asked. “Your folks must be excited.”

“Tomorrow,” I honestly replied. “And Pop’s already gotten-in a lot of petunias, pansies, phlox, scarlet sage, and geraniums, but more garden and lawn flowers are bein’ delivered later tonight. Also, there’s southern asparagus, strawberries, and tomatoes comin’ in at the Philly’ Food Distribution Center, and Grandpa Tony is gonna’ get us some to sell for tomorrow mornin’.”

“What’s happenin’ in the world?” I asked News as Hoss steered his Edsel east onto the White Horse Pike.

"Oh, not too much," T.T. remarked before reflexively yawning. "The musical *Bye, Bye Birdie* is openin' at the Martin Beck Theater in New York. The show stars Dick Van Dyke, Kay Medford, and Chita Rivera."

"I wish that some hot dame's legs were openin' at that theater," Goose laughed, "and then I might want to see the grand-opening of her hairy, pink snatcheroo."

News ignored Goose's derision and lewdness. "*Bye, Bye Birdie* is really a play about Elvis goin' into the Army and havin' his female fans go haywire during his absence from rock and roll."

"*Bye, Bye Birdie* sounds like a poor guy who had his dick cut off!" G.R. reacted in his typical vulgar, bawdy manner. "Yeah, the title sounds like the guy held his pecker too tight while jerkin'-off, and now the dumb-shit needs to find some *Elmer's Glue* in a hurry."

The three others in the Edsel robustly laughed in response to Restuccio's obscene sense of humor. News and I remained reticent.

Hoss Gregorio turned-up the radio's volume to WIBG playing the Platters' melodic rendition of "The Great Pretender", and I sat there wondering if the *great pretenders* really were the extroverts Goose, Hoss, and Little Joe on the one hand, or the introspective News and me on the other. When Hoss stopped at Al's Save-Way gas station to procure ten-gallons of thirty-cent high test, Hoss related a novel story about Ollie "Balls" Giordano as first told by Herc Juliano.

"If ya' clowns think that Goose and me are friggin' crazy," the driver proudly said, "ya' oughta' know about that damned mental case Balls Giordano. He ain't no relative of Little Joe and me, even though our last names both have four syllables. But a lot of the Blues think he's our insane cousin, but we don't mind that at all."

"Well, what about him?" I queried.

Hoss disclosed that Balls Giordano had gone rabbit hunting one day and encountered some bad luck. The dude decided to lay face down between two, tall pine trees, and pretended being dead. Two stubborn turkey vultures thought that Balls was human carrion, and then the famished dumb-ass birds landed to start pecking-away at his exposed pecker. Balls surprised the suddenly-startled buzzards by quickly reaching-out with both hands, and grabbing their legs as the Jersey condors began wildly pecking-away at the brawny kid's hands, wrists and shoulders.

"Why that's truly amazin'!" News exclaimed. "What cunning! What dynamic courage!"

"And then," Hoss continued his preposterous hyperbole, "Balls stood-up and started slammin' the turkey buzzards' heads against the nearby two big pine trees. The huge birds were scared shitless and squawked like hell, but Giordano kept at it until their brains oozed out of their friggin' heads. Soon, the stud had killed 'em both with his bare hands."

"Wow!" I admitted. "Two birds in the hands are worth a dozen in the sky." Only News Tomasello chuckled at my pun because Tommy was the only kid in the Edsel who knew where I was coming from. and what I had been alluding to.

"What happened next?" Goose demanded learning from Hoss. "Did Balls leave the nasty buzzards in the field?"

"Well," Hoss proceeded, "after Balls killed the fierce birds by bashin' their damned brains out, the St. Joe mauler took them home and skinned their feathers off, put 'em in an extra-large pan, broiled 'em in the oven, and ate them both for supper. He munched on the two vultures that was tryin' to eat him. What a barbarian!"

"It sounds like those two buzzards were real birdbrains," I added, while impersonating Bo Jalonec. "And Balls Giordano must've been so hungry that he ate his *fowl* dinner like a vulture."

The other four guys comprehended my *punny* language and all hardily chuckled. The gas station attendant had just screwed the cap back on, flipped the hatch closed, and then stepped to the driver's window to collect the three-dollars owed. A minute later, the five adventurers were riding down Bellevue on our way to Central, and soon Hoss was parking the classy Edsel in front of Joe's Barber Shop two doors down from the Gem.

"J. W., Goose tried insulting me. "Why are you so screwed-up in the head, constantly saying all of your dumb-ass bullshit?"

"Are you trying to castigate me?" I retorted.

"Why the fuck would I want to cut your balls off!" the Sicilian savage seriously reprimanded. "I don't collect tiny marbles!"

Bill Doggett's "Honky Tonk, Part II" was being emitted from the Gem's Wurlitzer jukebox, and the lively instrumental tune immediately made me think of Quinn and the music my former Diablo leader loved back in Levittown.

The five of us landed a booth near the juke, and not far from the main counter where Goose had "made reservations", even though none' of us were Indians. Rose Rita Errera, a spry, cute waitress with an affable personality came-over to take our orders. Hoss and Little Joe wanted veal parmigiana sandwiches; News ordered a meatball special deluxe on an Italian roll; Goose preferred a tuna fish seafood mix, and I ordered a Sicilian hoagie without any salami or baloney.

"Why no salami and baloney?" Rose Rita innocently asked.

“Because they might make my *liver worst!”* I laughed. Instantly, I was bombarded by a barrage of rolled-up paper napkins, since the offended guys had heard me use that simpleton joke once before.

“Are ya’ always this *goofy?”* Rose Rita asked.

“Only when I star on the Mickey Mouse Show with Daisy and Donald,” I quipped. Again, I was deluged with an array of rolled-up paper napkins obtained from the Gem’s table dispensers.

“What are you?” Rose Rita challenged, “a Loony Toon or a Merry Melody?” the doll quipped.

“Definitely a Loony Toon,” I calmly answered, “because I’m definitely more-crazy than I am queer.”

“Hey, Rose Rita,” Hoss interrupted. “We’re outa’ paper napkins to throw at this mongrel idiot!”

“Use the ones on the floor over again,” the bright waitress coyly suggested. “They’re reusable, ya’ know! Have yourselves a blast.”

Everything seemed as if it was back to normal. “Little Bitty Pretty One” by Thurston Harris was pulsating out of the rainbow-colored Wurlitzer. We all lit up *Camel* cigarettes to enjoy our marvelous camaraderie, and that was especially unusual, because Hoss, Little Joe, and News hardly ever smoked. Tranquility prevailed for a full ten-minutes, until six nasty Blues entered the neutral teen hangout. Gabe Gillette, Speed Mortellite, Ox Narducci, Hammer Bertino, Butch Lanza, and Pee Wee Lucca immediately noticed our presence, and sauntered over to aggravate us Reds in what we all had considered shared territory.

“Hey, what happened to your arms?” Goose questioned, pointing at the two casts adorning Pee Wee Lucca’s upper appendages from his wrists to his elbows. “Ya’ won’t be able to get a job at the post office until those stiff plasterboards are taken-off, so deliverin’ mail is off limits for a while.”

“Very funny!” Pee Wee uttered. “Ya’ oughta’ go on *Ed Sullivan* as a soda jerk,” the diminutive punk added, pointing to G.R.’s half-empty *Pepsi* cup. “Maybe even as a soda jerk-off!”

“Quit the mouth crap Pee Wee!” Gabe Gillette reprimanded his subordinate. “Goose, I have two shotguns down at the farm that I think might just belong to you. You’re welcome to come and get ‘em if ya’ want. They’re both still in good condition.”

“Naaa, I prefer machine guns to toy huntin’ rifles,” Restuccio smartly volleyed. “Shotguns are for faggot deer hunters. News Tomasello here has given me three Tommy guns, ha, ha, ha!”

“You’d rather shoot-off your foul mouth than shoot-off a shotgun!” Ox Narducci ridiculed. “Ya’ need your ugly nose tied around your face!”

Mr. Arturo Sorrentino had heard the commotion in the main dining-snack area, and the Gem proprietor rushed-out from the kitchen to investigate its source. We all sensed his adult incursion into our tense summit conference, so the emotional tempo shifted from hostility to civil discussion.

"Blueberry crop looks mighty good this year," Speed Mortellite indicated with a contrived smile. "Our first variety is Weymouth followed by Collins. Can't wait to get to those Blue Crops. We'll start harvestin' around mid-June. What about peaches?"

Hoss and News explained that the first peaches would be picked the last week in June, but that the money varieties like Loring, Blakes, and Rio-Oso-Gems would not be plucked-off of the fruit trees until mid-August. "The first three weeks of peaches are clingstones," News artfully elaborated, "and my family only has four orchards of 'em. After mid-July, production gets shifted into second gear when freestones start come in with the Red Havens."

Mr. Sorrentino was perceptive enough to realize the artificiality of the stilted conversation, so the owner cautioned that we should use moderation instead of feigned harmony. "Look fellas', I've already had my front window busted-up twice in the last couple of months," the irritated old man reviewed. "And I don't wanta' see it broken again today. If there's gonna' be any kind of trouble, then please take it outside. Otherwise, I'm gonna' call the cops."

"Oh no, what are we goin' to do?" Mortellite gasped while bending forward and cowering-down to fake-feeling excessive fright. "Please Mr. Sorrentino, anything but the po-po's!"

"Plunk your magic twanger Froggy!" News zanily exhorted from a kid's TV show to alleviate the pressure we all felt.

"I'll be good, I'll be good! I promise I'll be good!" yelled-out Little Joe as he wildly bounced and oscillated his body back and forth, imitating the impish Froggy the Gremlin on the popular *Andy's Gang Show*.

"I'm warnin' all of ya'," Sorrentino emphasized with bloodshot eyes, "any trouble is gonna' be done outside!" The disturbed owner wiped the grime from his hands onto the front of his white apron, and hastily stepped over to the counter. Thirty teen customers watched the flustered Gem owner lift a phone from its cradle and begin dialing the police station.

"Okay, then," Gable Gillette spoke. "You peach guys know where my farm on Weymouth Road is. Be there in twenty-minutes. We're gonna' have a contest to see which is the tougher gang, the Blues or the Reds. Are ya' afraid of losin'?"

"What kind of contest?" Hoss sneered as the human behemoth eyeballed his chief enemy, Ox Narducci. "The Reds ain't afraid of nothin'!"

"All I can tell ya' is that it's gonna' be fair and square, five against five," Gillette informed. "Are you peach guys chicken, or what? The Blues have challenged the Reds to a fair competition, and the fairy Reds wanta' know the rules before they go-out onto the playin' field. Are you' raunchy beef-jerkers pussies or what?"

"Okay Gabe," Goose returned and sneered. "We'll accept your dumb-ass challenge. We'll be at your farm in twenty-minutes. We're not gonna' back down to rank punks like you!"

The Blues all gave us the royal middle finger and then stormed-out of the Gem. The alluded-to mystery contest was the Reds next subject of conversation.

"I wonder what kind of event those knuckle-draggers have in mind?" Little Joe asked. "I could eat at least four-dozen blueberry muffins if I really had to. Hoss could probably eat eight-dozen."

"Guessin' ain't gonna' solve nothin'," G.R. very pragmatically hypothesized and stated. "We gotta' be shit-ready for anything and everything. That's how we gotta' think."

"Whata' ya' think, News?" Hoss asked the most academic kid sitting at our booth. "You know shit before its even digested!"

"I think I shoulda' stayed home!" T.T. wisely responded. "I sense big trouble on the horizon. That's what I think!"

Rose Rita brought over our food specialties, which we ravenously ate in ten-short minutes. There was little talking and no levity at the table. The Reds were all immersed in deepest concentration, thinking about what sort of mystery competition we were about to participate in, against the untrustworthy Blues.

Hoss drove us in his Edsel east on Egg Harbor Road until we came to the blinker light on the east part of town. The next thing we knew, the driver turned right and we were traveling past Morano Bag Company, and then over the railroad track bridge on Weymouth Road to Gabe Gillette's dad's thousand-acre blueberry plantation. Suspense was mounting, and anxiety was peaking. Not a word was uttered until the Edsel entered the main entrance to the enormous farm property.

Ox Narducci was seated on a colossal *John Deere* tractor and motioned with his left hand to follow him to a more remote part of the immense agricultural plantation. Our Edsel passed by at least thirty blueberry fields, and the same number of irrigation ditches and canals. 'Soon, the bushes will be budding and in another six weeks, and luscious blueberries will be growing,' I observed and thought.

I began telling the guys about the big 1959 *Labor Day* blueberry farm drag race between Quinn and Cummings, but Goose told me to "Shut it and zip it!"

The sandy farm road led to a canal with a thick wooden plank that served as a crossing bridge over it. Around a dozen Hammonton High Blues were standing next to the full irrigation canal. The five of us got out of the Edsel to learn more about the specific rules of "the anticipated contest".

"Glad you fellas' could make it," Gabe Gillette greeted with false pleasantry. "Welcome to blueberry country."

"Okay Gabe, quit the small talk crap!" Goose dramatically chastised in a perturbed tone of voice. "Let's get on with the action."

"Alright, if you insist!" Gillette snidely replied. "Get ready for an unforgettable tug of war, five against five."

Hoss and Little Joe smiled at each other, and then at News, at Goose, and at me. The stout brothers felt that our side would be superior in an evenly-matched five-against-five scenario that solely required pure strength.

"Are ya' retards ready for an unforgettable tug-of-war, five against five?" Speed Mortellite scornfully challenged. "Or are ya' five stooges queer yellow-bellied finks?"

"We're ready right now!" Hoss Gregorio confidently answered back. "What are the rules so we can get started?"

"That's great guys; that's just great!" Gabe Gillette repeated as the Blues commander opened a large wooden box and removed its frightening contents. "Don't worry, this here twenty-two-foot-long black water snake is already dead. Ox strangled the poor innocent serpent this morning with his bare hands." The twelve Blues let-out a loud cheer for their most gallant warrior Ox Narducci, as the five alarmed Reds stood there with our mouths agape.

While my friends and I stood by the muddy canal bank, stunned by the enormous size of the slimy, deceased reptile, Gabe Gillette calmly reviewed the rules of engagement. I listened attentively to his comprehensive instructions, while both of my eyes focused on the black, scaly, heavy creature that Narducci was casually holding in his lethal hands.

Gillette conveyed that the tug-of-war would feature five against five, with the snake being used "as the rope". Five Blues would be positioned on one side of the canal bank, and five Reds on the other. At the count of "three", both teams would tug the snake with all the power each squad could muster, and the first greaser gang to plummet into the canal would be designated the losers.

"Okay, Reds, which end of the snake do ya' wanta' pull?" Mortellite requested. "Don't be scared!"

"Er, the tail!" Goose answered while gaping at the hideous-looking scaly head and opened jaws.

"That shows us how stupid ya' peach knuckleheads really are!" Ox Narducci hollered. "Ya' can get a better grip of the skull than ya' can of the damned tail. There're more bones to hold on to in the snake's head! Ha, Ha, ha!" The dozen Blues all loudly laughed in unison as if the cretins were the audience, and then some TV network employee had held-up an idiot card in a TV studio reading the word: "Laugh"!

The Blues had achieved a great psychological advantage, and News, Goose, Hoss, Little Joe, and I were all feeling a little down in the dumps at G.R. being outsmarted. Gabe Gillette was ready with one final instruction.

"Since you Bozos chose which end ya' wanta' pull," Gillette said, "then it's our choice of which side of the canal to stand on. We choose this side. That means you five yo-yo's gotta' cross the plank and get on the other side of the water."

The five of us honored the rule that had been prescribed by Gabe Gillette and 'walked the plank' to the other bank of the five-foot-deep, six-foot-wide irrigation ditch. Ox Narducci threw over the tail of the long black snake to Little Joe, who neurotically inspected the slimy dead animal with a shocked face. News was second in line, followed by Goose, Hoss, and me as the anchor. The Blues' team consisted of Speed Mortellite at snake's head, followed by Dan "the Hammer" Bertino, Butch Lanza, Al "Sonny" Perone, and finally Ox Narducci.

Gillette slowly and clearly counted to "Three", and then the intense pulling struggle commenced. The grueling contest ebbed and flowed back and forth, and remarkably, the Reds were giving their advantaged rivals a very serious run for their money. I was finally adjusting to the horrifying feel of the snake's smooth, wet, scaly skin. Hoss, Goose, and Little Joe were grunting like wild boars during mating season. And then, something extremely sneaky was enacted by our obnoxious, unscrupulous foes.

Gabe Gillette rapidly jumped onto the flexible wooden plank, and began splashing brackish, putrid-smelling swamp water into the Reds' faces. Then, the wily rich punk got-out a peppershaker from his pants' pocket, twisted-off the cap, and flung the black particles into our faces, causing five immediate allergic reactions.

First, Goose sneezed on News, and then News released nostril debris onto Little Joe. After Hoss Gregorio let out a tumultuous nasal discharge, we all lost our composure and then also our balance. The next thing we knew, the five of us were tumbling into the stagnant canal. We all splashed and thrashed about in a frantic frenzy as if we were engaged in mortal combat with five deadly great white sharks.

"Ha, ha. Ha. Ha!" our diabolical tormentors laughed at their frustrated and defeated enemies. "Sorry, guys, but we ran-out of salt to go with the pepper!" Gabe Gillette condescendingly mocked. "Variety isn't the spice of life! Black pepper is! Ha, ha, ha, ha!"

The five drenched victims managed to ford the shallow canal and then wade onto the muddy, sloped bank. The Reds were in for another nasty surprise administered by our ruthless adversaries. Five fishnets were twirled and then hurled over our heads, and before we were aware anything else, my companions and I were viciously tackled to the wet ground and quickly rolled-up into our separate nets. We frenetically grappled and rolled-around on the sandy ground to escape our difficult snares, but to no avail. We were individually picked-up inside our 'prison-nets'. and then roughly deposited near the center of one huge military climbing-net that was large enough for us to be wrapped-up like sardines, wickedly trapped inside one massive prisoners' ball.

"What the fuck's goin' on!" Goose Restuccio screamed-out, almost-crying like an upset infant who had dropped its pacifier from a high-chair onto the floor.

"You're gonna' all pay for this!" Hoss promised from inside the middle of the giant human snare.

"That is if ya' lame jerkenheimers live through this ordeal!" Gabe Gillette taunted.

Ox Narducci climbed-atop the enormous green and yellow *John Deere* tractor, which the blueberry farm's equipment operators used to plow and cultivate fallow fields. Heavy chains were removed from the tractor's huge toolbox, and then threaded through the net, which was next tethered by other chains attached to the tractor's sturdy mainframe.

Gabe Gillette gave Narducci the signal to get rolling, and soon the *John Deere* was dragging the five hostages balled-up inside the military climbing-net across the dusty field that bordered the aforementioned canal. The five of us incessantly coughed, all the while receiving multiple bruises and lacerations as our bodies deflected off each other and scraped against stones, rocks, field weeds, and hard ground.

I was afraid of being crushed and suffocated by the weight of Hoss and Little Joe, and because we were moving and scraping against the ground, the overall punishment was far worse than being on the bottom of a pile of corpulent football players.

"We're gonna' die! We're gonna' fuckin' die!" Goose was shouting in a delirious, hysterical manner.

"I'm never gonna' listen to your ass again in my life!" Hoss yelled backed at Restuccio. "You either got shit or worms for brains!"

The field scraping excruciation continued for another five-minutes, which seemed like an eternity to its persecuted victims. The tractor finally stopped its forward progress, and before any of us could get our breaths, we were cut-free from our entrapment by sharp, blueberry bush trimming shears. We lay exhausted and a bit mutilated upon the dusty ground. I had the wherewithal to raise my dirty face above my shoulders, while temporarily resting on all fours like a dog would stand. I was astonished by our designed torture's next phase.

Four diesel-powered, front-end loaders were started, and the hulking machines began pushing piles of brush toward us, and soon, the circumference of trimmed blueberry bush branches was closing in. A jagged wooded fence had been maliciously formed to surround the five fatigued captives. Four walls of pruned blueberry branches soon encompassed our existence. The brush piles had been trimmed from the area field blueberry bushes during the winter off-season.

"If ya' can crawl out of that dense brush," Gillette hollered into the pile from the perimeter of the twelve-foot-high heap, "then ya' dipshits deserve to live and fight another day."

I heard the Blues talking merrily as the assailants entered several nearby vehicles, and then left us to endure our agony and our misery. Moans and groans abounded inside the tiny nucleus of the immense brush pile. Trucks, tractors, and front-end loaders could be heard leaving the area.

I had the presence of mind to tell Hoss to allow me to get onto his shoulders, so that I might escape the brush trap. I was elevated up through a clear space and could see several clouds of dust in the distance, signifying that the Blues' trucks, tractors, and front-end loaders had vacated the area.

Three turkey vultures were circling the pale gray sky directly overhead, and I instinctively knew that none of us possessed the strength to choke them to death as Balls Giordano reportedly had done to other hungry condors on the northern fringe of the Wharton State Forest.

"Hurry up J.W.! Please hurry-up!" Goose whimpered from inside the center of the all-confining pile. "I'll even pay for the recordin' of the Marvelons first album if ya' let me live!"

"I thought ya' once said there was no heaven or no hell!" I yelled down to the avowed atheist.

"There ain't!" Restuccio promptly returned. "That's why I don't wanta' die! There's ain't nothin' afterwards except nothin'!"

I managed to pull myself above the sharp, abrasive branches, several of which had penetrated the sensitive skin above my wrists. I told News to mimic my valiant effort and to also ascend above the heap, and soon Hoss hoisted Tommy up, also. Little Joe was the third to clamber to the mound's apex.

The three of us gingerly crawled on top of the perilous heap, getting scratched-up and pierced as the turkey buzzards glided across the gray cloudy sky, several-hundred-feet above our heads. The biggest chore remained to be undertaken.

The three escapees pulled and ripped blueberry branches from the brush pile until we managed to eventually dig a narrow tunnel and excavate Hoss from the rather peculiar enclosure. After an hour of assiduous labor, Goose Restuccio, the last Reds survivor, was finally extricated.

"What'll we do now?" Little Joe panted with his tongue hanging out of his mouth like a dog's does after strenuous exercise in the height of summer.

"Palace Diner is about two-miles from here," Goose remembered and declared. The scared wise-guy paused a moment to examine a bleeding wound on his right elbow. "We'll walk there down Weymouth Road and use the phone to call for help."

The five Blues victims trudged-off, heading south, and followed the wide canal, which we knew would ultimately lead us to Weymouth Road. Our human caravan took a shortcut through a dense woods', and then stayed under the cover of tall pines as we wearily trekked south on the sparsely-traveled county road.

"When traffic comes into sight," News advised, "duck into the pine tree forest. There's no tellin' what the Blues will do if the Neo-Nazis find us gallivantin' around, partially wounded in their territory." And then, to add to our accumulative aggravation, Tommy began talking about the Toni Awards going to *The Miracle Worker* for the best play, and then the awards committee having judged a tie for the best musical between *Fiorello* and *The Sound of Music*. "Anne Bancroft won the Toni for best actress in *The Miracle Worker,"* News aptly reported.

"We could use that bitch Ann Bank-craft to perform a fuckin' miracle for us right now!" G.R. exclaimed.

I was so tired and overwhelmed that I was giddy, and I idiotically answered News's trivia presentation by saying, "Ya' can rig an Oscar; ya' can rig an Academy Award, but ya' can't *rig-a-Toni!"*

"Shut the fuck up!" Goose screamed like an incensed bedlamite. "You two maggot dickheads are gonna' still be clowning-around on your goddamned deathbeds!"

Headlights were spotted off in the distance as we looked north on Weymouth Road. We all staggered into a wooded patch of trees to obscure our presence from the scrutiny of enemy highway traffic. The vehicle was proceeding very slowly, and a flashlight was scanning the trees on our side of the road.

"What the hell's goin' on?" Goose neurotically asked. "Are they the Blues lookin' to punish us some more? Is that that dirty bastard Gillette lookin' for more grief to give us?"

The automobile gradually advanced toward our secluded location. The driver was manipulating the steering wheel very deliberately. We all held our breaths as the headlights came closer to our observable hiding positions.

"The Palace Diner is still over a mile away," Goose softly regretted. "I might not ever see another fuckin' gum ball machine, ever again."

"Hey, I know that car!" I hollered as I dashed-out from behind a clump of evergreen trees. "It's Jives's Dodge Coronet!" I boomed to the guys as I madly waved my arms above my head to attract the driver's attention. The '57 Dodge stopped ten-feet in front of my imaginative highway semaphores.

"Hey J.W., we've been lookin' all over for ya'!" Jives greeted. "Ya' look like you've been beaten-up in a hairy sit-com by Marlon Branflakes and Gregory Pecker. What's with all the blood and dirt?"

I looked inside the Coronet and saw Fabian Midilli's familiar smile. "Hey guys," Sal said, "who won the contest?"

"How do ya' know there was a contest?" Goose asked the handsome stud.

"Jives and I went to the Gem after you guys had left," Fabian informed. "And then Joanne Berenato was in there, and she had heard from Rose Rita Errera that you five Edgewood freaks had gone out to Gillette's blueberry farm to go up against the Blues. We knew the farm was on Weymouth Road, so we took a shot in the dark, and here we are!"

"I never thought I'd be so happy to see you two wick-dicks again!" Restuccio confessed to Jives and to Sal. "I'm gonna' start believin' in fuckin' Santa Claus again!"

"If it weren't for Joanne Berenato and Elaine Hill bein' in the Gem," Fabian realized and reported, "then we would've never been able to show-up and rescue ya' five raunchy musketeers."

"Ya' mean Joanne convinced you to come out here in the dark on Weymouth Road to look for us?" I exclaimed in an amazed tone of voice.

"Sure did," Fabian verified. "And I honestly think she really likes ya', J.W. I think she likes you enough to care about your safety."

“J.W.,” Goose cautiously advised. “Don’t piss yourself until ya’ get safely home. Just remember, love sucks!”

Chapter Nineteen

"Goose's Gambol"

Goose Restuccio was rightfully enraged by his recent tribulations experienced at Gabe Gillette's immense blueberry plantation. The irate Sicilian rogue couldn't fathom how the Blues didn't care one iota about his Mafia or his Reds' affiliations. "I even got my James Dean jacket messed-up because of the ugly shit I suffered," the junior don bitterly complained before Frankie Arena dropped him off at his palatial home. "Good thing I bought three of 'em for myself! Ya' never know when ya' need a shitin' spare to survive the next horse-shitin' ordeal."

The next Tuesday in early May, Jives drove me home from school. In the front seat between us was Crystal Davis, a black neighbor of Frankie's over in Winslow Village. Crystal was a junior at Edgewood, and also the sister of Tyrone Davis, the starry-eyed lead singer and chief money-extortioner of the Marvelons.

"J.W., was that a colored girl in the car with Frankie and you?" Dad asked. "Who was she?"

"Yeah, her name is Crystal Davis. She lives three doors down from Frankie over in Winslow," I informed. "Jive's is just doin' a favor takin' her home from school, that's all. Crystal says she's gotta' get home early to baby sit her younger brothers, while her mom goes grocery shoppin' in Berlin."

"Oh," Pop said. "Be sure that that's all there is to it! Crazy things happen in this strange world, and I don't wanta' see ya' anchored-down with hardship and social problems that'll haunt ya' the rest of your life. Learn to enjoy your teenage innocence."

I dismissed myself to my room, trying to best decipher the code language Pop was attempting to communicate. Then, I called Goose on the phone to see how the mental wreck was doing.

"Hi, Goose," I began my inquiry. "How's your elbow healin'? Did it fall off yet?"

"It ain't gettin' any better! And I wanta' get you, Jives, Juice, and Fabian drafted into the Reds as soon as possible. I gotta' get even with Gillette and his punk amigos."

I couldn't believe that Restuccio had spoken two entire sentences without shouting one vile cuss word. 'He must be serious about this,' I reckoned. "Well, what did ya' have in mind?" I naturally asked. "*World War III!*"

"I gotta' show those bastard Blues I ain't afraid of their penny-ante shit," G.R. responded in his back-to-normal vulgar speech pattern. "I'm gonna' quickly get you four assholes initiated into the Reds so that Hoss, Little Joe, Herc, Balls, and the other members can use some of *your* ideas against Gillette and his faggot, scumbag creeps. My new red '60 Thunderbird just came in today. Did ya' hear what happened to Hoss's green and white Edsel?"

"No," I answered. "Did he ever get it back from the blueberry farm's custody?"

"The cops just found the car's remains two-hours-ago in the ......well, you know, in the the big brick oven over at the Winslow Brickyard," Goose stated.

"In the kiln?" I exclaimed in a loud astounded voice. "The HHS punks musta' baked his Edsel to a crisp, just like the jerks smoked your white T-Bird?"

"That's right, J.W.," Goose verified. "And Hoss wants you and your three hiney-munchin' amigos into the Reds right away. I already got your James Dean jackets from the Berlin Farmers Market, so it's just a matter of you dunces passin' the initiation."

"When is it?" I inquired. "What'll we have to do?"

"Tonight, at six o'clock sharp," G.R. reported, "I'm gonna' pick up Juice, Frankie, and Fabian. News and me will conduct the pledgin' rites. You four jerks be ready at six and either join the mix, or lose your dicks!" Click.

I told my parents after supper that Goose wanted to take me for a ride in his new red Thunderbird, and said that I would be home by ten to finish the final draft of my English essay on Washington Irving and Rip Van Winkle.

"What happened to his white car?" Mom questioned. "It looked brand new just the other day."

"Ah, ah, it overheated and got as hot as an oven," I creatively articulated, "and Ronald Restuccio has lots of money, so he just bought another new one."

"Be sure to be home at ten," Dad stressed, "because tomorrow ya' might have to go to Donio's Fruit and Produce over at the end of Old Forks Road to get some fresh produce that's just arrivin' in from the South."

Goose picked me up outside Pete's Market right on schedule, and after I exchanged pleasantries with Sal Midilli, Tommy News, Johnny Juice, and Frankie Arena, all squeezed inside the four-seater, the crafty driver turned left onto Walker Road and passed by the main peach orchards of White Horse Farm. I saw Joanne Berenato talking to her mother in the corner driveway, outside their Dutch colonial home, but the swarthy beauty was too preoccupied to notice the new T-bird, or any of its passengers zipping by.

"How ya' like my new wheels?" Goose asked everyone in general and no one in particular. "I can't wait to bury the numbers. I betcha' I can go over a hundred and twenty in this chariot!"

"Nifty, swifty, but not wifty," Jives coyly contributed. "What's the word, Thunderbird?"

"The ultimate red drivin' machine," Juice complimented and added. "The finest pussy-wagon around. Definitely orgasm city!"

"First class, just like the front of an airliner," Fabian Midilli rendered. "This car's a pussy magnet, and when on the prowl, it's the friggin' cat's meow."

"Hey, J.W., what do ya' think about my new dream wagon?" Goose queried, looking for more accolades.

"I think we'd better get this initiation business over with before it gets too dark," I replied sounding, like an authentic wet blanket. "I never want to run into that nasty hombre Gabe Gillette again, unless the Reds are organized full-force and ready for battle."

Goose insisted that the creature we had seen in the Wharton State Forest near the Blues' isolated hunting cabin was merely "an *optimal* illusion."

I insisted that none of us had been hallucinating during the confrontation, and that the guys there had genuinely been haunted by some evil, arcane, supernatural intervention. "We may be targeted by the Jersey Devil if we again enter the Wharton State Forest with rifles!" I warned.

"Naaa J.W.," News joked and smirked. "Most mirages hang-out up in the *Illusion Islands* between Alaska and Siberia, and not in the Jersey pinelands."

I didn't think that Tommy's absurd pun was humorous, but the other guys did. Even Goose's mouth slanted-down more than usual, and I knew that the driver had no idea of the nature of the absurd joke's punch-line, or had any clue as to where the Aleutian Islands were geographically located, or for that matter, the elusive non-existent *Illusion Islands*.

G.R. stopped at the Union-Walker Road crossing, and next drove across the dangerous intersection onto a dirt lane that meandered through the center of a small woods. On the left were fallow fields, ready for tomato and pepper planting, and also old man Berenato's Red Delicious' apple orchards, situated in a remote area of the farm that the local inhabitants called "Texas". On the right was the dark green, highly-fertilized, hybrid grass of Tuckahoe Turf and Sod Farm. Up ahead a half-a-mile to the left were several trails leading into the New Jersey Wharton State Forest, the legendary pine' barrens domicile of the mythical Jersey Devil.

Our unpredictable, flamboyant chauffeur stopped his new red T-Bird around fifty-feet from the first sandy trail that joined with other paths a thousand-feet into the thick pine forest, and then looped back again to another trail exiting the woods about five-hundred-feet north of our position.

Goose opened his trunk and showed us four loaded shotguns with safety locks. The gang's drill instructor distributed the four weapons to Juice, Fabian, Jives, and me. "Don't fuck up this time like some of ya' shit-heads did at the Blues' cabin!" the vengeful dago warned, using several of his trademark, obscene invectives. "Once you dimwits are all officially admitted into the Reds, then I'll give ya' the James Dean jackets ya' earned, and then we can have an honorable war against Gillette and his queer-bait gang of rich thugs."

"How come your red jacket ain't dirty and ripped like it was out on Weymouth Road?" Fabian asked Restuccio. "It now looks like it's good as new."

"Because I bought three of 'em at the same time for myself, just in case somethin' happened to one of 'em," Goose explained in an irritated voice.

"Ya' never know what might happen to your jacket when those Blues are on a *tear,"* I jovially injected. I was glad to see that Goose's explanation to Sal was consistent with what the gross prevaricator had chronicled to me over the telephone.

"Goose, maybe I'm missin' something here," Fabian disputed, "but what'll we actually have to do to qualify for the Reds."

"Ye' gotta' each kill a deer illegally, just like the Blues do," our taskmaster ordered. "And if two of ya' shoot the same deer, I'll even count that rare kill, because ya' all are lucky to catch me in a pretty good cunt-lickin' mood today. Now, where else are ya' four Winky-Dinks gonna' be able to find four deer to shoot, except right here in the fuckin' forest?"

Sal, Johnny, Frankie and I looked at one another, raised our eyebrows and then simultaneously shrugged our shoulders to indicate our reluctant unanimity. That particular moment was neither the proper time to show insubordination to Red' authority, nor to shirk our duty as prospective Reds' members.

Goose Restuccio led his pledges down the sandy pine-barrens-trail until the sun's rays were just about hidden by the tall tree canopy. "Shhh!" the head scout cautioned in the dark shadows with his finger pointed to his mouth. "The wind's blowin' from the opposite direction, so the dumb deer won't be able to pick-up our scent. This just might be you' bone-heads lucky day," our weird 'scoutmaster' whispered to his four anxious new recruits. "None of ya' jerk-offs are wearin' after shave lotion, are ya'?"

"Where's News?" Fabian asked in a quivering tone.

"I told Tomasello to stay and guard my red T-Bird," Goose related, "because he's already a Red like me. And if any of ya' pencil-necked Piss-heads shoot a buck, make sure he has a hard-on!"

"Why?" I gullibly asked.

"Because we'll get more meat to eat that way! That's why, jerk-off!" Restuccio smugly snorted and then giggled.

"Sounds like more venison from the denizen without Alfred Lord Tennyson," Jives rhymed in almost-standard English.

"Quiet Zit-tits!" Goose commanded. "I think I see somethin' like big antlers movin' up ahead!"

The four amateur deer hunters all followed Goose's lead and crouched-down as our suspect leader slowly and deliberately paced, with his head at waist-level, toward our quarry. "Shhh!" Restuccio again told us in a low baritone. "I think there's four horny bucks behind those ferns and sticker bushes up ahead. One for each of ya' rookie sperm shooters!"

The five of us advanced closer to our spotted prey. When we got to within twenty-feet of the targeted deer, the four animals were suddenly very visible, facing us in the center of the trail, directly in front of our rifles' crosshairs. "Ready, aim, fire!" G.R. commanded. The four greenhorn marksmen aimed and then fired our shotguns at our animal prizes. Much to our astonishment, the four bucks stood-up on their two hind legs', aimed *their* four shotguns at our scared-to-death bodies, and then began energetically blasting away.

"What the hell's goin' on!" Juice exclaimed in absolute terror. We all ducked-down in order to evade flying buckshot pellets whizzing by our ears. "Deer don't have fingers to pull triggers!"

"And the bucks sure don't have hands to hold shotguns!" I logically added. "And they don't have the physical tools to grip, hold, or shoot a shot-gun!"

"Those mother-fuckin' deer are still shootin' at us!" Goose frantically screamed. "Let's get outa' here while the getting is still good before I crap my new jeans three times!"

G.R. got-down on his hands and knees and began crawling over pinecones, fallen trees, pine needles, thorns, and dried leaves. We followed his lead until the group reached a dense, scrub tree cluster. Dragging our shotguns across the forest's cold damp ground, Juice, Frankie, Fabian, and I mimicked Goose's stellar example.

The five of us crawled a hundred-feet or so with our chests rubbing against the soggy earth, pine needles, and leaves. Goose stood-up from his haunches and then took-off like a bullet expelled from a rifle. A second later, Fabian, Juice, Frankie, and I dashed-ahead likewise. The five interlopers darted as fast as we could down a secondary trail that eventually took us out of the dense forest's dark interior. Shotgun discharges were discerned behind us as the vengeful, hostile bucks fired their weapons in our direction. We continued to fanatically flee the outlandish woodland scene, until we came to the Wharton Tract's outer fringe.

The five adventurers caught our second winds and had the stamina to sprint like Olympians to the safety of daylight, only to find two frowning forest rangers on patrol standing stationary, ready to arrest us on the spot. "Okay, you five junior hoodlums, put your hands in the air!" the first state official instructed as the officer waved his held handgun at us.

"Don't say a word," the second no-nonsense ranger dictated. "Anything ya' say could be used against ya' in a court of law. You hooligans are all under arrest for illegal deer huntin'."

I was never so mortified in all my life. How would I ever explain the outrageous circumstances that had just occurred to my disbelieving parents? The entire phenomenon the non-initiated Reds had experienced was too surreal to believe, let alone understand.

The militant forest rangers commanded that the four of us do a one-eighty spin, and place our hands on the roof of a patrol jeep, so that the officers could frisk us for concealed weapons. No sooner had we obediently performed the specified act, that Goose Restuccio and the two dedicated forest rangers broke-out into a wild burst of laughter.

"What's goin' on here?" Juice wanted to know. Our numb minds were totally perplexed by unknown variables that needed immediate explanation and definition.

"Ha, ha, ha, ha!" Goose boisterously bellowed, almost barfing-up his esophagus. "These two ridiculous goons of mine ain't no damned forest rangers. Take off your hats, guys," Restuccio instructed the uniformed men.

After the rangers removed their headgear, I recognized the two Sicilian impostors as Goose's father's chief henchmen, Frankie Fingers and Joe Zucchini.

"Forget the poop! What's the scoop, chicken coop?" Jives respectfully requested learning.

G.R. disclosed that he had rented the two forest ranger uniforms from a Berlin Auction' costume/novelty store. None of us recognized either Frankie Fingers or Joe Zucchini in their clever, unorthodox disguises.

“But Goose, what about the deer shootin’ away at us with their loud shotguns?” Sal Midilli interrogated the prankster. “What was that weirdness all about?”

Four chuckling figures in deer disguises, wearing brown, furry winter gloves, came ambling-out of the forest toward us, as we stood petrified near the green patrol jeep. Then, the cumbersome heads of the costumes were removed by each of the four masqueraders, who turned-out to be Hoss and Little Joe Gregorio, Herc Juliano. and irascible News Tomasello.

“While I was rentin’ the two ranger outfits over in Berlin,” Goose revealed, “I got a bright idea, which ya’ all know is as fuckin’ rare as four tits on a whore’s back.” After thirty seconds, of sustained hee-hawing from his almost captive audience, Restuccio continued his oddball monologue. “I decided to also rent the four deer costumes and buy me eight new shotguns to play this little trick on you four trigger-happy, ass-wiping fools.”

“News,” I coughed-out. “You were in on the crazy forest prank, too! How could ya’ betray me like this?”

“J.W., ya’ wasn’t betrayed,” G.R. interceded and insisted. “You was only hoodwinked by the one and only Goose Restuccio.”

“But what about the initiation?” Fabian demanded. “Are we full-fledged and full-pledged Reds yet?”

“Naaaa, not yet,” Goose said with a sly grin on his slanted mouth. “This *fee-ass-co* was only a fake initiation. It was sort of a trial to test your balls’ sperm count, which turned out pretty low. Next week, I’m gonna’ hit ya’ with the real thing, so be ready for anything and everything.”

Juice was extremely infuriated at being so shrewdly deceived after going through so much apprehension, travail, and struggle during our bizarre hunting expedition. “I’d hate to say it, Goose,” Johnny soberly accused, “but you’re far worse than the little boy who cried wolf!”

“You four pledges were running for *deer* life!” News giddily punned. “But as you know, Goose has all the *bucks* and *doe* wrapped in his pocket’s wad.”

Chapter Twenty

"The Reds' Initiation"

May on the 1960 calendar meant the arrival of warm weather, tedious farm market work, and the long-awaited, bona fide Reds' initiation rites of spring. I was more than a little peeved at Goose for making complete blockheads out of Juice, Fabian, Frankie Jives, and me during the fake forest initiation frolic. I was also disenchanted with News Tomasello, whom Goose had recruited as one of his costumed deer accomplices in the bizarre caper, along with fake forest rangers Frankie Fingers and Joe Zucchini.

I felt exploited and used, and I empathized with how Dennis Measley must have grieved every time some insensitive delinquent like Goose Restuccio or Gabe Gillette maliciously abused his sanity by throwing a hundred rotten apples, sounding like thunderclaps, against the poor kid's shabby, dingy, wood-framed shack.

I had to really put it on thick with Dad and Mom that I was being honored by dignified, outstanding, Edgewood and St. Joesph High students, who had asked me to join a prestigious "club", which had been established to pay tribute to the late James Dean.

"Alright, Son," Pop skeptically commended. "You can have Saturday afternoon off. I'm glad to hear you're joinin' a club and not some destructive greaser gang like those derelict Diablos you belonged to back in Levittown."

Goose picked me up in his red T-Bird at noon, and the sadist motored over to Spring Road "to bag" News Tomasello, the two opposites in personality being my joint sponsors into the noble Reds' organization.

"J.W., I got your coveted red jacket sittin' in the trunk just waitin' to be worn," G.R. indicated to News and me. "Just be cool under fire and make sure that there's no sticky, premature semen discharge," Restuccio ejaculated.

"What's that supposed to mean?" I nervously inquired. "What in the world do I have to do to be eligible *this time* to join the Reds? There was no such thing as an initiation before *you* had joined the peach gang," I protested to Goose.

"Don't worry a single iota, J.W.," News diplomatically comforted. "Everything's gonna' be peachy for ya'. And only fret if ya' own and play a guitar."

"That's so funny I forgot to laugh," I opined and smirked. "You and me used to be good friends. But after that fake huntin' initiation, I'm not so sure anymore."

"Cut the crap!" G.R. insisted as the future don wheeled his red machine from Spring Road onto congested *Route 30,* heading west toward Flemington Pike. "News, tell J.W. all about what's happenin' in this ass-backward world."

"Well, Dick Clark denied any involvement in the Payola scandal when the TV DJ testified before the Special House Subcommittee on Legislative Oversight," News aptly reported. "The Bandstand host claimed that *in his heart,* he has never taken Payola."

"I thought that the congressional *sub*-committee only discussed underwater ships!" I defensively inserted into News' current events dissertation. "Did the sub-committee meet in a hoagie shop?"

"What about *in his wallet?"* Goose cynically responded, ignoring my feeble attempt at sarcastic humor. "Ya' don't take Payola in your heart. Ya' put it in your goddamned wallet. What a slippery conniver! I can't stand guys that come across too nice on TV. They're more-fake standin' behind a freakin' microphone than the Wharton Tract huntin' expedition initiation was."

"Don't remind me of *that* planned farce!" I objected. "But getting back to the subject of Payola, the government's gonna' nail Alan Freed good," I added. "He's gonna' be the fall guy for the whole record industry. That J. Edgar Hoover and his hound-dog FBI wanta' destroy rock and roll because the government censors think the music causes juvenile delinquency."

"The new beat *is* rather rebellious," T.T. observed and contended, "and lots of church leaders have condemned rock and roll because the sanctimonious zealots think it promotes teens havin' sex."

"What's wrong with getting your noodle a little wet once in a while?" Goose injected. "I kinda' like the fish smell after the nooky juice dries on my pecker. And sex is much better than sittin' on your toilet and jerkin' your gherkin! If ya' keep too much sperm in your worm, ya' become too big and fat. Just look what the hell happened to the freakin' sperm whales!"

"That makes about as much total sense as the President, the Pope, or religion does," News laughed. "But the Southern Presbyterian Church's General Assembly recently declared that marital sex without the intent to have children is *not* sinful."

"Then, that means that havin' sex without bein' married *is* sinful, doesn't it?" I challenged, just when Goose turned left onto Flemington Pike in the direction of Winslow and Jives' house.

"Who the hell ever married Adam and Eve if they was the first man and woman?" Goose questioned. "There weren't any damned priests, rabbis, or prime ministers around back then. Only friggin' Adam and Eve."

"God married them," I futilely argued. "And He made them live happily until they committed Original Sin in the Garden of Eden."

G.R. was becoming quite perturbed with all of the Biblical rhetoric being exchanged. My direct opposition to *his* daily apostasy seemed to be jangling Restuccio's nerves. "What the fuck kind of stupidity is that!" my imminent sponsor into the Reds maintained. "An adult takes an apple from a tree; gives it to her husband, and God decides that a hundred-billion people gotta' suffer, get cancer, VD, and die, because of one damned apple. What a crock of bullshit that Garden of Eatin' is!"

"Stop cursin' so much," News chastised Goose.

"What makes ya' think I'm fuckin' cursin'?" Restuccio snapped back. "What ya' call cursin' is goddamned normal language to me. I hate all that holier-than-thou bullshit you're tryin' to lay on me!"

"Then ya' don't believe in God?" I asked G.R.

"The question really is," Goose replied and paused, "does God fuckin' believe in himself? I mean, if He's perfect and all that kind of shit, why the fuck didn't He create a perfect world, that stupid Asshole! He must have a double brain tumor, or a triple hernia, or some jazzed-up medical problem like that!"

"Goose," I predicted, "you're gonna' go to hell."

"I'm goin' into the ground at the cemetery and rot-away inside a steel box, just like everybody else does," the atheist said with certainty. "And if ya' have ever been to a funeral, ya' can plainly see that the dead person ain't in heaven, ain't in hell, or ain't in *perk*atory. He's lyin' there dead in the damned funeral parlor inside the expensive box, that's all! Nothin' else!"

"Shouldn't he be tellin' the truth in the box instead of lyin' in the box?" I quipped while thinking about Bo Jalonec. "I mean, it's hard for a dead person to think outside the box."

"Ya' know J.W.," Goose addressed and rankled. "You're really fucked-up! I really mean that *jar-gun.* And I also think that you're a real pro."

"Why, thanks, Goose!" I replied in sincere appreciation.

"A real *pro*phylactic, ya' fuckin' rubber head!" my shady sponsor facetiously exclaimed. "Ya' got a real bad case of constipation of the brain and diarrhea of the mouth. A true genius like me has just the opposite condition."

The red '60 T-Bird finally arrived at Jives Arena's modest home, and we were soon off to Hoss and Little Joe Gregorio's two-hundred-acre peach farm over in Waterford Township, situated at the edge of the Wharton State Forest.

"I'm a ready Teddy to rock and roll to save my soul," Jives rhymed some silly jabberwocky to his fellow passengers. "Let's do some movin' and a groovin' into the Reds. Solid Ted, enough said."

"Shut the fuck up!" Goose hollered at Frankie, sitting in the back seat. "I gotta' listen to the National Anthem." G.R. turned the radio knob to the right and blasted Bill Haley and the Comets' classic rendition of "Rock around the Clock". We all had to solemnly sit still without talking during the entire sacred rite. The song's catchy rhythm and beat was still relevant, six-years after hip D.J.'s in Cleveland, 'Philly, and New York City first had spun the classic tune in 1954.

When Goose pulled into the Gregorio farm, we were greeted by fellow Reds pledges Sal Fabian Midilli and Johnny Juice Illiani. The two urged us to step into a nearby red barn and witness Hoss performing a "discipline demonstration" designed to indoctrinate thirty newly arrived Puerto Rican migrant workers, who were gathered in a circle around him. A farm foreman acted as a packinghouse interpreter and translated Hoss's intimidating words into their Spanish dialect.

"Now, amigos," Hoss sternly commanded to his fresh crop of field employees, exhibiting a serious expression upon his chubby face. "I have two huge sledgehammers in front of me. I'm gonna' twist my wrists upwards, and lift the heavy sledgehammers off of the cement floor. Watch closely."

"Why's he doin' this?" I whispered to Juice.

"He likes to scare the daylights out of his field workers," Johnny answered. "They'll become afraid of Hoss once their eyes see his awesome strength. That way, none of 'em will give Gregorio any trouble durin' the whole summer harvest season."

Just when everything was quiet, Hoss twisted his powerful wrists upwards, and the two heavy sledgehammers were raised from the concrete floor to waist level. The stunned migrants were amazed at the giant's tremendous feat that none of them were capable of duplicating. Hoss next hoisted the weighty sledgehammers over his head and asked everyone to count slowly to a hundred in Espanol. Then, when *that* number had been reached, Hoss casually let the heavy objects fall to the floor, creating dual loud impacts.

While the thirty migrant workers stood there in great awe, Little Joe Gregorio entered the open packinghouse with two fierce Doberman Pinschers on chain-leashes. The canines were fiercely barking-away, baring ferocious, sharp fangs. The thirty migrants shouted a plethora of expletives in Spanish and swiftly dispersed in all directions, finally escaping being attacked and mauled by the vicious attack dogs.

"That'll teach 'em to respect their bosses," Hoss gleefully shouted as the human Titan lustily slapped Little Joe on the back. "Put 'em in line now, and our jobs will be easier in August."

I knew that Hoss Gregorio was just as strong as Ox Narducci was, and maybe ever stronger. During the growing season, he and Little Joe would stack fifty forty-pound cartons of peaches on skids, which the brothers moved by hand-jacks, and then race each other, dragging the two thousand-pound loads from the peach packing line into the farm's cold storage building. If Little Joe was powerful, then Hoss Gregorio was potent with a capital P.

"Hey, Hoss, it's time to get on with Goose's initiation," Little Joe reminded his older brother. "That's why we have all these fine guests visitin' our peach farm today."

On the drive from the packing facility out to the Wharton Tract, the selected setting for the Reds' official initiation, Goose related a story about the legendary Hoss Gregorio. The three-hundred-pound-hulk had brought an over-weighted truckload of peaches to New York City's Hunts Point Food Distribution Center. There were so many forty-pound boxes roped in on the tailgate that when Hoss Gregorio stepped-down from the cab's driver's seat at Hunts Point, the big rig's front wheels lifted six-inches off the ground.

"That's quite a story," I marveled and agreed. "It's a good thing Little Joe wasn't drivin' that overweight rig to New York, or he would've had to steer that truck with both front wheels ridin' a half-a-foot above the highway!"

Everyone inside the red T-bird got a good chuckle out of my timely comment. I glanced behind us and saw Sal Midilli's '59 white Chevy Impala with Juice Illiani riding shotgun. Hoss Gregorio and Little Joe were riding in the sparkling car's back seat. Three-hundred feet ahead on the dirt road stood other Reds' members from Edgewood High: Denny "Baker" Harrison, Guy "Moose" Marinella, Joe and Chickie Calabrese, Tony Passarella, Marty Ransom, and Pete Clarke. St. Joe's was well-represented too by the divine presence of Dave "Herc" Juliano, Ollie "Balls" Giordano, and Jake "the Brute" Maccarella.

Goose, News, Jives, and I exited the red T-Bird and sauntered over to the other guys, who were all crowded-around a peach farm flat-bodied water tank truck, which was there for some obscure purpose I could not fathom or determine. All of the assembled active Reds were proudly wearing their James Dean' jackets.

"How many gallons of water in that truck container?" Goose asked Herc Juliano. "Enough to drown an elephant?"

"Over a thousand," Herc answered. "And that's enough to drown any underground colony of rats. I drove it all the way over here from my farm, and the tank's full of *agua*."

"What's the water used for?" I wanted to know. "Is it for our initiation?"

"Yeah. We're gonna' baptize ya' four nincompoopers with the unholy water," Goose stated in a rather sacrilegious tone. "Juice, if ya' wasn't getting initiated into the Reds, we could easily make ya' into Johnny the Baptist," G.R. ranted, without getting *confirmation* from anyone being initiated.

All of the assembled Reds gave-out prodigious whoops, showing their strong approval of Restuccio's blatant irreverence. News Tomasello was then delegated by Hoss Gregorio to review the general procedure rules for the new pledges' formal installation rites. Our first task was that each of us had to kill an adult rat with a three-pronged, two-foot-long, hand hoe. Herc and Balls distributed the four garden tools to Juice, Jives, Fabian, and me. I carefully inspected the hand hoe's structure and configuration.

"How do we use these things?" I innocently asked as I continued examining the garden device.

"Oh, don't worry," Goose almost-evilly snickered. "The real *hoes* will show-up pretty soon."

"Don't listen to Restuccio," News cautiously advised. "Hoss is goin' to start-up the pump to the water tank. Balls is gonna' stick the hose into the big rat hole over there. When the underground tunnels and burrows become flooded, the trapped rats are gonna' start diggin' their way up to earth in order to breathe. When the rats stick their filthy, disgustin', ugly noses and heads through the ground to get fresh air and escape from drowning, then kill 'em with the sharp garden hoes."

"I'm used to stickin' my hose into lots of holes," Balls Giordano hollered and bragged for everyone to hear. "But they ain't been no rat holes! And that's exactly why girls are afraid of mice, 'cause mice always run to the nearest hole!"

Jives, Fabian, Juice, and I all looked at each other with expressions of consternation appearing upon our worried faces. It would be a test of courage to kill a desperate rat fighting for its life, and I didn't know if I would be equal to performing the horrible task.

"At least it's only killin' vermin and not murdering humans," Juice said trying to comfort me, "because murder is what ya' do to another human being, and killin' is what ya' do to an animal."

"I'll just pretend *those dirty rats* are the Blues bustin' up my Winslow Boatneck gig," Jives summarized while imitating Edward G.

Robinson. "*Those dirty rats* are gonna' be payin' for playin' with Frankie Jives Arena."

Ollie Balls Giordano inserted the long rubber hose into the rat's den; Herc Juliano activated the pump, and a torrent of water gushed into the cavity's main entrance. Some of the other Reds had clogged-up all of the escape burrows within a hundred-foot perimeter of the main tunnel, so the vermin were trapped inside their enormous subterranean domicile. The desperate rodents' only means to liberate themselves from their underground labyrinth would be by frantically burrowing-up to the surface, and inhaling vital oxygen before being drowned by massive flooding.

Two whole minutes elapsed without any sign of frantic rats, but then, pink nostrils and whiskers began penetrating-up through the soil. Jives, Juice, Fabian, and I savagely flailed-away and wickedly began thrusting our hand hoes into the ground, and soon into vermin flesh. I looked at my hand hoe's prongs and saw that I had butchered a baby rat, which did not count by Reds' standards as being acceptable. I disgustedly pushed the poor dead creature off of the middle and the left end prong with my left shoe, using my body's full weight as leverage.

In another thirty-seconds of smashing-away at the already panic-stricken farm pests, the four pledges had all accomplished our first assigned missions. Four dead adult rats had been savagely impaled upon our deadly hand hoes. A round of applause swelled from our Reds admirers, and quite frankly, I felt like vomiting my stomach's entire contents onto the ground, right then and there. Hoss Gregorio shut-off the water tank pump, and Balls Giordano removed the hose from the main tunnel.

"It is my pleasure," News announced, "to officially *rat*ify the four of you as successfully completing the first part of the Reds' new initiation ceremony."

"Now it's time for the real *hoes* I had promised ya'!" Goose sniggered. "Here they are, gentlemen; some of my finest prostitutes, imported direct from Pacific Avenue in Atlantic City."

I couldn't believe my eyes. Four of the most gorgeous women I had ever seen stepped-out of a brand new red and white Chrysler. The sex models were wearing mink coats and spiked high heel shoes. All of the gathered Reds began whistling and hooting like crazy pimps. The four voluptuous hookers then opened up their full-length mink coats, revealing magnificent naked bodies that left absolutely nothing to the imagination.

When the male hooting and whistling bravado did not subside, the models again covered their luscious nude anatomies with their luxurious fur coats. Wild cheering again commenced, urging the dames to expose their femininity a second time, but then Goose Restuccio raised his hands into the air requesting silence.

"J.W., ya' oughta' appreciate this the most, livin' out on the White *Whores* Pike," Goose teased me, much to the delight of the other Reds. "Now if ya' look to your right, you'll see four boards nailed to tree stumps, formin' four flat benches. Did ya' four dorks notice that each girl I hired from Jezebel's Den has different colored hair: a blonde, a redhead, a brunette, and a black-haired nude dancer. Did ya' four hammerheads notice that?"

Juice, Jives, Fabian, and I all nodded our heads up and down signifying "yes". Goose appointed News Tomasello to provide the remaining directions in standard English, so that the four candidates would fully comprehend the 'naked truth' ground rules. Tommy had our undivided attention.

"The four of ya' are gonna' lay on separate boards face-up on the four nifty benches we Reds had made. Next, you'll be blindfolded," News informed, "and then each of the four prostitutes Goose had hired will sit on your face and rub their crotches over your snotty noses. It's your job to guess what color pussy hair the doll has, either blonde, black, brunette, or redhead. The first guy who accurately guesses all four colors will be the first pledge to advance to phase three."

"What's phase' three?" I asked in total amazement while I still was evaluating the weird aspects of phase two.

"In phase three," News continued his directions, "you'll have to take-off all your clothes, and strip-down almost stark naked wearin' only your shoes and socks and nothin' else. Then, you'll have to dash as fast as ya' can a hundred-yards down that dirt trail over yonder and around the bend at the end 'til ya' get to the finish line. Just pretend you're scorin' a touchdown with no clothes on. The last guy crossin' the finish line will be the only one that will fail the initiation and not be admitted into the Reds."

My disheveled mind was swimming in an ocean of disbelief. "Well, News, the *Finnish line* is like four-thousand-miles away from here between Helsinki and Russia," I stupidly said. "Can't we just have the gorgeous girls sit on our faces?" I pleaded, because I didn't want to feel totally embarrassed running naked at full-speed down a sandy trail through a wooded area, and having my male friends make fun of my Saturnalian enterprise.

"Ya' gotta' do it if ya' wanta' join the Reds!" Goose injected. All of the guys hooted and shouted, and I, along with my fellow pledges, felt the real weight of peer pressure wrestling with our consciences. "And remember, if any of ya' get hard-ons while the exotic-erotic bitches are sittin' on your faces," Goose added, "you're disqualified! Ya' dig? Get an erection and ya' fuckin' automatically lose!"

The four of us laid-down horizontal on our backs; positioned ourselves upon the makeshift benches, and then, red blindfolds were quickly wrapped over our eyes and firmly tied around our heads. On the count of "three", I felt something like a *Brillo* soap pad rubbing against my nose as a naked doll stooped her fuzzy crotch down over my nostrils, and I yelled out "blonde" but was told by News's voice that my guess was wrong. After two more tries, "brunette" finally worked the trick. I could hear the other guys making jolly with my folly, but I was determined to triumph over their crazed adversity, even though my sense of morality was strongly being tested. What I had always imagined would be a sensual, pleasurable experience in a dream was suddenly turning-out to be a cruel and humiliating, perverted nightmare.

After around five more minutes of the *Brillo*-pad-bush treatment, I managed to finally yell "redhead" for correctly identifying the fourth hired prostitute's pubic patch. Someone officiating removed my blindfold. I quickly sat-up on the rudely-constructed plank and took off my coat, shirt, and pants in the seventy-degree May afternoon temperature. I observed that the strippers had already re-entered their red and white Chrysler, and were speeding-away from their triumphant gig. I then noticed that my three competitors were also rapidly disrobing in public, but since our audience was all male, it was just like taking off my clothes in the boys' gym locker room before showering at Edgewood.

I hesitated before pulling-down my jockey shorts, but I was buoyed in the wisdom that I had put-on clean underwear after I had showered that morning. I finally was naked except for my shoes and socks, and when I whirled-around, I saw that Juice, Fabian, and Jives had advanced to the exact same situation.

Goose Restuccio laughed, pointed his finger and hollered, "That way!" The four of us sprinted like decathlon champions onto the sandy lane. 'A hundred-yards is what's separating me from assimilation into the Reds,' I anxiously thought. I knew I could easily out-speed Jives, who was pigeon-toed, non-athletic, and awkward, but I had to be careful not to sprain an ankle or pull a thigh muscle in pursuit of the much-heralded finish line. I heard intense cheering coming from around the bend. 'Only fifty-yards more until pay dirt,' I excitedly thought. I put my head down and exerted my body and legs to the max.

When I rounded the bend, I saw that Juice and I were running neck and neck. I gave-out a loud yell as adrenaline fueled the glands and muscles all throughout my exhausted body. My lungs gasped for more air. My eyes noticed Herc Juliano and Balls Giordano holding a length of red crepe paper across the white dirt road, symbolizing the "finish line".

I gave it my all-out effort and victoriously whizzed through the thin red crepe paper. I was ecstatic! I heard cheering and shouting galore all around me, as I put my hands to my knees, inhaling as much oxygen into my chest as I possibly could.

When I stood erect, I was in for quite a shock. A mixed crowd of male and female high school kids were madly screaming and wildly jumping up and down, and right in the center of the jubilant teens was none other than Joanne Berenato. My dream girl held her hands up to her mouth and face, reacting in total astonishment at my indecent exposure.

Chapter Twenty-One

"The Atsion Lake Olympics"

I felt ashamed, humbled, and mortified. News Tomasello was on the scene and compassionately wrapped a new red bathroom around my exposed body to spare my already-fractured ego and additional embarrassment. Goose had purchased four identical cheap red bathrobes at the Berlin Auction to symbolize that Juice, Fabian, Jives, and I were new valid entries into the Reds' peach gang. "Here's your official James Dean jacket," Goose articulated after News had draped the red bathrobe around me. "Wear it with pride."

A crowd of sixty or so invited kids from Edgewood and St. Joe's gathered-around the four initiation survivors and applauded our savvy, determination, and admission. The sham that had been a debacle just moments earlier had been transformed into a veritable triumph for the four shell-shocked inductees.

I was still slightly confused and disoriented by the bizarre initiation. "I guess Frankie Arena didn't make it," I said to jubilant Goose Restuccio. "I think Jives was last in the race the last time I looked. Too bad for Frankie to have to go through all that agony without ecstasy again!"

"I bent the rules a little bit," G.R. genially confessed. "I only made-up that part where the last asshole crossin' the finish line would not be admitted into the gang. I did it so that everybody would bust his butt tryin' to win the naked sprint at the end. And I'm very happy to say ya' all did!"

I glimpsed over at Joanne Berenato, and she shyly waved and smiled at me, briefly showing her pearly whites. Herc Juliano ushered the four new Reds into his red Ford station wagon, and drove the neophytes back to the starting area where the prostitutes had capriciously smothered our faces with their various-colored pubic bushes. We retrieved our assorted clothes that had been strewn all over the ground, and took several private moments to re-enter our apparel behind some large elm and oak trees. The four new gang additions talked very little as we independently meditated, still collecting our clothes along with our wits.

Then, Goose approached the newly-qualified Reds. The initiation organizer told Herc to meet him back at the Gregorio barn. G.R. seemed rather amiable when the tyrant brought us in his T-Bird back to the red barn to smoke some *Camels* and to celebrate our full induction. All the gang's merry members drank-down several cases of *Schmidt's* beer. The party was exclusive, open only to Reds' members, so the other kids at the finish line eventually wandered home, fully entertained (except for maybe Joanne Berenato and Elaine Hill) from the rather eccentric initiation activities.

While the other Reds were lauding and reminiscing about the odd contest, my mind shifted into an introspective mood. I didn't like the way that Goose had been negatively influencing News Tomasello. Tommy was showing some bad attributes that I believed he had been acquiring from immoral G.R. And since Goose was decadent and thought that he could curry anybody's favor with either money or threats, I believed the teenage despot had been using his greenbacks and his arrogance to win over Tommy.

I also suspected that Frankie Jives Arena, Johnny Juice Illiani, and Salvatore Fabian Midilli would be the next ones in line to be contaminated by the selfishness of one corrupt Ronald Goose Restuccio. Then, I would in effect be isolated, becoming the final solitary target for my bigoted, conceited, haughty, dynamic, rich acquaintance to conquer.

The following Monday, things were not that propitious at school, either. True, I wore my red James Dean jacket proudly, but then Mr. Andrews informed me during fourth period class that I would be failing trigonometry and would have to either attend summer school in Haddonfield, or find a decent certified tutor to enhance my skills in *his* subject. I instantly became despondent and depressed. The failure notice would be going home from the guidance office in just a week, so that gave me a meager seven days of freedom before Dad would shift into his punishment' "grounded" mode.

"What's wrong J.W.?" Juice asked me at fifth-period lunch. "Did ya' forget to watch *Captain Kangaroo* or *Winky Dink* this mornin'?"

"Yeah, J.W.," Jives jumped in. "Meeska, mooska, mouseketeer, mouse cartoon time now is here! Are ya' drownin' in a stew, Jay Doubleyou? Is Joanne Berenato your new Princess-Summer-Fall-Winter-Spring special woman? I thought that your pretty Indian Princess was still dating Buffalo Bob!"

I completely ignored Frankie's ludicrous speculation. "Andrews gave me the dreadful hatchet word fourth-period," I somberly sniffed. "I'm failin' trig' and will have to go to summer school. That means at least a whole half a year stayin' out of college," I regretfully communicated my sorrow. "I was thinkin' about applyin' to *Glassboro State* over the summer, but I can't even take night courses if I don't graduate and get an Edgewood diploma."

"Things could always be worse," Fabian empathized, trying to elevate my spirits above depression. "Ya' could've gotten your penis caught in a rusty zipper and then needed a tetanus shot injected into the most sensitive part."

Goose Restuccio carried his tray of spaghetti and meatballs over to our daily lunch table. The instigator was in a very upbeat mood, and his cadence was unusually snappy and alert. "Hey guys, *I've got a secret!"* G.R. began as 'Mussolini" lowered himself into a seat.

"Who are ya' supposed to be?" I sneered in very apparent envy of G.R.'s uncharacteristic enthusiasm. "Garry Moore, the *I've Got a Secret'* TV host? Maybe Juice, Jives, Fabian, and News can be on the guessing panel, and I can be the show's mystery guest who will 'sign-in please'," I derisively uttered.

"Check-out this insane bullshit guys!" Goose exclaimed in an uncommonly excited voice that showed genuine emotion. "I got this here letter in the mail yesterday, and it's addressed to the Reds, Care of Ronald 'Goose' Restuccio. It's from none other than our enemy, Gabe Gillette!"

"What does that hambone want?" I nastily replied. "A couple of packs of *Gillette Blue Blades* for his electric razor!"

Everyone at the table found humor in my sarcastic reference to dual plays on words, even Goose, who was in a rare, jovial, non-combative state of mind. Restuccio insisted that I open the sealed letter and orally read its contents to my fellow Reds. I reluctantly complied with his request.

May 10, 1960

Dear Reds,

Congratulations on the induction of four new members into your fine organization. The Blues heard all about your great initiation from some of your invited guests. Now here's what we propose.

The Blues want to be friends with the Reds. You and we both now have twenty-four members each. It just so happens that there are twenty-four bottles in a case of beer. What a wonderful coincidence! I suggest a friendly little competition between the Reds and the Blues. Since *Route 206* divides blueberry country from peach country, I propose neutral territory for the first annual Atsion Lake Olympics to take place.

If you are interested in having some clean American fun, the Reds should accept the Blues cordial invitation by opening the inner envelope and reading the contest rules. If you are afraid to have some fun, games, and good socializing, then immediately destroy my second letter located inside the second envelope.

Gabe Gillette
President
The Blues

Everyone at the cafeteria table was intrigued with the contents of the first letter, so the six guys held an impromptu vote whether or not to open the second envelope.

"Why don't we show Hoss, Little Joe, and the rest of the guys over there at their table the letter, and let the jocks read it, and then we all could vote?" I constructively asked.

"Because J.W., the teachers on duty would see too many kids in a group, get suspicious, and take the letter away from us," Goose hypothesized and divulged. "Especially Andrews, who hates *your* stinkin' guts. We'll open the second letter right now, and if the rules are to our likin', we'll let Hoss and the others in on the gig."

"For once," News confided, "Goose sounds like he's right. We gotta' think strategically, and if we like what we read, then it'll be the Reds versus the Blues in the first annual Atsion Lake Olympics," Tommy convincingly argued. "I like the feel of those words."

All six guys seated at the table orally voted in favor of opening the inner envelope and scrupulously assessing the prescribed rules of engagement. Suspense was mounting as I ripped open the second, smaller white envelope.

May 10, 1960

Reds,

Okay, you've decided to accept the Blues friendly challenge to the first annual Atsion Lake Olympics. That's good! This event will help the two "clubs" get to know each other better. Here are the rules.

1) Event Number 1. (individual competition) Our best swimmer, Speed Mortellite will race your best swimmer across Atsion Lake. Two cases of beer, twenty-four bottles of *Pabst Blue Ribbon* for the Blues and two-dozen bottles of *Budweiser* for the Reds, will be drunk when the winner emerges from the race (one bottle for each member of each gang).

2) Event Number 2. (individual competition) #2 will be the Ball-Breaking Contest. Two almost identical huge rocks will be placed at the side of Atsion Lake, and Butch Lanza will challenge any Red to break the rocks down to sandstone, using two sledgehammers (one rock per contestant). Two more cases of beer will be drunk after the event during socializing time.

3) Event Number 3. (group competition) #3 will be the 100 Yard Crawl-a-Thon. The twelve largest Reds will get on hands and knees and the twelve smallest Reds on their backs. The Blues will do the same. Two cases of beer to be drunk at end of the friendly event.

4) Event Number 4. Competition #4 will be the Tree Chopping Contest. (individual competition). The Blues will provide the four axes needed for the event. Hammer Bertino and Bull Martino will compete against any two Reds to chop-down two twin oak trees next to Atsion Lake (one tree per gang). Two cases of beer to be drunk at end of event while socializing.

5) Event Number 5. (group competition) The Potato Sack Race will be event 5. The distance will be two-hundred-yards on two separate trails leading into the woods. Two Blues or two Reds per sack. Twenty-four sacks total. One leg in sack, one on ground while running and hopping. Reds down one path, Blues down the second trail. Two cases of beer and socializing at end of Potato Sack Race.

6) Event Number 6. (individual competition) The final event will be the much long-awaited Arm-Wrestling Contest. Ox Narducci versus the strongest Red. The event will take place at one of the Atsion Lake picnic tables. Two cases of beer will be drunk at end. Socializing.

No girls, cheerleaders, or guests will be invited to the First Annual Atsion Lake Olympics, which will be a closed affair to avoid any major distractions. The First Annual Olympics between the Blues and the Reds will be for gang members only! No spectators!

The Blues agree to pay for and supply the twelve cases of beer (six *Budweiser* for the Reds and six *Pabst Blue Ribbon* for the Blues). The Blues will also provide all the materials, sledgehammers, axes, identical giant rocks, and burlap potato sacks. No single Red or single Blue will be able to compete in more than one "individual event".

Be at Atsion Lake next Saturday morning just before high noon for the "Blue and Red Olympics". You can confirm your desire to participate by phoning any of my secretaries at my blueberry farm, Lois, Roseann, or Jeannie. Look our number up in the Atlantic County telephone book.

Very truly yours,
Gabe Gillette
President
The Blues

The six of us were absolutely dumfounded. I was amazed that Gabe Gillette's letter had featured impeccable English grammar and punctuation; Goose was astounded that the Blues had advocated cooperation rather than violence, and the four others were stunned that our former enemies now desired to live in peace and harmony.

"Why do ya' suppose the Blues wanta' buddy-up with us now?" Juice questioned. "This is all quite hard to swallow."

"I think the HHS rogues now see us as equals, twenty-four against twenty-four," I suggested. "Kinda' like a stalemate."

"What's that?" Goose honestly asked. "I thought a stale mate is a wife ya' get tired of screwin'?"

Everyone mildly chuckled. I had to explain the vernacular definition to Goose's slang-oriented colloquial mentality. After the six of us agreed to accept the Blues' challenge and their "fair rules" to the First Annual Atsion Lake Olympics, Goose conveyed the letter over to Hoss Gregorio's cafeteria table. In five short minutes, the other Reds' contingent endorsed the First Annual Atsion Lake Olympics, and supported the six listed major events.

Juice Illiani was a terrific swimmer and was chosen to compete against Speed Mortellite. Balls Giordano was selected to vie against Butch Lanza in the Ball-Breaking Contest, and according to Goose, "as long as Balls isn't *cast-rated* before competing". Little Joe Gregorio and Herc Juliano would compete against Hammer Bertino and Bull Martello in the Tree Chopping event, and Hoss Gregorio would at last be able to defeat Ox Narducci in a death-grip arm wrestling marathon.

"Did ya' notice," Fabian recognized and said at our table, "that one of the rules says that no single guy can compete in more than one individual event."

"Then, that means that none of us can compete," News joked, "because none of us are married. We're all *single* Reds!"

On the home front, I volunteered to drive the Pete's Market Special to Atlantic City to pick-up seventy-five watermelons on Sunday morning, if I could have Saturday afternoon off. Dad consented to my feasible offer, when I told him that I had some athletic competitions in which to compete against college bound students from Hammonton High School. Pop liked the false idea that I was finally associating with Hammonton college-bound students.

Saturday morning finally arrived. It was a beautiful, seventy-five-degree sunny day. The Reds all organized at Goose's mansion and were all enthused about participating in the First Annual Atsion Lake Olympics Competition. The rivalry appealed to our baser, primitive, survival instincts that dwell deep inside the human psyche.

"The two-group competition sounds like fun," Fabian evaluated and declared. "Pretty clever, a Potato Sack Race, and a cool Crawl-a-Thon. Those Blues are showing a little imagination, and aren't so dumb after all."

"And they're seemin' to become pretty decent kids after all," News added. "I hope there's no hanky-panky later on today."

"Sounds real hep," Jives Arena butted-in. "And no sweat with the twelve cases of brew. We're gonna' get totaled until we mushroom!"

"What the fuck's that big-mouthed jerk-off talkin' about?" Goose asked me. "Doesn't that horse's ass Jives know any damned college words I understand?"

"I think Frankie means we're gonna' drink beer until nighttime," I interpreted. 'Jives once told me that beer actually makes you smarter, because it made Bud wiser."

"Jives, man," Goose commented and snickered. "You've been readin' too many magazines about those asshole beatniks out in California. Why don't ya' just open up a goddamned coffee shop for Puerto Ricans and niggers in downtown Hammonton instead of dreamin' about drinkin' a six-pack of beer with the Reds."

Quickly changing the topic, Juice announced that he was ready to swim across cedar-water Atsion Lake against Speed Mortellite. "All I need to think about is that first cold bottle of *Bud,* and I'll be churnin' and windmillin' my arms and legs like crazy. I feel like I can even beat Tarzan today!"

"News, I still don't trust the Blues after all they've done to us," I considered and stated. "Why do they want a truce right now?"

"Because our rivals finally realize that hate and fightin' doesn't solve problems," Tommy speculated and offered as if he were a United Nations delegate. "And the blueberry advocates now know that violence only creates more problems."

“And besides,” Fabian contributed. “I can’t wait to see the final event between Hoss and Ox Narducci. That’s gonna’ be quite a classic to remember.”

“I still don’t trust those rotten bastards,” Goose concluded and remarked. “Especially with what the *bass-turds* did to my old white T-Bird and to us with the lousy billboard.”

“Ya’ might be right about them seeking revenge,” Juice agreed, “especially after what *you* had done to their huntin’ cabin.”

“Atsion Lake or bust!” I heralded, substituting our destination for Pike’s Peak.

“J.W., since when have ya’ grown tits!” Goose facetiously replied, rendering tit for tat.

Chapter Twenty-Two

"Deceived and Tricked"

Goose drove News Tomasello, Juice Illiani, Fabian Midilli, and me north up *Route 206* heading toward our slated appointment at Atsion Lake. As we passed by peach orchards on the left and blueberry fields on the right, we all felt anxious and nervous. Everyone in the red T-Bird had to shut-up for three solid minutes when G.R. turned the radio dial and found "Rock around the Clock" on W-ABC out of New York. But after the revered "National Anthem" ended, a momentary silence prevailed.

I looked behind from the front seat and saw Jives Arena's Dodge Coronet with five "Reds' gang brothers", and Frankie was trailed by four other Reds' cars, forming a neat caravan. 'All twenty-four of us are making the trip,' I observed.

Goose asked News to fill him in on some current events. A bit of trivial conversation would cut the emotional tension that filled the suddenly quiet red T-Bird.

"Well, guys," Tomasello began his standard line. "As ya' might know, Venetian Way won the 86th Kentucky Derby last Saturday with a time of 2:02 and two-fifth seconds. Bill Hartack was the winning jockey."

"Before Hartack was a jockey," I interrupted to honor my recollection of Bo Jalonec, "the midget was a featherweight fighter. That's when he went from wearin' boxer trunks to jockey shorts."

"Yes, and the horse had Venetian *blinders* on," News skillfully bantered back, obviously irritating our easily annoyed Mafia driver.

"J.W., do ya' stay up all night thinkin' about this stupid shit?" the junior don challenged. "Ya' know Punk, you're a moron waitin' to grow into an idiot." To shut up my drivel, Goose next asked News what else had been happening as documented by reporters in the journalistic world.

"Fellow Reds," my illustrious academic colleague resumed, "on May 10th, the same day that Gabe Gillette authored those two letters, the USS Triton made the first undersea around the world voyage," Tommy related more picayune information. "The Triton is quite probably the first known nuclear submarine."

Goose chided News for only knowing what he read in books and newspapers, or watched on television, or heard on the radio. "Don't ya' know any crap of local interest like in the Hammonton area?"

"Well, guys, we're leaving the northern peach line, which stops at the brim of the Wharton State Forest," T.T. blandly educated. "Peaches do not grow above *that* divide. And also, Hammonton goes way up *206* to where the Wagon Wheel Restaurant is, a full seven-miles north of the White Horse Pike."

"Wow!" I exclaimed in awe. "The town extends south about three miles to the Folsom line, so geographically, that makes Hammonton one of the biggest towns in all of New Jersey."

"I think so," News added, "next to Vineland in total square miles. But I'll have to research those particular facts and get back to ya'."

"That means," Juice elaborated, "that over half the town is in the State Pine Barrens, and that a living legend of the town is.....dun, dun, dun, da!....."

"The Jersey Devil!" the remaining four of us yelled out in sheer amazement.

"The monster is the town's most famous resident. That roving Fuck-head lives most of the time in Hammonton," Goose spontaneously realized and expressed. "What a stupid asshole *he* must be! Just like each of the friggin' fucked-up Blues!"

The red Thunderbird passed by the *Route 206* railroad crossing and turned left onto a sandy road that bordered half the circumference of placid Atsion Lake. The trailing cavalcade of Reds' cars copied our lead, and the picturesque road gently curved around the crescent side of the cedar-water-lake. Soon, we stopped near the deserted lifeguard stand and exited our vehicles.

"Memorial Day, this place will be hoppin'," Juice predicted. "This is just the right time to have the Red and Blue Olympics, right before the summer vacation season begins. The place is abandoned, except for us."

There was no sign of Gabe Gillette and his repugnant Blues anywhere, and that observation got us talking about the prospect of being deceived. But five-minutes later, just before noon, an old blue and white migrant labor bus sputtered-down the dirt road. The ancient vehicle was coming directly toward us.

"What the hell is this all about?" G.R. asked in awe.

"It's the Blues, all comin' to Atsion in a damned Farm Labor Transport bus!" Juice declared. "I think it's now time for me to die, because I believe I've seen everything."

Gabe Gillette and his rich-kid-posse disembarked from their strange means of transportation. The Blues' boss explained that the bus was big enough to accommodate twenty-four members, four axes, four sledgehammers, twenty-four empty burlap potato bags, and twelve cases of cold, freshly-acquired beer. "Ya' gotta' admit," Gillette eloquently and slickly communicated, "it's economical and convenient for us Blues to travel up here all together in one vehicle. It also kinda' allows us to identify with the lowlife Puerto Ricans and Jamaicans that pick our sweet berries every summer for the fresh market."

"Looks like a haul-ass day-haul clunker where dud-ly deadhead cubes could get their funky kicks groovin'," Jives Arena uttered. "That tank is rank."

"What the hell did he say?" Gabe asked News. "That guy with the red French beret is really way out there!"

"Frankie said that *you* arrived in a migrant-labor-day-haul-bus, where non-ambitious farm workers could have most of their fun riding in a vehicle that looks like someone's great-grandfather's dilapidated mode of transportation," Tommy interpreted.

"Oh," Gabe Gillette replied. "I didn't know what the hell that guy was sayin'. He was speakin' Martian or something."

"We don't know what he's utterin' half the time, either," I returned. "It's like a weird kind of code language that Jives speaks," I added. "It's enough to confuse King Arthur, Shakespeare or Queen Elizabeth, that's for sure."

The Blues removed the necessary equipment from the migrant labor bus, and News asked Gillette if he had any fears about being stopped by the police while being a minor illegally transporting twelve cases of beer. The twenty-three Reds listening to the conversation all thought that T.T. had raised a legitimate question that each of us was thinking.

"My Pop has great contacts high up in the state. And since he contributes to the county sheriff's election campaign and controls most of the local politics," Gabe boasted, "anything that says Gillette Blueberry Company on it, like this here bus, has a license to go wherever it wants and do whatever it wants."

Goose saw merit in Gillette's brazen statement, so G.R. told the guys to stop interrogating the Blues' President and help tote the beer cases and the games' equipment to the various pre-planned staging areas. Juice and I each grabbed a case of *Budweiser* and brought the cartons to the beach along Atsion Lake, placing the beer in the vicinity where the first two "Olympic" events would be conducted.

The Blues that were not assigned work responsibilities casually tossed-around *Frisbees,* pretending that the objects were flying saucers from alien planets. Several other idle Blues fooled-around with hula-hoops and fought over a pair of plastic 3-D glasses. After fifteen-minutes of additional preparation, all of the applicable materials were in their right spots, and so Gabe Gillette, sounding and looking like a stern high school gym teacher, blew a coach's whistle to obtain everyone's undivided attention.

“The first event will be the lake swim,” Gillette yelled into a Hammonton High School blue and white cheerleader’s megaphone that the thorough-and-efficient leader had brought along. “Speed Mortellite, in the interest of good sportsmanship, shake hands with you opponent,” Gabe requested.

Speed was already wearing his dark-blue bathing trunks. Johnny Juice Illiani removed his jeans, shirt, undershirt, socks, and shoes. He and Mortellite shook hands and walked to the sandy apron that bordered three sides of Atsion Lake. The two got into diving positions, ready to leap forward upon command.

“Since both of you gentlemen appear to be in excellent physical condition,” Gabe hollered into the megaphone, “you’ll have to swim the lake back and forth from the other shore to right here where we’re now standing,” the charge d’affaires directed. “Any questions? Then may the best man win the event. Ready, set, and go!”

The two champion swimmers dived into the chilly cedar-water-lake, which momentarily stunned their bodies’ energies, because of the water’s initial cold shock. Forty-six guys were yelling and cheering wildly as the champion-class swimmers churned their arms and propelled their bodies through the sixty-degree chilly lake. The competitors each touched land on the opposite side, swirled-around, and then thrashed their way back in our direction.

After the midway point of the return lap, the spectators were leaping and whooping in a wild frenzy, screaming, jumping, yelling encouragement, and many were enjoying their last few months of high school adolescence before enduring college rigors in September. The Blues were amazed that Juice was staying with Mortellite, who was the Atlantic County high school long-distance swimming champion. Much to their surprise, Johnny reached the shore at the exact time as Mortellite. A timekeeper’s stopwatch would have indicated a draw if one had been available.

“That was some contest!” Gabe Gillette genuinely gushed in an astonished voice. “Your guy almost beat Speed, who’s the best damned high school swimmer in our county. Congratulations go to both participants. Dry off, and then join the crowd in chuggin’ down two cases of beer.”

News, Goose, Jives, Fabian, Hoss, Little Joe, and I drank our *Budweisers,* but did not fraternize with the opposition. Balls Giordano and Herc Juliano did some kibitzing with Pee Wee Lucca, asking the neurotic runt why *he* was wearing casts on his forearms, but the chiders obtained no plausible explanation from the ‘Neanderthal boy’. We had a five-minute intermission to imbibe our beers and to return the empty brown bottles to their respective cardboard cases.

The second contest on the agenda, the Ball-Breaking competition was a real hum-dinger. Ollie Giordano and Butch Lanza were pounding-away with their sledgehammers, acting as if the rivals were a pair of human wrecking balls. Then, Balls went berserk and started hitting on Lanza's rock, and Butch saw merit in the mania and began smashing his sledgehammer against Giordano's boulder, and the event wound-up in a tie with both contestants effectively "breaking each other's balls".

During the second socializing session, there was a little more mingling between the Blues and the Reds, and perhaps it was because of the delicious flavors of the *Budweiser* and the *Pabst Blue Ribbon.* The two factions mildly integrated and interacted, and for the most part, the Blues and the Reds were pleasant and accommodating to each other, despite our former differences and misunderstandings.

The third event in the Atsion Lake Olympics was the hundred-yard' Crawl-a-Thon. I wound-up on Little Joe Gregorio's back. The chaotic race was a mad rush akin to the original Sooners charging into Oklahoma, but the forty-eight wacky participants were not in covered wagons or mounted on horses. This was a fun event and actually, not designed for serious competition. We all seemed to crash into one another like a stampeding herd of wild buffaloes smashing into a stone wall, falling and rolling all over the ground, in a scene of orderly civility gone amok.

As we imbibed our third bottles of beer, our normal inhibitions had loosened-up, and some of the Blues were becoming fairly chummy with a few of the Reds, and vice-versa. I struck-up a civil conversation with Bull Martello, and the HHS brute seemed to be an all-right kid once his tough-guy-façade had been cracked-open. Bull even enjoyed several of my ridiculous puns, and said that I had potential as a stand-up "*Steel Pier* comedian". The tasty beers were definitely having an impact in breaking the ice between the two gangs, and promoting peace on earth and good will toward teens.

The finish line for the hundred-yard Crawl-a-Thon had been two gigantic oak trees, and those stately objects were the focuses of Olympic event number four. Axes were distributed to Reds' Little Joe Gregorio and to Dave "Herc" Juliano, and also to Blues' Dan "the Hammer" Bertino and Mack "the Bull" Martello. I was almost inclined to root for Bull Martello because the jock had seemed like a decent kid when I had been conversing with him after the previous Crawl-a-Thon fiasco.

The four hackers pursued their objectives like veritable Paul Bunyans, ripping into both sides of the twin oak trees' barks, as if their axes were power saws. In ten-minutes, Little Joe and Herc's tall oak toppled-over to the ground, and the two Reds' lumberjacks emerged victorious in their quest for greaser glory. Even the Blues that were witnesses to the spectacle cheered the two Reds' mighty dominance during *their* fantastic exploit.

The forty-eight gang members congregated around the two new cases of beer and discussed the upcoming three-hundred-yard Potato Sack Race along with the highly anticipated Arm-Wrestling spectacular, scheduled between Hoss Gregorio and Ox Narducci. The two monsters were ignoring each other, despite all of the general conviviality occurring between the Reds and the Blues.

"I wouldn't be surprised if Hoss defeats Ox," Gabe Gillette confided to Goose. "Your guy's even bigger than that dude on *Bonanza* that he's named after."

"Oxen are usually bigger and stronger than horses are," News Tomasello interrupted with some scientific justification.

"Who asked your friggin' opinion?" Restuccio answered News in his typical sarcastic staccato. "Flake off with the ox-shit, er, I mean bullshit, will ya'!"

"Leave the poor kid alone, Goose," Speed Mortellite laughed as the charlatan put his arm around his former enemy. "He's just tryin' to pull your damned chain, rattle your damned cage, that's all!"

The fourth beers were making us all silly, groggy, and giddy, and being borderline inebriated, the Blues and Reds were behaving like we were long-lost fraternity brothers celebrating at a college reunion. Butch Lanza confided to me that he was greatly looking forward to the imminent arm-wrestling saga, but was half-wishing that Hoss would beat Ox, because Lanza and Narducci both liked and dated the same Hammonton High sweetheart.

"It's gonna' be a close hum-dinger," I predicted, "and Butch, don't be surprised if it's still goin' on when the moon comes up." I had never spoken to Lanza before, and now the two of us were all of a sudden blood brothers, acting so compatible that we would almost go to war for one another.

"Ya' ain't that bad a Turk after all," Butch informed as the young long-haired Samson gave me a mild pat on the back. "I have a feelin' we're gonna' be good friends someday."

"Great," I courteously answered. "You can teach me how to grow blueberries."

The five-minute pause elapsed, and soon it was time for the zany Potato Sack Race. Fabian Midilli selected me as his partner, and after we confiscated a burlap sack, I placed my right foot in the sack and Sal inserted his left. Two identical trails jutted into that section of the Wharton Forest, meeting again several-hundred-yards into the interior, where the next two cases of beer had been deposited for future consumption.

Gabe Gillette again blew his whistle like a strict football coach and took charge at the drawn-in-the-sand starting line. And all I could think about was guzzling-down my fifth bottle of *Bud* and enjoying more socializing with my new Hammonton High friends. I was nearly intoxicated, and so was everyone else in my company. The gangs' former enmity for the Blues was rapidly transforming into a mutual admiration society.

I was not too motivated to win the Potato Sack Race, so Fabian and I took it easy from the outset. Several hundred yards was a considerable distance to hop, and under the circumstances, there wasn't any trophy, award, or cash stakes involved, Sal and I simply frolicked-along the designated route, giggling, goofing-off, and lagging behind, like a pair of silly kindergarten kids.

"I think this is the most fun I've ever had," Fabian confessed and related. "I can't wait until next year's Second Annual Atsion Lake Olympics."

"You said it, this event is really hopping," I cackled like a real funny bunny or leaping lizard. "We oughta' do this at the next Edgewood *hop!"*

"I'd hate to have you and that Bo Jalonec kid in the same college dorm' room as me," Sal joshed, "or I might consider committin' suicide as a viable option."

Our merriment was interrupted by plenty of shouting originating up ahead. As Fabian and I approached the finish line, we both quickly sobered-up. With our legs still inside the burlap potato sack, our heads ducked-down, and we hid behind a wide oak tree to eavesdrop on distant conversations. My senses immediately went from numb to keen in a real hurry.

Two state forest rangers and a half-dozen state troopers had guns drawn, and the twenty-two Reds wearing their James Dean' jackets were observed leaning against pine trees. "They're bein' frisked?" Fabian whispered. "What's goin' on?"

"Okay, turn-around," one of the troopers ordered Goose.

"What's the rap?" Restuccio inquired.

"You're all bein' taken into custody for trespassin' on state property; for not havin' camping permits; for drinkin' beer and being intoxicated, and for destroyin' valuable state property," a second trooper informed.

"What valuable state property?" G.R. demanded. "This place was a dump when we got here!"

"Those two magnificent oak trees you idiots chopped-down over near the lake," the first game warden accused and revealed. "They're both historic treasures. Been there since the time of the *American Revolutionary War!"*

"Where are the Blues?" Restuccio insisted on knowing.

"The Blues?" a third trooper asked. "What are the Blues besides black jazz music from New Orleans?"

"Kids from Hammonton," Goose replied and explained.

"Sorry, but you're the only culprits in these woods, whether you're from Hammonton or not," the first austere trooper retorted. "We'll search the entire area and find that out soon enough."

"We've been set-up!" Goose exclaimed in heightened anger. "Set-up for a big embarrassin' fall by those damned Blues. And to think that I trusted those two-faced punks!"

I tacitly motioned to Fabian that we should crawl-out of danger to avoid being arrested. My good pal fathomed my intent right away, and after removing our legs from the cumbersome burlap sack, we slowly crawled like infants for a hundred-feet or so. Next, Sal and I stood and then rapidly sprinted to the vicinity of Atsion Lake.

Midilli and I heard a motor coming from around the crescent bend in the dirt road. It was the blue and white Farm Labor Transport Bus, heading directly toward Fabian and me. We froze like petrified deer being blinded by headlights. I could feel my legs shaking, my knees knocking, and my hands and lips quivering.

The bus halted, and I was ready to hit, scratch, punch and claw as many Blues as I possibly could. The swivel door opened, and I saw Gabe Gillette sitting in the driver's seat, laughing his buttocks off at the colossal prank the Blues had just masterminded. I foolishly leaped into the bus to grab the conniver by the throat, and choke his despicable tonsils and larynx out. The next thing I knew, Butch Lanza and Ox Narducci had collared me, and Bull Martello and Hammer Bertino had leaped outside the bus and were violently wrestling Fabian Midilli to the sandy ground. The two muscle-bound Goliaths finally subdued my frisky, exhausted friend.

"Welcome to the magical blueberry tour," Gabe shrieked-out before closing the bus door. "I hope you enjoyed the fabulous Atsion Lake Olympics as much as we did. Right boys!" the HHS bully shouted to his subordinates seated behind us.

"Right, boss!" his underlings bellowed like coaxed parrots.

For the whole seven-mile excursion south to downtown Hammonton, Ox Narducci had my neck wringed in a vice-like headlock, and Hammer Bertino had Fabian knotted-up in a painful full nelson. I was vaguely aware of the migrant labor bus crossing the

White Horse Pike, where *Highway 206* converts into *Route 54*. Then, I was cognizant of Gillette driving the unlicensed migrant labor transport through the center of town. The driver next turned right at Bellevue, onto Egg Harbor Road.

Gabe Gillette halted the bus at Vet's Bakery, and soon made a fast left onto Fairview Avenue. The out-of-place vehicle crossed the railroad tracks, and Gillette again jammed on the brakes.

"We gotta' move fast!" the Blues leader commanded. "Let's do it in two-minutes like we practiced. Pee Wee, you go outside and ya' can be our lookout. Direct traffic if any cars pass by, even though you can't raise your hands!"

In a matter of two-minutes, the Blues had dragged Fabian and me off the bus; knocked us to the asphalt; tied our hands behind our backs with thick electrical cords; hoisted us up onto the railroad gates, and tied us crucifixion-style to the vertical railroad posts.

"What the hell are ya' doin'?" Fabian screamed like a Banshee. "You psycho guys are even crazier than Goose Restuccio!"

"Those railroad gates might just as well be the gates of hell!" Gillette shouted from the bus's driver's seat. "Those gates are the only things that don't stop at railroad crossings! They rise to the occasion! Ha, ha, ha, ha!"

The blues all scurried back to their farm labor bus. I noticed that the pranksters had been carrying folding, collapsible stepladders, which enabled Ox, Hammer, Butch, and Bull to hoist Fabian and me up and tether us to the vertical crossing gates.

"Suckers! Idiots! Stupid shit-heads!" the Blues yelled from their opened windows as the blue and white bus pulled-away in first gear.

"Now what!" Fabian moaned, almost sobbing. "Goose's right. Ya' can't trust any damned Blue for anything."

"Ya' know, Sal," I grieved, my feet being suspended six-feet above the nearby tracks. "These are the same railroad tracks Grandpa Tony used to take me to see the freight trains rumble through town at three-thirty in the morning when I was a little tot."

"How old were you then?" he asked.

"About four or five," I lamented and answered. "Do ya' think anybody's gonna' notice us hangin' up here?"

"Maybe. They'll probably think it's some kind of college fraternity stunt, or somethin' stupid like that, and call the cops to come and get us down," Sal returned, looking much like one of the prisoners hanging on a separate cross with Christ at Calvary. "Say J.W., do ya' hear somethin' makin' noise in the distance?"

"Sure do, Jesus! It's the late afternoon freight train comin' through town."

Before any other words could be exchanged, red flashing lights were blinking, and the dual gates were descending from their vertical into their horizontal positions. Loud bells and shrill locomotive whistles were instantly discerned. I closed my eyes when the powerful locomotive went zipping by, its strong gust causing a vacuum that almost ripped me off of my horizontal railroad gate. All in all, my mind counted seventy-five freight cars, including the red caboose.

The bells clanged briefly, and then the red lights stopped flashing. The gates ascended again to their familiar vertical positions, with Sal and me still very much attached to them.

Automobiles approached from both directions, and the drivers simply stopped and gaped at the extraordinary sights. Then, an old peach farmer in a red pick-up applied his brakes. The elderly gent got-out and flagged-down a rusty, dirty black '47 Plymouth that was sputtering and passing by the Fairview Avenue railroad crossing. Incredibly, out jumped Dennis Measley to the rescue.

The elderly farmer had an old, wooden, peach tree picking-ladder lying in the rear of his half-ton. Dennis climbed-up the rungs, and using his trusty penknife, the valiant rescuer first liberated Fabian from his tethered predicament. The ladder was moved to the twin railroad gate, and then Measley freed me from my bonds.

"What happened to you guys?" Dennis asked, all out of breath.

"It's a long story," I panted, "but some nasty rotten apple throwers captured us, and showed that the pond scum know how to do other dirty stuff, besides chucking apples at innocent wooden houses."

Chapter Twenty-Three

"Anchors Aweigh, Bombs Away"

Dennis Measley drove Sal Midilli and me home in his archaic Plymouth jalopy. Fabian and I were glad we hadn't been arrested in the state police and forest ranger raid at Atsion Lake, but we were concerned about the others Reds' fate, and also about the future retribution and violence that were certain to occur against the Blues. I thanked Dennis and said "good night" to Sal. I walked up the front steps, and slowly entered the family's house, acting like the extraordinary Atsion Lake Olympics had occurred as part of just another ordinary day.

"How was the party with your new friends?" Mom asked. "Did you get to meet some new people?"

"Sure did," I fibbed. "It was quite an excitin' experience."

"Don't forget," Pop reminded. "You have to go to Atlantic City tomorrow and pick-up some more melons. Those Congos are big sellers at the market."

"Okay, I'm gonna' take a shower and rest up for tomorrow," I replied, really meaning 'I desperately need to rest-up from today.'

At nine the next morning, I received a phone call from vitriolic Goose Restuccio, who was still more than livid about being deceived and hoodwinked by cunning Gabe Gillette and the vindictive Blues. G.R. wanted to talk to me about "war strategy", so I offered to pick him up and drive the avenger to Atlantic City and get the needed load of watermelons. I steered the Pete's Market Special into his driveway at eleven a.m. I figured G.R. was infuriated that the future don had been fooled when the prankster normally cherished the role of being the one who did the fooling. The guy was fit to be tied.

"What happened to you and Fabian yesterday?" G.R. asked right before the incensed neurotic entered the cab. "I still haven't cooled-down yet from what the hell happened to me."

I explained all that had occurred; how Sal and I had narrowly escaped from being taken into custody by law enforcement authorities; I next depicted how our subsequent apprehension by the Blues had happened, and how our nightmare migrant labor bus trip down *206* to Hammonton had transpired. And finally, I revealed our symbolic dual crucifixions on the Fairview Avenue railroad gates. "Goose, what happened to you and the other guys?"

My passenger told me that the state troopers escorted the Reds in their five vehicles south on *206,* which formed a procession, and our gang followed the fuzz to the Hammonton Barracks. The game wardens rode behind the caravan in their jeep, making sure no Reds' cars broke rank and fled from the arresting state cops.

Everyone had been detained for three-hours at "the clinic", where Goose made a few vital phone calls to his father and to his father's criminal lawyer, and when the cops realized who and what they were up against, the state troopers eased-up on their rhetoric and released everyone, especially after G.R. had implicated the Blues in the disasterous Atsion Lake episode. The investigators wanted to keep the recent conflict a "minor difference of opinion" between the Reds and the Blues, and not five the arrests proliferate into an economic battle between Mafia gangsters and small-town farming millionaires.

"My Pop agreed to pay two-thousand-bucks and get everybody off the hook with all charges dropped," Goose related. "Now if I wasn't involved, News, Juice, Jives, Hoss, Little Joe, Balls, Herc, and the rest of the Reds would still be sittin' in the goddamned clinic bein' interrogated by a bunch of young, green, do-gooder state cops lookin' for crimes in order to be promoted."

"Too bad the forest rangers didn't turn-out to be Frankie Fingers and Joe Zucchini," I answered in a weak attempt to make Goose forget his need for 'sour revenge'. "And why did ya' have to pay two thousand *bucks* when you were arrested by state police, and not by female deer? Two thousand *bucks* is a lot of *doe*."

"Are you some kind of goddamned alien comedian from some other cunt-lappin' solar system?" G.R. ranted. "You musta' been born in a test tube on Planet Asshole or on Planet Retard, or some other shittin' asteroid like that!"

On the drive to Atlantic City, Goose disclosed that he didn't at all relish being tricked by Gabe Gillette, and that G.R. was planning to get even with the wily rich kid and his formidable "Blueberry Hill posse". I listened to the distraught maniac's goals and objectives very carefully, because I too was developing plenty of animosity towards our lecherous, bellicose enemies.

"Ya' know, J.W.," Goose said to me at the *Route 30* Elwood light. "I'm the one who calls the shots in my life, and not that rich jerk-off faggot, Gabe Gillette. I mean, I gotta' work for what the hell I got, bustin' my ass cleanin' out and restockin' candy and gum ball machines all over South Jersey," G.R. prattled. "I know the value of hard work, and I ain't shittin' spoiled like that bastard Gillette is. He's mung from the word go."

"Then, yesterday at Atsion Lake, there must've been a fungus a *mung* us!" I quite naturally jested.

"Get double-bent so that ya' then got a z-shaped dick to piss out of!" Restuccio rankled. "I'd have ya' assassinated by Frankie or Zuck if ya' wasn't so goddamned funny!"

I asked Restuccio if 'the avenger' had been scheming any particular shenanigans to soon play on the atrocious Blues. I learned that Frankie Fingers and Joe Zucchini had been dispatched on an important tactical mission to pilfer fifty bowling balls from Di Donato's Bowling Alley.

"Goose, I used to play Little League baseball for Di Donato's Bowling when I was ten-years-old," I gasped and objected. "And now I'm suddenly involved in a criminal theft against 'em. What are ya' gonna' do with fifty more bowlin' balls? Give them to Balls Giordano to break with a massive sledgehammer?" I challenged. "What about the hundred-ninety-nine bowlin' balls ya' still have sittin' on the racks inside your white box-truck?" I asked, just as we were coincidentally passing by Egg Harbor Lanes.

Goose heard Bill Haley and the Comets playing "Rock around the Clock" above the static on my truck radio, so instinctively, my rider yelled at me to "shut the fuck up during the National Anthem"!

"Now then," G.R. continued turning down the radio's volume. "I legally bought the hundred-ninety-nine bowlin' balls we already got, so that leaves us with the fifty DiDonato balls that are gonna' be stolen tonight. That's where you come in, J.W.," Goose emphasized. "Ya' gotta' think of a way to get those damned Blues in trouble with *all* the bowlin' balls."

I related to Goose how the Diablos had gotten the Kamikazes into trouble with the police by planting purloined goods in the Ks cars. I next disclosed that I would simply use the vast knowledge I had acquired from my Levittown "grand larceny" experiences, and skillfully transfer that sage wisdom to my dealings with the insidious Blues in Hammonton. "No sweat!" I informed my supportive colleague. "Don't worry, I know exactly how we have to take care of Gabe Gillette. He hasn't seen a schemin' expert until he goes up against me," I haughtily boasted. 'The fact is, bowlin' happens to be right up my alley."

"J.W., you're as cool as a lady Eskimo just wearin' a jock strap and a frozen used rubber on her clit on New Year's Day at the North Pole," G.R. simultaneously complimented and busted on me. "I'm callin' a bitchin' Reds' emergency meeting tomorrow night at my house. I expect twenty-four guys to be there. No excuses will be *excepted!* And J.W., ya' oughta' have this damned blue truck painted red! It looks like it belongs to the shit-fartin' enemy."

I steered the Pete's Market Special into the *Route 30* Atlantic City Food Distribution Center. I drove-around until my eyes located the

Fischer and Santelli Commission House. I backed-up the truck to load the seventy-five-green and black-striped Congo melons into the rear cargo compartment. Goose and I hopped-out of the cab to supervise the loading.

"Who do ya' guys think you are?" a commission house salesman greeted us. "James Dean?" the produce wholesaler commented with a grin, referring to our red zip-up jackets.

"Just get the damned melons loaded and cut the stupid bullshit," Goose snottily answered, "or we'll buy our damned watermelons from the hawker next door! We're here with this pick-up to pick-up seventy-five melons. That's why the friggin' truck is called a damned pick-up!" Restuccio inadvertently made a cute witticism.

The stunned salesman's smirk quickly transformed itself' into a grimace. 'Mr. Santelli', according to the I.D. on his badge, directed two black laborers to get busy on the watermelon loading detail right away. It really intrigued me how G.R.'s gruff, surly, crude demeanor yielded more immediate and satisfactory results than did my courteous and considerate approach to other human beings. His callous methods were much more effective than mine.

"Here's two five-dollar Jeffersons for your work," Goose said, handing the indigent black men their surprise bonuses. "Don't spend it all on watermelons! And save a little to buy yourselves some fatback and greens; grits; chitlins; Aunt Jemima pancakes, and some Uncle Ben's Converted Rice, which just changed their religion."

Instead of acting insulted at the venomous, racial, put-down stereotypes, the pair of black men gratefully smiled at us, showing piano-key ivory teeth, and each laborer personally thanked Goose for his magnanimous generosity. I raised the tailgate and inspected the mound of melons, making sure that the Congos had all been securely stacked. Then, my companion and I re-entered the blue, half-ton pick-up, and I gingerly maneuvered the Pete's Market Special out of the parking area, heading west onto the White Horse Pike.

I was telling Goose all about how the Diablos had spent Labor Day 1959 walking the famous Atlantic City Boardwalk and playing games of chance on the Million Dollar Pier and on the Steel Pier, right before the great blueberry farm drag race happened between Quinn and Cummings. G.R. seemed totally apathetic toward my past Diablos' adventure. We were approaching *the Route 30* bridge that served as a short causeway over the Atlantic City Canal, which was a part of the Inter-Coastal Waterway. Restuccio alertly spotted something familiar floating on the water, passing under the bridge.

"Stop the truck! Stop the goddamned fuckin' truck right now!" the madman screamed like a Bedlam patient in need of a second straightjacket.

I did as my incensed passenger commanded, and G.R. frenetically leaped-out of the cab. The possessed lunatic ran to the rear, and to my confounded confusion, the maniac selected two rotund Congos, and then dropped the first and then hurled the second watermelon onto the deck of an expensive blue and white cabin cruiser that was gently passing under the Route 30 bridge.

Then, my warped companion reached into his red jacket's pocket, found an explosive device, lit it with a match, and threw the sizzling-fused cherry bomb onto the cabin cruiser's deck. Male and female shrieks and screams could be heard, as pure panic set in on the sleek boat. Restuccio rushed back to the cab; quickly hurtled his body inside, and forcefully slammed the passenger door shut.

"What's goin' on!" I hollered in a rare display of lost self-control. "What was that craziness all about? If you thought that *that* small yacht going under the bridge was the *Caracas* again, then I say that you need some serious eye surgery, or maybe a new set of eyeballs!"

"That blue and white cabin cruiser belongs to Gabe Gillette," Goose divulged to me. "I would recognize that royal piece of shit anywhere. The Blues all keep their fancy boats up at Chestnut Neck Marina, over on the bay, near the Mullica River. That's about eight-miles north of here. Gillette's probably just out pleasure cruisin' with some rich bitches when I spotted and nailed his ass."

"But the explosion, and the watermelons!" I gasped as I shifted into second gear. "How do ya' know it wasn't his mother and father aboard the boat instead of him!"

"Because I saw only Hammonton High kids drinkin' beer, a couple Blues and their girlfriends," Goose answered. "One of the chicks, I think, was Joanne Berenato from Edgewood!"

"You're full of crap!" I screamed at the infamous demented delinquent. "Her strict father hardly even lets her go to the Hammonton Canteen Dances on Friday and Saturday night!"

"Only kiddin' ya', J.W., so don't get your bowels in an uproar," Goose laughed, just after creating a crisis situation in some other people's lives. "I always keep a couple of cherry bombs around for protection," the frightening, destructive, teen psycho continued. "I had left the one I just used home yesterday, and forgot to take it to Atsion Lake. Before we graduate, I'm thinkin' about blowin' up the toilets in the upstairs M-Wing Boys Bathroom at Edgewood."

"That was a blessing that you didn't kill anyone on the boat," I said with relief. "You were lucky!"

"That's right," G.R. admitted without remorse. "I was lucky to have the bomb with me today. I musta' walked in horseshit this mornin'. That mother jumpin' cabin cruiser hit the side of the bridge after the cherry bomb blast went off. I say the small yacht's been totaled, maybe fifty G's damage, at the very least. And guess what?" Goose rhetorically added. "Gillette was wearin' one of those ugly blue and white Boatneck shirts! Just wait 'til I tell Jives Arena *that* crazy shit!"

I was afraid that I had involuntarily become an accomplice to a major felony crime, and that a jail cell would be my future residence instead of a comfortable college dormitory room. My unstable traveling associate had a slightly different perspective of reality.

"It's just ordinary damage that an insurance company will pay for," Goose casually maintained. "And Gillette's not gonna' report the incident to anybody out on the street. If Gabe tells his rich Pop, he'll be botherin' the Mafia kingpin with his trivial chicken-shit, and old man Gillette will take it out on his kid for annoying his ass."

"What about a police report?" I stammered. "Ya' need one to collect insurance, don't ya'!"

"That's right," Goose acknowledged. "But Gabe Gillette will lie and say that the bridge crash was an accident. He wasn't payin' attention, or he was friggin' distracted by the on-board chicks' big tits, or some dumb-shit lame excuse like that," G.R. elaborated. "Gilette's not gonna' rat to the cops on us, because he'll want to personally settle matters with me without the po-po's outside help, just to show his Blues he doesn't need the fuzz to solve his problems. Get it? Real leaders don't need outside help, or they wouldn't be *cape-able* leaders, just like Batman and Superman in the comic books are."

"But you almost killed your rival and everybody else on that boat!" I argued. "Forget homicide. It was almost genocide."

"*Almost* only counts with gutless people that always fail," G.R. defensively stated. "News told me the other day that a shittin' asteroid *almost* collided with the earth. Well, it didn't. We're all still fuckin' alive. Gabe Gillette is still alive. *Almost* is a goddamned word for losers. That's all the hell it is! People that got brass balls never use *that* goddamned word!"

Goose demanded that I stop at White Way Farm Market, an Egg Harbor business similar to my parents' new place in Elm. Its landmark feature was a huge ten-foot-high chicken figure, roosting on top of the farm stand's front roof. The business's proprietor was shocked when Goose paid the gent twelve-dollars for two Congo watermelons, since we already had seventy-three twenty-five-pound "stripers" pyramided on the back of a truck that belonged to a *Route 30* competitor's farm market.

"That old White Way chicken-man is still scratchin' his bald-head," Goose related after producing an extended giggle. "I'll bet he's gonna' go to his liquor cabinet to see if he's already polished-off a bottle of booze before comin' outside again. Or, if the guy didn't already chug heavily outa' the damned whiskey bottle, then the drunk idiot might think he just saw a shit-eatin' mirage, a watermelon hallucination, or somethin' else fucked-up like that."

"You like getting shocked reactions out of people, don't ya'!" I assessed and accused. "What if that poor old man goes into the house, sees his liquor bottle still full, and then has a serious heart attack and dies."

"That old coot's too dumb to know it now, but he's better off dead than alive," Goose assured me. "Dead people don't feel no pain or sufferin' 'cause they're dead. It's that freakin' simple!"

I pulled into Pete's Market and G.R. helped Pop and me unload the seventy-five melons. Goose was laying it on thick, lying to Dad about how *he* amply loved hard, physical labor. Next, Restuccio falsely stated that he deeply appreciated the fact that I had allowed him to tag-along and help load and unload the melons. Goose was professing to love the cherished Protestant hard-work ethic, which I instinctively knew the lazy kid absolutely despised with a passion.

"I can't wait for Jersey cantaloupe season in order to do some decent exercisin'," Restuccio prevaricated. "Then, I could go with J.W. and fit five-hundred of them on the back of this here truck."

"You really enjoy workin' then, don't ya'?" Dad asked.

"That's what made this country great," Goose imaginatively fibbed, "and we're just helpin' to make it greater."

I felt like throwing-up after hearing the duplicitous series of devious falsehoods. Pop asked me to go into the kitchen for a private conversation. I shuddered, thinking that my parent had found-out about me failing trigonometry, and about my having to go to summer school in Haddonfield during the height of the farm market season. My heart was palpitating, and my forehead was beginning to sweat. I was surprised to note that Pop's facial expression was not as grim as I thought it would be.

"I want to talk to you, son."

"Yes, Pop," I fearfully answered.

"That Goose Restuccio fella'," Dad prefaced. "At first, I had thought he was a lazy, spoiled wise-guy, Sicilian brat. But now, I think he's a good, decent kid having fine work habits. It just goes to show that ya' always can't trust your first impression. Understand what I'm saying?"

"Yes, Sir," I formally and respectfully replied. "Looks can often fool ya', that's for sure."

Chapter Twenty-Four

"Bowlarama Madness"

The following evening at seven-thirty p.m. Goose held a big strategy meeting in his fabulous club basement. His folks were on a ten-day vacation out to Las Vegas, so the Reds had the whole place to ourselves. News and I were assigned bartenders, serving everybody shots of high octane *Seagrams 7, Old Grand Dad, Jack Daniel's, Southern Comfort* and *Canadian Club* before the big powwow commenced. All twenty-four Reds showed-up, sporting their James Dean *Rebel without a Cause* red haberdashery.

"Where's Moses?" I asked News at seven p.m. while pouring a triple-shot of *Jack Daniel's* for Hoss Gregorio, who insisted on drinking out of a dirty glass.

"Moses must be lookin' for *two* cold *tablets* up on Mt. *Sinus*," News double punned. "Why do ya' ask?"

"Because it looks like the Red Sea in here," I joked, referring to the two-dozen James Dean jackets.

Hoss gulped-down his triple-snort of Kentucky whiskey and aptly declared, "I'm gettin' to know *Jack Daniel's* pretty damned good, so J.W., kindly pour me another generous swig so I can get to know *him* even better."

The three of us laughed rather indulgently, since News and I had already sampled a few jiggers of the potent firewater ourselves. Ollie Balls Giordano and Dave Herc Juliano were feeling no pain as well as Little Joe Gregorio and Jives Arena. The guys were being converted from beer drinkers to hard liquor aficionados in a hurry.

"We should be musical instruments, because we're all gettin' tuned," Little Joe told me, standing at Goose's plush club basement bar. "Give me another double-blast of *Seagram's Seven.* This stuff's so powerful that I don't even remember the other six or seven bein' chugged."

"This hot gas moonshine sends me out there in orbit in the late sunshine!" Jives Arena indicated as the gang's beatnik imbibed another shot of *Old Grand Dad.* "This sweet juice is rocket-fuel, baby, and the booze has got me flyin' and skyin', and that's no lyin' or sighin'!"

News was telling me that the Southern Baptist Convention recently held in Miami Beach took the position that Roman Catholics should not be elected to high government office because the religious zealots wouldn't be able to separate strict church dogma from national political issues.

"Well, News," my voice boomed above the din while pouring shots, "if the Baptists don't want Roman Catholics, the river-dunkers must want in office Catholics that don't move around that much. The bigots with big guts must want stationary Catholics in high political offices, instead of roamin' Catholics."

Goose Restuccio's distorted ears were eavesdropping on our intellectual conversation and the opinionated Sicilian became a "butt-in-ski". "*Dog*ma!" he bellowed. "I can understand that word because God spelled backwards is dog. That's why whatever the Pope says is *dog* crap, soundin' like it came straight from your *ma!*"

"You should go to church more often," I teased Goose while pouring the lush another double-shot of *Southern Comfort*. "Maybe you could even mix whiskeys and drink *Jack Comforts* or *Southern Daniels,* too! Then ya' might learn how to pun half as good as News and me."

"J.W.," Restuccio slurred, "the next time ya' go to church just take the time to look at all the people prayin' around ya'. Then ask yourself if you'd like to spend the rest of eternity with those fake holier-than-thou assholes," G.R. pontificated. "Then look at the other half of the congregation and you'll see nothin' but bankers that'll take your house away tomorrow, if the creeps could foreclose on your mortgage. You'll also notice devout whores and sluts, and you'll also see a lot of envious shit-heads that would steal *your* eyes right from their sockets if the crooks could, just so *they* would be able to see better. And then the asshole kneelin' in front of you starts fartin', and then you realize why the wood benches are called pews!"

G.R.'s speech got quite a jolly response from the Reds assembled at the bar. News and I ignored the general braggadocio and continued our compatible repartee.

"Alan Freed's gonna' be charged by the government for acceptin' Payola," News related. "I read where the cops are gonna' get him on charges of commercial bribery. That guy's doomed."

"Even though it's late spring," I observed and verbalized, "Alan Freed's still gonna' be the *fall* guy for rock and roll."

"J.W., you really crack me up!" Goose enviously exclaimed for everybody's ears within hearing distance. "If I was a vase or a glass, I'd be fuckin' shattered by now!"

G.R. stepped-over to his own private jukebox and pressed down two keys. "Rock around the Clock" loudly started-up, and the two-dozen Reds all knew that the song was our default "National Anthem", and even though half-inebriated, we all stood quietly and respectfully at attention staring at the jukebox as if it were a tabernacle containing the American flag on the Fourth of July.

When the all-too-familiar song ended, Goose held his hands up to retain the silence and asked me to step forward and describe exactly how the Reds could implement fifty stolen DiDonato's Lanes bowling balls to successfully torment and aggravate the HHS Blues.

I came to the forefront and nervously reviewed how the Diablos had set-up the ruthless Kamikazes back in Levittown by using stealth and savvy. The Diablos had raided a police station; planted marijuana and pornography in the trunks of the Ks cars, and my gang had mischievously committed a series of minor crimes that made our avowed Kenwood enemies appear to be the guilty culprits in the eyes of the law.

"What other materials are we gonna' need besides bowlin' balls?" Juice asked. "Maybe some rope, if we're gonna' tie the Blues to railroad crossin' gates."

I waited for all of the laughter to subside. "Halloween masks, blue denim jackets, and we'll also need the services of a master lock-picker like Tinker was my pal with the Diablos," I answered.

"Don't worry, guys," Goose promised. "I'll make a special trip to the Berlin Auction, use some petty cash, and buy twenty-four identical Halloween masks and two dozen blue denim jackets. Those goddamned Blues are gonna' pay the price for givin' us all royal enemas over at Atsion Lake, and then hangin' Fabian and J.W. from the Fairview Avenue railroad gates. Let's give 'em all the big royal salami! What do ya' jerk-offs say?"

"Yeah! The big shafteroo!" News yelled and laughed. "Usually guys get suspended from school, but that damned J.W. and that stupid-assed Sal were suspended from railroad gates!" Tommy indulgently laughed.

The other intoxicated Reds thought that News' remark was humorous, but Fabian and I didn't. Goose was becoming such a bad influence on Tommy that I feared T.T. would soon take-up serious cursing instead of spieling current events as his primary interest.

"Okay," Goose orally concluded. "J.W.'s plan against the dip-shit Blues goes into action next Saturday night after midnight. I'll have all the stuff we'll need early in the week, and distributed to our different commando' squads by Friday. All in favor say 'Aye'!"

The Reds' decision was both democratic and unanimous. The following Saturday night, my imaginative scheme was going to be fully implemented. The "peach platoons" were determined to "even the score" against the dastardly Blues.

"Won't the Hammonton cops stick up for Gillette?" I asked Goose after the official planning conference had broken-up. "That's his territory, and his rich Pop has a lot of clout over there."

"J.W., the damned cops won't know what the hell to do except maybe scratch their fat asses with razor blades," G.R. stated rather confidently. "When the fire sirens go off in town, the dumb-assed cops gotta' hustle to a friggin' phone booth; fumble for a goddamned dime to call City Hall, just to find out what's happenin' in their dinky one-horse town."

"Yeah, but that's for the foot patrolmen walkin' the beat," I agreed and confirmed. "But what about the cops in patrol cars that have two-way radios?"

"J.W., we're gonna' have the fuzz so confused they'll all wish they'd been killed in *World War II!"* G.R. argued. "If Quinn and the Diablos ever hear about what mischief we're gonna' do, your former gang would be very jealous of the Reds after we pull *your* mother-humpin' caper off! There's gonna' be chaos all over friggin' Hammonton! I'll even bet my two assholes on it."

"You have two assholes?" News inquired in a puzzled state of mind.

"Yeah," Restuccio answered, "assholes are like tires. Ya' never know when you'll need a spare. The first one's for my constipation, and the second butt hole is used for diarrhea!"

Independent of the general levity, my conscience was seriously weighing the gravity of the specific events that were going to happen; the danger involved with each phase, and the great mischief that was going to be inflicted upon its recipients. I had only wanted to limit the shenanigans to our operations at Hammonton High School and at the usually quiet Hammonton Police Department, but Goose expanded my original plan into vandalizing private businesses as part of *his* general strategy. 'Oh well, Pop's gonna' already go through the ceiling about me flunking trigonometry,' I worriedly thought above all the peer pressure. 'Might as well go all the way and really give him something to explode and fume about.'

Before the planning session adjourned, Sal Midilli gave a tutorial course in locksmithing to everyone hiccupping, and Goose provided the essential tools and materials to be used in the scheduled raid, including the fifty stolen bowling balls Frankie Fingers and Joe Zucchini had recently purloined from DiDonato's Lanes.

On Friday night, the Reds had a final rehearsal inside Goose's basement to review all aspects of our mischievous project. Everyone received blue denim jackets and Frankenstein masks to wear during the surprise attack, and Restuccio, who loved chaos, appointed captains for the four teams that would simultaneously conduct four separate, clandestine, strategic "military operations" transpiring in downtown Hammonton. Restuccio conducted a roll call and then distributed four envelopes containing prescribed instructions, which I had prepared to the individual team captains.

"Herc will lead team one; Balls team two; Hoss team three, and J.W. team four," Goose orally designated. "The list of guys on each team is written-down in these four different envelopes, along with your important missions," G.R. remarkably announced without using a single curse word. Restuccio told the Reds that each commando unit would conduct its activities independently, and that each squad was under the leadership of its captain. "Remember what bullshit the Blues did to us at Atsion Lake!" our coordinator finished.

I hastened forward, obtained my leader's envelope, opened it, and reviewed that my six-member team consisted of Fabian Midilli, Goose Restuccio, Juice Illiani, News Tomasello, Jives Arena, and myself. I was happy with the composition of my squad. Our particular assignment was to terrorize the Hammonton Police Department, located beneath Town Hall on Central Avenue.

"I like everything about the four raids except the vandalism part," I told Goose. "I hadn't planned on doin' that prank! Now it's no longer just four pranks being played."

"That's the best part!" my destructive associate cackled. "There's somethin' about property being destroyed that makes people afraid and stay afraid. Terror makes victims and cops think fuckin' twice before they decide to mess-around with ya'."

"What do ya' mean by that? Aren't cops people?" I asked. "Ya' aren't makin' any sense! We're committin' a possible felony crime!"

"J.W., cops never go after the hard-core criminals because they worry about their houses being torched; about their families being hurt, and about them bein' killed," Goose insisted, pausing a second to gauge the impact of his statement. "That's why the fuzz spends most of their time givin' out parkin' and speedin' tickets to good citizens, and eatin' doughnuts in coffee shops instead of goin' after the Mafia or the local Cosa Nostra. Cops wanta' always stay-away from danger. And some pussy' Hammonton' cops might even be on our side against the Blues, without *you* even knowin' it."

The Reds had a pretty good spy network going, and through some St. Joe' girls who knew some Hammonton High chicks, we had been able to obtain earlier in the week the HHS locker numbers and combinations of Gabe Gillette, Speed Mortellite, Butch Lanza, and Ox Narducci.

The Reds went over our final attack schedule, and after we were satisfied with the adequacy of our team preparations, we removed our red James Dean jackets; donned the blue denim substitutes, and in order to develop false courage, we pretended to be intoxicated Blues, drinking final shots of *Jack Daniel's, Southern Comfort, Seagram's Seven, and Canadian Club.*

Four Reds' cars departed Goose's driveway on Saturday night, just before midnight. One of them was a brand new blue 1960 Buick, which team four had been assigned to take into Hammonton.

"What's with the blue Buick?" I asked Restuccio. "I like your red T-Bird better."

"I'll tell you on the way to *our* mission. We switched cars," G.R. explained. "Hop in and you'll learn a new wrinkle I added to *your* fucked-up plan!" the cocky insane asylum candidate chided in his normal, put-down manner.

The four Reds' vehicles cruised town once to evaluate exactly how our separate squads would conduct their individual forays. Everything we observed seemed tranquil and normal. G.R. explained that he and Fabian had "borrowed" the brand-new blue '60 Buick from a local car agency's parking' lot. Next, the two had driven the blue Buick to Gabe Gillette's blueberry plantation; sneaked into the unguarded supply yard; removed the license plates, from one of the blue and white farm labor transport buses; drove to G.R.'s house, and then attached them to the "borrowed" blue 1960 Buick.

"That's cool!" I commended and admitted. "The cops will think that *this* is a blueberry car in their reports."

"That's right, J.W.," Goose confirmed. "Just like ya' told me when the Diablos 'borrowed' Cummings' Ford to do some mischief, so that the Levittown cops blamed the pranks on the Kamikazes and not the Diablos."

Our part of the planned turmoil was to commence at 12:25. Goose had parked the blue '60 Buick in an unlighted municipal lot, situated behind the serene Hammonton Police Department. The instigator opened the trunk, which contained our six blue denim jackets; six Frankenstein masks; a long narrow funnel; two half-gallons, of sand blended with sugar, and ten DiDonato's Lanes' bowling balls.

Five of us quickly entered into our blue denim jackets, donned our Frankenstein masks, and each of us picked-up a bowling ball. G.R. closed the trunk and said, "Okay, fellas', good luck. I'm fuckin' excited about drivin' the get-away car just like in the movies," the junior villain said, putting-on his Halloween mask. "I'll pour the sand and sugar mixture into the two cop cars' gas tanks, while you freaks harass the goddamned po-po's with your ant-ticks," Goose directed in a voice muffled underneath his mask.

"Ya' look a lot better with the mask on!" I joked to alleviate the great tension we were all feeling.

The five of us trespassers cautiously descended the steps leading down to police headquarters and then, setting our five bowling balls down, removed bags of marbles and ball bearings from our blue denim jacket' pockets. We carefully and meticulously scattered the ball bearing and marbles on the tenth, eighth, sixth, fourth, and second steps. We next quietly picked-up our five bowling balls, and then flung open the police department's door. Two startled officers momentarily stared at us in absolute awe.

"Let's get rollin'!" I yelled though my mask.

"Have any *spare* change!" Juice hollered.

"*Score* another one for the Blues!" News bellowed.

Before the shocked officers could draw their handguns, the five of us rolled our bowling balls at the two still-stunned cops. One rolling sphere deflected off of Sergeant Benedetto's ankle, and another collided with Patrolman Anderson's lower shin.

The five of us turned and ran like frightened rabbits, still wearing our Frankenstein masks. Our team hightailed scampered to the steps leading-up to ground level, making certain that we used only odd-numbered steps one, three, five, seven, and nine.

The two antagonized police officers' pursuit soon reached the steps, but unfortunately, the chasers were unaware of our tricky numerical code. Upon stepping onto steps two and four, Benedetto and Anderson's bodies flipped up into the air, landing sideways on the hard metal incline.

"That hada' hurt!" I shouted through my mask to Jives Arena. "That was even painful to watch!"

"The po-po's are now the *peach* fuzz!" Frankie joked as the imbecile gasped for more air. The Frankenstein quintet wearing Dracula masks dashed across the City Hall parking lot and sprinted to the blue '60 Buick.

"Quick guys, here's the other five bowlin' balls!" Goose exclaimed while pointing to the parking lot's asphalt. "Let's see ya' get rollin' again!"

The five of us reached-down like synchronized human robots, and grabbed the purloined bowling balls. Sergeant Benedetto and Patrolman Anderson had partially recovered from their stairwell misadventure with the scattered marbles and ball bearings. The two keepers-of-the-peace were holding their aching ankles and shins as the disabled duo awkwardly ran and hobbled towards us, literally being hopping mad. We rolled the five bowling balls in their targeted direction. Sergeant Benedetto awkwardly jumped-up to avoid being struck, but soon landed on his already-sore ankle, spraining it some more. Patrolman Anderson was hit in his other shin, thus doubling the extent of his sustained pain and injury.

Goose fired-up the engine; we all swiftly piled-in, and the blue '60 Buick fishtailed out of the dark parking lot. The two disabled cops hobbled to the pair of parked patrol cars, but since Goose had poured a special concoction of sand and sugar into the gas tanks, those two vehicles weren't going anywhere soon. G.R. took all back roads home to his Winslow mansion, where we waited for the other three dauntless Reds' commando squads to return from *their* forays.

After all units returned safely to base, it was reported that Herc Juliano's team had masterfully placed their ten bowling balls into the trunks of five Blues' cars parked in town, one of which was Gabe Gillette's ice blue Corvette.

Balls Giordano's "team two squad" had been delegated to perform random acts of vandalism all over Hammonton, designed to distract attention from what the other three teams were doing. That squad indiscriminately hurled stolen bowling balls through the plate glass windows of the Gem, Joe's Barber Shop, Miller's Department Store, J.J. Newberry's Five and Dime, Ritchie's Army and Navy Store, Dan's Stationary Store, Kern's Drug Store, First Federal Savings and Loan, and Hammonton Auto Parts. The tenth bowling ball was tossed through the front living room window of Mr. Arturo Sorrentino's modest bungalow on Tilton Street.

Team three, led by Hoss Gregorio, had to really act surreptitiously. Their mission was to break into Hammonton High School; locate four Blues' lockers, and then plant the remaining bowling balls inside a classroom closet. The six raiders furtively entered the yellow brick building like professional burglars on the prowl. Hoss and his five comrades stealthily located the lockers of Gabe Gillette, Speed Mortellite, Butch Lanza, and Ox Narducci. After using the accurate locker combinations that had been learned through the Reds' female intelligence network, the encroachers "planted" a stolen bowling ball into each one.

Finally, using locksmith knowledge gained from Fabian Midilli, team three managed to break into Classroom 103. The marauders then deposited the remaining six bowling balls inside the sliding-door closet, leaving the doors partially open so that the homeroom teacher could easily detect and report the pilfered goods.

Upon exiting Hammonton High School, Hoss's team's presence was discovered by an alert night janitor, who chased the six intruders down a side corridor to the school's back door steps. Hoss and company used several "emergency bags" of marbles, and upon leaping onto the top step, the victimized custodian performed a full somersault into the air, and then tumbled-down the remaining concrete steps.

After all, four hit squads safely re-assembled back at Goose's suburban mansion, the Reds performed a special ritual to reinforce our brotherhood. The two dozen of us had a huge bonfire where we threw our twenty-four Berlin Auction blue denim imposters' jackets into the raging inferno, cheering wildly when each newly tossed piece of apparel ignited into flames. When the last embers finally died-down the gasoline-ignited blaze, the jubilant revelers celebrated our most recent accomplishments around the beautiful mahogany bar inside Goose's impressive club basement.

"Sergeant Benedetto and Patrolman Anderson will never be the same," I cackled to Goose. "That police station raid was a classic to tell our juvenile delinquent grandkids about."

"J.W., you had some really neat hairy-assed ideas to use against those freakin' Hammonton High dick-lickers," G.R. answered with plenty of rancor. "I have a feelin' we're gonna' need all of your smarts again to use against those pud-pullin' jerk-offs."

"I heard that Hoss's team nailed the Hammonton High night janitor, too, with the good old, reliable marble routine," Fabian hysterically related. "That must've been a real classic, too."

"And Balls's team kicked ass good, breakin' windows all over the downtown burg," Jives added. "I hear that the vigilantes even broke the Gem's front glass pane again, and then, the *pane* in the ass raiders visited Mr. Sorrentino's pad, and busted the crib's main lookin' glass, too."

"And it's all gonna' be blamed on the Blues," I injected into the dialogue. I informed the others that I had taken the liberty to mail an anonymous letter addressed to Gabe Gillette's residence. The missive stated that Pee Wee Lucca had leaked the locker combination' numbers to "the saboteurs". "So," I concluded my statement, "when the Blues confront Pee Wee with the accusation presented in the letter, there's gonna' be lots of questions being asked and answered over at Blueberry Hill."

"And guys, the license plate on the blue '60 Buick belongs to one of Gabe Gillette's migrant labor transports," G.R. contributed with a lusty laugh.

"I'm glad you weirdo freaks took-off your Dracula masks, because I was worried you fools were gonna' soon have hollow-wienies," Restuccio stupidly declared. "In fact, you' super-assholes looked better with the damned scary Dracula masks coverin' your *grow-tusk* faces!"

"Er, Goose," News reported while clearing his throat, "I'd hate to break it to ya', but we forgot to do one crucial thing."

"What's that?" Restuccio glumly wondered out loud.

"We forgot to return the blue Buick we had borrowed to the dealership," News reported. "It's still parked outside, in your driveway."

"Jesus Christ!" Goose screamed like a maniac. "J.W., I thought you thought of everything! We gotta' take a ride. I gotta' get my damned red T-Bird back, so hop like a frog on drugs into the blue Buick right now! How the hell did you think of everything *accept* the most-important part!"

Chapter Twenty-Five

"Mirror, Mirror on the Trestle"

Goose drove the "borrowed" '60 blue Buick back to the Hammonton GM Dealership with me as his sole passenger. I was concerned that the great teen fruit war between the Reds and the Blues was becoming Levittown revisited, all over again, and I expressed my gut-wrenching fears to apathetic Restuccio. As usual, the warped-minded hellion was non-compassionate and unperturbed.

"Don't worry, J.W. This is just a lotta' crap that's gotta' sort itself out, that's all," Goose believed and expressed. "The Blues can't cry too loud in public, because everybody in Hammonton is gonna' think they're a bunch of crybabies and wimps. The cops ain't gonna' make too big a stink because the town'll think *they* can't do their job if the fuzz bellyaches too much. And the Blues will wanta' settle the score against us all by themselves, without gettin' the goddamned po-po's, or their rich old man Gillette after our asses."

"And what if the cops do come after our butts on their own?" I argued. "What about fingerprints?"

"Ya' watch too much *Dragnet* and *Highway Patrol* on television," G.R. accused his audience of one. "J.W., ya' must think you're Jack Webb or Broderick Crawford! I'll buy ya' a black and white squad car with a loud siren, if that'll make ya' happy."

"No, but what about fingerprints?" I stubbornly insisted. "Please get serious about goin' to jail for a change!"

Goose laughed as if the Jersey Devil possessed his mouth and hemorrhoids. "J.W., I'm not returnin' this heisted Buick to the car agency. You're gonna' drive my red T-Bird back to my house, and I'm takin' this piece of shit back with me, too. Then, Frankie and Juice will get this new blue tank to a chop shop, and the tin pig will be dismantled by the 'South Philly boys in no time," the crazy kid related. "The parts will be sold in Mafia junk yards all over South Jersey, so there ain't no motherless fingerprints to worry about, except inside the goddamned bowlin' balls, and the fuzz are too stupid and lazy to look inside the shittin' finger and thumb holes."

I didn't sleep well for two whole nights, scared that the police would be knocking on the front door. But nothing of the kind happened, and the sun rose as usual the next two mornings, and the world hadn't ended. I boarded Mr. Priestley's school bus, and was never so glad to see News Tomasello after old Herman picked him up on Spring Road.

"Read any good books lately?" Tommy asked.

I was ashamed to divulge my latest literary sampling to my curious companion. "I've been readin' *Through the Looking-Glass* by Lewis Carroll," I confessed, fearing that it was too juvenile for a high school senior.

"That's a fantastic book!" News exclaimed. "Lewis Carroll is the pen name for Charles Lutwidge Dodgson, who lived from 1832-1898."

"I read on the back cover that he lived in England, and I can't help but thinkin' that Goose and Gabe Gillette are like Tweedledum and Tweedledee," I joshed.

"That's funny J.W.," News agreed. "So damned funny that it's absolutely true."

"I like to read classics, since I get a lot of my ideas from them," I disclosed to my good friend. "Ya' never know when an idea from an excellent book like *Through the Looking-Glass* will be used."

"Do ya' think that Goose will ever appreciate intellectual activity?" T.T. asked. "An unconscious chimpanzee has more academic curiosity than our cursing amigo does."

"No," I curtly replied. "G.R. only knows how to use people who have imagination to help him reach his own wicked goals. He reminds me too much of Tinker and Bruno Popeye Messina back in Levittown. But News," I continued my analysis, "Goose Restuccio is smarter than us in many ways. Restuccio's very practical. He understands the real adult world. We see it as we wish it oughta' be. He sees it as it is."

"Ya' know J.W.," News mused. "Scholars have been studyin' Lewis Carroll's books for a century now, tryin' to make meaning out of what seems to be nonsense."

"That's us, News," I realized and admitted. "We're tryin' to make sense out of nonsense, and Goose and Gabe Gillette think that the world is just nonsense, with nothin' needin' to be made into sense."

"Wow!" News exclaimed. "Aristotle and Plato must've been your genetic ancestors!"

"Afraid not," I grinned. "I'm just a poor, little, mixed-up mongrel kid, half-Sidgee and half-Pollack."

News pondered my erudite revelation for a minute, but then Tommy began getting onto his customary tangent by telling me that the Joint Commission on Mental Health stated that emotional illness afflicted twenty-five percent of all Americans, who required professional help at least once in their lifetimes. I was glad to hear his irrelevant side-talk. It allowed me to escape the clutches of reality's fierce talons in regard to the Reds versus the hostile Blues.

"I think Goose, Gabe Gillette, all the Reds, and all the Blues need mental help right now," I answered my informative friend.

"You're probably right J.W.," News concurred. "But where's the craziness all gonna' end? At Ancora State Mental Hospital, or maybe in Trenton State Prison?"

I knew the answer to T.T.'s query right away. "It's gonna' end in regular hospitals, morgues, and cemeteries," I bluntly replied. "I've been to this scene before, and it's gonna' get uglier before it gets prettier. You can bet your life on it!"

"Goose say's he wants you, Fabian, and me at his house tonight at seven p.m.," News whispered and related. "Be there or be square."

I cautioned that I might not be able to make the engagement if Pop received my final trig' failure notice from the guidance department. "Then, I'll be grounded until pigs and rhinos start flyin' in bat caves," I maintained.

"The letters ain't goin' out 'til tomorrow, so you'll have at least one more night of fun," News informed.

School that day was somewhere between a bore and a bummer, and so, I was glad to see News pull into the farm market's driveway at seven p.m. My pal volunteered helping Dad, Mom, and me cover the exposed outside produce with quilts and blankets; shut the overhead garage doors, and close the place down.

"Be home by eleven," Dad warned. "Ya' got an important day at school tomorrow."

I was fearful that Pop had already received a phone call from Mr. Andrews or Mr. White. My apprehensive mind pictured the strict math' instructor gloating over the official presentation of the bad news to Pop'.

When News and I arrived at G.R.'s opulent palace, Goose was downstairs in his family's club basement conferring with Fabian, Hoss, and Little Joe Gregorio. "How ya' doin' J.W.?" G.R. greeted while ignoring News' presence. "We need your brains to do somethin' big to the Blues. I wanna' hit the space aliens hard while they're still reelin' from the great Bowlarama roll off! I know from experience that they're plannin' some goddamned wicked counter attack, but I wanta' hit the homos again hard in the balls, and cut-off their peckers before the dolts can ever take a piss at us."

"What did ya' have in mind?" I uneasily asked. "Haven't ya' done enough damage already?"

"No way, Jose," Goose replied as Hoss and Little Joe snickered in the background. "You're the most intelligent asshole I know anywhere," Goose sincerely complimented, "and now's your big chance to shine."

I asked my superior exactly what the scoundrel had in mind, and his response was rather imaginative for a guy of his academic dynamics. "J.W.," the nitwit said, "I want ya' to be creative. Look around this here club basement and come-up with an idea that'll cream those jerk-off, blueberry cootie-munchers. Hey guys, I've heard the Blues have finally graduated from eatin' cooties to chompin' on and swallowin' dingle berries," Goose jested to his appreciative, red-jacketed, gang brothers.

My brain had to think fast under extreme pressure. My eyes surveyed the party room and its paintings, beer steins, mahogany bar, fancy glasses, chairs, stools, tables, and wall mirrors being the most conspicuous objects. Then, I had a most-wonderful inspiration. "Hey guys," I said. "Do ya' know t*hat* old railroad trestle over on Flemington Pike."

"Goddam it, speak fuckin' English for Hoss, Little Joe, and me to understand, and stop pretendin' you're just talkin' to News and Fabian," our petulant host rankled.

I decided that I should be less esoteric in my revelation. "Okay, the railroad bridge built over on Flemington Pike," I repeated. "Do ya' know what I'm talkin' about?"

"What about it?" Fabian asked. "It's just a normal railroad trestle. Nothing special."

Goose gave Sal a dirty look because Fabian had used the seldom-spoken word *trestle*. G.R. then waved and rotated his hand, signifying that he wanted me to elaborate on my grand scheme.

"See that big long mirror ya' have hangin' on that stucco wall over there," I indicated. "That's what we're gonna' use." I next told the guys that Hoss and Little Joe could take the huge mirror up on top of the railroad bridge, and then cover it with a dark cloth or sheet. Somehow, we would get a carload of Blues to chase us down Flemington Pike. The Reds would safely pass under the trestle while Hoss and Little Joe would be suspending the covered *looking-glass* from the bridge.

"I get it," Fabian excitedly interrupted. "When the Blues are speedin' after the rest of us, Hoss and Little Joe release and drop the dark cover. The Blues see their own headlights glaring in front of them. The pursuers slam on their brakes, and then skid and crash into the side of the bridge."

"I'll be damned," Goose concluded and declared. "They'll think it's an approachin' car, and to avoid a head-on collision, they'll panic, jam on the brakes, and veer-off and slam into the friggin' *trestle*. Those stupid asses won't know what hit them."

"Or, what they'll hit," News coyly added. "How are we gonna' get the buffoons to chase us?"

"That's' easy," I replied. "We'll play the hidden rope trick on them." After I explained the intricacies of the Diablos hidden rope trick, Goose Restuccio was amazed at my creative acumen. "If Hitler had *you* on his side," Mussolini junior said, "that fucked-up bastard would've won the goddamned *Civil War!*"

Everyone including Hoss and Little Joe found humor in Goose's obvious deficiency in history. But the paragon of educational illiteracy quickly recovered from his erroneous, chronological, war knowledge in a jiffy by saying, "I've got too fast *Harleys* in my garage. Fabian and News will be ridin' on one, and J.W. and me will be on the other. Hoss and Little Joe," Goose continued his flamboyant lunacy, "I'll find a long black blanket I have stored somewhere in the tool shed. You two Einsteins know what to do with the mirror, don't ya'? Okay then, let's roll baby!"

Goose and Fabian walked the two black *Harleys* out of the garage; News closed the overhead door, and the two honchos skillfully fired-up the bike engines. T.T. hopped onto Sal's 'buddy seat'. I did the same onto Goose's motorcycle, and then we barreled-out of the driveway on the two noisy hogs, looking for our next adventure. I was thrilled by the machine's power, and I felt my hair blowing wildly in the wind. Goose, followed by Fabian, buzzed by Winslow Junction and took Spring Road to the White Horse Pike. We passed the *Route 30* and *206* traffic light, and then G.R. made a sharp left onto Middle Road. I turned my head, and Fabian and News were keeping pace directly behind.

"We're now in blueberry territory," Restuccio yelled over his left shoulder. "A kid named "Spoonsy" DiMeo has a berry farm near the end of Middle Road, and he's good friends with Speed Mortellite. We'll check-out that place first."

I was enjoying the exhilaration of speed and sharp turns, but was wholly unprepared for the mania that fate had in store for us. Goose brazenly pulled into Spoonsy DiMeo's U-shaped driveway and motored over a section of lawn to the back of the kid's house. Gabe Gillette was caught seated inside his ice blue Corvette, talking to Spoonsy, Butch Lanza, Ox Narducci, and Speed Mortellite. I noticed that Speed's white Thunderbird was parked in front of Gillette's mint-condition 'Vette. Our two Harleys startled our adversaries as we again looped to the back of Spoonsy's pad via the well-manicured lawn. G.R.'s wheels squealed when his boss cycle hit the asphalt driveway and skidded to a halt.

"You clowns need any bowlin' balls!" the ball-breaker hollered in their direction. "Ya' lousy jerk-offs need all the balls ya' can get!"

Restuccio and Fabian wildly peeled-out of there, and the five Blues, regaining their testosterone, shouted a series of derogatory expletives in our direction, while vigorously shaking their fists. When

I glanced backward, the five incensed blueberry barons were jumping into the blue 'Vette and the white T-Bird.

The twin *Harleys* made a left onto South Union Road, motored past the Penza and Rizzotte Farms, and then sped across *206* at fifty-miles-an-hour without honoring the cautionary 'Stop' sign. I glimpsed behind, and observed that the blue 'Vette and the white Thunderbird had to stop to avoid colliding with *206* traffic.

"Now we're into peach country," I yelled to Goose as our bike advanced onto the northern part of Union Road. "Don't forget what we do at the bend."

G.R. and Fabian completed the difficult curve and stopped their *Harleys* on opposite sides of North Union Road. News and I hopped-off our respective bikes to enact the "Invisible Rope Trick," which the mischievous Diablos had often employed back in Levittown.

News stooped on one side of Union Road, and I was crouched-down on the other. When Gabe Gillette's blue 'Vette came speeding-around the curve, News and I pretended we were pulling a rope across the road. This unexpected sight caught Gillette by surprise. The confused driver slammed on his brakes and skidded to a halt. Just as he and Spoonsy DiMeo were about to leap-out and chase us through a fallow field, Speed Mortellite's white T-Bird came whizzing around the precarious bend. Mortellite applied his brakes too late, and his car slid into and dented the back fender of Gillette's 'Vette. The five crazed maniacs leaped-out of their dented vehicles and pursued News and me on foot.

T.T. and I hopped onto the backs of the two black Harleys that were waiting for us, and Goose and Fabian took-off in a blur. "You dirty mother fuckers!" Gillette was screaming. "Look what you've fuckin' done to my wheels!"

Now that the Blues were beyond livid, we had to make it fast to Flemington Pike to execute our scheme's final phase. Goose and Fabian turned-up the speed as our cycles, stayed on Union, and flew by Basin Road. A series of peach farms dotted both sides of Union. A half-mile later was Pine Road, and a half-mile after that was Oak, both very dangerous intersections. Our machines zipped past the crossings without stopping, and I could feel my heart racing almost as fast as the *Harleys* were speeding. A half-mile past Oak was Walker Road, and my concerned eyes glanced-back and saw headlights gaining on us. "They're comin' up fast behind Fabian's machine!" I loudly shouted into Restuccio's ear.

"We're passin' Spring Road now," Goose hollered-back over his right shoulder, "and then we'll be on Flemington."

"Yeah, but we have to cross *Route 30* to reach the railroad bridge," I yelled. "Ya' better slow-down and stop! There's always lots of traffic on the Pike!"

Goose opened-up full throttle, and Fabian duplicated his mentor's feat. 'If we fall off now and slide and skid on the asphalt,' I prayed, 'there won't be any skin left on our bodies.' When we approached the always-busy White Horse Pike, Goose lowered the speedometer down to sixty. But instead of halting, the careless lunatic zoomed through the intersection. I heard horns loudly blowing. I opened my eyes, and was glad that I didn't see archangels tooting them. I twisted my neck to see Fabian's motorcycle, and the audacious Red crazily had mimicked Goose's more-than-risky maneuver, as Midilli's *Harley* flew through the treacherous intersection.

"You almost got us killed!" I cried. "Are you trying to defy the Grim Reaper?"

"Remember what the hell I friggin' told ya' about the dumb-ass word *almost!"* the Sicilian loony-tune reiterated and reminded me.

At last, the dim outline of the Flemington Pike railroad trestle was visible a thousand-feet-ahead. We flashed under the bridge, and ten-seconds later, so did Fabian and News. The two bikes stopped a thousand-feet beyond the overhead, waiting for the results of our great stratagem to transpire.

"Did ya' see Hoss and Little Joe up on the bridge?" Restuccio asked.

"No, it was too dark!" I answered, breathing heavily.

Headlights with their high beams shining came speeding toward the railroad overhead. Suddenly, the first vehicle slammed on its brakes and skidded, veered to the side, and then smashed into the right stone wall supporting the trestle. The second car skidded and veered left into the stone wall on the opposite side.

Five outraged passengers leaped-out of the two severely damaged automobiles. The former car occupants apparently were unscathed but very distraught. A loud sound was heard as Hoss and Little Joe dropped Goose's huge club basement mirror onto Flemington Pike, temporarily scaring the feces out of the five enraged Blues standing below. The two burly Reds huffed and puffed their way down an incline, falling and tumbling the last ten-feet to ground level. Hoss and Little Joe hopped into a nearby red pick-up, fired-up the engine, and we all then safely returned to G.R.'s rustic mansion to celebrate our most recent success.

"Those sons of bitches got what the hell they deserved!" Goose gloated. "Those *un-screw-polis* pricks are really seeing *red* now!"

"What do we owe ya' for the mirror?" Hoss innocently requested. "Joe and me didn't plan on droppin' it. We got so excited that we lost our grips."

"Nothin'," Goose replied. "That was like the cherry on top of the sundae. It was worth the price of a hundred goddamned expensive mirrors, just to watch those crazy mothers shit their pants."

"But Goose, things are only gonna' get worse," I predicted, "and the next time, someone's liable to get killed!"

"J.W., just do the goddamned thinkin', and forget about doin' the worryin'," Restuccio recommended. "And forget about *almost*. Just think about almost *after* I get ya' goddamned killed!"

The six of us exchanged jolly anecdotes about what had happened at Spoonsy DiMeo's house; at the Union Road bend; at the *Route 30* and Flemington Pike crossing, and at the infamous Pennsylvania Railroad trestle. I forgot my mental troubles by downing three shots of potent *Southern Comfort*.

News drove me home past Winslow Junction and then down Spring Road to the White Horse Pike. The academic wizard was telling me about a study soon to be released by the American Heart Association, to which I half-heartedly listened, in light of what we had recently experienced with the Blues.

"J.W., the American Heart Association has found that death among middle-aged men who are heavy smokers is a hundred- percent higher than among those men that don't smoke at all," News irrelevantly informed me. "It's all statistically justified. Heavy smokers die quicker and younger."

"I'm glad I only weigh a hundred fifty-five pounds," I said, as I took a long drag on a *Camel* cancer stick. "That makes me a light smoker and not a heavy one."

"Ha ha, you're a real jester," News chided. "Your Dad's a big smoker. I've seen him puffin' away like a chimney the few times I've visited your place."

"I think I make him very nervous," I remarked in my feigned, relaxed state. "Pop smokes to get his mind off me," I bragged. "Dad's afraid I've gonna' become a juvenile delinquent someday. That's the main reason why we moved outa' Levittown back to Jersey, because of my involvement with the Diablos."

"Your Pop really cares about you," News emphasized. "Goose's old man doesn't give a crap what *he* does. He wants his son to grow-up and become a loan sharkin' egomaniac criminal just like him."

I contemplated News's sagacious words for the remainder of the drive home. My deep meditation was interrupted when we approached

Pete's Market. Red blinking lights were flashing, and immediately, several guilty thoughts entered my mind.

"News, do ya' think the cops are investigatin' what happened to the Blues? Now I'm really in deep trouble!"

Tommy stopped his red and white Ford Fairlane in the middle of the gravel driveway in front of Pete's Farm Market. We got-out and walked over to the emergency scene.

"It's an ambulance and a police car," News recognized and stated.

I saw Mom sitting inside of the ambulance with my father lying on the stretcher. "What's happened?" I gasped, my mouth trembling.

"Is that your dad in there?" the cop asked.

"Yes!" I acknowledged, almost crying.

"He's gonna' be all right," a paramedic said. "We believe he's had a minor heart attack. We're takin' your dad to Cooper Hospital for tests. He'll be laid-up in Camden for at least a month."

"Mom, are you alight?" I sincerely asked.

"Yes," my mom sadly answered. "Your father became a little overwhelmed. His heart started wildly palpitating. After he spoke with Mr. Andrews on the telephone, his heart suddenly went into cardiac arrest!"

Chapter Twenty-Six

"A Tale of Two Drive-ins"

My whole life suddenly became convoluted. Nothing had clarity or definition. Pop stayed in Cooper Hospital for four-days. I visited him in Camden three-times, once with Juice, Fabian, and News on separate days, respectively. Goose told me that Dad would recover and that *his* stay was more of a false alarm than an emergency, so G.R. preferred diligently scouring South Jersey and emptying-out and restocking his coveted candy and gumball machines, than accompanying me to see my father.

"Are you a licensed doctor?" I challenged Goose over the phone.

"The best doctors are those that never went to medical school," Goose answered, "and the rest are worse crooks than the Mafia, lawyers, or even judges."

An ambulance was scheduled to deliver Pop home on a Tuesday in late May. I thought about how much grief I had caused him both in Levittown and in Hammonton, and I felt rather remorseful, feeling that my misery had been more than a mere product of educational and peer-related circumstances. I had instigated area teen chaos by choice, and not by chance, even if those choices were influenced by Red' peer pressure.

My mind recollected the stories Dad used to tell me about his family history where his father had been a hardworking lumberjack immigrant from Krakow, Poland, who brought his family to Alpena, Michigan, seeking a new start in America, the land of opportunity. My paternal grandfather had leased timberland from the federal government to operate a lumber camp. A huge winter fire devastated the lumber location. No insurance had been purchased to cover the staggering losses, and grand pop's spirit was broken by the calamity. He contracted pneumonia and died a defeated man at an early age, his hopes and dreams crushed by the grotesque social and economic realities that guys like Goose Restuccio and Gabe Gillette knew much better than academic types like News and I did.

I tried wearing a happy face around Edgewood High, but I was crying on the inside while attempting to reflect a contented external façade. Tyrone Davis approached me in the hallway outside the main office. I was not too thrilled to have to interact with the money-solicitor at that particular moment.

"J.W.," I just got a call from Mrs. Pagano over in Hammonton," Tyrone mentioned rather enthusiastically.

"Mrs. Pagano?" I answered, showing the extent of my cluttered and beleaguered mind.

"Yeah, Dude, Mrs. Pat Pagano, the lady who runs the monthly Canteen Dances at Hammonton High. She called me to say that the Marvelons are scheduled to appear the third week in June. You're invited to attend our gig, since you're the manager."

"Are ya' gonna' do the gig for free?" I asked.

"She's gonna' give us twenty-dollars travelin' expenses," Tyrone excitedly conveyed. "We needs the stage experience, especially performin' before an all-white crowd. We wanta' see if the cracker kids dig us as much as our own kind do!"

"Okay, Ty," I replied with a forced smile. "Keep in touch about the Hammonton gig. I'm glad ya' didn't need any more money advances right now."

I was really disconsolate about certain reprisals and punishments that went into effect because I had failed Mr. Andrews' hallowed trigonometry class. I either had to attend summer school in Haddonfield, or find myself a certified local trig' tutor fast. According to steadfast rules laid down by Pop before his mild heart problem, I could not go to the Edgewood prom or enjoy the senior class Washington Trip if I failed the subject. Worst of all, Mr. White informed me that I would not be allowed to graduate on stage with the senior class.

My mind was pretty depressed that day during cafeteria period, and the other Reds fully understood why. I was also angry because my average in Mr. Jenkins' physics class was higher than my average had been in Mr. Andrews' trigonometry class, but my science teacher had the decency to pass me with a D, while Andrews quite vindictively put the screws to me with an F.

"I think it was all because of that idiotic 'Meet the Press, Face the Class' remark I made in his classroom when I first came to this school," I lamented at our exclusive Reds' cafeteria table. "I was really stupid making that rude comment. Andrews took it personally, and never forgave me," I grieved.

"That's alight," News comforted. "Someday, you'll do great things like authoring novels, and Andrews will look like a complete numbskull for failin' a true literary genius."

"Ha, ha, ha!" Goose gleefully reacted. "Don't worry J.W. Mr. Andrews is walkin' around over there' struttin' like a peacock, but he's payin' the price for flunkin' ya' right now!"

"Whatcha' mean, jelly bean?" Jives Arena inquired to the human scourge. "Tell me the truth, Baby Ruth!"

"Just this, Asshole," Goose sneered. "St. Joe had a half-day today because of conferences, exams, or some other stupid school shit like that. Anyway, I told Herc Juliano and Balls Giordano what that shit-eatin' Andrews was gonna' do to J.W., and guess what?"

"What?" Jives, Juice, Fabian, News, and I all asked in unison.

"Don't piss yourselves all at the same time," Goose whispered as his football-shaped head leaned to the center of the table. "But Herc, Balls, Jake Maccarella and some other St. Joe seniors that wanta' be Reds are out in the faculty parkin' lot right now, takin' Mr. Andrews black '60 Ford into the *woods*."

"What?" we all gasped in unison.

"Assholes," G.R. sternly admonished, "where's your smarts? That's why this dump's called Edgewood. It was friggin' built on the edge of a goddamned woods."

Goose told us he was impressed with the story I had once related of how the Diablos had stolen Father Malcolm's brown Volkswagen, carried it to a nearby woods, and wedged the Beetle upside-down between three trees. "Herc, Balls, and the boys are probably jumpin' up and down on the chassis right, now getting that upside-down car stuck between some trees, just like the Diablos had done to that jerk-off Cardinal Reagan priest. That Father Malcolm salami sounds a lot like Andrews does."

"You're damned crazy?" I yelled in a rare, mild display of cursing. "I never asked for this vandalism to be done?"

Mr. Andrews suspected that something was awry at our table, so the martinet patrolled our section of the cafeteria until some of us obediently brought our trays back to the washing room. Then, some loud noise and "slate spanking" was originating from Hoss Gregorio's table, so that diversion attracted the attention of Mr. Andrews, Mr. Jenkins, and Mr. Rebeck.

"And so, guys," G.R. proceeded with his lecture. "Herc and Balls told me that the boys had two more stolen bowlin' balls left from DiDonato's they didn't use, because Balls had acted with a mallet to break a couple of windows in downtown Hammonton during the Bowlarama job," Goose clarified. "So, the last two stolen balls are now inside Mr. Andrews' trunk."

There was a moment of silence as everybody at the table digested the essence of Goose's profound disclosure. Then, News thought of something very essential and pertinent. "Er Goose," Tommy T. began, sounding like he was choking and struggling to breathe. "Are ya' sure the black '60 Ford wasn't Mrs. Murphy's car?"

"Damned straight," G.R, confidently replied without thinking twice. "I gave the St. Joe' Reds that freak Andrews' license plate numbers just to make sure. This is gonna' be a clean hit job, no doubt about it. And besides," Goose smugly continued, "Mrs. Murphy just bought a new white '60 Ford because she had such bad luck with her black one."

News was not so convinced about the foolproof nature of G.R.s thorough and efficient plan. "Er, Goose," T.T. said, clearing his throat three distinct times. "I hate to break it to ya', but Mr. Andrews liked Mrs. Murphy's white Ford so much, that *he* sold his black one to Mr. Jenkins, and then Andrews bought a white one just like Mrs. Murphy's."

"What!" Goose bellowed in absolute disbelief. "Why would *he* do such a stupid-assed thing like that!" Restuccio boomed in a vain effort to transfer blame for mistaken vandalism from himself to Mr. Walter Andrews.

"Because," News explained in a very shaky voice. "Mr. Andrews is very superstitious, and I heard him tellin' Mr. Rebeck yesterday in the S-Wing that black Fords were bad luck, and *he* didn't want the same kind of trouble that Mrs. Murphy had with hers."

"Jesus Christ come down from the cross and do three circus flips!" Goose shouted like a berserk maniac, while flinging his arms up into the air to appeal to heaven. Most everyone in the cafeteria turned-around to gawk at our raucous table. Mr. Andrews came-over and reprimanded, "Mr. Restuccio, even though this is not a Catholic high school, I feel that it is my explicit duty to assign you three days of office detention for using unacceptable profanity. Please refrain from employing derogatory and vulgar remarks in public in the future. Do you hear?"

Mr. Jenkins' new black car was indeed sabotaged by Herc, Balls, and the St. Joe boys as an ugly case of mistaken identity. Mr. Andrews had once again escaped the Reds' wrath by sheer lucky coincidence, and Goose put it very aptly when the perpetrator stated, "That jerk-off Andrews must walk in horseshit, cow shit, chicken shit, dog shit, bullshit, dinosaur shit, and angel's shit, every damned mornin' the bozo takes a dump!"

Juice Illiani sensed my malaise, so my handsome friend concocted a viable plan to allow me to escape "the Blues", as Illiani called it. Johnny appeared at Pete's Market two weeks after the Edgewood prom and gave me the details of his mental dynamics. "Ya' know J. W.," the non-famous Fabian prefaced, "Elaine Hill was tellin' me that Joanne Berenato wanted ya' to ask her to the prom."

"Yeah, I sensed that possibility," I sadly responded. "But her narrow-minded father wanted her to go to the big dance with a peach kid. The likely candidate happened to be Herc Juliano, who has already messed my mind up with what he did to Mr. Jenkins' black Ford, and to downtown Hammonton, which looked almost as devastated as Hiroshima after the atomic blast." I paused for a second to gather my fleeting thoughts. "I could see Herc, Balls, and the rest of his rowdy chums jumpin' up and down on the wrong upside-down chassis as if it was a trampoline. Juice," I continued with guilty conviction, "I'm causin' juvenile delinquency by just breathin' air and failin' trig'!"

"Don't worry, J.W.," Johnny confided. "I'm gonna' make ya' happy. I've been talkin' on the horn with Elaine Hill, and she's gonna' arrange somethin' special to your likin'. Can ya' come with News and me to the Circus Drive-in on Friday night? Elaine's got a real corker planned."

"What movies are playin'?" I asked.

"Forget the small stuff," Johnny firmly replied. "I'll pick ya' up at six-thirty. What do ya' say, anchors aweigh!"

"Okay, I'll ask Mom if I can go," I said. "Pop's ready to start doin' some light work around the farm market tomorrow, and my sister Annie can fill-in for me and do some retailin'. I'm sure I can make it. Pop's accepted the fact I'm not graduatin' and have to attend summer school, or somehow get a bona fide tutor."

"Great! See ya' six-thirty on Friday night," Juice summarized as Johnny helped me stack a dozen boxes of Washington State rowed Bing' cherries, along with a dozen cartons of southern corn, inside the farm market's cinderblock cooler.

Friday night rolled-around, and News pulled his washed and polished '57 red and white Ford Fairlane into the driveway with Juice as his privileged passenger. Dad was back into the adult work routine, but he couldn't do any lifting or hard labor, so I had made sure most of the physical chores had already been taken care of. The guys were in a hyped-up, festive mood, and their exuberance soon wore off on me.

"Who's playin' at the Circus Drive-in?" I asked. "John Wayne or Charlton Heston?"

"Neither. It's an Alfred Hitchcock double-feature," News replied. "*North by Northwest* starring Cary Grant, and *Vertigo* with James Stewart and Kim Novak."

"Wow, Alfred Hitchcock's the greatest, and I really love double features!" I exclaimed. "Even on Goose Restuccio's sour puss!"

"Yeah J.W.," Juice chuckled. "That's why ya' like lookin' at fat people's chins and cheeks all the time, especially the double cheeks on obese female asses!"

"Isn't it a little strange havin' three guys goin' to a drive-in movie?" I asked. "What am I supposed to be doin' while you two jive turkeys are makin' out in the front seat?"

Juice and News filled me in on the essential details. We were going to link-up with Elaine Hill, Esther Phyllis, and Roseann Scolia at the Circus Drive-in Movie Theater, which was a teen' Mecca located a mile east of Hammonton on *Route 30* in Devonshire. Juice and News would quickly pair-off with Esther Phyllis and Roseann Scolia. I would then drive Elaine "the reputable Matchmaker" Hill twelve-miles west to the *Route 30* Atco Drive-in' passion pit, in News's red and white '57 Fairlane.

"But Elaine doesn't have any romantic interest in me," I argued, "and she's really madly in love with that muscle-bound loony tune Herc Juliano. He's not a bad guy, though, since I've gotten to know him pretty well in the Reds."

"J.W., let Juice finish tellin' ya' the arrangements, and then make your outrageous opinions known," News insisted as the '57 Ford waited in line at the Circus Drive-in for admission. "And ya' won't even have to hop into the trunk this time to be successfully sneaked into the Circus."

Johnny gave me the missing parts of the intricate social cryptogram, and suddenly my heart became ecstatic. "J.W., when Elaine and you get to the Atco Drive-in, you'll link up there with Herc and Joanne Berenato. Herc really has the hots for Elaine, so you'll be together with Joanne in Elaine's Plymouth, and she'll be with Herc in his hydrogen bomb, until the double-feature playin' over in Atco is done."

"What's playin' over at the Atco passion pit?" I asked.

"Marilyn Monroe is starrin' in *Some Like it Hot,* and Paul Newman, Burl Ives, and Elizabeth Taylor in Tennessee Williams' *Cat on a Hot Tin Roof,"* News reported. "Got your *big daddy* ready to erupt?" Tommy asked, employing some rare sexual innuendo.

The guys split a gut while I blushed in the back seat, my cerebrum still contemplating the most optimistic and thrilling set of circumstances that had imaginatively been coordinated by helpful Elaine Hill.

I was very anxious, so after we entered the Circus Drive-in and paid our dollar a carload special admission fee, I alertly spotted Elaine's green and white '58 Plymouth sedan. After exchanging the usual small-talk greetings, Johnny and Tommy hopped into the Plymouth with Esther and Roseann, and Elaine entered and sat in the red and white Fairlane with me.

"I wanta' thank you for all you've done, linkin' me up with Joanne," I sincerely related to Elaine. "You're a terrific friend."

"Glad I could help ya' out J.W.," Elaine happily said with a grin. "As you know, Joanne's father will only allow her to go-out with peach farm boys. I like Herc, and he likes me, so it all seemed like a reasonable solution, once I spoke with Johnny about it, and learned where you guys were goin' tonight. Once I knew where Herc and Joanne were headin', the rest was easy to figure-out."

"Did ya' hear what happened to Fabian Midilli?" Elaine asked as I prematurely exited the Circus Drive-in, piloting Juice's reliable red and white '57 with Elaine as my passenger.

"No, Sal wasn't in school yesterday, so I thought he had the flu, or played hooky and went down to Ocean City or Wildwood, because of a bad case of Senioritis," I answered.

Elaine related that Sal Midilli had taken a girl and another couple from Williamstown High over to Glassboro to buy some liquor at a bar carry out that catered to kids having false IDs. When Fabian tried pulling-out of the bar's parking lot with a case of beer in the trunk, Midilli had to stop his car on a slippery surface. The driveway and the road both were slick, because of a constant light drizzle. Instead of hitting the brakes, Sal was gloating about how easy it had been to purchase an illegal case of beer, and as a result, his right foot accidentally mashed-down on the accelerator. His auto wildly skidded between two cars going in opposite directions, and then plowed into a barbershop, breaking the front glass-pane window. Two flowerpots with geraniums inside came crashing-down on the hood of Sal's auto.

"Did anybody get hurt?" I asked. "Is Fabian okay?"

"Fortunately, nobody was injured. The barbershop was closed, so no one was in it," Elaine explained. "But when everyone leaped outa' the car, the engine hadn't been shut-off, and the wheels kept spinnin' around. So, Sal, being mechanical with cars, had to reach-in and shut-off the ignition."

"What about the case of beer? Did Fabian get in trouble when the police came?" I inquired.

"Well, I gotta' admit that Fabian really thought fast," Elaine said. "So, Sal opened the trunk; lifted-out the case of beer, and handed it to the delighted town drunk, who was about to enter the liquor store."

"The rum pot musta' been shocked," I added.

"Sure was," Elaine "the Matchmaker" affirmed. "And I heard that the town drunk looked-up to heaven and thanked the Lord for answering *his* prayers."

I drove the red and white Fairlane into the Atco Drive-in's entrance, and indeed, the marquee indicated that *Cat on a Hot Tin Roof* and *Some Like It Hot* were the feature films, just like Juice and News had described. Nanette Banks worked nights at 'the Atco'. collecting the admissions' money, but I had to pay the hefty sum of three-dollars for Elaine and me to be able to advance inside.

"Hi, J.W., hi Elaine," Nanette greeted. "Elaine, make sure *he* doesn't hop into the trunk. This is News Tomasello's car, isn't it?"

"Yeah, it's a long story, too long to explain right now," I replied. "But either Elaine or I will give ya' the full lowdown at Edgewood on Monday."

"It wouldn't involve Herc Juliano and Joanne Berenato? Would it?" Nanette prodded, whetting my emotional appetite.

"Maybe," I confided. "Either you're a great guesser, or a terrific observer."

"Both!" Nanette admitted. "Watch-out though; there's also some rowdy Blues from Hammonton High inside. I don't wanta' see my place of employment all bustin' up over a bloody feud about peaches and blueberries."

I nonchalantly drove the red and white Fairlane into the Atco Drive-in. I thought about three things: Joanne Berenato, Sal's unique accident over in Glassboro, and unsavory Blues invading Reds' territory, even though drive-in theaters were generally regarded as "neutral turf". I drove up and down between the rows of parallel-parked autos until we sighted Herc's red and white De Soto. Fortunately, there was an empty space to the left of Juliano's father's high-finned cruising tank.

"Hi, J.W., hi Elaine," Herc and Joanne jointly greeted.

We waved, acknowledging the odd couple's presence. Elaine and I exited the Fairlane, while the pre-feature coming attractions were still showing. A few inconsiderate patrons honked their horns for us to duck-down, so Elaine and I readily piled into the back seat of Herc's De Soto.

"Before we split-up into separate cars," Herc said rather seriously, "Speed Mortellite gave me this here envelope in the concession stand about fifteen-minutes ago. The messenger said that Gabe Gillette had sent one guy to the Circus Drive-in and one courier to the Atco with identical letters. That way, the information inside was sure to get to *you*, 'the farm market kid'."

"I hope it's not bad news," Joanne said with beautiful sad brown eyes. "J.W., I really wanted to go to the prom with you, and Elaine wanted to double-date with Herc."

"Let's just pretend it's *after* the prom right now tonight," I winked and smiled. as my hands ripped-open the envelope. I examined the contents rather hastily, and then let out a shriek.

"Holy crap!" I yelled. "What a nightmare!" I bellowed after I read the message delivered by Gabe Gillette's liaison.

"What's wrong? What is it? What's it say?" Joanne, Elaine and Herc chorused, all strongly desiring to know.

"It says that I gotta' drive to Royale Crown Custard over in Hammonton and retrieve Fabian from the garbage bin in the back of the ice cream stand," I stated. I glanced at my three listeners, who all seemed shocked at hearing the *initial* bad news. "Then, I gotta' take Fabian to Larry's Pier IV Seafood Restaurant to discover Goose Restuccio lying on his back, shackled inside the lobster tub.

"The lobster tub?" Joanne and Elaine gasped.

"Yes, that's where customers pick out the lobsters the diners want to have broiled," I stated. "And the Blues are gonna' have Goose lyin' in the metal tank bein' pinched and crawled all over by dozens of disgustin' crustaceans."

"Crusty what?" Herc asked, his eyes bulging from their sockets like those on a hungry crab.

"Crustaceans is a fancy word for shellfish like lobsters, shrimp and crabs," I loquaciously elaborated. "At least I learned somethin' in four-years of science classes. I guess I know more biology than physics or chemistry."

"Won't there be people eating inside the restaurant? "Joanne asked. "How could Goose Restuccio be lying in the lobster tank in a crowded seafood restaurant?"

"My family eats at Larry's Pier IV all the time," Elaine indicated, "and there's a bigger metal lobster tank in the diner's storage area. The lobsters are transferred from the storage area's giant tub to the restaurant's tank every afternoon before the place opens."

"That means that Goose is lyin' in the big storage tank right now, probably screamin' and cursin' in the dark," I exclaimed. "And I gotta' first get to Royale Crown over in Hammonton to get Fabian, who is the only one who could possibly pick the lock to the lobster storage room. Herc, we have no choice. We gotta' save Fabian and Goose from dyin'."

"You're right J.W.," Herc agreed. "Sorry girls, but Reds' life and death situations are more important right now to J.W. and me than either love or women!"

"What!" Joanne screamed, rather insulted. "This is insane. Can't we come along for moral support?"

"Too dangerous for fragile chicks," Herc Juliano answered. "J.W. and I might have to commit a couple of homicides if any Blues are hangin' around. Sorry Elaine, but I gotta' take a rain-check."

"Sorry Joanne," I softly apologized, nearly sobbing. "There will be a better time and place for us."

"You guys care more about your Reds' friends than you do about us," Elaine alleged. "This fiasco is down-right sickening!"

"Our good friends are in trouble facin' great danger, but you girls aren't," I diplomatically countered. "Sorry, but we have to rescue Fabian and Goose. Blame the Blues for what we gotta' do."

Joanne and Elaine exited the car in disenchanted, melancholy moods. When the two "stood up", confused chicks reluctantly entered News's Fairlane, I hopped into the front seat of Juliano's car. Herc fired-up the De Soto's engine; put the gearshift into reverse, and jerked-out of the drive-in parallel parking space. A loud clanking followed by two thuds was clearly discerned.

"What happened?" Juliano asked me.

"Herc, I think your window just pulled the damned drive-in speaker and the portable heater out from the stand!" I yelled in astonishment.

"Holy shit! Let's get the fuck outa' here!" the anxious driver screamed like a bona fide psycho. Herc put the red and white De Soto into gear and sped down the lane with the extracted speaker still blaring. I looked behind and observed the window heater box stationary on the ground with its wire yanked-out from the drive-in stand.

"You're lucky ya' didn't break your window when you jerked the heater from the stand," I related to Herc. "The speaker was still workin' on the ground, though."

"Damned heater musta' been made in Japan!" Herc complained. "My De Soto's window was made in the good old USA. That's why it didn't break."

"What about Joanne and Elaine?" I questioned Herc. "They feel left-out and stood-up!"

"Look, J.W., are their lives hangin' by a thread?" Herc rhetorically reasoned. "No, but Fabian and Goose's lives are. That's why we gotta' help the guys right now, and not be makin' out with the friggin' girls. We gotta' think with our heads, and not with our stupid dicks."

Ironically, Herc and I zoomed east past Larry's Pier IV Seafood Restaurant, which was located only a mile from the Atco Drive-in. I turned on the radio to break the heightened tension I had felt. Herc and I listened to "Searchin" by the Coasters, "Come Go with Me" by the Del-Vikings, and "I'm Stickin' with You" by Jimmy Bowen. All three song titles reminded me of what was going on in real life, and so, since my objective was to escape reality and not reinforce it, I angrily extinguished the radio's volume.

"Goose was in the lobster tank in that seafood restaurant we just passed back in Atco," I commented to Herc.

"Yeah, but we gotta' first rescue Fabian at Royale Crown before we can think about getting' Goose outa' the lobster tub," Herc responded. "We gotta' do things in *astrological* order."

"You mean chronological order," I emphasized.

"Whatever bullshit you say," Herc conceded. "Ya' know what the hell I meant, no matter how the hell I said it."

When we neared the intersection of Flemington Pike and *Route 30,* I told Herc, "Slow down! Sometimes, some crazy kids on motorcycles come flyin' across the Pike without even lookin' or stoppin."

"Well, I don't give a shit! They'd better watch-out for me," Juliano warned, "or else this here De Soto is gonna' send 'em to either Greenmount or Oak Grove Cemetery. That Goose Restuccio is really somethin'," Herc proceeded to say. "He's the only damned kid I know that's got a new Thunderbird and two new *Harleys,* all to himself. Not even Gabe Gillette has that kind of luxury."

"Shouldn't ya' be goin' a little slower," I suggested. "This is a congested area the next four-miles to Royale Crown. You're doin' seventy on the speedometer."

"Don't worry," reassured Herc. "I gotta' radar detector on my dash. Only trouble is, the damned thing doesn't work!"

I slouched-down in the front seat as we sped past Pete's Market, fearing that my parents might recognize me as a passenger in a speeding automobile. Juliano went through an amber light at *206,* sped around the dangerous Hammonton Lake bend going sixty-five, and a minute later, made a sharp left onto Moss Mill Road. We took the shortcut' back entrance into Royale Crown Custard. Juliano and I swiftly leaped out to inspect the business's rear trash bin. Standing on our toes and peering-down, we saw a pathetic human figure with hands and feet hog-tied. The encumbered person squirming and wriggling-around was basically lying in the familiar prenatal position. A blue handkerchief had been stuffed into Fabian's mouth.

Herc and I climbed on the top corners of the bin, and heroically jumped into a mound of Dixie cups, soda cartons, and sundae and ice cream cone waste. Juliano removed a penknife from his dungaree pocket and cut Sal free from his bonds. I yanked the blue bandanna from my close friend's gasping mouth.

"Thank goodness you guys showed-up!" Fabian panted. "Those green-headed flies buzzin' around my head were really nasty critters. I thought the nasty suckers were goin' to devour me alive!"

The three of us clumsily clambered-out of the trash dumpster, ready for more chaotic adventure. "Look!" Fabian pointed-out. "Inside the phone booth. There're two of the Blues who had tied me up, and I heard them chattin' about kidnapping Goose."

"How many of the skunks were here?" Herc asked.

"Six," Fabian answered. "Three assaulted my ass, and three tackled G.R. Do ya' guys know where *he* is?"

"Yeah," Herc replied, "but before we go, I wanna' do somethin' neat to Butch Lanza and Ox Narducci, who are hidin' over in that phone booth."

The three of us stepped to Herc's red and white De Soto. The always prepared pugilist flipped-open the glove compartment; removed a large roll of tape used for odd jobs on his peach farm; and gave two sentences of specific instructions. The three of us quickly surrounded the phone booth, and passing the roll of tape between us, and kept rotating the adhesive tightly around the rectangular, vertical cubicle six-times, before the two Blues ever knew what was retribution was occurring. Butch and Ox were soon unhappy prisoners, cleverly trapped inside the glass and metal phone booth chamber.

"Hey, Assholes! Let us out!" Ox yelled as the irate behemoth wildly pounded his huge fists on the glass walls and door.

"You'll pay for this!" Butch futilely boomed. "Ya' dirty mother-fuckers will pay for this!"

Herc, Fabian, and I furiously dashed to the red and white De Soto, and in less than thirty-seconds, Juliano was steering his wheels west onto *Route 30* in the direction of Atco.

"The Circus Drive-in is only a mile east of Royale Crown," I related, "and Fabian, would ya' believe that's where I started the evening?" I had to describe to Sal the chronology of events that had transpired since News, Juice, and I had met Elaine Hill and her two scheming girlfriends at the Circus Drive-in Theater.

As Herc sped past Flemington Pike heading toward the Ancora overpass, Fabian described his bad fortune in Glassboro, and how the stud managed to demolish the barbershop window.

"Fate's really unfair at times," Sal philosophized as if he was Diogenes or Socrates. "I was all set to have a good time; had a beautiful blonde Williamstown High chick in the front seat with me, and then I had to ruin it all by showin' off. J.W., my wheels are gonna' be in the repair shop for at least ten-days. What a bummer!"

"At least you're still alive," I comforted. "Things could always have been a lot worse. And now, Herc and I both know that ya' don't only *fuel around* at your father's Flyin' A' gas station," I joshed.

"Now ya' sound a little like Plato," Fabian smiled as Sal recalled a historical personage he had studied in his sophisticated, sophomore Western Civilization class.

"My little brother has got some *play dough,"* Herc sincerely added, "but it don't sound or look nothin' like Fabian."

Sal and I stared wonderingly at each other; raised our eyebrows, and briefly smiled and giggled. Herc Juliano didn't have a clue about the identity of a great ancient Greek's myriad contributions to modern government organization and to modern day logic.

The on-a-mission driver finally swerved his De Soto into the main parking lot of Larry's Pier IV Seafood Restaurant. Juliano swung around the back, hanged a left, and halted next to the business's nautical-looking storage room.

"Lucky those Blues' freaks didn't steal my tools," Sal informed while reaching inside a side pocket of his red James Dean jacket. He removed a small case containing six precious tools that would allow him entry into any room or chamber.

Sal uncorked the storage room's lock in less than a minute, Herc flicked-on the overhead lights and I shut the squeaky door. Before us, inside a colossal metal tub was Goose Restuccio, lying face-up, stark naked, with his hands and feet hog-tied as had been Fabian's in the raunchy, putrid Royale Crown trash bin. A blue handkerchief had been stuffed inside G.R.'s slanted mouth. His eyes had a glassy look, and his pupils appeared to be both disoriented and panic-stricken.

Six giant lobsters with untied claws were crawling-around and over his defenseless body. Herc latched onto one creature prowling around Goose's mouth, I grabbed one that had been nipping at *his* left big toe, and Fabian saved the day by gripping and removing a crustacean that was about to slit open the head of Goose's sensitive penis's glans. All three hungry lobsters were immediately dropped to the gray-painted, cement floor. I removed the blue bandanna from G.R.s quivering mouth, while Fabian and Herc used their personal cutting knives to free the traumatized victim's tied hands and feet.

The three rescuers gently lifted the hysterical, wet Red leader from the odor-laden tank, and set nude Restuccio down on the cold cement floor. We frantically gathered his scattered clothes that had been thrown all over the lobster storage room, and then dried-off G.R. with some loose rags and an old blanket we had found inside a pile of junk. Then, we allowed Goose to return to dignity by assisting and dressing his rear-end in his underwear and socks, and by the time those accessories had been put onto his maligned body, the lobster-tank survivor was finally capable of donning his pants, shirt, shoes, and soiled James Dean jacket all by himself.

"Do ya' like misty weather?" I asked a totally confused and still-disoriented Goose Restuccio.

"No," th 'Italian Stallion' muttered, still tottering down Weird Street, somewhere in Strangeville.

"Well then, let's get the *fog* outa' here!" I recommended in honor of the memory of my old Levittown pal, the inimitable Bo Jalonec.

Chapter Twenty-Seven

"The Marvelons"

Memorial Day came and went on the 1960 May calendar. Edgewood seniors had just gone on their Washington trip the last week of May, and I had to stay in school and help four other kids including Tyrone Davis paint the football bleachers green. Pop thought that the hard work would be good punishment for lazily not applying myself in mastering trigonometry, and would permit me to reflect on why I should make all attempts in the future to avoid harsh, arduous consequences for failure.

June of '60 was a heartbreaking month for my ego. I was introspective, and my mind and soul did a lot of soul-searching. I couldn't go on the senior class trip, and I had to live with the stigma that I couldn't graduate on stage with my classmates. My self-esteem had plummeted to a new low depth.

Mom had heard of a superb retired Hammonton High math' teacher and persuaded me to give the instructor a ring. Much to my delight, Mr. Charles B. Sipley agreed to tutor me over the summer months, so I didn't have to take a Public Service Transit bus back and forth from Hammonton to Haddonfield, Mondays through Fridays for twelve weeks starting mid-June.

Mr. Sipley was a masterful pedagogue, and his patience guided me through the fundamentals of sine, cosine, tangent, co-tangent, secant, and co-secant, one-step at a time. Eventually, I developed a base of understanding, and as July progressed, I became proficient in the same subject that had befuddled me under Mr. Andrews' helm.

"Do you intend to go to college?" Mr. Sipley asked me during my first visit to his modest Grape Street home. "You'll have a better future in store for yourself if you do."

"Yes, I want to be a teacher," I replied, "so I'd like to apply to Glassboro State College in September so that I could be admitted next January."

"If you can harness the discipline to allow subject matter to go into your brain instead of thinking about what *you* want to come out of your mouth," Mr. Sipley wisely suggested. "I believe you'll make stellar advancement in trig' in no time."

"Could you explain that advice again in words I can understand?" I meekly asked.

"Well, when you speak, you only show others what little you do know," Mr. Sipley declared. "But when you listen and forget about what you'd like to say, ideas are absorbed quickly into your head, and you add to what little you do know. You then don't interfere with your own learning," Mr. Sipley explained. "You then become your best friend instead of your worst enemy. Basically, learn to listen instead of speaking! Use your ears instead of your mouth."

"I'll try to remember that method," I promised. "Keep my mouth shut and my mind and ears open."

Goose Restuccio was still in shock from his Larry's Pier IV Seafood Restaurant trauma, so I figured I would give the mental case a call to cheer him up.

"Hi Goose, how's your red T-Bird doin'?"

"Those dingleberry Blues smashed my headlights over at the Royale Crown," Restuccio stated, "and it's a good thing I had my wheels parked in the light near the ice cream stand, or those freaks might've destroyed the whole damned car before the punks kidnapped my ass and took me to Atco. J.W., there's somethin' I wanta' tell ya'," the usually arrogant ingrate confided. "Shit like this is hard for me to say. I hate cryin' and sadness, and crap like that."

"I hear ya' loud and clear," I acknowledged, "and now I know the reason why you've been *crabby* the last two weeks. How about if ya' take me over to Larry's Pier IV and treat me to a nice lobster tail dinner," I joked. "Then, we can enjoy chewing-on those same *crusty nations* that almost ate you!"

"J.W., listen to me," G.R. requested in a low voice. "I'm tryin' my best to be serious. I was nothin' before I met you. Everybody hated me, but I pretended not to care," Goose confessed. "After you came to Edgewood, things changed in my life. People began respectin' me. I became popular in the Reds. Do ya' get what I'm sayin'? I'm a changed asshole all because of you."

"Goose," I jovially answered, "do ya' know what I used to call ugly dragons with zits on their faces back in Levittown?"

"No, what?"

"Mince-meat," I responded, trying to cheer-up my melancholy friend. "And do ya' know what I used to call fairly attractive Cardinal Reagan chicks?"

"No, what?" Restuccio asked in almost a mantra-type utterance. "Tell me, and make it quick."

"Hamburger meat," I humorously replied. "And the better-lookin' girls the Diablos used to call roast beef. And above the decent-lookin' dolls, we described those girls as sirloin steak, followed by the next higher level, luscious filet mignon."

"No kiddin'," my despondent Italian paisan answered as if I had been genuinely educating him about an aspect of the female gender he had never before comprehended.

"And do ya' know what succulent, gorgeous babes were called back in Levittown?" I queried.

"No, ya' gotta' tell me!" he demanded. "I can't believe I'm interested in this *whore-end-us* mouse-shit you're layin' on me."

"Goose, are ya' tryin' to bait and *alienate* me?" I fired back.

"Look, J.W. I think ya' need a triple brain transplant," the distressed Mafia kid's voice defensively boomed through the kitchen wall telephone. What the hell kind of *jar-gun* are ya' sayin?' I ain't no cannibal space alien that had eaten you for supper!"

I completely ignored Goose's grossly erroneous English class vocabulary word interpretation, and proceeded with explaining my 'ideal girl' food analogy. "The cream of the crop of teen womandom was what the Diablos referred to as *lobster tail!* See ya' later, aggravator!" Click. I must admit, at *that* moment, it felt pretty good for a change, being the confident predator rather than the intimidated prey.

Five-minutes later, the kitchen phone rang. Mom said, "J.W., it's for you. Don't tie up the line too long. Your father is expectin' an important call from Aunt Marie in Baltimore."

I lifted the phone to my ear and was almost glad to recognize Goose's high-pitched staccato voice. "J.W.," his slanted mouth began. "Believe me, it's really hard for me to say this, but I'd like to thank ya' for savin' my life from those damned crusty nations."

"That's alright," I uttered, trying to dismiss my apparent heroism. "You'd do the same for me, wouldn't you?"

"After *that* horrible night at Pier IV, yes I would," G.R. answered. "*Before* that seafood problem, I was a wise-ass. But I know ya' feel bad about what Herc, Balls, and the St. Joe' jocks did to Mr. Jenkins's black Ford that used to belong to Mr. Andrews, don't ya'?"

"Why yes," I stammered. "I do feel bad about that error, I mean *that* mistake. I'm even scared to tell the priest in confession. I mean, where do I even begin to explain it?"

"Well," Goose continued in a depressed tone, "I'm gonna' give ya' five-hundred-dollars to put in an envelope with a typed letter of apology. Don't sign any names. Make it *synonymous,* just like the one ya' sent to Mrs. Murphy. Ya' understand!"

"Yes, I think so," I replied. "Thank you. I'll mail it from 'Philly. I have to take a drive to the Food Distribution Center to pick-up some produce for the market tonight."

"Can't join ya'," Goose returned. "Gotta' do somethin' with my Pop. He's back from Vegas. Had some big deals to do out there."

My next statement surprised Goose by asking the apologetic caller if his real biological father was really a priest as *he* had hinted in a previous conversation. His credible reply was rather staggering.

"J.W., don't tell a soul, not even News or Juice," my contrite friend pleaded in a solemn voice.

"I promise with a double pinky finger cross, hopin' to die if I break my sacred word," I pledged.

"Good. I gotta' get this monkey off my chest and tell someone, so it might as well be you," Goose confessed, even though I wasn't a priest. "In 1940, my father was in a bad car accident up on *206* near Atsion Lake. A deer ran out in front of his headlights, and the high beams blinded the buck. Pop swerved off the road, and veered into the pine woods."

There was a pause while Goose collected random thoughts and amassed the courage to put them into the right words. I respectfully gave the penitent caller the space and time he needed.

"Well," I finally said, "what happened to your father in the nighttime accident?"

"He smashed-up his testicles against the collapsed steerin' wheel, and *they* had to come-off at the hospital."

"Oh, sorry to hear that," I answered, not knowing what else to say. "Is there more to this story?"

"Well, I wouldn't tell this to anybody else," Goose confessed, "but I was born on September 7, 1942, exactly nine months after Pearl Harbor. Pop was away on business in Florida the whole month of December, when the Japanese attack happened. Mom was very religious and went to church and communion every day. She became friendly with a young priest, and that's how I came into this fuckin' world."

I heard Goose nearly sobbing at the other end of the line. "How did ya' find all this out? Is it just a theory of yours?" I wanted to know. "Who told you?"

"My two best friends before you came around told me the scoop," Goose related. "Frankie and Joe gave me the lowdown. That's how I know about it."

"Goose, you're now my good friend," I said. "Thanks for tellin' me that secret. And thanks for the five-hundred-dollars for Mr. Jenkins' car. I'm glad ya' have a conscience."

"Thanks, J.W. I'll never forget this! I owe you more than money." Click.

Goose did cough-up the five-hundred-dollars, which to him was mere pocket change. I put four-hundred in the envelope and mailed it from Philadelphia to "Mr. Jenkins, Edgewood High School, Coopers Folly Road, Tansboro, New Jersey". The other hundred-dollar bill I kept for emergency seed money should the Marvelons need another cash advance. I felt a little guilty keeping the "Ben Franklin" in my wallet. However, I did not feel as guilty as when I had neglected to put the five-dollars Grandma Annie had given me to pin on the Lady of Mt. Carmel statue in the Sixteenth of July procession. I finally rationalized that I needed the hundred-dollars more than Goose did, and I would repay him the money after the Marvelons cut their first successful hit record album.

The third week in June, I received a phone call from Mrs. Pat Pagano, coordinator of the Hammonton Canteen Dance held inside the high school gymnasium. "Can you have the Marvelons there at seven-thirty?" Mrs. Pagano asked. "We'll put the group on and see how the crowd reacts. If the kids like their songs, we'll let your group do more than two numbers."

"Sure thing," I excitedly replied. "They have great harmony. They're gonna' bring the roof down!"

"That's what I was afraid of!" Mrs. Pagano gasped. "Let's just have a nice, pleasant performance. Remember, they'll be singing in front of an all-white audience."

"Alright," I guaranteed. "We'll keep it down to an acceptable level. You won't be disappointed."

On the next Friday night in June, I drove Pop's '55 green and white Chevy Bel Air and picked-up Tyrone Davis in Winslow, several doors down from Jives Arena's place. We went to New Brooklyn and got the other four members of the Marvelons, Leroy, Gary, Clarence, and Little Floyd, a thirteen-year-old midget phenom' who could play the piano without being able to read music.

"Well, guys," I prattled after picking-up Little Floyd, "it's off to Hammonton High's gym and the big Canteen Dance."

"We's a little scared about this gig in Hammonton," Tyrone nervously admitted, "because a lotta' cats in that town don't like black people."

"Just be yourselves and don't try changin' your act to suit them," I advised. "Music is the universal language, and the Hammonton kids will relate to it, just like white kids around the country like Fats Domino, Chuck Berry, and Little Richard."

"You makes it all sound too easy," Leroy asserted. "I hope's there's no riot or rumble. We'll have to come back with the brothers and tear the town-up. I's real nervous, man. I mean, I might hit a few of them prejudiced Italian wops on top of their heads, if the dago jerks bug me too much! Most of 'em ain't too cool!"

"Wops!" I laughed. "That's an old slang abbreviation for Italian immigrants meaning *w*ith*o*ut *p*apers. W-O-Ps. And you guys are gonna' be doin' Doo-Wop! That's really both ironic and funny!"

Arriving in downtown Hammonton, I parked in the Acme Market lot across School House Lane from Hammonton High. The Marvelons anxiously got-out and stretched their arms.

"Hey, J.W.," Tyrone said, "ain't ya' gonna' lock your car?"

"Tyrone, this is Hammonton," I replied. "Nobody needs to lock their cars in this town. Where do ya' think we're at? North Philly' or New Brooklyn?"

"I don't trust nobody with my personal property!" Leroy added.

"Me neither," Clarence mimicked in his deep bass voice. "What's mine stays mine!"

The six of us crossed School House Lane and walked the Central Avenue pavement in front of the high school, arriving at the gymnasium door. Mrs. Pagano was there to greet us. I asked if a piano was available for Little Floyd to play, and Mrs. Pagano said we could roll an upright console model down the main hall from the auditorium floor and into the gym. That mission was accomplished rather easily with six guys contributing to the moving effort.

Tyrone introduced me to Jack Steins, a music producer for Marquee Best Records. The impresario was also the Marvelon's greedy business agent.

"Hi J.W.," Jack said, "good to meet you. I think this group has a lot of potential. With a few breaks and my many contacts in the industry," the fat Jewish promoter continued, "Tyrone and the Marvelons could zip to the top of the charts and make it to the bigs' in no time."

"That would be great," I hoped and commented.

"Well, J.W., I'm their agent, as you might know," Mr. Steins repeated, "and we're gonna' need another hundred bucks to cut a demo' with Marquee Records. If the big boys in the main office like what they hear, I believe that the first big record release is only a couple of months away."

I reached into my pocket and removed the crisp hundred-dollar-bill I had skimmed from Mr. Jenkins' mailed envelope for the damage done to *his* inverted black Ford, which had been wedged between three trees in the woods next to Edgewood High. "Here's the dough ya' need," I said to Mr. Steins, pretending to be a big shot.

"You're a good money man," Jack Steins told me, slapping my right shoulder. "You're more reliable than most of the managers I gotta' deal with."

"Thanks," I awkwardly answered, feeling like I had again been fleeced by big promises from a fast-talking con artist.

I surveyed the Hammonton High gym, festooned with blue and white crepe paper; blue and white balloons, and flaunting a giant Blue Devil, the school's mascot and logo. Two-hundred acne-faced teens were milling around the polished wooden gym floor, and I saw Joanne Berenato and Elaine Hill worriedly speaking with Herc Juliano and Balls Giordano. Feeling like an important invited guest, I stepped-over to their company to generate some small talk.

"Hi guys," I began. "Looks like a big dance tonight."

"J.W.," Joanne interrupted. "I hear you're the Marvelons' manager. They're supposed to be really good."

"Well yes," I replied, blushing all over my face. "Herc, I'm glad to see there's no Blues wandering-around in here. That's odd, isn't it? Hammonton High is *their* school."

"You know it," Herc suspiciously agreed. "Those slime-balls are up to no good. I'd rather see them in the flesh and keep an eye on them than not see them, and have to trust their pretend good behavior, if ya' know what I mean."

"Don't worry, J.W.," Balls Giordano confidently contributed to the conversation. "Those freaks won't crash the Canteen and ruin the Marvelons debut performance. No way! Herc and I won't let them cause trouble. Herc and I will guzz all their toothbrushes if they do," Balls laughed. "Then *their* breaths will smell like *our* assholes!"

"That's very comfortin' to know," I thankfully responded.

"Good luck J.W.," Elaine wished. "Ya' got guts! I admire that!"

I recalled something that Quinn once said to Bo Jalonec when we had left the Atlantic City boardwalk on Labor Day of '59. "When you're good, Elaine, you don't need luck." I then winked and waved 'so long' to the four very impressed listeners.

Mrs. Pagano welcomed everyone to the Hammonton Canteen Dance over the microphone, and next the coordinator presented the "fabulous Marvelons". Tyrone put the mike back onto its stand, and the other back-up singers stood in a semi-circle behind a second microphone stand. Little Floyd adroitly pounded-out the intro' to the Marvelons first slow number, "Kathy Don't Leave Me," which featured Tyrone's smooth, baritone, lead voice.

The lights dimmed. I gazed-around the darkened gym and was happy to see heads swaying to and fro to the ballad's serene rhythm and melody. The group's harmony was terrific, and when the first misty-eyed selection had been completed, the appreciative audience emitted a resounding applause.

The second song was a nifty rendition of the Five Satins "In the Still of the Night," which was followed by the Marvelons version of "My Prayer", originally recorded by the Platters. Next was "Silhouettes on the Shade," a song which had been put on hot wax by the Rays. Amazingly, the audience was really warming-up to the group, and Mrs. Pagano seemed relieved that the black Edgewood kids were being well-accepted at the Hammonton dance. Little Floyd banged-away at the upright piano console, sounding a little like Jerry Lee Lewis, when the Doo Wop group switched-into their stellar rock and roll segment.

First was a great presentation of Frankie Lymon's "Why Do Fools Fall in Love?" which was followed by Chuck Berry's "School Day". The Hammonton kids were going wild, and when the crowd all repeatedly screamed "encore", the Marvelons brought the house down with their Little Richard medley of "Tutti-Frutti," "Good Golly Miss Molly", and "Keep a Knockin'."

I really felt proud to be associated with the talented group I had reluctantly invested in. Even Jack Steins and Mrs. Pagano were enthusiastically clapping their hands at the medley's climax. I looked over to Joanne Berenato, and she and Elaine were elated at the tremendous performance being given by *my* group.

Amidst all the boisterous Hammonton teen adulation, I jubilantly congratulated Tyrone, Leroy, Clarence, Gary, and Little Floyd. It was a most triumphant moment, and I felt such exultation that I stepped-up to the microphone and took a bow with the then-admired five singing wonders.

The six of us began rolling the upright piano, returning it from the gymnasium to the school's main corridor, and then back to the auditorium. Mrs. Pagano gave us the twenty-dollar stipend and invited the Marvelons to come back and perform at the August Canteen dance. I graciously accepted the *Andrew Jackson* from the event's organizer, and consented to have Tyrone's band reappear at the August gig, if *we* weren't profitably touring "on the entertainment circuit in Las Vegas or Los Angeles".

Tyrone, Leroy and the rest were all in such a jovial mood, certain that our imminent success was just around the next corner. The Marvelons and I exited the gym via the side door, and cut across the high school campus around the back of the yellow brick building to the Acme Market parking lot. We were laughing and celebrating so hard, reviewing the details of the great live performance when a horrible observation shut us all up in a hurry. I couldn't believe my shocked eyes.

My father's green and white '55 Chevy Bel Air was loaded with at least a hundred-pounds of loose vanilla custard and a hundred-pounds of chocolate ice cream. Also, smeared inside was a hundred-pounds of melted vanilla ice cream; at least twenty-pounds of hot fudge stained all over the upholstery, and at least two-hundred unwrapped chocolate-covered ice cream pops.

"I told ya' to lock your doors," Tyrone Davis reminded me. "This sort of crap doesn't even happen in New Brooklyn or in Philly'."

"It looks like the skunks dumped a whole *Good Humor* truck inside your daddy's wheels," Leroy added.

My heart was filled with venom as I stepped to the windshield and savagely removed a note held under the wiper' blade.

"Hey nigger-lover, better run for cover,
To you and your black-faced pricks,
Black and white, just don't mix.
Tonight, you'll have a bad dream,
About drowning in tons of ice cream.
J.W., you know you're gonna' lose,
Whenever ya' wanta', fuck with the Blues."

"J.W.," Tyrone apologized, "we're sorry about what happened to your car, man. But I hate to break it to ya' cat. We ain't never gonna' do another gig in Hammonton. How we's gonna' get home now?"

News Tomasello had been at the Hammonton Canteen and had come out to the Acme parking lot to congratulate the Marvelons and me on a great piece of musical entertainment. "J.W.," Tommy said, "ya' gotta' call Sal Midilli from that phone booth over there to drive his tow truck out here to get your molested Chevy. I'll drive the Marvelons home."

"Thanks News," I softly replied, nearly crying. "You're a true friend when I really needed one."

Chapter Twenty-Eight

"The Polaroid Camera"

I was extremely scared to tell Dad about his Chevy Bel Air being vandalized and devastated by four-hundred-pounds of misplaced ice cream. Fabian drove me home and he told Pop the bad news. I was afraid of my father entering into a major coronary. Instead, Pop surprised me with an unexpected statement.

"That was the best thing that could have happened to that damned car," Dad attested. "It was on its last legs ever since *you* blew the engine up returning that March night from Levittown. The insurance should cover its true value, so I'm gonna' go over to Blatherwick Chevrolet in Berlin and get us a new '60 white Impala. I'll call the Hammonton police and have a damage report filled-out."

After Fabian drove his tow truck back to his pop's Flyin' A gas station in Waterford, dad gave me some adult advice. "Son, I know you're very idealistic," my mentor said, "but the car was destroyed because you're hangin' around with those Negro boys. I realize they must be nice kids, but try to limit your contact with colored kids. Our house and farm market might be torched if ya' keep seein' them. Those Hammonton High delinquents you're messin' with are as bad as the KKK."

"Then ya' aren't mad that your car's been ruined?" I incredulously asked.

"J.W., you honored my rule," Dad reminded me. "The car was parked in the Acme lot next to the high school. I told you back in March not to drive the car outa' Hammonton, and ya' kept your word. How could I be mad at you under those circumstances?"

I dared not tell Pop that I had picked-up the Marvelons with his '55 Bel Air in Winslow and in New Brooklyn. "Thanks Dad," I answered. "It sure pays to be honest."

The last week in June, I received an interesting phone call from Jives Arena. "Hey J.W.," the unmotivated high school beatnik greeted in a jovial tone of voice. "How's it hangin'?"

I then used one of my analogies from my Levittown repertoire. "Long and straight, but not for queer bait! I'm just happy to be a homo erectus!"

"That's some boss sauce without moss or loss," Jives weirdly admitted. "How about trippin' over to Atlantic City. Today's Saturday, and Dion and the Belmonts are giggin' over at the Steel Pier. News and Juice are already keen, ya' dig, jellybean? Pick ya' up at nine if ya' give me the sign!"

"Okay, what about Goose? Is he goin', too?" I asked.

"Naaa, he's too busy makin' money and stashin' his cash for a new speedboat that'll do more than float," Jives informatively returned. "I think he also has to guzz his own toothbrushes."

"Look, if I can't make it, I'll call ya' back in five," I told the hipster. "It's really hard for me getting-away from the farm market on a Saturday."

"I dig your gig like Porky Pig," the impudent goofball pathetically rhymed. "See ya' later, prevaricator."

I was surprised that Mom and Dad let me have the whole day off, it being the last Saturday in June. Since I was doing well with my trig' lessons, and because Mr. Sipley had given me a fine progress report in a conversation with Pop over the phone, I was allowed to accompany my friends to the 'Queen of Resorts'. I think that Dad was also glad to know that I was traveling to Atlantic City with some white boys and not getting into more trouble with the Marvelons.

As I waited for Jives's black and white Coronet to pull into the driveway, I considered how unfair life at times could be. I knew more math' than Goose Restuccio ever did, but the "General Student" had graduated from Edgewood and I didn't, simply because the numbskull was not going to college and passed taking easy courses that an advanced orangutan could have mastered. The inequity of it all boggled my mind. 'Andrews almost ruined my future,' I thought, 'but I'll show him by becoming a teacher and then becoming a member of the Edgewood faculty in five short years.'

I was thinking about how Jives had been accepted at Pace College up in New York City. News was going to Rutgers, and Juice to Villanova. And I was going to Mr. Sipley on Grape Street, all because of Andrews' militant classroom discipline. My deep meditation was interrupted by the appearance of Jives's familiar Dodge in the Pete's Market driveway.

"Hey J.W., let's make the scene, Daddy-o!" Frankie insisted. "We're gonna' buddy-up with Juice over at News's pad, ya' dig my jig, better than trig', don't ya', big wig?"

"I'm understandin' trig' better than ya' think," I maintained. "By the end of the summer, I'll know as much about it as Andrews does."

"It's all over with Andrews puttin' the screws to your noggin," Jives joked.

"Yeah, I guess it's now the after *math*," I jested back.

Jives eased his Dodge into News's place over on Spring Road, and the "current events' kid", along with Juice Illiani and Fabian. were there to meet us.

"Hope ya' don't mind if I tag along," Fabian asked Frankie. "I've been working pretty hard over at the Flyin' A, and since I just got word in the mail that I've been accepted into Glassboro State, my dad was so happy he gave me the whole day off."

I felt badly that I was the only one in the group that wasn't going off to college, but I had the decency to commend Johnny on his recent good fortune.

News Tomasello invited us all into the house to enjoy some refreshing *Pepsi's* and to see his newly-finished Hammonton area landscape down in his basement. We all obliged and followed our host downstairs.

"Wow! What a neat layout!" I marveled as I admired the beauty and the detail of the miniature version of Hammonton and vicinity that had been meticulously constructed on plywood platforms.

"It looks cool beyond ridicule," Jives verified and rhymed. "It's neater than the Jolly Green Giant's peter!"

News picked-up a pointer similar to the one used by Mr. Andrews in his classroom, and the self-appointed lecturer demonstrated exactly how the magnificent model had been built to scale by his dad and him. "Here's *206,* and I'm gonna' follow the exact route that Goose, Fabian, J.W. and me took on the great motorcycle chase with the frustrated Blues in hot pursuit," Tommy prefaced. "Here's Basin Road, and notice that at precisely half-mile intervals on Union Road are: Pine Road, Oak Road, Walker Road, Spring Road, and finally Flemington Pike, which we'll follow all the way down to and across *Route 30,* right here," News carefully reviewed. "Now, here's the railroad trestle where Hoss and Little Joe held the covered mirror from, and where the Blues had their nasty car collisions."

"Amazing," Juice acknowledged. "And look at the detail of all the buildings. There's the Atco Drive-in, and there's the Circus over in Devonshire," Illiani recognized and described. "And there's Wooster's Funeral Home, and Edgewood High, over on Coopers Folly Road, and then there's Hammonton High next to the….."

Juice paused for a moment, realizing what he had incidentally identified, looked at me hesitantly, and then the junior beatnik finished, "next to the Acme Market parking lot."

"And look," Fabian noted. "There's the *Route 54* 'Welcome to Hammonton' billboard, the Gem, St. Joe High, the Rivoli Theater, the Hammonton Police Station under Town Hall, Augie's Burger Paradise, Royale Crown Custard, White Horse Farm, Dual Motors, the Midway Diner…."

"Why do they call that grungy greasy spoon the Midway Diner?" Jives interrupted.

"Because it's in Hammonton, midway between 'Philly and Atlantic City," News informed Frankie. "Even a dumbbell like Mr. Andrews knows that."

"And DiDonato's Lanes and Hammonton Lake Park are situated here and there," I observed and orally identified, "and Bruni's Pizza, and the Palace Diner way over to that far corner on the Black Horse Pike. What's that big empty patch of blue?" I asked.

"That's where we're goin' this morning before we zip over to Atlantic City," News informed. "It's Gabe Gillette's thousand-acre blueberry plantation."

"Why are we goin' there?" I asked. "Won't we be trespassin'?"

"No way, Jose," Jives clarified. "We're gonna' be in the woods to take some pix of trees, of naked Mother Nature, and maybe even some *animules* like deer and skunks. Dig this new camera I got for bein' accepted into Pace up in New York."

"Wow!" I exclaimed being impressed. "It'a a *Polaroid!"* Does it take color pictures?"

"No, just black and white photos'," Jives laughed, "so, that means I can capture you and the Marvelons on film."

"Thanks," I glumly answered. "Ya' really know how to make me feel better about livin' happily in this screwed-up world. As long as we don't set foot on the blueberry farm, I guess it's alright to take pictures in the woods. I don't wanta' end-up incarcerated in a massive brush pile again."

"Or in a treacherous lobster tank," News added.

We finished drinking our bottles of *Pepsi Cola* and then piled into Frankie's primitive Dodge. Soon, Jives was motoring on *Route 30,* our innocent destination being Weymouth Road. "I really groove on Mother Nature," Jives related, "so I'm gonna' snap 'til I crap."

"Hope ya' aren't constipated," Juice laughed, "or you'll never run out of film, and we'll never make it to the Steel Pier. Get the picture, Matthew Brady?"

"Who's playin' at the Steel Pier this week?" I asked.

"Dion and the Belmonts," Juice reminded me, "and next week the major stage attraction is...."

"Fabian!" Juice said turning, pointing, and laughing at Sal Midilli, smiling and sitting in the back seat with me.

"Turn Me Loose", man, 'Like a Tiger'!" Jives added, referring to the rock singer Fabian's two biggest hits. "Sal, ya' can hop up on the stage and be the real Fabian's double."

"No thanks. I'd rather pump gas; fix transmissions, and commute to Glassboro," my modest, good-looking friend replied.

News started jabbering about how Floyd Patterson had knocked-out heavyweight Ingemar Johansson on June 20th in the fifth-round. "Patterson became the first fighter in boxing history to regain the heavyweight championship," News boringly elucidated, "and not even Joe Louis had done that feat. But Floyd Patterson is not a big guy by heavyweight standards. In fact, he's kinda' little."

"I thought Little Floyd played piano for the Marvelons," Juice joked. "Isn't that right J.W.?"

I asked Jives to turn-on the radio, so we listened to WIBG 99 and heard the Everly Brothers' "Bye, Bye Love", which made me think about Joanne Berenato and me. Then, the guys were treated to Bill Doggett's "Honky Tonk, Part II", which automatically made me think about Quinn's love of instrumentals back in Levittown, and finally, we listened to Fats Domino's "Blueberry Hill", which made me uneasy thinking about our contemptible rival Hammonton gang. "Let the Good Times Roll" by Shirley and Lee was blasting from Frankie's radio when we passed Morano's Bag Distribution Company on Weymouth Road, and my mind slowly shifted from having a hot romance with Joanne Berenato to having a good time in Atlantic City with my fellow stags.

Frankie made a quick left onto New Creek Road, which the Blues affectionately called Third Road, suggesting that powerful Gabe Gillette owned that entire section of Hammonton and vicinity. The Coronet entered a dirt path, and was furtively parked behind a cluster of pine trees, which were obscured from any occasional vehicle that traveled-down gravel-surfaced, New Creek Road.

"Hey, did ya' guys hear what the Blues did to Pee Wee Lucca?" News asked.

"No, what happened?" Juice inquired as Frankie stopped his '57 Dodge beside a thicket. "Pee Wee's a true Blue. Why would his buddies do anything harmful to him?"

"Because Gabe Gillette calls the shots with the Blues," Fabian stated, "and the big Blue honcho decided that Pee Wee had leaked some secret information to the Reds, and was like a double-agent spy, which he wasn't!"

News Tomasello further divulged that Gabe Gillette and Speed Mortellite had accused Pee Wee Lucca of treason for conveying certain Blues' secrets to the Reds, so then the blueberry' thugs made the accused elf to strip-down to his jockey shorts inside Ox Narducci's storage building. The crazy loons stood in a circle and then squirted their diminutive victim with fifteen squeeze containers of sticky blueberry syrup. Next, the Blues escorted their hostage upstairs in Narducci's red barn, and pushed the "Benedict Arnold" through the hayloft door onto a heap of smelly fertilizer. Poor Pee Wee was corroded from head-to-foot with a 10-10-10 mixture of potash, potassium, and nitrogen.

"Where did you hear all of that gossip?" I asked Juice as we exited the Coronet with the intent of experimenting with the novel *Polaroid.*

"Hoss Gregorio had heard the story from Herc Juliano and Balls Giordano over at the Gem," Johnny related. "But ya' haven't heard the best part yet."

Juice told us that after the Blues had drenched poor Pee Wee with fertilizer and indignity after "betraying" his gang, the detestable hooligans further destroyed his self-esteem by transporting the helpless runt late that night in the trunk of Gillette's blue Cadillac to Ancora State Mental Hospital. The malevolent rich kids strapped Pee Wee's legs together, and then taped basketballs to his right and left hands, so that the disabled wimp couldn't use his fingers. The unsavory fiends left Pee Wee in the courtyard between two state hospital buildings, and next lit three sticks of dynamite several hundred-feet away. The cruel tricksters left Lucca behind to hear the loud explosions that would eventually wake-up the mental hospital patients and the facility's resident staff members.

"They would even turn on their own kind," Fabian suggested and maintained, "and Pee Wee was probably the Blues most loyal member."

"The Blues would eat their own kind," News corrected Sal. "Absolute power corrupts, and absolute power corrupts absolutely. Thank you, Mrs. Murphy!"

The five of us exited the Dodge Coronet and breathed in the pristine, early summer country air. The pine trees smelled fresh and nicely scented. The entire rustic environment was quite healthy and inspiring. It was the Jersey pinelands being experienced and savored in all its glory.

Jives told us, "Stay still. I think I see a squirrel I'm gonna' nab in a pic'." We all inched forward, but instead of a squirrel, we came across a silver fox with a dead bird hanging in its mouth. The size of the creature frightened Frankie, who dropped his *Polaroid* camera without even taking a candid snapshot. "I woulda' got the fox," Jives reckoned, "but you guys scared the friggin' frisky critter away."

"Sure, Jives," Juice joked and grinned. "That's why ya' probably now have seven additional shit stains in your damned underwear."

The five of us trespassing explorers proceeded-down a narrow sandy trail, and Frankie managed to get some still shots of a blue jay in a pine tree, and a splendid male cardinal in a blue spruce. We slowly advanced onward to a clearing, searching for an unwary deer that might be foraging for food in the late morning sun.

"Wait!" Frankie cautioned. "There're two adult cats talkin' turkey in that blueberry field up ahead."

"That's Mr. Gillette and Goose's old man," Fabian recognized and whispered as we all simultaneously crouched-down behind some sticker bushes and wild ferns. "What's in the damned suitcase?"

"Probably money," Juice verbally speculated. "Illicit money of some sort, I'll bet."

"A payoff, maybe," I nervously wondered and shared in a low, soft voice. "An illegal deal!"

Jives motioned for the rest of us to stay put while the amateur photographer crawled forward to a lone huge tulip tree, situated at the fringe of the newly-planted blueberry field. The camera enthusiast snapped three *Polaroid* photos' from behind the tulip tree, about two-hundred-feet from his lens.

After Mr. Restuccio entered his new blue Mercedes and quickly drove-away in a cloud of dust, Mr. Gillette removed a shovel from his blue Rolls Royce's trunk and dug a hole between two rows of tiny blueberry bushes. The agricultural tycoon placed the attache' case into the shallow cavity, and then covered the stash with loose dirt. Gillette then counted to thirteen, the number of rows from the corner of the field to the recently buried loot. The blueberry czar next entered his Rolls Royce, and being satisfied that his clandestine activity had gone undetected, the plantation mogul looked in both directions, and then slowly drove his luxury automobile out of the remote farm field.

"The five of us scampered-out of the woods into the vacant field. Jives waited for the last of his *Polaroid* pictures to develop, and then removed the photo' from the camera, and quickly separated the negatives from the actual photos. "Look at these babies!" the excited hipster exclaimed.

Two revealing photos' had captured Mr. Restuccio and Mr. Gillette making a surreptitious transaction, and the third showed an abundance of cash that had been secretly concealed inside the black attache' case.

"Let's dig-up the illegal bread," Jives impetuously urged. "We'll all be rich as Rockefeller!"

"How do ya' know it's illegal money?" I challenged. "It's not ours, whether it's legal or illegal."

"Look," said Juice. "If it's illegal to begin with, then Mr. Restuccio has probably already gotten his share if he's givin' the rest to Mr. Gillette. And if it's Gillette's money, we can either steal it or destroy it. I'm not afraid to get my hands dirty when found treasure is involved!"

"Why can't we take it to the police station?" I inquired as News and Fabian got-down on their hands and knees to start excavating the shallow buried treasure.

"J.W., are ya' stupid or somethin'?" Juice admonished. "If the money's legal, we'll look like fools diggin' it up and takin' it to the cops. If it's illegal," Johnny continued his perceptive analysis, "then the not-too-innocent cops might be in on the illicit dough deal and might charge us with handlin' and transportin' stolen goods that were never reported to the IRS."

"Here it is," Fabian informed. "Let's open up the latches and see how much dough is inside."

The excess dirt was rubbed-off of the black leather attache; the overhead snaps were popped, and inside the small traveling case was a cache of hundred-dollar-bills that had been stored. Jives counted a stack of a hundred bills, and the discoverers estimated that the case contained the phenomenal sum of around seven-hundred-and fifty-thousand-dollars.

"Well, what are we gonna' do with all this found money?" I anxiously pressed the others for an answer. "I have a feelin' we gotta' get outa' here soon," I concluded and recommended. "I don't wanta' wind-up naked at Ancora State Hospital with blueberry syrup and stinking fertilizer smeared all over me."

The five of us 'Long John Silvers' held an impromptu vote, and by unanimous agreement, we elected to destroy the cash and put a minor dent in the Gillette and Restuccio family fortunes.

"J.W.," Juice imperatively nominated. "You're hereby appointed to come-up with the idea of how we can dispose of this here loot."

Chapter Twenty-Nine

"The Steel Pier Excursion"

The five obsessed 'Treasure Hunters' had to be crazy possessed teenagers. We rushed to Jives's Dodge, and Fabian, who had been carrying the attache case, gently deposited the pilfered, heisted 'treasure' into the Coronet's trunk. Frankie drove the thirty-miles down *Route 30* to Atlantic City with the stolen cash stashed in the rear storage compartment. I promised the guys that I would have a definitive solution of how we would dispense with the purloined money by the time we finally returned to Hammonton.

Jives' was wearing his trademark red cap, a tilted French beret. Juice worked the non-conformist over pretty good, when Johnny berated, "Why don't ya' graduate from that red cloth to a Davy Crockett coonskin hat? The furry head-dress has only been out of style for three-years. Jives, that grotesque thing you're wearin' on your enlarged noggin," Juice Illiani continued articulating his personal commentary, "is old enough to have been sewn by Betsy Ross's great-grandmother."

"Stop makin' front burner square jive outa' back burner dumb threads barf," Frankie Arena cryptically replied.

"What did *that* illiterate jabberwocky mean?" Johnny asked News, Fabian, and me. "Frankie needs a team of translators from Pluto, because this guy's way out there in his own unique orbit."

"Jives meant," News interpreted, "that silly, stupid jokes about his noteworthy hat shouldn't be given a second thought."

"Oh!" Johnny Juice interjected. "Mr. Fashion Plate has spoken. Pardon my French! Kindly pass the collection baskets, please."

"Guys," I objectively piped-in. "There's seven-hundred-and-fifty-thousand bucks in the trunk of this three-hundred-dollar car, and you two nitwit turkeys are only concerned about Jives's red beret. Won't Goose be pissed at us when he finds out we stole the cash that was once his father's dough?"

"He ain't gonna' find-out because nobody in this car is gonna' squeal, comprende amigo," Juice expressed. "J.W., do ya' think everybody on this corrupt planet is as honest and naïve as you are?"

"Si, yo comprendo," I answered as I exhausted most of my Spanish vocabulary. "But I didn't know for sure that Goose's Dad and Mr. Gillette were in cahoots. It's like there's no difference between a legitimate commercial business and an illegitimate rackets' enterprise, anymore."

"Now at last, J.W., you're finally learnin' about real life," Fabian indicated, alluding to his impression that I was basically a quixotic dreamer. "Mafia are illegal crooks, and millionaires and lawyers are legal crooks. It's all that simple," Fabian sensibly indicated. "They didn't all become rich by workin' in factories as common laborers."

Jives drove his Dodge into a familiar-looking Virginia Avenue parking lot. "Hey knuckleheads," I perked-up. "This is the same lot where the Diablos parked our cars before the big blueberry farm drag race last Labor Day between Quinn and Cummings. That was the beginnin' of the end for the Kamikazes."

"Well, whoopty-doo and peek-a-boo," Jives cynically ridiculed. "Instead of the Steel Pier, let's go home and watch *Ozzie and Harriet* and *Leave It to Beaver* on the boob tube. Then, maybe faggot maggot J.W. will be happy and comtented like Elsie's cows."

Jives received the parking stub from the lot attendant. The five Jersey shore visitors walked up the Virginia Avenue wooden ramp to the world-famous Atlantic City Boardwalk. The quintet shook hands with a costumed person dressed as Planters' *Mr. Peanut,* who was positioned in front of the Steel Pier, and we all got a good laugh when Juice pointed to the giant overhead marquee which read, "Appearing Next Week, Fabian".

"Looks like you're here seven days too early," Johnny cackled to a slightly-miffed Sal Midilli.

Then, we bought our general admissions tickets, played some games of chance and next had our pictures taken at an "Old Tyme Photo Gallery". After a dip in the Atlantic Ocean inside the world-renown "Diving Bell", followed by a visit to the "Diving Horse" spectacular, both of which were located near the end of the quarter-mile-long pier, it was time for the Reds to see Dion and the Belmonts performing on stage.

The scarlet curtain was raised inside the Steel Pier's main theater, and Dion's musical performance was really terrific. The group started-out with their newest release, a slow number called "Where or When", which was followed by upbeat numbers "Teenager in Love" and a terrific upcoming record cut titled "Lonely Teenager". I was thinking about the Marvelons during the great stage presentation, and I suspected that Jives was having a mental newsreel reviewing his ill-fated roller coaster association with the now-defunct Boatnecks.

The enjoyable show was over in less than an hour, so we bought some caramel popcorn and slices of tomato and cheese pizza; drank some *Pepsi's,* and headed back to the Virginia Avenue parking lot. After paying the parking attendant two-dollars, we all piled into the black and white Coronet. My distrustful, dubious nature suddenly prompted me to state something on the doubtful side.

"Hey, Jives," I distrustfully began. "Shouldn't ya' check the trunk and see if the case of money is still in there?"

"J.W.," Jives nastily retorted. "If some jive chickenhawk made off with the stolen bread, then ya' don't have to worry about gettin' rid of the loot. Do ya', Dingle-head?"

"No, you're absolutely right," I agreed, nodding my head. "That was a stupid thing to ask after seeing a great show before eating caramel popcorn and delicious pizza. Anybody got any *Alka-Seltzer* for dessert?"

Just as Jives was about to turn right onto Virginia Avenue, the air-headed driver suddenly halted his automobile. A beautiful white '60 Thunderbird came down the Steel Pier's concrete *VIP* ramp and gracefully entered onto Virginia Avenue. The boss machine passed by us in a blur, but Jives got a good look at the T-Bird's occupants.

"Was that Speed Mortellite and some Blues?" I sarcastically asked. "Did Speed get his T-Bird fixed-up already?"

"No, Asshole!" Jives screamed like a fanatic with his fingers caught in a mousetrap. "That was Dion and the Belmonts in that car. They just finished their last gig at the Steel Pier, and I'll bet my red beret and a visit to the sacred *Howdy Doody Museum* that they're headin' back to Brooklyn to see if any trees are still growin' there."

Jives took his role as chief tracker quite seriously as the cretin tailed the white Thunderbird down Virginia Avenue to *Route 30.* We stayed close behind the popular celebrity singing group through six traffic lights, all the way down to the White Horse Pike. All the while, Juice Illiani related an interesting story about Goose Restuccio that had taken place in the Men's Room at the Starlight Ballroom Skating Rink in Devonshire, directly across from the incomparable Circus Drive-in.

"I was in the Men's Room with Goose about a year ago," Johnny recounted, "and right when we were about to leave to go out to the dance floor, this chunky black fella' came into the lavatory. He looked into the mirror and asked me if I had a comb he could borrow. I reached into my pocket and lent him my groomer."

"So, what's wrong with that?" I asked. "He needed his rug adjusted and you accommodated the kid."

"Well," Juice continued his mediocre anecdote. "After the heavy-set black kid left the Men's Room, Goose told me to 'throw the damned comb in the trash can to avoid getting cooties or deadly venereal disease inside my scalp."

"Did ya?" Fabian inquired. "I've heard of segregated bathrooms, but never segregated combs in bathrooms," the mechanic joshed.

"Yes, I chucked it. I didn't want to have Goose snide remarks go crazy on me," Johnny confessed. "But then, when we went back into the dance hall, the lights dimmed, and the announcer introduced a future rock star, none other than Chubby Checker."

"No shit!" Jives exclaimed. "That wig-divider might've been valuable someday if ya' had just kept it."

"Real smart," I interrupted. "Here we have three quarters of a million dollars sittin' in this jalopy's trunk, and we're playin' private detective followin' Dion and the Belmonts to who knows where, and now you brain-dead Neanderthals are all bent out of shape about a five-cent comb that might be worth five-dollars now."

"Hey, J.W.," Fabian got my attention. "Have ya' thought about how you're gonna' destroy the money Mr. Restuccio gave to Mr. Gillette yet? How about havin' a massive dumpster bonfire?"

"I'm still workin' on it," I admitted. "It's not everybody like me that's got money to burn," I joked.

Dion and the Belmonts pulled into a futuristic-looking pizza palace on the White Horse Pike in Absecon, just beyond the Atlantic City line. Jives mimicked the singing group's T-bird and turned into the second entrance (which was really the exit) to avoid the rockers' detection. The place was rather empty of diners, munching on pizza, so Frankie eased-up to the linear counter stools and sat next to Dion. Myself, News, Juice, and Fabian occupied the four stools to Jives' right.

Dion and the Belmonts ordered two medium pepperoni pizzas, and *we* were so neurotic and pumped-up that we couldn't think of anything else to say to the waitress except "two medium pepperoni pizzas," even though that's exactly what we had just eaten an hour before at the Steel Pier.

And then Jives, acting like a complete impulsive idiot, noticed a product packaged inside a box displayed on a ledge behind the serving waitress. "Miss," the imbecile said, "could I have a pack of that Beechnut Spearmint Gum, the one wrapped in green, made for a teen," as the garrulous hipster quoted a familiar slogan often-mentioned by the popular Saturday night television host of "The Dick Clark Show".

I had seen Dion and the Belmonts sing "Teenager in Love" on the highly-rated "Dick Clark Show", and so, Jives' attempt to be super cool inside the *Route 30* Absecon pizza parlor was rather embarrassing, and almost nauseating at that particular moment.

Dion obviously had heard Jives' attention-getting comment. The thoroughly amused singer turned to the Belmonts and said, "See fellas', that television advertisin' stuff really works. Dick Clark says *that* Beechnut line all the time on *his* show."

The five Reds made sure that we ate our pepperoni pizzas faster than Dion and the Belmonts ate theirs, and we were the first group out the door. Our contingent patiently waited in the Coronet for the famous Laurie Record Company artists to exit the futuristic-looking, UFO-shaped, pizza palace.

"Let's just offer Dion three-quarters-of-a-million bananas to come to Hall Street in Winslow and do a private concert at Jives' house," I outrageously suggested. "Say Frankie, how did you ever get those two hundred screaming honeys to show-up on your front lawn for the imitation Boatnecks?"

"I have two blabbermouth, chatterbox chick cousins, one in Pennsy' and one in Delaware," the obnoxious kid revealed, tilting his red beret while glancing into the rear-view mirror. "I gave the broads a cool hundred bucks apiece to get their babe buds to come to the Winslow disastrous shindig."

Dion and the Belmonts finally left the futuristic-looking pizza establishment, and Jives followed their impeccable T-bird out of the restaurant's parking lot and onto busy *Route 30*. The white Thunderbird soon veered right onto the ramp leading to the *Garden State Parkway*. Jives duplicated the T-Bird's maneuver with his black and white Dodge.

"See, I told ya' that the Belmonts was goin' back to Brooklyn," Jives observed and joked. "There's no joint like home."

"I hope it's got more to offer than New Brooklyn does," I retorted, referring to the Marvelons' village. "How far are we gonna' follow them?"

"All the hundred-miles to New York, if I have to," Jives declaratively maintained. "I still got three-quarters of a tank includin' the *mucho* gas comin' outa' your mouth and ass."

Dion and the Belmonts cruised over the *Parkway Bridge* that spanned the tranquil *Mullica River,* and the Coronet trailed the T-Bird a quarter mile behind. "Hey, there's Chestnut Neck Marina on the right," Fabian identified. "That's where Gabe Gillette keeps his cabin cruiser and his speed boat."

"Well, Sal," I answered. "Gabe Gillette probably just keeps his speed boat there now because Goose took good care of the blue and white cabin cruiser with two accurately-thrown Congo watermelons and an explosive cherry bomb," I added. "The detonation sent the expensive craft smashin' into the pillars supporting the *Route 30* bridge over the Atlantic Canal."

After paying a toll and passing by a *Garden State Parkway* Service Area. Fabian urged and then dared Jives to catch-up to the Belmonts and intrepidly race them all the way to Brooklyn. I noticed the speedometer registering ninety-five when we pulled alongside the white T-Bird. Dion must have thought our vehicle had been a state trooper's cruiser, because the T-Bird had slowed-down in the passing lane, enabling us to eventually straddle it on the right.

The rock and roll singers soon realized that we were simply a group of excited fans or autograph seekers, wanting a little highway action, and so the driver floored the white 'Bird, and Frankie did likewise inside his Coronet. After about a quarter of a mile, the T-Bird left us literally smelling its exhaust fumes.

"Nice try Frankie," Fabian sympathized. "Next time bring a kiddy fire engine with ten pedals. Ya' must've learned how to race at the Indianapolis Kiddy-Way 500 Meters!"

"Make sure you don't break the head gasket and blow the entire engine block," I shouted, recollecting my old speeding experience.

Frankie had no time to answer Sal's critical remarks nor my cautionary exposition. There was a loud "boom", and suddenly, the Coronet's front wheels began shimmying and then wobbling at sixty-miles-an-hour. The Dodge swerved left, right, left, and then right again. The flustered driver managed to get the car to shake its way to the parkway's shoulder, and Jives finally was able to stop its forward momentum before zooming into a guardrail.

Expert mechanic Fabian Midilli took charge of the right front tire changing, and had the spare put on within fifteen-minutes. A state trooper stopped his cruiser with its red lights flashing, and when he saw that we were neurotic kids, the officer became suspicious of our nocturnal activities.

"Where are you kids headin'?" the trooper sternly asked.

"Up to Asbury Park to visit my cousin, walk the boardwalk, play pinball, and stay overnight," News intelligently lied.

"Yeah, we just got a flat tire," Fabian said extending his hands to show his grimy fingers. The cop shined his flashlight on Sal's palms, which were indeed greasy and dirty.

"Okay, just show me your license and registration, and I'll let ya' be on your way," the trooper requested.

Jives complied with the state cop's demands, and with all requested documents being satisfactory, the trooper declared, "Have a safe trip and take it easy. Asbury Park is still another thirty-miles from here. Be careful. There's a lot of crazy speeding kooks zipping-around out here at nighttime."

After the five of us hopped back into the Dodge, Jives rotated the wheel, and we were again on our way traveling north. With no more Belmonts or Dion to race, Frankie entered the next Service Area, and then swung around and took the *Parkway* south toward Atlantic City. I inhaled a breath of relief.

"That was a close call!" I exhaled while wiping the excess sweat from my brow. "News, how did you come-up with that great Asbury Park lie? It sounded so convincin'."

"I have an uncle who lives up near there in Long Branch, so if the trooper asked me any questions about the geography of the place, or about any specific landmarks," News bragged, "then I was ready with the right responses."

"Quick thinkin'," Juice commended our friend with an appropriate new nickname, *TNT*. "And Sal, that was smart showin' the cop your grimy hands. He forgot all about inspectin' the trunk and accidentally seein' more than a dirty flat tire."

Jives exited the *Garden State Parkway* at the Bass River ramp, and after paying a ten-cent-toll, headed west on the back route toward Hammonton through historic Batsto Village. "Sweetwater Casino is on the other side of the *Mullica River,"* News reported.

"Do people gamble there?" I innocently asked.

"No Dummy," Tommy chastised. "Sweetwater Casino is a large restaurant and marina business alongside the *Mullica*."

When Jives passed the historic stone Batsto Playhouse, the slang-authority soon stopped, and then made a left-hand turn onto Pleasant Mills Road, which meandered through blueberry country into Central Avenue and downtown Hammonton.

"Thank goodness we're outa' the main part of the pine-barrens," Juice sighed. "The Jersey Devil hangs out there!"

"Okay J.W.," Jives challenged. "What do ya' have to say about magically poofin'-away the seven-hundred-fifty-grand. Is your middle name Houdini or Mandrake?"

I thought about my severe case of indigestion after eating an overabundance of pizza both, at the *Steel Pier* and at the *Route 30* tomato and cheese palace, all the while accompanied by a bevy of annoying Reds along with Dion and the Belmonts. I had just finished reading Ray Bradbury's science fiction novel *Fahrenheit 451,* and since I enjoyed plagiarizing plots from literature, and marketing them to my friends as original ideas, I ingeniously combined the idea of pizza with the notion of a blazing inferno, and came-up with a rather remarkable solution.

"Listen, Guys. I've just got done reading Ray Bradbury's *Fahrenheit 451,* "and it gave me a great idea."

"What's that?" News remarked. "Call the Hammonton Fire Department and have *them* incinerate the money?"

"No!" I angrily replied in reaction to Tommy's blatant cynicism and sarcasm. "I learned from reading the novel that paper and books burn at four-hundred-and-fifty-one degrees, hence, the book title," I elaborated. "So, paper money must also burn at around five-hundred-degrees temperature," I assumed and estimated.

"Are ya' gonna' put the seven-hundred-fifty-thousand clams in the brick kiln at the Winslow Brickyard?" Fabian joked in reference to Goose's recent automobile misfortune.

"No, Silly," I replied. "We're gonna' break into Bruni's Pizzeria on Twelfth Street. I understand that Mr. and Mrs. Bruni are on vacation for two weeks visitin' relatives in Sicily, and the shop is presently closed."

"Holy Moley!" Jives yelled. "We're not only cookin'. We're now shakin' and bakin'!"

"Those new pizza ovens Mr. Bruni has can get-up to six-hundred-degrees," News informed us. "That's one reason why Bruni's has the best pizza in South Jersey."

"And if Ray Bradbury is right," I theoretically added, "the new crisp *Ben Franklins* oughta' burn when those ovens hit five-hundred-degrees Fahrenheit."

Jives instantly and irreverently yelped, "Holy Ash Wednesday! It's just like crematin' Ben Frankin thousands of times over and over!" Fifteen-minutes later, the 'colloquial kid" dimmed his headlights and drove-around the right side of the pizzeria into the empty rear parking area. Frankie opened his trunk, and I was assigned to carry the attache case into the neat and tidy eatery. Fabian got-out his hand tools' packet, and deftly picked the lock on the back door.

In five minutes, the cold cash was entered inside the soon-to-be hot oven without any pepperoni or anchovies sprinkled on top. Sal rotated the dial to six-hundred-degrees, maximum temperature, and then closed the oven's door. "Okay, let's cut outa' here before the fuzz smells what's cookin'!" Jives astutely recommended.

After we inelegantly hopped into the Coronet and swiftly closed the doors, Juice asked me a vital question. "J.W., do ya' have any other bright ideas?"

"Why, yes," I casually replied, winking my right eye. "Jives, take Weymouth Road to New Creek Road. Park in the woods where ya' did before. Fabian and I will bury the empty attache case in the unlucky thirteenth blueberry row, right where it had been dug up."

After that scary 'field mission' had been accomplished, Jives drove the other guys to their respective homes. When we finally pulled-up to Pete's Market, perpetual rhymer amazingly asked in standard English, "J.W., are ya' sure that money's gonna' burn in that pizza oven?"

“Sure,” I answered, faking certainty, a frail habit I had learned from Goose. “Only a few ashes will be left from the embers. Good night, Chet!” I signed-off with a smile, alluding to the closure of a popular NBC News program, the *Huntley-Brinkley Report*.

“Good night, Dave!” Frankie Arena mechanically answered.

“Jives, we ain’t good enough to be Walter Crankcase on CBS! I suppose we’re permanently stuck on NBC without News!” I jovially finished.

Chapter Thirty

"An Unfortunate Pedestrian"

On July 1st, Goose Restuccio pulled into Pete's Market on an unexpected visit. I was unloading forty fifty-pound bags of potatoes from the Pete's Market Special, but I kept an eye on G.R., who was engaged in a genial, extended conversation with Pop. Five-minutes later, Goose ambled-over to the blue truck.

"Need any help?" the lethargic chronic liar asked. "I seldom do any damned physical labor. That kind of hard work is for Puerto Ricans, niggers, and Mexicans."

"Maybe I can get the Marvelons or Sammy Davis Jr. to help me with these potatoes," I joked. "The main difference between you and Tyrone Stevens' group is that the Marvelons have black skin, and you've got a black soul."

"Stop with all of the moral bullshit," Goose snapped. "If ya' could show me a picture of my soul, I'll give ya' a thousand bucks right now outa' my pocket. There ain't no such goddamned animal, but ya' believe it, or I think ya' wanta' believe it."

"You should've been a priest," I laughed and then wiped my brow. "You're very persuasive, almost convincin' most of the time! If ya' had paid more attention in your low ability General English class, ya' would've learned that *soul* is an abstract noun, like love or justice. Ya' can't have a concrete noun *picture* of anybody's soul."

"Look, J.W.," G.R. angrily lectured. "When you was a kid, everybody told ya' there was a Santa Claus, and when ya' found out that there wasn't any such silly-assed gift giver, you got mighty pissed off, didn't ya'!"

"Well, yes," I answered, trying to figure-out Goose's modus operandi.

"You was pissed-off because ya' was lied to by your parents; lied to by your school, and lied to by the whole damned society, ain't that the truth!" G.R. persisted.

"Why yes, I guess so," I responded. "So what?"

"Well then, there ain't no God, just like there ain't no Santa Claus," my chief tormentor maintained. "God didn't create man; man created God to serve *his* own purposes." G.R. went on to say that the laziest and weakest people in ancient villages made up stories that capitalized on the natives' fears and hopes, so that "the prehistoric village priests and witchdoctors" wouldn't have to toil and work for a living. According to my atheist acquaintance, the priests and witchdoctors soon found-out that they could survive on the labors of others through contributions and donations. "People would rather be lied to and believe in those goddamned lies than accept the truth that there ain't no God, or no damned heaven or hell," G.R. concluded and argued. "Most people like to be used and manipulated! The damned bishops carry staffs like shepherds do! If you follow those con-artists around a shit-manure pasture, then that makes you a damned sheep!"

I figured I would change the subject because my fellow Red was becoming a little too vociferous, and Mom would then become offended if any farm market customers were insulted by Goose's propensity for being a foul-mouthed religious anarchist and a vulgar moral iconoclast.

"Why don't ya' get the Blues rubbed-out by Mafia machine guns?" I asked my jaded pal. "One target session could eliminate all of the pests!"

"J.W., first of all, ya' watch too many *Untouchables* episodes on television," wily Restuccio commented. "It's all sort of like royalty. Kings and queens don't mess around with jacks and jesters. The rulers only fuck with other kings and queens. Princesses only marry peasants and frogs in fairy tales, and religion is just one big fucked-up fairy tale. Get it?"

I maintained that in America, social and economic mobility were highly possible realities because modern democracy and free enterprise had taken civilization out of medieval feudal times, when governing queens and kings were then especially important to the society's survival.

"J.W.," Goose gruffly lectured, "my old man believes that I shouldn't hang-around with lower class peasants like you, but right now, I happen to like ya'," the volatile despot insisted. "My old man believes that the only reason for *our* connection is for me to make money off of you and your dad's business. Get the message?"

I told Goose that business should be based on mutual trust and respect, and not on mere exploitation. The Mafia prince had other ideas that refuted and shook the very premises that supported my interpretation of the basic Biblical reason for man's existence.

"J.W.," G.R. debated. "My Old Man wants me to solve my problems on my teen level, but if I get hurt bad or get killed by the Blues, then Gabe Gillette and Speed Mortellite will soon know that the jerk-offs stepped over the line, ya' understand?" Goose loudly raved. They'll pay the price with their lives, and the main Blues know it. The smart-asses can only go so far."

Restuccio then informed me that he had recently started several new businesses, and that the braggart was saving money to acquire an expensive speedboat in which to race-around on the Mullica River. I thought I would switch topics again, never realizing that such a maneuver was impossible when having a frustrating dialogue with G.R.

"Goose, what were ya' talkin' to Pop about?" I inquired. "Are ya' lookin' for a summer job?" I joked.

"J.W., I'm getting into bigger business enterprises, since I ain't goin' to no friggin' college to learn how to masturbate and wipe other people's asses for four freakin' years," Restuccio insisted, believing that he had outgrown gum-ball capitalism. "I'm graduatin' from gum-balls. Your Pop has agreed to get a soda machine and a cigarette machine in the stand here. The money he'll make from the soda and cigarette dispensin' will help pay for *your* college education," Goose emphasized. "Of course, ya' gotta' get your high school diploma before ya' can go the Glassboro and learn how to masturbate and wipe other people's asses for four wasted years."

Surprisingly, Goose helped me unload the remaining twenty-five fifty-pound potato sacks from the truck, and stack the items into a neat pyramid. I thanked my volunteer for his assistance, fully realizing that physical labor was contrary to G.R.'s habits and to his perverted, decadent, immoral philosophy.

"J.W., I've worked-up an honest sweat," Goose indicated. "Do ya' wanta' go get a custard before it gets dark?"

"Sure, I'll go ask Pop," I replied. "He'll be happy that the truck's been unloaded."

"No need to do that," my spoiled pal remarked. "I've already asked him for ya'."

It greatly bothered me that Goose could manipulate Pop with his high-pressured jargon, just like the conniver could contortion my personality almost by whim. People were gullible, and their vulnerable wills were malleable, according Goose's egocentric perspective. Other people were simply existing, there to be used; to be deceived, and to be exploited by greed, by money, and by power. Those three factors were G.R.s lowest common denominators that could go into and divide any human relationship.

"Where are we goin'?" I asked as the two of us jumped into his red Thunderbird just before dusk.

"To Mr. Bill's, over on *Route 73*."

"Why not go to Royale Crown on the Pike, or to Toni's Custard on *Route 54?*" I challenged.

"Because I ain't got no damned soda machines and cigarette machines in those shit-eatin' dens yet," Goose volleyed-back rather defensively. "And besides," the junior entrepreneur continued, "those jerk-off Blues hang-out at Royale Crown, and the last time I was there,

I wound-up naked, floating in that shit-hole lobster tank at Pier IV over in Atco."

"Are ya' gonna' start-up the car?" I wanted to know. "It's getting dark, and that back road to Mr. Bill's is dangerous and unlit."

"I don't like takin' orders from a pipsqueak of your low social-*echo-nominal* caliber," the spoiled rogue curtly answered. Then, Goose attempted to demolish the very core of my value system; endeavoring to suck-out the essential part of my moral conscience, and trying to verbally hammer and pulverize my sensitive ego. The adamant tyrant returned to his theme that there wasn't any God in Heaven, because there isn't any Santa Claus at the North Pole.

"Goose," I argued, "don't ya' think we were put on this planet for a purpose?"

"Naaa, J.W." We're on this asshole planet for the same damned reason ants and elephants are on this goddamned friggin' planet. We're here to live as long as we can; to enjoy eating and screwin' females, and to financially screw others of your species that try to interfere with you screwin' their females."

"Very interestin'," I observed and remarked. "But besides biological pleasure, aren't we also here to have children and enjoy raising them."

"You're more of an asshole than I thought you were," G.R. criticized. "Look at *your* parents. They got married; had three kids, and now your mom and dad have to work the rest of their sufferin' lives to pay for their stupid mistakes."

"You're sayin' that I'm nothin' more than a stupid mistake?" I lividly questioned.

"Yes, I am," Goose answered quite matter-of-factly. "Your parents have the wrong values that will just always keep their noses above water," Restuccio insisted. "If your folks thought like me, they wouldn't have to struggle to make a livin'. Cigarette and soda machines, and flunky Puerto Ricans and niggers, would do all their damned work for 'em."

I was defiant in defending my general position. I argued that my parents were decent, hard-working people, and that I was worthy of being cared for and loved. My friend had a much different perception of the universe.

"J.W., ya' probably couldn't beat-up a crippled midget in a wheel chair," the self-centered chided.

"Why would I want to? And why would *I* be in a wheelchair with a crippled midget?" I jested, desiring to inject an element of humor to change my companion's argumentative mood.

"Your problem is," Goose' said with a smirk, "ya' got the balls, but ya' don't got the sperm."

"What's that accusation supposed to mean?" I questioned.

"It means that ya' have the guts to act, but ya' don't have the money or the power to back it up. People like the Blues know that I have the bucks and connections in high places," Goose proceeded, "so folks take me more seriously than they take you, even though ya' seem to have lots of courage and honesty. It's all that friggin' simple. People respect money and power!"

At last, feeling victorious in our fruitless debate, G.R. finally fired-up the Thunderbird's powerful engine; backed up; went forward, and crossed the Pike heading west toward Camden. I was a little disturbed that uneducated Restuccio had neutralized my Socratic method of reasoning, which I had diligently studied in Miss Hunter's Western Civilization class.

"Do ya' really think that kids have no reason for bein' born into this world?" I persisted. "Don't ya' believe that each person is a special gift?"

"Kids are stupid accidents that just result from people screwin'," G.R. argued. "The only reason kids happen is because nature gives adults the urge to wanta' fuck. So, stupid people screw and have kids, and then screw some more and have more friggin' kids," Goose insisted. "Most men ain't smart enough to know that havin' blow-jobs is more excitin' than screwin' their wives for five-minutes, and then havin' kids that are gonna' cost them their whole lives to pay for. No wife or whore has ever gotten pregnant for just givin' a guy a good blow-job."

"Don't ya' believe in God?" I asked, deliberately aggravating the avowed atheist.

Goose went on a total, wild, out of control tangent, saying that if there were a God, all animals, including humans, would only eat plants, grass and vegetables. The Devil incarnate discussed that crocodiles eat other crocodiles, and snakes eat other snakes without thinking twice about their meals, and that animals would not be "cannibals" if there really were a real God out there. "If there was a God," my demented friend speculated and editorialized, "all animals on the damned planet would behave like wimpy lambs and sheep, and not like lions, bears, and wolves. And that's exactly what your priest wants ya' to act like," Goose angrily continued his tantrum. "A weak, lame lamb or sheep is what religion tries to groom. In fact, the word pastor means 'shepherd', so the priest treats ya' like you're a goddamned stupid sheep grazing in a goddamned stupid pasture," G.R. ranted in his hostile diatribe. "And the damned bishop is just a bigger, more powerful sheepherder than the local fucked-up parish priest is. Baaaaaa!" the demented maniac bleated.

The driver was so engrossed in what his distorted mind thought, and what his corrupted soul was dictating to his lips, that the devil's advocate almost missed the left turn onto Flemington Pike. The enraged fiend was almost in a hypnotic trance as his red T-bird sped ahead. "J.W., if there was a God," the crazed driver grunted, "all animals would know that man was a special creation. Sharks would not kill and eat ocean swimmers, and lions wouldn't kill and eat African hunters, or alligators wouldn't swallow-up little kids in Florida. That proves there ain't no God out there in the sky or in space, and it shows that things just happen by accident, by coincidence, and by fucked-up chance."

Goose was proving to be a bigger intellectual obstacle than I had thought he would be. His ideas were so diametrically opposed to all that I had been taught and led to believe.

"J.W., if you was lyin' dead in the road right now, turkey buzzards and crows would fly-down and eat the damned flesh right off your bones," Goose declared. "Ya' would be fuckin' road kill, just like any cat or opossum that gets run over. If there was a God, the buzzards and the crows would know to leave your ass alone and not eat ya,' because you are supposed to be God's special creation."

I couldn't believe that Goose was getting the best of me. I had always prided myself on being academically gifted in certain subjects like history and morality, but there I was, getting the crap beaten-out of me by someone who never opened a textbook.

"But Goose, God created men with free wills," I stated, "and ya' make it all sound like God had a lot of marbles, threw them into space, and one accidentally became the earth. Then, God walked-away and forgot all about his creation. That's called you bein' a disgruntled agnostic!"

Goose chuckled for a moment as the street-wise Edgewood graduate formulated his response. "That's right. J.W.," he agreed. "God's either got amnesia or mental illness, or some shitty brain disease like that. The Guy doesn't know what the hell He's doin'. I mean," Goose prattled while searching for the correct words to express himself, "I mean, God needs a beatin', a real good spankin' for havin' the balls to create such a fucked-up world!" G.R. emphasized as the apostate forcefully mashed his foot-down on the T-Bird's accelerator.

"Er, aren't we goin' a little too fast?" I worried and asked. "I wanta' live to see tomorrow!"

The incensed driver ignored my entreaty while habitually pursuing his anti-Christian point of view. "J.W., just imagine how bored God must be havin' to live forever," Goose claimed, almost in a self-imposed, deep hypnotic trance. "Most people get bored in less than a human lifetime, but poor God's gotta' live forever. He must be bored to death from sheer *monopoly!"*

"I never thought of that possibility," I acknowledged. "But can't ya' slow down a bit. It's really getting dark out."

"And J.W.," Goose countered his wild narrative. "If there was a friggin' God, only good men like your father would become rich, and only bad men like Hitler would suffer. Ya' dig? Either there is no damned God, or *your* damned God doesn't give a flyin' shit about what really matters! The damned Jerk must have a shittin' brain tumor the size of Jupiter!"

"Goose, you're goin' entirely too fast. That's Dead Man's Curve up ahead!" I shouted in a panicked voice.

"And if there is a damned God," Goose continued without being fazed by my emotional alarm, "when I go to heaven, He's gonna' tell Jesus to get the hell up from the table and give me *His* damned seat. God will know I never allowed no fuckin' flunky Romans to nail me to any silly-ass damned cross. So, then *They* both can listen to a smart guy who knows what the frig' he's talkin' about!"

"Goose, slow down!" I screamed and demanded. "Look ahead! Deadman's Curve! Remember!"

"I ain't stoppin' for no damned injured nuns in an overturned Volkswagen trick, ever again!" the nutcase yelled, as our red T-Bird screeched around the bend at sixty-miles an hour.

'It's a good thing there wasn't a car coming the other way,' I thought, 'or we would have had a certain head-on collision.'

Happy with his intimidation and verbal bludgeoning of me, G.R. put the pedal to the metal and accelerated from sixty to ninety-miles an hour. "Slow down! Stop it!" I raged. "Watch out for that man!"

The speeding Thunderbird had veered to the right side of the Flemmington Pike, and as Goose was showing-off his prowess behind the wheel, his right front fender hit the pedestrian, who instantly flipped-up onto the hood. The victim's eyes were wide-open, eerily staring in at me through the cracked windshield, and blood was oozing out of his mouth and nose.

"Stop the damned car! Stop the damned car!" I vainly and deliriously repeated to the entranced driver, who cackled and laughed like a lunatic on a bizarre rampage. I lifted my left foot and thrust it down on the brake pedal. The T-Bird skidded left, right, left, and then right again, and just before the vehicle halted, the man's body rolled off the hood and windshield, and thumped-down upon the road's right shoulder.

I opened the door and ran a hundred-feet back to investigate the pedestrian's condition. As I sprinted with all my might, a vision of Quinn flashed across my mind, and I recalled how brave *he* had been when he felt a dead pilot's pulse after a small plane had crashed, and how *he* had pronounced Worm dead after a deadly automobile accident in Croydon.

I arrived at the bloody, prone body. I knelt-down and touched the man's twisted wrists. They were still warm, but no blood was surging through his veins. I turned the figure so that I could view his face, that same horrible face I had seen pressed against the partially shattered windshield. My quivering hand felt his neck. There was no evident pulsation. I turned and glanced upwards and saw Goose Restuccio standing next to me, snickering and chuckling as if something funny had just occurred. I stood and looked the insane madman in the eyes.

"What the hell is wrong with you?" I shouted. "You just killed a man going ninety-miles-an-hour! He's dead! Do you hear me! The man's dead!"

"He's just a worthless spic farm worker, no big loss," Goose said, laughing in a haunting tone of voice, sounding like a complete psychopath. "Probably doesn't have five damned dollars in his cheap rubber wallet, if the stupid bastard has a wallet!"

"You're cruel! You're wicked! You're evil!" I accused. "Ya' have no heart for other people! This man might have a wife and family back in Puerto Rico."

"He probably was walkin' to a liquor store to spend his week's salary on some cheap booze," Goose hypothesized and verbalized. "That's what all these stupid sons of bitches do; blow all their dough on fucked-up bad habits."

"You feel no guilt or sorrow for killing this man!" I returned. "You committed manslaughter, do ya' understand! You committed cold blooded manslaughter!"

"J.W., listen to me," the acrimonious kid without a conscience imperatively said. "Remember when I told you that most people were nothin' more than crabs in a bushel."

"Yes, but what does *that* analogy got to do with recklessly sideswipin' and killin' a man on a dark road?"

"Plenty," Goose declared, "because this spic' slime-ball is just like any nigger or Jamaican migrant. He's worse than a crab in a bushel. He's nothin' more than a fuckin' shrimp in a basket!"

"You're a disgraceful fraud! What the hell are ya' really sayin'?"

"I'm sayin' that if I ran over somebody important like John Wayne, or J. Edgar Hoover, then I'd feel a little bad about it," Goose clarified.

"But since I ran over a dumb asshole scumbag fifty-dollar a week alcoholic, I really don't give a flyin' shit!"

Headlights appeared rounding Dead Man's Curve. An old, dusty black '47 Plymouth chugged and stopped at our location. Dennis Measley opened his driver's side door, and hustled-over to the accident scene.

"Oh no! What happened?" Dennis cried out.

"This guy tried crossin' the road in front of me," Goose lied, "and I couldn't avoid hittin' him."

"Is he still alive?" Measley asked.

"No, I believe he's dead," I sighed.

"I think that's old Hector Rodriquez," Dennis identified the corpse that had a thick gray mustache. "He works on the small farm next to my house. In the winter time, Hector does odd jobs to send money back to Puerto Rico."

"What's he doin' walkin' alone in the dark on this road?" Goose asked Dennis.

"Hector works so hard seven days all week long," Dennis revealed, "and then once a week, he walks to Mr. Bill's and treats himself to a custard. That's how he rewards himself."

"Who the hell are you kiddin'!" Goose objected. "This guy collects unemployment all winter, just like all the other spics around Hammonton. He's out lookin' for his next cheap bottle of wine."

Dennis Measley told us to remain at the accident scene while he would drive to Mr. Bill's and have the local Winslow Township Police notified. The poor kid jumped into his relic Plymouth, and took off toward the custard stand, a half-mile ahead at *Route 73.*

My eyes looked-down in sympathy at the unfortunate dead pedestrian. "I still can't believe you killed him!"

"I didn't kill no man," Goose insisted. "I just accidentally killed a little spic shrimp inside a big spic shrimp basket."

Chapter Thirty-One

"Goose Gets Outsmarted"

News drove Juice, Fabian, and me to the Gem the night of July 2nd. Gratefully, No Blues were around because blueberry season was at its height, and everybody that grew the luscious blue fruit was involved packing eighteen-hours a day because the wholesale market prices were high. So temporarily, the four of us felt safe from surprise aggression being initiated by our fruit war adversaries.

I was telling the guys about how Goose had killed Hector Rodriquez on the way to Bill's Custard, just beyond Deadman's Curve on the Winslow-Williamstown Road, which locally was known as "Flemming Pike". Before anyone could ask any relevant questions, none other than G.R. stepped into the establishment.

"Hi jerkenheimers," the speeding menace sarcastically greeted. "Mind if I sit down and park my can?"

"Er no Goose, have a seat," I uncomfortably reacted. "Glad to see ya' in a pleasant mood."

"Well, J.W., I guess your tiny balls are still all shriveled-up after last night's minor accident," G.R. continued without any sign of showing remorse. "I suppose you other turds know what happened to Victor Rodrico."

"His name was Hector Rodriquez," I corrected.

"Yeah, thanks J.W.," Restuccio acknowledged with a frown. "Anyway, the cops finally came to the accident scene, and right away threw a sheet over Hector until the *corner* arrived. J.W. and I had to wait two whole freakin' hours until Hector's carcass was finally hauled-away to the county morgue."

"Are you gonna' go to Hector's funeral?" Juice innocently asked Goose. "That would seem the proper thing to do."

"Are you shittin' kiddin'?" the reckless egotist replied. "You expect me to fly all the way to San Juan for a scummy dirt-bag like him? I never told you guys, but I'm a little afraid of heights!"

"What about the funeral? Are you going to pay for it?" Sal asked.

"I agreed to pay four-hundred-dollars to ship *Victor's* body back to Puerto Rico in the cargo hull, and to partially pay for his funeral expenses," Restuccio revealed without regret. "There goes a damned week's profit on my new cigarette and soda machines. I also had eight-hundred-dollars damage to my new T-Bird."

"Do ya' mean that you aren't goin' to jail for runnin' him over?" News inquired. "It sounds like you committed manslaughter!"

"Why should I?" G.R. protested. "The Winslow cops knew who the hell I was, and wrote-up a decent accident report sayin' that *Victor* stepped out of the shadows and into the path of my T-Bird. Everything's been neatly swept under the carpet."

Goose then changed the subject and related that his father was having a major problem with Mr. Arturo Gillette about money being stolen, and the crazy Sicilian kid wondered if any of us had heard anything about the conflict. We all denied any knowledge of any such disagreement being gossiped. Restuccio then gave us curious perpetrators a a brief background.

"Why did your father have to pay Mr. Gillette money?" News intelligently asked. "Did he borrow it, or did your old man lose big in Vegas and owes a mucho grande gamblin' debt?"

"Neither," Goose said. "My old man ran out of spare loan sharkin' money, so he borrowed a bundle from Gillette. He paid the money back in full with interest, but then Gabe's old man hid it somewhere, and then the cash was stolen. I understand that Gabe's old man is really pissed about the *synonymous* theft."

"Your father could've paid Arturo in Gillette blue blades!" Juice foolishly joked.

"Then, your father's off the hook free and clear?" Fabian seriously stated before Goose could call Juice "a dumb-shit little shaver".

"Yeah, Sal, ya' might say that," Goose replied to Midilli. "But the money had been skimmed by Gillette from secret cash businesses he's involved in, so the blueberry czar can't claim it as an insurance loss, because then the *IRS* will wanta' know where and how the hell he got it. It's all a big mess."

Then, I had to open my big mouth and I was sure that Goose didn't appreciate my comment after I had haphazardly blurted it out. "This sounds like a classic case of a loan shark borrowin' money from another loan shark. I've never heard of double-loan sharkin' before," I asserted.

Juice and News laughed at my humorous evaluation, but G.R. definitely had gotten his horns twisted. "J.W., what makes the world go around is money, blow-jobs, and pussy in that damned order, and you're fuckin' poverty-stricken in all three cat-a-gore-ease."

I was instantly insulted, so I figured I would make Restuccio jealous by pulling off a Bo Jalonec' telephone scam with one of the two new waitresses on duty at the Gem. "I'll show *you* who has the knack with chicks," I angrily reacted, not realizing that I was going to embarrass an inexperienced waitress to make Goose know exactly how cool and masculine I could be. I exited the teen hangout and paced-over to the payphone across Central Avenue, outside Olivo's

Supermarket. I deposited two nickels and waited for the Gem carryout phone to ring.

"Hello, Gem restaurant," inexperienced-but-savvy Carmella Salvatore respectfully answered.

I put a white handkerchief over the phone to muffle and disguise my distinguishable voice. "I'd like to order a large tomato and cheese pizza to go, please."

"It'll be ready in twenty-minutes," Carmella predicted. "What's your name?"

"Richard Sgro," I fibbed.

"Thanks Richard, see ya' in twenty-minutes," the new waitress cordially finished.

I casually sauntered across Central Avenue and returned to the Gem, and everyone at the booth was wondering exactly what I had said over the telephone. I told the guys my "magic name", and Goose claimed that if my trick worked, he could duplicate it with "no sweat".

"This prank worked fifty-percent of the time back in Levittown," I disclosed, "so let's see what happens."

Carmella Salvatore brought some bottles of *Coke* and orders of French fries to our table, while her new colleague on duty, Terry Ingemi, a real snotty bitch on wheels, attended to individual patrons seated at the side counter. To kill some time, I asked News what was happening in the headlines.

"Well, J.W., on the Fourth of July, the new U.S. flag is gonna' be unveiled showin' fifty-stars now that Hawaii is officially admitted to the Union," Tommy proudly proclaimed.

"That's good, because the *49ers* were in California and not in Alaska," I jested, deliberately confusing Restuccio with my rhetoric.

"Hey what's wrong with that new bitchy waitress, Terry," Goose declared. "Somebody oughta' put a flag over her face and fuck her for Old Glory."

Nobody thought that Goose's uncouth remark was funny. Juice thought he would invent a believable explanation for Terry's apparent moodiness. "I'll bet she's havin' her damned period," Johnny suggested.

"I can't understand girls," I said, faking seriousness. "I think I told you guys once before that in school we guys all have eight-periods a day, and chicks get one extra period a month and then go haywire." Then, I conveyed to my pals what Bo Jalonec used to do to the Feed Bag waitresses that the Diablos suspected were having their periods.

"What did Bo Jalonec do?" Juice questioned. "He sounds like a pretty cool guy."

"Bo would go to the jukebox and play Johnny and the Hurricanes version of 'Red River Valley Rock' twenty-five times until the waitresses finally comprehended the *bloody* message," I answered, impersonating a Brit's accent.

My little commentary inspired Goose to march-over to the jukebox and deposit a handful of quarters into the slot. The slow-reader researched the appropriate instrumental title, and his two fingers kept mashing-down the upbeat tune's selector buttons. When G.R. ambled-back to our booth, "Red River Valley Rock" was already blasting throughout the Gem. I looked-around and saw other customers nodding their heads and snapping their fingers to the catchy, lively beat.

"J.W., I'm still smartin' from that damned lobster tub prank Gabe Gillette played over at Larry's Pier IV," Goose confided. "I *wants* ya' to come-up with something cool to do against the Blues. I know ya' got lots of ideas."

"A joint activity will definitely bring us five *pro*tagonists closer together," News admitted. "Our fraternity will be more fraternal," Tomasello ended, sounding a trifle redundant.

"I'm in favor of a little excitement, as long as we all live to talk about it," Fabian agreed, while Goose was apparently wondering what an *amateur tagonist* was.

"Okay, I'll think of a plan and tell ya' about the scheme after we leave this greasy spoon," I complied.

Mr. Arturo Sorrentino came-out of the kitchen's swinging doors, carrying a large tomato and cheese pizza in a box "to go". "Red River Valley Rock" was playing for the fifth consecutive time on the Wurlitzer, and the patrons and the waitresses were becoming weary of the monotonous melody. Then, Carmella Salvatore did her stuff.

"I have a hot carryout pizza for Richard Sgro. Where are ya' Richard?" Carmella called-out.

There was no immediate response forthcoming, so Carmella repeated her inquiry a little louder. "Tomato and cheese pizza for Richard Sgro. Where are ya' Richard?" the new waitress beckoned.

Still no answer, so the five Reds looked at each other, smirked and rolled our eyes, waiting to hear Carmella's final frustration.

"For the last time," the worried waitress barked, "I have a tomato and cheese pizza to go for Richard Sgro. Who's Dick Sgro?"

The five Reds all shouted simultaneously "Mine, mine, mine!" Several other tables of male teens caught on to our mischievous antics in a hurry, and instantly mimicked our general excellence. Carmella Salvatore immediately realized her inadvertent sexual allusion, turned three shades of scarlet, and then fled through the swinging doors into the shelter of Mr. Sorrentino's kitchen. I walked to the counter and volunteered to buy the pizza should Richard Sgro not show his face in the place.

"Red River Valley Rock" was playing for the eleventh straight time when our gang finished devouring the pizza. Goose Restuccio had to honor his promise to replicate my telephone success with the probability of Terry Ingemi answering the Gem's horn. G.R. asked me for a workable name in order for him to employ in his fraudulent pizza order, and I told him, "*Himan Akes* often worked well for the Diablos back in Levittown."

Goose nonchalantly stood-up from the booth and exited the restaurant without anyone other than the Reds paying attention to his furtive departure. The veteran prankster crossed Central Avenue and sauntered-over to the familiar phone booth outside Olivo's Supermarket. Restuccio dropped a dime into the slot and dialed the designated number listed in the booth's telephone book.

"Hello, Gem Restaurant," Terry Ingemi snottily greeted.

"I wanta' order a large pepperoni pizza with anchovies," G.R. began his ruse in an oddly uncharacteristic, polite voice. "How long will it take?"

"It'll be ready in just twenty-minutes," Terry Ingemi nastily replied. "What's your name?"

"Himan Akes," Goose answered rather courteously.

"Who's Himan Akes?" Terry demanded.

"Terry Ingemi's *hymen aches!"* Goose guffawed, feeling very triumphant about his exceptional telephonic accomplishment.

Terry Ingemi was not to be outdone by any sleazy prank pizza caller. "Well, Asshole," the livid hussy yelled into the telephone's receiver. "If your *Himan Akes* like ya' say ya' are, you freakin' male queer, you oughta' change your name to Christina Jorgensen! And for your information, I'm not havin' my damned period until next week, no matter how many damned times ya' play *that* stupid song on the jukebox!"

Everyone inside the Gem burst-out in a loud roar. Goose returned to the burger joint with his head crestfallen, a vanquished and verbally battered victim of a reverse prank.

"Boy, Terry Ingemi really turned the tables on you," Juice giggled at G.R,'s emotional expense.

"Go ahead, bust my balls good," Goose sulked. "I don't give a shit. Say News, who the hell is Christina Jorgensen, anyway?"

"He's a guy that had a sex operation and is now a woman," News laughed. "His infamous sex operation made scientific history, and all the newspapers, too."

"Red River Valley Rock" was still-being emitted from the Gem jukebox for the fifteenth time. "Come on guys, let's get the fuck outa' this dump," Restuccio rose from the booth and demanded. "And I never wanta' hear that goddamned stupid song ever again!"

* * * * * * * * * * * * *

Somebody had to go with Goose to calm the vindictive brat down, so I reluctantly volunteered. The five of us Gem patrons agreed to meet at Tommy T's house to conduct an important Reds strategy session. On the way to Spring Road, G.R. was still seething about his embarrassing negative encounter with Terry Ingemi.

"Ya' know, J.W.," the spoiled brat began his soap opera spiel. "That bitchin' broad really turned me on when she took the heat over the phone. Then she *cruise-a-fied* me."

"I think it's all about power over people with you and nothin' else," I evaluated and volleyed back. "Ya' couldn't control her, and that makes ya' want to have her more than ever, so that eventually, you *could* control her. When that happens, you'll want to dump the broad, leaving her for the next uncooperative dame to conquer."

"Ya' know," Goose intimated, motoring north on Bellevue Avenue. "Your brains ain't in your ass, even though you fart out of your mouth. You're a pretty smart cookie. That's exactly what's goin' on in the bottom of my goddamned brain."

"Your subconscious mind," I further defined with a smile.

"Yeah, my sub*conscience,"* Goose tried to repeat. "I think I musta' injured my *Medusa oblong-gotta* in the damned car accident. Anyway, J.W. I wants ya' to come-up with a super shit-assin' plan to get back at Gillette and Mortellite for havin' those damned hungry lobsters almost claw the balls right-out of my scrotum."

I told Goose that I would work on devising a shrewd scheme, but I also related that *he* was being too vindictive. "You've already demolished Gillette's 'Vette and Mortellite's T-Bird with the train trestle mirror stunt, and all you've received has been two smashed-in headlights at the Royale Crown in return."

"You make everything sound too friggin' simple and easy," my diabolical, paranoid pal concluded and assessed. "But J.W., ya' just don't understand. This whole damned thing is about power, and I can't back-down and lose face. If I don't fight back, I'm disgraced, and I couldn't live with that monkey on my back," Goose disclosed. "Don't worry. Gillette and me ain't gonna' fuckin' kill one another. We're just seein' how close we can come to *that* point, 'til somebody finally says *uncle."*

Goose drove by the landmark White Horse displayed on the farm market's red pedestal, and keenly noticed that the white stallion's reproductive organs had again been painted polka-dot blue. "See J.W., if its balls and dick were painted red, then *that* would now be funny. Those friggin' Blues are encroachin' into our peach territory," the mercurial driver vehemently complained.

"Look, Goose. There's the peach float over there inside the storage building, all ready for the Fourth of July parade in downtown Hammonton," I pointed-out.

"Are you part hound dog? Didn't your parents ever teach ya' it ain't fuckin' polite to point," G.R. rankled. "So, who gives a crap?"

"So what?" I repeated part of his apathetic statement. "Joanne Berenato is this year's reigning 'Peach Queen', and she's gonna' be ridin' on that float in the big parade."

"J.W., I'm gonna' buy ya' a damned suck-u-tron machine to give ya' instant blow-jobs, so that you'll stop dreamin' and day-dreamin' about that stupid chick all the time."

When the sarcastic paranoid kid turned right from the Pike onto Spring Road, the junior Mussolini continued his one-track monologue. "Gillette and Mortellite just bought two black *Harleys* like the ones I got."

"Why do ya' think they did that?" I naively asked, realizing that Goose could explode any second like a disturbed beaker of combustible nitro-glycerin.

"They have some ugly trick planned, I betcha'," Goose theorized and shared. "That's why I need *you* to think up somethin' quick to beat the creeps to the punch. I want a knockout, ya' understand, no goddamned TKO," G.R. emphasized. "And besides, I'm pissed-off that a new fender and windshield from the *Victor* accident cost me eight-hundred smackers this mornin' at a 'Philly chop shop. Wasted my whole fuckin' morning waitin' for the friggin' job to get done."

"I'll have to find a quiet *room* where I could *ruminate*," I alliterated, much to Goose's consternation.

The five of us reorganized in News' paved driveway, behind his spacious, upper middle-class ranch home. I couldn't help but detect a foul odor, so I inquired about its origin. "What's that horrible peculiar smell?"

"It's rotting peaches," News informed. "We forgot to spray an orchard of clingstones. We pay more attention to the August freestones because they bring more money in the fresh market later in the season."

"Why not just let them rot on the trees?" Fabian suggested.

"Can't do that," News maintained, "because bacteria from *the hangers* will infect the trees next year. So, we gotta' pick 'em like regular peaches, but then dump ‘em, all eighty-thousand-pounds of ‘em. Missin’ one spray was a costly mistake.”

I asked News where he and his dad were disposing of the rotten fruit. His answer illuminated a dark corner of my mind.

“J.W., we’re dumpin’ the stench in a hollowed-out pit at the end of our farm near the Wharton Tract,” News reported. “It’s all bio-degradable, and we might get lucky if a few deer get trapped goin’ down in there after the bait. The wind’s blowin’ from the north, and that’s why we can smell the decayin’ stench!”

“Can ya’ drive us out to the pit so that I can look at the size of the cavity?” I asked.

“Are you pretendin’ you’re some kind of dentist or gynecologist now?” Juice laughed.

“No, but I think I have a scheme brewin’ in my brain, and when I see the rotten peach pit,” I explained, “I’ll be able to decide whether or not my plan will work.”

The five of us desperados hopped into News’s red and white Fairlane and sped onto the other side of Union Road, where his dad’s northernmost peach orchards were located. A sandy trail exited a neck of the pine forest, leading directly into the dump, which was partially filled with stinking, rotten clingstones. We all got out to survey the situation. Thousands of fruit flies were flitting-around inside the pit, and some even ascended to harass us.

“How deep is it?” Fabian asked.

“About fifteen-feet,” News indicated. “But after all the ruined peaches are dumped in, it’ll only be about ten-feet-deep.”

I expressed what my plotting mind was wondering. “News, do ya’ think a motorcycle could jump this here pit?”

“That’s a tough one,” the boy genius answered. “I’ll have to get out my slide-rule and do some estimates. If two small ramps were built, one for takin’ off on one side of the pit, and the other ramp for landin’ on the other side, then I think I can come-up with the right speed to be able to zip from one ramp to the other.”

“News, is there a wholesale produce market open anywhere on the east coast tomorrow?” I asked.

“No, because of the gala Fourth of July holiday,” Tommy communicated. “New York and ‘Philly will re-open on the fifth.”

“That’s all I need to know. We have the rest of today and the 3rd to get ready. Okay, guys, I have a plan,” I disclosed. “It’s gonna’ be a little complicated, and some things could possibly go wrong.”

“The more complicated the better,” said Juice, who, like fictional Tom Sawyer, relished the prospect of serious, complex adventures.

“Let’s get it goin’,” Goose excitedly endorsed, anticipating us employing ample revenge on the Blues.

“Let’s talk about our strategy at News’s house,” I suggested. “This plan is gonna’ be as good as any that the Diablos pulled-off against the Kamikazes back in Levittown.”

Chapter Thirty-Two

"Rodders' and Blues on the Rampage"

News drove us back to his house on Spring Road. The five of us drank some *Pepsi's* out of bottles, ate some pretzels and potato chips, and then descended the stairs to Tommy's magnificent Hammonton area miniature landscape. Everyone was anxious to hear what kind of ingenious prank I had designed.

"Say, Goose," News addressed the illiterate, Edgewood graduate, slow-learner. "Did you know that Martin Luther had a Diet of Worms," Tommy jested, intentionally Americanizing the German pronunciation of the word *diet.*

"If the stupid asshole was smart, instead of swallowin'-down disgustin' wigglin' worms, the dumb-fuck would've been like Mussolini, and eaten a lot of *cow-zone!"*

"Well, actually it's a dual prank, or maybe even a triple prank if ya' think hard about it," I boasted, getting back to my revenge strategy. "It's really quite complex, and yet very simple."

"Just give us the important nuts-and-bolts details without all the other bullshit thrown-in," Goose complained. "You're all smoke and no fire, ever since I've known ya'."

I asked Juice if Hoss, Little Joe Gregorio and some other Edgewood High Reds would be available on the night of July 3rd, and Johnny attested that all definitely would be, if the Reds and the Blues were involved in a wild adventure.

"Great," I said, "because this plan is so tremendous that it'll also involve the insane Ramrodders. And we'll definitely need the services of Herc Juliano, Balls Giordano, Jake Maccarella, and the other St. Joe athletes, too."

"What the hell did ya' have in mind, needin' all those rough Turks?" G.R. questioned. "Ya' gonna' be doin' *D-Day II!"*

News stated that he was going to use his trusty pointer to identify, on his scale-model, all of the sites I would be describing in my presentation.

"First of all, Goose," I formally commenced, "you and me are gonna' have to take a preliminary trip to the Berlin Auction and buy two black leather jackets, four skeleton masks, and two blue denim jackets."

"We burnt all of the friggin' blue denim jackets in the bonfire outside my house the night of the Bowlarama," G.R. objected. "We shoulda' kept two of 'em for this hit job. J.W., you're runnin' me broke," the repugnant Sicilian finished, faking aggravation.

News pointed his indicator at the Berlin Auction on the landscape model to illustrate my reference.

"Juice, I want ya' to get Hoss and Little Joe and the Edgewood Reds to build two small ramps, so that a *Harley* with two passengers can zoom over Tommy's peach dump near the Wharton Tract," I assigned. "The boys will have a whole day to get the job done and have the sturdy ramps placed exactly where they gotta' be."

News pointed to the Gregorio farm on the Old White Horse Pike in Waterford, and then to the section of News' farm where the utilitarian ramps were to be placed on level ground.

"Goose," I emphatically instructed. "We're gonna' have to get in touch with Herc, Balls, and Jake to get some St. Joe' musclemen to handle ramp number two, or better known as the landing ramp."

News pointed his stick at where ramp number two was to be situated. "Tommy, do ya' want J.W. to give ya' a few *pointers!"* Juice joked, much to News' chagrin.

"That wasn't funny," Tommy replied with an authentic grimace exhibited on his florid face.

"Now, I need your undivided attention for the rest of my plan," I requested. "It'll involve one set of Walkie-Talkies; two telephone booths; Goose's two motorcycles, and two Ramrodder black leather jackets to begin with," I prefaced. "Then, we'll also require two blue denim jackets; four skeleton masks; one state police barracks; one gas station; one bus terminal; one blueberry Fourth of July parade float; two decent cherry bombs; two small wooden ramps; one peach dump, and a lot of luck. Who's game?"

Everyone was curious about the plethora of specifics of my ruse, so the Reds all raised their hands. "Fabian, you got an A in art, and you're always tellin' me how artistic ya' are," I praised.

"You mean autistic instead of artistic," Juice laughed.

I ignored Johnny's inane bantering. "All you'll have to do, Sal, is draw the Ramrodders' big R with a piston and rod on the back of the two black leather jackets, which Goose and I will deliver from the Berlin Auction," I eloquently specified. "Those Ramrodders' jackets will be worn by News and Juice." Then, I divulged the particulars of my plan, and the other intrigued participants loved every phase of it.

* * * * * * * * * * * * * *

Goose and I motored over to the Berlin Auction to purchase the two blue denim jackets; the four skeleton masks, and the pair of ordinary black-leather motorcycle jackets. My partner in crime was quite impressed with the glorious magnitude of my stellar project.

"Where do ya' think of all this crazy shit?" G.R. asked inside his re-conditioned red T-Bird on the way to Berlin.

"I become more intelligent when I play cowboy trivia quiz games," I frivolously answered. "It makes my mind sharp as a razor, sharper than a Gillette blue blade. Remind me to buy those four skeleton masks, too. They're usually pretty effective, and ya' can really scare the crap out of a grown adult a lot easier wearin' one, especially when it *ain't* Halloween."

"Okay, let's play your silly little game, and I'll see if I can think any better after it's over with," Restuccio half-heartedly replied. "I think my *Medusa oblong-gotta* is finally healin'!"

"Who has the leading role in *Bonanza* on television?" I quizzed.

"Lorne Greene," Goose proudly responded. "Who plays Hoss and who plays Little Joe on the show?" my comrade-in-crime asked.

"That's a snap," I declared. "Dan Blocker and Michael Landon. And don't forget Pernell Roberts, too."

"Who is the actor that stars in *Rawhide?"* I demanded.

"His real name is Clint Eastwood," Goose said, "but I don't think he'll ever amount to anything except bein' the star of *Rawhide.* He ain't got no swell personality, and the guy's a big, wimpy sissy, too without any future in acting. J.W., I watch a lot of cowboy shows. Who's the main actor on *Johnny Ringo?"*

"Don Durant," I accurately replied. "Stop givin' me such easy ones. Ya' gotta' dig deeper."

"I thought that guy Don Durant was starrin' on *The Rebel,"* Restuccio weakly challenged.

"Sorry Goose, you're wrong," I countered. "Johnny Yuma, the Rebel, was played by none other than Nick Adams. Who is the star of *Swamp Fox?"*

"*Lesbian* Nielson," Goose proudly and sincerely answered. "That guy could never be a comedian in a million years. He's too goddamned serious, just like that friggin' Clint Eastwood is."

"That's stretchin' it all the way to Mars," I commended. "His real name is Leslie Neilson."

"That's just what the hell I said," Goose insisted.

My demonic buddy and I walked-around the Berlin Auction three times. We found some good bargains on our desired merchandise; ate a couple of hamburgers and two bags of popcorn, and then completing our special mission, delivered the two black leather motorcycle jackets and two of the skeleton masks to Fabian at his dad's Waterford *Flyin' A* gas station.

"Make these two things look just like Ramrodder jackets," Goose instructed. "And make the skeleton masks look like Adolph Hitler's skull does right now!"

"And meet the Reds at News's place at eight p.m. sharp tomorrow night," my voice added. I felt that my entire preparation had to be precise, since I had put my reputation as a military strategist on the betting line. "And don't forget to give Juice and News the two skeleton masks, too."

"Don't worry," Sal dependably assured. "I wouldn't miss this escapade for all the *Monopoly* money in the world."

Goose and I stared at each other in reaction to Sal Midilli's absurd comment. Then, we jumped back into the red T-Bird, left the Flyin' A, and headed east on *Route 30*.

"I'm assumin' that you and me are gonna' be ridin'on one of your *Harleys,"* I deducted and concluded. "Is Fabian gonna' drive the other one?"

"Naaa," Goose answered. "I'm gonna' let News have a turn at some *traumatic* excitement this time around. Tommy has an old *Triumph* bike he drives around the farm, so I'll let him drive somethin' more-classy for a change."

On the home front, Pop was glad that I was going to be in the company of Goose Restuccio, who according to Dad, had a two mild-mannered-workmen crew named Frankie and Joe deliver the new soda and cigarette machines to Pete's Market that same afternoon. "I was wrong about your friend Ronald Restuccio," Pop confessed. "He's a fine young man who truly believes in the practice of American free enterprise."

At eight p.m. on July 3rd, fourteen Reds assembled in the basement of News's ranch home for "a brief club meeting". Tommy had told his parents that we were going "deer spottin" over in Winslow, and that some of the Reds were thinking about joining the Boot Hill Gunning Club, of which his father was a charter member. From that moment on, Tommy's pop was proud of our "club's" activity, and gave us his full support.

"We could always use some new blood in our gunnin' club," Mr. Tomasello confided, "and especially young, energetic lads such as yourselves." When Mr. Tomasello stepped upstairs to attend to his own private interests, News used his military pointer and reviewed the various "staging areas" where everybody should be at precisely nine p.m. In five-minutes, our briefing had been completed. At eight-fifteen, the energized Reds all eagerly migrated to our prospective "battle stations".

Goose fired-up his favorite black *Harley Davidson,* and I hopped on the "buddy seat". News started-up the other black motorcycle with Juice as his partner, sitting directly behind him. Fabian drove his white '59 Chevy Impala to Al's Save-Way gas station on *Route 30* with a Walkie-Talkie and a handful of dimes for phone calls.

G.R. carefully observed the speed limit as the "demolition kid" maneuvered his *Harley* down the White Horse Pike; then around Hammonton Lake, heading east toward Devonshire. Next to the Starlight Ballroom Roller Rink was Burdick's Public Service Bus Stop, where passengers would exit and stretch their weary legs, midway between Philadelphia and Atlantic City. A snack bar was inside, and two bus loads were utilizing the fast-food stop when we had arrived. Goose and I immediately commandeered *the designated telephone booth,* so that we could receive a call from Fabian at Al's Save-Way right before *our* vital phase of mission was to commence.

My eyes looked across the four-lane-pike at the Circus Drive-in and remembered the crazy adventure I had recently had there and also at the Atco. G.R. was staring west at the Starlight Ballroom Roller Rink, and the numbskull started telling me the same old story of Chubby Checker asking to borrow a comb inside the place's Men's Room, when the phone suddenly rang. G.R. picked-up the receiver, and after several brief exchanges with Fabian, he turned to me and announced, "It's a go!"

We both paced briskly to his bike. Goose started it up, and steered the powerful machine onto the Pike. Our destination was not too far away, the Hammonton Barracks of the New Jersey State Police, which was situated to the left of the Circus Drive-in. Restuccio stopped his machine at the mouth of the barracks' driveway. "Make sure the fuzz gets a good look at your blue denim jacket," the mission's captain reminded me. "That's why we're wearin' em."

"They're gonna' think we're both Blues," I returned.

"If we can pull this one off," Goose said, "we could both pull our dicks off and still be able to cream a load. Ya' got the cherry bomb and the lighter on you."

"Yeah, right here in my pocket," I answered. "Ya' got your skeleton mask?"

"Sure do! Let's roll!" G.R. concluded.

Everything was peaceful outside the state police barracks, and up to then, it had been just another lazy, ordinary, summer evening for the uniformed, prospective troopers. I remembered thinking how Tinker used to say that the cops were just another gang of adult punks wearing blue apparel, instead of outstanding Diablo' black leather and blue denim.

Goose stopped his bike at the side entrance. I jumped-off, opened the door, and G.R. eased his *Harley* through the opening. We then donned our "Adolph Hitler" skeleton masks. I hopped back on, and my lunatic friend buzzed down the straight, three-hundred-foot-long corridor. Several astonished cadets heading to the shower room with towels wrapped around their waists got the surprise of the lives as we sped by them on the *Harley*. Their shouts aroused the attention of other trainees inside the building, but most of the commotion was already left a hundred-feet behind us.

At the main front entrance, G.R. screeched to a stop, swerving sideways on the neatly kept, polished, tile floor. Several actual troopers were sitting at desks reviewing paperwork. I removed the cherry bomb from my blue denim jacket, lit it on the first try with the reliable lighter, and flung the small explosive in the direction of the two shocked troopers. It fizzled as the scared pair ducked under their respective desks. Just before the tiny bomb exploded, Goose took-off down the remaining stretch of corridor. His *Harley* blasted through a door on the Hammonton side of the barracks, and the "wild Goose chase" was on. The *Harley* was opened-up to full throttle, and the thrill of being the prey, while the antagonized predator chased behind in a patrol car, surged through my entire nervous system, sending spine-tingling chills up and down my back.

While a state police car desperately pursued our *Harley* toward the Hammonton line, News and Juice were having their own classic adventure. The duo had done a drive-by of Waff Scaffidi's Blueberry Farm, situated three growers down Middle Road from Scaff DiMeo's operation, and two farms down from Spoonsy DiMeo's homestead. Since Waff and Scaff were new Blues' pledges, the twosome had been in charge of supervising and constructing the Miss Blueberry float for the upcoming Fourth of July Parade down Bellevue Avenue.

From the beginning, here's what actually went-down. After staking-out the float construction site, News and Juice were in for a bonus. Gabe Gillette and Speed Mortellite's new black *Harleys* were parked behind Waff Scaffidi's home and in front of the main packinghouse, where the float was being ornamented. News and Juice took it easy, passing slowly by on Middle Road, so that the engrossed float decorating committee would not be paying any attention to the passing motorcycle.

At the intersection of Middle and Union Road, News, undetected, stopped, and Juice whipped-out his Walkie-Talkie. His voice contacted Fabian at Al's Save-Way gas station, and Sal was restlessly waiting inside his designated phone booth for the special Walkie-Talkie message on his receiver. Fabian then called Goose at Burdick's Bus

Stop, over in Devonshire and the dual raids had been officially initiated.

News and Juice almost duplicated the type of foray Goose and I had executed inside the Hammonton State Police Barracks, but the dynamic duo performed the same procedure with the Blues (instead of the local state police) as their targeted opponents. Wearing their "Ramrodders" black motorcycle jackets and accompanying skeleton masks, News and Juice blitzed into Waff Scaffidi's U-shaped driveway. Horrified girls screamed their tonsils out at the sight of the grotesque skeleton masks the two trespassers were wearing. The phantom rider in the buddy-seat lit a cherry bomb and hurled it onto the gaudy blueberry float. The small grenade exploded, sending-out another wave of terror shrieks from the panicky females.

News and Juice sped-around the house and skidded out of the driveway. Thinking that the blueberry float party had been interrupted by arrogant Ramrodders, Gabe Gillette and Speed Mortellite leaped onto their black machines and took off in intense pursuit of their greaser molesters.

A familiar itinerary was enacted to South Union Road, across *206,* and then into peach country on North Union Road. News and Juice were vigilant in their frantic, escape passing by Basin Road, Pine Road, and Oak Road at half-mile intervals. However, upon accelerating west and reaching Walker Road, Gillette and Mortellite were gaining on the two fleeing Reds' rascals disguised as Ramrodders. At Spring Road, News hung a sharp right, his foot scraping the dusty farm field's surface.

It was only three-hundred-yards until the *Harley* would enter a sandy dirt path meandering between two pine-tree woods. Then, the cycle would zoom-up the wooden ramp at forty-nine miles an hour, which was the speed that News had precisely calculated to safely span the gap from ramp to ramp, gliding over the peach dump.

The *Harley* zipped up the west ramp and hurtled over the rotten peach pit. Immediately, Herc Juliano, Balls Giordano, Jake Maccarella and some other St. Joe' Reds' recruits dashed out of the pine woods from opposite sides and dragged the second ramp twenty-feet backwards, away from the stench-laden hollow. The "stage crew" scampered-back into the dark pine tree cluster as the roar of Gillette and Mortellite's black bikes could be heard approaching on the dark, dirt farm road.

Gillette followed by Mortellite zoomed up the obscure ramp and shouted several unsavory curse words as their motorcycles awkwardly hurtled into the air. The second surprise came when the two cycles could not clear the other side. The unfortunate blueberry princes crashed into a putrid, soggy mound of rotting peach slush. Moans and groans were soon originating from inside the cleverly concealed pit.

Herc Juliano, Balls Giordano, Jake Maccarella, and the rest of the St. Joe contingent rambled-out of the pinetree woods, picked-up the portable second ramp, and then dragged the heavy object back to its original location.

Goose and I had taken the White Horse Pike west through the entire diameter of Hammonton, being chased by a determined state trooper inside his high-speed patrol cruiser. Restuccio zipped past White Horse Farm and cut a wide-angle right onto Walker Road. I was exhilarated as adrenaline rushed into every vein, artery, and vital organ inside my body. I turned-around and observed that the police cruiser with the whining siren and flashing red light was rapidly gaining on us.

G.R. slowed-down to fifty and then looked beyond several fallow fields on both sides of Walker Road, assessing that no traffic would be crossing in our path across Union. Restuccio didn't honor the Stop sign, opened-up the throttle, and fishtailed across Union Road. A gravel trail passed between woods of mostly deciduous trees on both sides, and soon we were flying first past "Texas" on our left, and then by the Tuckahoe Turf Farm on our right. The stubborn state trooper's vehicle was only about a thousand-feet behind us.

"Fifty-three miles an hour!" I yelled into G.R.'s ear, for according to News's calculations, the increased speed was necessary for a motorcycle with two riders to successfully clear the entire peach dump, since Restuccio was forty-pounds heavier than News was.

Goose made a quick left just beyond old man Berenato's "Texas apple orchards", and established a direct beeline for the ramp on the eastside of the designated peach pit. I remember dust blowing-up into my face from the sandy road, and twenty-seconds later, I was holding onto Restuccio's waist as our *Harley* raced up the incline, and then catapulted into the air. I closed my eyes and heard a loud thud when the tires miraculously touched-down on the second ramp.

"Touch-down, without a football!" I screamed into my driver's ear.

After our *Harley* had successfully cleared the rotten peach pit and landed safely on the other side, the roaring police cruiser entered the dual woods and approached the dark incline. The cop unknowingly sped and progressed up the first ramp, and before the trooper could apply his brakes, his vehicle was launched into the lower atmosphere. Gabe Gillette shouted, "Duck!" and Speed Mortellite screamed-out "What the fuck!" inside the pit, as the police cruiser hurtled-over their heads and impacted with the opposite bank of the peach dump. We all ran to the pit to evaluate the result of the dual chases. The groggy state trooper managed to awkwardly climb-out of the passenger side window, and staring directly at Gillette and Mortellite while shining his flickering flashlight into the dark peach pit, the fuzz rep' declared in a stammering voice, all out of breath, "You two punks in the blue denim jackets are under arrest!"

The two committees of ramp movers quickly dismantled the main sections with hammers and crowbars. Hoss drove one truck around the back of the pine-woods and backed-up to the east ramp, and Little Joe repeated the process with another truck for the recently moved west ramp. The "stage crews" worked assiduously and loaded the two disassembled inclines onto their respective trucks. Everyone assisted in the endeavor, making sure to throw all telltale evidence into the box trucks' storage areas. Then, Hoss and Little Joe closed the back panels, got into their cabs, and zipped-off in different directions.

Most of the participating Reds had their cars and trucks hidden in back of the two pine-woods on both sides of the sandy trail. The ecstatic Reds all ran to their autos, and very quickly evacuated the peach dump.

Goose took a shortcut through a fallow field, and I thought I was going to go flying off the "buddy seat" when the *Harley* riveted over irregular curvy ground. Restuccio finally cut-over to a flat dirt road just before Little Joe's "ramp truck" reached that point. When G.R. stopped at the junction of Spring Road and Union Road, my peepers looked-back over my left shoulder and witnessed a rapidly moving procession of Reds' vehicles still escaping the incredible scene.

"Should we call the cops about the accidents?" I asked my unpredictable motorcycle chauffeur.

"There's already a damned cop in the pit with a friggin' radio in his car!" my petulant companion gruffly answered. "Let the state cop call the goddamned local cops and an ambulance!"

Goose put the *Harley* in first gear and sped south down Spring Road. I had to ask the driver another question. "Won't the fuzz come lookin' for the ones who built and removed the ramps?"

"Naaa, don't sweat the small stuff!" G.R. yelled back. "That state cop doesn't want to look like a stupid kindergarten kid in the newspapers, landin' his patrol car in a remote peach dump pit."

Goose made a quick left turn onto *Route 30* heading toward Pete's Market, soon cruising into the driveway, and next parking his cycle behind the farm market.

"Ya' know J.W.," G.R. pontificated as we dismounted. "Those friggin' blueberry kids have real weird names like Waff DiMeo and Scaff Scaffidi."

"You mean Waff Scaffidi, and Scaff DiMeo," I clarified.

"Yeah, those are the two fucked-up hammerheads I was talkin' about!" Restuccio replied. "Shouldn't their names be Waff DiMeo and Scaff Scaffidi? Some Italians really have screwed-up first and last names! And don't forget that Spoonsy jerk-off, too!"

As we entered the farm market via the back door, three police cars and a Hammonton ambulance zipped by, speeding west on the White Horse Pike.

"Wonder what happened?" Pop said to Goose.

"Probably some dumb kids wrapped-around a telephone pole," Restuccio verbally decided. "Most teenagers don't know their limits, especially their speed limits."

"Too bad high school kids all aren't as mature and as wise as *you* are," Pop praised Goose. My father paced to the front of the market, heard other sirens approaching from Hammonton, and then waited to watch the new emergency vehicles flash by.

"The Blues are on a *ramp*age," Goose whispered, trying to show me that his lips could utter clever words.

"If this were a novel," I whispered back, "then the reader would be on the ramp page."

"How do ya' think of this stupid, silly shit?" my irascible companion incredulously asked. "You must be *Mark Twine re-jew-van-ate-it!"*

Chapter Thirty-Three

"The Mullica River"

The Fourth of July came, fizzled like a dud firecracker, and quickly vanished into history. I had just put in a weekday visit with Mr. Charles B. Sipley, who told me I was making such splendid progress in trigonometry that by the end of August, I would be capable of teaching the subject myself. Since I liked Mr. Sipley and my trig' mentor praised my gradual performance, I busted my buttocks and soon started to academically excel. Sugar seemed to work a lot better with me than Mr. Andrews' sour vinegar had, and Mr. Sipley used plenty of the sweet stuff.

On the Monday after the Fourth, Pop directed me to drive the Pete's Market Special over to Stella's Farm in Berlin and pick-up fifteen-hundred-ears of Silver Queen white corn. On the way to the country farm, I decided to stop at Mr. Bill's for a medium vanilla custard cone. Goose Restuccio was inside the restaurant section of the establishment admiring a new pinball machine.

"How do ya' like it?" the show-off asked me.

"Pretty nifty," I replied. "Do ya' wanta' play a few games? I'm pretty good at pinball, ya' know!"

"J.W., why the hell would I wanta' play a dumb-ass pinball machine?" Goose nastily replied. "I happen to own the damned machine! Pop just set me up in the amusement distribution business, in *edition* to havin' cigarette and soda machines. Do ya' wanta' buy my gum ball machine route?"

My ears pricked-up at the prospect of going into real business without ever going to college. "How much?" I inquired.

"Twenty-five-thousand, cash on the barrel-head," G.R. said, "and I'll even tutor ya' the first two weeks so that ya' don't make any rookie mistakes that I've learned to *a void* from experience."

"Er, no thanks," I sighed. "That's a little out of my modest affordability range."

I was generally depressed because I had had an argument at the Rainbow Room Nite Club over in Sewell several nights before with Tyrone Davis and Jack Steins. The Marvelons had made a terrific guest appearance and received a standing ovation from the patrons. Then, Tyrone and Jack laid the wood to me, and I became antagonistic because I was already in over my head.

"I tried to call you three times yesterday, but you were unavailable!" I sincerely informed.

"Why the hell did you call me *yesterday* instead of by my fuckin' real name!" Edgewood grad' G. Restuccio hollered. "What did those two clowns want?" Goose asked.

"They want to record the song 'Kathy Don't Leave Me' on the A side of a 45, and 'The Night is Still Young' on the B' side," I sniffed, nearly beginning to weep.

"So, what the hell is wrong with that?" Goose challenged. "Why are ya' so bent out of shape over somethin' so goddamned minor?"

"Because Jack Steins asked me for a thousand-dollars to finance the record cut, and I didn't have it," I sobbed, tears welling inside my eyes. "So, we had a big argument, and they voted me out as the manager."

"Jesus Christ! I told ya' not to get involved with those fuckin' shines and that *Jew* bastard'. And cheatin' Jew bastards are just as bad as spooks," Goose admonished. "Those black clouds and that *paris-site Moses* musta' taken ya' for all your life's savings? Didn't the leechin' pricks?"

"Yes," I whimpered, "and I have nothin' to show for it except a few fond memories and a car full of melted chocolate, covered ice cream pops, and mounds of vanilla and chocolate ice cream."

Goose put his arm around my shoulder and gave me some comfort. "J.W.," the hooligan predicted, "someday the world is gonna' know what kind of a great guy ya' are. Ya' have a real good mind and a lotta' word talent. I don't quite know how to explain it, or put it into *lang-wedge.* Ya' have strange, weird talent that I envy, if ya' know what I mean."

I thanked Goose for his much-needed vote of confidence, and then the paragon-of-non-virtue revealed that his father had been in a good mood and had bought him a high-powered speedboat that was berthed at the Sweetwater Casino Marina on the south bank of the historic Mullica River.

"Wanna' go for a ride tonight?" Captain Goose asked. "You need a fuckin' change of scenery!"

"Sure," I sobbed and sniffed, in need of an ideal escape mechanism. "What time?"

"I'll pick ya' up around four this afternoon," G.R, indicated. "We'll have dinner at the casino restaurant. I'll call your dad and get the okay, so ya' don't have to humble yourself and ask him permission to go. He likes me, and thinks that my shit doesn't stink, so in my book, right now, your dad is an alright guy."

"Thanks, Captain Kangaroo, er, I mean Captain Goose," I facetiously replied. "Ya' meant a lot to me today. I saw a human side to you today that ya' never showed me before. I feel I can really trust ya' now."

"Forget the emotional chicken crap. Remember what I just predicted about you," Ronald Restuccio answered, "because every word of it was true. Ya' better believe it! Once ya' believe in yourself, then soon the other dumb-fucks around you, will too."

The red Thunderbird appeared in the farm market's driveway at quarter to four. I was overwhelmed and busy. The stand was having "a rush", with eight retail customers demanding personal service. Goose even waited on a fussy old lady patron who insisted on opening all twelve-ears of Silver Queen' corn before buying a dozen. The hectic pace finally slowed-down, and at last it was time to visit Sweetwater Casino.

On the way down Pleasant Mills Road, I asked G.R. a really inane question just to bust his chops. "I've never been to a *casino* before," I kidded. "Will the greedy owners let me play the slot machines? I don't think I'm old enough."

Goose had never been as amused as the ingrate had been at that very moment. My escort gave-out a very genuine laugh, not because I had made a total fool out of myself, but because he had honestly felt like laughing from his normally black heart.

"J.W., Sweetwater Casino is just the name of the restaurant and marina," the driver explained, thoroughly enjoying his rare encounter with clean and genuine humor. "There just ain't no goddamned slot machines, roulette wheels, craps tables, or any five-card-stud tables in the whole damned place. Legalized gamblin' is in Vegas, and no-where else, not even in the sleaziest cellars and *done-gins* in Atlantic City."

I too enjoyed my own intentionally-naïve *casino* remark, thinking all the way to Sweetwater that life and people were good, in spite of the Marvelons, Jack Steins, and Goose Restuccio. News, Juice, Fabian, and Jives had set me straight about Sweetwater Casino when we had passed by it on the way back from the Dion and the Belmonts high-speed chase up the *Garden State Parkway*. I was simply playing mind games with G.R.

While Goose took a secret shortcut to the popular area eating place, I remembered I had read in a magazine where the Mullica River was the scene for several skirmishes between British warships and American privateers, particularly up at the river's mouth at Chestnut Neck near Smithville. The British were also interested in making it downstream to maraud and plunder Batsto Village, which in colonial times, forged bog iron into cannonballs and also into cauldrons, which were used for the Continental Army to cook their food. I tried educating Goose about those historical references, but the former General Ed. student was always inclined to view academics as being a synonym for “unimportant”.

“J.W.,” my demented pal gloated and suggested. “Someday, I’m gonna’ take ya’ to that goddamned fancy whorehouse in Atlantic City. It ain’t no fleabag hotel, ya’ know,” he emphasized. “And when you’re there, you’ll get to shoot off your own damned cannon, and you’ll even get to fire-off your own cannon’s balls. Ha, ha, ha.”

I slunk-down in my front seat inside the four-passenger vehicle, fully aware that Goose had vacillated back into his wicked sarcastic mode. Luckily for me, a sign read: “Sweetwater Casino, Turn Left One Mile”, so I would only have to endure the driver’s ridicule for another minute or so.

“That’s okay, J.W.,” Goose proceeded with his oddball lexicon, intermittently coughing during a mild allergy attack. “History is history, and now is now, so stop livin’ in the damned past with a lot of dead people and learn to live your own damned life as J.W.”

I noticed a wooden-arrowed sign that read “Leeds Point”, which was the legendary birthplace of the Jersey Devil, but I dared not bring that subject up in conversation, fearing the full brunt of my companion’s probable scorn and derision if I attempted to discuss it.

G.R. parked his fine red auto in the establishment’s spacious parking lot. His first objective was to flatter himself by showing me his expensive gift received from his father, an eighteen-foot-long red *Fiberglas* speedboat that was moored at a dock.

“Ain’t it a beauty? It’s cigarette shaped,” the owner bragged. “This sucker can do over fifty on the water if it has to. The salesman over at Egg Harbor Boat Company says it has around fifty horsepower.”

“Wow! It sure is a doozy!” I marveled and flattered. “Where did ya’ learn how to navigate it.”

“Ain’t nothin’ much to it,” G.R. boasted and answered. “If ya’ can drive a motorcycle, ya’ can drive this thing. It’s easy as chocolate cake. Right now, J.W., let’s go get a bite to eat. Then, we’ll tour this two-bit river in style.”

My itinerant guide and I entered the exquisite restaurant, which featured a nautical, knotty-pine, country look. We passed the main bar, and a hostess seated us at an attractive table for two, overlooking the scenic river. The items on the dinner menu were quite costly compared to the regular hamburgers and hot dogs I was used to eating when away from home.

“Don’t worry about prices,” Goose allayed my fears. “You’re my friggin’ guest, and ya’ can order any damned thing ya’ want.”

G.R. ordered a "filet mignon end cut, well done". I was going to order lobster tail, but I remembered what had happened to G.R. with crustaceans at Larry's Pier IV over in Atco, so I decided on prime rib au jus, "medium rare".

The matronly waitress brought us a basket of bread and rolls and soon showed-up with plates of salad with choices of dressing. I was not used to such opulence, but was savoring my initial exposure to it. In fifteen-minutes, a large tray was next carried-out to our table, and our fabulous meals were served.

"This food is delicious," I commented as I sampled the prime rib au jus. "It sure beats Italian hoagies and meatball sandwiches."

"J.W., if ya' listen to my common sense shit I tell ya' all the time," Goose bragged, "then ya' could have and afford prime rib au *juice* any damned time ya' want. Tell me, what do ya' like about Joanne Berenato's body that ya' got the hots for her so much?"

"I think her pearly teeth and her big brown eyes are very attractive," I replied.

"No Dip-shit," Goose objected. "I meant what part of her sexual apparatus attracts ya'? Her tits, her cunt, or her ass?"

"Well, now that you're puttin' everything is a biological context," I related, "I guess I like her buttocks."

"Her buttocks! Ha, ha, ha!" Goose boisterously laughed as if I had described something hilarious. "Just like ya' to like a girl's ass, the most stupid part of Joanne's skinny body that her shit comes outa'!" the gross nutcase loudly commented.

My eyes looked-around and noticed that the rest of the people seated inside the restaurant had suddenly acquired acute laryngitis along with keen hearing. I bit my tongue, and my face turned crimson. Feeling publicly embarrassed, I quickly slouched-down in my comfortable chair.

As we cheerfully maneuvered our forks and knives, I noticed that a family from Hammonton had entered the dining room's portal and then passed by our table. "Hey Goose, that's Pee Wee Lucca. He's finally gotten the casts off his arms," I identified.

"Probably his damned birthday today," Restuccio sneered. "Must be at least eleven. I've seen better lookin' pineys' hangin' out in local deer clubs."

For some odd reason, I thought Goose's cynical statement had been comical. "But Pee Wee has detected our presence, I know he did," I added. "Smaller kids tend to observe their surroundings better. They're more aware of dangerous predators and bullies because of their size."

"So, what?" Goose mildly exclaimed. "He's just a little Mama's boy out with his family celebratin' his introduction to *poo-burt-tee.* Who knows? Maybe he'll get his first hard-on tonight."

"But remember what the Blues did to him?" I reminded my irascible host. "They nearly killed Pee Wee over at Ancora Mental Hospital on suspicion that the dwarf had conspired with the Reds?"

"Stop using all these fuckin' big college fifty-cent words!" Goose yelled a little too boisterously for sophisticated clientele seated at other tables to appreciate. "He's just out with mommy and daddy, that's all! A lousy jerk-off in search of his first boner."

"But what if the runt wants to get back in thick with the Blues?" I reasoned and suggested. "What if Pee Wee reports us to Gabe Gillette to get back into *his* good graces. He must feel like he's a traitor, a sort of Benedict Arnold."

"Who the hell is Benedict Arnold? Is he a stupid cartoon character? Ya' must read too many comic books," Goose answered and accused, again getting over formal diners' attention. "I'll have to get ya' a couple copies of *Playboy* to get your mind on more practical matters."

For dessert, I regained my composure and consumed a hot fudge sundae with lots of whipped cream, and G.R. devoured two scoops of spumoni. Pee Wee Lucca passed by our table on his way to the Men's Room, pretending not to see us.

"The munchkin deliberately ignored us," I mentioned to Goose. "He's up to somethin', I just know it."

"J.W.," my skeptical mentor replied. "Ya' have quite a *lou-sid* imagination. That squealin' asshole has to take a piss in the Men's Room urinal, and he's afraid of us bein' here without Gillette, Mortellite, Lanza, and Narducci bein' around to protect his lily-white ass. So, because Pee Wee's feelin' *in-tents* fear right now, the timid midget can't fuckin' show it with eye contact, or by makin' threats. Get it?"

"Okay, you win this time," I conceded. "The ostracized punk's probably lookin' around to find a new set of hands after failin' miserably at mailbox baseball demolition! Let's go out on the Mullica and enjoy some fresh wind and air."

"I don't think that pee-wee has an *ostrich-sized* neck," my language-deficient comrade declared. "His thimble-sized neck looks more like it belongs on a baby turtle!"

Goose gave the elderly waitress a ten-dollar tip, and she was thrilled, praising his admirable generosity, which was really an extension of his general propensity for doing most everything in excess. "That's okay, Hon," G.R. told the old dame. "My ship's come in!" the notorious blowhard hooted, pointing outside the window to the picturesque marina and his newly-acquired, cigarette-shaped speed machine.

On the way out of the restaurant, I brought to Goose's attention Pee Wee Lucca surreptitiously talking in the *Ma Bell* payphone booth. My comrade had a unique interpretation of what I had just witnessed.

"J.W.," G.R. stubbornly addressed me. "The worried runt is probably talkin' to his psychiatrist, or to his babysitter. Maybe his high chair is broken, or somethin' fuckin' dumb reason like that. Why don't ya' just go into the Men's Room and jerk-off. You'll feel a lot better after ya' do! I'm thinkin' about goin' in there and poppin' a load myself. I haven't gotten laid yet this week, and I'm horny as hell!"

My gregarious host and I walked-down the dock to where his speedboat *Goose's Gadget* had been moored. We carefully entered the magnificent red marine-machine, with Goose going first. The river pilot activated the powerful outboard motor; untied the aft and stern ropes, and our sleek dream boat gently glided-away from the dock, and then drifted out of the marina.

"How much did this baby cost?" I inquired.

"More than your friggin' house and farm market combined," the self-appointed navigator boasted. "Cigarette *Fiberglas* speedboats don't come as prizes inside *Crackerjack* boxes, ya' know."

"Did ya' take any required courses or lessons on how to drive this boat?" I asked.

"All ya' gotta' know is ya' pass other boats on the right side close to the green marker, and they pass you on their left," he related.

"You mean on the port side," I clarified.

"J.W., what the fuck's the matter with ya'?" my *Mullica River* tour guide protested. "There's ports on the left side and ports on the right side, too, all over this damned river, and all over the whole shit-eatin' coastline."

"In other words," I clarified, "ya' always keep to the right, no matter which way you're goin'."

"That's right Jerk-weed!" G.R. sarcastically agreed. Goose then gave me a brief lesson on channel markers, claiming that certain parts of the *Mullica* up near Sweetwater were shallow, and that sailors had to stay in the center of the river to avoid shoals, or their boats would scrape thc bottom. "Notice the markers on those long poles planted in the river. They're called 'day markers'," my cruise director lectured. "Notice that the red markers are on the left, and the green ones are on the right. They mark where the main river channel is, and we gotta' keep between those markers, or this here speedboat will become a death anchor."

"I get it," I understood. "Ya' gotta' stay closer to the green marker to stay to the right, and the red markers are probably green on the other side for traffic goin' toward Sweetwater. I *fathom* what you're sayin'," I jested."

"J.W.," G.R. admitted with a grin. "You oughta' manage a big city sewer plant, because you really know your shit!"

"Where are we headin'?" I asked.

"Down to Chestnut Neck Marina, just past the *Parkway Bridge,*" Restuccio informed. "It'll be a nice ride for an amateur boat's man like yourself. Say, where's your blue and white Boatneck shirt?"

"Chestnut Neck!" I exclaimed. "Isn't that where the Blues keep all their boats?"

"Boats!" Goose yelled. "Ya' mean yachts. Those guys run cunt-grabbin' cabin cruisers with huge inboard motors. The Blues don't fart-around with penny-ante speedboats like this piece of shit."

"Chestnut Neck was the scene of a *Revolutionary War* battle," I recalled and said, as I shifted into my academic gear, since News was not present to expertly elucidate on the matter. "American privateers had a warehouse there, and auctioned-off goods the pirates stole from British ships. The buccaneers advertised the auctions in Philly' and New York newspapers," I related to deaf ears. "The British got angry and leveled the town, but the Red Coats never made it down to Batsto to torch the bog iron cannon ball factory."

"J.W., who gives three turkey turds about what the hell happened at Chestnut Neck in your little kid's history book," Goose criticized. "I don't' give a diarrhea shit if corn was a *buck an ear,* or what! I just wanta' know about what happened to Gabe Gillette and Speed with the peach pit."

"Well, I heard from reliable sources that Gabe Gillette has a broken right leg and that Speed has a fractured left arm," I reported. "Their bikes were banged-up pretty good in the peach pit caper. So, I guess they're immobile with you destroyin' Gabe's blue and white cabin cruiser at the Atlantic Canal; his blue 'Vette at the railroad trestle; demolishin' Speed's T-Bird at the railroad trestle, and now obliteratin' their two *Harleys* in News's peach dump. Goose, why are we slowin' down?"

"This is a 'No Wake Zone' on the river," G.R. stated. "You're only supposed to go five-miles an hour under this here bridge."

"No *wake* zone. Is everybody sleepin'? Probably never have any funerals or burials here, either!" I joked. "Where are we?"

"This here place is called Green Bank, and there's another bridge just like this one five-miles or so down the river at Lower Bank. Then, the channel gets deeper and wider as we move out to the bay."

"Look at the gorgeous forests and the sky," I remarked. "It's all really quite peaceful and beautiful out here. It's sort of like communion with nature. It's like the wicked world has stopped, and we're the only two creatures enjoyin' this river all to ourselves."

"J.W., you're a goddamned dreamer," Goose derided, "and ya' gotta' make big bucks out there in the real world to be able to have the luxury of cruisin' this river and gettin' away from friggin' *syphilisation.*"

"You're too materialistic," I seriously argued. "There's more to life than money, and sex for money."

"You're right J.W. There's power, too!" Goose yelled as the speedboat throttled-up to twenty-miles per hour beyond Green Bank. "Have ya' ever been in a department store?"

"Yeah, it's easy once ya' get beyond the revolvin' door," I answered, amusing just myself.

"Well, J.W., life's full of revolvin' doors, and your' life is now stuck in a maze of 'em. Revolvin' doors are power objects," G.R. declared.

"Power objects? How?" I queried.

"Well, everybody tries to trap you in *their* revolvin' door, just to make themselves feel powerful," Goose indicated. "Mr. Andrews has you trapped in his; Joanne Berenato in hers; your parents in theirs, and the Blues want to intimidate us into bein' *in-car-sir-rated* in their friggin' revolvin' door," Restuccio elucidated. "If ya' learn how to stay outa' other people's revolvin' doors, ya' can then trap people inside yours, and become rich, powerful, and famous."

I assessed the insights that Ronald Restuccio had conveyed, and I saw a degree of merit in his unique hypothesis. The speedboat again slowed-down for the Lower Bank Bridge and associated 'No Wake Zone', and several signs anchored in the river alerted us to that fact.

"I think I remember News saying somethin' about an International Waterway Code," I shared, "and this 'No Wake Zone' business must be part of it."

"Only seven or eight more miles to *the Garden State Parkway Bridge,* and then we'll hit Chestnut Neck," Goose laughed. "But don't worry, J.W. I'm not gonna' pull into that marina. I know the Blues keep most of their boats there. The rest of their navy the freaks keep at Oyster Creek, two-miles south of Chestnut Neck. I just wanta' open this baby up when we get near the *Parkway' Bridge* and then…"

"The *Parkway Bridge!* That's where Jives began racin' Dion and the Belmonts," I interrupted. I began describing how Jives, Fabian, News, Juice, and I had gotten involved with Dion and the Belmonts when I perceived three pleasure yachts heading our way at intense speeds. As the small armada approached, I had a funny feeling that some significant problem was about to occur.

"Yeah J.W.," G.R. said. "Right here is about where the salt water line from the ocean ends and the fresh water begins."

"Er Goose," I alerted. "Aren't those boats comin' towards us a little too fast?"

"Jesus Christ!" Goose shouted. "That's Narducci's, Mortellite's and Lanza's yachts comin' right toward us."

Restuccio swung his red, cigarette-shaped speedboat around, and turned the lever to full throttle. The three pleasure crafts had to momentarily slow-down because of the *about-face* wake that *Goose's Gadget* had created, which gave us a temporary advantage in the chase.

"Those mother-fuckers ain't gonna' catch me!" Goose screamed like a raving lunatic.

"Watch out ahead! We're trapped!" I yelled as I pointed to the closed Lower Bank Bridge.

"We're not trapped!" G.R. cackled like a zany, insane warlock. "The Blues are trapped. It's high tide, and we can make it under the lowered bridge, but their yachts are too high, either for high or for low tide. They'll have to wait for the drawbridge to open, and we'll be back in good old Sweetwater by then," Goose snickered. "They're not stupid enough to have three yachts smash into the pilings and the bridge supports. That'll be over a half-million in damages."

The crazy speedboat operator didn't diminish his velocity one iota, and the watchman in the bridge's lookout house nearly fell out of the open observation window as we zipped underneath, squeezing through the narrow space at about fifty-miles an hour, wildly zipping between the bridge's concrete supports.

The three pursuing yachts had to slow-down and stop on the Mullica, until the scared-to-death bridge operator was able to open the draw to let them through.

"Ha, ha, ha!" Goose screamed, nearly expelling his thyroid gland from his throat and out of his mouth. "Those dirty bastards were outsmarted by us again!"

"Are ya' sure they don't have their own speed boats hidden in one of the side-creeks that feed into the Mullica?" I asked as the wind blew my greasy hair into my face. "This river has a lot of tributaries."

"Who the hell cares!" G.R. hollered as spray from the river splashed up into our faces. "They'll never catch us, and besides, we're havin' fun breakin' the law and scarin' the shit out of those old poop-heads standin' in the bridge towers."

Restuccio kept the speedboat skimming over the Mullica at fifty-miles-an-hour so that the three yachts couldn't possibly gain on us, and intercept *Goose's Gadget*. Not honoring the "No Wake Zone", the pilot zoomed under the Green Bank Bridge at top speed, just like the violator had done at Lower Bank. "Only six more miles to Sweetwater!" 'Captain Ahab' yelled, featuring a very self-satisfied grin upon his face.

Just when I thought that we had escaped our formidable enemies, a late afternoon shadow was cast over *Goose's Gadget*. The fleeing captain and I looked-up and saw a black helicopter, easily keeping the fifty-miles an hour speed that our marvelous swift boat had been maintaining.

"Are they the state police?" I shouted out.

"Shit! That's one of the Blues' helicopters that the punks use for sprayin' the berry bushes," Goose yelled. "They're buzzin' our asses pretty good!"

"Look! That's Speed Mortellite sittin' up there with the pilot!" I yelled into G.R.'s right ear. "There's no way you're gonna' outrun that chopper! I think we're cruisin' for a bruisin'!"

The helicopter opened-up its jet-nozzles and began spraying us with a foul-smelling substance. Then, the flying machine elevated into the sky, angled left, and soon disappeared from view.

"What the fuck did they dump on us!" the *Goose's Gadget's* incapacitated captain asked his only mate.

"It stinks like urine!" I grimaced and sneered. "And we're both drenched head-to-toe with piss. I'll bet it's probably raw sewage taken-out of the main cesspool at the farm labor camp."

Goose wiped his face with a convenient towel and stubbornly kept his fifty-mile-an-hour speed, and the boat was hopping and skipping the river surface as if it were a fast-propelled flat stone.

"Just three more miles to Sweetwater!" Goose yelled. "I'll keep her at fifty-miles all the way in."

"Don't ya' mean fifty-knots!" I bellowed back, still closing my nostrils from the horrible urine odor.

"Ya' just say knots when you're out in the ocean," Goose clarified. "Ya' say miles per hour when you're toolin' on the river, or haulin' ass in the bay."

Our dialogue was interrupted with the appearance of a second helicopter, suddenly shading the stern of our rapidly moving *Goose's Gadget*. The noisy aerial machine had effectively distracted the vociferous captain. Our craft erratically whizzed-by too close to two stationary fishermen standing inside a skiff and casting their lines. The petrified river anglers lost their balances, and plunged with their fishing rods into the *Mullica*. I looked skyward and saw a gloating Gabe Gillette sitting in the seat next to the chopper's very skilled pilot.

I presumed that the Blues head-honcho must have switched to a second chopper at his expansive Weymouth Road plantation, only ten-miles-away.

The second whirlybird's pilot deliberately allowed G.R. time to negotiate a sharp river bend at top speed. Then, the chopper caught-up to us, and before either Goose or I could scream-out any derogatory cuss words, the flying machine ejected a thick white spray onto *Goose's Gadget's* two unfortunate victims.

"What the shit's happened now?" Goose cried in discomfort. "I can't see a fuckin' thing! I've been blinded!"

"Stop the boat! Stop the damned boat!" I shrieked. "I recognize the smell! They've also bombed us with insecticide spray. Maybe D.D.T. It's toxic and can kill us! We might have to jump into the river to get this toxic crap off of us!"

"Jesus Christ! I can't swim!" Goose ranted as the boat slowed-down and finally stopped. "Those fuckin' scumbags!"

For a whole minute, the two of us stumbled and fumbled around, trying to locate rags and several fresh water bottles to wipe the irritating debris from our burning eyes. I could vaguely perceive light, darkness, and shadows, but could not distinguish colors or any geometric pattern definition.

"We're gonna' be captured," Goose remorsefully predicted. "J.W., I shoulda' listened to ya'. You was right about that friggin' Pee Wee Lucca phonin' Gabe Gillette to get on his better side again. I still can't see shit, even though I'm covered with it!"

Around five-minutes later, our presence was detected, and the sound of engines was discerned, approaching on the river. The three Blues' expensive yachts soon surrounded our neutralized speedboat. Our ears perceived laughter and merriment abounding aboard the victorious cabin cruisers.

"You two assholes are under arrest!" commanded Butch Lanza's very distinct voice. 'This is not playin' 'Truth or Consequences', only consequences, ha, ha, ha!"

"You're gonna' have the special donkey and pig treatment," Ox Narducci's baritone informed from another direction.

"But that'll be preceded by the highlight of the evenin'," Dan "the Hammer" Bertino, the triumphant captain of the third vessel predicted from *his* bobbing yacht's deck.

Chapter Thirty-Four
"Dual Indignities"

Goose and I were grabbed one at a time by our arms, roughly manhandled, and then violently lifted onto one of the Blues' exotic fishing boats, becoming captives of blue-fruit tyranny. The other two ecstatic captains hopped-aboard and temporarily joined Ox Narducci and our captured company.

"What about my new red speedboat?" a semi-blinded Goose Restuccio yelled in all directions at our humored captors. "Where is it? It's brand new!"

"It'll be taken to Chestnut Neck," Ox Narducci's voice laughed. "I can't want to try it out for a joyride! But if I was you, I'd be more worried about my life than bein' concerned about my stupid, damned, little-red toy speedboat."

"What are ya' gonna' do *with* us?" I pleaded, blinking my blue eyes in an attempt to effectively view my surroundings. "We were just out sightseein' on the *Mullica*."

"Ya' meant to say what are we gonna' do *to* ya'!" Butch Lanza's crude voice ominously cackled. "First, we'll rinse ya' off and get the cruddy insecticide off your crummy bodies. The spray was diluted, so ya' won't die or nothin' like that," the disreputable greaser assured us. "But your eyes will be irritated for about an hour. Then, we'll have a little advanced fun with our two nice guests."

"Yeah," Hammer Bertino's voice agreed. "We think ya' two jerks are responsible for a few things that have happened to the Blues lately. We now have two wars goin' on, one against the Reds, and thanks to you jerk-offs, and one against the Ramrodders," Bertino emphasized. "You're both gonna' pay dearly for defyin' *our* control of Hammonton. And when we figure-out exactly which gang has done what to us, either a few Reds or a few Ramrodder culprits are gonna' pay with their testicles. Ever been castrated before?" Hammer Bertino asked as the barbaric Goliath brandished and then placed a butcher's knife against my neck.

"What have we done?" I challenged before wiping my eyes with a clean towel that one of the subordinate Blues on board had given me. "I told ya', we're just out for a pleasure ride on the *Mullica!* I wanted Goose to show me Batsto Village."

"If I were you, you lowly farm market punk, I'd keep my damned trap shut! Ya' have the bad habit of talkin' too damned much," Ox Narducci's voice asserted and determined. "Everything was fine between the Reds and the Blues 'til *you* moved into town! Now, there's a great teen fruit war goin' on, and you're to blame for it all!"

The Blues' three-boat armada turned-around in the middle of the Mullica and made its way to Crowley's Landing, across from Sweetwater, on the Batsto Village north side of the river. By that time, my eyesight had almost returned to normal vision. And as I turned my head and looked behind, I could see the other two pleasure crafts following the one in which Goose and I had been kidnapped, and I then observed that Ox Narducci was piloting our ocean-worthy yacht.

"Hey, who's drivin' my speedboat?" Goose yelled as the scared Sicilian began regaining his vision.

"Sonny Perone is takin' it over to one of our berths at Oyster Creek," Marty Gillette, Gabe's chief surrogate informed G.R. and me. "I can't wait to take that red baby out in the Atlantic all by myself! Maybe I'll drop anchor, and do a little *Blue*fish anglin' near the surf, just off the Ocean City boardwalk."

Marty Gillette's mentioning of "Blue" generated a huge laugh from his loyal audience. The five half-drunk blueberry kids (on deck guarding Restuccio and me) were being vastly entertained. I was so mad and frustrated that I felt like sticking my index finger down my throat and vomiting a partially digested hot fudge sundae and a full-course prime rib au jus supper right into the center of the little obnoxious squirt's face.

Zeke Errera appeared behind me holding two changes of clothing. "Be sure to come out of the bathroom wearin' your blue denim jackets," the bearded gladiator said into my ear, cherishing the utterance of each syllable. "You guys are gonna' be officially initiated into the Blues, and you're both gonna' love every bitchin' second of it."

I descended seven steps and entered the boat's tidy bathroom first, before Goose's turn to also change apparel. I washed some of the crud off of my extremities; used the toilet facilities, and five-minutes later, exited, wearing blue jeans, a blue cotton shirt, and the other gang's trademark blue denim jacket. Goose then descended the steps, entered the bathroom, and likewise, changed into his informal Blues "initiation uniform".

Upon returning to deck level, G.R. had to sit on a bench on the opposite side of the fancy fishing boat, facing me, and we were not allowed to communicate with each other. Eye contact convinced me that G.R.'s mind and heart were fuming on the inside, just as much as mine were.

"Hey Goose," Zeke Errera beckoned. "Did ya' ever get caught jerkin'-off in the closet?"

"The closet's a good hidin' place for the faggot Blues to work their sticks!" I impetuously interrupted. "Goose has all the women he wants.

He doesn't have to put it on automatic like you goons have to!" I cleverly interrupted.

"Look, you weak farm market fairy, if ya' butt-in one more time," Marty Gillette threatened, "your ass is goin' overboard into the drink. Tell me the truth J.W., did ya' ever eat shit on a stick?" Marty insultingly inquired.

"Do ya' think J.W. is like you' impotent ball-busters?" Goose injected, without committing any verbal errors. "J.W.'s got fussy eatin' habits. He doesn't like the taste of sticks!"

"Don't knock the Blues," Marty returned. "You're gonna' be one in about an hour-and-a-half, whether you like it or not. If ya' fail the gang's initiation, designed especially for you two homos, then you'll both be dead meat. Buzzards' material, I guarantee it!"

Goose and I remained reticent the rest of the way to Oyster Creek, fearing that our physical welfare might be in jeopardy. The Blues seemed content drinking *Pabst Blue Ribbon* beer bottles, and then littering the *Mullica,* and later the bay, with their empty brown-glass bottles. Just before twilight set in, the four boats all docked at Oyster Creek Marina, several miles down-bay from Chestnut Neck.

"Okay, wick-dicks! Come with us!" little-squirt Marty Gillette, Gabe's appointed lieutenant, commanded. "Take a good look at your cheap speedboat. It might be the last time you'll see it in one piece."

G.R. and I were escorted to a nearby white box truck and directed to climb into the empty rear storage compartment. The back panels were then shut tight, and quickly locked from outside. We were futilely imprisoned inside a large, dark cube. The truck's diesel engine started-up, and the vehicle began its short journey back to Hammonton. The noise from the loud muffler reverberated up into our totally black area of confinement, and the noxious fumes from the neglected exhaust system made me want to regurgitate.

"How could the enemy get-out and be on the river so quickly from Hammonton?" I asked my fellow captive. "Are they magicians, or what?"

"The helicopters certainly came from Hammonton, no fuckin' doubt about that shit," Goose inferred and stated in the dark. "But the blueberry guys must've gotten a day off from work because berry prices usually crash after the Fourth of July holiday. When the price per crate rebounds in a few days, those assholes will be back workin' on their farms. The snot-noses probably were partyin' at Chestnut Neck when Pee Wee Lucca called Gabe Gillette, who then sent the three boats out from the marina. Gotta' give the Blues credit for puttin' together a slick scheme in little time," Restuccio surmised and reluctantly praised.

"Do ya' think they'll kill us?" I nervously asked. "I know they'd like to kill us!"

"Naa, they'll just try to outwit us and put a scare into our asses that'll make the shit turn-around in our butts, and travel back up to our stomachs," G.R. exaggerated. "Then, I think they'll be satisfied. Those flunkies know that if they hurt or kill me, they've writtin' their own death sentences. Now, with you, that's a whole other story," Goose indicated. "The shit-heads might make ya' eat a live porcupine or poisonous snake, or put you in a cage with three raccoons that have cancer and rabies, or somethin' stupid like that."

"What's goin' on between the Blues and the Ramrodders?" I asked. "Have ya' heard anything? There seems to be some major friction there, too."

"The Blues are now at war with the greaser punks, and also at war with the Reds," Goose informed. "Thank goodness the *fan-attics* think the Rodders' had played the last motorcycle prank on them at the peach dump, or those fucked-up Blues would really take their anger out on the two of us."

"Is there no justice in this world!" I questioned.

"Not in this world, and definitely not in the next," Goose concluded, bouncing up and down inside the dark enclosure, "because there ain't no next world to have any justice in. That's why that jerk-off Darwin guy I studied about at Edgewood was right. Survival of the fittest rules, and right now J.W., the Blues are the most-fittest, up on the big fruit war scoreboard."

The box truck exited a smooth paved road, and the ride in the back suddenly became excessively bumpy and disconcerting. G.R. and I bounced-around off of the floor and against the walls, as if we were both pinballs banging-around and against bumpers, inside a souped-up, amusement, flipper-device.

"I'm really pissed-off!" Goose futilely exclaimed. "We're caught in the Blues revolvin' door, and I can't do a damned thing about it!"

"You could always pray," I suggested.

"Religion is another fuckin' revolvin' door that traps millions of assholes every shittin' Sunday!" G.R. yelled in the dark.

Three-minutes later, the box truck halted; the rear panels were opened, and when we clambered-out, I immediately recognized by the sky's light that the time of day was around dusk. I also realized that we were situated inside the same blueberry field near New Creek Road, where Mr. Gillette had clandestinely received an attache case full of hundred-dollar-bills from Mafia man Mr. Restuccio. I observed Gabe Gillette standing on crutches, and Speed Mortellite in attendance, with his left arm hanging-down in a sling. Twenty-one other nasty Blues stood in a circle, appearing like a hungry wolf pack ready to strike and pounce.

"How many rows are we from the end of the field?" Gillette cleverly asked Goose and me.

Neither of us answered, knowing that if we quickly and correctly had responded "thirteen", which we very easily could have done, then we would be admitting that *we* knew something about the missing three-quarters of a million dollars. I pointed to the rows with my left index finger and systematically counted, "One, two, three, four…"

"That's enough!" Speed Mortellite sternly commanded. "You jerk-offs luckily passed the first test. It musta' been the Ramrodders that stole the friggin' money."

"What money?" Goose asked, pretending that the 'Mafia-Kid' was unaware of any large heist.

"Never mind," disappointed Gabe Gillette yelled. "We ask the shittin' questions around here! You're just our stupid-assed hostages in our custody. Now, I want you two fucked-up Edgewood degenerates to please respect the rules of civilized warfare," Gabe continued his prosecution. "And if ya' two side-show freaks would please accompany me, we have a little special treat for ya' both to appreciate," Gabe promised, his face sporting a sinister, false smile. "You're both gonna' be rewarded for cooperatin' with us, and for not stealin' the buried loot."

Ox Narducci, Hammer Bertino, and their fellow Hammonton High defensive and offensive linemen grabbed Goose and me, and paraded us to our left, as if we were kidnapped barbarians. We soon had a rendezvous with the first row of yet to be harvested blueberry bushes, which were laden with clusters of luscious blue fruit. The limbs of the plants were bent-over, and the heavy fruit actually weighed some of the lower branches down to the sandy ground. I looked to my feet, and got the absolute shock of my short life. I was totally horrified.

Lying in the dirt and wriggling-around in the sand was a stark-naked Crystal Davis, Tyrone's younger sister. Her clothes were strewn alongside her sweaty and twisting, chocolate-brown body.

"We kidnapped this here nigger bitch a few hours ago over in Winslow," Gabe Gillette informed, "and the first one of you two assholes that gets a hard-on gets to screw the black whore in public."

"This is a serious felony, kidnapping and rape!" I yelled. I looked down at the pathetic black girl, still squirming and gyrating about. Crystal had a blue bandanna stuffed inside her mouth, and her four limbs had been tied-down with strips of clothesline, tethered to stakes that had been driven deep into the soft earth. Her legs were spread eagle, and my heart felt great empathy for the dehumanizing torture

Crystal was enduring at the hands of the dirt-bag Blues. "You can all go to federal prison for what the hell you're doin' to her!" I vehemently protested. "The local cops can't protect you there!"

Someone in the mob didn't savor my remark, and the pugnacious punk attacked me from behind with a blackjack. I felt a terrible pain above the nape of my neck, and then, I must have gone unconscious for five-minutes or so. When I finally regained my sensibilities and cleared the cobwebs from my disoriented brain, I realized that I had been lying face-down on the sandy soil. I felt a terrible ache throbbing on top of my cranium. I strained to raised my head, and when my eyes glanced to my right, I heard and viewed the Blues jeering and cheering. Apparently, Goose had gotten an erection and was in the process of having unwarranted, forced sex with Frankie Arena's encumbered Winslow neighbor, Crystal Davis.

I saw tears of humiliation streaming-down from Crystal's sorrowful eyes, with the 'windows of her soul' revealing her extreme emotional anguish. And I witnessed the beleaguered girl wrenching her hips back and forth to free her body and spirit from the diabolical embarrassment, but her resistance was futile. Several more minutes of the ungodly, brutal agony elapsed, and finally, Goose climaxed amidst the cheers, shouts, and derogatory barbs shouted his and Crystal's ruthless persecutors. I thanked God that the demonic debauchery had finally terminated.

A gleeful Gabe Gillette instructed Goose to put-on his boxer shorts, undershirt, blue jeans, and blue denim jacket. Then, G.R. and I had to watch as Marty Gillette and Zeke Errera poured a bottle of lighter fluid, and then ignited our dirty James Dean jackets in a miniature bonfire, while the Blues wildly celebrated and liberally drank whiskey and beer in what constituted a bizarre Saturnalia.

"Ya' two lucky jerk-offs passed your Blues' initiation with flyin' colors," Gabe Gillette proudly announced. "I got the idea when I read in a history book about the medieval ordeals that knights and accused criminals had to endure to keep on livin'. Congratulations," Gabe sarcastically stated. "You two lucky fuck-heads have passed the ordeal exams!"

"Please untie the girl and show her some mercy," I begged. "Give her back some of her dignity. She never did anything to any of you!"

"You talk too much for a nothin', cock-suckin' farm market kid!" Gabe Gillette vulgarly accused. "Curb your goddamned tongue, or you might not have it for long!"

I saw Ox Narducci clobber a semi-conscious Goose Restuccio on the back of his skull with a blackjack. Next, I felt an intense blow smash against my scalp and head, and then everything blacked-out, and my abused mind instantly went blank.

Chapter Thirty-Five

"Donkeys and Pigs"

When I finally regained consciousness, I found myself sitting in a western saddle on top of an old, stubborn donkey. I glanced to my left and observed Goose, also on a saddle, sitting atop a twin donkey. Our hands were virtually immobile, tied to each saddle's pommel. My eyes cautiously surveyed my immediate environment, and my failing spirit was disappointed to discover that G.R., the twin donkeys, and I were situated inside a makeshift rodeo, with twenty-three Blues and their mocking girlfriends in attendance.

A leather pouch had been attached to and inserted next to the pommel, and when I looked over and analyzed Goose's saddle, a similar arrangement had been connected to his.

"Now that both of you two new Blue recruits are awake," Gabe Gillette hollered to us, "we'll now begin the donkey phase of your Blues initiation, which will be followed by our favorite recreational activity, the hog-feedin' session. I hope you, J.W., and Goose is cooked Restuccio, don't mind bein' the stars of our little circus."

The first event, the "donkey phase", was the jousting competition. Long wooden poles were placed inside the leather pouches. Goose was sitting there in some kind of hypnotic trance, incapable of any kind of action or exchanging of words with anyone.

The two donkeys were led to opposite ends of the makeshift arena. The obstinate animals were pointed toward each other; two Blues' members raised the long wooden lances inside the pouches, and on the count of three, Ox Narducci slapped my beast on its rear end, and Butch Lanza hit Goose's in a duplicate manner.

The lethargic donkeys slowly advanced toward each other. I pushed Restuccio's long wooden lance out of the way, but my pole glanced off of his already-distorted forehead. A round of applause was emitted from the entertained audience. The jousting competition had ended in a draw, with Goose in a stupor, sustaining a deep gash across his forehead.

Everyone watching our repulsive plight cheered Gabe Gillette's master-of-ceremonies' announcement that the second event would be much more exciting. The ringmaster, on crutches, then directed Ox Narducci and Butch Lanza to insert the same long poles into the rugged pouches attached to our pommels, and then carrots were hooked onto the ends of the long wooden rods. The donkeys reared forward, trying to munch the tempting food that was suddenly tantalizing their formerly dormant appetites.

"Why can't I move my arms and legs?" I dully asked everyone in general. "What have you' blueberry swine done to us? Why can't Goose say anything?"

"Because you've been drugged by a strong sedative," Gabe Gillette wickedly laughed like Bela Lugosi. "Let's just call it a powerful muscle relaxer. Ox administered you a dose in your rear end with his favorite hypodermic needle, but I think your buddy over there got a much bigger injection because he's hardly awake."

My mind was swimming in a half-dazed state of distorted sanity. I glanced-over at Goose, who appeared to be comatose, sitting in his saddle with his head slumped-down upon his chin. Butch Lanza climbed the rungs of a wooden ladder, and placed mock cardboard crowns, colored-in with crayons, on both of our heads. I felt completely mortified, which to me at the time seemed a trifle better than being hideous and evil like the satanic Blues were.

The left side of my butt really hurt badly from the potent injection. Although I felt weak from the "muscle relaxer", I still had the presence of mind to survey my immediate surroundings. Judging from a gathering of well-fed hogs off in the distance, my afflicted brain registered the composite visual data, and I vaguely understood that Goose and I were situated inside DiGiacomo's Pig Farm at the end of Eleventh Street, not far from the Hammonton Town Dump.

My pupils looked-up at the sky and recognized that it was dusk. I tried to identify several constellations I had studied at Cardinal Reagan High in the astronomy section of a science textbook, but the only object I could accurately identify was the moon. My dizzy mind conjured-up a strange notion that I had been removed from the *Milky Way,* and was somehow mysteriously struggling on another Earth in a distant galaxy.

I stared-over at Goose's face, which had glazed eyes, and his limp body was showing very slow reflexes. 'His coordination must be hampered by that extra strong dose of muscle relaxer,' my fuzzy mind reckoned. 'Despite his head wound, he's drugged-up and better off than I am, because the poor devil doesn't know what in the universe is happening to us.'

The first time around the circular track, Ox Narducci, Butch Lanza on my team, and Zeke Errera and Hammer Bertino on Goose's squad, held onto the temperamental donkeys' bridles. The beasts-of-burden were guided around the corral's track, which was about a hundred-yards in circumference. When Goose and I reached the finish line flag, which was also the starting line, the poles with the uneaten carrots dangling from the ends were removed from their leather pouches. I hadn't at first realized that event number two had several perilous segments to it.

Ox, Butch, Hammer, and Zeke inserted the two long poles into holes drilled into a wooden frame. The frame was attached to the rear of a blue farm utility jeep. Marty Gillette hopped inside the vehicle as the driver, and his brother, Gabe, was already-seated as the passenger. I turned my head to again view Goose, but his body was still limp, and his facial features were so morbid-looking that I preferred staring upward at the crescent moon. I thought of howling at the moon like an Ancora State Hospital *luna*tic, but then my addled brain considered how frivolous and foolish such a notion was, while sitting on a donkey in the middle of a sprawling pig farm.

When the jeep took-off in first gear, Speed Mortellite fired a pistol with his good right hand. That loud noise frightened the formerly lazy donkeys. The animals bolted forward, nearly dislodging my body from my saddle, and my feet from their stirrups.

The jeep accelerated in first gear, and the hungry donkeys pursued the two tantalizing pole carrots as if the vegetables were the last remaining food morsels on planet earth. G.R. and I were like two bobbing-head manikins, detached from reality, and trapped in the culmination of an ugly nightmare. When Marty Gillette sadistically shifted the jeep into second gear, the harnessed beasts began trotting even faster than before.

Goose's body and head were bobbing-up and down, to and fro, and from side to side, and his mental inaction resembled something between a zombie and a space alien. *The Headless Horseman of Sleepy Hollow* he was not, and Ichabod Crane, no doubt, was much more graceful in the saddle of old *Gunpowder* than either of us had been while riding upon our famished donkeys. The jeep eventually reached the finish line, but instead of stopping there, the incredible charade continued for another lap around the pig farm track.

The jeep driver shifted into third gear, and my stomach began churning. Restuccio and I were still both tied to our saddles, and I had the wherewithal to glance-down, and for the first time, noticed that a rope had been draped around the donkey's, neck and also tethered around my waist.

Speed Mortellite fired-off his revolver three more times and yelled out, "Way to go, you Reds' *lappers!*" The uncouth kid's comment engendered a tumultuous roar from the twenty-three assembled Blues and their fully-amused girlfriends.

My donkey's erratic running and the incessant bouncing-up and down triggered a reflex response within my upper digestive tract, and before I could burp, belch, or hiccup, a sour taste squirted-up to my mouth from my esophagus.

The jeep slowed-down and finally came to an abrupt stop just beyond the arbitrary start/finish line. The excited crowd dashed-over to my victorious donkey, and Master of Ceremonies Marty Gillette declared me the winner. My mouth was barfing all over the saddle and the ground from my lips and also from my nose, and *that* disgusting phenomenon stimulated a wild ovation from my thoroughly appreciative audience.

"Well, J.W., before ya' move back to Pennsylvania," Gabe Gillette hollered, "I want you and your fucked-up partner to feel like you're both *home on the range*. And your pal, Goose, might have a *nigger baby* inside a black oven already! Ha, ha, ha, ha!" Gillette insulted my temporarily brain-dead friend, the punk referring to a popular black licorice candy.

Ox Narducci cut my bonds with a blueberry bush branch-trimmer, and Butch Lanza held another cutter, and did the same thing to Goose. Next, G.R. and I were ripped from our saddles and carried to an old, discarded, gas stove. After our carcasses were deposited onto the four burners, Gabe Gillette announced so that all his disciples could hear, "Look gang, J.W. and Goose are *home on the range!* Ha, ha, ha, ha!"

I couldn't take the psychological abuse any longer. My nerves were jangled, but when I focused my attention upon G.R., my fellow Red was still a human vegetable, an unconscious prisoner listlessly existing in another dimension. 'He'll never believe this story if I ever live to tell it, and if he ever lives to hear it,' I thought and lamented.

"Okay, J.W., welcome to hog heaven," Gabe loudly giggled. "Now that you've thrown up your Sweetwater Casino dinner all over this exotic hog farm, it's now time for ya' to really pig-out! Is everybody ready for some more clean, wholesome country fun?" Gabe Gillette solicited to his congregation, much to the delight of his faithful apostles and their HHS chicks.

Ox and Butch lifted me off of the rusty, decrepit stove, and Zeke Errera and Hammer Bertino hoisted-up Goose. We were then both hurled onto the ground as if we were two sacks of rotten onions. Our denim jeans and underwear were rolled-down over our buttocks, and Ox Narducci, relishing his phony role as doctor, administered two more doses of "muscle relaxer", which in two-minutes paralyzed *our* vulnerable neuro-muscular systems. I was so fatigued from enduring the ordeal that I could barely stick my parched tongue out of my extremely dry mouth.

The contemptible Blues then transported Goose and me to a long wide pig trough, where we involuntarily joined two dazed Ramrodders, Mark Benedetto and Warren Watson, who had also been victimized by the despicable Blues, seeking random vengeance for the motorcycle-peach pit incident. Goose and I were recklessly tossed into the long wide slop tube and we, like the two helpless Ramrodders, simply lacked the dexterity and the stamina to clamber-out of the hogs' stinking eating receptacle.

"Okay, you four tough guys," Gabe Gillette ridiculed. "It's time for all of ya' to thrash around and *pig* out!"

The assembled Blues set-up a single-file straight line, forming a weird bucket brigade. The psychopaths passed pails of slop and rotten fruit including blueberries, peaches, plums, raspberries, cherries, and blackberries along to Ox Narducci, who merrily filled-up the pig trough with us four humans moaning and groaning, our tortured heads tilted inside. Gabe Gillette and Speed Mortellite, being injured, supervised the "Chinese slop-passin' fire drill".

"It's time to fatten ya' guys up before the slaughter, oink, oink, oink, oink!" Gabe satirized our sadistic debacle. "You four dim-wits must all live in goddamned pigsties. In fact, that's what ya' should wear to church with your Sunday suits, pigs' ties. Ha, ha, ha, ha!"

"When we release the squealing pigs, don't *pork* any *Petunias,"* Speed Mortellite's voice bellowed, alluding to two popular 1960 television cartoon characters.

"Pay attention J.W.," Gabe advised, "so that you'll learn how to bring home the bacon when ya' finally become a man. Now, Asshole, you can be a real ham when you move back to Pennsylvania."

A side corral gate was flung opened, and a bevy of thirsty and hungry swine came running and snorting-over to the convenient slop trough. The hogs were squealing, gobbling and spitting putrid-smelling food all over and around Goose, Mark Benedetto, Warren Watson and me. It was a most dehumanizing experience to be the unfortunate recipient of the two-dozen pigs' affections.

"Don't climb on top of one another unless ya' wanta' go piggyback!" Gabe shouted for the merriment of his already-blithe colleagues and their chicks. "J.W., ya' stupid swine, you can become a professional wrestler and go up against the Butcher," Gillette cackled as the cruel molester referred to a popular TV wrestler.

"J.W., one of the girls will make your long greasy locks into a pigtail!" Butch Lanza disrespectfully called-out. "And if ya' enjoy your company, ya' have enough slop in the trough to eat to really make a hog out of yourself! Ha, ha, ha, ha!"

A rather sophisticated, philosophical thought surfaced in my totally confused mind. 'Even crabs in a bushel or shrimp in a basket is better than pigs in a trough,' my psyche conjectured.

Goose, Warren, Mark, and I had to endure a whole hour of scornful catcalls and obscene allusions. The excessive scoffing continued until the Blues and their girls finally consumed four cases of *Pabst Blue Ribbon.* Tired of their hackneyed burlesque rodeo, the satisfied Blues and their dates decided to quit their droll travesty; ambled through a cluster of fir trees to their flashy vehicles, and abandoned the peculiar debacle that had been their source of preposterous levity.

Another hour of loneliness passed by in frightful, eerie silence. The only sounds I heard were crickets and bullfrogs in the distance, and an owl hooting on a limb in a far-off tree. I hoped and prayed that no bloodthirsty, red-tailed hawks were in the secluded vicinity, for I once saw one fly into a tree and easily rip a squirrel to pieces with its powerful talons and razor-sharp beak.

Then finally, Goose began to stir and breathe deeply; Mark Benedetto started coughing, and Warren Watson sounded as if the nasty Ramrodder was choking and gasping for oxygen. We were all panting with our chests heaving, and me, being face-up, had a good view of the other three occupants' predicaments, since they were all lying face-down in the slop-laden pig trough.

An amusing idea filtered-up from my subconscious into the cerebral section of my brain. 'At least the Blues didn't make us wallow in pig crap,' I thought as my beleaguered mind searched for some consolation to justify me surviving my extraordinarily bizarre pig farm travail.

Two sets of headlights flashed across the trees and bushes, and then the approaching beams focused directly on the four of us, still incarcerated at the disgusting, lengthy, pig trough. 'Oh, the police have arrived at last,' I imagined. 'Thank God for the police.'

The cars' high beams illuminated closer, and the sound of the two automobile engines became more distinct. 'I'd recognize those motors anywhere,' my dizzy mind concluded.

Soon, four doors opened, and then quickly slammed, and three figures hustled to the scene of *our* dilemma. Frantic, familiar voices resounded and echoed off the surrounding tall pine trees.

"J.W., are ya' still alive?" Elaine Hill asked.

"J.W., what happened to you and Goose and the two groggy Ramrodders," Dennis Measley interrogated. "How did ya' ever get yourselves into this awful mess?"

"J.W., please say something," the third melodic voice pleaded. I looked-up to determine the possessor of the magical tongue. I lapsed off into a state of semi-consciousness after my eyes discerned that the beautiful sensitive voice belonged to my Ivory Tower dream girl, St. Joe Prom Queen Joanne Berenato.

"Oh J.W., this is horrible," Elaine evaluated as her eyes examined the filth and slop-sludge floating inside the loathsome pig trough. "How do ya' always get yourself into these crazy tortures?"

"It's really easy when ya' know guys like Goose Restuccio," I answered. "It's *terribly* easy."

Dennis Meade was used to grime, manure, and pungent odors, so the experienced rescuer dirtied himself up pretty good, dragging my butt out of my inhospitable entrapment. Then, I mustered-up enough strength to help Dennis roll Goose, Warren Watson, and Mark Benedetto, one at a time, out of the stenchy, narrow, horizontal pig-food receptacle.

Out of the three survivors that I had helped Dennis salvage, Goose was still the most incoherent. I was going to slap him across the cheeks to revive his dazed condition, but then I reconsidered that G.R. would possibly remember my act of aggression in the future and seek violent retribution.

A minute later, I was sitting on the ground and leaning against the trunk of a tall oak tree. The herd of pigs were oinking and snorting about fifty-feet away, socializing on the other side of a chain-linked fence. I asked Joanne and Elaine how the girls had found-out about *our* unfortunate misadventures at DiGiacomo's Pig Farm.

"Joanne and I were sittin' in the Gem sippin' cherry *Cokes* and enjoying our burgers," Elaine Hill began, "and Dennis was in there to pick-up a carryout pizza. It all seemed like just another ordinary, boring night in downtown Hammonton."

"Then, I visited the Girls Room," Joanne joined the conversation, "and I saw Brigette DiMeo in there crying her eyes out. I asked her what was wrong. She couldn't keep the pig farm a secret any longer. As soon as my HHS friend mentioned Goose and you, J.W.," Joanne paused, "Elaine and I had to do something quick."

Near the rancid pig trough, Joanne informed Warren, Mark, and me that Brigette had become upset, because Joanne, Elaine and her had been good friends since elementary school, and the girls also had sung in the St. Joseph church choir together. When Brigette DiMeo saw Joanne and Elainc seated chatting inside the Gem, the Hammonton High student suddenly felt very guilty.

"Brigette told me she had been with Sonny Perone and her older brother Scaff at the pig farm and saw what Gabe Gillette and the others had done to Goose, Mark, Warren, and you," Joanne continued her background story, "so I got out of the Girls Room in a hurry. The only one I thought I could trust in the whole place besides Elaine was Dennis."

"That's right," Dennis verified. "And when Joanne asked me to follow her and Elaine and drive out here with my Plymouth, I did just what she asked me to do. Say, J.W., do ya' want any pizza. It's a little cold right now, but you're welcomed to a slice or two."

"Er, no thanks, Dennis," I responded, holding my irritated stomach and swollen abdomen to avoid me regurgitating. "Maybe by Christmas, I'll be able to eat again."

Elaine filled me in on some negative activities that had been happening in and around Hammonton during my day's absence. Juice Illiani and Jives Arena had taken a day trip to Clementon Lake Amusement Park. Six Ramrodders led by Sam Olive, Frank 'the Tank" Ordille, and Joel Salvo accosted them inside the "Haunted House". The Rodders had accused the two Reds of being involved with kidnapping Mark Benedetto and Warren Watson, who obviously had been detained and thoroughly persecuted by the all-too-malicious Blues.

"What happened to Juice and Jives?" I asked Elaine and Joanne.

"Well," Elaine anxiously explained. "The Ramrodders cruelly arrested Frankie and Johnny, and transported them to the Hammonton Brewery. Your friends were put in a huge vat with their hands tied together. The nutcase Ramrodders then threw two sand sharks into the beer tank, but the creatures died either from lack of oxygen or intoxication, or maybe both."

"How do ya' know all this?" I asked.

"Two of the Ramrodders that were at Clementon, a new kid named Petey Santelli, and another one named Teddy Tell, had nervous consciences, so the decent guys called News Tomasello, who then called Fabian Midilli. Those two brave knights drove-over to the brewery and rescued Jives and Juice from sufferin' death by intoxication."

"But where did the Ramrodders get the two sharks?" I wanted to know.

"Frank 'the Tank' Ordille was at Chestnut Neck Marina this mornin'," Joanne reported gossip she had heard, "and a fisherman had caught four large sand sharks. Frank the Tank bought two of 'em; put 'em in separate large tubs filled with seawater, and kept 'em alive until he figured-out what to do with 'em. Frank met-up with the other Ramrodders at the Gem; went to Clementon Lake Park to hustle some girls; saw and recognized Jives and Juice enter the Haunted House, and kidnapped the two Reds back to Hammonton."

"How did the Rodders' break into the Hammonton Brewery?" I asked. "Did the idiots use a can opener?"

"Gee J.W., you've only been out of Hammonton for one day and it's like you had gone to Mars or something," Joanne said with a cute smile. "The brewery's been closed since the Fifth of July because of a labor dispute, and so nobody was there when the crazy Ramrodders broke into the building."

Mark Benedetto and Warren Watson had become alert-enough to absorb most of the conversation. The new facts prompted Benedetto to speak.

"Now that Warren and I know the true facts," Mark said, sounding a little like Inspector Joe Friday on *Dragnet,* "and since the Blues have pulled a lot of crap tonight on the Reds and also on the Rodders', I want to make an apology. Warren and I are very sorry for what the boys did to your two guys at Clementon Lake Park and at the brewery."

"Yeah," Warren Watson promptly agreed. "We thought that it was the Reds that had the state cops investigatin' about Gabe Gillette and Speed Mortellite flyin' their *Harleys* into a peach pit near the Wharton Tract. When the fuzz mentioned something about a peach pit, right-away the Rodders thought about the Reds bein' the culprits and not the Blues."

"So, it looks like Elaine is a Clara Barton and Joanne is *my* Florence Nightingale," I concluded and gratefully declared. "Thanks girls, for helpin' us out of a tough jam. And thanks, Dennis, for being Denny on the spot."

Goose was finally coming out of his dramatic three-hour stupor. The ornery Sicilian moaned; spit-out some distasteful fruit morsels; sneezed rather egregiously, and then inhaled a deep breath while opening his bloodshot, dark-brown eyes. "What the fuck happened?" the partially-traumatized scoundrel impetuously asked. "Oh, sorry girls, I didn't realize I was in mixed company," G.R. added as the rogue rubbed a big bloody lump on the side of his forehead, which had been received from my wooden lance during the inane, inane jousting contest.

"Are ya' okay?" Dennis asked. "I can drive ya' to the Atlantic City Hospital!"

"Naa," Goose declined. "I'll be just fine once I wake-up from a real-bad nightmare I was havin'. The whole bullshit seemed so real in my mind! I dreamed that the Blues had this colored girl pinned on the ground in a blueberry field, and that the blueberry jerks made me..."

"Er, Goose," I diplomatically interrupted. "Gather your senses. It was just a giant annoying nightmare, a really bad giant annoying nightmare. The Blues drugged ya' up worse than the crazies drugged me up, so I think you were doin' some serious hallucinatin' on that donkey, and also in that slop bin. I'll bet tomorrow mornin' you'll be able to think clearer and remember exactly what the heck happened to you and to me."

"What donkey are ya' yappin' about!" G.R. demanded. "I don't remember any damned donkey! Are ya' tryin' to make an ass outa' me?"

"Maybe things will be more lucid for you tomorrow," I suggested. "Right now, you're pretty exhausted! I think that the best prescription is lots of rest!"

"But the colored girl on the ground seemed so damned real!" Goose exclaimed in awe. "Hey, what the hell are all of us doin' in the middle of a goddamned pig farm? Are we all in some lousy, low-budget black and white movie?"

Chapter Thirty-Six

"The Swimming Pool Fiasco"

Almost a full week had passed, and I was so stressed-out that I desired to remain incommunicado. I was afraid of being investigated by the police; of being terrorized by the reprehensible Blues, and of being brutalized by the formidable Ramrodders. News had called me once on the phone to tell me about a big fight in downtown Hammonton between the Blues and the Rodders'. That probability made me feel as though the Reds had *temporarily* escaped *our* participation in the double peach pit escapade, which also could have been a major felony if we had been caught obstructing the administration of justice.

"J.W.," News eagerly began on the phone. "I heard all about what happened to you and Goose on the *Mullica River* and at the smelly pig farm."

"I learned that Juice and Jives nearly got bottled into premium beer at the brewery," I answered. "Those guys were lucky, too! Who told you about the Mullica River boat chase and the pig farm incidents?" I asked.

"Elaine Hill," my good friend amiably replied. "She seemed to know a lot from speakin' to Brigette DiMeo. They've talked a few times on the phone this past week."

"Did ya' hear anything about a perverted Blues' prank at Gabe Gillette's blueberry farm?" I curiously probed. "I heard that the hoodlums nearly killed a couple of kids."

"No, what happened there?" Tommy requested to know.

"It's a long story, and I'll tell you everything when I have a lotta' time," I related. "I have to unload a truckload of produce that's sittin' out behind the market."

"Okay J.W., but could ya' be at my house around noon?" my amigo asked. "I'm havin' a little Reds' committee meeting."

"Sure, I haven't been out in about a week, so my parents will understand I need a little recreation time."

I unloaded the half-ton pick-up, which had been filled with fifty boxes of peaches; twenty-five boxes of red-ripe Jersey tomatoes; ten crates of cucumbers; five bushels of radishes, and two cartons of zucchini squash, which Dad had purchased at the 'Philly Distribution Center overnight. After getting permission to drive over to News's place, I hopped into the Pete's Market Special and made the visit. I was surprised to see Goose's red T-Bird and Jives black and white Coronet parked in the driveway.

"How you guys doin'?" I asked everybody. "Haven't seen any of ya' in almost a week. I felt a need to stay-away from the teen scene."

"Great," News mechanically answered, nodding his head. "J.W., we're here to talk some strategy that we'd like to use against the Blues. Goose just told us about the *Mullica River* fiasco and the pig farm disaster, but G.R. said he needed *you* here to explain everything that happened in between."

"Er, Goose," I acknowledged, clearing my throat. "What happened with your Thunderbird? I saw it sittin' in the driveway in perfect condition. Do ya' mean to say that the Blues never put a scratch or a dent out at the Sweetwater Casino?"

"That's right, J.W.," Goose confirmed. "And the morons never touched my wheels. Frankie Fingers and Joe Zucchini took me over to Sweetwater the next day, and my car was in A-1 condition. Good thing I had another set of keys, because I lost my first set somewhere, either on the boats, or at the pig farm, or wherever else *we* might have been."

I asked Goose if he recalled what had happened to his fancy, red, cigarette-shaped speedboat, and my companion that day told me that the Blues had chopped it up with axes, hatchets, and sledgehammers, diminishing it into "a pile of toothpicks and splinters". "The dirty bastards then had the nerve to put the remains on a dump truck, and unload the fuckin' mound of broken-up *Fiberglas* fragments and wood splinters in the center of my newly tarred driveway. My old man was home from *sin-dick-kit* business in Miami and had a friggin' fit. The only thing left intact was the damned outboard motor, which was filled with Blues' piss."

"Just like the first helicopter spray-blast," I remembered and declared. "Do ya' remember that happening?"

"Yeah, kinda'," my weird-but-vindictive pal recalled. "But that's where ya' gotta' fill in the blanks."

I was shocked at hearing about the gross vandalism done to *Goose's Gadget.* I felt guilty living with the knowledge of Crystal Davis's rape, and now the rapist was asking me to enter his forced aggression into *his* memory. Since Goose had apparently been suffering from a form of amnesia in regard to the repulsive incident, and since everyone in News's cellar evidently wanted revenge on the dastardly Blues, and since G.R. and the others insisted that I tell them all the ugly horrific details, my conscience felt compelled to divulge exactly what I knew about G.R. and me being held hostage.

"Goddam it, J.W.!" Goose cursed. "You've refreshed my memory a little. Now, I remember very *dis-stink-ly*. I thought it was all a bad friggin' dream. But it did happen, me on the ground with the colored girl, and the shit-faced Blues all thought it was funny!"

"Crystal Davis is all bent outa' shape and is really frosted about you and her doin' ebony and ivory rock and roll," Jives Arena, the aforementioned black girl's neighbor revealed.

"What the hell did Jives just say?" G.R. asked Johnny for clarification of Frankie's slang reference.

"Jives said that the black girl is very upset and angry about the abnormal incident," Juice evasively interpreted.

"Guys, before we leave here, I gotta' tell ya' that I went to the Berlin Auction and bought some new James Dean jackets," Goose informed us. "I got new ones for Juice, Jives, J.W. and me for what the Blues did at the pig farm, and for what the Ramrodders did to those *sweethearts* Frankie and Johnny at the brewery."

"In the 1940s song 'Frankie and Johnny'," News described and corrected, "Frankie was a female, and Johnny was a guy."

"Holy shit! Frankie Arena might be a *fast-titty-us* female, foolin' us about her sex *mask-queer-raid!"* Goose considered and stupidly stated, much to Jives's humiliation.

No one laughed at G.R.'s preposterous commentary. Everyone agreed that the Blues' rape caper gossip was utterly abominable, and had to be answered by swift and decisive retaliatory action on the part of the Reds. But none of us wanted to elaborate on the 'naked truth' in Goose's presence.

"The Blues went over the limit this time, way over," Juice decided and maintained. "We gotta' turn the tables on the goons, Big League get-even style."

Fabian Midilli, who had been all ears up to that moment, finally contributed to the discussion. "Why won't the local cops' step in and arrest someone about all that's happened?" the gas station heir inquired. "What's wrong with the law?"

"Because big money runs little towns," Goose smartly answered, "and when ya' got blueberry farmers, peach farmers, and Mafia involved, the fuzz and the politicians do the old ostrich head in the sand act. The police are *cow-wards* and don't wanta' fuck with the big area taxpayers that pay their dip-shit salaries."

"Let's dig the gig and do somethin' oddball kookie, yeah baby; actin' Dr. Demento-like to the Azuls," Jives suggested.

"What the hell did *he* say?" Goose inquired.

"Jives said he wants us to do something crazy to the Blues," Juice deciphered for G.R. "Frankie wants to punish 'em for wildly molestin' and torturin' you and J.W."

Goose then proceeded to out-of-character praise and compliment me in front of the others. That commendation made me feel like a VIP in the Reds' organization. Then, 'the psycho' really put me on the spot.

"J.W., I want ya' to think of somethin' light to do to aggravate the Blues today, and I wanta' see ya' come-up with somethin' big to bust their stones good during next week's 16th of July carnival."

"Okay, just let me think," I verbally accepted, obviously stalling for time. "Give me a minute to assess things. Do ya' want it to be something *nostalgic* that you'll remember fifty-years from now?" I asked G.R. like he was a contestant on a TV quiz show.

"No, J.W. I don't use any nose spray," Goose seriously articulated. Everyone thought that Restuccio's comment was fairly hilarious, except the orator of it, who actually believed that he had made a candid statement.

News mentioned that Mr. and Mrs. Bruni had returned from vacationing in Sicily, and upon opening-up their magical pizza oven, the Italian proprietors discovered a prolific heap of mysterious ashes inside. "The Hammonton police are seein' if the Mafia had cremated somebody in the oven," Tommy Tomasello informed and laughed. My idea light bulb suddenly illuminated inside my dense head.

"That's it!" I proclaimed. "Thanks, News. I now know what to do," I revealed. "All we'll need is six sturdy square soda cases and a garden hose with a functional spray attachment. Here's what I have in mind."

I withheld certain information from my Reds' companions who were in attendance. My plan was really a duplicate of one that the Diablos had played on Angie Palermo and Bubbles Messina back in Levittown, but I scrupulously presented it to my colleagues as an original foray worthy of *their* application. In his furnished basement, News got-out his pointer and indicated the general location of the raid, and then identified the specific, targeted Second Road house on his comprehensive Hammonton-area platform.

"That's a really tremendous idea," Fabian instantly praised and acknowledged. "Where do ya' get these great plans? J.W., ya' oughta' write comic books!"

"He reads enough of 'em," Restuccio criticized.

"I get most of my ideas from meditatin' on donkeys and hangin' out in pig troughs," I naughtily giggled. "They're terrific sources of inspiration."

"We're gonna' have some kicks with some chicks out in the sticks to fix those pricks with tiny dicks!" Jives concluded and orally rhymed.

"What did *he* say?" Goose asked the rest of us.

"Frankie said that the Reds are gonna' have fun out in the country getting even with the Blues," Tommy News accurately interpreted, exhibiting enviable clarity.

"Well, why the fuck didn't *he* say that in fuckin' normal English!" G.R. rankled. "Frankie could be fuckin' dyin', and I'd think he'd be talkin' about getting' laid, or somethin' stupid like that!"

Goose and Frankie drove us in their cars to G.R.'s rustic palace to acquire the particular materials I had stipulated. Restuccio only had three wooden soda crates in *his* garage, so we rolled-up and put the lengthy garden hose, with its spray attachment, in *his* trunk, next to the three wooden beverage boxes. Frankie, and the other pranksters followed Goose and me to Mr. Bill's Custard Stand on *Route 73,* where we easily obtained from the cooperative proprietor the other three needed empty soda cases.

"Now it's off to Second Road and blueberry country," I said to my fellow raiders. "I know the exact house where we gotta' pull the job. Let's put our little scheme into motion!"

"This is gonna' be fun," Juice predicted. "I can't wait to see the looks on their faces. It's cool to pester people. Sometimes, I wish I was a mosquito, so that I could be a pest it all the time."

"Come on, baby, let the good times roll, and I have chicky fools in pools in my peepers, 'cause *splish-splash,* little darlins' is takin' a bath," Jives injected before we left Mr. Bill's.

"What the hell did that idiot say just now?" Goose asked Juice.

"Your guess is as good as mine," Johnny Juice replied with a grin. "Sometimes, Frankie goes into the *stratosphere* and never comes-down to Earth. I think Jives now believes that he's Bobby Darin!"

"I don't give a shit what freakin' kind of *fear* he's got, *status* or no status; *he* shouldn't have to talk like that!" Goose vulgarly insisted. Soon, the zany, spoiled Sicilian paisan, and the rest of us, finished our Mr. Bill's vanilla custard cones.

The six Reds hopped into our two cars. Frankie's Dodge carried three soda cases in its trunk, and Goose's red T-Bird had the other three. As we passed by Rosedale and then Angelo's Store heading toward Hammonton, the curious driver had a few pertinent questions that required clarification.

"How do ya' know that Mr. and Mrs. Bruni aren't home right now?" G.R. quizzed me.

"Because they're at the pizza parlor," I replied, "and today's Tuesday, and the pizza joint is only closed on Mondays."

"Yeah, that's right," Goose agreed, "but it's only two in the afternoon. Bruni's doesn't open 'til four."

"I talked with News at your place while you were rummagin' in your garage for the three empty soda boxes," I told Goose. "And Tommy said that Mr. and Mrs. Bruni were goin' in early to work to clean-up the oven that had plenty of mysterious ashes smeared inside it. The mess had been made while the owners were happily away for two weeks, visitin' their relatives in Italy."

"The Hammonton police think the ashes are a cremated human body," G.R. laughed. "The goddamned cops always have half-baked ideas," Goose said, not realizing he had made a pretty decent pun regarding the operation of the pizza oven. "Not even Mr. Wooster's funeral home has a *cream-or-tory* in it."

"You had meant to say crematoria!" I corrected.

"What was that word you just said?" Goose asked.

"Cream *a tory!*" I exclaimed and giggled. "That's what General George Washington told his men to do at Valley Forge. And the military commander even said to one patriot, 'Chicken, catch-a-Tory!"

"Why would Washington yell to his men 'funeral home', or tell them to chase a damned chicken? That's really dumb shit!" Goose exclaimed. "Sometimes, J.W., ya' say the most fucked-up things that make no goddamned sense at all. Washington would have yelled 'charge' instead of hollerin' cream-a-toria, or catch a chicken!"

Mr. and Mrs. Bruni lived on Second Road, right next to Jill Errera, Zeke's pretty sister, who was a HHS junior. Jill was the incumbent captain of the Hammonton High cheerleading squad. Since it was early afternoon on a sultry mid-July day, I figured that Jill and her friends would be having a little fun reclining on pool chairs and gossiping around the family pool. I had figured correctly.

Goose and Frankie stopped their autos in front of the Bruni' residence. A six-foot-high, blue-painted fence separated the girls' privacy from our scrutiny. We stealthily gathered our equipment and furtively ambled to the Bruni's well-manicured back lawn. News and I attached the hundred-foot-long garden hose to the back wall spigot, and then we stretched the hose over to the blue fence, where we could hear the rhythm of the Royal Teens' "Short Shorts" song blaring from a portable radio.

The six soda crates were quickly turned upside down. We stood atop the wooden crates, allowing our eyes to inspect the unsuspecting femininity casually chatting and lounging-around the pool. Some of the blueberry chicks were sunbathing face-down on large beach towels with their bikini tops unfastened. Several of the dolls showed a nice amount of breast flesh sagging on each side, where the detached bikini tops were loose.

I mentally counted 'one, two, three,' and then I opened the spray attachment. A strong jet of cold water was directed to the backs and posteriors of the unwary Hammonton High young ladies. I pointed and moved the hose, squirting as many girls as I could.

Several gorgeous females leaped-up in disbelief and shock, exposing beautiful boobs for our appreciative visual inspection. Amidst all the screaming and shrieking, the Royal Teens' rendition of "Short Shorts" was being completely-drowned out. Panic and chaos were evident everywhere within the trusty hose's shooting perimeter, and judging from all of the clamor and hysteria, an uninformed observer might have thought that *Mt. Vesuvius* was in the process of destroying Pompeii.

"Only two more girls had to be doused, so I directed the spray nozzle and skillfully blasted the delirious dolls. As I thoroughly enjoyed my delectable enterprise, my gleeful activity quickly turned from hanky-panky to grave concern. The final two young ladies who were frantically searching for their bikini tops turned-out to be Elaine Hill and Joanne Berenato, who both were hiding their exposed chests with crossed arms, as I proceeded to blast them with the intense water treatment.

"J.W.! How dare you!" Elaine yelled at me.

"Brigette DiMeo invited *us* to Jill Errera's birthday pool party!" Joanne loudly yelled. "Now you've ruined everything!"

"Brigette thought it would bring the Hammonton High and Edgewood Regional girls closer together after graduation!" Elaine elaborated as the other half-naked girls finished scurrying into the Errera residence.

"Quick, guys! Let's get the heck outa' here while we still have legs!" I strongly recommended. "This chick-crash has turned into a total disaster!"

The six of us scooted out of the pandemonium rather swiftly. The raiders were so anxious to abandon the premises that we left the six wooden soda boxes and the hundred-foot-long garden hose, with its excellent spray attachment, on the Errera and Bruni back lawns. In ten seconds, we were inside the two cars and peeling-out of the clamorous chaos like six rats desperately fleeing from a sinking ship.

"That was one of the coolest stunts I've ever seen played," Goose congratulated. "J.W., when it comes to shit like this, you're the best, and second place ain't nowhere in sight," the inimitable driver concluded and praised without swearing or cursing.

"Goose," I guiltily stammered. "That was Joanne Berenato standin' there at the end, half-naked, and I totally wrecked a decent birthday party where the Edgewood and Hammonton High girls could become better friends."

"Listen to me closely," G.R. commanded. "*You* were the hit of their dumb-ass, shitty party. Now, the bitches got somethin' excitin' to tell the Blues, and get Gillette and his goon squad all riled-up. A bunch of

Reds raided the house with a silly garden hose prank, and saw the Blues' women without their bras and panty hose, and now you're fuckin' worried that your favorite Edgewood High bitch is gonna' yank off *your* hose! Ha, ha, ha, ha!"

"That wasn't one bit funny," I adamantly disapproved. "And it wasn't right to do what *I* had done."

"What the hell do ya' mean?" Goose disagreed. "What you did made those squealin' bitches so hot and so goddamned horny that they're probably lyin' all over the freakin' house right now, and masturbatin' like crazy. Maybe ya' made 'em all so hot and so horny that they're fondlin' each other's tits, and actin; like lesbians, eatin' each other out right now."

"You're a real sicko, ya' know that!" I angrily accused. "Don't you understand? I embarrassed the girl I love in front of her new friends, and I completely wrecked her new friend's pool party."

"J.W., tell me somethin' *con-fee-dent-shall,"* G.R. said, as his red Thunderbird sped past Greenmount Cemetery. "If ya' didn't know any of the girls around the pool, would it have made any difference if ya' squirted complete strangers?"

"Why, er, I guess it would have," I answered. "But that still doesn't make it right to squirt them, does it? Well, I mean, *we* have to start livin' moral lives and begin acting like adults."

"That's a crock of horse-shit!" Goose tersely replied. "During the Reds initiation, Joanne Berenato saw *you* fully naked after you stupidly ran in your birthday suit through the mother' jumpin' woods, and then just stood there in the nude, right in front of her."

"So, what's that analogy supposed to mean?" I challenged. "You're so damned headstrong that you can't even relate to my embarrassment!"

"It means, J.W. that you're still one-half naked body up on her," Goose profoundly deduced. "And in the final *anal-a-sis,* good buddy, ya' won't be even with Joanne until ya' get to also see her naked from the waist-down."

Chapter Thirty-Seven

"The Summer Carnival"

I met News at his house several afternoons after the swimming pool catastrophe. I was encouraged that my friend was understanding and sympathetic, unlike Goose Restuccio, who only thought about Goose Restuccio, money, power, and raw sex in that order. News took me to downtown Hammonton where the Amusements of America carnival was setting-up for its annual visit in conjunction with the Lady of Mt. Carmel 16th of July feast and procession.

"I remember that once the *Clyde Beatty Circus* came to the carnival grounds," News mentioned, "and I worked all day like an ambitious handyman, helpin' put the bleachers together, and getting the tent raised up on the poles."

"Did they pay ya' by the hour?" I asked.

"Naa, Juice and I were only twelve-year-old kids," Tommy recalled and informed. "And we each got paid two admissions tickets to the Big Top."

"Wasn't much compensation, was it?" I asked. "Sounds like a violation of child labor laws."

"The experience was well-worth the effort," News admitted. "Say J.W., do ya' wanta' know what Goose calls the Mt. Carmel Feast?"

"Yeah, what?" I asked.

"The Mt. Caramel Feast, as if the mountain was made out of taffy or confections," News laughed. "Maybe G.R. lives on a candy mountain palace in Switzerland, when he's not livin' in his stately Winslow mansion."

"He does get plenty of words confused," I concurred. "And I think the non-scholar tries to impress us with sophisticated vocabulary because our senile friend feels academically inferior to us. I mean, Goose has some good ideas, but the stubborn guy doesn't have the verbal finesse to put them into the right order."

"At least Goose graduated from high school," News kidded. "And some wise guys like Tyrone Davis and somebody else I know didn't walk the stage on time."

If anyone else had made *that* statement, I'd want to separate their head from their neck and shoulders, but Tommy was different than the rest. Tomasello usually had compassion and goodness in his heart, and when News made what seemed to be, on the surface, a disparaging remark, it was only meant to generate fun, and not be malicious or sarcastic in intent like if Goose, or Gabe Gillette, or Speed Mortellite was saying the exact same words.

"How ya' comin' along with Mr. Sipley?" T.T. asked. "That guy was once principal of Hammonton High School back in the early forties, ya' know."

"I'm learnin' an awful lot fast," I related. "And when I go back to Edgewood for my diploma, if Andrews wants to give me his hardest exam' in his trig' arsenal, I'm gonna' ace it with a capital A."

News then began expounding about how the U.S.S.R. was claiming that it had shot-down a U.S. reconnaissance high-altitude spy-plane, flying over Russian air space, with the international incident occurring over Arctic waters near Siberia.

"The Russian communists claim that the Air Force plane shoot-down represents a case of American espionage," News concluded and conveyed, "and that's why the dirty dogs shot it down."

The fate of the downed U.S. surveillance plane made me contemplate something else much closer to home. "I was shot-down at the HHS girls' pool party," I acknowledged and regretted. "Bein' shot down is even worse than bein' *put down* by crude raunchy bullies like the Blues or the Ramrodders."

"Why do ya' say you were shot-down? Ya' did somethin' cool that backfired, because your stunt happened to the girl you happen to like, that's all," Tommy logically stated. "No one was injured or killed by your prank. It was only teen mischief, and not teen malice."

"Because I shot myself down, News, and that's plenty worse than somebody else shootin' me down," I candidly remarked. "It's a lot worse when ya' make a fool outa' yourself than when somebody else makes a fool outa' ya'."

News drove his red and white Fairlane off of Third Street down Pratt to Tilton, where we stopped and checked-out the carnival personnel setting-up the giant Ferris Wheel and the familiar Octopus ride on the Third Street end. The side show tents, the midway, the Salt and Pepper ride, the Haunted House, and the mini-roller coaster were being erected on the Tilton Street side of the gravel carnival grounds.

The driver steered over to the French Street curb, next to the St. Joseph High School nun's convent, where we watched the entire beehive of activity. We were fascinated, like two seven-old-kids seeing a carnival for the first time. I began recollecting that the same touring Amusements of America show visiting Levittown in early June each summer.

"Goose and his long neck wants ya' to come-up with some dynamic plan involvin' the carnival," News commented and reminded. "Do ya' think ya' got it in ya'?"

"I know all about it, and I'm tryin' to think of a good scheme that'll publicly humiliate the Blues," I promised. "I gotta' defend my reputation for bein' inventive and fast thinkin' when under pressure. That's one thing I take pride in."

At that moment, I felt motivated to tell News about how the Diablos had used the same roller coaster ride that was presently being constructed to stifle Popeye Messina in Levittown. "My pal Carnie's dad had some concessions on the midway," I disclosed, "and the Diablos borrowed an old wooden chair from him. We captured our chief enemy, Popeye Messina, tied the bully to the chair, and stuffed a handkerchief in his mouth."

"That prank sounds mighty interestin'," News evaluated and commended. "What happened next? Did some local judge issue a gag order?"

"Well, when the roller coaster zipped-down the first hill, we lifted the chair up and stuck Popeye's head through the parallel tracks. If Messina didn't curse out loud out of fear of dyin', we promised to hold him up there so that the Kamikaze punk would be decapitated," I recalled and described.

"Did he curse like Goose does?" newsy News wanted to know.

"Did he?" I giggled and smiled. "I'll say! Popeye cursed like the devil's apprentice to save his life. His black soul knew he was goin' straight to hell if he died right then and there."

"Maybe we can do the same thing to Gabe Gillette or to Ox Narducci," Tommy suggested having a rerun. "Your roller coaster chair scheme sounds more effective than the electric chair."

"If I can't think of anything better," I answered, "then that's precisely what we'll do. But News, ya' gotta' promise that when I present the roller coaster-chair caper to the guys, you gotta' give me your word that ya' knew nothin' about it, and that my ploy's just as original to you as it will sound to them."

"I know exactly what ya' mean, jellybean!" Tommy agreed.

On Monday evening, the Amusements of America Carnival opened for business. I walked the midway with Goose Restuccio, with Jives Arena, and with Fabian Midilli. I became hooked and scammed on throwing three softballs into the bushel-basket game. It was really weird. When the attendant told me to try it for practice, I could easily get the three balls to gently bounce and stay inside the distant bushel, but every time I paid the operator a quarter to play, one of the softballs would always carom out.

"Let's get outa' here," Goose advised. "This game's as crooked as Nikita S. Khrushchev's erect C-shaped dick!"

I didn't heed Goose's sage advice. I wasted eighteen hard-earned dollars attempting to get those three uncooperative softballs inside the bushel. My eyes were focused on a large kangaroo I had planned to win and give to Joanne Berenato to make amends for what turmoil had transpired at the First Road pool party fiasco.

What Goose lacked in showing common morality, the chronic sinner made up for in basic generosity. The gang's pragmatist called the bushel-ball-game operator on the side; explained that I had "pissed away" twenty-dollars; threatened that his father was a bigwig on the town chamber of commerce, and that his pop was also a prominent figure active in the local Mafia crime syndicate. "Ya' don't wanta' be pushin' up daisies over a stupid stuffed animal, do ya'?" my audacious Sicilian pal asked, rattling the bushel game barker. Then, after threatening the carnival employee, G.R. bribed the shill with twenty-dollars. The shocked and outmatched fellow, who introduced himself as Harold Cassabone, merrily climbed-up on a small ladder, lifted the giant kangaroo from a hook, and handed the enormous stuffed plush animal to me.

"Thank ya' Mr. Cassabone," I happily said.

"Think nothin' of it. kid," the concessionaire replied. "Kid, ya' more than paid for this cheap piece of crap four times over."

I saw Elaine Hill talking to Esther Phyllis over near the cotton candy booth, so I ambled in their direction to say a polite "hello". I was surprised that Elaine wasn't the least bit spiteful over my recent pool party misdemeanor.

"J.W., where did ya' get that beautiful kangaroo?" Elaine desired knowing, forgetting about the pool party calamity.

"Er, I, well Goose…" I stuttered.

"You're so talented," Elaine commended. "No wonder why Joanne likes ya' so much. Not every stud walkin' the fair-grounds can get three softballs inside a rigged bushel and win a fantastic prize like that one you're holdin'."

"Err, I know what ya' mean, but it was all…"

"And J.W., Joanne's not here tonight because she had to go shoppin' in town with her mom," Elaine informed. "But ya' know that trick ya' pulled the other day with the garden hose?"

"How could I forget that stu…"

"After we got over the initial shock of you seein' us half-naked," Elaine prefaced, "Joanne and I thought that it was one of the neatest pranks we've ever seen or heard of."

"Ya' don't say!" I exclaimed as my heart fluttered and did a full hundred-eighty-degree pivot on the emotional spectrum. "I figured you'd like it once ya' seriously thought about how darin' it all was to attempt. I'd like to give this cute kangaroo to Joanne if she was here. I really worked hard to win it! It's not an Edgewood High Eagle, but it's a St. Joe Joey!"

"Oh, don't worry about that," eavesdropping Esther Phyllis chimed-in. "We're gonna' stop in at her place later tonight, and we'll be sure to give it to her."

"Thanks a million," I cheerfully replied. "This means a whole lot to me," I claimed as I handed Esther the king-size kangaroo.

After I left the girls' friendly company, Goose, Jives, and Fabian came sauntering over to me while I was eating some popcorn from a bag in front of the Tilt-a-Whirl ride.

"Hey J.W.," Fabian commenced his kidding drivel. "I thought that kangaroo was reserved for Joanne Berenato. You datin' Elaine Hill and Esther Phyllis now?"

"Naw. Elaine and Esther are gonna' give the marsupial to Joanne for me later tonight," I answered. "Sal, I trust those girls almost as much as I trust you."

"That's what the hell Elaine told you!" the always-skeptical Goose Restuccio commented. "She's probably gonna' give it to Herc Juliano! Elaine really has the hots for him, so I hear."

"That marsupial is gonna' fracture your ga-ga queen at the next Hammonton hop, so don't be surprised if the target chick shows-up with a new nest that you're gonna' eat the poop outa'," Jives uttered.

"What in the world did that nutcase turkey say now?" Goose asked Fabian, because our normal jive interpreters, News Tomasello and Juice Illiani, happened to be missing from our glorious companionship.

"Jives said that Joanne will really love the kangaroo prize, and that she might even get a new hairdo before the next Canteen Dance, just to please J.W.," Sal adroitly translated.

"Well, J.W.," Goose resumed vociferating his challenging salvos, "ya' have until ten o'clock tonight to tell me a decent plan to use against the Blues. I'll never forget about the donkey and the pigs' *mayhem,* even though it happened in July. And I forgot all about havin' imaginary sex with Crystal Davis," Goose guiltlessly stated. "And I think the Blues are pissed about us drenchin' their women with the garden hose, which looks and sounds better and better every damned time I think about it."

I walked with the guys all around the crowded carnival grounds for five circuits, avoiding the annoying hawkers ballying and yelling-out their fantastic deals and solicitations. I was in an introspective mood, weighing, assessing, thinking, analyzing, and evaluating. I wasn't too conversant until I heard Fabian say something I immediately valued as being relevant.

"Hey Goose, where are all the Blues tonight?" Sal inquired. "Ain't seen any around nowhere?"

"That's what the hell *I* wanta' know," G.R. concurred. "I trust those slimy bastards more when I can see 'em than when I can't see 'em. But they're usually actin' like flies on shit, and there's a lotta' shit happenin' right here and now between Pratt and French Streets."

"The Blues ain't pilin' up any z's," Jives jived, "and your peepers can't see those mushrooms nowhere, ever since ya' got smog in your noggin', rockin' and rollin' with Petunia over in swine-land."

"What the fuck did that faggot jerk-off say now?" Goose demanded to Sal Fabian Midilli, as the frustrated listener nervously clenched his hands, forming two fists.

"Jives said that the Blues aren't exactly sleeping because they're essentially night people," Sal very aptly decoded, "and ever since DiGiacomo's Pig Farm, *you* haven't been the same because you got your memory lost, having sex at slop haven with a female pig."

"Look you' crazy asshole," G.R. threatened Frankie. "I think I did have sex with a female pig, but it happened to be a well-built nigger girl, and not a goddamned fat sow at the pig farm," the irate sociopath with the mercurial temper screamed in Jives's frightened face. "Get on my nerves again, and I'll hit ya' in the mouth so hard that your teeth will be stuck inside your asshole!"

I looked at Fabian, and both of us were deeply embarrassed by Goose's loud, foul, public tantrum. I had to get the insane lunatic onto another topic before Restuccio continued his obscene tirade.

"Er, Goose. I think I've got the right plan to use against the Blues. Do ya' wanta' hear it now?"

"Sure, why the hell not?" G.R. assented. "Give me some good idea to think about, and I'll let Frankie live at least until tomorrow."

I disclosed my stratagem to the guys, who appeared to relish my plan's simplicity, along with its complexity, both at the same time. "Now all that Hoss, Little Joe, Herc, Balls, and the Calabrese brothers gotta' do is somehow capture and kidnap Pee Wee Lucca and Marty Gillette. I now know from trigonometry that the rest of the operation is all mathematically feasible," I declared.

I noticed a familiar face over near the candy apple barrel, so I left the guys' company and approached my old pal Carnie's dad, who immediately recognized me from the time the same carnival had visited Levittown in June of '59. After exchanging introductory small talk with Carnie's deadbeat father, I was happy to learn that my old Dogwood Hollow buddy was still alive and doing well, and that Carnie often mentioned my name to his pop. Then, I asked my former friend's dad for a small favor, and the wheeler-dealer con-artist said that for two-hundred-dollars, the secret project would be "a go".

I returned to Goose, Fabian, and Jives, and I relayed some wonderful information that I had negotiated with the shrewd, traveling barker I had known from Levittown. "Ya' say it'll cost me two-hundred-bucks?" Goose uttered while twisting his long rubber-like neck back and forth. "Tell ya' what I'll do, J.W.," G.R. wryly smiled and conveyed. "If it works like ya' say it will, it'll be worth five times that much dough just to see it all happen."

On Tuesday, in the late afternoon, six Reds' patrol cars scoured Hammonton and vicinity to sight and apprehend our two targeted Blues. With the cooperation of Elaine Hill, Esther Phyllis, Nanette Banks and their good friend Barbara Noto, our surveillance and reconnaissance teams coordinated their data and successfully tracked-down the two paranoid Blues.

Hoss, Little Joe, and the Calabrese boys cornered and bagged Pee Wee Lucca in a compromising position, while the midget was taking a carnival beer leak behind the nun's convent across Third Street from St. Joseph Church. Marty Gillette was nailed by Herc Juliano, Balls Giordano, and Jake "the Brute" Maccarella when the elf was coming-out of the Palace Diner after buying a pack of cigarettes. "Johnny Mac" subdued Marty with "the Brute's" notorious "sleeper hold," which by reputation could have put King Kong to bed in an all-girls' dormitory.

At midnight, the carnival rides, booths, and midway all shut-down, and by twelve-thirty, all the colorful bright lights on the rides had been switched-off. It was time to release the two smallest Blues from their temporary cage, which happened to be Goose's red Thunderbird's accommodating trunk. News, Juice, Fabian, Jives, and I all participated in the last crucial phase of the clever kidnapping.

"It's a good thing I saved a couple shovel-fulls of splinters and *Fiberglas* shavings from my speedboat," Goose laughed. "The junk was thrown into my trunk before Marty and Pee Wee were tossed inside," Goose inadvertently rhymed, "so, I guess the two dwarfs feel like doin' plenty of itchin' and scratchin'."

Our two diminutive prisoners were un-gently lifted out of the trunk. The intimidated pair had had their hands tied in front of their waists, and red handkerchiefs had been stuffed into their mouths to prevent the munchkins from screaming and attracting attention.

"Are you two dwarfs ready to fly over to Snow White's place?" News asked the confused, neurotic runts.

The six of us tugged our reluctant captives across quiet Pratt Street, and then dragged the squirming duo between two carnival tractor-trailers, where we met Carnie's itinerant pop at the designated rendezvous point.

"So, these are the two lucky guys," Carnie's dad remarked. "They seem to be just the right size."

"They're the only two that perfectly match the exact physical requirements," I added. "It just so happens that all the height and weight pieces fit together just right."

"Good," the cooperative carnival barker reacted. "Here comes Floyd right now."

Carnie's pop quickly introduced us to Floyd Miller, a rather discontented carnival drifter who never could hold a job for more than a month, because of severe, chronic alcohol problems. Floyd would get into wild arguments with his superiors no matter where he had worked, and the Amusements of America traveling show was no exception. Miller had just been fired by the A of A rides manager; needed immediate booze money to support his ugly habit, and required sufficient revenue to blow town and make it with a few dollars to spare to begin a new life at his next temporary gig in upper New York State.

"Do ya' have the two-hundred-smackers?" Carnie's pop anxiously asked Goose.

"Right here," G.R. complied as the rich investor unraveled two *Ben Franklins* from a wad of at least fifty. Restuccio handed the two crisp new bills to the traveling concession stand owner.

Carnie's pop gave one of the "century notes" to grungy-looking, bearded Floyd Miller, who then graciously accepted the payment for *his* end of the bargain. We all stepped across the secluded midway, four of us escorting hostage Marty Gillette, and four latching onto captured Pee Wee Lucca. The group stopped right next to the brown and black canvassed Caterpillar Ride, making sure that the final phase of our mischievous, clandestine operation could be successfully executed.

"Now fellas'," Floyd Miller addressed us. "I know how to shoot off the dual cannons, but exactly how they work I don't rightly know." The carnival drunk had a trace of bourbon emanating through his decayed brown teeth, and the putrid odor was wafting out of his pallid, swollen lips. "I think it involves pistons or heavy springs inside, but I'm not exactly sure how the cannons function, but they do," old Floyd indicated and hiccupped.

"Just pretend you're little St. Martin and that you're tiny St. Pee Wee," Goose laughed, ridiculing Gillette and Lucca. "Because both of you' wimpy, junior jerk-offs are about to be *cannonized* by Pope Goose Restuccio."

"These two kids are about the same size as The Great Atomo and his wife, Queen Protona," Floyd observed and related. "Anybody ten-pounds bigger than those two humanoids would fall short of the nets."

"That means that Ox Narducci and Butch Lanza would just trickle and then plop outa' the cannons," Juice noted. "If the huge imbeciles could be shot out of cannons, then those two monsters could easily destroy a pair of battleships, or maybe Rescignio's candy store over on Third Street."

"Everything has to be just right and calculated according to exact mathematics, just like the motorcycles' ramps were at the peach pit," News realized and added.

"Let's stop shootin' off our mouths and start shootin' off the cannons," Jives suggested in near-normal English. "I wanta' see these jive turkeys fly in the sky, and that's no lie!"

"Now you're finally jive-talkin' my fuckin' language," Goose emphasized to Frankie. 'If Jay Dubya never learned trig' from Mr. Sipley, none of this great shit would be possible!"

The eight of us scuffled with and pulled the pathetic Blues' duo over to the two parallel cannons, their dragged feet making shallow furrows in the gravel ground. One by one, the short, skinny Blues were elevated-up and deposited into the loading chambers. The resisters tried screaming and shouting, but their muffled calls for help went unheeded. The distressed pair still had their hands tied at their waists.

Floyd Miller lit-up the two fuses to the twin cannons, and then we all waited for the dual explosions to occur. Two loud booms were distinctly heard; smoke flew-out of the cannons' barrels, and remarkably, so did Pee Wee Lucca and Marty Gillette's frail bodies. The human projectiles propelled in two neat arcs through the air and clear across the midway, and then the mortal rockets landed face-down, directly into the center of two awaiting safety nets.

The six Reds instantaneously made mad dashes across the midway and through the tractor-trailers, sprinting to our respective cars. Floyd Miller exited the Mt. Carmel carnival grounds in a jiffy, en route to the nearest bus stop on Bellevue Avenue. Carnie's father scurried to his mobile trailer's office, where the co-conspirator pretended to be awakened by the sudden loud explosions.

As Goose drove me home down North Third Street, the wily, methodical schemer asked exactly how I knew that St. Marty Gillette and St. Pee Wee Lucca would be ideal candidates to be "canonized".

"That was easy," I divulged. "I had watched The Great Atomo and his dwarfish wife get shot-out of the cannons five times this week. I soon realized that the two were almost identical in size and weight to Marty Gillette and Pee Wee Lucca," I related. "Those were the only two Blues who could've been used in the prank. Any others would've been killed because of bein' too big and too heavy."

"But J.W., what if it didn't work?" Goose interrogated. "How did ya' know it would? Was it worth the damned risk?"

"It *was* a calculated risk," I confidentially shared. "Thanks to Mr. Andrews failin' me in trig', I had to take lessons from Mr. Sipley, who is a great teacher. I simply applied several standard trig' formulas in my head that Mr. Sipley had taught me, and bingo, Marty and Pee Wee become super carnival stars," I indulgently laughed. "To tell ya' the blessed, Gospel truth, Goose," I breathed-out very deeply, "I was really quite glad and relieved to see those two knuckleheads land safely into those safety nets."

Chapter Thirty-Eight

"Mausoleum Messes"

The Reds wisely stayed-away from the St. Joseph Church's carnival grounds for the rest of the week. Our intelligence sources informed us that the Blues were conspiring to commit some vile, atrocious acts against us, and my gang was considerate and civil enough that we didn't want to give the Mt. Carmel celebration a bad reputation in the local newspapers. Still, I imagined the enactment of some future capers the Reds could use to stymie the Blues, while still cherishing our last dual cannon exploit, involving involuntary pipsqueaks Pee Wee Lucca and Marty Gillette.

The following Thursday morning of carnival week, I had to pick-up a load of tomatoes and peppers from a Williamstown farmer at eleven, and right when Pop was handing me the money to pay for the high-quality produce, the Pete's Market kitchen phone rang. News was on the other end talking-up a storm. Luckily, mom and dad were inside the market, sorting and packing produce items.

I told Tommy I was on my way to Williamstown to transport some vegetables back to the market to resell. Tommy claimed that he had a "few hours to kill" before dropping three-hundred-baskets of peaches into his peach washer and grading and sorting line, before packing the fruit into forty-pound cardboard boxes. So, News and I agreed to meet at Mr. Bill's for lunch.

"Hi, J.W.," Tommy greeted as the nice guy entered the popular eatery and approached a table I had reserved. "I called Juice and he's gonna' join us for a few *snake* sandwiches with *marijuana* sauce."

"Are ya' sure ya' don't want a cheese furburger with brunette pubes instead?" I joked, mimicking Bo Jalonec's memorable wit.

I really valued News's friendship because the kid was "book smart", and because there was nothing secretive or contrived in what Tommy said and did. His only Achilles heel was that the avid reader magnified trivia all the time. I was an integral part of the general problem, since I always would ask the studious bookworm about current events.

"What's new News?" I inquired.

"Well, while we were busy shooting Pee Wee and Marty outa' fake cannons," Tommy began with a grin, "the Democratic National Convention nominated Senator John F. Kennedy of Massachusetts for President of the United States. He's only the second Roman Catholic candidate, the first being Al Smith, who lost a close election to Herbert Hoover in 1928, right before the devastatin' great stock market crash."

"I guess Hoover didn't give a *dam* that Al Smith had lost," I routinely jested. "In fact, the whole cotton-pickin' country was so dejected over Al Smith's election loss that most everyone experienced a great depression."

News would not give me the satisfaction of saying something clever, so the aggravator persisted in deluging my presence with his glib, boring prattle. "And J.W., if ya' haven't heard," Tomasello proceeded in his pontification, "the National League won the second summer All-Star Game, defeatin' the American Leaguers."

"Didn't the National League win the first All-Star Game, too?" I asked the super know-it-all.

"Sure did J.W., by a score of 5-3 on July 11th," my encyclopedic buddy delivered.

"Goose really came through with the necessary two-hundred-bucks to send Pee Wee and Marty airborne," I laughed, wanting to get off of baseball and discuss something more personal and meaningful. "I suppose Gabe Gillette is all cranked-up over what *we* deftly did to his baby brother."

News heard me mention Goose's name, and that allusion sent him off on a tangent that would have impressed one of Mr. Andrews' co-tangents or co-secants. Tommy related that a mangy mongrel dog would often trespass onto Restuccio's property every day at exactly noon, and then lift its leg and take a leak on one of G.R.'s *Harleys* parked in the driveway. "Restuccio became so pissed-off that the paranoid ingrate hired an electrician to rig-up a device so that when the dog's pecker made contact with the metal kickstand," News chuckled, "an electric shock would zip right up the dog's dick, and go straight to and electrify its brain."

"Did the electrical solution work?" I asked.

"It sure did," News acknowledged. "And that mangy mutt never returned to haunt old Goose again."

"Ya' gotta' agree that G.R. is one of a kind sick pup," I insisted, "and thank goodness the mold was destroyed after *he* showed-up to stake his claim in the world."

"Goose is a very unique individual," News concurred. "Fabian told me that once G.R. was in Wildwood with Chickie and Joey Calabrese sittin' in beach chairs near the surf. Two Hare Krishnas walked barefooted over three-hundred-feet of hot scorchin' sand, just to hand Goose a religious magazine in exchange for a solicited token donation."

"Well, what did Goose do?" I asked.

"He grabbed the magazine from the bald-headed, pigtailed freak and yelled, 'How come this friggin' magazine doesn't have any dirty pictures in it! I wanta' see some open beaver shots and some wet pink pussies. Do ya' two scumbags have any pictures of hairy virgin pussies I could look at? I like to lick the color photos'!" News laughed. "And sometimes, I like lookin' at pictures of bald-headed freaks in orange gowns givin' each other sixty-nine blow-jobs'!"

"What did the shocked Hare Krishnas say after that?" I curiously responded.

"They said, 'we, er, no'," Tommy laughed. "And then Goose finished them off by sayin', 'What the hell's wrong with you' stupid asshole jerk-offs? Next time, bring me over some hot *Playboy* magazines to look at. or don't freakin' bother comin' over here and annoyin' me anymore!"

"That's choice G.R. all right," I cackled. "Real choice vintage Goose Restuccio, for sure."

Our repartee was temporarily interrupted with the arrival of Johnny Illiani, who was the courier bringing sketchy descriptions of negative encounters that some of the Reds' charter members had recently had with the petulant Blues. There was no doubt that pranks were increasing in number and in magnitude, and push was rapidly coming to shove between the stubborn rival fruit factions. The tenor and tone of our conversation soon turned from levity to seriousness.

"Yesterday, Chickie and Joey Calabrese were takin' rented canoes out in Hammonton Lake lookin' for some snapper turtles," Juice commenced. "The guys were mindin' their own business paddlin' along in the middle of the lake, proudly wearin' their red James Dean jackets."

"Yeah, then what happened?" News yawned and asked Johnny.

"Ox Narducci and Butch Lanza sped-up in a motorboat and threw four heavy cinderblocks into the canoe," Johnny reported. "Chickie and Joey fell overboard, and worse yet, the cinder-blocks had made two big holes in the little canoe. The boat sank, and the boys had to pay a twenty-dollar down-payment for damages to the boathouse keeper, and the fellas' still owe eighty more bucks for complete compensation, which the pugnacious Blues were actually responsible for creating."

"It looks like the fruit war is escalatin' to new heights," News accurately deduced. "J.W., what should we do?"

I was still pondering what Johnny had conveyed when Juice hit us with another not-so-funny-anecdote having the cruel theme of Blues' brutality. "And guys," Johnny proceeded. "The Blues later corralled Marty Ransom, Pete Clarke, and Denny Harrison outside the carnival grounds, and kidnapped our friends for bein' suspects involved in the human cannon conspiracy. Those three Reds didn't know nothin' about what had happened on the midway to Pee Wee and to Marty!"

"What did the Blues do to our three loyal members?" News asked the harried messenger. "Our three guys were innocent victims."

"Marty, Pete, and Denny were tied-up, slapped-around a little, and then transported to the Little League park's visitors' dugout over at Hammonton Lake."

"That's significant," I theorized and related, "because Marty, Pete, and Denny went to Edgewood, so they're like the *visiting* team over in Hammonton."

Juice ignored my unsolicited interruption and continued with his latest revelations. "Well, the Blues sat our three guys down on the visitin' team's dugout bench, and then tied the Reds to the pinewood," Johnny revealed. "Of course, Marty, Pete, and Denny were already tied-up, and had blue bandannas stuffed in their throats before bein' tied-down to the visitors' bench," Juice meticulously reviewed.

"Well come on, now," News prompted. "Don't keep us in wild suspense."

"Then, Gabe Gillette let Pee Wee Lucca and Marty Gillette have the honors of cloggin' up the dugout drain pipe with rags, and then fillin' up the dugout with two industrial garden hoses," Juice reported. "When the water level reached-up to chest level, the Blues shut-off the valves; took the hoses with 'em, and ran off of the premises. The Hammonton cops didn't discover our three members sittin' and shackled inside the dugout until late this mornin'."

"Wow, I sat the bench in Little League when I was ten, playin' for DiDonato's, but I never sat overnight in chest deep water!" I marveled and conceded.

News and Juice both frowned at the utterance of my cute mental association, so I decided to provide them with some of my more mature perceptions. I gave my opinion that the Blues were adopting and imitating *our* proven methods, and that the more ideas the Reds would come up with, the more aggression would occur between the gangs on more dangerous levels. And throw the Ramrodders into the explosive mix, and Hammonton and vicinity would have a lethal combination of matches, gasoline, and nitro-glycerin.

"Any other bad things happenin'?" I asked, expecting that what I had already heard was more than enough.

"Unfortunately, yes," Juice glumly reported, shaking his head in disbelief. "You're absolutely right J.W., the Blues are copy-catin' our special methods."

"Monkey see, monkey do," News injected. "What are the Simians doin' that we *don't* have patented? At least, the Blues should be payin' the Reds royalties for copy-cating *our* ideas, that the gorillas are now effectively usin' against us."

"This last one is really a hard pill to swallow, because it's hittin' some of our closer friends," Juice indicated. "Some Blues broke into the Edgewood band room and stole a dozen parade uniforms. Mr. Pinkerton is bent-out of shape as if the school principal was made outa' Turkish Taffy."

"Well, how does *that* theft affect or involve the Reds?" News desired to learn.

"Six of the heisted uniforms were put into Hoss and Little Joe's barn, and the other six were placed in the Ramrodders' clubhouse on Egg Harbor Road, in back of Vet's Bakery," Juice disclosed. "Two anonymous phone calls were made to the fuzz, and Hoss and Little Joe were hauled into the clinic this mornin' to be interrogated."

It was quite evident that the Blues suspected both the Reds and the Ramrodders for Gabe Gillette and Speed Mortellite's recent motorcycle flirtations with death. I feared that the Blues would eventually ally with the Rodders', and have a big numbers' advantage fighting "the James Dean' gang" in a fierce rumble.

"Well, the only good feature about all this is that Hoss and Little Joe are innocent, and can't tell the cops nothin' about nothin'," I commented. "Here's some money to cover the steak I ate and the tip included," I told News, who already had his greedy palm out. "I gotta' run to Williamstown and pick-up the produce order Pop had made."

"Three paltry dollars?" News strenuously objected. "J.W., you're really parsimonious!"

"It's better to be Parson Monius than to be Rabbi FreeBee, Pope Pius the Pauper, or Minister Measly," I responded. "I'll get in touch with Goose when I get back from Williamstown, and meet you guys at the Gem when everything's fully coordinated."

All afternoon to and from Williamstown, my mind pondered recent developments. Even while I unloaded the Pete's Market Special back in Elm, my brain was drawing closer to the only inevitable conclusion it could reach. I knew from my past history with the Kenwood Kamikazes that the only way to combat the aggressive Blues was to outsmart them and to out-punish them. Up until mid-July, I was generally content imitating Bo Jalonec's wit; Quinn's cool leadership, and Carnie's nice-guy image. The only good weapon that would now really be effective against the indefatigable Blues was to mimic the hell-bent-for-black-leather and blue denim' style of the most implacable, merciless, depraved, teenage villain I had ever known, my old evil Diablo pal, Tinker.

I called Goose at around three from a town payphone and gave him instructions on how our next scheme would materialize. Restuccio couldn't believe his elf-shaped ears. The "Mafia kid" said he could arrange to pick me up and meet Juice, News, Fabian, and Jives at the Gem at seven on Sunday evening, the last night of the carnival. I could tell that G.R. was excited about the magnitude and the cunning of my newly-blueprinted commando raid. The obnoxious, flamboyant, future Sicilian don was virtually flabbergasted when he hung up the phone.

Several boring days passed, and at quarter to seven on Sunday evening, I was looking into the mirror and making mean grimaces while trying to intimidate my scrawny-looking reflection. I also performed some strenuous "towel exercises," simulating the 'Dynamic Tension' lessons advertised in muscle-building magazines, and marketed and sold to skinny wimps like me by the legendary Charles Atlas.

The front doorbell rang. I hastily descended the steps so that I would not keep my impetuous friend Goose Restuccio waiting. Standing there was good old G.R., and the crazy kid was cradling a tabby kitten in his hands.

"Here, J.W.," Goose said, holding the tiny creature out towards me. "Your sex life with Joanne Berenato hasn't been too good, so I thought ya' needed a little pussy."

"Real funny!" I protested. "You'll go to any crazy extent just to destroy somebody's ego!"

"That's exactly why ya' need somebody like me around to go up against the Blues with ya'!" Goose argued. "Evil beats *wicked* every single time."

"Where did you get the tiny kitten, at the SPCA?" I asked.

"Sorry to say, I just found it meowin' on your front porch," G.R. clarified. "Its mother either got killed on the highway, or she's huntin' in the nearby fields for mice. Give it a plate of milk, and the poor *a-band-done* little orphan will be perfectly happy."

I enacted what Goose had suggested; carried the tabby through the house, and left the frightened kitten and a dish of fresh milk on the back steps. The hungry kitten immediately began licking the milk, and soon shifted into a much calmer frame of mind. Several minutes later, the tabby responded to its mother's call, and the stray was again reunited with its next of kin.

"Well, that starts the night off right," I remarked. "Are ya' ready to do some dangerous indirect battle."

"Yeah," Goose readily *confirmed,* without having any seminary credentials. "And you're a real tough taskmaster, I must say. But I got swell connections, and Frankie and Joe are keen on participatin' in this secret operation," G.R. informed us. "Your neat plan was all put together in three short days. Hoss and Little Joe are really pissed over the stolen Edgewood band uniform' bullshit, and the fuzz questionin' the brothers about something they know nothin' about," Restuccio elaborated. "And last but not least, Fabian has a mechanic from his father's garage, and also one of the Reds, ready to drive the two flatbed trucks. All we really need right now is a little lady luck," the vulgar Sicilian summarized, without utilizing one obscene expletive.

"Great!" I exclaimed, feeling my friends' staunch support. "I've jumped off the divin' board, and there's only one way I can possibly go. Let's kick some royal Blue' butt! Pick me in a couple of hours."

On the ride to downtown Hammonton, I saw a familiar road sign and said to the T-Bird driver, "Goose, this is a bad place for dogs as well as for cats."

"Why do ya' say that?" the preoccupied driver asked.

"Because that sign on the Pike reads: 'No *Litter!* $50.00 Fine'!" I coughed and jested.

"Where the hell do ya' think of all this crazy, jazzed-up shit?" the driver asked. "Do ya' work part time in the goddamned Hammonton sewer plant? Is your family pool a cesspool?"

I dared not tell Restuccio that my entire joke catalog came from one Bo Jalonec, and that my whole destruction of enemy property behavioral pattern had been acquired from Tinker. Levittown had more to do with my evil genius, which the gullible Reds perceived I genuinely and naturally possessed.

Brian Hyland's "Itsy Bitsy Teenie Weenie Yellow Polka Dot Bikini" was playing on the car radio, and that tune made me remember the aborted Reds' pool raid into blueberry territory on Second Road. Thankfully, the song ended, and then the Four Lads' "Standing on the Corner" was spun on WIBG, just as we whizzed by Vega's Drugs and saw the Blues faithfully guarding the east side of Hammonton, and the Reds patrolling in front of the Rivoli Theater, proudly defending the west side of town.

Goose cruised the crowded Bellevue Avenue downtown business district, joining at least a hundred other cars loaded with kids doing the exact same monotonous circuit thing, while trying to discover that elusive special soul mate. After two full downtown rotations, we found a parking spot not far from Olivo's Supermarket, and parked directly behind News's red and white Fairlane. After scooting across busy Central Avenue, Goose and I entered the main portal into the Gem.

The slow song "Maybe" recorded by the Chantels was throbbing from the jukebox's speakers, and as I surveyed the faces in the place, my eyes made contact with Joanne Berenato's big browns. The Sicilian doll was seated in a semi-circular booth with Elaine Hill, Esther Phyllis, and Nanette Banks. I sauntered over, trying my best to be civil, suave, and flirtatious.

"Hi, J.W.," Elaine greeted. "Glad ya' could make it tonight."

"Er yeah, so am I," I awkwardly and shyly answered.

"Thanks for the wonderful kangaroo," Joanne warmly greeted. "It's sittin' on my bed right now, and every time I look at it, J.W., I think of you."

"Why that's terrific," I stammered. "Glad ya' like it."

"J.W.," Esther chimed-in. "We're plannin' on pairin' off with some of you studs later tonight. We really groove on your James Dean jackets. They're the ginchiest!"

I should have known that bad luck was on the horizon when Jimmy Clanton's "Just A Dream" filtered-out from the Wurlitzer's speakers. I stared at Joanne's big brown eyes and her radiant smile.

"Yeah," Elaine agreed. "I'm thinkin' about goin' to the submarine races with Herc out on Snake Road, and Joanne's wantin' to do some hitchin' up with you, J.W. And Nanette and Esther wanta' double date with two of your hot friends."

I glanced-over at Juice and Fabian, and I guessed those Reds were the two hombres that Elaine had been alluding-to. "Is today Sadie Hawkins Day on the town calendar?" I laughed. "If this is what Sadie Hawkins Day is like, it oughta' happen every day of the year. Romance would be a lot easier for everybody if girls did all the askin'."

By the time I finished making *that* appropriate comment, Elvis Presley's recording of "Wear My Ring around Your Neck" came pulsating over the hamburger joint's jukebox speakers. Those lyrics also haunted my susceptible psyche, because I was thinking about asking Joanne to go steady and for her to wear *my* Edgewood ring around *her* sexy St. Joe neck, but since I hadn't graduated from high school, it was like I owned an illegitimate ring for her to wear. That fact made my heart sink deep into my stomach.

Goose was standing behind me, his elf-shaped ears listening to the entire conversational exchanges with the gabby girls. It was his privilege to throw a massive monkey wrench right through the center of *the big picture* window. "Sorry girls, but J.W. and all the Reds have important club business to do tonight," the insufferable social vandal related to the instantly-disappointed dolls. "Maybe some other night J.W., Herc, Juice, and Fabian will be available for small stuff like neckin' at the Circus, or makin' out at the Atco."

I felt that I had shrunk-down to the height of a Lilliputian. My heart, soul, and ego had all been crushed by one sarcastic summary from the unruly mouth of despicable Goose Restuccio.

G.R., Herc, and I shuffled our feet to another booth to sit with Juice, News, Fabian, and Jives at the largest table inside the Gem. I glanced over at the girls' booth, and perceived that the chicks were not too keen on the idea of Reds' business taking priority over affairs of the heart. And when the Everly Brothers' rendition of "Bird Dog" piped through the jukebox's sound system, I felt so small that even a Lilliputian could have cast his or her tiny shadow over me.

"Okay, guys," Goose proceeded with his imperative narrative. "We just order *Cokes* and fries. At nine we gotta' meet Frankie Fingers, Joe Zucchini, and Fabian's flatbed drivers at the Greenmount Cemetery. Hoss and Little Joe will be there with boards for ramps, if we need 'em. Balls Giordano and Jake Maccarella are on the prowl lookin' for the right merchandise to heist. J.W.," Goose commended, "ya' really have the greatest battle ideas I ever heard of. This friggin' fruit war is turnin' me on more than any decent cunt havin' big firm tits and a hairy muffin ready to be buttered!"

I cupped my hands to my face to conceal my intense agony. Connie Francis was then belting-out "Everybody Is Somebody's Fool" over the Gem jukebox, and as I took a glimpse over at Joanne Berenato and the other "nice girls", I quickly realized that my cemetery raid might be ending what might have been the start of a wonderful, lifelong amorous relationship.

At quarter to nine, the assembled Reds rose from our booth and surrendered the space to the next batch of anxious, acne-faced teens that just entered the hamburger haven. I glanced back at Joanne's table, and our eyes made one final contact. Ironically, the Drifters were singing "There Goes My Baby" through the jukebox's sound system when my friends and I readily left the premises.

I noticed that Jives had been uncommonly silent up to then, so I asked the hipster why he hadn't discussed anything weird or abnormal all night.

"Larry Gytis is in my throat," the aspiring beatnik whispered. "And the dude's really rattlin' my cage. I'm so down that the dumps look like paradise right now, and man, I can hear the *dull drums* beatin' like crazy."

I figured that Frankie was scared and suffering from a bad case of nerves, because when I would also get *that* throat condition, I would lose my voice, too. "Just hope that frog in your throat doesn't turn into an alligator!" I warned as we crossed Central Avenue on our way to the Reds' cars. "And Jives, if ya' swallowed a small pony this afternoon, I could understand why you're a little *hoarse* right now," I finished, repeating a silly joke I had used once before.

I was with Goose, Herc, Juice, and Fabian, all squeezed inside the Red T-Bird "sardine can". We cruised around Bellevue Avenue for ten-minutes, and then crossed the railroad tracks and drove-down Twelfth Street to First Road. Everyone was silent, thinking about our individual roles in executing the highly-complicated, soon-to-happen graveyard enterprise.

When the Thunderbird reached the last entrance into Greenmount Cemetery, Goose slowly entered and drove all the way up to the central *Civil War Memorial.* The overall atmosphere inside the place was eerie and spooky, but not as frightful as the night of the scavenger hunt, because at *that* particular moment, there were a lot of Reds in the immense, dark, gloomy scene.

Goose, followed by News, drove the Reds' cars up to two impressive mausoleums that were still under construction. All of the stonework had been completed, except that the white marble roofs had not yet been cemented on top. Waiting for our arrival was Frankie Fingers, standing by a Mafia-owned cement truck. Joe Zucchini was leaning against a septic tank "honey wagon", and Fabian's loyal mechanic, who was nervously smoking a cigarette, was standing alongside *his* flatbed rig. Gabe Gillette's spanking new ice blue Corvette was sitting on the flatbed. Balls Giordano had driven a second flatbed to the town cemetery, which had been obtained by Fabian Midilli at the Flyin' A. The vehicle had Speed Mortellite's brand new blue '60 Thunderbird situated upon its rear.

Hoss and Little Joe Gregorio were there, too, waiting in a farm truck with a pretty hefty forklift on it. When Goose gave the signal, Hoss drove the forklift down the sturdy ramp boards onto the asphalt surface. Everyone went to work as if we were programmed robots, for time was of the essence.

"Who do these stone *temple* pads belong to?" Jives's larynx strained to say. "Zeus, or that Greek heel, Achilles?"

"Mr. Gillette and Mr. Mortellite," I tersely answered. "Each one of the mausoleums is almost as big as *Temple University*."

Hoss went into action. First, the Titan raised the ice blue Corvette up off of Fabian's flatbed, and lifted the giant forks as high as they could go. Next, the muscular farm-boy tilted the blades down, and then Little Joe and the Calabrese boys (who had come to Greenmount in one of the trucks) climbed-up onto the forklift's guard and pushed with all their might. The 'Vette slid off the tilted forks and fell into the Gillette family mausoleum's interior. The same process was soon repeated with Speed's new blue T-Bird, which snugly fit into the Mortellite family's palatial tomb.

Then, Frankie Fingers and Joe Zucchini went to work. Frankie backed his specialized truck up to the Gillette mausoleum; fired up the cement mixer, and Herc and Balls diligently angled the chute so that the cement poured-down onto Gabe's ice blue Corvette that had just been buried inside his family's mammoth tomb. Joe Z. had backed *his* sewage disposal truck up to the Mortellite' sepulchre, and the Calabrese boys, who wanted revenge for what had happened to them in the canoe incident at Hammonton Lake, actively participated in *our* grand vandalism. Chickie and Joe stood on top of the septic truck's circular receptacle tank and pointed "the honey-wagon's hose" into the middle of the Mortellite family's sacred mausoleum.

"There goes Speed's new blue T-Bird," Goose solemnly orated like a country minister with his right hand held over his heart. A foul stench was smelled by all, but none of the septic waste penetrated through the walls of the well-constructed mausoleum, so the marble structure was apparently waterproof in addition to being "feces proof".

Those specialized activities went on for a full ten-minutes until the first mausoleum was filled with liquid concrete, and the second one was brimming with human waste. With our nefarious plan being efficiently completed, all of us felt that vengeance had been served in retribution for what the Blues had maliciously done to Goose, to Hoss, and Little Joe, and to the rest of us during the turbulent course of the great fruit war.

The Reds all hopped into our respective vehicles, and we exited the vast Greenmount Cemetery, all taking different routes and directions.

"Whew, that was so super cool!" I yelled from the red T-Bird's tightly-crammed back seat to Goose, Herc, Juice, Jives, and Fabian. "What a tremendous mission!" I panted. "Definitely, my biggest one ever, and that includes everything I ever did with the devious Diablos back in Levittown."

"It's a good thing the Mt. *Caramel* carnival's still in town," Goose reminded everyone. "All the local people are either attendin' it on its last night, or are vacationin' down the Jersey shore."

"And all the Blues are probably illegally getting drunk at the Mt. Carmel Beer Garden, and roamin' the carnival's gravel lookin' for Reds as prey to bust-up," Herc added.

"And all the damned cops are at the carnival, too, keeping peaceful law and order," I added.

"That was the most orgasmic gig I've ever dug," Jives chortled with his raspy voice. "It was a dynamo trip and a half plus seven mini vacations."

"J.W.," Juice began his compliment. "You're the most-clever guy I ever had the displeasure of knowin', and I just hope that you're never my enemy, or I'll be sure to quickly move to northern Siberia."

"Juice, ya' could then live with the *Abdominal* Snowman," Goose sincerely stated. "That fuckin' guy has a lot of *guts*."

The five of us were enjoying terrific camaraderie, telling jokes, making wisecracks, and insulting the intelligence of our principal blueberry enemies, mercilessly mocking each fully-hated name and personality individually.

Goose took a roundabout back route to Elm. The new area pinball machine distributor traveled down Union Road to Walker, to leave *me* off first, so that I could help my parents close-down the farm market, while pretending that it had just been another ordinary night in somnolent "Dullsville", as Frankie quite aptly called and described downtown Hammonton and vicinity. Juice was reviewing certain details of my stellar commando raid when our boss automobile passed-by old man Berenato's garbage bin.

"Goose, hit the damned brakes!" I yelled.

The red Thunderbird skidded to a stop. G.R. backed-up and peeled some rubber, so that we were parallel to the full and overloaded packinghouse fruit dumper. On the very top of the rejected peach heap was the plush kangaroo that I had given to Joanne via Esther and Elaine. My heart sank when I gazed at the pathetic sight.

Tears formed in my eyes. I theorized that Joanne had interpreted what had happened in the Gem between the Reds and her and her girlfriends had been a permanent rejection of the girls from the guys and me, all inspired by Goose and the Great Teen Fruit War.

"J.W., don't worry about it!" Goose advised in his normal caustic voice. "No bitch could ever give ya' the excitement the Reds gave all of us tonight at the town cemetery."

"But Goose," I said almost crying. "That kangaroo was special between Joanne and me. Now it's in the garbage heap."

"Goddam it, J.W. Goose yelled. "When the hell are ya' gonna' grow-up and stop wastin' your time on courtin' that friggin' peach queen! And remember, if it wasn't for me, ya' would've never gotten your paws on that cheap five-dollar kangaroo to give to your precious lady friend."

"You mean my *former* lady friend," I sobbed. "Right now, I think I'd be more desirable to Joanne if I had bad dual cases of leprosy and small pox."

Chapter Thirty-Nine

"Uncle Clyde's Place"

My head was spinning like a top. The Blues were on the warpath, so I didn't venture far from the safety of the farm market for several days. Goose confidentially conveyed to me over the phone that the Blues and the Ramrodders had made a truce, and that the former rival gangs had formed a pact and were planning to ally against the Reds. Our chief enemies were still Gabe Gillette's gang, and until the Rodders' did something detrimental to the Reds, I personally felt we had no real grievances with Mark Benedetto and Warren Watson's greaser gang.

The last week of July, Goose Restuccio visited Pete's Market to see how I was doing. Pop had planted two acres of his own tomatoes in late April behind the stand, so G.R. and I stood in the middle of the weed-infested vegetable field to confer and commiserate. The disreputable instigator related to me that the Blues had ascertained that the Reds were the villains who had ruined the twin mausoleums and had demolished Gabe Gillette's second ice blue Corvette, along Speed Mortellite's replacement blue Thunderbird.

"How did the cave-dwelling, knuckle-draggers ever figure that out?" I asked my inimitable colleague, who should have had Phd's in vandalism, cursing, and exaggeration.

"Easy, Jerkenheimer," Goose chided. "The friggin' Ramrodders only got hot rods and motorcycles to ride-around in. The Rodders' don't got no goddamned forklifts, flatbed trucks, or access to cement mixers and smelly honey-wagons. Only farm teens, gas station kids, and Mafia delinquents could get and use those kinds of neat cunt-lappin' things!"

I was still devastated and heartbroken from the kangaroo in the dumpster scenario behind Joanne's house, and I believed that nothing Goose could possible say could placate my emotional despair. I was surprised to learn that my evaluation of my personal romantic situation had been as wrong as wrong could be.

"J.W.," my roguish alter-ego continued his prattling. "I was talkin' to Elaine Hill and Esther Phyllis over at Mr. Bill's yesterday, and that's why I'm here talkin' to you right now."

"Oh, great Goose, what were you doin'?" I nastily jumped to conclusions. "Were ya' collectin' donations for kangaroo and wallaby animal preserves in Australia? Ya' always gotta' be a butt-in-ski all the time. Back off, will ya'!"

"Just hold your goddamned horses right there, Buffalo Bob!" G.R. admonished as if he were Mr. Bluster speaking to Mr. Bob Smith on the *Howdy Doody Show*. "Don't jump the gun 'cause ya' don't know all the facts yet. If ya' ever screw Joanne, you'll probably have a damned premature ejaculation."

"Just like *you* had with Crystal Davis in the blueberry field," I angrily retorted, feeling like I wanted to knock the wise guy's block off while getting the crap knocked out of me.

"J.W., I can tell that ya' just wanta' be another small tombstone in the cemetery, and that's exactly what you're gonna' be; just another tiny tombstone in Greenmount or Oak Grove Cemetery," Goose reiterated.

"Everybody on this earth is gonna' die, and that includes you!" I replied rather emphatically. "What's this B.S. about me bein' just another tombstone!"

G.R. defended his brilliant deduction by saying that the only important people that ever lived have the really big monuments in the cemetery, like the Gillette and Mortellite families, who could afford to build new mammoth monuments, even if their old ones had been destroyed in the great teen fruit war. "Goddam it," the junior don argued. "Those poor souls that spent their entire lives believin' in a fake afterlife wasted their entire lives on nothin', hopin' and prayin' that some greater force was gonna' save 'em from nothin'. J.W.," Goose claimed, "there ain't no damned afterlife. There's just now, and only now, so start buildin' your big *mass-soul-leum* right now, or ya' ain't gonna' ever accomplish much in this life; the only fuckin' life there really is."

"I wish you wouldn't curse all the time," I humbly replied. "And I don't know why I talk at all to you. We've been down this path before. Ya' don't believe in God, do you? The only almighty ya' know is the almighty dollar."

"Look J.W.," the peeved atheist rankled. "What kind of God has to send the Holy Goblin down to earth to knock up an innocent virgin for him? Ya' fuckin' answer that *miss-terry* for me!" Restuccio screamed. "If God wanted to get laid, He shoulda' had the balls to do it himself. He must be one of those perverted voyeurs, or something, sendin' the Holy Ghoul as his hit-man, so that *He* could watch from the damned sky. Get real now!"

"First of all," I said very loudly, "it wasn't the Holy Goblin or the Holy Ghoul. It was the Holy Ghost. And second of all, it wasn't a different Person 'cause God, Jesus Christ, and the Holy Spirit are one and the same Person."

"Now that's the biggest bullshit lie ever *invented* besides the Immaculate Deception!" G.R. irreverently blasphemed and bungled simultaneously. "J.W., are ya' me? Am I you? No two people can be the same friggin' person! How fuckin' stupid are ya' to believe such crap! It's just not friggin' *lodge-a-cull!* I mean, what kind of fucked-up religion do ya' have when you go to church each Sunday and eat your God! It sounds like religious cannibalism to me!"

"If ya' can't speak about anything else that doesn't offend me," I said, while almost crying, "then hop into your red T-Bird! You're enough to turn heaven into hell."

"Anyway," Restuccio continued in a less-heated tone. "Elaine Hill and Esther Phyllis told me that Joanne still likes ya'. Her old man found-out about the plush kangaroo, and since he doesn't know ya' from Adam, or from Jesus Christ, he's the one who chucked the damned thing into the trash dumpster. Joanne didn't do it. Her old man was the jealous culprit."

"She didn't throw the kangaroo away?" I asked in disbelief, seeking verification from the Reds' Hermes.

"The villain wasn't Captain Kangaroo or Mr. Ed," G.R. joked. "No, in fact Elaine said that your girl Joanne cried all this week, and hasn't spoken to her mean old man since *that* night," Goose elaborated. "Joanne's on the verge of a nervous breakdown because her *re-cent-full* pappy is too damned strict with his beautiful daughter. Joanne's pop forbids her to see any other friggin' guy other than a *boner fide* peach grower's son."

Goose then divulged the real reason for his unannounced visit. August was approaching on the 1960 calendar, and soon blueberry season would be over. G.R. asked me if there was any way that I could solve a triple problem. First, I had to get Joanne involved in a special Reds' project to win back her admiration and favor. Second, I had to devise a way for the Reds to "crash" the Blues' gala end of harvest party at their slick clubhouse, a converted barn secluded near a pine forest, not far from New Creek Road. "Third, J.W., I wants ya' to figure-out a way to use the two-hundred bowlin' balls I bought from Egg Harbor Lanes. Those son-of-a-bitchin' things are still sittin' in my Old Man's white box truck, and he wants 'em outa' there before Labor Day."

"That's a lot of problem-solving to think-about at one time," I acknowledged. "Let me find my thinkin' cap."

"Ya' got just about one week to come-up with the solution to the three ass-suckin' riddles," Goose commanded. "The blueberry farms are almost done with their Blue Crop, the last good fresh market variety. We gotta' hit those mung-heads good before the cock-suckers have more time to think-up an idea that might kill us both before we get to build our big *mass-soul-leums.*"

I told Goose he'd better study the dictionary and learn the English language. "The word is pronounced 'mausoleums'!" I corrected.

G.R. pointed his middle fingers on both his hands while closing the other eight, and the chronic pessimist pressed those two middle fingers directly to his temples and moved them back and forth, simulating the sex act. "Ya' know, J.W., ya' give me a *fuckin'* headache! I ain't ever gonna' get trapped in any of Gabe Gillette's revolvin' doors anymore!"

I couldn't help laughing at my deranged pal's brazen impudence. We compromised and shook hands. Goose departed the property as if nothing at all had happened, or had been debated or argued between us. I thought about what G.R. and I had talked about, and then I recollected how the lunatic had killed Hector Rodriquez, and how the Puerto Rican's death hardly bothered G.R. as if *he* had only stomped on an ant, or a beetle, or a cockroach, with his shoe. Then, I walked through the high weeds, out of the rear tomato field, and joined the rest of the family as we sorted-out thirty baskets of peaches that hadn't been sold the day before.

I kept a low profile the whole following week, but managed to have time on Wednesday to briefly visit Jives in Winslow, on my way to Turnersville to pick-up a load of corn and squash. Frankie intimated that he had almost gotten pneumonia and was on heavy-duty prescription drugs.

The garrulous hipster told me he had been leaving the Hammonton Post Office, wearing his James Dean jacket, and suddenly had been violently accosted by Butch Lanza and Ox Narducci. The two nasty gorillas dragged Jives across South Third Street and tossed his butt into the small water fountain, situated in a quaint triangle at the corner of Vine and Central, right across the intersection from the Hammonton Police Department. Frankie had already been feeling sick the night of the spectacular cemetery mausoleum raid, and was just recovering from his flu malady when Lanza and Narducci decided to play the roles of Mr. Nemesis and Dr. Destructo.

It was soon a new month, and as Pop aptly put it, "We're now into the dog days of August." News called, saying that his farm was in between peach varieties, and that my fruit friend had some free time on his hands. That morning, G.R. had been in touch with Tommy over the telephone. By Goose's imperial decree, a Reds' strategy session had been scheduled in the basement of the Tomasello' residence on Spring Road at 7 p.m., the first Thursday in August. Tommy's parents, free of daily farm work, had planned to visit Atlantic City to stroll the world-famous boardwalk, so we didn't have to worry about adult supervision or interference.

I was the first Red to arrive at News's place on Thursday evening. "Hi J.W.," T.T. greeted. "Destroyed any unoccupied mausoleums, or shot any midget Blues out of carnival cannons lately?"

"No, I've been too busy sortin' peaches and tomatoes and slappin' annoyin' fruit flies. Stuff really gets rotten quick later in the summer," I admitted. "There are fruit flies and mosquitoes flittin' around all over the market. I think I accidentally inhaled two of 'em this mornin'."

"Do ya' have your' next special plan devised and ready yet?" Tommy asked. "You'll have to go some to beat that last cemetery gig. It sure was a double blast."

"Sure do, News, and I had to disintegrate my brains to sort things out, but I came-up with a terrific scheme when I was sortin' peaches into three piles: good ones, soft ones, and rejects. That's when I developed my three solutions. What's new, News?"

"Well, J.W., as you might've seen on TV, last week the first Polaris missile was launched from a submerged submarine, the USS George Washington," News reported. "The rocket was able to fly 1,150 miles down range."

"Wasn't the first Polaris missile from a submarine fired earlier in the year?" I recalled and challenged. "Ya' told me *that* fact a couple of months ago."

"Yes, J.W., you're right about that," Tommy conceded. "But this time a missile was fired when the submarine was actually underwater. The last time the Polaris missile had been fired was when the submarine was afloat in the *Pacific*. Ya' weren't payin' attention to every word and detail I had said."

"Sorry, News, I was thinkin' about my new plan I'm gonna' tell the guys, and you're right, I should pay more attention to exactly what ya' do say," I apologized.

"And also," News added. "The Republican National Convention just nominated Vice President Richard M. Nixon. Senator Barry Goldwater from Arizona only received ten token votes."

"That's wonderful," I responded, still meditating my grand military operation soon to be implemented by the supreme Reds. "Nixon seems like a sincere, decent man, with a good conscience. I think he'll make a good, honest president. Even a great president."

I heard Percy Faith's melodic "Theme from a Summer Place" playing from a radio in the background in News's basement, and the beautiful melody made me think about Joanne Berenato and me lying alone, romancing on a tropical beach, drinking pina coladas at a classy Hawaiian resort.

"J.W., I just thought of something. If Joanne Berenato went to Edgewood High, how did your girl ever become St. Joe Prom Queen."

I explained to T.T. that the St. Joe administration wanted to have more harmony existing between Hammonton High, Edgewood, and the Catholic School, so the rules were changed to allow any girl attending the prom from any of the three schools to be eligible to be selected the queen. The same rule modification was true for any guy from any of the three area high schools, escorting a St. Joe girl, to be qualified to become the Prom King.

A moment passed without any conversation. "Guess what, J.W.," Tommy sternly declared, breaking my momentary tropical island fantasy. "Color television is coming within the next year. I can't wait to watch the Phillies and the Eagles playin' on a big 18-inch color screen!"

* * * * * * * * * * * * * *

All twenty-four Reds showed-up for the big powwow, even Jives Arena, who sounded like the raspy-throat nutcase should have been hospitalized in intensive care. Jives's recent water fountain misfortune at the hands of several aggressive Blues provided the gang with added incentive to want to swiftly retaliate in a big way.

I presented my "triple idea scheme" to the "Reds' war council", and I was surprised at how well it had been received. After the cemetery dual mausoleum expedition had been cleverly enacted, all the Reds gave me more respect and prestige, and the guys had the utmost confidence in my grandiose preparations, which were really only variations of stuff that the Diablos had practiced against the Kamikazes back in Levittown.

As I finished outlining my next project to the assembled Reds, News looked like a contemporary Napoleon as the "Reds' General" moved his "military pointer" to different "staging areas" displayed upon his topographically-accurate Hammonton and vicinity miniature landscape. Everyone knew the exact locations of the various settings News and I had been describing.

"Wow, J.W.," Jives commended in a zombie-like ventriloquist's voice. "I liked the way ya' got *Joanney B. Goode* involved in this boss prank. This gig is gonna' be the cat's meow, maybe even bigger than the cool Bowlarama, the el neato peach pit dilly-do, the pizza oven dough burn-off, and the boss mausoleum honey-wagon crapola."

"Jives, what do ya' really think about J.W.s new plan?" Juice asked the mentally and physically sick extrovert.

"It's such a cool dude-like gig that I gotta' see *Dr. Pepper* right this sec'! I can't wait until this pneumonia turns into *old* ammonia," Frankie cryptically answered.

"What did that forked-tongue hand-job say this time?" Goose asked the other twenty-two befuddled Reds in attendance.

"Frankie said that he needs a cool soda to make his throat and bad cold feel better, and that in a couple of days, after seeing Dr, Pepper, he'll be feelin' back to his normal, abnormal self again," Juice interpreted.

"I think I'd understand that word mangler better if he spoke Russian or Shakespeare, or some other asshole languages the coons and spics speak in New York," Goose seriously remarked. "We don't need no army or navy to defend us if fucked-up space aliens from Planet Piss accidentally land in Hammonton and run into Frankie first," G.R. finished.

Everyone laughed as Jives made his way upstairs to the Kitchen refrigerator to locate his favorite soda. The focus of discussion returned to the intricacies of our next Blues' mission, which quickly gained the endorsement of the entire gang.

"I like how J.W. got the two-hundred remainin' bowlin' balls involved in the operation," News praised. "This one is gonna' be the cream of the crop, and I don't mean Blue Crop blueberries, either."

Tommy's brief "get-even" speech got a good laugh from the gang, especially from Hoss and Little Joe Gregorio, who were both still smarting from the Edgewood band uniform heist.

"I like the way Herc is gonna' get Joanne outa' the house to be with Elaine at the Blues' harvest party," Balls Giordano remarked. "Gabe Gillette will never suspect that Joanne's gonna' be secretly actin' as an important Blues' enemy."

"And what about how we're all gonna' crash the Blues' harvest party when the low I.Q. dolts least expect it," Fabian added, "right in their own backyard. Just like a band of medieval crusaders takin' it to the Muslims in their own main tent!"

"Good!" I exclaimed. "Goose, News, and I are goin' up *Route 9* to Manahawkin late next Saturday afternoon, to start phase one. I'll arrange for the seafood pick-up. My contact in Manahawkin is sure to fill our order and have the supply ready."

"The Blues' harvest beer blast is scheduled for Sunday night startin' at eight, just before dark," Juice Illiani reminded everyone. "So, everybody should be ready to strike, and be at your assigned stagin' areas a half-hour before eight. All in favor of J.W.'s excellent plan, say 'aye'!"

"Aye!" all attending Reds yelled in unison.

On Saturday afternoon, Goose and News showed-up at Pete's Market in Restuccio's big white box truck. I hopped into the passenger side with Tommy sitting in the middle.

"How's it hangin'?" G.R. greeted before loudly farting and stinking-up the entire cab with the windows closed.

"It's so long it's hangin'-out at the Gem!" I laughed.

"Goose can't wait until he gets old," News said to me as Restuccio entered the Pike and grinded and brought the truck's gears on the floor-shift into second.

"Why's that?" G.R. asked as the preoccupied driver wound-out second and popped-in his clutch for third. "I don't wanta' get old."

"Because when you get old, you'll have strong arthritis in your fadorkenbender," News laughed, "and it'll be hard all the time."

Restuccio was a little pissed-off at News' s clever comment, so the resentful asshole farted again rather wickedly, but before G.R.s non-academic mind could respond with a flurry of salacious words, I double-teamed the mannerless driver.

"You're absolutely right, News," I added. "And watch-out when Goose goes into fourth gear. He has a reputation for bein' a pretty *shifty* character."

"Goddam it, ya' two corny fuck-heads!" the ornery, cantankerous driver hollered, before loudly and deliberately farting a third time. "Stop bustin' my fuckin' balls!"

"Speakin' of balls," I mentioned, "I hope the two-hundred bowlin' balls from Egg Harbor Lanes aren't still in the racks on the back of *this* noisy tank."

Goose informed News and me that Frankie Fingers and Joe Zucchini had transferred the two-hundred bowling balls from the white box truck into the posterior of an enormous dump truck that "the boys" had borrowed from a Mafia associate, who was partners in a Sicilian construction company's "*front money launderin' business*". "Since the *boys* are on the payroll," G.R. surmised and reported, "and since Frankie and Joey like me and know I'll slice their balls off if they don't do what the fuck I ask 'em to do, those two bone-breakin' grease-balls transferred the bowlin' balls into the Mafia dump truck."

"Won't somebody see the bowlin' balls in a big mound sittin' on top?" Tommy plausibly questioned. "It's mighty hard to hide two hundred stacked bowlin' balls."

"Naaa," Goose calmly uttered and grinned. "Frankie and Joey have the balls covered with a big *tarp-pullin,"* G.R. related.

"You couldn't drive this truck with the road's tar-*pullin'* against the tires," I jested.

"And Goose," News added, ignoring my stupid *pun*ishment. "Frankie and Joey are gonna' have two-hundred-and-four-balls with 'em on Weymouth Road tomorrow night. Add it up. Two-hundred bowlin' balls and two sets of brass balls."

"Can't ya' two stupid clowns jerk each other off or somethin'!" Goose shouted at us in a booming voice, that in ancient times would have frightened either Zeus or Hades. "You're givin' my headache a fuckin' headache!" G.R. yelled as the non-conformist stopped the truck to make a left turn from Basin Road onto *206*.

Soon, we were passing by several peach farms on the left and rows of blueberry bushes on the right, as the Mafia transport truck traveled north past the Red Barn Restaurant. I figured News and I ought to get serious or be forced to hitchhike home, so we deftly *shifted* into more mundane conversation that our driver would appreciate and fully understand. 'Pop used to tell me, I thought, 'if ya' listen to and make somebody feel important, they'll talk for an hour about themselves, and how wonderful they are. And then when they're finished their proud stories, they'll eventually do whatever *you* ask them to do, just because *you* made the person feel good by your not saying anything while he or she was talking.'

"Won't the cops start intervenin' in the fruit war?" I asked. "How come nobody's been arrested or questioned except Hoss and Little Joe about the Edgewood band uniforms? In my opinion, the fuzz ain't doin' their job."

Goose explained that the Winslow and Hammonton cops only did a casual investigation because the pilfered band uniform crime involved two separate police departments, and each police jurisdiction wanted to make it look like *they* were promptly responding to the practice of mild juvenile delinquency occurring in a rural area. "The uniforms were recovered and returned to the Edgewood band director," G.R. remembered and maintained. "And nobody was hurt or killed. It was a wash, a fuckin' clean slate as far as the area cops were concerned."

"But sooner or later, the fuzz is gonna' discover that it's not the fruit game goin' on here, but it's now the fruit war," News injected. "Somebody's gonna' get really hurt or killed, and then it's gonna' be too little too late."

"Cops are like hungry sharks swimmin' around in the ocean," Goose generalized and stereotyped. "The pred-a-tory fuzz only go after the small weaker fish. Sharks know better' than to screw-around with mean-ass killer whales, or fuck with a school of barracudas. They leave the mean fuckers alone, and swim the other way to harass and eat a little sea bass, or a small lost octopus."

"But what about when Gabe Gillette broke his leg and Speed Mortellite busted-up his arm?" I asked. "Those injuries had to be close calls with the law that needed skilled medical attention."

"You're right J.W.," Goose concurred. "But since the Blues wanted revenge, and since the dumb-shits didn't know exactly who'd done the motorcycle prank, Gillette and Mortellite wanted to even the score without the fuzz or the cops' hairy hand-job' clinic getting involved in the complex mix."

Goose stayed on *206* up to the Red Lion Circle; headed east on *Route 70* for a few miles, and at another circle, veered onto *Route 72,* which then took us in the direction to Manahawkin. A right on *Route 9* soon had us in front of a dilapidated, in-need-of-paint seafood place, that catered to black customers.

The three of us stepped inside the ramshackle establishment, and a gray-hair, elderly black gentleman immediately recognized me from my phone call and from a past meeting. "J.W., good to see ya' again," the old Negro pleasantly greeted.

I introduced "Uncle Clyde" to Goose and News. I educated the fellas' that the aged black gent was the uncle of a notorious friend I had known back in Dogwood Hollow by the name of Marcus "Sugar Ray" Spellman, the first black kid to move into formerly all-white Levittown, Pennsylvania.

"How's Sugar Ray doin'?" I asked. "Haven't seen him since I moved from 'Pennsy half a year ago."

"Great, J.W.," Clyde Spellman answered. "My nephew's quittin' auto' mechanics and goin' to school to become a barber. He's learnin' how to blast wigs now."

"You wouldn't happen to be the new manager of the Marvelons!" Goose cynically said to Uncle Clyde, because G.R.'s black humor was really black ridicule in disguise.

"Never heard of 'em!" Clyde honestly remarked. "Are they magicians?"

"No, they're a popular singin' group back where we come from in Hammonton," I told the affable seafood distributor.

"Hammonton!" Clyde exclaimed. "J.W., ya' all live *there* now! I hear there's a big fruit war goin' on down in that crazy town. Somethin' about blueberries and raspberries."

"Blueberries and peaches," I corrected. "Now Uncle Clyde," I said respectfully, "let's get-down to business here."

"How much are these *crusty stations*," Goose interrupted, pointing at a heap of *crabs in a bushel,* while trying to impress us with his extensive vocabulary, which the tricky word-stealer had learned from News and me.

"Five-dollars a bucket, which is a peck, or a half of a half-bushel in the peach world," Mr. Clyde Spellman indicated.

Goose, News, and I inspected "Uncle Clyde's" inventory and concluded that we would purchase twenty-five plastic buckets of dead shad; fifty-pails of crabs, and fifty-pounds of shrimp. We decided to go with the "plastic pecks" because the containers had handles and would be easier to pour or dump.

Restuccio had the opportunity to again play the important big shot. The exorbitant seafood bill came to over three-hundred-dollars. G.R. peeled off five *Ben Franklins* from his wad, and the arrogant kingpin told "the Kingfish" that *Uncle Clyde* could keep the change.

"Holy mackerel!" the exhilarated fish store entrepreneur fittingly exclaimed. "I can now afford to go to barberin' school with my ambitious nephew Marcus!"

We thanked Uncle Clyde for his benign cooperation, loaded our seafood acquisitions, and finally entered the white box truck's cab. Then, Goose took *Highway 9* south to Bass River.

"How come we aren't goin' back to Hammonton the way we came?" I asked. "It takes less time."

"Because Asshole. No Mafia guy in his right mind ever takes the same route twice," Goose divulged and snickered. "Enemies see your patterns and habits, and before ya' know it, ya' fuckin' wake-up dead the next mornin'!"

"That's humanly impossible!" I challenged. "Ya' can't wake-up dead!"

"Ever tried it or done it?" G.R. vociferously fired back.

"No!" I succinctly replied.

"Well, Shit-head. Don't knock it until you've tried it," the junior Mafioso effectively chastised.

I then made a rather huge verbal blunder. I asked News what was happening in the big wide world, and my educated colleague boringly elucidated that a new X-15 experimental rocket plane, piloted by civilian Joseph A. Walker, had recently broken the world aviation speed record of 2,196 mph.

"If this pilot guy delivered pizza," I said, "Joseph A. Walker could be a big star in the fast-food delivery business."

News gave me a dirty look, and then verbally regurgitated about the latest scientific phone experiment where American researchers had successfully bounced human voices off the moon. I suggested that those scientists could make more money at a popular bar, bouncing obnoxious drunks out the door for management, and Tommy gave me a second nasty frown as Goose scratched his testicles through his dungarees and chuckled his *"cool-yune-ees"* off.

Then, irrepressible News discussed how the first payload from orbit around the earth had been sent into space, and had been lifted by a U.S. helicopter from the *Pacific Ocean,* just when our Reds' seafood express box-truck was passing by the historic *Mullica River* and Batsto Village, while heading southwest towards Pleasant Mills Road.

"Well, why didn't the government just send the helicopter to the *Pacific Ocean* in the first place, drop the payload into the drink, and then lift the damned object outa' the sea," I giddily recommended. "The bureaucrats in Washington could've saved the taxpayer's a lot of money if the leeches hadn't wasted *their* valuable time sendin' that expensive rocket into orbit with the dumb payload," I reckoned and elaborated. "Why didn't the stupid Feds just put the payload in the local bank in the first place, instead of in the ocean? The crazy, delusional Republicans are right. No wonder why this country's goin' super-bankrupt fast!"

It was a good thing we were almost home. The three of us were emotionally exhausted, thinking about the big foray planned against the Blues' clubhouse on Sunday evening. However, we only had seven-hours to organize our resources in order to initiate *my* intricate scheme's vital, first, dangerous phase.

Chapter Forty

"The Seafood Brigade"

It was really hard working almost every day at Pete's Market; seeing Mr. Charles B. Sipley for mentally draining, one-hour trigonometry crams, and hanging-out with Goose, Juice, News, Fabian, and Jives. I really didn't have too much free time to myself, except when I was sleeping, and I never could remember what I had been dreaming about. And so, I would daydream a lot, preferring each special reverie to the daily grueling, harsh reality most 1960 humans had to contend with each and every day.

I called Goose late Saturday afternoon to see when our squad leader was coming-over to pick me up, and the demented rebel told me over the phone to do something I had never tried, so I followed his wise advice. I stepped to my bathroom medicine cabinet, opened it, and found a bottle of aspirins. I swallowed-down three pills, and recalling G.R.'s words, "Take the aspirins *before* the big job J.W.; that way ya' won't have to take them after." I honored Restuccio's oral commandment and gulped-down a full glass of water to wash the 'Moses tablets' into my stomach.

As I waited downstairs for Goose to arrive, I studied a calendar hanging in the hall closet, where I usually kept my treasured James Dean jacket and my old Diablos' black leather one. Each month on the calendar featured a popular Norman Rockwell painting, and I began wondering which America I was really living in, or wanted to live in, Norman Rockwell's clean, wholesome version, or Ronald Goose Restuccio's corrupt, decadent one. Idealism versus reality; good versus bad; and morality versus evil were distinct polarities that dominated *my* teen universe.

'Oh well,' I thought. 'I've cut-down on my smoking. That's one positive.' Most of the Reds didn't smoke because the football guys like Hoss and Little Joe, and the wrestling Calabrese boys were conditioned athletes. 'Even my clothes smell fresher,' I admitted as I donned my Reds' jacket in preparation for the big early-August raid. 'I'm beginnin' to dislike second-hand smoke comin' from other people's mouths, even from my friends' mouths,' I healthily thought and believed.

While I was sitting in a living room chair, impatiently waiting for G.R. to pull into the driveway, I thought about him, Fabian, and Frankie, being the biggest smokers in the gang, but in addition to nicotine, Goose also cursed, swore, manipulated, and threatened people. So, in many respects, the tall, stocky Sicilian was a New Jersey rich version of Levittown's criminal-minded Tinker.

Gabe Gillette also liked Joanne Berenato, but I knew in my heart her loyalty was to me and to the Reds, despite her cantankerous father's protestations. Elaine Hill connived, arranged, and helped me implement an important element of my latest plan, which featured three basic creative themes: crabs, marbles, and bowling balls.

Goose finally arrived and picked me up in the red Thunderbird to avoid any suspicion from my parents about leaving Pete's Market again in a big white box truck. The devious dude drove me over to his Winslow palace, where the rest of the gang would be assembled. On the way, I asked G.R. what he thought of Norman Rockwell.

"He'll never stay in the major leagues that long because he's a lousy hitter and can't field worth a damn," Goose fibbed and fabricated. "That shit-head should be playin' in the minors."

Bobby Rydell's summer hit "Wild One" was playing on the car radio, right before Restuccio entered his driveway, and that lively tune got my dormant hormones flowing, and set the fast tempo for the rest of the evening.

All of the other Reds were ready to contribute to the huge military mission. Like a tactical attack squad, most of the prepared commandos piled into the back of the white box truck wearing their red jackets, which gave us all secure feelings of unity and solidarity.

"Be sure to load the twelve-foot-plank," Goose reminded Hoss and Little Joe. "I had to have it cut special over at Crane's Lumberyard. And don't forget the tall ladder, too. Everything's gotta' go like clockwork."

"These crabs, fish, and shrimp really stink," Juice complained from inside the truck's cubed rear. "The air smell's almost like a big city sewage plant."

"What grows on a sewage plant?" I asked. "Is a sewage plant like a pepper or tomato plant?"

"Just think of how that seafood is gonna' smell to the Blues tomorrow night," Fabian laughed. "The Blues are gonna' have to wear clothespins on their nostrils."

Goose and I closed the back panels, temporarily sealing the twenty-two warriors inside the truck's rear compartment. Soon, we were rumbling-out of the driveway on our way to New Creek Road, via Second Road and Weymouth Road.

"Is Joanne goin' to the big blueberry bash tomorrow night?" Goose seriously asked.

"Yes," I replied. "Herc Juliano asked her out, so her old man thinks that she's goin' on a date with a peach farmer's son."

"What about Elaine Hill?" G.R. asked.

"Elaine's the key cog in our dating wheel game," I stated. "Elaine got Brigette DiMeo to set her up with Speed Mortellite tomorrow night. Mortellite just broke-up with his girlfriend, who's goin' to the affair with Sonny Perone. It's all very complicated," I explained. "But Speed wants to just use Elaine to make his old girlfriend jealous. Elaine knows she's involved in a love triangle, and bein' used by Mortellite."

When I said the word "triangle", *that* math' term automatically made me think of trigonometry, but Mortellite's triangle had no secants, sines or tangents.

"J.W., do ya' think I'm a fuckin' moron or somethin'!" Goose scolded. "I can follow a shit trail all the way to somebody's asshole. I'm a real *sloth* when it comes to that."

"You mean *sleuth,"* I corrected.

"That's just what I meant and just what I said," G.R. injected. "I'm a stubborn hound dog. I read that word 'sloth' in a Sherlock Houses' story my dumb-ass class read in Mr. Rebeck's English *semen-hour*."

I avoided discussing Goose's misuse of the word *seminar*. Instead, I elaborated to my uncultured companion that on Saturday night, Herc Juliano was going to pick-up Joanne, take her to the Gem, and then leave her with Elaine until Gabe Gillette and Speed Mortellite showed-up to escort the girls to the blueberry gangs' festooned clubhouse.

"Now I get it, J.W.," Goose realized and declared. "Joanne and Elaine are like our spies operatin' in foreign territory. The chicks conned the two big *blue* fish right smack-dab into the center of your scam's net," G.R. orally concluded. "Gabe and Speed have been tricked and set-up by T and A, good old tits and ass."

"Exactly," I quickly agreed. "Joanne and Elaine are like a couple of Mata Hari's."

"Why would Joanne and Elaine be mad at Harry?" G.R. inquired. "And who the fuck is Harry, anyway?"

"I'll tell ya' the whole scoop later, after we finish tonight's clever shenanigans," I replied.

"J.W., ya' make more fuckin' sense when ya' don't say a damned thing," Restuccio decided and admonished. "But what about the friggin' fireplace?"

"Tomorrow night, Joanne and Elaine are gonna' tell Gabe and Speed that a nice fire is the most romantic thing to a woman," I chuckled as the white box-truck passed Angelo's Store and entered Chew Road, which would eventually change to North Second Road. "When the jerks light some wood in the fireplace and open the flue, that will be *our* signal to start crashin' their end of harvest party."

"And that's when the rotting seafood odor will stink-up the freakin' room," Goose laughed. "Until then, the damned rotten smell will be trapped inside the chimney."

Goose took Second Road to Weymouth Road, made a right turn, and the box-truck slowly rumbled over the familiar bridge that arched across the busy *Atlantic City Expressway*. Right across from Arrow Paving Company was the north section of Gabe Gillette's father's expansive blueberry empire. No traffic was coming in either direction, so Goose dimmed his headlights and made a left onto gravel-surfaced New Creek Road. A thousand-feet down from Weymouth Road was a sandy trail that meandered behind a dense pine tree woods'. The path was the same dirt lane that Frankie Arena had taken the day *we* had witnessed Goose's dad handing the black attache case full of genuine hundred-dollar-bills to Mr. Gillette.

"Here's the most crucial part," I told the reckless driver. "Go down around a thousand-feet, and then turn this monster around. And whatever ya' do, don't get stuck in the soft sand."

"Big deal," Goose argued in his typical haughty, rebellious style. "I got twenty-two warm bodies standin' in the rear that could push this tin cock-sucker outa' a manure pit, or pull it outa' quicksand, or even slow-sand if they had to."

The truck stopped. The driver and I opened the cab's doors, and jumped-out onto the ground to unlatch the back panels. The twenty-two anxious marauders leaped-down to assume their designated "battle stations". Hoss and Little Joe removed the twelve-foot-long plank, lifted the lumber vertically, while standing next to the bank of an irrigation canal. And then the brothers plopped the wide, sturdy board onto the opposite bank of the canal. "We now have a good solid bridge to walk across, just like J.W. sketched it out," G.R. admiringly verbalized to Hoss and Little Joe.

Restuccio momentarily lit a flashlight to allow everyone to see the board's exact location. The distance from the other side of the canal to the Blues' clubhouse was around four-hundred-feet. Herc Juliano and Balls Giordano were the first ones who "walked the plank", with both St. Joe Reds gingerly carrying the tall wooden ladder across the makeshift canal bridge. Then, most everyone else crossed the recently constructed span, and those Reds that had gone to the other side positioned themselves around twenty-five feet apart for the entire distance from the canal to the clubhouse. Each member would be an integral part of the Reds' seafood bucket brigade.

Juice and Fabian possessed good equilibriums, so Goose and I had delegated Johnny and Sal to be stationed at either ends of the plank. G. R. instructed me to clamber-up onto the truck. The foul odor from the decaying fish, shrimp, and crabs was rather horrendous. I felt that my hands and my palms were rather *clammy*. 'Quite appropriate for the seafood brigade,' I thought. I could feel blood pulsating through the veins and arteries in my neck, as I nervously anticipated the initiation of our glorious prank.

"Okay J.W., you pathetic asshole, start unloadin' the *merchants dice*," G.R. commanded.

"I began with the fish, passing a bucket at a time to Goose, who handed each one to Juice, who carefully moved his feet to mid-plank and then handed the container to Fabian, and then the fish pail was passed to News and so on, all the way to the Blues' clubhouse. Herc Juliano and Balls Giordano had climbed the wooden ladder up to the clubhouse's roof. There, the trespassers quickly located the chimney, and slowly-but-surely, dropped all twenty-five pails of fish down the flue chute.

"Those Blues are' gonna' think that none of their dates washed their crotches," Goose theorized and laughed. "That place is gonna' smell like a Martian whorehouse. I can't wait until tomorrow night. Stinkin' pussy really turns me on."

"What's a Martian whorehouse smell like?" Juice asked. "Are you from Mars?"

"It smells just like rotten fish does, ya' stupid asshole! Ain't ya' never licked any unwashed pussy before, you Italian Dip-shit!" Goose un-chastely chastised.

"We oughta' call that chimney a *chum*ney," Juice joked in reference to chopped-up deep-sea fishing bait.

"Why call it a *chum*ney?" Goose responded. "I see. It's because our good friends Herc and Balls are up on the roof."

"Exactly," Juice laughed as Johnny and I both buckled-over from giddiness, stimulated by G.R.'s lack of mastery of basic English poly-semantic words.

"Juice, can your bird reach your ass?" Goose asked.

"Yeah," Johnny proudly bragged.

"Well, then go fuck yourself!" G.R. snorted.

After the bucket brigade had finished passing the twenty-five containers of dead ocean fish, the twenty-four of us started handling the fifty pails of smelly blue crabs, passing the containers the full four-hundred-feet distance to the clubhouse's chimney.

"I hope these here blue hard shells are gonna' give Gillette and Mortellite a bad case of the crabs," Goose laughed as the idiot joined our zany silliness. "I hope both those jerk-offs in the clubhouse get *crusty stations* all over their friggin' balls."

I was really getting exhausted, running back and forth inside the box truck, even though I had lots of similar experience unloading produce on the rear of the Pete's Market Special. Sweat was cascading down my back, so I took twenty-seconds to remove my cherished James Dean jacket, and then continued handing down buckets of rotten seafood to Goose.

Finally, at last, I got to the five-pound containers of shrimp, which was like the culminating point of our outrageous, mischievous surreptitious activity.

"These putrid shrimp samples are especially for Pee Wee Lucca and for Marty Gillette," I imaginatively said to Goose and Johnny. "Little shrimp deserve little shrimp."

"J.W.," Goose objected. "Just remember that this is what Joanne Berenato and any other pretty girl's cunts smell like if the bitches don't take baths when they're havin' their periods! So, just remember that the next time ya' wanta' play that son-of-a-bitchin' 'Red River Valley Rock' song on the Gem's jukebox, just think about what pussies smell like when they ain't been washed and scrubbed for a while."

Chapter Forty-One

"Marbles and Bowling Balls"

After the fifty pounds of shrimp had been dumped down the Blues clubhouse chimney, falling on top of the decomposing crabs and fish, Herc and Balls descended from the clubhouse's roof. The other Reds' members gathered-up all of the plastic buckets, leaving behind no telltale evidence. Then, the high ladder and the red pails were brought back to the canal. Everyone being elated with the night mission being accomplished, the "Red Raiders" crossed the temporary wide plank bridge. Hoss and Little Joe dragged the heavy board across the canal's surface to the box truck. The brawny brothers lifted the plank onto the truck to again be used the following evening.

The ecstatic twenty-two tricksters quietly hopped into the rear; Goose and I closed the back panels, and ten glorious minutes later, the Reds were victoriously crossing back into peach country. Soon, the merry contingent had returned to G.R.'s club basement drinking *Southern Comfort, Canadian Club, Jack Daniels,* high-octane combination *Jack Comforts,* and finally, *Budweise*r beer.

"Goose," I said while stirring a *Southern Comfort* on the rocks with my left index finger, "where are your parents? They're never around."

"They're too busy makin' money all around the country than to hang-around here and babysittin' me," the rich egotist somberly answered. "I think they're either in Chicago or Miami, don't know which. Pop's makin' some deals, and mom's taggin' along as usual, goin' shoppin' and countin' some newly collected cash."

"Goose, don't ya' miss them?" curiously asked Juice, who was eavesdropping on our conversation.

"Not really," G.R. replied, shrugging his shoulders. "My folks give me all I want when I ask for it. That's all that really matters to me. And I got fuckin' freedom; no debts; my own businesses, motorcycles, lots of money, a new car, and just about any goddamned thing I need. Aren't you guys envious?"

"Well, yes," I honestly confessed. "Ya' sure got the *Life of Riley,* even better than William Bendix does."

"Who the hell wants to live in a dumpy shanty that looks like that Chester A. Riley's shack on TV?" Goose opined, while referring to a popular '50s television show. "But J.W. and Johnny, let me tell you somethin' else. Ya' both got folks that really care about ya'. Ya' both better fuckin' always remember that," G.R. emphasized, his lips quivering and his eyes almost in tears. "My folks care about *things* and they give them to me. Your parents care about *you.* That's one big goddamned difference between you two guys and me. I'm the one that oughta' be fuckin' envious."

Goose cleared his throat and mustered-up the wherewithal and the courage to yell out, "Okay, guys. This is your last firewater drink, and most of you dumb fuck-heads aren't even Indians! Tomorrow's a big day, so I don't wanta' see ya' get too drunk tonight," the junior Mussolini bellowed as best as he could, his voice faltering, still a little shaky. "Everybody, remember to keep your dicks inside your pants tonight so none of ya' jerk-offs get too cocky."

I slept pretty well Saturday night. I first thought about the abundance of seafood filling the Blues' clubhouse chimney; about the upcoming Reds' crashing of the scheduled blueberry harvest party, and about vivacious Joanne Berenato being a recruited Reds' spy. Then, I journeyed off to slumberland.

The next morning, I woke-up at six. I ate a quick breakfast, which constituted a bowl of *Wheaties, Breakfast of Champions,* and drank a tall glass of orange juice. I had to drive up to Indian Mills to get a load of Jersey cantaloupes, twenty-five boxes of 'orange regulars', and twenty-five crates of green-inside Jenny Linds, a combo cantaloupe and honeydew, having a dome on top that resembled a woman's breast. Jenny Lind had been a world-famous 1800s Swedish opera star that the sweet Jersey cantaloupe had been named after.

After I completed my first major daily chore, I had to again drive the Pete's Market Special to Stella's Farm in Berlin to purchase another load of corn. I was glad not to have too much contact with my parents, fearing that I was so nervous I would spill the beans about the intensifying fruit war going on in and around Hammonton. I decided to turn into Mr. Bill's when I saw Fabian's Chevy Impala parked outside the popular ice cream joint.

"Hi Sal, whatcha' doin'?" I asked when my feet arrived at the customer counter.

"Buyin' a custard, and thinkin' about last night and tonight," Fabian replied. "J.W., I've never been involved with excitin' shit like this before. Never."

"Your Impala still looks as good as new after the Glassboro accident you had," I complimented. "Pop just bought a new white '61, and it'll be at Blatherwick's in a few days. Had to come special from Detroit."

"Can I buy ya' a custard?" Sal offered. "I gotta' tell ya' somethin' really big."

"Okay," I agreed. "When it's free, food always seems to taste better."

Fabian Midilli purchased two medium vanilla cones and we ambled-over near his Chevy Impala so that we could have some decent privacy. Sal told me that News had called him on the phone earlier that morning.

"What did Tommy say?" I asked as I licked the top of the velvety vanilla custard. "Did he tell ya' somethin' trivial about Mars, Jupiter, or Saturn?"

"You know how News is," Sal laughed. "He's gotta' preface everything until the fink gets to the meat of the conversation. He chews the fat first, ya' get what I mean?"

"Sure, I have that same faulty tendency," I confessed.

"Anyway, News began talkin' about a racial discrimination problem in Troy, Michigan," Fabian related. "At first, I was inclined to ignore it all."

"Do any Trojans live there in Troy, Michigan?" I joked. "Is that where they make rubbers for those quarter wall-dispensers that you see inside all the Men's Rooms?"

"J.W., this is serious stuff I'm tellin' ya'," Fabian cautioned, "so just please listen. Receive and don't send, comprende amigo."

I consented to honor Fabian's request. The messenger informed me that News was concerned about the Troy, Michigan story, because the body of a Winnebago Indian, George V. Nash, was not allowed burial in a Troy cemetery.

"Why?" I innocently asked.

"Because the guy was not white," Sal answered. "This guy George V. Nash was a *World War I* veteran who served his country with honor, and then *he* had to be buried in Pontiac, Michigan instead of in Troy, Michigan, where he wanted to rest in peace."

"Well, Sal, that seems right and proper because Pontiac was an Indian chief up around the Michigan peninsula," I casually remarked, "and this guy George V. Nash was an Indian, too. If ya' ever notice, the emblem for a Pontiac automobile is an Indian chief."

"J.W.," Fabian breathed deeply, showing his exasperation, "please let me finish. News was usin' the case of racial prejudice to get to his real topic. Tommy had learned from Jives, who is a neighbor of Tyrone Davis, that…"

"That Tyrone wants *me* back as the Marvelons' manager?" I gleefully joked.

"Damn it, will ya' just shut the hell up and listen!" Sal vehemently admonished. "What a yo-yo you are, sometimes! Pardon me. Most of the damned time!"

"Okay," I assented, while being a trifle disappointed that I was still no longer the Marvelons' Caucasian manager.

"Do ya' remember Crystal Davis, Tyrone's younger sister?" Fabian rhetorically asked. "Well, she's pregnant; missed her period by three weeks, and she's now claimin' that Goose Restuccio is the daddy of a little chocolate *Hershey* bar."

I nearly choked on my vanilla cone with some of its crust particles getting stuck in my throat. I had to cough three times to dislodge the flaked-off fragments, and spit them into the napkin I had been holding under the base of my cone. "This isn't gonna' flush too good down G.R.'s toilet," I commented. "He'll be steamed more than those shrimp and crabs we dumped down the Blues' clubhouse chimney last night."

"Jives, News, and I all think that you're the best one to break the bad news to Goose," Fabian suggested. "You can talk and relate better with him than the rest of us can."

"Okay, Sal, thanks for handin' me the lit sizzlin' dynamite stick," I commented. "I'll talk to G.R. sometime after tonight's big raid. And if ya' find-out any more raunchy *good news* in the meantime, like the world has ended, do me a super large favor, and keep it all to yourself."

* * * * * * * * * * * * *

The blueberry harvest crash was slated to go-off at precisely nine o'clock Sunday night. By then, Elaine and Joanne would have surely been picked-up by Speed Mortellite and Gabe Gillette at the Gem, and be socializing with bad company Hammonton High graduates at the Weymouth Road clubhouse shindig. Goose again picked me up at seven-thirty in his newly-waxed red Thunderbird.

"Did ya' take your three aspirins again?" the persistent pest asked. "*Pretention* is always better than *cure,*" the grammar dunce cited, attempting to impress me with his special vernacular.

"Tell that one to a smoked ham," I laughed.

"Sometimes, I don't know what the fuck you're talkin' about," G.R. admitted with a forced smile. "All I know is that it's always some kind of corny bullshit, if *I don't* know *egg-act-ly* what the hell ya' mean," the neurotic driver insisted as he gently pulled out of Pete's Farm Market's driveway, heading west onto the Pike.

"Goose, how will Speed Mortellite and Gabe Gillette be able to dance with Elaine and Joanne?" I asked. "Do Speed and Gabe still have their *casts* on? It's a little late for the dolts to star in the high school play, in that they've both already graduated from Hammonton High. Ya' only need one cast for a play, ya' know."

"I heard that *that* bastard Speed Mortellite got his cast off his arm yesterday," Restuccio informed, "and that annoyin' prick Gabe is off his crutches, and now has to walk with a cane."

"That's good," I concluded, "because if Joanne has to get-away from him in a hurry, she'll be able to easily escape. because Gillette is somewhat handicapped, and can't run too fast."

"Ya' always think of the dumbest, most stupid shit!" Goose related. "Just learn to relax. Ya' took your aspirins today, right? Everything's gonna' be cool."

"Er, Goose, there's something I wanta' tell ya. I was…"

"Does it involve tonight's big Reds' crash?" G.R. asked. "If it doesn't, then tell me later. I only wanta' think about bustin' the Blues chops tonight, and nothin' else right now. You *Sob-bee.* Sorry, but that's all the fuckin' Spanish I know!"

The driver turned-up the volume on the car radio, and WIBG AM was spinning "Everybody's Somebody's Fool" by Connie Francis, so immediately, that bouncy tune made me contemplate the integrity of my opposing relationships with weird Goose Restuccio and with charming Joanne Berenato.

Just like the night before, twenty-two Reds were waiting in the driveway. Their seven cars were parked over near a well-maintained yew hedge. We all marched inside "the Mafia Palace" to review final instructions and assignments. I could tell that all twenty-four guys were enthusiastic about taking it to the Blues inside *their* territory, and invading the enemy gang directly on *their* home court.

"Okay, men, listen up!" Goose hollered like an austere Marine drill sergeant at Parris Island. "Hoss and Little Joe, did ya' cut the second plank the way I told ya'?"

"Affirmative!" Hoss boomed back. "Any person over fifty-pounds will crack that baby in two."

Everyone who was present inside the club basement laughed in anticipation of the board splitting with a few Blues' a*board.*

"Where are the two-hundred bowlin' balls?" Juice analytically asked. "I'm asking you troops this, even though your dirty minds are always in the gutter?"

"They're in the damned dump truck that Frankie and Joey are takin' to Weymouth Road," G.R. reported. "The guys are gonna' turn-around at *Nude* Creek Road around ten of nine, and wait in the dark there. Then, when *they* see us pull-out from the farm with all you guys stashed inside the back of the white box-truck, they'll let us go by, and then take the dump truck to the *Atlantic City Expressway* overpass. Fingers and Zucchini will sit in the dump truck on top of the bridge, until the Blues come after us in their expensive cars."

"What if the Blues show-up before the white truck does at New Creek and Weymouth Road?" very astute and erudite News Tomasello questioned.

"That will never happen," I answered stepping forward. "The Blues are gonna' be in turmoil tryin' to get organized. The victims won't know what to do. They'll be in shock for a couple of minutes, just like people are after bein' in major car accidents. It'll take 'em at least three-minutes to figure-out what actually happened, and then decide to chase after us."

"Okay, men," Goose finished. "We hit the friggin' road in fifteen-minutes. Get all the stuff we need loaded aboard the damned box-truck. If anybody's gotta' drain their radiators or take a healthy shit, then do it now."

At eight-fifteen, just before full dusk, the white truck with Goose and me in the cab, and with twenty-two courageous Reds in the rear compartment, were traveling on the familiar route: passing Angelo's Store and veering onto Chew Road, which then becomes North Second Road, officially leaving Rosedale and entering Hammonton. I dared not bring-up the sensitive subject of Crystal Davis's announced pregnancy, so I discussed some specifics of the night's maneuvers with the volatile-tempered driver.

"Er, Goose, I just thought of somethin'," I prefaced. "How are you, Juice, News, Fabian, and me gonna' be able to get upstairs to the loft if the party's goin' on downstairs?"

"Are ya' tryin' to test my *dig-nitty* or somethin'?" the volatile driver objected. "I solved that simple problem when I spoke with Herc and Balls last night after I took you home," G.R. disclosed. "There's a trap door, a hatch up on the roof near the chimney. We use the same tall ladder tonight; get up on the roof; open the hatch, and slide into the loft where we can spy on the party," G.R. described. "J.W., I just thought ya' left that point out of your presentation for me to fill in. And Herc and Balls tested the hatch last night while up on the roof, and there's no lock on it."

"Okay, but how do we escape?" I stammered, showing a degree of self-doubt in my own plan that everyone else had wholeheartedly endorsed.

"Herc and Balls are the lookouts, just like ya' told us in the club basement," Goose related. "The St. Joe boys move the ladder from the chimney side to the hay loft side. That way we got seven less rungs to climb down. J.W., why are ya' bustin' my balls askin' this simple-ass stuff we've already figured-out?"

"You should join the Army," I commended. "You could be a court-martialed general within a year."

"Yeah," Goose agreed. "I'll be General Nuisance. But J.W., the shit will start hittin' the fan when Joanne and Elaine convince Gabe and

Speed to light some wood in the fireplace to warm-out, even though it's only August."

"For romantic purposes," I jealously said and half-smiled. "Then, the Blues will probably have to open the clubhouse windows, not only because of the hot temperature, but because of the smell when the fire warms up the fish, crabs, and shrimp that have been stuffed down the stone chimney."

The box-truck stopped at the intersection of Second Road and Weymouth Road, made the right turn, and passed over the crowded *Atlantic City Expressway*. Soon, we were once again at New Creek Road, and in five-minutes, the truck transport was stationed exactly where it had been the night before, hidden in the pine woods, and facing north on the sandy road, in order to facilitate a quick escape.

G.R. opened the back panels, and our twenty-two confederates slowly and quietly leaped-down to ground level. Hoss and Little Joe lowered the plank we had used the night before, and next placed the improvised bridge exactly where the sturdy board had previously been put over the canal, and the brothers laid down the second "cut plank" five feet away from the first portable bridge, on the "north side".

Herc Juliano and Balls Giordano again successfully carried the wooden ladder across the wide, strong plank, and Juice, News, Fabian and Goose followed the St. Joe commandos across the plank, through the newly-planted blueberry field, their path heading straight toward the Blues' isolated clubhouse. Hoss and Little Joe did the tightrope act across the canal, each carrying a full five-gallon metal gasoline can. I was the last of the nine 'pirates' to "walk the plank".

"Good luck!" Frankie Arena told me before I skipped over the board. "Don't forget to cream farty-Marty."

I again remembered something that my hero Quinn had told Bo Jalonec in Atlantic City before the *Labor Day* big blueberry farm drag race, when Bo had stated the same words that Jives had just spoken. "Jives," I turned and spoke as calmly as I could. "When you're *good,* ya' don't need any damned *luck!"*

Hoss and Little Joe had been instructed by Goose to stop and stay with the ten gallons of combustible fuel, midway between the canal and the clubhouse. "You guys do what ya' were told," Rostuccio reminded the small, overzealous platoon.

Shouting, hooting, raucous merrymaking, and loud music could be heard emanating from the Blues' secluded clubhouse. The remaining seven of us stealthily approached our principal objective. Herc and Balls positioned the tall wooden ladder next to the chimney. The smell of seafood was hardly detectable, since it was all confined within the high, stone, vertical funnel.

Juice, News, Goose, Fabian, and I ascended the ladder's rungs onto the roof. The hatch was carefully opened, and one by one, we all slid through the opening, down into the loft, which overlooked the gala festivities going on below.

Most of the Blues were drinking hard whiskey, and some were imbibing *Pabst Blue Ribbon* beer, and a few others were sampling a potent combination of both beverages that Ox Narducci and Sonny Perone always called "boilermakers". I checked my watch, and it read five-minutes to nine.

"In five minutes, Joanne and Elaine are gonna' ask Gabe and Speed to light some logs in the fireplace," I whispered to Juice.

"Then, that's our signal to go into action," Johnny answered.

"Shhhh!" Goose warned and whispered. "Not a fuckin' word. Just stay low, ya' hear!" our commander very quietly advised and gestured with his hands as Fats Domino's fabulous "Blueberry Hill" finished playing below.

A slow dance number next started-up on the phonograph. I immediately recognized the melody because the arrangement was my favorite slow song, "A Thousand Stars in the Sky", sung by Kathy Young with the Innocents. Jealousy surged through my soul and body when my eyes witnessed Gabe Gillette and Joanne dancing slowly and closely to the romantic lyrics. I had to control myself from jumping down from the loft onto the floor and smashing the half-crippled jerk directly in the snout with a solid right-cross. Even though Gillette had to dance holding a cane in one hand, I still almost went ballistic right through the clubhouse's roof, where I had just recently entered the loft. My greatest fantasy was to be doing the exact same waltz with Joanne, to the exact same song, as Gillette was dancing to with her, right there and then.

It seemed like an eternity of emotional suffering for me until the formerly endearing ballad finally ended. The girls then asked Gillette and Mortellite to light a romantic fire "for atmosphere", and the two creeps pretended to be gentlemen and accommodated their dates' wishes. Everything was normal for about three-minutes, until the smoke had trouble rising up the clogged chimney, and fumes began escaping from the hearth, billowing-up to the wooden-beamed ceiling, and then saturating the clubhouse. Windows were opened on all walls because of the intense heat being released, and soon, an unpleasant odor was detected, which a minute later, smelled like thousands of dead clams and oysters, rotting on a beach. My eyes were tearing-up in the loft from the extreme malodor.

"Now!" Goose yelled.

The five of us stood-up and threw opened bags of marbles and ball bearings onto the wood-planked floor below. At least a thousand small circular objects were bouncing and scattering, thrown from twenty opened pocket bags. Every time a Blue would try to walk or move, that gang member would wind-up flipping up into the air, and then landing on the seat of his blue jeans.

"Up there! They're up there!" Gabe Gillette screamed like a crazed banshee, pointing-up to the hayloft.

The five brave crusaders opened the loft's storage door, climbed-down the reliable ladder, and rejoined Herc and Balls. Pandemonium reigned supreme inside the clubhouse, and the horrible stench of the seafood combination rotting and burning inside the stone chimney was enough to make everyone *outside* the converted barn feel like incessantly puking.

"Quick, let's get the fuck outa' here!" Goose yelled. "I ain't got no clean underwear at home, in case I have a damned accident!"

The seven of us sprinted in the direction of the canal, leaving the ladder behind for the Blues to have as an official souvenir of *our* splendid expedition. Winded, we stopped after running at full speed, halting where Hoss and Little Joe had been stationed, midway between the clubhouse and the canal. Ten Blues, led by Hammonton High linemen Butch Lanza and Ox Narducci, came hustling toward us, and when the livid pursuers were about fifty-feet away, Goose yelled "Now!"

Hoss and Little Joe lit the ten-gallons of gasoline the brothers had poured into a hundred-foot-long furrow, which had been dug in the ground with the farm boots the boys were wearing. The gas ignited, sending a five-foot-high fence of raging fire bursting into the air, temporarily scaring the devil out of the ten nasty, husky incensed predators.

The nine of us then dashed as fast as we could to the canal, and in thirty thrilling seconds, singularly took four strides each on the pliable plank, to successfully span the stagnant water. The fire in the furrow had died-down, and the ten irate, mean-spirited Blues shouted like barbarian warlords as the maniacs tripped and scuttled onward in our direction.

Hoss and Little Joe grabbed the first plank on the box-truck side of the canal, and then tugged the heavy board out of the water. The brothers threw the lumber onto the north-side bank, leaving the Blues with a second souvenir of *our* illustrious trespassing,

The remaining twenty Reds frantically hopped into the rear of the truck. Goose fired-up the engine and drove fifty-feet down the sandy road. I hopped-out of the cab to close the back panels, but before I did,

I gave all the rear passengers a good view of Ox Narducci, followed by Butch Lanza and several other Blues, running onto the second, weaker, cut board, that was spanning the canal. The first five pursuers tumbled into the canal when the cut plank snapped from their weight, with the enemy Blues being vastly outsmarted by the Reds' superior, brilliant strategy.

Laughter abounded inside the truck's rear compartment as I closed and latched the panels. I rejoined an extremely jubilant Goose Restuccio inside the cab.

"Brains usually wins-out over brawn every time," I panted, quoting a familiar maxim to the especially-jovial driver.

"I had a backup plan ready just in case yours failed," Goose giggled as the Sicilian barbarian made the left off of the dirt trail, onto the dull, orange-color gravel of New Creek Road.

"My plan only called for nine members," I realized and related, "but you had all twenty-four Reds involved. Why? For gang spirit?"

"Well yeah, sorta'," Goose admitted. "But I wanted all two dozen of us there in case somethin' major went wrong. Then, instead of us havin' the big fuckin' trick backfire, I figured we coulda' had a big fuckin' gang fight with the two sides bein' even. As it turned-out, J.W., we didn't need the big fuckin' gang fight."

"Wow!" I exclaimed. "Goose, you're smarter than the average John Q. Public. We coulda' got killed fightin' the infuriated Blues nine on twenty-four!"

The box-truck turned right onto seldom night-traveled Weymouth Road. Goose stopped and waited for headlights to become visible speeding around a curve. When four sets of high beams appeared close together coming from behind, G.R. put the gearshift into first and quickly popped the clutch. The white truck jerked forward toward the Weymouth Road overpass of the newly-constructed *Atlantic City Expressway*.

Waiting near the crest of the overpass were two junior Mafia men sitting inside an enormous dump truck, which left just enough room for the white box-truck to squeeze by. Soon, after our vehicle had passed, G.R. applied the brakes. I again exited the cab, jumped-out, and then opened the back panels.

As the four speeding cars approached the dark country overpass's incline, Frankie Fingers hydraulic lift raised the tail section. The dump truck's back chute flipped-open, and suddenly, two-hundred Egg Harbor Lanes' bowling balls dropped-out onto the asphalt, and then rolled down the hill into the oncoming Weymouth Road pursuers.

When the lead car jammed on its brakes, a terrible chain-reaction collision occurred. Four Blues' cars had been wrecked-up at the base of the *Expressway* incline.

"Those Blues are really accident prone," I stated to Restuccio.

"If any of 'em die," Goose answered with a wink, "it's gonna' be *your* damned fault."

The Reds hung-around for a minute until all twelve occupants climbed-out of the dented-up, badly damaged autos, and staggered-around Weymouth Road in a bewildered state, trying to clear-away their drunken cobwebs, while tripping over errant bowling balls. Then, Goose and I closed and locked the back panels, and the Reds' entourage victoriously returned to Goose's club basement to celebrate our most-recent triumphant battle in the great teen fruit war.

Chapter Forty-Two

"The War Council"

Word had spread like wildfire all over Hammonton and vicinity about a major traffic accident involving drunken teenagers on Weymouth Road. Fortunately, none of the Blues involved in the collisions had been seriously injured. The local barber and beauty shop rumor mills circulated gossip that all of the blueberry boys were intoxicated, so according to the mechanics of local politics and law enforcement, no major charges would be pressed against anyone, since no one had been injured, maimed, or killed. 'Just like in algebra and trigonometry,' I thought, 'factors cancel each other out. Mr. Sipley's absolutely right. Life is often a lot like advanced mathematics,' I concluded.

Monday morning, Pop had been down the Pike to Moe's Market near Fairview Avenue to purchase some lunchmeat and sliced cheese, and dad had heard some scuttlebutt about antagonism going on between the peach and blueberry boys. Naturally, my father was concerned about the possibility of my involvement in what he described as "the great teen fruit war".

"J.W., Mr. Sipley called yesterday and gave me a very favorable progress report on you," Dad diplomatically began his interrogation in a complimentary fashion. "Your tutor says you're rapidly becomin' an expert in the subject."

"Thanks, Dad," I modestly replied. "I could definitely use all of the encouragement I can get."

"Now, Son," Pop continued, shifting into a less praising mode. "There's talk in town of some kind of crazy fruit war goin' on between the blueberry kids from Hammonton High and some of the peach kids from Edgewood and St. Joe. Are you involved in it? Do ya' know anything about it?"

I knew that when Dad addressed me as "Son" instead of "J.W.", then my parent was more in a punishment mood than in a commendation one. "Well, Pop," I answered. "My closest friends are Goose Restuccio, Sal Midilli, and Jives Arena. None of 'em or their dads have anything to do with growin' peaches or blueberries."

"Well, what about that News Tomasello?" Dad challenged. "His father has a peach farm over on Spring Road. We've bought some softs and rejects from that farm."

"You're right, Dad. News' does work really hard and long hours in his Pop's peach orchards," I agreed. "But out of all my friends, I think he's the most stable. Don't you?"

"Well, you're right there, I guess," Dad agreed. "He's a fine boy, and very knowledgeable about world events, I must say. But J.W., those red *club* jackets you fellas' are wearin'. They aren't gang jackets, are they?"

"No, Pop. We're just honorin' the memory of James Dean, that's all. What a tragic loss!"

"Okay, Son. But remember the main reason we moved outa' Levittown was because of you belongin' to the Diablos, and all the trouble that was goin' on with the Kamikazes. Enough said!" my father tersely finished.

Pop assigned me a special task. I had to buzz over to Swedesboro in the Pete's Market Special to pick-up a mixed load of green vegetables at a farm to transport back to Elm.

I made two phone calls before departing for Swedesboro. The first was to Goose, and the second was to News. I arranged to meet Goose at twelve-thirty at his place, and News at one p.m. at Mr. Bill's, under the pretense that I only had a half-hour to spend with each because I was on a "work order schedule" from Pop. I told my parents I was going to eat lunch on the road, so not to worry since my presence would be about an hour longer away from the market than normally expected.

I arrived at Goose's estate at twelve-twenty-five. Restuccio seemed in a congenial frame of mind, so I decided to amass sufficient courage and break the bad news to him.

"Er, Goose," I prefaced after our friendly salutations. "Do ya' remember that black girl Crystal Davis?"

"Yeah, vaguely. Did she get killed in an automobile accident or get *sift-less* or *mal-air-ia,* or some stupid-assed sex disease like that? That's what happens to most shines and coons, ya' know."

"No, Goose, she didn't," I firmly responded. "Do ya' recall I once broke it to ya' that the Blues made ya' have sex with her in the blueberry field, right before the donkey parade and the pig trough adventures at DiGiacomo's Farm?"

"Well, J.W., I remember the pig thing a little bit, and I partially remember the shit-eatin' donkey *fee-ass-co.* And I do remember ya' tellin' me about the nigger bitch and me goin' full tilt," Goose paused for a moment. "But I thought maybe you was makin' that part up to *em-bell-wish* the story, and make the *fix-shin* all seem bigger and uglier than it really was."

"No, Goose," I disagreed. "You and Crystal Davis did have sex, but it was forced sex, or else the Blues would've murdered you, her, and me. I think ya' really did it to protect me, at least in your subconscious mind," I skillfully suggested. "Then, I think we were both drugged-up for the donkeys and the pigs' part of the disgrace at DiGiacomo's. You were a hero that day!"

"Well, alright," G.R. answered. "Let's say that me and the nigger bitch did have sex like ya' say we did. That's not the first time I've ever done it with a coon," Restuccio boasted. "I mean, I've been in the sack with a few good-lookin', clean, colored prostitutes in Atlantic City at that cool expensive whorehouse I had been tellin' ya' about."

"Well, Goose, I really don't know the best way to break it to ya'," I stammered, "but Crystal Davis is a month pregnant, and she's claimin' that *you* are the father."

"What the fuck is that you're sayin'!" the mercurial-tempered Edgewood graduate ranted. "I ain't admittin' to any bullshit like that. This is all a goddamned, lowdown scam for her to get *ex-tour-shin* money outa' me, and I ain't fallin' for it. No way, Jose."

I next told Goose that Crystal Davis might have had sex with other white guys, and if the baby is mixed, or on the white side, a judge might rule in her favor, because Tyrone's sister had accused G.R. of being the biological father.

"J.W., what will *you* fuckin' say at the trial?" Goose demanded to know. "Will ya' lie for me and say it never happened? If ya' don't, you'll get the Blues in trouble by squealin' on them, and get all the Reds in trouble for their part in the fruit war," G.R. angrily yelled in my face while jabbing his index finger deep into my chest. "All of that legal bullshit with expensive lawyers and judges will happen, just because *you'll* want to tell the truth to some fuckin' *prostitutor* to protect an ugly pregnant nigger bitch! You're a real stupid fuck, J.W., ya' know that! Only stupid assholes like you tell the truth to judges, cops, and priests!"

"I just thought I'd tell ya' the facts, that's all," I replied, nearly crying from the dire consequences G.R. had said would result if I had to testify in court against him.

Goose then went on a tirade about how the Blues probably paid Crystal Davis fifty-dollars to pretend she had been flagrantly raped, and next, how *he* had been set-up to be like the Holy Ghost making the Virgin Mary pregnant, and how the Blues were "playing God".

I finally realized that when Goose became angry, Restuccio also became hostile, vindictive, accusatory, and irrational. And the insulted kid habitually transferred blame to others to protect his frail, underdeveloped conscience from feeling guilt, shame, or remorse.

"Okay, let's say you, me and Crystal were all set up by the Blues," I agreed. "The girl's still pregnant, and if the baby is white or half-white," I stressed under stress, "you're the one that's fryin' in the pan. And if Crystal Davis accuses *you* in a court in Trenton or Camden, or some other place far away from Hammonton or Winslow Township," I continued my description, "then there's a good chance you'll be found guilty the way the Civil Rights' movement is gainin' strength all across the country."

"Okay, J.W., get the word to Frankie Jives that I'm willin' to pay for an abortion. Also, tell that goofball Winslow neighbor that I know the girl's a damned whore, and has had sex at least a hundred and fifty times with guys of all colors."

"That's a possible *defense* solution," I concurred. "And I promise that News, Juice, or me will tell Frankie to give *that* option to Crystal."

"I told ya' many times when you' was pissing-around with those fuckin' Marvelons, you needed to stay away from fuckin' niggers. I shoulda' followed my own goddamned advice."

"Goose, Northern Africa isn't that far away from Sicily," I indicated, "just across the Mediterranean Sea. It's a good chance that you and me have some black blood flowin' in our Sicilian veins, because you're dark-skinned to prove my point."

"Get the fuck outa' here before I cut your dick off, plant your Oscar Mayer wiener up your' freakin' asshole, and then sew it inside to *funk-shin* as a goddamned cork!" the incensed fanatic screamed.

When I left "the dago palace" and slowly ambled-over to the blue truck, Goose came to the back kitchen door and boisterously and insanely yelled, "I ain't gonna' be fuckin' set-up for a pregnant bitch like that stupid-assed *Holy Ghoul* was!"

I drove the mile to Mr. Bill's on schedule to confer with News under what I hoped to be more pleasant and amicable circumstances than those that had existed at my bizarre encounter with G.R. 'It's a good thing I swallowed-down those three aspirins before I visited Goose,' I thought. 'At least *he* was right about one thing.'

News Tomasello was faithfully waiting for me at Mr. Bill's. I parked the Pete's Market Special next to his red and white Fairlane. We stepped inside the restaurant part of the establishment to sit and talk over lunch. After ordering hamburgers and *Pepsi's*, I wanted to get down to business, but first I had to listen to Tommy tell me all about current events.

"Ya' know J.W.," T.T. began his familiar Homeric catalog. "The friggin' Russians just sentenced Francis Gary Powers to ten-years in prison. I think they're lookin' for trouble."

"Francis Gary Powers, the U-2 spy pilot?" I asked, my mind still being in a heavy fog over my intense verbal interaction with Goose Restuccio.

"Yeah," Tommy verified. "Powers was the U.S. spy pilot shot-down by a missile while flyin' over Russia."

"I think Nixon will straighten-out Khrushchev when he becomes President," I predicted. "I don't think Kennedy is *that* experienced. The Russians will think J.F.K.'s still wet behind the ears, and then try somethin' major. Anyway, I can relate to Francis Gary Powers because I seem to get shot-down all the time. In fact, I feel *power*less!"

"That's what I think, too, about myself," Tommy commiserated. "We're alike in many ways, ya' know!"

"News, I gotta' change the subject, but not the theme. I was just *shot down* by Goose at his place."

"Did ya' tell him about Crystal Davis?" Tommy inquired.

"Yeah, and it wasn't too peachy-keen either,"

After I reviewed all that had transpired at Ronald Restuccio's mansion, News agreed to discuss the matter with Frankie Arena about Goose's being willing to pay for Jive's neighbor's abortion. Meanwhile, I had my own emotional problems.

"News, do ya' know what ever happened to Joanne last night?" I caringly asked. "I mean, I didn't even think of what might've happened to her after *our* excitin' escape from Blueberryville."

News began parody-singing the lyrics to his favorite Fats Domino song. "I found my thrill, at Blue Berry Ville."

"That's not funny," I angrily yelled, getting the attention of several other tables of lunch patrons at Mr. Bill's. "Are ya' referring to Crystal and Goose, to Joanne and me, or to all of *us* by your singin' of those coincidental lyrics?"

"Cool it, J.W.," News advised. "Joanne's okay. I got the lowdown from Juice, and also from Herc Juliano."

"Well then, what happened *Dummkoff?"* I asked, demanding more salient information. "She's my girl, and I'm the last to know. You coulda' had the courtesy of callin' me. You are *News,* aren't you?"

I soon learned from Tommy T. that the Blues didn't return to the clubhouse, because five of the gorillas had fallen into the canal when the cut board broke, and the rest of the Simians had been delayed at the *Expressway* surprise bowling ball accident scene. A major police investigation ensued, but after the cops learned that the Blues were involved, and that no one had been seriously hurt or killed, and that the influential Blues were all drunk, then all major charges were quickly and conveniently reduced to minor infractions.

"Elaine Hill intelligently called the Gem from the clubhouse," News related, "and Esther Phyllis and Nanette Banks were inside the joint havin' snacks and sundaes. The two friends drove-out to the stench-laden clubhouse, picked-up Joanne and Elaine, and then took the stranded girls back unscathed to the Gem at about eleven," Tommy reported. "Joanne was then reunited with Herc Juliano, who obediently drove your girl home as pre-planned. What an unbelievable night!" T.T. assessed and shared.

"Thanks for sharing the good news," I said in a simmered-down tone. "I felt bad that I thought about everything in the raid except Joanne and Elaine's safety, after the historic Reds' clubhouse 'crash' had occurred. I coulda' kicked myself for not thinkin' of her, and only worryin' about the Reds and me survivin' the perilous raid."

"Well, J.W.," News orally summarized. "If it's any consolation to ya', Joanne told Herc that the clubhouse siege was the most excitin' thing that ever happened to her in her dull, parent-dominated life. I believe she likes ya' more than ever now," Tommy communicated, grinning like a satisfied shark. "She likes the way ya' don't accept the reality *she's* forced to live in."

"Thanks, News," I replied. "And I liked what ya' told me so much that I'll gladly pick-up today's tab."

I drove to Swedesboro, loaded the ordered green vegetables at the designated time and place, and then returned to Elm to unload; to quietly ponder some more thoughts about the classic blueberry farm attack, and to swallow-down more aspirins. After my exhaustive physical labor and emotional duress passed, I stepped into the house to take a much-needed shower. After dressing, the living room phone rang. Pop was in the house, picked the receiver out of the cradle, and answered the call.

"J.W!" Dad called upstairs. "Get the phone. Some kid named Gabe Gillette wants to speak with you."

I couldn't believe my ears. Why would a rich, powerful kid like that lucky blueberry heir ever desire to say "hello" to me? I rushed downstairs to see exactly what my wealthy adversary had to say. However, I didn't want Pop to catch-on to my important involvement in the great fruit war.

"Hello," I tentatively answered.

"J.W., I'm gonna' make this short and sweet, a gentleman's agreement, ya' understand?" Gillette began his extraordinary rhetoric.

"Sure, go ahead, shoot," I replied, while doubting the veracity of every word the caller was speaking.

"Here's the real deal," Gabe proceeded with his tough-talk monologue. "The Blues wanta' have a rumble with you guys to settle things once and for all. Speed, Butch, Ox, and me wanta' have a meetin' with you, Goose Restuccio, News Tomasello, and Hoss Gregorio. We think you four guys are the key Reds that's been given' us a ton of crap lately. Where and when can we meet to arrange a decisive rumble?"

"Er, Royale Crown and the Gem are on the Blues' side of town," I mentioned, stalling for time while assiduously thinking about a neutral rendezvous location. "And Joanne's Luncheonette, Bruni's Pizza, and Mr. Bill's are on the Reds' side of town. What about Toni's Custard on *Route 54* near Folsom?" I suggested.

"That's fine with us," Gillette indicated. "What time?"

"Eight tonight," I returned.

"Be there or be queer. I wanna' see your face in the place!" Gillette finished. Click.

I hung-up the phone, a little overwhelmed and puzzled by the unexpected call from *my* wealthy arch-enemy. Dad was hanging in the kitchen, waiting for me to finish speaking with Gillette.

"J.W., that Gillette boy; doesn't his father have a big blueberry farm outside of town?"

"Er, yes," I uncomfortably answered.

"What's a rich kid like that want with someone like you?" Pop suspiciously asked.

"He wants to know if Pete's Market wants to buy any blueberries next year," I imaginatively contrived and fibbed. "The kid is in charge of the farm's wholesale and retail department, and Gabriel wants to know if we're interested in doin' business with 'em. I said I'd meet him tonight at Toni's Custard, and we'd talk all about it."

"Nice of him to call," Pop conceded, changing his tone. "Tell him tonight that we're definitely interested in a good blueberry source for next summer."

After Dad stepped outside to the farm market, I immediately phoned Goose, News, and Hoss about the urgent eight p.m. war council powwow at Toni' Custard. All three were motivated by hate and curiosity, and were also anxious to see what would result during and after the emergency "war council meeting". G.R. agreed to pick us up around seven-thirty to honor our appointment with our formidable enemy's executive committee.

I entered the back of Goose's four-seater Thunderbird and sat next to News. My mind recollected that I had been to one other "war council meeting" at the Feed Bag back in Levittown, right before the big quarry fight between Quinn and Cummings, so I did have a frame of reference with which to equate *that* 1959 April night's meeting with the slated August 1960 session at Toni's Custard.

"Let J.W. and me do all the talkin'," G.R. recommended. "Too many *chiefs* spoil the broth. And J.W.," Restuccio proceeded. "Don't fuck-up too bad, or I'll have to take ya' to a Mafia butcher in South 'Philly to give your dick and balls plastic surgery, and make them into a workable cunt."

"Why would I want to have a vagina?" I argued.

"You'll have no freakin' choice in the goddamned matter," Goose sneered. "And anyway, if ya' had a friggin' pussy, ya' could screw-around all ya' want!"

The other two guys in the T-Bird laughed, so I went along with Goose's absurd bravado charade. I knew that G.R. was trying to loosen me up before the impending negotiations' session, in spite of the fact that I had again consumed three aspirins as prescribed by Dr. Restuccio in order to alleviate all confrontational possibilities with the dastardly Hammonton Blues.

Goose turned-off the Pike before the *206'* light onto Bellevue Avenue, which also was the end of *Route 54*. We virtually crawled through congested downtown Hammonton, and G.R. honked his horn and we all waved at some familiar cruisers, casually content on motoring around the all-too-familiar circuit. After crossing the railroad tracks, the red Thunderbird was on Twelfth Street, which like Bellevue Avenue, also magically co-existed as *Route 54*.

"What do the Blues actually want?" Hoss asked.

"I believe they're gonna' request a rumble between the two gangs," I replied. "I just feel it comin' on."

"Ya' can't trust those dirty bastards as far as ya' can shit a turd out of your dick while constipated," Goose warned. "I'll bet those skunks have somethin' rotten up their dirty blue sleeves."

"Let's see what materializes," I recommended. "But if ya' want my honest opinion, I smell an enormous rat in the woodpile."

"Yeah," Goose verified. "There's somethin' rotten in *Hall mark*, I betcha'."

News looked at me, and we both snickered at Goose's malaprop, because we had heard the prevaricator say many other verbal errors like "neon (nylon) stockings," "Pearl Island," "polo bears" and "polar shirts" many times before. Hoss Gregorio looked back at us. The tough Red was unaware that 'infallible Goose' had violated any grammatical or logical communication rules.

The red Thunderbird arrived at ten of eight at Toni's Custard, and the four ambitious warriors got-out to stretch our legs. Soon, a royal blue Cadillac Fleetwood entered the parking area. Gabe Gillette, Ox Narducci, Speed Mortellite, and Butch Lanza exited and haughtily walked-over to Goose's T-Bird.

Mr. Ed Martinelli, the alert proprietor of Toni's Custard, was staring-out at us from his service counter, and if a brawl were to suddenly erupt, the owner would surely get on the hotline to notify the state police.

"You still need a cane?" I cleverly asked Gabe Gillette, comparable to me making the first strategic move in a chess match.

"Yeah, the doctor says it'll be another week until I can walk normal, Now, I wanta' cut-out the small talk and get some facts straight, point blank. The Blues want a rumble. It's now *your* privilege to give us the time and place."

"Well, Gabe," I countered. "Don't ya' think the Blues oughta' rumble with the Reds when all your guys are a hundred percent?" I suggested. "I mean, *you* got a busted leg; Speed has a broken arm that ain't all healed yet, and I understand a few of your bigger guys got messed-up a bit in a strange auto accident on Weymouth Road out near the *Expressway*."

"Ya' do have a valid point there," Gillette admitted, and the other three Blues nodded their heads in agreement. "Tell me, J.W. What else do ya' have in mind to settle the issue besides a rumble?"

I loved challenges that required instant solutions, so my active brain quickly sifted through all of the mental files and scenarios it had registered in my lifetime. Then, I thought of Levittown and the fantastic quarry fight between Quinn and Cummings, and it all came to me as if my cerebrum had been especially magnetized to attract ideas that were actual answers.

"Yeah, J.W.," Goose prodded. "Give us all a solution that'll be *pallid*able to both sides."

"Here's what I think," I calmly and deliberately stated. "We'll have the strongest guys from each gang. Hoss Gregorio and Ox Narducci will compete in a contest. Hoss and Ox got the right to choose their opponent's partner from the rival gang, and they'll then also compete, two against two, two Reds against two Blues."

"That sounds fair so far," Gillette surprisingly acceded. "So, tell us the rest of your grand scheme. We're listenin'."

"Well," I continued after clearing my throat. "The two teams of two guys each will have to climb the rungs to the top of the Hammonton Water Tower on Lincoln Street, just off of Bellevue. The first team of two that climbs to the walkway near the top, and then climbs back down to the ground wins."

"And," Goose cleverly interrupted, "whatever gang wins the climbin' contest gets to choose whatever the *vic-tours* want the other gang to do, or not do."

"Sounds fair to me," Gabe Gillette established. "What do ya' think, guys?"

Ox, Butch, and Speed all endorsed the terrific contest idea. Only several details still had to be ironed-out. "Which Red do you choose to be Hoss's partner?" I asked the Blues.

"Goose Restuccio," Gabe instantly answered. "No question about it, Goose Restuccio!"

I looked at Goose, who seemed just about as astounded and flabbergasted as Hoss and Ox, who were also about to be suddenly thrust into the limelight.

"And Goose," I added. "It's now your call as to which Blue is gonna' be Ox's partner. Gabe and Speed are ineligible, simply because they have injuries and can't compete."

"Errrr," Goose answered, all confused, trying to regain his lost composure. "Since Gillette and Mortellite are in-*legible,* I say the second Blue oughta' be, Butch Lanza."

"Great, the only other thing that has to be settled is the time and place," I swiftly deduced and established. "I say, tonight at ten-thirty. If we schedule it too far in advance, the cops might get wind of it."

"Okay, that sounds reasonable," Gabe confirmed. "Do we need any materials to take along?"

"Yes, each team will need a ten-foot-high ladder to bring so that the bottom rungs on both sides of the water tower can be reached," I declared. "Any further questions?"

No one had any additional questions to ask. All of the terms had been negotiated and understood, so the dueling executive committees shook hands on the final arrangements.

"See ya' men at ten-thirty at the water tower," Ox Narducci reminded our Reds' delegation. "Goose, you'll never *get over me,* because I'm gonna' always be above ya'!"

"And remember," Gabe Gillette added to *our* chagrin. "You peach pissants will always be admiring my behind from behind!"

"Okay, you're on!" Hoss forcefully replied in response to Gabe Narducci's arrogant claim, since Ronald Restuccio's slanted mouth seemed totally paralyzed, unable to speak.

Chapter Forty-Three

"The Water Tower Contest"

The Blues gleefully departed Toni's Custard's parking lot, and as *we* pulled out of the driveway, I could still see Mr. Martinelli peering-out from his service counter, making certain that no violence or fisticuffs had occurred on his precious property. Goose was ready to wrangle, but not with the Blues.

"Damn it, J.W.," the warp-minded Sicilian began articulating his irritating diatribe. "Why the fuck did ya' have to get me involved in this tower-climb bullshit? I got *aquaphobia* and am fuckin' scared-to-death of heights."

"I didn't get you involved," I clarified. "Gabe Gillette selected ya'. He could've chosen any of the Reds' guys, but the blueberry head-honcho wanted *you* to be Hoss's dependable first mate. It was his choice, his privilege."

"That's a lot of stupid bullshit," G.R. maintained, "because there's gotta' be some gimmick somewhere to give the Blues an advantage. The cheaters went along with the deal a little too easily. I know, because I make deals all the goddamned time."

"Look," Juice interrupted. "There'll be the exact same number of Reds that show-up at the water tower as Blues. The sides will be even, if a wild rumble suddenly breaks-out."

Then, the real reason for Goose's reluctance to participate in the tower climb came-out. "Guys," the worried and insecure tyrant uttered in an uncharacteristic, low tone of voice. "I ain't no fuckin' athlete! I'm as graceful as a wounded lame duck without wings. And I'm fuckin' scared of heights!"

"Just be the best ya' can be, ya' awkward son of a bitch!" Hoss yelled-over from the front passenger side. "I'm scared of heights, too, but I'm gonna' do my best 'cause I'm representin' the Reds. Stop jabberin' and start performin', or I'll have to rearrange your teeth, voice-box, and nose!"

Hoss Gregorio had effectively shut Goose up by employing *his* persuasive, blunt oratory that was backed-up by a huge, clenched, right fist. Being intimidated, Ronald Restuccio silently drove his red T-bird to his place, and since nobody dared speaking after Hoss's forceful declaration, when Bill Haley's classic "Rock Around the Clock" came on the car radio, we were already silently honoring the "Reds' official National Anthem.

At Restuccio's Winslow mansion, each of us took turns talking on the horn, and in less than a half-hour, all our members had been contacted by the self-appointed "executive committee", or had heard from other Reds about the scheduled "great water tower climb". Goose and Hoss were a little nervous, so the partners each chugged-down a double shot *of Southern Comfort* at the club basement bar.

"Goose," I said to build the contestant's faltering confidence, "you're gonna' be a tower of power, I just know ya' are!"

"J.W., go fuck yourself' up your woo-woo with your dick and a monster dildo at the same time! I'm about as graceful as a flyin' pig wearin' four concrete blocks for shoes."

"Pigs don't fly!" Hoss realized and commented.

"That's what the fuck I mean!" Goose emphatically exclaimed. "I'm an awkward piece of shit!"

At twenty after ten, Goose parked his red T-Bird behind Bruni's Pizzeria, which, according to the crowded parking lot, seemed much busier than usual. When the four of us walked a block north and then crossed Twelfth Street, at least fifty kids had already congregated around the metal legs of the town's main water tower. Little Joe had brought Hoss's favorite ladder from their peach farm, and the blueberry gang was using the wooden ladder the Reds had hastily left alongside the seafood-infested, clubhouse chimney.

Marty Gillette had parked his mother's royal blue Fleetwood behind the small, white-brick *Hammonton News* Building, and the annoying munchkin and Sonny Perone came-over to join the growing throng. The Ramrodders had heard about the contest and were also on the scene, too, and so were some girls that had been gossiping inside the Gem, including Elaine Hill, Esther Phyllis, Nanette Banks, and luscious Joanne Berenato.

"Good luck," Joanne wished me. "You're very brave."

"I'm just a spectator, just like *you* are tonight," I confessed. "It's gonna' be Hoss and Goose versus Ox Narducci and Butch Lanza."

Lieutenants Speed Mortellite and News Tomasello summoned me to the tower's base. "Okay, J.W," Speed reluctantly acknowledged my presence. "Let's get this show on the road before the fuzz gets here."

I checked to make sure the ladders were in place under the tower's bottom rungs, and then signaled Hoss and Goose to the left ladder, and Ox Narducci and Butch Lanza to the one on the right.

"Okay, men, on your marks, get set,....go!" I yelled without the aid of a starter's pistol.

Hoss Gregorio and Ox Narducci clambered up their respective ladders, followed by their nervous partners, Goose Restuccio and Butch Lanza. There must have been a hundred metal rungs to ascend in order to reach the walkway near the summit of the water tower, so after G.R. latched onto the first rung, I yelled-up, "Way to go Goose! Only ninety-nine more up, and a hundred more down."

The crowd of cheering teenagers must have, by that time, swelled to about two-hundred screaming rooters, with most of the Bellevue Avenue cruisers being temporarily diverted to a more entertaining venue occurring at the Hammonton Water Tower. Everyone was enthusiastically yelling and shouting words of encouragement and catcalls of derision, and the entire spectacle seemed like a bizarre high school pep rally with both competing schools in attendance.

Hoss and Ox finally made it to the halfway mark up the first rigorous fifty rungs, and Goose and Butch were right beneath the two behemoths' active feet on opposite vertical rungs. Endurance, strength, stamina, and coordination were all needed in the dual ascensions, and it appeared that G.R. had miraculously overcome his original phobias, and was over-achieving his athletic limitations out of fear of losing, and also out of fear of being rejected, of being shunned, and of being labeled a local loser.

The euphoric crowd was becoming ultra-boisterous. When Ox and Butch soon got midway up to the fiftieth rung, *they* surprisingly started descending amidst the booing and jeering of the assembled bystanders, the crowd looking-up into the star-filled night sky.

"Hey, the Blues are cheatin'!" Joanne loudly exclaimed into my ear. "Ox and Butch are already coming-down."

"Then, the Reds will win by default!" I confidently answered my dream girl's concern. "But Joanne, something mighty strange is goin' on here."

All the while, Hoss and Goose heard the great clamor originating from below, and the fatigued participants interpreted the human noise as being good American cheering and coaxing. The two determined Reds proceeded climbing upward, and were remarkably only twenty or so rungs from the tower's walkway. I was certain that the two courageous pals were destined to win the great contest.

Suddenly, blinking lights appeared in the eastern night sky. At first, I thought the distant glows were from a police helicopter, but as the flying machine advanced closer, I realized that the object was a chopper all right, but a blue one that belonged to Gabe Gillotte's family's blueberry corporation.

Everyone pointed to the eastern night sky, and as the helicopter came nearer, a spotlight shone directly onto the apex of the water tower, precisely where Hoss and Goose were both immediately blinded by the bright illumination.

The chopper circled-around and passed-over the left side of the tower, and as it hovered over Hoss and Goose with its intense spotlight focused on their position, the noisy machine emitted a quantity of insecticide from its spray nozzles.

Panic ensued. Girls screamed and shrieked, while everyone scurried for shelter to escape from the descending liquid-spray chemicals. I looked-up and witnessed Goose and Hoss, hanging from separate rungs with their encumbered hands. Their dangling feet were desperately feeling for lower rungs upon which to rest their body weights. I also caught a glimpse of Gabe Gillette's disgusting face, laughing incessantly inside the helicopter's passenger seat.

Descending Ox Narducci joyously applied his feet to the top rung of *his* gang's ladder. Butch Lanza soon thereafter duplicated Narducci's successful descent. When Ox triumphantly reached ground level, the football lineman was immediately spun-around by Little Joe Gregorio, who was infuriated about "the cheating gimmick" that had just happened to *his* big brother. Little Joe smashed Narducci squarely on the chin with a stiff uppercut, knocking the brute out cold, even before the notorious bully fell onto the ground. Little Joe repeated the stellar boxing exhibition with startled and exhausted Butch Lanza, who was spun-around and instantly leveled, as if the punk were a fallen redwood being disposed of by Paul Bunyan.

A wild gang fight suddenly broke-out between the Reds and the Blues, as Ramrodders joined in the fracas, and sided with the Blues. I gave Pee Wee Lucca and Marty Gillette good shots to their jaws that knocked each wise-ass to the ground. But then Zeke Errera clobbered me from the right side, and I joined Pee Wee and Marty on the turf.

Police sirens were heard, and red flashing lights were soon seen. Cops arrived, blowing whistles and twirling nightsticks. The crowd dissipated in a hurry, and kids evacuated the combat scene in all directions to escape arrest and fuzz' interrogation. I observed some of the Blues escorting Pee Wee, Marty, Ox, and Butch, diagonally cutting across some neighborhood lawns, and quickly heading toward Passmore Avenue.

Goose and Hoss had somehow recovered on the tower from their near-death experiences, and half-blinded, both managed to slowly descend one rung at a time, all the way down to their ladder. News and I were the only remaining Reds, so I climbed-up the wooden rungs, carefully grabbed and guided Goose's feet to the top ledge, and gingerly assisted him down. News did exactly the same kind of assistance for Hoss. When all available cops arrived on the scene, only the four of us were still there.

"Okay boys," Sergeant Tom Versacci yelled. "That was a crazy stunt to pull. Ya' clowns almost got killed up there. Now I think you're all in a bit of hot water!"

"But what about all the kids that were here, and the other climbers, and the big fight," I vehemently protested upon deaf ears, "this is definitely police discrimination against my three friends and me, and also, the…"

"Listen, Kid," Lieutenant Joe Frederico hollered into my face. "We don't wanta' make this report too complicated, ya' understand, Pal. It'll be too much paperwork! We caught you four guys trespassin', causin' a public disturbance, breakin' the peace, and illegally climbin' the town's water tower."

"But what about everybody else that was here?" News rightfully balked.

"Listen, Kid. We caught *you* four bozos in the act!" Officer Tom Versacci snapped. "That's all we gotta' know, and that's all we really care about!"

"Okay, you four criminal wannabes'. Let's head on over to the station for some intense questioning," Lieutenant Joe Frederico advised. "Hop into the patrol cars right now."

Chapter Forty-Four

"Tuckahoe Turf Farm"

Gabe Gillette had cunningly hoodwinked the Reds. Hoss Gregorio and Goose Restuccio almost had fallen from the water tower, and could have been killed like blueberry field gnats by helicopter insecticide spray. And after Little Joe went berserk because of family allegiance and flattened Ox Narducci and Butch Lanza, the stage had been set for a massive royal rumble between the Reds and the Blues, and maybe even the Ramrodders loyally allying with our despicable arch-enemies.

My idea of a modern David versus Goliath match-up had evolved into a miserable failure. I had been only thinking of avoiding multiple injuries occurring during a wild gang rumble, but the best of intentions had proved to be a dramatic, bad-judgment, personal defeat.

The cops hauled the remainder of the brawlers into "the clinic". But since no one had been seriously injured other than bumps, bruises, shiners, and irritated eyes, the charges were minimized to simple "trespassing on town property and causing a public nuisance". Our parents were notified, and Pop wasn't too thrilled to get the phone call from the Hammonton Police Station. He drove his new white '61 Chevy Impala to the fuzz's headquarters to liberate me from custody.

"Whatever you were involved in tonight cost me fifty bucks," Dad stated to me on the way home. "And ya' have a black eye, and you're all dirtied-up like a tramp. You're grounded for a month. No outside night activities for thirty days, is that clear?"

"Yes, Sir," I obediently agreed as I cautiously inspected Dad's new white '61 Chevy Impala that smelled just as fresh as the automobile actually was. "My friends were in trouble and I tried to…"

"I don't wanta' hear it," Pop insisted. "Unless ya' wanta' see your penalty extended to two months, then don't say another word to me for the rest of the evening. You're an embarrassment to the entire family, and a poor example for your younger sister and brother to model after," Dad lectured. "You're allowed to see your friends durin' the daytime, or talk to them on the telephone, that's it. End of conversation."

My true loyalty was to my friends, as much as I tried to honor and respect my father's authority. I realized that Pop was trying to insulate and isolate me from trouble, but I felt that if the Reds desperately needed my dedicated services, then I would have to honor and accommodate their beckoning.

Goose Restuccio showed-up Monday afternoon and talked with Dad to soften and butter him up, while I seethed in the back of the farm market sorting and grading late summer tomatoes. Ten minutes later, the crazy "Mt. Etna kid", who held some kind of mysterious, sinister power over my free will and good judgment, approached my rear sector of the farm market.

"Wow, how did ya' get that nasty-lookin' shiner?"

"I ate too many black-eyed peas," I sneered back.

"J.W.," G.R. said in his normal, condescending tone of voice. "There's gonna' be a big rumble between the Blues and the Reds, I'm tellin' ya', it's gonna' be a real big shittin' rumble."

"That makes a heck of a lot of sense after all that happened last night," I muttered as I examined my lacerated left elbow. "You and Hoss just about got your pores clogged like insects, and almost wound-up dyin'," I articulated. "So, the idea of a big rumble makes an awful lot of sense, yes, it does."

"J.W., the Reds need your smarts right now, really bad," Goose pleaded without either cursing or swearing. "Hoss and Little Joe wanta' kick Gabe Gillette's butt all the way to the moon, and Ox Narducci and Butch Lanza wanta' get even with Little Joe for 'sucker-punchin' them and hurtin' their public tough-guy images, and all the rest of the Blues hate all the rest of the Reds, and vice-versa."

"Goose, we almost went to jail last night," I countered. "And Pop's grounded me for at least a month of nights' out with the guys."

"Who says we got to have the damned rumble at night?" Goose maintained. "Do ya' have any special trips ya' gotta' take with the Pete's Market Special?"

"Yeah, this comin' Thursday at high-noon I'm supposed to go to Marlton and get an ordered shipment of apple cider gallons and half-gallons with preservative in 'em. Twenty-five cases of each, I think."

"Well, J.W., ya' just wrote-out the day and time of the rumble," Restuccio complimented me, "Thursday at twelve noon. We can't fight this one without ya', J.W. I'm still pissed about the insect spray makin' me see red," Goose grieved. "That means the Blues are gonna' see Reds, get it. See Reds! Ha, ha, ha, ha. I did one of your stupid-shit jokes, ha, ha, ha."

Goose helped me sort through ten half-bushels of messy, red ripe canning tomatoes. I knew my visitor must have been serious because the clean-hand-addict would never want to get his fingers grimy over anything like overripe tomatoes, under normal circumstances. G.R. asked me to devise some imaginative rules for the rumble. I informed the instigator that I had woken-up in the middle of a "rumble dream" the night before, and remembered the entire sequence from beginning to end. I related the details to Restuccio, and my unexpected farm market guest said that he loved my recommendations.

“I don’t know anybody who takes dope or smokes marijuana who has ideas anything as good as yours,” Goose commended. “This one may be the best one yet. It’s simple, but real fuckin’ creative.”

“Don’t forget to bring the golf clubs, and get a nine-iron for the best accuracy,” I advised. “And don’t forget to tell the Blues to each get a nine-iron, too. Since Gillette’s gang challenged us to the rumble, we get dibs to set-up the official ground rules.”

“Okay,” Goose consented. “All the guys are gonna’ jerk-off at least twice after hearin’ this baby. I’ll drive over to the Berlin Auction and get you an authentic gym coach’s whistle, too.”

* * * * * * * * * * * * * *

Thursday morning arrived, and at eleven a.m., I obtained payment for the Marlton apple cider order from Dad. I eagerly hopped into the Pete’s Market Special, which I drove to Walker Road, and next across Union Road and through the two sets of woods to the massive Tuckahoe Turf Farm, located next to “Texas,” the setting that I had chosen for the upcoming, spectacular rumble. ‘What a place for a turf battle!’ I thought and worried. ‘A *turf* farm! I hope nobody commits *sod*omy out here during the big fight.’

The Reds all entered the lush green ‘altercation arena’ from the Walker Road side, and the Blues all came to the battlefield down Oak Road; crossed Union; followed the linear hedgerow, and parked their expensive machines on the dirt lane next to the woods on the opposite side of the immense sod farm. I met Goose, and keeping his promise, Restuccio handed me my official silver-plated, gym coach’s whistle.

“Make sure ya’ give this thing a good blow-job!” G.R. laughed, thoroughly appreciating his own risque-but-primitive form of humor.

Gabe Gillette, Speed Mortellite, and Ox Narducci were the Blues’ captains, and the trio met Goose, News, and me in the center of the velvet-green, grassy turf field.

“Still got your cane,” I pointed-out to Gillette. “It’s against the rules to use it as a weapon.”

“Get on with the silly rules, Pecker-head,” the blueberry head honcho snidely remarked. “I’m not payin’ any attention to a high school flunky like you.”

I reviewed the rules, and everyone listening fully understood the simple instructions. The captains shook hands and retreated to their respective teams. Two huddles formed on opposite sides of the turf field, just like on a football gridiron, and then the teams dispersed to separate golf tees on either side of the turf farm’s verdant grass field.

Just before I blew the starting whistle, a caravan of Hammonton cruisers entered the arena area from both Oak and Walker Roads. All in all, about three-hundred spectators had heard of the imminent rumble and showed-up en masse to witness the battle.

Each Red had to tee off a red golf ball, and each Blue a blue one. Goose was the first to tee off, and his red ball sliced to the right. Then, the shanker surrendered the nine-iron to News Tomasello, the next driver, and then Restuccio paced the distance to his red golf ball's landing. Gabe Gillette did the same from the opposite side of the turf farm field, and handed his club to Speed Mortellite, who could only use one hand and hit his blue golf ball about fifty-feet.

The rules were that after all forty-eight gang members drove their golf balls with the two gangs' nine irons, and ambled-out to their hit balls' location in the center of the field, then when the official whistle blew, each combatant had to square-off with the opponent having the closest different colored ball nearest to him.

I looked-around the cheering bystanders and saw Joanne, Elaine Hill, Esther Phyllis, and Nanette Banks on the Blues' side with their fingers crossed on both hands, symbolically wishing my gang good luck. A weird thought passed through my mind. 'As Elvis once sang, it's now or never,' I sentimentally thought. I again looked-around the area of my red golf ball's position, and the closest blue one belonged to Pee Wee Lucca. I couldn't wait to get into action and savagely strangle and mangle the neurotic pipsqueak.

I blew the coach's whistle, and everyone squared-off and immediately started pummeling and pounding a member of the opposing gang. Formal rules soon disintegrated into total mayhem, and piles of six and eight bodies mounded-up all around me. Still, I managed to tackle Pee Wee Lucca, knock the runt to the damp ground, and squeeze his neck until the kid started turning *blue.* I felt someone grab me from behind, and Ox Narducci quickly gave me a forearm smash that sent me reeling off of Pee Wee, who was gasping for oxygen like a polio victim inside an iron lung.

The assembled crowd cheered even more boisterously as the melee continued into its second minute. As I rolled-over on the turf, I saw Hoss smash Ox Narducci in the mouth, and blood squirted-out from the ruthless monster's ruptured lips. Little Joe and Butch Lanza were duking it out toe-to-toe like heavyweight boxers, inflicting some serious damage with uppercuts to each other's solar plexus, and exchanging left hooks and right crosses that were definitely connecting. Pandemonium was happening all around me, and my senses had to be acute in order to avoid a possible concussion administered by belligerent Hammonton High linemen gone amok.

I took a good left jab to the back of my head from Marty Gillette, who then fled when I pivoted to swing at *my* formerly anonymous aggressor. I then saw Dennis Measley run-out from the sidelines, tackle Marty, and begin putting a decent hurting on the midget troublemaker, repeatedly smacking *his* face left and right.

My eyes next observed hobbled Gabe Gillette using his cane, and Speed Mortellite cheating by swinging his gang's nine' iron at three Reds that were horizontally banging-away on the turf in a colossal scrum pile with three Blues. I sprinted twenty-feet and hurtled my body into the air, jolting Gillette into the center of the pile of wriggling, clawing, and punching bodies. I was in some sort of survival trance where the only thing that really mattered was putting a hurt on any available Blue, with my heightened animosity starting with intolerable Gabe Gillette, and in the meantime, with my survival instinct protecting my sense of mortal existence.

Just when it appeared that the Reds were gaining momentum in the bitter battle, twenty-four Ramrodders surprised everyone except the Blues, and the crazies charged like maniacal savages out of the woods on the Oak Road side of the turf farm, joining the Blues in fighting the Reds. I saw greasers Mark Benedetto and Warren Watson leading the assault, with Petey Santelli, Joel Salvo, Sam Olive, Teddy Tell, and Frank 'the Tank" Ordille screaming and running like barbarians not far behind. The fresh greaser recruits entered the wild fray, ripped Reds off of Blues, and then injured News, Fabian, and Juice pretty badly with tire irons and chains, the new weapons being illegally introduced into the escalating altercation.

No sooner had the advantage swung in the Blues/Ramrodders favor that another surprise unfolded, much to the joy of the curious cruiser-crowd bystanders, but also to the appreciation of the beleaguered Reds, who were much in need of immediate reinforcements. Tyrone Davis led a platoon of thirty black kids out of the west woods on the Reds' Walker Road side of the turf field, and as the invaders ran toward the brutal battle scene, the "black Cavalry" shouted and scared the feces out of the startled Ramrodders and Blues.

"Tyrone grabbed Gabe Gillette around the neck, flung the wise-ass to the ground as if the blueberry prince had been a rag doll; then livid Davis leaped on top of the impudent punk, and kept thrashing and wind-milling his arms into Gillette's lily-white face. The tide of battle quickly tilted in the Reds/Marvelons favor, and after three-minutes or so of bloody hand-to-hand combat, the Blues and the Ramrodders called it quits, and the craven wimps made a hasty retreat to their cars. The two Hammonton gangs had surrendered the final battle of the great teen fruit war to the Reds and their new-found black allies.

I was winded, bleeding from my mouth, nose, and knuckles. Juice, News, Fabian, and I staggered-around, ascertaining that all of our gang members had survived the incredible donnybrook. Everyone I saw was pretty well banged-up, but no one so badly that the member required an ambulance or hospitalization. I looked across the field, and all of the Blues and the Ramrodders were making dust clouds with their vehicles and motorcycles, abruptly frantically turning, and then fishtailing back toward the safety of Oak Road.

"Wow! What a fight!" I coughed and gasped. "Better than any the Diablos and the Kamikazes ever had back in Levittown."

I looked to my left and saw Goose, hobbling toward News, Juice, Fabian, Frankie, and myself.

"What the fuck happened?" G.R. asked in a disoriented voice. "Don't those asshole Ramrodders know that they're *not* supposed to use tire irons on us, and *are* supposed to use chains on winter tires, but not on us! Stupid fucks!"

"Man, I'm in cookoo clock land," Jives Arena asserted, holding a large lump on top of his head. "My noggin is foggin', smoggin', joggin' groggin', and cloggin'."

Juice reached his hand inside his James Dean jacket, removed a bottle of aspirins, and distributed tablets to the guys and me. "I learned this cute trick from J.W.," Johnny confessed.

News held his head and irrelevantly uttered, "Say, guys. Did I tell ya' that the United States Weather Bureau is predictin' that Hurricane Donna is formin' out near West Africa, and might just be the biggest storm to hit the East Coast in years?"

"News," Juice criticized, "why don't ya' take a trip to Paris and buy yourself some cheap plaster."

"Or better yet," Fabian added, holding his swollen jaw. "Take a plane to the Philippines and buy yourself a damned Manila envelope."

I turned to my right and saw Tyrone Davis standing there, and deeply panting like an exhausted football linebacker. I warmly shook his hand.

"Thanks, Ty," I gratefully acknowledged. "*We* woulda' gotten the crap kicked out of us if you and your friends didn't come to the rescue."

"Hot damn! J.W. I really organized the boys to come here for my sister," Davis admitted. "Crystal told me that Goose did the rape crap because the Blues woulda' killed him if your cat didn't do it to her. Goose might've gotten Crystal pregnant, but when ya' compare what he had to do that the raunchy Blues and Gabe Gillette made *him* do, your oddball pal looks like a friggin' saint when standin' beside any of those blue jacket creeps."

"How did ya' find-out about the rumble?" I asked Tyrone.

"Crystal told me about it when we were talkin' to that big-mouth neighbor of ours, Jives Arena, standin' over there. It's a wonder sissy understood a word that weird cat was jivin' at her."

"Why didn't ya' come outa' the west woods earlier?" Goose asked the Marvelons' lead singer.

"Because as long as it was twenty-four against twenty-four, it was a fair rumble," Tyrone declared. "But when the Blues startin' hittin' you dudes on the topside of your skulls with that cane and that golf club," Tyrone said, shaking his head, "we got the notion of chargin' in. But when we saw the Ramrodders' comin' outa' the opposite woods thinkin' they're Spartans, or Nazis, on somebody like that, we jumped right in to whup their fannies good."

I turned my head and noticed Joanne Berenato standing close by, next to Elaine Hill, Esther Phyllis, and Nanette Banks. I instinctively opened my arms, and the beautiful, brown-eyed girl ran into my embrace. No sooner had that transcendent, triumphant moment occurred that News Tomasello gave us all an unwanted alarm.

"The fuzz is here! Thc fuzz is here!" News screamed like a colonial town crier.

"Let's get the hell outa' this fuckin' wicked *turf* war!" Goose Restuccio characteristically yelled. "Who needs this *editional* shit?"

Two Hammonton police cars with flashing red beacon lights and wailing sirens rumbled into the Tuckahoe Turf Farm green battleground from the Oak Road side. Everyone panicked and raced to their respective vehicles to cut through apple and peach orchards, and pepper, squash, and tomato fields bordering "Texas". And some of the more adventurous escapees even drove their trucks into the Jersey Devil's haunted Wharton Tract pine barrens.

Mt eyes saw Joanne rush to Esther Phyllis's classy '56 red and black Ford Crown Victoria. I then sprinted to the blue Pete's Market Special and took several shortcuts I knew through "Texas" onto Flemington Pike, which lead straight to the White Horse Pike.

As I passed the familiar Renault Winery's tall three-dimensional champagne bottle in Elm, just before the Ancora Bridge overpass, I wiped some sweat and dirt from my brow. I glanced into the rear-view mirror. My left eye was swollen really badly, and dried-up blood was caked under my nostrils.

'I'll stop off at Fabian's Flyin'-A' gas station in Waterford and clean-up a bit,' I thought. 'Then, I'll detour over to Marlton and get that load of apple cider.'

I again solemnly peered at my grotesque-looking reflection in the Pete's Market Special's rear-view mirror and soberly said, "J.W., thank God that the great teen fruit war has finally ended. Long live peaches. Long live the glorious Reds!"

Chapter Forty-Five

“Then and Now”

The great teen fruit war had ended that late 1960 August day at the Tuckahoe Turf Farm. In early September, News was off to *Rutgers,* Juice to *Villanova,* Fabian to *Glassboro State,* and Jives to *Pace College* in New York City. Most of the other Reds also left to attend their respective colleges and technical schools. Goose Restuccio and I didn’t bother too much with each other after then, probably because we had no common enemy to focus our mutual attentions and hostilities upon.

Also, in early September, I made a visit to Edgewood Regional High School with a “Letter of Recommendation” signed by Mr. Charles B. Sipley. The handwritten missive stated that I had mastered the fundamentals and mechanics of trigonometry, and that I should receive a minimum average of “B for the course”. I took my tutor’s note to the main office, showed it to the principal, Mr. Pinkerton, who then shuttled me up to Mr. Andrews’ dreaded M-Wing classroom.

I handed the stern pedagogue Mr. Sipley’s complimentary letter, and after reading its benign content, Andrews said that the note might have been a counterfeit, and that I still had to pass *his* awesome final examination. The mean-spirited martinet chuckled as the trig’ instructor directed me to park my body in the last desk in the last row near the window, the same seat I had occupied the previous semester. Then, Mr. Andrews handed me his toughest test.

It took me twenty-minutes to solve the formerly complicated mathematical riddles, and after spending an additional five-minutes double-checking the exam items, I marched to the teacher’s desk and handed my answers to Andrews. The inflexible pedagogue appeared momentarily alarmed by my excessive arrogance and by my abundant self-confidence.

The trig’ teacher intensively scrutinized my paper, closely eyeballing every answer with his mouth agape. I instinctively knew that I had gotten every problem correct, but the obstinate math’ instructor did not put any grade on my test paper. Instead, the Edgewood Mathematics Chairman scribbled his name on Mr. Sipley’s letter and wrote to Mr. Pinkerton, “Give this student a C average”.

Andrews handed me his notation jotted upon Mr. Sipley’s letter, which I read. I looked the man straight in the eyes and somehow, his former dominance of my future no longer seemed to validly exist. I felt like viciously punching the human obstacle in the face, but I restrained myself and thought, ‘I’m gonna’ go to *Glassboro State* and become a teacher, so that I can help kids learn instead of tryin' to destroy them like some people I know.' I accepted the altered letter, promptly brought it to the main office, and then an administrative secretary inserted a "C" for trigonometry on my transcript.

I shook hands with Mr. Pinkerton, who like Mr. Andrews, seemed diminished in stature and potency, now that I had also escaped *his* jurisdiction. I left the high school building with a new lease on life, anticipating a future devoid of mortal obstacles such as Andrews and Pinkerton had been dominant in my mediocre academic past.

In early October of '60, business at Pete's Market slowed-down to a trickle, so Pop got me a job where he worked as a welder in Norristown, Pennsylvania. It was a long commute of an hour-and-a-half to the Martin and Quade Stainless Steel Fabricating Factory, and then back to Elm, five days a week. I soon realized that I didn't want to breathe-in horrible gas welding fumes for the rest of my adult life, so the following September, I enrolled-in and attended *Glassboro State Teachers College*.

In 1965, I graduated from *Glassboro State* as a junior high school English and Social Studies teacher. In '65, Hammonton High School moved its faculty and students from the 1925 yellow brick building on Central Avenue to a new edifice on North Liberty Street. The old high school instantly became the *new* middle school. I taught English to over four-thousand students in a thirty-four-year career, retiring from the profession in June of '99. Ironically, I had taught English in the Hammonton Middle School, Room 103, the exact same room where in 1960, the Reds had planted stolen bowling balls in the classroom's closet at the then Hammonton High School.

In 1966, I married Joanne and we now have three grown sons. We live on the White Horse Pike in Hammonton, about a thousand feet on the Hammonton side of the landmark White Horse. Every time I pass the statue, I recall what Goose Restuccio and Gabe Gillette had mischievously done to the farm's majestic symbol with red and blue paint, and now I am a guardian of what I had once vandalized.

My present home is actually located in two counties, Atlantic and Camden, but since most of it is situated in Hammonton (all but the west-side porch), I pay my property taxes to *that* municipality, and also some minor land taxes to Winslow Township. It seems that my entire existence has always been hanging on the cusp, and my current residence is no exception, being a tale of two counties.

Goose Restuccio and I eventually went our separate ways, as did the rest of my Edgewood and St. Joseph High School friends. I see my former Edgewood pals every five-years at high school reunions. At the last celebration, Goose had flamboyantly showed-up in a white Rolls

Royce, escorting two beautiful black models as his guests, causing quite a commotion of gossip, which I knew the Italian Stallion intentionally wanted to generate.

I feel that a lot of my past has been erased from history, and sometimes I even wonder if the great teen fruit war of 1960 had ever really happened. Levittown's Bishop Reagan High has been torn-down and no longer exists. Edgewood Regional High School is now Winslow Regional High, and *Glassboro State Teachers College* is presently *Rowan University*. Mr. Andrews, Mr. Pinkerton, Pop and Mom are all dead. Dad passed-away in September of '74, and Mom in July of 2004, and my parents are buried behind Grandpa Tony and Grand-mom Annie in Oak Grove Cemetery, which was a stop in the 1960 scavenger hunt, which had been conducted by avid joy-riders News Tomasello and myself.

In the late 1960s, Goose Restuccio established himself with boardwalk businesses in various New Jersey shore resorts. I understand he rents and owns over thirty boardwalk operations in Atlantic City, Ocean City, Seaside Heights, Cape May, and Wildwood. G.R. has expanded his enterprises into condominium developing, and the prominent multi-millionaire serves on the board of directors of three prestigious banks. I always knew Goose Restuccio would be very successful, but never expected him to be so legitimately wealthy.

Goose is still a legend in and around Hammonton, not only from his 1960 exploits, but also because of his prosperous boardwalk retail store and amusement arcade operations. One story has a motorcycle gang from Vineland entering one of his Jersey shore bars. Goose asked the gang leader why the members all had *Harley Davidson* tattoos on their chests as free advertisements, and none of the motorcycle rebels could satisfactorily answer *his* question.

Restuccio then made the twenty-five rough and tumble motorcycle gang members offers the ruffians couldn't refuse. According to the legend, G.R. promised to pay each of the bikers three hundred-dollars to visit a tattoo parlor and have the name of *his* bar engraved on their chests in blue and red ink. The next morning, the twenty-five motorcycle gang members proudly entered Goose's boardwalk bar displaying their new tattoos, and without blinking an eyelid, Restuccio distributed seventy-five crisp *Ben Franklins* to the very happy road warriors.

Another story has Goose wearing a gorilla costume and hiding inside a boardwalk haunted house *he* owns. When another motorcycle gang was touring the attraction, G.R. leaped-out in his King Kong costume, instantly frightening the bikers into a rage. The black leather gang proceeded to pound the living daylights out of Restuccio until the motorcycle bullies finally discovered that Goose had been just another human cleverly disguised in an artificial gorilla costume.

Goose is reputed to live the summer months just off the Wildwood boardwalk in an apartment that has a back bathroom window facing an amusement ride area. G.R. reportedly enjoys sitting on the hopper and watching thrilled passengers riding in the Wild Mouse roller coaster ride come zooming on metal rails straight at his apartment's bathroom window, and then zipping-down a hill, much to G.R.'s own personal *amusement*.

Over the last forty-two years, blueberries have decisively won the economic fruit war over peaches in the Hammonton area. Only several small peach farms can now be found around town, but in 1960, the two crops were running neck and neck in popularity and profitability. Then, in the late 1980s, large California farms started growing the O. Henry peach variety, and the competition from the "prettier fruit" doomed the future of the New Jersey peach industry. One by one, the Hammonton area peach farmers began uprooting trees and eliminating orchards by the hundreds of acres, and then planting blueberries.

Hammonton is now rightfully called the "Blueberry Capital of the World", and the logo and slogan appear on all the town's police cars and on the *Route 30, Route 54,* and *Route 206* billboards leading into the rural community. Two modern-day reminders of the great 1960 teen fruit war still exist on the White Horse Pike for visitors to the farming community to view. The Blueberry Crossing and the Peach Tree Plaza shopping centers are only a traffic light apart on now congested *Route 30,* better known to local residents as the "uptown White Horse Pike".

On Monday morning, December 24, Christmas Eve of 2001, I ambled out to my White Horse Pike mailbox to retrieve my usual bills and junk mail. I awkwardly sorted through the handful of procrastinators' late arriving Christmas cards; unwanted credit card solicitations, and separated various magazine sweepstakes' offers. Among the assorted usual envelopes was one item promptly that stood-out from the rest. The hand-written envelope had been addressed to me, with the language appearing in formal, cursive lettering, and the unexpected missive had Goose Restuccio's return address indicated in the standard, upper left-hand corner. My immediate curiosity was definitely peaking. Experiencing great anticipation, my hands hastily ripped-open the envelope, and I was immensely curious to see exactly what my former 1960 friend had to say or announce. I earnestly read the following letter.

December 20, 2001

J.W.,

How the hell are ya'! I hear you're retired from teaching and are married to Joanne with three kids and four grand-kids. That's really great! I always knew you would contribute something good to our American society.

J.W., on Saturday, January 5, 2002, I am going to be honored by the New Jersey Chamber of Commerce for my success in my boardwalk and resort enterprises in Atlantic City, Ocean City, Seaside Heights, Wildwood and Cape May. The award ceremony will be held in Conference Room B at Harrah's Casino Hotel, near the Brigantine Bridge, at eleven a.m. on Saturday, January 5.

J.W., I would be deeply honored if you could attend the event, so that you will fully see that I have grown into a legitimate, successful businessman, and I believe that I owe a lot of my success to you and to our past friendship.

Thanks for teaching me so much about people and about life.

Sincerely,

Ronald "Goose" Restuccio

I stepped to the pantry's closet, removed next year's calendar, circled the date Saturday, January 5, 2002, and wrote-in the date's square, "Award ceremony for G.R., Harrah's Casino, 11 a.m." I was extremely happy that Goose Restuccio had miraculously matured and evolved into a successful and reputable businessman.

Chapter Forty-Six

"Harrah's, Atlantic City"

New Year's Day, 2002 came and vanished into history, and after the traditional bowl games and *Pasadena Rose Bowl Parade,* my mind couldn't think about anything else except Saturday, January 5, 11 a.m., Harrah's Casino Hotel, Conference Room B, Atlantic City. I couldn't sleep the night before Goose's upcoming award ceremony, tossing and turning, thinking about Ronald Restuccio, the Reds, and the dramatic great teen fruit war of 1960. Finally, the alarm clock buzzed at seven in the morning, and my feet sprung out of bed as if I was an eager bullfrog on steroids.

"I have to go to Harrah's Casino to see Goose Restuccio," I reminded Joanne from inside the master bathroom. "He's bein' honored by the New Jersey Chamber of Commerce."

"Your black suit is dry-cleaned and hanging in the closet," my devoted wife yelled through the bathroom door. "I have to go to the hairdresser's, visit my mother, and do some light grocery shopping. See you later on today."

"Okay. I'll come right back after the Harrah's ceremony. I can't wait to see Goose honored. It's hard to believe that forty-two years have passed since I first met him at Edgewood, along with the rest of the Reds."

"In your mind," Joanne thought and laughed, "you're still livin' in high school."

I donned my black suit, put on my best red tie, socks, and shoes, and stepped through the family room to the two-car garage. My eyes admired the handsome '57 green and cream Chevy Bel Air, a treasured gift that my old Levittown pal Bo Jalonec had left me in his will. Bo had died from leukemia in the summer of '94, but at the Diablos' December 28, 2000 reunion in San Diego, Quinn had presented the classic car surprise to me. I was so thrilled that I canceled my Continental Airlines return flight ticket to Philadelphia and drove the magnificent vintage automobile from California three-thousand-miles east to New Jersey.

'This car easily puts me back in time, to a most wonderful time, to magical 1960,' I nostalgically thought. I pressed the electronic garage door opener, backed out into my driveway, lowered the garage door, and stopped the sparkling-clean '57 Chevy to allow traffic to pass by my residence on the all-too-familiar White Horse Pike.

'I think I'll drive around Hammonton a little bit,' I sentimentally decided. 'I have more than an hour-and-a-half to burn before I have to be at Harrah's Hotel.'

I turned the radio on and tuned into Philadelphia's WOGL-FM, Oldies 98.1. The silly novelty number "Kookie, Kookie, Lend Me Your Comb" by Ed Byrnes and Connie Stevens was playing, and the song brought back memories of Jives Arena and the weird words and phrases the unique hipster used to practice on News, Juice, Fabian, Goose, and me.

And then Johnny Preston's "Running Bear" was spun, but my naughty mind associated the song's words into "Running Bare", and I quickly chuckled thinking about the fake Reds' initiation Goose had contrived, with Joanne and the other girls shocked and blushing while the dolls were standing, staring at my nudity, at the pre-arranged finish line. And when Duane Eddy's guitar was featured in "Because They're Young", which was soon followed by Fats Domino's classic solo "Blueberry Hill", my mind mystically time-traveled back to the year 1960, and my brain mentally relived the very real great teen fruit war.

As I drove around town, I thought about some of the new buildings that had been erected in Hammonton since 1960. The new high school is presently being constructed and situated on the corner of the White Horse Pike and Old Forks Road, which had been a peach orchard opposite Oak Grove Cemetery when the scavenger hunt had taken place. Kessler Memorial Hospital is now at the intersection of *Route 30* and Central Avenue, right at the bend where Hammonton Lake meets the Pike. Also, in front of the First Union Bank on Bellevue Avenue, the Reagan Rock is situated, the spot where President Ronald Reagan came to Hammonton and inspirationally spoke to local citizens on September 19, 1984.

Plenty has changed in Hammonton and vicinity since the year 1960. The old yellow brick high school is presently the middle school, but the faculty and students of HMS will soon transfer to the present high school building located on North Liberty Street. The new high school will be on Old Forks Road and the Pike, and will open in September of 2002. Ironically, St. Joseph High has purchased the old original 1925 "Winslow-yellow-brick" Central Avenue Hammonton High building.

Winslow Junction, at the end of Elm's Spring Road, is now an empty depot station where rusting freight cars and hulking, unwanted and unneeded railroad cars are temporarily stored. The old Rivoli Theater, which for decades was a town landmark at the corner of Bellevue Avenue and Third Street, is presently a modern-looking office building. The Atco Drive-in had been razed in recent years, and a state-of-the-art Multi-Plex Cinema exists in its place at the juncture of *Route 30* and *Route 73,* and the Circus Drive-in's rusting screen can still be seen from the White Horse Pike in Devonshire, just east of Hammonton.

The old Hammonton Fruit Auction block had been knocked-down on Washington Street. Dual Motors on the Pike is now the renovated Village Mall. Next door used to be the Midway Diner, but now the building's been converted into the Midway Medical Center. The Hammonton Brewery is presently mostly used for warehousing, and the area that once was the Gem Restaurant on Central Avenue is now the setting for several small business offices. Augie's Luncheonette and Burger Paradise has been torn-down on Bellevue to allow for downtown parking, and Olivo's Super Market is no longer in business on Central Avenue.

Al's Save-Way gas station has gotten a facelift and is currently Al and Rich's Texaco, the biggest retail gas supplier in town. Still highly visible on the White Horse Pike are Square Deal Farm Market, Pete's Market, White Horse Farm, DiDonato's Bowling, Royale Crown Custard, and Burdick's Bus Stop in Devonshire. The little white house (now painted gray) that I lived in when I was young has been moved a half-mile west on the Pike, from next to Square Deal to a site near the new Hammonton High School.

Some other area 1960s' businesses still around are Angelo's Store in Rosedale, Morano Paper Supply Company on Weymouth Road, Vet's Bakery on Fairview Avenue, and Bruni's Pizzeria on Twelfth Street, which is under new ownership, but still has the same great pizza.

As I merrily drove the '57 green and cream Bel Air all over Hammonton, I fondly observed the buildings and businesses that existed forty-two years ago, and happily recollected the wonderful memories associated with each of the structures. I was so caught-up in my reverie that I hadn't realized that it was nine-forty-five on the car's dashboard clock, so I left downtown Hammonton and steered the classic '57 Chevy onto *Route 30,* heading east toward Atlantic City.

I laughed to myself, thinking about Jives Arena following Dion and the Belmonts down *Route 30* out of A.C. And when I passed by the former Starlight Ballroom Roller Skating Rink, which is now a manufacturing concern in Devonshire, I again recalled something minute that seemed relevant to my past. Johnny Illiani told the guys in Frankie Jives Arena's black and white Dodge Coronet how Goose had admonished Juice for lending Chubby Checker *his* comb in the skating rink's Men's Room.

I passed by the giant 3-D Renault Winery champagne bottle east of Egg Harbor, and that made me again remember the adventurous scavenger hunt, and how Gabe Gillette and Speed Mortellite had been detoured sixteen-miles by simply adhering to Joanne's worthless, listed directions. A sign outside Egg Harbor City read "Sweetwater Casino," and my brain vividly recollected the once-in-a-lifetime *Goose's Gadget's* speedboat escapade up and down the historic Mullica River, with the three streamlined Blues' pleasure boats and two versatile helicopters in hot pursuit.

Finally, I arrived in Atlantic City, passing over the Atlantic Canal where Goose had bombarded Gabe Gillette's fishing/pleasure yacht with two Congo watermelons and a small-but-powerful cherry bomb. I soon steered onto Brigantine Boulevard, and was not too far from Harrah's Casino Hotel. I gave the parking valet my keys, and entered the hotel via the active and noisy casino.

I stepped inside a Men's Room, and when I exited the lavatory, my urge to gamble made me reach in my pants' pockets and find some spare change to burn, along with a cash reserve, should my limited number of quarters expire inside the slot machines. Twenty-minutes and forty-five dollars later, I made my way to the escalators just off the hotel's main lobby, and soon I was eagerly ascending up toward Conference Room B.

After entering the large chamber, my eyes took a quick search toward the right rear, not wanting to draw attention from anyone I might know, for I have always basically been a very shy, withdrawn person upon initial contact, even when first conversing with an old acquaintance. The large conference chamber quickly filled-up, and by five-minutes to eleven, all three-hundred or so chairs had been occupied by attendees.

The master of ceremonies stepped to the podium's microphone and introduced the important businessmen seated at the head table, and one was the distinguished guest of honor, Ronald Restuccio. Goose looked a little thinner than I remembered him being as a rebellious teenager in 1960, but the Sicilian multimillionaire still possessed a unique swagger and spunk in his demeanor, as the boardwalk czar flashed his distinctive smile out of the left side of his slanted mouth. Finally, the time had come for Ronald Restuccio to receive his highly coveted Chamber of Commerce award. My friend graciously accepted the beautiful plaque and stepped to the podium's microphone.

"Thank you all very much for this very high honor," Goose began in a very appropriate, humble and modest manner. "I've never been a good public speaker, so I wanta' make this *dessert-station* short and sweet. There are some wonderful people sittin' in the audience that have greatly helped me become who I am today, and I would like to recognize those special folks at this time. There is no way that I can *renumerate* them enough for what these people have done for me, and for my career."

G.R. removed an envelope from his black tuxedo's inner pocket, took a gulp of water from a glass, and then proceeded with his presentation. "Could Dennis Measley come forward to the podium please?"

A gaunt, frail bearded man, wearing an old shiny black suit, rose on the opposite side of the conference room and awkwardly proceeded toward the front dais. I hadn't seen Dennis in over thirty-years, but I could tell it had been him by his ungainly gait, and by his general self-conscious mannerisms.

G.R. was handed a bushel of fancy waxed apples by a hotel attendant, and then presented the special fruit to Dennis, along with the large envelope. "Dennis, you came to my rescue several times when I was a reckless teenager, and I was not the kindest person in the world to you in our younger days. Please accept these gifts as a token of my *depreciation* for helpin' me in the past. Please do not open the envelope until after the meeting."

Dennis Measley thanked the presenter for the unusual gift that Goose had pressed inside the bushel, and recipient carried the cumbersome container of apples, along with the mystery-envelope, to his comfortable seat.

Goose paused for a moment, again taking a healthy gulp out of his water glass. "Could Mrs. Hector Rodriquez come forward please," the guest of honor formally requested. A heavyset, elderly, Hispanic woman rose on the opposite side of the conference room and timidly stepped to the front.

"Mrs. Rodriquez, you are one of the bravest and finest women in this whole wide world," Goose praised. "Your *diseased* husband was a fine man, who actually helped change my life in later years because of my first contact with him. Please *except* this small gift as a token of my sincerest *depreciation*, and please don't open it until after this meeting is over," the obvious, nervous speaker requested.

Ronald Goose Restuccio handed Mrs. Hector Rodriquez a sealed envelope, and the woman returned to her seat to join seven family members that had recently accompanied her (at Goose's expense) from San Juan, Puerto Rico to Harrah's Casino Hotel.

"Will Crystal Davis step forward please?" I was absolutely shocked because I knew the real significance of Crystal's Davis's life in relation to Goose Restuccio's teen years, but everyone else in the audience apparently seemed ignorant of any past relationship between them, so the attendees all politely applauded.

"Crystal, you have to be one of the most *curr-rageous* woman in the whole-wide-world," Ronald Restuccio commended. "You've sacrificed immensely over the past forty-two years, given of your-self, and have raised a fine son, Preston, who has grown to become a brave New Jersey State Trooper. I would like to express my pleasure and present you with my personal gift in honor of your great dignity and compassion. Please accept this token of *depreciation* from me to you. Crystal, I believe I owe you much more than what is inside this envelope. Please don't open it until after the meeting."

Crystal Davis and her strong handsome son, Preston, slowly ambled to the head table, accepted their unexpected envelope, and then returned to their seats amidst gentle applause.

"Now, I'd like to call to the podium to receive an *a-pro-pre-it* gift, Crystal's older brother, Tyrone," Goose requested. "This man saved my life in late August of 1960 when he and his friends came out of nowhere to rescue several of my close friends and me from great danger. Tyrone, please accept these gifts as a token of my sincerest thanks, and don't open the envelope until after the *confer-rents*."

Tyrone Davis, who had put on about a hundred-pounds since I had last seen the former Marvelons' lead singer, reluctantly approached the podium. Goose reached behind a red curtain, and much to my astonishment, presented Tyrone with a lidless bushel of eggplants with a large envelope stuffed inside. Tyrone graciously smiled, grinned, laughed, and then shook Goose's hand, and only he, I and G.R. knew the true symbolism of the eggplants, even though some members of the audience laughed, thinking that the peculiar vegetable gift had been very uncommonly funny.

"And now ladies and gentlemen," Goose announced, clearing his throat, "it is my pleasure to introduce to you the man who has been the most positive *in-flew-ants* in my life. And," the uneasy honoree continued, "I can't begin to tell you how much I respect this gentleman, and how he has helped me change into a decent, good person, and an *effy-cow* citizen. All my life, I have had anything I wanted: money, cars, jewelry, speedboats, anything at all. But I really lacked common good, and also terrific idea things like trust, honor, kindness, truth, respect, and *curt-tessi,*" Goose publicly confessed. "All of those special, emotional growth *qual-titties* I have learned from this special gentleman," the slightly-flustered speaker orated. "J.W., would ya' please come forward and *except* your gifts."

My knees were knocking and tears formed inside my eyes. I cautiously advanced toward the head table, not wanting to trip and embarrass myself before such an eminent audience. When I arrived at the Harrah's podium, Goose reached behind the red curtain and handed me a furry horse's tail, three softballs, and a giant stuffed kangaroo. I was flabbergasted by the articles associated with past 1960 memories. I suddenly felt quite sentimental and nostalgic.

"And now ladies and gentlemen," G.R. un-eloquently elucidated, "I wanta' tell ya' all that J.W. taught English in a public school for thirty-four difficult years; survived the torture, and is now an author. He's gonna' record everything that happened between him and me in the year 1960, and then publish it all in a book and make big *royal-tease,* I just know that's gonna' happen," Goose predicted with a trembling voice. "Then, everyone will understand why the people who have been recognized by me this mornin' are all present here today in Atlantic City."

Goose gave a few waiters standing behind him a signal; the red curtains behind the speaker opened, and room dividers that separated Conference Room B from Conference Room A were instantly visible to all. The dual-room partitions were swiftly opened, and inside the newly revealed chamber were my wife Joanne, Elaine Hill, Esther Phyllis, Nanette Banks, and all the supportive girls I had known from Edgewood High School, class of '60.

I turned to my left while holding the stuffed kangaroo, three softballs, and the 'White Horse furry tail, and was enthusiastically greeted by News Tomasello, Juice Illiani, Fabian Midilli, and Frankie Jives Arena, along with their wives and friends. To my right were Gabe and Marty Gillette, Speed Mortellite, Butch Lanza, Ox Narducci, and all of the other former Blues and their wives and guests. Everyone gave me a thunderous round of applause, and I never before had ever felt so proud and so humble at the same time. Goose's honorary awards ceremony was merely a marvelous pretext to recognize my grand influence upon his fascinating life.

Crystal Davis opened her white envelope, and then came-up and gave me a big hug, for she had received a check for one-and-a-half-million-dollars. And then, Mrs. Hector Rodriquez did the same to me in appreciation for her check of an equal amount. Tyrone Davis was thrilled with his bushel of shiny eggplants and a cool five-hundred-thousand-dollar bonus.

Dennis Measley came over to me, his eyes full of tears. The good-hearted fellow had also received a check for a half-million-dollars. and also, the keys to a 2002 Chrysler Concorde to complement his bushel of fancy apples.

I handed Joanne the giant stuffed kangaroo, a replica of the one from the 1960 Amusements of America Carnival that had regretfully wound-up in her father's packinghouse dumping bin. A familiar melody originated from the Harrah's Conference Room A's sound system, and tears filled my eyes as Kathy Young with the Innocents began the stirring introduction to "A Thousand Stars in the Sky".

Goose Restuccio motioned for Joanne and me to begin slow dancing, and after we initiated our old "American Bandstand" routine, my former Reds' friends and their spouses, along with *our* former Blues enemies and their wives, all joined the wonderful experience, and Hammonton was at last healed and united with the great teen fruit war finally reduced to a bad ancient memory.

"This is really great, Joanne," I commented to my supportive Sicilian wife. "This reunion is 1960 revisited, and we're reliving it the way it should've been lived way back then. All my dreams have finally come true."

"All *our* dreams have finally come true," Joanne aptly clarified and corrected. "I'm so glad that you're still alive, after all that teen danger that had happened to you back in all-too-memorable 1960!"

About the Author

Jay Dubya is author' John Wiessner's pen name. John is a retired New Jersey' public school English teacher, having taught the subject for thirty-four years. John lives in Hammonton, New Jersey with wife Joanne and they have three grown sons.

Jay Dubya has written other adult fiction besides *The Great Teen Fruit War, A 1960 Novel. Black Leather and Blue Denim, A '50s Novel* depicts J.W.'s experiences as a greaser' gang member in Levittown, Pennsylvania from 1954-'59. *Frat' Brats, A '60s Novel* completes the adult action/adventure trilogy. *Ron Coyote, Man of La Mangia* is a satire/parody on Miguel Cervantes' *Don Quixote*, published in 1605. *Pieces of Eight*, *Pieces of Eight, Part II*, *Pieces of Eight, Part III*, and *Pieces of Eight, Part IV* are collections of eight novellas each featuring science fiction, paranormal and humor' plots and themes. *Nine New Novellas, Nine New Novellas, Part II, Nine New Novellas, Part III* and *Nine New Novellas, Part IV* have science fiction and paranormal plots and themes. *So Ya' Wanna' Be A Teacher* is an autobiography of Jay Dubya's public school teaching career.

Thirteen Sick Tasteless Classics (books one to four) are collections of satirized famous fiction' works. *The Wholly Book of Genesis* and *The Wholly Book of Exodus* are parodies of the Bible's first two books.

Fractured Frazzled Folk Fables and Fairy Farces (Parts I, and II) and *Mauled Maimed Mangled Mutilated Mythology* are adult satire/ parodies on famous children's stories and classic Greek myths respectively.

Jay Dubya has also written a young adult fantasy trilogy, *Pot of Gold, Enchanta and Space Bugs, Earth Invasion. The Eighteen Story Gingerbread House* is a collection of imaginative children's stories. All of the author's books are available in Adobe Reader, Mobipocket and in Microsoft Reader e-formats. eBookstand.com has Print-On-Demand paperback editions of fifteen of Jay Dubya's e-books.

Jay Dubya likes '50s music, and he enjoys listening to pop songs by the Beatles, the Beach Boys, ELO, Doobie Brothers, Fleetwood Mac, the Eagles, John Mellencamp, the Rolling Stones and John Fogerty. When not enjoying popular music, Jay Dubya likes watching *76ers* basketball and *Phillies* and *New York Yankees* television baseball games.

Author Biography

Born in Hammonton, NJ in 1942, John Wiessner had attended St. Joseph School up to and including Grade 5. After his family moved from Hammonton to Levittown, Pa in 1954, John attended St. Mark School in Bristol, Pa. for Grade 6, St. Michael the Archangel School in Levittown for Grades 7 and 8 and then Immaculate Conception School, Levittown, Pa. for Grade 9. Bishop Egan High School, Levittown PA. was John's educational base for Grades 10 and 11, and later in 1960, the aspiring author graduated from Edgewood Regional High, Tansboro, NJ. John then next attended Glassboro State College, where he was an announcer for the school's baseball games and also read the nightly news and sports over WGLS, GSC's radio station.

John Wiessner had been primarily an English teacher in the Hammonton Public School System for 34 years, specializing in the instruction of middle school language arts. Mr. Wiessner was quite active in the Hammonton Education Association, loyally serving in the capacities of Vice-President, then building representative, and finally, teachers' head negotiator for a period of 7 years. During his lengthy teaching career, John had been nominated into "Who's Who among American Teachers" three times. He also was quite active giving professional workshops at schools around South Jersey on the subjects of creative writing and the use of movie videos to motivate students to organize their classroom theme compositions.

In addition, John Wiessner was very active in community service, being a past President of the Hammonton Lions Club, where he also functioned for many years as the club's Tail-Twister, Vice-President and Liontamer. John had been named Hammonton Lion of the Year in 1979 and in 2009 received the prestigious Melvin Jones Fellow Award, the highest honor a Lion can receive.

John also was a successful businessman, starting with being a Philadelphia Bulletin newspaper delivery boy for two-years in the late 1950s in Levittown, Pennsylvania. After his family moved back to New Jersey in 1959, John worked at his grandparents and his parents' farm markets, Square Deal Farm (now Ron's Gardens in Hammonton) and Pete's Farm Market in Elm, respectively. He later managed his wife's parents' farm market, White Horse Farms in Elm for three summers.

Also in a business capacity, for 16 summers starting in 1967 John Wiessner had co-owned Dealers Choice Amusement Arcade on the Ocean City, Maryland boardwalk and also co-owned the New Horizon Tee-Shirt Store for eight summers (1973-'81) on the Rehoboth Beach, Delaware boardwalk. In addition, "Jay Dubya" was a co-owner of

Wheel and Deal Amusement Arcade, Missouri Avenue and Boardwalk, Atlantic City. And then, for 18 summers beginning in 1986, John had been the Field Manager in charge of crew-leaders for Atlantic Blueberry Company (the world's largest cultivated blueberry farm), both the Weymouth and Mays Landing Divisions.

After retiring from teaching in 1999, writing under the pen name Jay Dubya (his initials), John Wiessner became the author of 75 books in the genre Action/Adventure Novels, Sci-Fi/Paranormal Story Collections, Adult Satire, Young Adult Fantasy Novels and also Non-Fiction Books. His books exist in hardcover, in paperback and in popular Kindle and Nook e-book formats.

In January of 2022, John Wiessner (Jay Dubya) was nominated into Marquis Who's Who in America, and in April of that same year, was one of nine distinguished Who's Who in America members honored with receiving Lifetime Achievement Awards, all nine sharing a news article of recognition appearing in the Wall Street Journal.

Google: Jay Dubya, books
Google: Walmart, Jay Dubya

www.ingramcontent.com/pod-product-compliance
Lightning Source LLC
Chambersburg PA
CBHW020557310726
48979CB00008B/1241/J
* 9 7 8 1 5 8 9 0 9 1 3 1 3 *